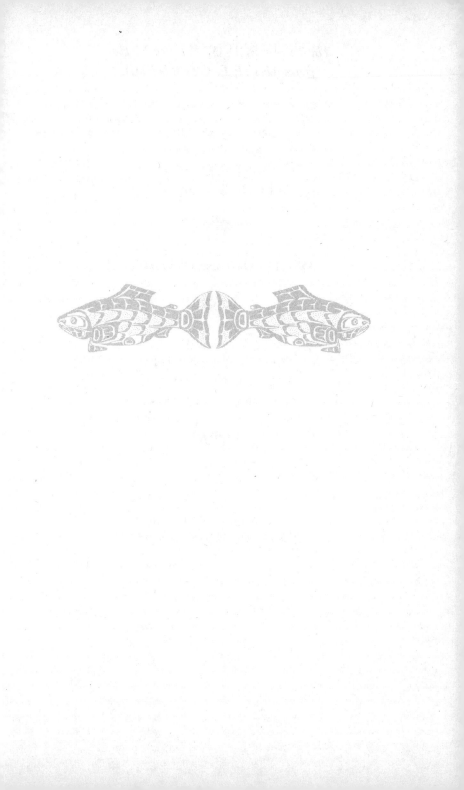

REGENERATION

Species Imperative #3

JULIE E. CZERNEDA

DAW BOOKS, INC.

DONALD A. WOLLHEIM, FOUNDER

375 Hudson Street, New York, NY 10014

ELIZABETH R. WOLLHEIM

SHEILA E. GILBERT

PUBLISHERS

For Roger . . .
Always.

Acknowledgments

Wrapping up a story three books long took some help, and I'm grateful to all those who contributed to the effort. First, I must thank the folks at DAW Books, starting with my editor, Sheila Gilbert, who managed to calmly offer constructive comment regardless of venue or timeline, and those in production, who've borne the brunt of that timeline. I hope I never impose on you again this badly. I don't dare promise! You were great. Luis Royo came up with another fantastic cover, true to everything I'd imagined. I'm spoiled, I admit it.

Sam Schrant, Sebastian Jones, Doug Court, Kevin Maclean, and Michael Gillis are real people who dared lend their names to this book. Gentlemen, I hope you enjoy the result. Feel free to claim the good bits; anything else I made up. Kevin also acted as my local New Zealand resource, while Lance Lones kindly provided his "stranger in a new land" perspective. I'd also like to thank Ivars Peterson of *Science News* for his willing patience while I finished this book.

While writing this, I was privileged to travel extensively and would like to thank some of my hosts: Stan Gardner, Ron Vick, and their Willycon committee; the concom for Eeriecon, Duckon, Toronto Trek, and Cascadiacon; while in the breathtaking Yukon: Joyce Sward and the incredibly talented students of the Writers Festival, Lori Schroeder and Claire Eamer of the Yukon Science Institute, (Whitehorse), Sebastian Jones, Dan Davidson, and students/staff of Robert Service School (Dawson City); Christine

Royce and the Pennsylvania Science Teachers Association. Yes, there's more, but I can't thank everyone I should without doubling this book. Please know I'm beyond grateful for your kindness and interest.

Jana Paniccia, Jihane Billacois, Janet Chase, and Jennifer Czerneda read this book in manuscript for me and offered comment and encouragement. Doranna Durgin checked my puppies. Those who urged me on through posts and e-mails? Thank you, too. Always helpful. And this book marks the first time, but I trust not the last, that I'll wave happily to the "Biogeeks," avowed fans of Mac and the biology in my books.

Last, but never least, my family. You put up with more than the usual angst from me on this one, and I appreciated your support every minute. Thank you, Jennifer, for your help with the last chapters and the ending. Poppa? Hope you'll like it. I know it's a little big, but—stuff happens.

- Table of Contents -

- CONTACT -

THE PORTENTS WILL COME. And Change will follow, to take the landscape, to bring death.

Those who can flee, will.

And still that which is Dhryn must wait—too frail to risk confrontation—too slow to race others from the doom.

Only in the lull time, when the emptied land has finished dying around them, will the Dhryn venture forth. Scouts first, to taste the land, seek routes to what the Progenitors will crave. They will find where the great forests rot, bring the feast to sustain.

That which is Dhryn shall cleanse the land, removing debris, clearing blocked rivers. All will sustain the Progenitors as they *move* behind the rest.

Most will not complete the Great Journey, spent by the effort, worn by toil. Lost. Left. Remembered.

All that matters is the Progenitors reach Haven, the place of safety and plenty. There They will rest, setting the Path in memory, bringing forth new generations who will not know Change in their lifetimes.

Until it begins again.

(Inscription found at southern hemisphere haven site 9903-ZA,
pre-alloy Dhryn ruin, Planet Myriam)

- 1 -

BEER AND BOTHER

"**A**RE YOU THINKING what I'm thinking?"

Dr. Mackenzie Connor, Mac to those she intended to talk to more than once, gave her closest friend a wary look. She'd learned the hard way where such conversational gambits could lead. *Especially when Dr. Emily Mamani was* this *bored.* "That," she ventured, "depends on what you're thinking."

That tilt of the elegant head, with that smile, spelled pure mischief. "Then you are!"

"Am not." As this didn't seem a particularly adult retort, Mac added primly, "I never think such things."

Emily's laugh, as rich and contagious as before, as always, warmed Mac's heart. She wished it could erase the shadows clinging to the other woman's cheekbones, haunting her eyes. *Time might do that.*

Or not.

"You're allowed, you know," Em continued, leaning closer. They were both sitting with their elbows propped on the dark, polished wood of the bar. The bar that stretched in a friendly manner right to the door.

The door Mac eyed wistfully. *She'd left so much work . . .*

"Oh, no, you don't," Emily protested. "You promised."

"So now you think you're thinking what I'm thinking?" Mac asked, dragging her attention back to her beer. "Hah!"

"Hah, yourself. We get a night away from that bunch of loons. You promised."

"They aren't—" Mac stopped as Emily raised a shapely, black, and highly expressive eyebrow. True, Wilson Kudla, author of *Chasm Ghouls: They Exist and Speak to Me,* was presently conducting the third night of what boded to be a prolonged—and already very sweaty—exorcism attempt, having, like the rest of the Origins Team, become convinced the Ro were not beings to welcome under one's roof. Or inside one's tent.

Not that the rest of the team had tents, Mac corrected hurriedly. Particularly tents full of perspiring Humans chanting themselves hoarse. "Not all of them are loons," she qualified. "Archaeologists simply have their own approach to the work. You'll get used to it." This last hope echoed inside her half empty glass as Mac lifted it to her mouth. She took a long swallow, thought about it, then took another. A local brew. By now too warm by her standards, but with an excellent aftertaste. She squinted into the foam. *Honey?*

Despite its colorful name, *The Takahe Nest* was little more than a long room, two thirds filled with wooden tables and assorted chairs. The floor was wood as well, rough and scarred by hiking boots—from the look of the trail leading past the bar, soaking wet and muddy hiking boots. The bartender, a big friendly man who'd introduced himself as "Kevin MacLean but not the actor," claimed it had rained every day of the first fifty years the *Nest* was open. The occasional sunny day since hadn't helped much. Mac and Emily had been directed here to experience firsthand a slice of the unique Fiordland atmosphere.

It had that. Mac surveyed the eclectic and dusty mix of objects suspended from every exposed beam and wall. Perplexed-looking stags' heads, antique hunting weapons, and odd-shaped drinking cups vied for space with what could only be bits and pieces of skims—most broken. The tip of a helicopter blade—Mac's curiosity had made her ask what it was—easily two hundred years older than the pub itself, held place of honor behind the bar. Nor'easters ripped down the mountain valleys without warning, Kevin had explained cheerfully. The wind took its tithe from anything that dared be in the sky.

The clientele matched the bar. *Well, except for themselves.* Emily—in her long black shawl and yellow top, with a full red skirt swirling around her calves—stood out like some exotic flower transplanted in the wrong place. Mac herself, in dark pants, blouse, and sweater, had attracted only slightly fewer stares when entering. She eased her toes in the dressy sandals Emily had insisted she wear, missing her boots. The few folks here looked to be straight off a hiking trail or farm—people who worked with their hands and weren't afraid of a little deluge.

Felt like home. Although she'd never had a beer as a namesake before. Mac tipped the rest of her bottle of "Mac's" into her glass and smiled.

"How long are we going to stay here?" Emily demanded in a low voice, with a gesture including more than *The Takahe Nest.*

Back to that again? Mac held back a sigh. "Your guess is as good as mine, Em," she said, truthfully enough.

The Gathering, the collaboration of every Dhryn expert the Sinzi could find within the Interspecies Union, had been— *disbanded wasn't the right word,* Mac decided. Sent packing was more like it. The synergy provided by their being in the same place, namely housed at the IU Consulate for Sol System, had been irrevocably outweighed by becoming a single, convenient target. The Dhryn assault could have eradicated not only life on Earth, but the best chance of coming up with a defense for the rest of the IU—those thousands of worlds linked by the transects that permitted instantaneous travel between star systems.

"The sum," Mac mused into her drink. "More than the parts, you know."

"Gods, Mac. Philosophy on the second beer? Way too early."

Mac's lips twitched. "Sorry." She ticked her glass against Emily's. "Bad habit."

"I'll say. Kev!" In answer to Emily's urgent summons, the bartender hurried over with two more bottles, lingering to trade smiles. *Mistake.* When Kevin turned away to serve other customers, Emily leaned well over the bar for a better look, lips pursed to whistle. Mac hauled her back to her seat. "Two beers are way too early for that," she muttered under her breath, hoping no one else had noticed. Luckily, few of the tables were inhabited this early in the evening. A couple held what had to be groups of regulars, engrossed in their own conversations; the rest of the patrons stood around tables at the far end, where each solid *thunk* of dart into cork was followed by a roar—frequently accompanied by jeering comments about coordination and the lack thereof.

Emily settled peacefully. Then she leaned closer, her shoulder against Mac's. "We don't need to be here, Mac," very quietly. "We shouldn't be here."

No chance she meant the pub this time either. For all of Em's insistence on a night out for the two of them, "just like any Saturday at Base," this was looking more and more like a night out to air grievances Emily didn't feel like discussing with anyone else. *One grievance in particular.*

Mac swallowed the dregs of beer number two before taking a healthy swig of beer number three straight from the bottle. Nice and cold. "I know," she admitted at last, pouring the rest slowly into her glass. "The Sinzi-ra—"

"The Sinzi-ra has already sent every other research team through the transects, each to a secret destination. Smart move. The right move. Mac. *They* know this place."

There was only one "they" to Emily, anymore. Her by now familiar stress on the pronoun sent a chill down Mac's spine.

In the six weeks and handful of days since Emily's reawakening, her scars had healed, flesh had reappeared over her bones, and her skin had regained its normal golden glow. The streaks of silver in her glossy black hair were new, but she'd never been one to avoid an attractive contrast. The repairs to the damage left by the Ro— the new arms, abdominal wall, portions of her back, one cheek, internal organs—had been made with an ability to match detail beyond current Human medicine.

Only the way Emily flinched from naming the Ro aloud showed what hadn't been fixed. So far, she'd remembered nothing of her time with the aliens. *It wasn't her memory that had failed,* Mac corrected, studying her friend. Noad, Anchen's physician-self, believed Emily's mind continued to struggle for some means to process those experiences, based as they were on stimuli from an environment no Human sense had evolved to understand. No-space. The chosen realm of the Myrokynay, the Ro.

Emily did recall, with devastating accuracy, everything else. How the Ro had used her to help destroy the very life she'd thought she was sacrificing herself to protect. How, through her actions, the Dhryn had been unleashed . . . to decimate worlds . . . to threaten Earth herself . . . and now, to wait like some hidden plague, ready to strike anywhere in the Interspecies Union.

They'd lied to her.

They'd discarded her.

That simmering rage deep in the eyes meeting hers, even here and now, above the cheerful smile Emily shaped with her lips? Mac knew what it meant.

They would pay.

Mac recognized Emily's fury because it matched her own. No matter what anyone else thought of the Ro, no matter that there was division in the IU, the same evidence maddeningly taken as proof by both sides, she knew the Ro were the true enemy. They'd turned a sentient species into a deadly weapon, one they'd used to scour the Chasm worlds of life, one they were using again.

Some night out. Mac looked away, letting her gaze travel the labels of the truly bewildering array of bottles lined up behind the bar. Single malt scotch, most with names as long and unpronounceable as those for local streets.

No luck. After a moment's struggle, she gave up. *Shouldn't drink and read,* Mac chided herself, refusing to blame her still-tenuous ability to sort meaning from the written word. *No wonder the devout kept lists.* "Here," she said at last, patting the bar. "Somewhere else. It doesn't matter where we are, Em. Whatever gets the job done. At least here we have resources—the backing of the Ministry as well as the IU. A little patience, okay?"

That drew a steady look, a nod, and finally a chuckle as Emily let go for the moment. "Patience? Oh, please, Mac. Not *that* word again." She wiggled her long fingers, gloved in textured black silk, in front of Mac's eyes. "If they made these things properly, it wouldn't take ridiculous, monotonous, 'patience, patience, Dr. Mamani' exercises! One dose of sub-teach, and I'd be performing solos on my cello."

"Cello?" Mac snorted. Emily's taste in music ran to a driving, heavy beat and flashing strobes, preferably delivered over a hot, crowded dance floor. She wrapped her own artificial hand around her glass and raised it, the faintly blue-tinged pseudoskin glistening as if with sweat. *Trick of the bar's light.* Mac glanced at her friend and stiffened.

Emily was staring at her own hands, as if suddenly transfixed by them, her eyes wide and unblinking. "They missed one," she mumbled in a strange, unsteady voice, bending then straightening each finger and thumb in slow motion, one after the other, again and again. "I told you, Mac. This isn't right. They missed—"

"Emily, no." Mac took Emily's nearest hand, gently pushing it down to rest on the polished wood of the bar. "Em. Em!"

She shivered, then gave Mac a thoroughly sane look of annoyance. "What's the matter with you?"

"Had a vision of you playing a cello, that's all," Mac lied.

She'd thought Emily had stopped this fuss over her fingers, the absentminded counting she'd continue until interrupted. *This quiet place was a mistake,* Mac decided. *Emily needed that hot dance floor, ideally crowded with young, athletic men. Distraction.*

Then again, her fellow biologist was once more making come-hither eyes at their dubious but willing bartender, who, to be honest, was a few years past young and looked to lately watch more athletics than he performed.

Dancing was one thing. *This could get complicated.* "Em," Mac warned.

"He's cute." Emily, perfectly capable of flirting and arguing at the same time, circled back to her subject like a shark circling blood spoor in the water. "Hollans. Ask him to get us out of the consulate."

A bubble fought free of the cream-tinged foam as Mac watched. She helped another burst with a fingertip.

"Well?" Em prompted.

"We aren't exactly on speaking terms at the moment."

"And whose fault is that, Dr. Tact?"

Mac pressed her lips together. Bernd Hollans, humanity's representative on the IU's council dealing with the Dhryn, was an important, capable individual of considerable influence who had, she gave credit where it was due, proved himself willing to listen and take action in a crisis. But with the immediate threat seemingly over, Hollans had reverted to the rule-following, overly cautious, pompous annoyance she'd initially judged him.

Who hovered *over her shoulder while she worked*, she grumbled to herself.

They didn't do well in meetings together. Not well at all. Mac winced. In fact, at the last one, she'd come close to throwing her imp at his head.

Hadn't let go. That had to count.

Out loud: "And I thought Oversight was bad."

"Old Charlie's all right," Emily asserted, taking a drink herself as if in toast.

While Mac agreed, she made a point of keeping any fondness for her former adversary to herself. They both preferred it that way. *But still* . . . She couldn't help herself: "He hates 'Charlie.' "

Emily grinned. "I know."

Mac's lips twitched. "No wonder you and Fourteen get along."

"Fish of a scale, my dear Dr.—" Emily began archly, then stopped, looking toward the door. "I see your friends have arrived."

"Who—?" Mac turned to answer her own question, then hurriedly looked away again. *Too late.*

She'd been spotted.

"Dr. Connor!"

"She's not here," that worthy muttered, glaring into her beer. "Not. Not. Not."

Emily's elbow dug into her ribs. "As if that's ever worked."

Stools and chairs complained as they acquired oversized passengers, the bar now filling up on either side of the two women. Kevin the bartender hesitated. Either he didn't know who to serve first, or he'd never been faced with so much gloom at one time in his entire career. Mac gave him a sympathetic look.

She wasn't entirely sure why the Sinzi-ra would choose Grimnoii to act as, well, she wasn't really certain what they did for the Sinzi either, other than wander about in groups of seeming misery from dusk till dawn. Intimidating groups of seeming misery, even without the ceremonial axes, knives, and spikes they were entitled to wear on consular grounds. Massive, furred, cloaked-in-brown misery.

Depressing giant teddy bears. Who'd have thought?

"Glad we found you, Dr. Connor," said several Grimnoii at once. Completing their doleful effect—on Humans, at least—they had low, melancholy voices, capable of instilling the most cheerful greeting with funereal undertones.

Mac lifted a suitably limp hand in acknowledgment.

The Human minority sent up another series of raucous jeers as a *clink/plunk* announced a significant failure of aim. Several Grimnoii rose to head in that direction, as if determined to possess the entire building. *Or,* for all Mac knew, *their apparent fixation on pointy things extended to darts.*

Mac caught Em's eye, gave the "last call" look honed through years of practice, and picked up her beer. She poured it down her throat with one easy motion, replacing the glass on the bar with a firm thump to cover a less-than-discreet belch. *Always, when she rushed.* "Just leaving, Rumnor," she informed the alien who'd taken the stool to her left. "Have fun."

"No." A thick, pawlike hand trapped her arm in its warmth as she stood. "You must stay and drink cider with us, Dr. Connor. Much cider."

"Cider," echoed the rest in their sad voices. "Dr. Connor." "Cider." "Stay with us."

The snicker was Emily's.

Keeping her face as straight as possible—*one never knew which being could read Human expressions*—Mac improvised. "Sorry. Gotta go and—go and give blood," she nodded briskly. "Late for our biweekly drain." That said, she used her free hand to remove Rumnor's. He didn't resist, though his pale brown eyes wept copiously. *Nothing to do with her or cider.* The tearing seemed a species' trait, producing crusty yellow tracks down the fur of both cheeks and dribbles over the mud-brown cloth that covered a Grimnoii's rounded chest. "You know Humans when we don't expel our erythrocytes on time," Mac continued glibly.

Which was #22 on the *Favorite Myths About Humanity* list published by the consulate, but she'd bet Rumnor wasn't the brochure-reading kind.

Sure enough, he grunted something inexpressibly sad, his attention drifting to the tray of cider the bartender was carrying past. One paw wavered out to engulf a mug, endangering the rest.

"Let's settle the—" Mac began, then realized Emily was halfway to the door. *Smart woman.* She stood to follow. "Put us on their tab, Kevin!" she called to the bartender, who raised a brow but nodded.

She caught up with Emily on the sidewalk, standing below the sign that read "Warning: Wreckers at Work" complete with an image of several large parrotlike birds in yellow construction helmets, each using a jackhammer to demolish a parked skim. *She'd forgotten to ask Kevin about that one.*

Mac and Emily crossed the street in companionable silence, sandals crunching through the remnants of late-winter leaves. This part of Te Anau had wide, quiet roadways lined with tidy buildings, each with a small patch of garden out front. Trees, most with no intention of dropping leaves despite the season, overhung the pole lamps. Their soft shadows blurred the circles of light beneath. Shivering at the difference from the too-warm indoor air to the evening's nip, Mac shrugged into the sweater she'd tied around her waist. Em had tossed her black shawl over her head as well as shoulders, the ends still brushing the backs of her ankles.

A skim passed in the distance, but otherwise the town appeared deserted. Lambing was starting, according to Kevin, an event guaranteed to keep a majority of the local population preoccupied for the next few weeks.

Emily didn't say a word until Mac paused to squint up at the road sign, trying to decide which lengthy assortment of vowels was which. Then, quietly but with conviction: "I told you we couldn't leave the consulate without being watched."

Of course not, Mac thought smugly. They had their protectors— out of sight, out of mind, until now. *Just not teddy bears on the town.* She shook her head. "You're reading too much into it, Em. There are only two bars within walking distance from the lev station. Rumnor's lot probably drank the other out of cider." *Making* The Feisty Weka *the place for us,* she promised herself. *Not to mention it boasted a dance floor.*

The third and hasty beer was trying to make itself felt, so Mac decided not to guess at the vowels lined up on the sign. She pulled out her imp to display directions in the air above her hands. The light from the map etched bone-thin lines back into Emily's face. Mac turned it off quickly. "Thaddaway," she announced, pointing.

"Wait. I see a shortcut."

Shortcut? Mac shook her head again, but willingly followed the taller woman as she picked a narrow lane overhung by vines, clearly not heading toward the *Weka*. She puffed as they passed through the glow from a back porch light, admiring the little cloud of condensed vapor her breath produced. Oh, yes. Winter. *Remarkable notion, winter in August.*

Mac gathered her thoughts. *She hadn't had that much beer, surely.* No, it had to be the deliciously familiar sensation of sneaking off making her giddy, of letting Emily lead her where she'd never—as a serious person with responsibilities she took, well, seriously—ever go on her own.

No point asking where they were going.

"I should have asked where you were taking me," Mac complained some time later. She was perched on the flattest of several large tumbled stones, trying to deal with the sodden mess that had been her new sandals. *Never,* she vowed, *go out in anything but sensible boots.* She finally managed to pull and twist the now-loose straps into some kind of knot, hopefully to stay on her feet until they got home.

"You know you like it here."

Mac grinned. "You had any doubt?" She leaned back, supported by her hands on the damp rock behind her, and admired the view.

Pasture climbed from the opposite side of the river in smooth waves of darkness that appeared to break against the distant silhouettes of trees marking the forest edge. All it would take were pale swirls of morning mist to complete the illusion of land become sea. For now, the moon, only a quarter full, picked out the rapids mere meters from their feet, split by long, fingerlike gravel bars: gray on black, the presence of driftwood and boulder suggested by faint, pale streaks of foam.

The pile of rock she was using for a seat must be the ruins of an old bridge support, a very small bridge, likely for four-footed traffic and trampers. New Zealanders, Mac had been told, loved nothing more than walking their countryside, carrying lunch. The support's abandoned partner huddled on the opposite bank, undercut and ready to fall into the water.

Mac drew a slow breath in through her nose, dismissing the honey-note of beer, the wet richness of grass, that pungent whiff of equally wet sheep. *There*. That smell. The river itself. *Its life*.

Mac doubted anyone but Emily appreciated how thoroughly she hated being stuck indoors. Then again, Lyle Kanaci could wax almost poetic about his research station on the lifeless Dhryn home world, now officially renamed Myriam after his late wife.

Amazing what Oversight could accomplish with a flood of officious memos on a topic, Mac thought fondly.

Emily stood to the right of Mac's stony perch, in this meager light as ephemeral as the rest of the landscape, as liable to shift or disappear as any shadow. Mac tasted the old dread. The damage left by the Ro had been extensive; the reconstruction of Emily's body a challenge to the Sinzi's skill. But it had worked. Emily lived. *She* was *here*.

"How did you know about this place?" Mac asked, pleased by the calm tone of her voice. *Mind you, she'd had practice there, too.* Calls to her father and brothers. Emily's sister. Kammie Noyo back at Base. Telling them what she could, without revealing what she couldn't: *yes, Emily's been found . . . she's been ill and needs time to recover . . . I'm staying with her . . . bit of vacation for both of us . . . you know me, catching up on some research, too . . . call anytime.*

She'd finally learned to lie, Mac thought with a mix of regret and grim pride. *Maybe not up to Emily or Nik's standards, but enough to forestall inconvenient questions.*

Emily gave a soft laugh. "I didn't." A pause. "You know me, Mac—always looking for the more interesting path."

As that path, from the end of the laneway, had involved several unseen but deep puddles—hence the ruined sandals—followed by a scramble up a rocky slope and down again until they could no longer see the lights from the town, "interesting" seemed a bit of an understatement. Mac stretched contentedly, giving the situation deep thought. "I don't suppose you brought beer."

A chuckle, then: "Tell me. Our Nikolai. Were you lovers before he left?"

Vintage Emily. Shocked sober, if she wasn't before, Mac was grateful for the darkness that hid her flaming cheeks. "I don't think that's any of your—"

"No, then." Another pause. "Trust me. It's just as well."

Not so vintage. Mac tried to avoid temptation but failed: "This," she asked, "from the woman whose motto is 'a night alone is a night wasted'?"

"Mac. You're such an honest fool," kindly. "Sex is the oldest excuse. Even low-class hotels keep vidbots out of their rooms."

Mac lost all interest in the river. She stared at the tall, slender shadow of her friend, trying not to think what she was thinking, trying not to let anything else *change.*

As usual, the universe was oblivious to the wishes of a certain salmon researcher. Emily spoke again, the words as calm and inevitable as the dew forming on the grass around them. "You alone, Mac, haven't asked me to explain what I did. Why I did it. Don't you think it's time?"

A night out like the old days? Hah!

Emily's invitation, this conversation with the two of them faceless and in the dark, snapped closed around Mac like a trap. They weren't supposed to have it. She'd gone out of her way to make sure they didn't. *Forgive and forget.* That was the way it should be.

She shook her head. Not to deny the ambush. *Oh, if anyone knew the risks of an Emily Mamani Patented Pub Crawl Shortcut, she did.* But at herself.

Emily had been debriefed by seemingly everyone else on the planet—and quite a few off. Mac had avoided those sessions. She'd chosen to accept Emily back without questions, give her what peace she could. *Forgive and forget.* She trusted the Sinzi, or the Ministry, would tell her any facts she'd need for their work.

For Emily's peace? Mac wondered with unexpected guilt. *Or her own?*

"You're back," she protested, knowing it was in vain. "That's all I care about."

"Don't be afraid, Mac," Emily replied ever so gently. "The truth—it's not going to change things. You won't lose me again."

Emily had asked for Mac's forgiveness. *She'd already given it.* Mac shook her head again. "I don't need to know."

"I need you to. Please, Mac. Don't be difficult."

She'd love to be difficult. Instead, Mac pulled one knee to her chest and rested her chin on it, staring into the dark. "Suit yourself."

CONVERSATION AND CONSEQUENCE

"IT BEGAN WITH FEAR," Emily told her. "I was only a child when I first heard about the Chasm, a place where all life had been mysteriously wiped from its planets. Only a child, but I understood too well. I had nightmares of everything around me disappearing. Over and over. Finally my mother gave me books about the Chasm. She insisted I read them; told me the only way to stop fear was to learn its cause. My fear turned to obsession." Her voice became rueful. "I grew up planning to save the rest of the universe."

Somehow, Mac wasn't surprised. Of course, she herself had grown up ignoring the universe, blithely confident it would return the favor. *Look where both attitudes had landed them,* she thought grimly.

"I continued to study everything I could find," Emily went on. "Until, one day, I stumbled on the key, Mac. Some believed a sentient species from the Chasm had escaped its destruction. Such a species would have my answers. All I had to do was find them."

"The Survivor Legend," Mac acknowledged. Brymn had told her Emily had been researching it when they'd met. *A scrap of truth within the lies.*

Emily's secret quest had succeeded. She'd found the Ro—or they'd found her. As far as Mac was concerned, the difference was academic.

Not a healthy topic of conversation. Not away from trained help, with Emily's mind fragile enough. There could be worse things than compulsive finger counting. "Good thing you went into fish biology instead," Mac offered, her voice strained to her own ears. "How did that happen?"

"I didn't. Not instead. Because."

Trust Emily to dangle the right bait. Worried or not, Mac couldn't help herself. " 'Because?' "

"I haven't lost it." Emily's laugh was too hollow to be reassuring. "Believe me, Mac, there's been good, legitimate science behind the search for a lost civilization from the Chasm, unlike your chanting friends. But . . . I felt it prudent to have a day job, to keep my private research exactly that. To this day, my sponsor—even my sources—don't know the full extent of my efforts. Just to be discreet around you."

Sponsor? Sources? Mac floundered after what confounded her most. "Around me? Who?"

"Who did you think I was with on Saturday nights?"

Anyone willing? Mac thought of the innumerable partners Emily had drawn from dance floors and bars during their times together. Was information for sale the common denominator she'd missed amid the loud shirts, lack of shirts, tattoos, suits, and the "only a mother could love" still-breathing? "There were quite a few," she concluded, feeling every bit the fool Emily'd named her.

A real laugh this time. "They weren't all sources, Mac."

Mac blushed in the dark. "Oh. Of course." *She was* not *going back through her mental list.* "I assume you had to pay them—the sources, I mean," she added quickly.

"Hence the sponsor. How do you think I knew about Kanaci's little group?"

She hadn't, Mac realized. *Given it thought, that is.* She'd gladly left the details of that grisly day to others, her attention divided between Emily's recovery and her research group. *Interspersed with daydreams about a certain absent and altogether yummy spy.*

Mac coughed. "Okay. How did you know?"

"Sencor Research funds us both. I had access to Kanaci's data, such as it was." Emily's voice grew amused. "Which reminds me. Bureaucrats have this lovely inertia—want to bet they've kept crediting my account?" The amusement faded. "Before you start on me, Mac, don't. The Ministry of Extra-Sol Human Affairs has everything I've done to date for Sencor—I gave your formidable Dr. Stewart my codes and contacts weeks ago. Surprised she didn't demand an impression of my teeth at the same time."

Mac refused to be distracted by Emily's opinion of 'Sephe, stuck on the improbably normal. "You had a sponsor," she echoed. "A real sponsor. To chase a—a myth!"

"Yes, Mac." Em's tone was the impatient but fond one she used fairly often during their discussions. *Usually when Mac was being willfully obtuse about some offworld topic.* "The Group very quietly supports a number of research projects into the Chasm. Their interest in the Survivors matched my own. They've funded my work for over fifteen years."

Mac snorted. The snort turned into a giggle. A giggle that multiplied until Emily interrupted, sounding rather offended: "I don't see what's so funny—"

"I know you're persuasive, Em, but how on Earth did you manage to talk these people into supporting you for years, pay for clandestine sources, send you offworld—" Mac stopped, considering what wasn't funny to her after all. "That's a great deal of funding." *Enough to finance every project at Base for a year, if not more.*

With trademark Mamani arrogance: "The goal was worth it. And so was I."

The goal had almost killed them both. Mac eased her bottom on the stone, stretching out her legs. *It still might.* "I don't get it," she said bluntly. "To start with, you're a fish biologist, like me."

"Haven't seen you studying salmon lately."

Not her idea. Aloud, and letting her exasperation through: "Putting aside the whole issue of searching for a species no one has ever proved existed in the first place, supposedly in hiding where no one can find them for the last three thousand years, why would Sencor sponsor you, of all people, to look for them? What could you possibly have had to offer? And, please, no innuendo."

"Spoilsport." Mac could hear the grin in Emily's voice.

The tone, the banter, was Emily at her most relaxed. Mac didn't buy it. Her friend hadn't moved since they'd arrived. She stood looking out over the river, a slip of darkness. The moonlight barely caught the fringes of her shawl, tugged by the light breeze. It didn't reveal her face.

The Emily Mac knew was restless and prone to pacing, said pacing typically accompanied by dramatic gestures liable to threaten both lab equipment and incautious vases. Her entire body could become an exclamation point. This new ability to remain still—it wasn't right. Mac curled up to hug both knees. *They should have stayed in the bar despite Rumnor and his pack.* "Well?" she prompted reluctantly.

"Weeellll," repeated Emily, stretching the word. "Tonight's supposed to be fun, Mac." That coaxing voice. *Emily the troublemaker voice.* More than anything, Mac wanted to be relieved by the sound of it. "C'mon, Mac. Take a guess."

Or maybe not. "Guess?" Mac repeated blankly.

"Guess. Don't worry. I'll give you a clue. Dr. Mackenzie Connor has left her salmon to follow aliens migrating across the stars, *si*? Dr. Emily Mamani did the opposite."

Gods. It struck too close to what hurt between them: that Emily came to work at Base, befriended Mac, only to lay the Ro's trap for Brymn.

Old, old news. Mac shook her head, impatient with herself and easily frustrated—as usual—by Emily's penchant for games. *It was that. Nothing more. Forgive me, Emily'd asked.*

She'd forgiven her.

What more *did she want*?

"You, Emily Mamani," Mac said through tight lips, "can be the most incredibly annoying—"

"Lazy, are you? Think! You haven't had that much beer."

Pity. "Fine," Mac surrendered for the second time. "That's the clue? You did the opposite to me, in terms of choice in research fields? I suppose that means you started with this obsession about Survivors and only later switched to fish biology, eventually developing technology to follow trophic movement in benthic-feeding fish species in the Sargasso Sea by identifying and tracing individuals. Promising topic," she added wistfully. "I don't suppose your sponsor was interested in that."

"Oh, yes, they were. Because I was interested. Think, Mac," Emily urged again, the hoarse emphasis in her voice abruptly making this anything but a game. "I need you to understand me."

Understand? Mac felt the hairs rise on the back of her neck, on her real forearm. Her stomach twisted to remind her it currently held an unfamiliar blend of sausage in thick pastry, plus three "Mac" beers. *She could almost feel Seung's hands on her shoulders . . . hear Denise complaining about the com system . . . see Norrey's . . .*

Understand *that level of betrayal?*

When Mac didn't—couldn't—speak, Emily pushed: "Why do you think I developed the Tracer device, Mac?"

Shivering free of ghosts, Mac found her voice, lips numb. "To record genetic information for individual fish in a moving group." *To find and track Mac's own DNA through the labyrinth of tunnels beneath the surface of Haven, to the Progenitor's Chamber, so the Ro could target their prey.*

Why? Mac puzzled, gladly distracted by the familiar problem. To set the great Dhryn ships in motion? They'd hardly needed to strike a specific portion of the planet for that. There had to be another purpose, some reason one Progenitor had been the target.

A question high on Nik's list to ask, for it was this same Progenitor he'd left to find. Mac looked up at what stars showed between the sheets of moon-grayed cloud. *Not that she'd the faintest idea where he was.* As few as possible knew where he'd gone and why. His mission with the Dhryn was a secret even from Emily. Though, given she'd already found out more about Nik than Mac had intended, it seemed only a matter of time till she learned the rest.

"Mac."

Emily's impatient voice dragged Mac's attention back, reluctantly, to the here-and-now. She scowled. "If you've something to tell me, Emily, I wish you'd do it. I hate games."

"I know. But this time, it's important to me. *Por favor?* I need you to feel something of what I felt, when I first recognized the potential of my approach. I want you to—"

"—understand," Mac snapped. "I heard."

"Is that so hard, my friend?"

"Yes!" The word was hard and sharp, like a weapon launched in the dark. Mac shuddered and hunched her shoulders. "Em—Emily, I'm sorry. I didn't mean . . ." *Forgive and* forget. *Why wasn't Emily cooperating?*

"Of course you did." Pure triumph. "About time, too."

" 'About time,' " Mac repeated. *Something was wrong here.* "What are you talking about?"

"Poor Mac. You've held on to me, to our friendship, with that incomparable will of yours. It saved me; I love you for it. But it isn't real—"

"How can you say that?" Mac whispered, feeling the burn of tears. "Emily—"

"It's not—not if you can't bring yourself to admit the Emily you thought you knew was someone different. Mac, if you can't understand me, and still call me friend, you might as well give in to that anger you're holding just as tight."

"I'm not angry—"

"And I'm a cod. Honestly, Mac, you're the only one who doesn't see it. You're furious with me. You've every right to be! Look what I've done!"

"No," Mac exclaimed. "I know it wasn't your fault—"

Emily's voice turned cold: "No, Mac, you don't. You're hoping it wasn't my fault. You're doing your utmost to avoid any evidence that might prove you wrong. Damn poor science, if you ask me."

"I didn't ask you," Mac lashed out.

"Which is why we're here," Emily responded with equal passion. "I can't stand to have you like this, Mac. Clinging like grim death to an Emily you fear never existed. Refusing to find out if this Emily—" a low thud as Emily thumped her chest with a fist, "—is the friend you thought you had. Gods, Mac. Anyone else would have demanded answers the instant I was conscious. I waited. I wondered if it was that place—being among aliens, strangers. But even here, by water . . . ?" Emily stopped, then went on in a husky voice: "Must you always do things the hard way?"

Mac licked her lips, tasting salt. "I lost you once."

A heavy sigh from the dark. "You haven't found me yet."

The words were half accusation, half challenge. Mac rubbed her eyes with her real hand, feeling abruptly weary. *Hadn't found her?* Nonsense. Her friend was standing right there.

Or—was she? Wasn't that the root of Mac's reluctance to know more about Emily and her past?

That she didn't know this woman at all?

"Give me a minute," she pleaded. "I need to think."

"That would be a nice change."

"Shut up, Em," Mac muttered distractedly. She focused on one thing at a time, did her best to keep her thoughts free of emotion.

A brilliant, ambitious mind . . . a seemingly intractable puzzle. Emily and the mystery of the Chasm. A good fit, attracting the support of Sencor.

Perhaps good enough to attract the Ro as well. *There was irony for you.*

Mac flinched, circled back to Emily's obsession. Why switch to fish biology? Why that particular field . . . *unless* . . . She crowed: "You believed the Survivors were aquatic! You built the Tracer to find them!"

"Must you shout?" Emily complained.

"The sheep won't care," Mac observed dryly. "I thought you wanted me to react."

"React. Just no shouting." From her tone, Emily was making a face. "Humor me. It's not easy giving up my ace, even to you."

Ace? Mac shifted restlessly. *More old news.* The real Survivors had been found. "It's not easy sitting on this rock."

"I'm trying to unburden my soul here."

Wasn't her idea. Mac made her own face, but settled again. "What made you so sure the Survivors existed in the first place?"

"There was evidence from the Chasm itself, if you knew where to look. I did. You have to realize, Mac, at that time research was devoted to planets with ruins or potential for mining. Interest was sporadic at best; support, the same. It's not as if the IU lacks living worlds to explore, thanks to the Sinzi. And the Chasm—it's not a comfortable place."

Neither was a rock. "What evidence did you find?" Mac prodded, thinking wistfully of the warm, crowded pub. Not to mention barstools. *Easier to stop that hint of rain in the air than Emily on a roll.* Especially when that roll was for Mac's enlightenment.

"The anomaly," Emily said with relish. "The only system connected with the rest of no interest to archaeologists or miners. Chasm System 232. Oh, it had a world capable of supporting life. Once. It became so much orbiting rubble—by my dating, three thousand years ago, give or take a decade." She paused as if this was significant.

"One of us," Mac hinted, "didn't take astrophysics."

"Think about it, Mac. We know the Chasm worlds were destroyed by the Dhryn three thousand years ago; by your Brymn's estimate, that's the Moment, when the Ro locked his kind in the Haven System." Emily's voice held unusual patience. "Here we have a planet destroyed at the same time, in a completely different way."

"And no else one noticed?" Mac pursued. "C'mon, Emily."

"The team who originally mapped Chasm 232 pegged it as a natural disaster. There was no reason to look at it more closely—not with all those planets with ruins waiting to be explored. But we both know the Dhryn aren't *Their* only weapon."

Oh, they knew. The Ro had toppled a mountainside to cover their tracks. Sing-li Jones, chief among the Ministry personnel still assigned to her, admitted they didn't know how the aliens had done it. Mac shifted to another rock. She was no more at ease talking out loud about their invisible enemy than Emily was.

She always listened. The wind ruffling the grass. The scurry of something small and careful. The cheerful babble of water over stone. Nothing unusual.

Nothing unusual now. Mac didn't quite shiver.

What she didn't understand was where Emily was going with this. "Say I accept your dating," Mac suggested. "I don't follow what this has to do with aquatic aliens."

"Not so fast, Mac. This one world wasn't destroyed by the Dhryn. Think what that means."

"You think the inhabitants of Chasm 232 had some way to protect themselves. There's an easier explanation, Em," she frowned. "That world could have been home to—to *Them*—and discarded when they were finished with it."

"*They* abandoned orbiting rock before humanity stood up." As if uneasy, Emily moved at last, to pull her shawl tighter as the breeze lifted its edge. "It couldn't have been *Theirs*. But it was a world that somehow evaded the Chasm catastrophe. So I studied long-range scans of the rubble, looking for anything to set this place apart from the others. Insufficient. I had Sencor divert a salvage ship to collect samples for their experts to analyze. You should have been there when the first results came in, confirming my remote dating, showing refined materials. It was quite a thrill."

Given her intense lack of interest toward anything off-Earth in those days, Mac sincerely doubted that, but made a noncommittal noise to be polite.

Emily continued. "We found abundant evidence the world in Chasm 232 had supported a technologically advanced civilization during the same time span as the others. Perhaps they'd died with their world. But what if they hadn't? There was legend, other hints. So if these were the Survivors, the question became: how could they have escaped? *They* controlled the transects; the Dhryn attacked through the gates." Her hand lifted skyward. "Leaving sublight. Maybe they had ships from a time of exploration before the transects; maybe they were warned to build them. What matters, Mac, is where they could have gone. Chasm 232 doesn't have many neighbors. At one-tenth light, we're talking almost a thousand years to the nearest world suited to you or me. Multigeneration ship—or stasis."

A raindrop hit her nose. Mac looked up in reflex and another hit her in the eye. She pulled her sweater over her head, feeling nostalgic.

"Long trip," she commented.

"If you need our kind of planet. But there's something closer. Much closer. Within a couple of centuries. A system with a similar star, a planet of the right mass. But with no signs of civilization or technology. On land, that is. But it has oceans. Lovely, deep, wide oceans."

"You don't have to be aquatic to live underwater," Mac observed. "We do it."

"For three thousand years?"

"There's that." As hypotheses went, Mac had heard flimsier ones. *Not much flimsier.*

Meanwhile, she discovered she could tuck a remarkable amount of herself inside her sweater. *Human Becomes Sheep—had to be in some brochure.* "I take it your buddies at Sencor checked it out?"

"Mac, were you not listening to a—"

"Using a scan from their ship in the Chasm," Mac interrupted.

"What did you think I meant?" she asked innocently. "That they'd closed their eyes and clicked their heels? 'Poof' go the light-years?"

"Nothing," Emily said with exasperation, "from you would surprise me."

The familiar complaint was oddly comforting. Mac grinned to herself. "I presume your next step is to ask Anchen for a transect-initiating probe."

"*Aie!* Mackenzie Connor. Okay, that surprised me. When did you start caring about transect technology?"

The night you disappeared from Base, Mac almost said. She settled for: "When I started using it."

"You're right. We need to send a probe. Assuming there's a civilization there, and it's still space-capable, they can use the probe's instructions to build a transect gate on their end. When they do, we'll be connected. They'll know what happened. Just think of the possibilities." The satisfied warmth in Emily's voice only made what Mac had to say harder.

"I know how I'd react to a transect opening in my system," she began cautiously. "Not well."

"Bah. The Sinzi have made successful first contact with thousands of species. They'll be able to reassure the Survivors."

So much for caution. Mac bristled. "Reassure them about what? It's not as if we can stop the Dhryn from using the transects."

"It's worth the risk. If there's a chance the Survivors can help us—"

"Then the Ro will destroy their new home, too. Do you want to find more victims for them to slaughter?" Mac regretted the words the moment they left her lips, but didn't apologize. *The truth didn't come in an easier format.* "The Ro don't need gates. If your Survivors exist and have been left in peace until now, it's only because the Ro haven't considered them a threat."

Unless they were discovered—by someone or something else first. "That's why the Ro noticed you in the first place, isn't it, Emily?" Mac breathed. "You were looking for what they didn't want found."

Instead of answering, Emily said, very quietly, "It began with fear. It became obsession."

The rain chose that moment to go from teasing random drops

to a steady, if light downpour. "Emily—" Mac's fingers tightened their hold on her sweater, "—you said that already."

"I know. It's the truth, Mac. You see, the day came when I received data from a new, unnamed source. Out of the blue. Wonderful, fresh information. Different from anything I'd seen before—than anyone had seen—about the technologies of that world in Chasm 232, about the planet itself. And because of my obsession, I kept it to myself."

The trap the Ro had set for her. "Why, Em?" Mac asked, frustrated. "You must have realized something was wrong."

"It didn't matter. What mattered—" a swift, indrawn breath before Emily rushed on: "Mac, it wasn't enough to find the answer. I had to find it first. Do you understand? I'd worked on this all my adult life. To see the end—a discovery of such magnitude, just waiting? Oh, Mac, I could taste it. It was mine. My work, my life, my family—my friends? Nothing compared to being the one to do it—to solve the greatest riddle of our time."

Mac stood, stretched, and walked to the river's edge, cautious of the footing in her tied-together sandals, leaving Emily behind.

"Mac? Don't you understand?"

That word again.

She didn't turn, instead stooped to feel for a pebble to throw at the dark water, adding its sound to the faint drone of the rain. *Plonk.* "No," she said at last. "I don't. Discovery is a process, Emily. Looking for questions that can be answered; using those answers to choose new questions." Another pebble. She thought of Little Misty Lake and put muscle into the throw. *Plink PLONK.* "There's no end to it. There's no first. And certainly no 'mine.' You forgot that."

"And look what it got me?" Soft, bitter.

"I didn't say that—"

"You don't have to—I'm reminded every time I look in a mirror. Or at you. So is everyone else." Footsteps, then another rock followed hers into the dark. *Plonk.*

Was that what this was about? "No one doubts you, Em," Mac said firmly.

"You do. And we're staying here, rain or no rain, until you hear me."

"I've been listening," Mac pointed out. *Plonk* went her next toss. "You were hunting the Survivors, you received information from a mysterious source . . . then what?"

"Then a man—a Human—approached me. Gordon Stanislaus. He claimed to have sent me the data, to have more to offer. You know him as Otto Rkeia."

"The man killed under Pod Six," Mac breathed, turning to try and see Emily's face. But all she could discern was a darker shadow, taller and still. "Glued thirty meters down to a pod anchor. Ministry called it 'death by misadventure.' "

"They told me at the consulate," Emily said. "No surprise. *They* don't like to leave loose ends. Poor Gord—Otto. He was . . . within any field, Mac, there are those who warn of the consequences of success. You know the type. Whistle-blowers. Cassandras. That was Otto."

"Rkeia was a criminal," Mac objected. "Nik told me."

"Was he?" She could make out Emily's shrug. "We didn't talk about our day jobs."

"Emily Mamani!"

"It's raining, Mac. Can we move past your irrelevant morals?"

When Mac didn't bother to reply, Emily went on: "Otto told me he feared the Survivors were responsible for the Chasm. He wanted to find them, all right, but in order to prevent the same thing happening to us."

"Smart man," Mac muttered under her breath. *For a crook.* Louder, to be heard over rain and river: "But you didn't buy it."

"Not at first," Emily admitted. "The technology in Chasm 232 was no more advanced than the rest; there was no reason to assume they could have devastated the other worlds. Now we know it was the Dhryn. But then—what evidence Otto could offer was compelling. Details about the order in which the destruction had advanced across other systems, how quickly it had occurred. I checked everything I could—the data was solid, Mac. I still didn't believe the inhabitants of Chasm 232 were anything more than fugitives, but Otto did convince me whatever—or whoever—had destroyed the Chasm worlds so long ago might still exist."

Emily spoke more slowly, deliberately, as if this was something Mac had to hear, but hard to say. "That's when my obsession became—it became my mission. I was in a position to track down that threat; I would. Suddenly, secrecy wasn't about being first with a discovery, Mac. It was about staying out of sight of an enemy I couldn't be sure existed. About protecting those around me. And," a low humorless laugh, "there remained the very real possibility I was chasing my own imagination in steadily decreasing circles."

"But you weren't," Mac acknowledged, heart in her throat. "Emily, the Ro might have killed you then and there!"

"*They* prefer to manipulate." For a wonder, Emily sounded calm, as if they now discussed lab results. "And I made it easy, Mac. Once convinced I could be trusted, Otto revealed his secret. Far from fearing the Survivors, he claimed to be working with their descendants, that they'd been guarding against the true threat from their hiding place. Oh, I swallowed every word. After all, poor Otto believed it, too. I insisted on meeting them. He told me it was impossible—but they could communicate directly with me, if I was willing. The first . . . the first implant . . . Otto told me it was a translator. From the moment I let it be put under my sk–skin—" At the break in Emily's otherwise controlled voice, Mac's fingers clenched around the cold pebbles in her hand. "From that moment, I felt part of something important, something critical to the survival of every living thing I knew. I gave myself to *Them,* Mac, body and soul. There wasn't room for doubt. There wasn't room for anything but the mission. I was so . . . sure." A long pause.

Mac waited without moving. The rain softened to a mist she blinked from her eyelashes, tasted with her tongue. All the while, her heart hammered in her chest. *Gods, Emily . . .*

"Then," Emily said at last, "I found myself climbing rocks and sleeping in tents with the original woman of doubt. You questioned everything: yourself, your ideas, everyone else's ideas—everything, it seemed, but me. Me, you absorbed into your life as if I'd always been there. What were you thinking?"

"What was there to think about?" Mac shrugged and threw another pebble. *Plonk.* "You're good with salmon dynamics. A bit flighty, maybe, but I could put up with that."

"Flighty?" Emily choked on the word. "I was trying to save the universe and you made me count fish!"

Her outrage was so thoroughly "Emily," Mac had to smile. "You made me go dancing," she countered.

"You made me sleep on rocks."

"You got me thrown out of *Carly's Pig and Whistle*. Twice."

"Three times." Emily reached out and tugged Mac's hair. A pause that, for the first time in forever, felt comfortable. Then: "I didn't know *They'd* attack Base, Mac. I swear I didn't. *They* warned the disappearances along the Naralax Transect marked an imminent threat . . . *They* claimed the Dhryn had come from the Chasm, even as Kanaci's group confirmed finding the Dhryn home world. *They* kept insisting the Dhryn—who seemed harmless enough—were connected. There was growing pressure to spy on any Dhryn in reach. A desperate need to somehow penetrate the Dhryn home world. It was confused, unclear. Urgent. That, above all."

Words tumbled from Emily, more and more quickly. "When Brymn first mentioned your work, Otto and I, the others, we had to act. We knew it. *They*—always difficult to hold an idea—clearly Brymn's interest in your work was something *They* wanted to understand. We had to learn about you; I was the right choice. Brymn's coming to meet you couldn't have been better timed. Don't you see? I was already here. And once the IU and the Ministry forced your hand, Mac, everything fell into place. But—Mac, the plan was to lure you offworld in search of me, to draw you and Brymn to Haven, not chase you there." Emily faltered. "I'd never have done anything to hurt you or anyone else. It should have worked—"

"Should have?" Something inside Mac snapped. "You made me believe you'd been kidnapped!" she said fiercely. "I had to go through your room, see the blood on the walls. I sent divers looking for your body! I had to call your sister, Emily. Do you hear me?"

"I'm sorry—"

"Sorry?" Mac's harsh voice sounded strange to herself. "I had to find out from a stranger—a spy!—that you'd been—damn it, Emily, that you'd been lying to me from the start."

"Mac—"

Abruptly spent, she rubbed her hand over her eyes. "Shut up, Em."

Stiffly. "So that's it? You've made up your mind, and nothing I can—"

"I understand," Mac interrupted wearily.

A tiny gasp. *Just as well they couldn't see each other's faces.* "You . . . do?"

Mac nodded. "You got yourself into this by being who you are. And who you are . . . well, it's pretty much who I thought you were. I get it." *And she did, finally,* she thought with a relief that made her tremble. She'd been right to believe in Emily.

"You realize that made no sense whatsoever, Mackenzie Connor."

It would with more beer. Aloud: "Anyone else would have passed the mess to the authorities. Anyone else would have realized she couldn't save the universe by herself." Mac found herself close to smiling. *Odd, given the tears running down her cheeks.* "If you cared less and thought more, you wouldn't be Emily."

"Don't you dare make me into some damn hero," her friend snapped. "It was the worst mistake of my life."

Typical Emily, Mac thought. *Contrary.* "Your motives—"

"Motives mean nothing. *They* left me to die, so now I'm the noble victim to beings who fear *Them.*" *Plonk.* "But so far as others are concerned, I helped *Them* almost succeed in killing the Progenitors on Haven. You know who loves me for that." *Plonk.* "Both factions at me nonstop, trying to suck me into their scheme of things . . . I'm sick of being told I had the right motives, Mac. I was arrogant. There's no prize for that."

Mac understood Emily's frustration. There'd been no stopping the interrogations, the tests, the visits from anyone with clearance from the IU. How could there be? Emily Mamani was the only survivor. The rest of the Ro's informants? They'd found their ruined bodies throughout Sol System—seven, so far. When the Ro had withdrawn their technology from the hulls of retreating Dhryn ships, opening them to vacuum, that same call had ripped the Ro's devices from the flesh of their—*what did you call someone who'd risked their lives to become eyes and ears for the alien?*

A hero, Mac decided. "Motives count with me," she assured Emily.

Plonk. "Stubborn. And a fool."

"I prefer to think of myself as internally consistent." Mac squatted to find more pebbles, using her nonflesh hand. The local spiders were opinionated.

"You're that," Emily said quietly, a hint of a quiver in her voice.

Mac stood with her handful and tossed the largest. *Pluuush.* "How's the ratio so far?" she asked. *In how much danger were they all?*

"I've lost track." A little too flippant.

Mac rolled the small, hard stones around in her palm. "You mean the idiot faction is growing."

Plonk. "You don't let me call them names," Emily protested mildly.

"That's because you'd do it to their faces—or whatever," Mac countered. "Things are tense enough."

"They aren't going to get better."

"They will, Em. We'll find evidence—proof that will convince even the idiots of the Ro's real intentions." *Evidence that couldn't be reinterpreted to suit species' self-interest,* Mac vowed to herself.

"It's not as though I've been any help." *SPLASH!* Emily must have tossed in a minor boulder.

"You could kill something that way," Mac chided gently. This land was full of odd birds wandering where an outsider wouldn't expect them.

"Haven't you noticed? Life's going cheap these days."

The despair in the faceless voice was too familiar. Mac let the rest of her pebbles fall to the ground. "We really need more beer," she concluded. Suiting action to words, she turned from the river and rolling pasture, squinting to pick out the path back to town from the shadows.

Emily took her arm, the grip tighter than natural. *Then again,* Mac thought, *the arm she gripped wasn't natural either.* "I've tried to remember, Mac," low, urgent. "I swear I have."

"I know." Mac covered the hand with her own. "We both heard Noad. Your mind may find a way. Or not. That's the way of it, Em. It's not your fault."

"It's not that I don't have any memories. I have too many. Being here, in the dark. This empty, open place. My pulse the loudest sound. It feels—" Emily fell silent. Mac held her breath, hoping for more, for anything, but Emily only sighed: "—familiar. A place I've never been before." She gave a short, hard laugh. "Little good that does."

"It's a start. Now, about that beer." Mac hesitated, squinting again. "Ah, Em?"

A tug on her hair. "This way."

"Whatever you do, don't use the washroom," Mac advised, slipping into her seat in the booth. "Trust me."

Emily grinned. "That bad?"

There was something terminally sticky on the soles of her sandals—clearly destined to be another set of footwear that would not survive a night out with Em. She abandoned them and tucked her bare feet underneath the curl of her legs on the bench. "Proves the Grimnoii were here first," she commented. Cider in, much worse out. *You'd think,* Mac sighed to herself, *they'd learn not to drink the stuff.*

Em wrinkled her nose. "Who'll foot the bill for cleanup?"

"The consulate, I'm sure. The bartender doesn't look worried."

"Probably has his own toilet. What say we find out where?"

Mac laughed at the eager look on Em's face. "Give him a couple of minutes first. You've got the poor man in a sweat."

The other woman nibbled the fingertip of her glove, eyes bright with mischief. "Like you make your poor Nikolai sweat, *si?*"

Mac arched one eyebrow. "For me to know, Dr. Mamani, and you to hypothesize."

"Bravo."

The Feisty Weka was larger and livelier than the *Nest,* although its tropical resort motif seemed a little embarrassed. The fake palms with their stuffed parrots were pushed into dark corners and the pineapple-printed tablecloths were covered with obscure local sayings in indelible ink Mac assumed were rude, given how much Emily had enjoyed them.

It was larger, livelier, and possessed not only these comfortable private booths, with soft benches, but an actual dance floor. Or Mac guessed that was the function of the area where people held their beer in their hands rather than sitting down at a table. Emily's face had lit up like one of the lanterns at the doorway. They'd finally found where all those not tending sheep were spending Saturday night.

Mac studied a cartoonish drawing of a small bird running off with a bag, wondering why it was considered funny.

"Can I interest you lovely ladies in a dance?" The voice was deep and smooth.

And male. Mac looked up and scowled; Emily beamed. Mac's "No, thanks" was overruled by Em's warm: "And here I thought I'd sit here all night."

"Not in Southland. We take care of our guests."

There was a friendly smile to match the voice. A perfectly normal Human male body to match the smile. *Okay,* Mac admitted, a tall, blond, ruggedly handsome Human male, wearing, of course, some kind of ruggedly handsome clothing that emphasized all the right bits.

Mac scowled harder.

"Em," she hissed under her breath. "Don't you dare."

Tossing aside her shawl, Emily smiled as she stood, hips already finding the beat of the music Mac only now noticed coming from the dance floor. Her creamy bare shoulders tipped into the arm-covering black silk of her gloves, an exotic look for a New Zealand pub; Mr. Ruggedly's eyes were about to pop. "C'mon, Mac," Emily said, leaning over the table to smile at her. "You know you're thinking what I'm thinking. Someone this good-looking must have a friend."

Mac muttered something hopefully incomprehensible under her breath. "Broken sandals," she confessed brightly, trying for a rueful smile. *Technically also permanently stuck to the floor, but details weren't essential.* "You go. I'll order another round."

They abandoned her without argument, as she'd expected. Once Emily and Mr. Ruggedly were safely absorbed into the mass pretending to dance, Mac let her forehead drop to the table, hiding a yawn. *She usually caught a nap during their nights out.* She turned her head to press her cheek against her glass, one eye peering through amber at the couple. Emily was smiling. He must be a good dancer. Whoever he was.

The pattern of so many Saturday nights. *Why didn't it feel the same?*

Mac watched a bubble struggle toward the surface and knew why. It wasn't learning about Emily's sources, or her poor choice in obsessions.

This time, she was the one with a secret.

Why was the Origins Team still on Earth? Because she'd refused to let them leave with the rest. Those in charge wanted Emily close to medical treatment and protection. Then there was the ever-hopeful wait for Emily's brain to process anything useful about no-space and the Ro.

And if Emily had to stay, so would Mac.

Something plaid got in the way of the dance floor, and Mac waved impatiently until it was gone. She spotted Emily in the arms of Mr. Ruggedly and relaxed.

Mac yawned again and sat up, wondering if it was time to order coffee instead.

She smiled at a familiar laugh, loud and abandoned. *Points to Mr. Ruggedly.*

It wasn't only the attractive stranger willing to tango to anything. As realization hit, Mac's smile faded. It was this thoroughly Human place bringing the old Emily back, from the stale air to the seats worn comfortable by the personal attention of generations of posteriors shaped like theirs. *Okay, some several sizes larger,* Mac corrected absently, shifting on the lumpy bench. Emily had needed—

"Watchit!"

The outcry was a signal for pandemonium to break loose. Mac snatched her beer glass to safety as a body, in plaid, landed on the table in front of her. She blinked as Mr. Plaid scrambled to his feet, teeth bared in a wild grin and shouting something highly improbable about someone else's mother. He vanished into the mêlée.

For that's what now filled the pub as far as Mac could see. Beer in hand, she climbed to stand on the bench, wrapping her other arm around the post behind it in case Mr. Plaid flew her way again. *Or someone else.* She tried to spot Emily in the press of bodies.

As barroom brawls went, this was starting out an orderly affair. Everyone seemed happily paired with a sparring partner of equal gusto, and the furniture was staying on the floor. Mind you, Mac hadn't bothered to check if the chairs and tables were bolted down as a precaution. No sign of what had started it. *There rarely was.*

As a precaution, she finished her beer in three quick gulps and, gently, rolled the empty glass under the table where it could keep her sandals company and not become a weapon if things turned nasty. She lurched over the table to grab Emily's shawl, a move involving a somewhat precarious dance with one foot on the table and the other planted firmly in sagging upholstery.

With a crow of success, Mac stood upright on the bench again, absently rolling her prize into a tube to tie snugly around her waist. She craned her neck.

There! Mac caught sight of glossy black hair and shouted: "Em! Over here!"

Somehow, Emily heard. She waved her arm, pointing at the door. Mac nodded and grinned. She considered the pair currently wrestling beside her table, albeit with little success and significant grunting, and chose to swing her legs over the back of the bench, dropping into the next booth.

Which wasn't empty.

" 'Just a quiet evening out,' " Sing-li Jones quoted mildly.

Mac almost fell, keeping herself upright only by quickly sitting on the narrow rail dividing the booths. "This," she informed him with what dignity she had left, gesturing at the brawl, "is not our fault." The belch that punctuated the last word wasn't her fault either. *Chugging beer did it every time.*

The Ministry agent was slouched comfortably in the shadowed corner, for all the world like someone too drunk to care about the fight. He coughed a couple of times before saying: "I see."

"And I'm not drunk," she informed him. Mac eyed the half full glass in front of Sing-li. "Yet," she clarified. *A shame, that.* She could feel the weight of responsibility sliding back, as inevitable as the morning after. Despite being perched on the back of a bar bench, surrounded by the good-natured thump and crash of Humans being themselves, her mind helplessly began to ticktock through means to avoid tomorrow's meetings while setting priorities for the day's research.

"You've lost your shoes."

What else was new? Mac wiggled her bare toes, eyes searching the dark room for the door and Emily. Odd the bartender hadn't upped the lights to illuminate the fight. "Emily's heading for the exit," she said, abruptly uneasy. Sliding down to the bench, Mac scooted sideways to the edge of the table, preparing to launch herself into the crowd.

"Wait." Gone was the slouching, casual Sing-li, replaced by the version she knew better—tough, capable, and determined above all else that if he couldn't keep Mac out of trouble, he'd at least get there first.

On the scale of recent troubles, a bar fight barely registered so far as she was concerned, but Mac let the man do his job. Bare feet were a disadvantage. Not that sandals would have been much better. *Next trip out? Solid sensible boots,* she decided.

Sing-li was a good size by most Human standards, although Mac noticed *The Feisty Weka* was overly endowed with large men. Very large, annoyed men. *Maybe being annoyed only made them seem larger,* she thought hopefully, sticking close to Sing-li as he made his way after Emily. She winced as the Ministry agent took a low blow, then winced again as the person who'd struck him mysteriously faded to the floor with a shocked look on his face. "That's hardly fair," she hissed to his back.

Fair or not, her companion cleared their path. Mac stayed up on the balls of her feet as much as possible, grimacing as she stepped on, or in, who knew what. *Hopefully not glass,* she told herself, firmly banishing thoughts of Grimnoii and their reaction to cider. *Ugh. Slimy.*

The wide door was open to the night, although stuffed with patrons enjoying the spectacle from its safer perspective. Sing-li lowered his shoulder as if to ram his way through, but the others parted amicably, pushing back into the doorway the instant Mac squeezed through.

"Well, that was fun—" she began cheerfully, looking around for Emily.

The road and sidewalk were deserted, except for a trio supporting each other as they stumbled away.

"Em?" Mac's eyes widened. "Sing-li!"

"You stay here. Right here." Sing-li's tone brooked no argument.

He didn't wait for her nod as he strode off, his wrist to his mouth as he gave orders, doubtless bringing others into the hunt. Mac wrapped her arms around her waist and waited, standing within the overlapping circles of light at the entrance to the *Weka*. The sporadic bedlam from within made the outside world colder and too quiet.

No. No. No. Mac realized she was shaking her head repeatedly and stopped. She did her best not to think either, knowing she'd only blame herself for bringing Emily out too soon, which meant assuming the worst. And the worst meant . . .

No.

A few people passed her where she stood, on their way into the *Weka*, where the sounds of brawling had been replaced by music, loud and danceable. *Must be a typical Saturday night here,* Mac decided. An older woman hesitated, giving her a searching look. Mac did her best to look fascinated by the street.

"Are you all right?"

Mac the Transparent, Em called her.

"Waiting for a ride," she said, hoping to forestall any questions.

As if on cue, Sing-li was back. He took her elbow, offering the other woman a smile. "And the wait's over," he announced with just the right mix of chagrin and cheer. "I've found the skim. You were right, dear, I'd parked it down that alley. Good night." This to the woman, who hadn't left, still not convinced about Mac's situation.

Mac forced a smile. "Thank you," she said, meaning it. "But I'm really all right. Have a nice evening—just stay out of the washroom."

The woman rolled her eyes, relaxing. "Again? Appreciate the tip." She went into the bar.

Sing-li bent to put his lips to Mac's ear. "I found her. Steady—" This with concern as she sagged, his grip firm on her arm in support. "She's okay, Mac. C'mon."

He led Mac into the shadows along one side of the building, around a corner to where overgrown shrubbery formed an arbor-like opening. Seeing two silhouettes within that shelter, Mac stopped. "Wait," she whispered. "It's Mr. Ruggedly."

"Who?"

Mac could feel the blush heating her cheeks and was once more grateful for the dark. "We should probably leave them be," she suggested. "For a while."

"You've got to be kidding," he protested.

She snorted, albeit quietly. "And you don't know Emily Mamani."

"No wonder she gets along with Fourteen."

Mac nodded. "Don't I—Wait." *Something was wrong.*

One of the figures had broken away, now coming toward them: the taller one, walking quickly as if about to break into a run. *Mr. Ruggedly?*

He didn't appear to see them, so Sing-li stepped in front of Mac at the last minute, preventing a collision. "Out of my way!" the man ordered, despite being startled. He tried to get past; the Ministry agent persuaded him otherwise. *Amazing,* Mac thought distractedly, *what an ability to loom intimidatingly could do, even in dim light.*

"We're Emily's friends," she said with haste. "We've been looking for her."

"Good. I was coming to find you." The relief in his voice sent an alarm through Mac. "Something's—something's wrong with her. It's nothing I did, I swear—"

Mac pushed by both men, hurrying to the unmoving form in the shadows. Sing-li's reassuring: "We'll take care of her," as he dealt with Mr. Ruggedly barely registered.

Emily was like a statue, staring at her gloved hands, their fingers outstretched and rigid before her face.

"—I tell them," she was saying. "They missed one. This isn't right."

Mac caught her friend's hands in hers. Emily resisted, making a fretful sound, but Mac held on until the other woman was still. "Time to go, Em," she said then, keeping her voice light with an effort, aware of Sing-li as a silent, distressed shadow at her side.

Making another of those lightning recoveries, Emily tugged her hands free and laughed. "We can't go home," she asserted, whirling in place. Her skirt brushed Mac's legs. "The dancing's started again. C'mon, Mac. Night's young!"

Suddenly, everything about this night and Emily crystallized in

Mac's mind. She considered the result. *Could it really be that simple?* she asked herself with wonder.

First, to get Emily away from *The Feisty Weka*. "Mr. Jones insists," she claimed, knowing Sing-li would have already done so, if he'd thought it would work.

Next?

It remained to be seen if "simple" translated into Sinzi.

- CONTACT -

"**I**T'S A GHOST."

Meme spread his aural folds, a dismissive display to imply that no matter how much of his Human scan-tech's verbal utterances he collected to process, they would never make sense. His predecessor had failed to convince Meme such species-specific gestures were not comprehended by the aliens.

Meme was sure this lack of comprehension had more to do with his predecessor's unusually small aural folds. During the entire change of command ceremony, he'd needed all of his self-discipline not to stare.

Meme's own aural folds were magnificently broad, their skin kept well-oiled and supple. He had brought—

"Or maybe it's not."

The Human's strident voice intruded on Meme's pleasantly semidormant state. Worse, she—the matter of the creature's gender having been settled contrary to expectation, costing a fair sum in wagers—did not appear to have noticed Meme's display. *Nothing for it,* the Ar sighed, *but to actually pay attention.* "What are you mumbling about, Scan-tech?"

"Oh. You're awake?" The Human sat straighter and appeared confused. "Sorry, Captain. I've been following a tick in the aft sensor. Might be something."

"Define 'something.' "

"A ship, sir. Shadowing us."

"No. There is no 'something.' No ship." Meme closed his aural folds. *Annoying Human.* Their patrol area was days out from the transect gate—well beyond the orbit of what remained of the Dhryn world. Nice and safe and boring. No one and nothing came here. As if anything could get past the eager clusters of ships farther in.

Peaceful. Just the way he liked it.

"Captain?" Merciful silence. Then: "You can't just ignore this!"

He certainly could.

What Meme couldn't ignore was the shocking pain of his left aural fold being yanked open. "Captain! We must investigate any intrusion!"

Eyes watering, mouth working, Meme gestured helplessly at his tormentor.

She released his fold and Meme shuddered with relief. But the Human wasn't done. She leaned forward until her hideous eyeballs almost touched his. "Or should I contact the Trisulian?"

Meme shuddered. At last count, there were fifteen hundred and sixty-four ships orbiting Haven's sun, courtesy of the anxious governments of systems along the Naralax. Most were like this, quick, sensor-laden scouts capable of squealing a near-light com signal to the packet ships waiting by the gate, crewed by those willing to sit in the darkness and wait.

The Trisulian warship was the exception, a bristling mass of threat that gave the Ar hives to even contemplate. *As for her grim captain?* "Let's not contact them unless we're sure," he pleaded, well versed in the reckless nature of females.

The Human gave him one final glare, then returned to her station. Meme took several calming breaths as he fingered his abused fold. Obviously Human females were no more stable than Trisulian. He could only hope she was capable. The Ar weren't a wealthy or adventurous race. When the call had come for ships to watch Haven, the Sinzi-ra of the IU consulate on Arer had thoughtfully hired this Human ship and its crew, asking only that the Ar provide a volunteer of their species to captain.

Meme was the fourth Ar to so serve, while the three Human crew remained unchanged. *It was as if they didn't need a captain at all.*

"Gotcha," the scan-tech announced. "Transferring to the bridge monitor. And yours, Captain."

Meme's aural folds clenched in dread at the sight of the large ship floating almost in his lap. He drew up his toes and began crooning to himself, the sound echoing inside his skull and nicely drowning out any Human voice.

He'd underestimated the decibels available in a Human's lungs. "IT'S DEAD!"

Meme paused in his croon, letting his folds unfurl slightly. "You're sure?"

"Scans read null," the scan-tech confirmed at a more reasonable volume. "Relax, Captain. Munesh is going to squeal a pulse about our claim while I collect as much data as possible."

" 'Claim?' " Meme frowned.

"Sorry." The Human turned an interesting pink hue. "Old habit. We operated a salvage operation—before the Dhryn. I meant, Munesh is notifying the other ships."

Meme kept his toes close, away from the black hulk slowly spinning in front of him. "Is this—is it one of theirs?"

The Human pressed a control, studied the result, then stroked another. With that, a placid voice began to speak in Instella, the common tongue.

"This is an automated distress call from the freighter *Uosanah,* registered out of Cryssin Colony. Any ship receiving this message is required to render assistance under the provisions of the Interspecies Union. This is an automated distress call from the freighter *Uosanah,* registered out of Cryssin Colony. Any ship receiving this message is required to render assistance under the provisions of the Interspecies Union. This is—"

The Human lifted her hand from the control, silencing the voice, and turned to look at Meme. "Cryssin was a Dhryn colony. If this ship came to join the other Dhryn, why is it still here?"

"Ships break down all the time," Meme replied with the innocent conviction of someone who had no idea how his oil warmer worked. "Probably junk they left behind."

She shrugged. "The experts'll check the logs."

Feeling this settled matters nicely, Meme stretched out his toes and stood, edging around the display the Human had left wheeling in front of his chair. It wasn't easy. The bridge was cramped compared to where the navigator/pilot and com-tech worked. Meme often wondered why the captain's chair was here instead of there. *Likely a Human design flaw.* The nearby galley, however, was most ample and their success deserved a celebration.

"Another contact, Captain," the scan-tech said, interrupting Meme's happy consideration of appropriate treats.

"One of the others, come to see our prize," he guessed, flaring his folds triumphantly. "Who is it?" If it was Me'o, the Cey, there was a distinct possibility of young nerbly cheese. Its nip would go very well with—

"Not ours. Another drifter. Freighter. Dead like the first."

The Ar considered two an alarming number, fraught as it was with change. And unresolvable arguments. *Not that he'd lured a female into argument yet, but . . .* "Are you sure?" Meme demanded. "Two? Check again."

She did, then gave him a stranger look than usual. "You aren't going to believe this," she said. "I don't believe this."

Meme couldn't imagine what a Human would find unbelievable—he had to ask. "What don't you believe?"

"You're right. There aren't two."

His aural folds spread with pride. "You see—"

"Captain. There must be dozens, maybe more, along this vector." She put her hands flat on the console, then stood, turning to face him.

"We're in a Dhryn graveyard."

- 3 -

PROPOSAL AND PROMISE

THE INTERSPECIES CONSULATE for Sol System sat on a coast where mountains plunged into abyssal depths, part of a system of fjords that rivaled any on Earth for breathtaking beauty, in a country so remote from any other on Earth its residents were like a model for humanity within the IU itself: vaguely interested in what went on "outside," but believing themselves both isolated and self-contained.

None of them had a right to believe any such thing, Mac fumed to herself, for once oblivious to the view from her ocean-side terrace.

She laid her hand on the cool white roughness of the outer wall. "Request." The air might not hear, but a touch on any wall, plus the word in Instella, gained the attention of the hordes who serviced the consulate. "I need to see the Sinzi-ra. Immediately."

Mac strode through the doors to her quarters, into the bedroom, to be exact, unsurprised to find a member of the staff already waiting. She was beginning to suspect they had their own, equally discreet, doors and hallways. The staff, a female humanoid with the characteristic brush of red-brown hair shaved into elaborate whorls over her scalp, bowed slightly. Her uniform, like those of her fellows, was the same earthy tone as her hair, a change from the bright yellow they'd worn when Mac first arrived.

Sinzi seemed incapable of offering knowing offense to any visitor, even their common enemy, the Dhryn.

There had been other changes, less obvious. The consulate had swarmed with alien construction workers for a time after the Ro were found to be misusing the Sinzi-ra's fish tank. Guests were welcome. Uninvited ones were not. Mac didn't know the details; she accepted Sing-li's assurance she could sleep at night.

Most nights.

"The Sinzi-ra has been informed," staff announced calmly. "She will attend you later this afternoon, Dr. Connor."

By which time she'd have lost her nerve. Mac shook her head. "Is Anchen in her office?"

"The Sinzi-ra does not have an office, Dr. Connor."

Taken aback, Mac realized she should have known. The Sinzi had always come to her, or to where she worked. More formal meetings were in the Atrium or the larger room down the hall. "Then where is she? Right now."

"The Sinzi-ra is in her quarters, Dr. Connor."

Good. She knew where those were. "Thanks," said Mac, heading for the door.

The staff's eyes widened in an alarm response they shared. "Dr. Connor—where are you going? There are protocols."

Mac smiled over her shoulder. "I'm sure there are. Remind me on the way."

The consular staff knew Mac by now, well enough the other being didn't attempt to argue.

Her sigh, however, was almost Human.

The Sinzi-ra occupied a suite of rooms almost identical to Mac's. Glazed French doors from the hall opened into a large bedroom. There was a similar set of doors, clear this time, to a terrace overlooking the sound and ocean beyond. To the left, as Mac entered, was the archway leading into what she thought of as a sitting room. Mac's version was now distinctly her office, complete with anything that could be carried from Pod Three—her friends were literal sorts. The Sinzi's was white on white, simplicity itself, four jelly-chairs facing a white stone table, deep creamy sand on the floor, white walls windowed to the sky beyond.

The perfect frame for complexity. Mac stopped so quickly the unhappy staff behind her almost ran into her back.

The Sinzi-ra was busy.

Her left hand—or rather the trio of meter-long fingers that constituted the Sinzi equivalent—was adding blue and clear gems to a circular mosaic on an easel, the result scintillating like cold fire. Her right hand, meanwhile, worked some type of keypad. The faint outlines of three workscreens flickered in front of her face, each angled to favor a different segment of her eyes. Not that Mac's Human eyes could make out details. The Sinzi—and their servants—had a broader spectrum available to their sight.

To top it off, Anchen was humming in a minor key.

Normally, Mac would have been fascinated. The alien rarely gave any indication of the distinct individual minds, six in number, inhabiting her willowy form. Only the changing attention of her complex, compound eyes hinted at how many were participating in a conversation. Anchen: Atcho, the precise and careful administrator for the consulate; Noad, the curious physician, interested in all things alien, particularly the mind; Casmii, who preferred the background, not least on the IU Judicial Council; Hone, youngest or most recent, as such minds went, but already a notable transect engineer; Econa and Nifa, scientists who currently shared a passion for Earth, the former a gemologist, the latter a cultural historian, studying, to Mac's dismay when she'd heard, the incidence of familial homicide among Humans, with a side interest in cannibalism between neighbors.

You tidy the house for company, and they trip over the dirty laundry every time.

"The Sinzi-ra must compose her selves," said a quiet voice from behind. "Please do not speak, Dr. Connor, until she addresses you by name."

Mac nodded. She could use some composure. It was one thing to charge forward, sure she was right.

Quite another to be reminded who she had to convince.

"Feel free to enjoy the Sinzi-ra's collection while you wait, Dr. Connor." With this, the staff touched a portion of the plain white wall.

"What col—" Mac started to ask, then closed her mouth as every wall turned dark blue, honeycombed with small, bright openings. She stepped closer.

The openings were cubbyholes, each containing one object suspended in its midst, gently lit from every side. As Mac looked into the nearest cubby, the object inside seemed to jump at her. In reflex, she stumbled back a step, shoe filling with sand, then realized it was an illusion.

Entranced, Mac experimented. She found if she looked directly at any one object, it would become enlarged until she looked elsewhere. *A technology well-suited to the Sinzi's multipart eye,* she decided. Personally, she found it disconcerting to have item after item appear to launch itself toward her face.

It didn't help that the items were hardly art. A mug advertising a pastry shop. A crumpled snakeskin. A nondescript coin. A purple alligator with a snow globe stomach. A pebble. A pink kazoo. The entire room was walled in an eclectic array of Human trinkets, souvenirs, and odd devices. There was no apparent order. A studded cat collar was displayed beside a vial of sand. A ticket stub from a museum accompanied a package of candy.

Mac winced involuntarily as a miniature Human head in a bottle—hopefully a replica—invaded her personal space. She quickly stared at a section of harmless dark blue wall.

"My dear Mac," Anchen greeted her, coming to stand at Mac's side. "I apologize for being preoccupied." Her fingertips played with a sapphire and Mac spared an instant to wonder which personality might still be preoccupied. Her guess was Econa, the gemologist. "What do you think, Mac?"

She started. "About what?"

"About my collection."

"I've never seen junk treated so well," Mac admitted, then winced for the second time. *Tact. She needed lessons.*

"Junk?" Anchen's fingers rippled in a laugh, their coating of silver rings tinkling against one another like rain. "One species' junk, Mac, is another's treasure."

Really? Mac glanced into another cubby. Its contents, a tiny plastic fish bottle with a dark sauce inside and a bright red nose, obligingly enlarged itself to palm-sized for her inspection. "So long as no one charged you for them, Anchen," she said fervently. "I'd hate to see you cheated."

"Worry not, Mac. These—" Anchen spread her fingers out to

their full length, as if to gather in her collection. "—were gifts. As for their value? To me, objects derived from a particular journey are beyond price."

Mac imagined the regal, distinctive alien wandering a beachfront souvenir shop and grinned. "I didn't think you left the consulate."

"Too rarely," Anchen told her. "These are from Nikolai. Whenever he travels on my behalf, he brings me a treasure. Thus." A languid fingertip indicated a cubby on the next wall. Mac walked over to look inside. A salmon leered back at her. A cross-eyed lime-green rubber salmon, to be precise, with the name of a restaurant glowing down one side.

Probably where he'd taken Mudge to find out more about a certain salmon researcher. Forgetting the illusion, Mac reached out her hand, only to curl her fingers around empty air.

She found herself utterly distracted by the knowledge that Nik had selected each of these things. He'd carried it here, in a pocket, in a pack. He'd explained its place in his past as he gave it to the curious Sinzi.

There was more of Nikolai Piotr Trojanowski in this alien's collection than Mac knew herself.

Not hard. Mac gave herself an inward shake. *Spy, remember? Mysterious past, tendency to consider anything a secret until proved otherwise. Annoying as hell.*

And she missed him, Mac realized with some astonishment, *the way she missed her salmon.*

The walls turned white again. "Forgive me, Mac," the Sinzi-ra said as Mac blinked at the change. "I should not waste your time with indulgences. Please, let us sit and you can tell me why you needed to see me right away." She led the way to the jelly-chairs.

Mac blushed at the polite reminder. "My fault," she explained, taking the chair indicated by the elegant tilt of the Sinzi's tall head. "I was in a hurry. Not that this is urgent."

Anchen settled herself, the pleats of her white gown falling perfectly over her long toes. Her eyes blinked. "A contradiction."

Score another for interspecies communication, Mac sighed inwardly. "Yes," she said, then corrected herself: "No. What I mean is—I need to speak with you. It couldn't wait. It's about Emily."

"You should feel no anxiety, Mac. Noad examined her last night following your return. She was tired, but otherwise fine. Overall, he believes your excursion was beneficial."

"I know." Mac wiggled so she could lean forward, wishing the alien chairs weren't so all-encompassingly comfortable. "Em's downstairs now, working with the others. That's why I'm here. Last night, Emily made me listen—" Mac couldn't subdue the twinge of guilt: *to what her best friend wouldn't listen to before . . .* "I understand now how the Ro involved her. The Survivor Legend. She was obsessed by it. I think she still is."

"The legend is speculation at best, Mac," Anchen said, her small triangular mouth tilted down in mimicry of Human disapproval. "I remain unconvinced this is a worthy line of inquiry, despite Dr. Mamani's persuasion."

Mac shrugged. "One thing I've learned. Living things are messy. They do the unexpected. In some ways, I find it more incredible that the Ro could completely eradicate life from the Chasm worlds than one species might escape them."

"This has become your obsession also?"

"No, Anchen. I've riddles of my own, starting with the Dhryn themselves." Mac took a deep breath. "I agree the Survivors could be wishful thinking—but they've been Emily's focus, her passion, for decades." *With a side interest in salmon,* Mac reminded herself. Kammie would approve of such cross-pollination of fields; poor Case Wilson, the deepwater fisher she'd plopped into a study of tidal ecosystems, would doubtless sympathize with Em.

Anchen's fingers rose to her shoulders, a positioning Mac had learned to read as mild distress. "She has asked for a probe. I have delayed a response. It has not been our way, to attempt to contact an unknown species by giving them the means to reach us in return. The risk is incalculable. And you, Mac, appreciate the moral obligation. Opening a transect gate may well doom any life there."

"You're opening new gates right now." Mac might not like meetings, but she valued the information they—rarely—provided. Such as the continuing expansion of the transect system to new worlds in every direction. The Sinzi might not approve, but they were involved. Every system connected by a transect became part of the Interspecies Union. To be part of it meant hosting an IU consulate—with a Sinzi-ra in residence to oversee the transect gates, because key parts of that crucial technology remained theirs alone.

Mac didn't concern herself with the details. Someone had to have a hand—or finger—on the switch. And the diplomatic, pragmatic, irreproachable Sinzi had the only fingers every other species trusted.

The Sinzi inclined her head in acknowledgment. "It has not been forbidden." The "yet" was implied. "Other species within the IU may expand the transect system from their gates, but they do so only where there is evidence of a thriving civilization capable of space travel."

And good manners. That Sinzi attitude permeated the IU: from the adoption of Instella, the common language used between species, to ships' hatches that matched regardless of origin, to the use of their consulates to indoctrinate visitors on local customs, before those customs could be violated. You could muddy your own backyard, but please wipe your feet before stepping inside the house.

The transects didn't carry war.

Until the Ro had unleashed the Dhryn.

"There is no such evidence from this world of Dr. Mamani's," Anchen finished. "I see no purpose to a probe without it."

"I'm not here to ask for one." Mac sensed confusion and pressed on: "Anchen, Emily's request—it means she wants to help. We couldn't stop her if we tried. I've had her working with my team, but what we're doing—what I'm doing—is a constant reminder of the Ro. Of what they put her through—of her mistake in trusting them. But what if she continued her work on the Survivors? Whether they exist or not—it doesn't matter. So long as she believes . . ." *Was any of this getting through?*

"I see." Two fingertips met, forming an arch. "I have been concerned how best to occupy Dr. Mamani's excellent mind during her recovery. Her Tracer device is part of her search, is it not?" At Mac's nod, she continued, "A novel application of life-form scanning techniques. Quite impressive. As is her incorporation of relevant principles from Myrokynay technology. While we have yet to discover any clues from that technology, the effort continues." The Sinzi dipped her head in a slight bow. "I applaud your wisdom in this matter, Mac. Dr. Mamani may have any resources she requires."

Mac swallowed and sat up straight. "Not here," she said. "At Norcoast."

"Why?"

That was the crux of it. Mac hesitated. It was the right answer for Emily. She knew it. But she couldn't explain why to herself—let alone to another Human. *How could she explain to the Sinzi?* She blurted out the first reason that came to mind: "She'll need an aquatic ecosystem to further develop her Tracer."

Brilliant.

Of course, Anchen lifted a long finger to indicate the view out her window. "Is this an insufficient body of water?"

"No," Mac sighed. "And before you say it, Sinzi-ra, I realize you can provide all the facilities Base has plus some. Emily's original equipment is already here, in my closet." In several pieces. *A minor point.*

"Then why risk moving her?" Anchen's head tilted so the eyes Mac had come to associate with Noad, the physician, were most directly aimed her way. "I have concerns. Both for her recovery, and what she may yet remember."

Mac nodded. "I know. I share them, believe me. But if you could have seen her . . . she was happy last night, Anchen. Her old self, mostly. For the first time since—since coming back. In that crowded, smelly bar—" She stopped, unable to read compassion or confusion in those sparkling amber eyes.

"Where everyone around her was Human," Anchen finished. Ever the consummate diplomat, the Sinzi formed a gentle, Human-looking smile. "What could be more natural, Mac? We can accommodate anyone you wish to invite here. A wonderful idea. I will arrange for an entire building to be Human-only, until Dr. Mamani is more comfortable. Is this acceptable?"

She should have expected nothing less; Anchen took particular pride in being a good host. Even so, it was an overwhelming offer.

Too bad.

Mac took a deep breath. "No, Anchen. I'm grateful, but what Emily needs isn't just to be around Humans—she has me and Oversight, Kanaci and his people, Sing-li, 'Sephe, and theirs. She needs a Human place. Base . . . it will be familiar, she'll have friends, distractions. Her sister could visit." Mac tried to keep the urgency from her voice. *This was right.* "Nik told me you have someone there," she went on. " 'Sephe has a job waiting for her. It's protected from the media. It's—"

"This is where you wish to be, Mac, is it not?"

Irrelevant, Mac told herself and almost believed. "This isn't about me. Emily's been told what the Ro did to Base—the attack on the pods; the earthquake on shore. She knows she helped them do it. She might rationalize it wasn't her fault, realize people have gone on with their work and their lives, but that's not enough, Anchen. Humans—we have to be in a place, touch it, breathe its air, in order to know it." She firmed her voice. "That's why I have to go as well. But not to Base, Anchen. To the Chasm, to Myriam. With the Origins Team."

The Sinzi rose to her feet with a swiftness that suggested some strong emotion. "Mackenzie Connor," she started, her voice unusually high, then stopped, fingers lifting well above her shoulders. *Distress?* "You strike at the essence of my selves."

She'd done it now. "I didn't mean to offend—"

"Offend?" Anchen's triangular mouth shaped a tremulous smile, imitating the Human expression with devastating accuracy. "My dear Mac. I am overcome . . . the harmony of what you would achieve . . . I ask your patience while I compose my selves."

Mac's confusion must have been apparent even to the alien, for she waved her own comments aside with a long finger, sinking back to her seat. "This is what I have longed to propose to you and Dr. Mamani, but did not dare."

"You did." Mac closed her mouth, guessing she'd been gaping like a fish out of water. *So much for marshaling arguments.* "Why didn't you?"

"I had to assume you would resist this, as you have resisted every suggestion you be separated. Yet now, you offer to make a personal journey to achieve community." The Sinzi-ra gave an almost orgasmic shudder. "Can a Human possibly appreciate the significance of this to Sinzi?"

This Human? Mac resisted the urge to laugh. "Em at Base, me with the team—it just feels the right thing to do. I know it's not thoroughly logical or rational."

"Both admit limits," Anchen dismissed. "Limits are not useful in accommodating disparate ways of thought." She seemed calmer, though still intent. "Based on my studies of your species, I see your proposal as a Human need to put affairs in order. You plan a leave-taking, a change of magnitude and risk. Part of this plan deals with what you leave behind, so you are free to go. Is this accurate, Mac?"

Mac sat back in the jelly-chair, letting her shoulders sink into its' soothing warmth. "I hadn't thought about it that way." She nodded slowly. "Yes."

"This is not how it 'feels' to me, Mac. In Sinzi terms, your proposal instills profound circularity by its plan to reattach sundered connections. The importance of any connection is demonstrated by the effort—the distance traveled—to accomplish it. Thus, this is a proposal I find aesthetically as well as fundamentally, worthy. 'Right,' in your terms. In our different ways, we seek the same result—to restore what was broken. To build harmony."

Mac held her breath, feeling close to grasping something innate about the Sinzi, about the transects and the IU itself. "The Atrium," she said finally. "The layout is inefficient by Human standards—researchers have to use a lev-platform or walk halfway around the consulate to meet face-to-face." More than inefficient, Lyle considered it a slight, as if they didn't belong with other scientists—*archaeologists were touchy that way*. Mac hadn't been sure. "But it isn't inefficient to you as a Sinzi, is it? Because the act of physically seeking each other matters." Perhaps explaining why the Sinzi-ra, despite being in charge of the consulate, constantly roamed its halls and rooms. *Intriguing*. Mac wriggled to sit straighter again.

Anchen tilted her head sharply left, as though Mac had drawn the profound attention of one of her personalities. "You are unusually perceptive today, Mac. Yes. To move to a common meeting point is the highest of courtesies. Effort reflects the significance of the desired meeting. Even symbolic travel, as done using the platforms, helps set the appropriate tone of connection."

"That's why you brought experts from all over the IU here, to the Gathering." Mac took the plunge. "Having them move through the transects was a message to all Sinzi. Or from the Sinzi. Or both. A demonstration of the significance of the Dhryn threat."

"We felt a profound need for congruence on this issue," Anchen replied, giving a gracious bow as her fingertips sought one another. Mac wasn't sure if it was agreement or explanation. *The danger with interspecies communication,* she cautioned herself, *wasn't when it went wrong, but when it seemed to make sense.* "We value the synergy of coming together. The Gathering proved insightful, as you know."

"But now you've had to send everyone away. What message does that give?" *Probably not the most tactful question,* Mac realized, too late.

"Message? It is the essential reflection, Mac. That which must take place after congruence. Circularity is movement. Congruence grants momentum. The farther we dare go from one another, while remaining always part, the stronger we—" The Sinzi tilted her head the other way and made a soothing gesture. "My apologies. I have lapsed into language inappropriate for discourse with an alien."

"If we stick to shrimp, we'll never understand one another," Mac assured her.

This drew a laugh, but when Anchen's fingers settled, she pursed her small mouth in a less happy expression. "I will miss our conversations."

The words took a moment to sink in. Then Mac struggled to her feet. "We can go?"

"Yes. However, there must be preparations."

Mac nodded and sank back into her chair, already thinking ahead to her own. Her heart was hammering. She'd wanted this outcome—it was another thing entirely to have it. Then, something in the alien's emphasis caught her attention. "What preparations, Sinzi-ra?"

"Although Dr. P'tool makes progress developing a teachable pattern for the Dhryn language, with the cooperation of the Vessel, it will not be ready for some time. We may need you." Two fingers lifted as Mac opened her mouth. She closed it. "For this reason," Anchen continued, "a transect-capable ship will remain in orbit while you are on Myriam. I trust it will not be required. There is considerable circularity in using that world for any negotiations, should we achieve that stage."

Mac swallowed. "You'd rather bring the Dhryn to me," she said, numbly contemplating the immense power and scope of the Inter-species Union, focused on one, out-of-water, salmon researcher.

It made sense beyond the Sinzi aesthetic. The Chasm worlds were already dead. Myriam was as close, through the Naralax Tran-sect, as any other world connected along its reach, including Earth. *There was just one small problem.*

"I study salmon," Mac repeated aloud.

That tiny smile and a gentle correction, "You study life, Macken-zie Connor. But don't worry. In the event you are needed to trans-late, there will be senior diplomats to handle every aspect of the negotiations."

"Great. You'd better send someone to translate them for me," Mac muttered.

Anchen ignored the mutter, bringing her fingers together in a complex arch. *New topic*, Mac guessed. Sure enough. "You realize several here will protest losing their access to Dr. Mamani."

"The idiot faction," Mac identified without thinking. "I didn't mean that," she said hastily, then winced. *How confusing could she be?* "I do," she admitted. "I just didn't intend to say it. I apologize."

"There is no need." Anchen made a soothing gesture. "I envy your ability to speak what you mean."

Mac had to laugh. "Trust me, it's not a gift."

"You could start a war by yourself," the Sinzi agreed with re-markable complacency. "Hence the urgent need for diplomats." Before Mac could protest, the alien smiled at her. "A joke. You have shown gratifying restraint under difficult circumstances."

Well, she hadn't thrown anything, Mac thought. *Lately.* Despite temptation. She took advantage of the Sinzi's mood to ask what she hadn't dared before. "You agree with me, don't you? About the idiots."

"I agree that some of my colleagues on council have failed to overcome species' bias when interpreting the actions of others." The alien swayed to the left, then back. "It is more common than not, Mac."

"Interpretation?" Mac couldn't help herself: "The Ro are the threat, not potential allies! Their actions proved it!"

"Through your eyes." A lifted finger silenced Mac's response to that. The Sinzi went on: "Through other eyes, other minds, Mac, the same actions encourage differing conclusions. Actions alone, facts alone, are never enough. They must be considered within the species imperative. What matters to the Myrokynay? What is their nature? All of us must learn to see as they see before we can grasp their true motivations. That is why your exploration of the past is so important."

Mac scowled. "I deal in facts. The Ro are the enemy. Everything I've discovered supports that."

"Are the walls of the consulate featureless and white?" The Sinzi steepled all of her fingers, their rings cascading down with a sound like rain on ice. "Is this a fact?"

Checkmate.

If she said yes, the Sinzi would correctly inform her they were white only to her Human eyes. If she said no, she was admitting the Sinzi was right—that knowledge about an alien species was crucial to interpreting the actions of that species.

Mac shrugged it aside, not ready to surrender. "What if the imperative for the Ro is to destroy all other forms of life, starting with anyone who dares tamper with no-space?"

"Then our survival will depend on how quickly and well we answer that question, Mackenzie Connor." The Sinzi stood and two staff appeared in the doorway as if this had been a summons. "You know what to do, I trust."

Mac rose to her feet, but stayed where she was. "My team's ready to go," she stated. *More than ready.* Kanaci kept his clothes packed, according to Oversight. "But, Anchen. About Emily. I'd like to talk over the arrangements—"

Instead of responding, Anchen beckoned to her staff. One, a male, passed her a silver ring, just like any of the hundreds adorning her fingers from shoulder to final joint. Light reflected in a quick flash as her fingertip rolled to hold it. "Perfect," she said, her voice pleased. The finger, with its contents, reached toward Mac. "For you."

Mac took the smooth ring in her hand. Already warmed by the Sinzi's touch—*implying a higher body temperature*—it was a plain circle of precious metal. When she tried it on, it slipped over her right ring finger, fitting as if made for it. *A good-bye gift?* "Thank you, Sinzi-ra," she said, nonplussed.

The staff glanced at Anchen for permission. At her nod, he said: "It is a Sinzi *lamnas*—a private communications device, Dr. Connor. Each *lamnas* accepts only one message, intended for a sole recipient."

Which meant . . . Mac's eyes widened and she stared at Anchen's ring-coated fingers. She couldn't begin to imagine why a Sinzi would want to carry his or her mail this way, yet the small devices were obviously designed to be worn, perhaps at all times. And were the ones Anchen bore messages received or those waiting to be sent? She couldn't see any outward differences.

Before she could frame her curiosity into questions, the Sinzi gestured to the ring in Mac's hand. "This arrived today, in a transect com packet from the *Impeci*. You are the recipient."

The ship name wasn't familiar. *Which didn't mean anything.* "Why would you think it's for me?" Mac asked, proud of the evenness of her voice. Hope wasn't familiar, either; her heart began to pound with it.

With a left finger, Anchen stroked the rings on a right, setting up a faint cascading chime. "Each Sinzi-ra carries a supply of *lamnas,* uniquely marked, with which to send information," she explained. *Explaining those she wore.* "That is one of four Nikolai asked of me before he left."

Mac's fingers closed around the gift, her mouth forming a silent: *Oh.*

Anchen pulled free one of her rings. "It functions thus. To record." She brought the ring, encircled by her flexible fingertip, to touch her pursed triangular lips. She blew gently, then opened her mouth further to place the ring on her tongue. Her lips closed over it. After an instant in which Mac couldn't see anything happening, Anchen removed the ring and gave it to the waiting staff. "At first, Mac, I doubted. A Human, even one with so disciplined a mind as Nikolai, imprint a *lamnas*? But he insisted on making the attempt, and I could not refuse him. We share a deep and abiding connection." Fingertips touched. "The results were—interesting. Be aware, Mac, this is not a message which can be decoded and sent to another device. This is an imprint, affected by intent as much as event. I cannot say how your mind will interpret the result."

"So—it might not work at all," Mac ventured, her hope of an instant before fading.

"Oh, it will. But how? That only you can discover. To receive, act thus." The Sinzi chose another ring, identical to the rest as far as Mac could tell from a distance, and repeated the same initial movements, touch to the lips, a breath through the ring, but finished by holding the ring to one of her eyes, looking through its tiny circle. As if to avoid distraction, Anchen brought this ring down again quickly and replaced it on her finger, shaking it up to join the rest.

"Now, if you will excuse me, Mac, I am reminded of an appointment—"

Somehow, Mac wrenched her mind to the business at hand, preparing to stand her ground. *Emily.* If there was one thing she'd learned in dealing with bureaucracy—or aliens or most particularly alien bureaucracy—it was to never leave without a final answer. *Ideally signed and sealed.* "We need to talk about Emily."

Anchen turned so all of her eyes were directly on Mac, one finger sending her staff to other duties. "Be assured I have given this considerable thought. Dr. Stewart appears capable of monitoring Dr. Mamani's recovery, given instruction. I myself will be available to Dr. Mamani at any time via secure com to discuss her memories. What remains an issue . . . Mac, as you yourself said, there are many in the IU interested in your friend's relationship with the Myrokynay, 'idiots' and otherwise. I expect more delegates later this week. Sending her anywhere else on Earth ends their access except through your Ministry. I must consult with Mr. Hollans. There must be arrangements in advance, mutually agreed—"

"Or one lev, tonight," Mac interrupted, taking a step closer. "Discuss the details after she's gone. You can arrange vid meetings with Emily for those who want to talk to her. In the open, with you present. Whatever it takes."

Anchen bent until the tops of her eyes were aimed at Mac. It was so unusual a posture Mac guessed she'd attracted the particular attention of Casmii, the IU judge.

That wasn't, she decided, *necessarily good.*

"Relations between the Frow and Trisulian delegations have been strained over this issue," the Sinzi-ra mused. "There is merit in distancing the source of contention. It could serve to return attention to the problem at hand: developing a defense against the Dhryn."

Or, it could be good. Mac brightened. "We can be out of your way in no time."

" 'We,' Mac?"

"I have to go with her," she explained, although surely it was obvious even to an alien with tentacle fingers. "I'll need to talk to Dr. Noyo and the other senior staff—make sure Emily's settled."

"How long would this process take?"

Mac pushed aside wistful thoughts of visiting field stations, inspecting the new anchors, and generally being a nuisance to Kammie and Tie, who were doubtless looking after all of the above and more. "Three days," she proposed and did her best to look regretful. "I realize I'll miss some meetings."

"I doubt that troubles you," the Sinzi commented shrewdly. "But, yes, so long an absence would be noticed." She paused—*consulting her selves?* Mac wondered—then tilted into her more usual posture. "It is not impossible. I should be able to schedule your team's departure for the Chasm to allow time for you to 'settle' Dr. Mamani and still meet them in orbit. The meetings—I will arrange a means of obtaining your input even while you are on Myriam." *Of course she would,* Mac sighed to herself. "You," Anchen finished, "face the more difficult task."

Mac, in the midst of congratulating herself for everything but the meetings, gave the Sinzi a suspicious look. "What might that be?"

"Convincing Dr. Mamani."

No problem.

Emily, Mac told herself, *would love the plan.*

Permission to free Emily from the consulate. Away from reminders and questions.

A private message from Nik.

And a return to Base!

If she'd been impatient before, Mac was nigh on to frantic now.

Her mind whirling with plans, arguments, and the tendency to simply stall in possibilities, she somehow managed not to run down the ramplike hallway. Not quite, anyway. Her low-impact lope couldn't have been mistaken for a walk by any being. *Maybe it would stop anyone from pestering her on the way.*

"Ah! There you are, Norcoast."

Or not.

Mac growled under her breath but waited for Mudge to catch up to her. There wasn't a window, but diffuse light filled the hollow core of the building. If she walked to the corridor's edge, she would see how its gentle slope spiraled to connect the main floors. *And probably startle a few pigeons.* "In a bit of a rush, Oversight—" she began.

As well talk to the walls. Charles Mudge III had successfully fought his end of their interminable arguments about Base's access to his Wilderness Trust for fourteen years. His recent career change to Mac's admittedly invaluable assistant, administering all the business and com traffic of the research team they ran—truth be told, together—hadn't softened his approach. *That she'd noticed.*

Now, predictably, he ignored her protest, instead shaking a crumpled mem-sheet under her nose. "Look at this!" Mudge fumed. "Dr. Kanaci knows how I feel about proper lines of communication. I've made it abundantly clear. Submissions must go through the main system. I'm telling you right now, Norcoast—"

Mac was acutely conscious of the *lamnas* around her finger. "Can't you tell me later?" she pleaded.

"Certainly not." For no apparent reason, he stopped at that, giving her the oddest look.

Maybe Mudge was *more annoying than Hollans.* "Oversight?" she prompted, shifting her weight from foot to foot. "What can't wait?"

He leaned forward and lowered his voice. "There's a message from Stefan."

"Nik," she corrected automatically. For all Mudge paid attention to Nikolai Trojanowski's real—or at least official—identity, she might not have bothered telling him at all. On the other hand, Mac assured herself, she no longer had to worry about using the right alias. They all seemed to work. *Spies.*

"You know who I mean." His eyebrows rose and fell suggestively.

While Mudge's attempt to be clandestine was entertaining, in a bizarre sort of way, Mac refused to be distracted. "Yes, I know who you mean. And I know about the message. The Sinzi-ra mentioned a com packet arrived today. It's being decoded."

"Done."

Mac stopped trying to escape and snatched at the mem-sheet in Mudge's hand.

He pulled it away. "Not this," he *harrumphed,* crumpling the mem-sheet into a ball. "I'll have you know I had to go in person to get a copy. Security reasons."

Mac nodded impatiently, barely restraining the impulse to search his pockets. "Where's the message?"

"I had to get it from that Myg." He waited.

Oh. Mac reined in her temper. "I trust he cooperated."

"I didn't take the chance." Stiffly. "I brought a Ministry agent with me. The one with no sense of humor. Selkirk."

She'd have to find a way to deal with this. Unfortunately, Fourteen's intellect either soared with brilliance or hung around bathrooms looking for entertainment. Which meant Mudge.

Give the alien credit, Mac thought with reluctant admiration. *He applied his genius.* The "mirror image" switch had involved not only every item on Mudge's desk but also each and every file accessed by his imp. Then there was the time Fourteen replaced the backside of Mudge's pants with a material that could be rendered transparent by remote.

The trick was to keep Fourteen busy, or the two of them apart. *Easier said than done.*

"You can't keep avoiding him," Mac insisted aloud, despite her utter lack of success on this point with Mudge to date. "It only makes him worse."

She couldn't very well explain that what made Mudge such an irresistible target for the Myg wasn't the Human's gullibility or his tendency to bluster. *Although they helped.* It was Mudge's constant, steady usefulness to her.

Not jealousy. She'd worried at the situation, observed their interaction long enough to believe she had it right. In their own species-specific and personally idiosyncratic ways, Fourteen and Mudge competed for the opportunity to serve her.

Mac frequently wanted to strangle them both.

Later. "Just give me the message, Oversight. Please."

His eyes widened dramatically. "Here?"

"Why not here?"

Mudge lowered his voice. "Someone could be listening."

On the verge of exasperation—*the man had vidbots on the brain*—Mac reconsidered. Mudge had a point. Given the open structure of this hall, and the variety of aural capabilities possessed by those roaming it, there was no way to know if someone could overhear them. *And there were idiots.*

"Fine. We'll go— What time is it anyway?"

"Don't tell me you've missed breakfast again."

"When I want someone fussing over my eating habits," Mac countered absently, "I'll call my dad." *That late?* She shoved the hand with its ring into a pocket. "Let's take a walk."

Mudge kept pace, even when Mac lengthened her stride. They were of a height, though he outmassed her by a few kilos. Less now—there wasn't much time behind a desk for either of them, especially with the Sinzi's predilection for distance between meeting places. Being needed had agreed with Mudge, put a sparkle in his eyes.

Being under threat of species annihilation had deepened the worry lines beside those eyes, and added gray to his already peppered hair.

Mac had some herself.

"What's Lyle after now?" she asked once they reached the lift and sent it heading down.

Mudge gave the ball of mem-sheet in his hand a surprised look, as if it should have filed itself, then scowled at her. "Same as always. He wants to know when they can get back to that rock of his—claims the IU station on Myriam isn't cooperating. This time he tried to go over your head to Director Hollans, whose secretary promptly sent everything back to me." He grew smug. "Protocol has its purpose."

Protocols. Politics. Mac was grateful to have someone who actually relished both on her side. "Use your power for good," she advised as the doors opened on the main floor.

Mac didn't say anything more until they stood outside on the terrace, overlooking the grounds of the consulate. Winter was losing the battle here, helped along by the eager efforts of a small army of gardeners. There were swathes of green beside the patio stones, color peeking shyly from the mulch. But in the distance, upslope, snow clung to ridge and treetop.

It wasn't raining, but the feel was in the air. The sky sported flags of cloud, torn loose by the westerlies that raced straight from the Antarctic to this shore. They were protected by the consular building and by the shoulders of ridges higher than this, but the wind tossed debris around below them—to the frustration of the staff sweeping the stones.

The vast research complex called the Atrium lay deep beneath those same stones, quiescent now save for a cluster of irritable archaeologists and the usual groups studying the market impact of technology alien to Human and vice versa. The most active area was the Telematics section, where the Sinzi—and Earthgov—monitored comings and goings through the transects.

And watched for Dhryn.

Rooted above the bustle of science, giant graceful trees lined the sides of the patio, a tame forest laced with secluded paths and inviting entrances. Beyond them and the buildings, the cliff face plunged into the sound, where life usually found in mid-ocean depths came within reach of land.

No time left for exploring. Mac laid her hands on the cold, wide stone that topped the rail edging the terrace. "I'll be back," she vowed.

"Back from where?"

"The message, Oversight," she reminded him.

He unfastened the upper of the two pockets that bulged at his waist, fumbling inside. Before he pulled whatever it was out, Mudge gave her a wary look. She knew that expression, very well. He was bracing for her reaction.

"What is it?" *Nik had been discreet, hadn't he?*

Instead of answering, he finished the motion, passing her the result between two fingers. "Don't blame me," he said grimly. "It was that Myg."

Mac pressed her lips firmly together, determined not to smile, and took the folded piece of glittery pink paper. She sniffed appreciatively. *Lily of the Valley.* Her favorite.

Saying anything would only make it worse.

She opened the folds. It was real paper, not a mem-sheet, inscribed in block letters. Fourteen remained convinced she found large type easier to read. At the moment, Mac didn't care. She scanned the message three times to be sure, then stared at Mudge. "That's it?" she protested, her voice rising. " 'Continuing as planned; situation nominal?' What kind of a message is that?"

He gave a faint *harrumph.* "Succinct?"

Unable to say another word, Mac crumpled the fragrant pink paper in her hand and glared at Mudge, seriously considering where to put it.

Mudge threw up his hands. "See? This is exactly why I didn't want to give it to you indoors. You do better with—space—to calm down. A great deal of space. I knew you'd be upset."

"Upset!" Realizing she'd shouted, Mac took a deep shuddering breath. Then another. *Fine.* She had the *lamnas* on her finger, with Anchen's promise it contained a private message from Nik. *This?* Mac straightened out the paper. "Why would I be upset?" she asked more calmly. "It does get the point across. But surely there was more than this in the com-packet."

"Nothing I thought you'd want. Language modules for the translation project. Private mail from the others." Mudge snorted. "Knowing Fourteen, he's tucked away a copy of anything embarrassing for later use."

Mac shocked herself by immediately wondering how she could gain access to any mail from Cinder, Nik's partner, and what it might reveal. *Not that she expected anything to have changed for the better.* Cinder had admitted she wanted nothing more than a chance to kill Dhryn. Any Dhryn. Including the Vessel, on whom everything depended.

When she hesitated, Mudge frowned. "Was I wrong, Norcoast? Did you want the rest?"

Mac noticed he didn't ask why she might. *Gods, the spy mentality was contagious.* She shook her head. "Let's leave snooping to the pros. We have enough to do."

Mudge gave her one of those too-keen looks. Mac thought her

expression nicely neutral, but he *harrumphed* anyway. "Do? What's going on?"

Moving offworld? Mac found herself not quite ready to say the words. Instead, she began: "It's Emily—"

"I knew it!" Mudge pounced. "You shouldn't have gone out alone last night. What were you thinking?"

Are you thinking what I'm thinking? Mac's lips twisted, but aloud she said: "It's not about last night, Oversight." Once she told him, there'd be no turning back. Mudge with a mission was a force of nature. *So be it.* "We're leaving for Myriam. As soon as Anchen makes the arrangements."

"Who's 'we?'" he demanded, unwittingly echoing the Sinzi.

Mac reached out to tap the ball of mem-sheet clutched in his hand. "Everyone. The entire team. You, me, Fourteen, the archaeologists. We'll—"

"And when were you going to ask me, Norcoast?" Mudge drew himself up. "I don't recall agreeing to this."

She blinked. *Go without him?* The mere notion sat like a stone in her empty stomach. "You have to come," she blurted.

"I have to do no such thing." He wagged his pudgy finger at her. "And neither do you."

For a heartbeat, Mac believed she had that choice. She imagined returning to Base with Emily to stay, back to work, back to her life.

Home.

Then she imagined, all too easily, what the Dhryn could do.

Mac shook her head. "I'm not finished, Oversight. I've too many questions, questions only that planet can answer. But if you want to stay here," she added evenly, "that's fine."

"You wouldn't last a week without me," he huffed.

She wasn't sure if he meant her, or the Origins Team, or both. *Probably right on all counts,* Mac told herself. *Didn't matter.* She shrugged. "I'll manage. Fourteen can help me."

Mudge frowned at her. "Don't try to manipulate me, Norcoast."

"I know better," Mac assured him. She rested her elbows on the cool stone and turned her head to study him. "What do you want me to say, Oversight?" she asked quietly. "Admit I'm afraid? That returning to that world will be the hardest thing I've ever done?

I'm still going." She considered his face, cheeks blotched with angry red. "It would be easier with someone I trust along. To watch my back."

A living friend when she faced the dead, she added to herself. *Brymn.*

His *harrumph* sounded mollified, although his eyebrows still glowered at her. "Well, it doesn't have to be me. The Ministry will send its lunkheads with you."

"It's IU jurisdiction. I don't know if they can come."

"What about Dr. Mamani?"

Mac ran her artificial fingers over the stone, finding some moss to poke. "Emily," she said carefully, "will be returning to Base. To work on her Tracer device."

"What? You can't be serious. Whose stupid idea was that?" Mudge's voice rose to a regrettable volume. A gardener glanced up.

"Shhh," Mac hushed him, not bothering to be offended. *He could be right.* "Mine—and the Sinzi-ra's. And it's—Emily needs to be away from here, Oversight. It was the only way I could think of that would keep her safe."

"It's where you belong. You know it. You're out of your league here, Norcoast. Offworld? The Chasm? It's ridiculous. You can't go. I certainly won't."

Mac pressed her lips together and returned glare for glare, willing to wait all day if necessary.

It took three and a half minutes. Then Mudge *harrumphed.* Twice. "I'll have to round up some proper packing crates. The toss to orbit will wreak havoc with the equipment. You know who'll complain about that," he added, growing almost cheerful, a bundle of daunting efficiency about to be unleashed on his victims.

"Oversight—" Mac began, her voice unsteady. She straightened and turned to face him.

Mudge edged back, as if suspecting intent to hug. "I'll confer with Anchen's staff and book a meeting within the hour about the details—don't miss it," he warned. "We'll keep things close to the chest until the schedule's set."

She had to be sure. "You'll come with me?"

He feigned surprise. "Of course I'm coming, Norcoast. Who

else could spot when you were about to fly off on some idiotic tangent? Or just wrong," he added magnanimously.

Mac grinned. "I'm so comforted."

"As you should be. Now. About the meeting. We should hold it—"

"Wait. Give me a chance to tell Emily before she hears the news from anyone else."

Mudge's mouth dropped open. "You mean—you went to the Sinzi—arranged this—without asking Dr. Mamani first?" He shook his head dolefully. "Norcoast. What were you thinking?"

"There was nothing to ask her about until I'd talked to Anchen," Mac snapped.

He stared at her, then heaved a distinctly theatrical sigh as if the entire matter was beyond him. "I'll go and get started with the rest, including Fourteen. It'll be easier than what you'll be doing."

As Mudge walked away, Mac threw up her hands. "Why does everyone keep saying that?"

Emily would love the plan.

- 4 -

OBSTACLE AND OBSCURITY

"ANCHEN LOVES THE PLAN."

Mac heard the pleading note in her own voice and winced. *Not the right approach.*

Sure enough, Emily spat out a frustrated string of Quechua Mac didn't want translated. "Of course she does," she finished in English, throwing her gloved arms skyward in emphasis. "Don't you see, Mac? It splits us up. Means you'll do whatever she wants."

"No!" Mac protested. Her friend would have to rediscover physical expression for this conversation, she sighed to herself, neck sore from following Emily's relentless pacing. Just as well they'd met in her quarters rather than outside. "That's not true. She—to Anchen your returning to Base would be—" *profoundly circular?* Somehow, she doubted spouting alien philosophy was going to help, even if Emily could be convinced that she, Mac, had any idea what she was spouting. *Not likely.* "She loves the plan," Mac repeated lamely.

"While I hate the plan. I'm not going. End of discussion."

Anchen and Mudge had been right, Mac realized with some disgust. The way it stood, if she had a month, she couldn't argue, cajole, or rationalize Emily into doing things her way. *That left . . .* Mac steeled herself. "You owe me, Em."

Emily stood still. "Owe you?" A shapely dark eyebrow rose—curiosity, not offense. *Yet.*

"Yes. And I'm collecting. You're going to Base. I need to know it's running." Mac didn't bother adding: *and you're safe.*

Here came the offense, right on cue—that proud flash of Emily's eyes, the passionate outrage. "I don't believe it. You—it's revenge, isn't it? Bizarre, twisted revenge! Aie! You're abandoning me. To—you want me to work on your damned fish for you! Well, I won't!"

"Good. Because I want you to work on your damned Survivors!"

They faced off, both furious. Then Emily's expression shifted to shock. "What did you say?"

"You'll have to rebuild your Tracer. But you'll have every resource." Mac considered this, then hastily qualified: "Short of interfering with the field season."

"Heavens forbid I do that." But Emily's slowly expanding smile took the sting out of the words. "You actually talked the Sinzi-ra into this. Supporting my research. Now that I don't believe."

"She owes me, too," Mac said succinctly.

"You always were dangerous in a corner, Mackenzie Connor." Emily shook her head, her hands spreading in a gesture of surrender. "Okay. I love the plan."

Mac tried not to sound smug. "I knew you would. Now. We don't have much time."

After sending Emily to prepare her "shopping list" for the Sinzi-ra—doubtless to be long and costly, judging by the other scientist's intense air of concentration when she'd left Mac—Mac sat behind her desk and began a list of her own.

She'd committed herself now, she thought, studying the 'screen hovering before her eyes, drawing a finger through a lower quadrant to retrieve her field station inventory. Emily at Base; Mac in space.

There was a switch.

She'd learned a few things about travel offworld. Mac didn't bother deleting any items, given she had no idea what she might face and now knew better than to believe anyone who said they did. Tools, dissection kits, syringes, specimen bottles, scales—anything might be useful. And they fit her hands. She'd become all too aware of the dearth of Human-oriented technology outside this system.

On that thought, she added a distillation kit and several collapsible jugs for water to her list.

Myriam was a desert. Never an overly moist world, lacking the large oceans cradling Earth's continents, what water remained on the Dhryn planet ran through underground rivers and lodged in aquifers. This was, in fact, another and troubling facet of the Chasm puzzle: the dust-dry ruins. What they now knew of the Dhryn feeding—Mac shuddered—did not include the removal of surface water. Oh, Dhryn didn't care for the stuff. For some reason they'd done their best to drain their new home, Haven, and chosen colonies that were arid and desolate by Human standards. But that didn't explain the rest of those worlds.

For a fleeting instant, Mac thought of Emily's Survivors. *What if they did exist? What if they were aquatic? Did the Ro remove any ocean that might have sheltered them?*

Did the Ro fear them?

She shook her head. *More likely the Ro had been their thorough selves and simply finished the sterilization of each world begun by the Dhryn.*

Because it was nothing short of deadly, that hope there was a species out there with the answers, more advanced than the Sinzi, ready to save everyone else out of the goodness of whatever passed for their hearts.

It had seduced Emily into believing the Ro.

It threatened their efforts even now.

Mac closed her 'screen and pushed herself to her feet, thoroughly unsettled. "The sooner we're away from here, the better," she told the empty room.

The *lamnas* glittered on her finger, as if in reassurance she hadn't lost it. Mac had a regrettable history with jewelry—something along the lines of her ability to keep dress shoes intact.

Was now the right time?

Mac glanced out the window. The sun was shining, doing its best to hurry spring along. Not quite as helpfully, the wind had picked up to a howl, and she didn't need to walk out on her terrace to know its protective membrane would be in place. *Where was the fun in that?*

Sing-li had refused to show Mac how to turn it off. He'd insisted a safety feature designed to keep guests of little mass—or sense—from being blown out to sea or worse, given the rocks below, was not to be treated lightly.

She'd only wanted to feel the rain. *Okay, and maybe toss her imp with the latest meeting notes into it.*

Spoilsport.

Mac tucked her imp into its pocket, and surveyed her room. Strange how putting a few personal belongings around had made this alien space hers. "Okay, more than a few," she admitted aloud, eyeing the salmon swinging overhead and the filled shelves on every wall. She hadn't asked for all of her belongings from Base. They'd just . . . arrived. Sing-li's doing. "It's going to take a while to pack all this."

If not now, when?

Mac heaved a sigh of resignation and went into her other room. The bed beckoned—too risky, given the struggle she'd had to leave it this morning. The jelly-chair by the door was promising, but it lacked a certain privacy.

Which was the problem, she abruptly realized, fingers wrapping around the tiny device.

A moment later, Mac sat on the floor of her closet, its door closed, content in the knowledge that, while undignified and likely silly, she was as alone as she could manage. She leaned against a storage bag, wiggling until its contents stopped digging into her spine. From the feel, tents.

Now.

She took the ring between forefinger and thumb, lifting it—

"Mac! What on Earth are you doing in here?"

Closing her fist over the ring, Mac glared up at the man in the doorway. "I'm meditating," she said stiffly.

"Meditating." Lyle Kanaci gave her a doubtful look. "In your closet?"

"I thought it would be peaceful," she grumbled, climbing to her feet. "What is it?"

"Not even you would call a meeting of this importance and not attend." His voice rose and he waved his hands. "Weren't you even planning to be there?"

Mac held back any number of retorts. While she'd known Lyle

to be testy—and Fourteen knew he had a temper, *although the alien had deserved what he'd got, using Lyle's depilatory cream that way*—he'd never burst into her rooms before. Not to mention she usually heard about her attendance, or lack of it, from Mudge.

"I don't need to be there, but I was coming." *Eventually.* "What's wrong?" She waved him out of her closet and followed behind. "Besides, you're better at those things than I am," she added honestly. *And enjoyed being in charge.*

Like Mudge, Lyle Kanaci was Mac's height, but with an academic's tendency to slouch that made him appear the shorter of the two. It also made it easy to see the red mottling the pigmentless skin of his scalp and neck. *Something's definitely up,* Mac decided.

He whirled on her the moment they were through the door. "You could have at least warned me!"

"About what? Oh." Mac nodded. "The move offworld. Things fell into place—" she made a helpless gesture "—fast."

"I don't like it."

Déjà vu. She felt like grabbing Lyle by the shoulders and giving him a good shake. *While she was at it,* Mac decided grimly, *she'd shake the rest of the universe with him.* "You've been complaining for weeks about not returning to Myriam," she pointed out. "I'd have thought you'd be thanking me."

"Not when it's some trick by the Sinzi to make you cooperate."

Was he worried about her? Mac wondered. She scowled. "This was my idea. There's no trick, the Sinzi-*ra*—" the emphasis on the honorific a rebuke, "—and I are in complete agreement as to the benefits to everyone, especially Emily, and what made you walk into my closet anyway?" *Oh, for doors that locked,* she thought wistfully. *Just once.*

"You weren't anywhere else." He had the grace to look embarrassed. "Emily said you were still in your quarters."

She scowled a moment longer, just for effect. "I'd better have privacy on Myriam."

"You'll have your own tent," he promised, then half smiled. "Middle of a sandstorm, you'll be alone for days."

Mac rolled her eyes. "Don't remind me."

"Mac." Lyle lowered his voice. "Are you sure about this? Myriam, the Chasm. It's not what you're used to—we'd understand—"

Ouch. She decided to be equally blunt. "I do my best work in the field, Dr. Kanaci. As do you. A little—a great deal—" she amended, "—of sand doesn't change that. We can't learn what we must about the Dhryn here."

This drew a measuring look from his pale eyes, followed by a short, quick nod. "Then let's get going. Charles has the specs for the flight—if you're finished meditating?"

"All done," she assured him serenely, feeling a growing impatience herself.

Field season. Not to a river or her salmon, but the potential for discovery was there nonetheless. It quickened the heart, steadied priorities into one. *Move.*

"Let's go," she told Lyle.

If she replaced the ring around her finger, turning it twice with regret, that was no one's business but her own.

Familiarity couldn't breed apathy. Not here. As always, Mac slowed when she entered the Atrium, taking a good look at its remarkable space. The vast underground research facility beneath the IU consulate deserved it.

Aerial platforms filled the inverted cone that was the Atrium's core. Most were rooms without walls, linked in various temporary configurations to better serve the needs of the researchers using that space. Some were docked against the steplike levels that formed the outer walls, if you'd call a wall what resembled more the side of a giant pyramid under excavation, studded with entrances to still more rooms and facilities. Other platforms were in motion in every direction. Mac had yet to see a pattern to the traffic, although she had to admit she hadn't seen a collision either. *A few near misses.*

The ceiling, high enough to feel like sky, was the underside of the stones forming the patio, itself in the lee of the main consulate building. Tree roots formed wisps of brown cloud, the plants seemingly unharmed by finding air rather than rock beneath. Mac suspected extra care by the gardeners.

Space, bustle, changing shapes, but what Mac noticed most each time was the din. Her ears rang with voices from varied throats, machinery, and the incessant beeping of whatever felt obliged to beep. She'd only experienced silence here once, when they'd waited together for the Dhryn.

When they'd expected to die.

The Origins Team, as they styled themselves, had been granted space between the permanent researchers here, those who looked for the best fit between approved alien technologies and humanity. And vice versa. The trade in knowledge and invention went off-world as well. To reach their little pocket of xenoarchaeology, one had to take a platform into the center, then rise to the far back, uppermost level.

Mac reconsidered its location from her new understanding of Anchen's perspective. *If the farther you traveled to consult, the greater importance that consultation had . . . ?* "In that case," she mused aloud, trailing Lyle to the waiting platform, "she thinks pretty highly of our work."

"Who thinks highly of it?"

"Anchen." Mac shook her head at his incredulous expression. "Don't ask. I'm not sure I could explain."

One of the advantages to being the last remnant of the Gathering was, to Mac's not-so-secret delight, a reduction in ceremony and fuss. They weren't expected to hold their meetings at the Sinzira's long table—although Mac herself continued to be called there far too often. For Origins, meetings had become practical affairs. Staff would bring food, she and her group would curl up in jelly-chairs, and they'd finish discussion and dessert at roughly the same moment. *Relaxing and effective.*

Except, obviously, for today. Mac and Lyle stepped from their platform to confront a maze of crates and bags, most stacked in piles reaching well over their heads. They exchanged a look. "Oversight," Mac guessed; Lyle nodded in complete understanding.

Consular staff were busy removing items from the maze to waiting platforms docked to either side, forcing the two of them to thread their way between. The entrance to the research area was equally cluttered. Its door had vanished, along with most of the wall to either side, to allow larger equipment to be rolled through.

"Is this a meeting or are we already packing?" Lyle shouted at her over the clang and clatter.

"Staff are packing," Mac observed, then lifted her hand to return a wave. "Looks like we're meeting."

The wave had been Fourteen's, whose head, shoulders, and wildly moving arm could be seen over the ranks of shifting crates. Mac used him as her guide, the room they'd worked in these past weeks being essentially gone.

Including the comfy chairs.

Luckily they still had a table, Mac discovered once she and Lyle passed the remaining obstructions. Fourteen was jumping on it, as if to be sure she'd seen him. "Idiots!!!!" the Myg shouted cheerfully. "Over here!"

"Do we have to take him with us?" Lyle whispered in her ear.

"Oversight would miss him," Mac whispered back. She'd already spotted Mudge, seething in the background. Given the alien's onslaught on the furniture, she was relieved he was only seething. "Fourteen," she called out before worse could happen. "Don't break the table. I need it."

"Bah!" the alien grinned down at her. "You are trying to stop Charlie from strangling me with his bare hands." But he obliged.

Like other Mygs of Mac's acquaintance—granted, a small number, including six tiny offspring, the xenopaleoecologist who might be their mother, and Fourteen's uncle, who'd visited last week—Fourteen was a stocky humanoid, similar enough in body plan to shop locally. Currently, he was challenging the optics of every other species in Origins by wearing fluorescent green, yellow, and mauve striped pants with an orange tank top emblazoned "Go Native!" in red across its stretched chest. He'd taken off the formal wig the moment his uncle had left; his brush of reddish-brown hair spiked wildly in all directions.

Mac was quite fond of him. *So long as he stayed away from her things.* Her family cabin on Little Misty Lake would never be the same after one of Fourteen's creative spells.

Lyle's words ran through her mind just then. Leave him? *Not an option.* Fourteen had declared some kind of Myg debt to her. He'd probably buy his own ship and follow anyway. Or hand her an offspring.

Who were cute—just not that cute.

Mac sighed. Ever since he'd failed to stop the Ro signal, for which she'd never blamed him, he'd been worse.

"About time you showed up, Norcoast," Mudge accused. He looked harassed, but in the "busy moving the world, coming through" way that meant he was enjoying himself thoroughly. *Not that he'd admit it,* Mac smiled to herself. "We had to start without you."

"Oh, I never mind that," she said calmly. "Hi, everyone."

The chorus of "Hi Macs" that ensued ranged from bass to soprano, with a "Hiiii Maaaaac" elongation in the tenor offerings. Extra vowels meant the Sthlynii were not enjoying themselves. *No surprise there.* She'd learned they didn't care for change, not at the pace Humans moved, anyway. The switch to the Atrium, even with better facilities, had twisted Therin's mouth tentacles into a foul knot for days.

You couldn't please everyone, Mac reminded herself, silently counting heads. *Speaking of which . . .* "Where's Kudla?" she sighed.

"Irrelevant!"

She sent Fourteen a quelling look. The Myg didn't play tricks on the author or his followers. *It wasn't a compliment.* "You can brief him later, then," Mac ordered, hopping up to sit on the near end of the table. When no one else moved, she made an impatient summoning gesture to gather them around her in a semicircle.

A semicircle Mudge immediately burst through in order to confront her, brandishing his imp like a miniature sword. "I protest, Norcoast. Even by your standards, this is no way to run a meeting!"

Mac brought a finger to her lips. He subsided, barely, and the others grew still, obviously expectant. "Oversight has the transport details," she informed them. "I dare say you've gone ahead without us to calculate the optimal allocations of effort and resources for everyone?" This directed at Mudge. He gave her his patented defiant scowl; Mac smiled peacefully back. "There," she exclaimed, rubbing her hands together. "Who needs a meeting? Oversight will give each of you your assignments, send any bills and additional requests to consular staff as usual, and then? We're out of here."

There was a verbal explosion as everyone tried to talk at once.

Mac ignored them, swinging her legs back and forth. After a moment, the uproar sputtered, then died away. "You know we'd come around to his way by the end," she reasoned. "Think of all the time I just saved."

The easy victory clearly upset Mudge, doubtless armed with arguments for every point and particular. He *harrumphed* vigorously. "We should at least discuss sleeping quarters on board the transport. At least!"

"Really?" Mac raised an eyebrow at those assembled, collecting a few chuckles and one interesting hue change. "I think they can handle that. Now. If that's all?" She jumped down. "See you in orbit."

The wall of bodies didn't budge. Mac stood, confronted by anxious looks—or body tilts of the same meaning—and realized what was bothering them.

Emily.

She'd made quite an impact, even while recovering. Some here were smitten. Others, friends. And others . . .

Mac focused on Fourteen's small, flesh-enclosed eyes.

Others saw Emily as a tool.

They'd have their separate reasons for worrying about Emily being removed from the team.

Not one of which mattered now, Mac told herself grimly.

As if warned by some change in her expression, those blocking her path silently moved aside.

Mac stalked through the opening, thought, and turned abruptly. *For the friends and the smitten, and as a warning to everyone else.* "The Dhryn have been quiet. Do any of you think that's going to last?" She kept it calm, but some of them flinched. *Easy to forget fear, safe in the Sinzi-ra's snow-white palace.* "Dr. Mamani has work to do," Mac continued, letting them see her exasperation. "Work backed by the Ministry of Extra-Sol Human Affairs, as well as the full resources of the IU consulate on Earth. As do we."

With that, she left.

Or tried. Mudge caught up to her in the midst of the maze of crates. "Norcoast. Norcoast! Wait."

Mac stopped, narrowing her eyes at him. "You're ruining a great exit line, Oversight. I don't get many of those."

"Giving me carte blanche to make arrangements. Yes, yes. But what kind of an example do you set by not waiting for your own assignment? Hmm?"

She blinked. "Pardon?"

"Hold out your imp and I'll transfer your duty list."

Wordlessly, Mac did as asked. Mudge in this mood? *As well argue the arrival of spring.*

They shifted closer to a stack of bags to avoid being run down by a hand lev. Mudge leaned toward Mac as he fiddled with their small workscreens, presumably sending her the list. Presumably, because he seemed to be more interested in who was nearby, sending anxious looks in every direction. Then, as if satisfied, his hands stilled and he met her eyes. "I'm scheduled on the shuttle with the rest." A hoarse whisper. "I should be going with you, Norcoast."

Mac frowned. "Do any of the others know I'm taking Emily to Base myself?"

"No. They'll find out on the shuttle. But I must—"

"I'll meet you at the way station, Oversight," Mac assured him, resisting the urge to lay her hand on his arm. Such gestures made Mudge break out in a sweat, entertaining but hardly kind. *And he deserved kindness.* "I'll be fine. Don't worry. They aren't letting me stay more than a few hours. A day at the most. You can contact me anytime." *Unless she switched her com off,* but Mac didn't see any point in bringing up that habit. "Sing-li will be his annoyingly overprotective self."

He pursed his lips, eyes still troubled. "The defenses here, on the transport—I don't like you being outside them. Bad enough last night."

"Last night went quite well, all things considered," Mac asserted, pocketing her imp now that the transfer was complete. *If there'd been one at all, and all this wasn't a ploy to keep her listening to Mudge's protest.* The spy mentality was catching.

"The Ro won't have forgotten you. It was a foolhardy risk, Norcoast. Foolhardy!"

"No, it wasn't." She paused to let three staff pass, arms filled with empty bags. "A little secret, Oversight, between you and me. Last night? An experiment." She watched the color drain from his florid cheeks and gave a curt nod. "Everyone believes the Ro are waiting for something. No one knows what—yet. I needed to convince certain pigheaded committee members it wasn't for Emily or myself to be in easy reach. Or we'd wind up virtual prisoners here." *Or bait.*

"What if you'd been wrong?"

She shrugged. "Worth knowing."

"Norcoast!"

Mac gave a tight smile. "If it makes you feel better, I was sure nothing would happen. The Ro pulled out, remember, taking their technology with them." *Leaving twenty-three Progenitors and millions of their kin dead.* "I have no reason to think they'd bother with two Human scientists."

"One came to watch you die. I'd call that 'bothering.' "

There had been something personal, or its alien equivalent. *She wasn't a fool.* But Mac shook her head again, dismissing Mudge's concern. "The Ro have more on their minds," she said, to him and to herself, "however sane or insane those might be. Our little encounter could have been nothing more than an opportunity—a voyeur's chance handed to the Ro by the Sinzi's new no-space technology. We can't attribute Human reactions to the alien. Believe me, I've learned that lesson."

"You've learned a great deal more, Norcoast," Mudge agreed, surprising her, then predictably: "but not enough by a long shot."

She reached out and poked him in the chest with a forefinger. "Which is why I have you."

He *harrumphed,* color returning to his cheeks. "We'll have to work flat out to be ready by the Sinzi-ra's launch date."

"There's a date?" Mac demanded, startled. The trouble with making suggestions to Anchen was how quickly she acted on them. The floor suddenly felt like a river, rushing by underfoot. "When?"

Mudge held up his imp. "You've the details."

No doubt she did. On discovering Mac was to practice reading, retraining her mind to that skill, Mudge had taken to sending her daily message summaries with annotations. *Innumerable annotations.* To be honest, his comments were often perceptive and some outright funny, whether Mudge had intended them that way or not.

Time. "This week, next month?" Mac insisted. "When?"

He glanced around, again checking for listeners. *A reasonable precaution*, Mac fumed, *if they weren't by now almost shouting to be heard over the racket from all sides.* "You leave tonight, 21:00. The trip by lev takes about six hours; you can grab some sleep. That means you'll arrive at Base 8:00 AM their time, but the day before—"

"I can do the conversion," Mac muttered. *Just after the second wave of breakfast through Pod Three.* She made a note to take some of the consulate's superb coffee in case Kammie hadn't finished her ritual: three cups to conscious, fourth to converse.

Mac's heart began to pound. Anticipation, dread, or a mix? She couldn't be sure.

Change. That at least.

"What about you and the team?"

"It's in—"

"Oversight, please?"

His *harrumph* was kinder. "The Sinzi-ra wants us out by tomorrow morning. We'll transport to the Antarctic station, hop to orbit from there, catch the shuttle to the way station, and meet you the next day."

She'd hoped to spend three days settling Emily, had been glumly sure she'd be lucky to get two. *One?* "Looks like we'll all be busy," Mac said, mind whirling. "Can you look after—?" She waved vaguely in the direction of the Origins Team.

"Don't worry. I'll get them to the way station. You get there, too."

Mac smiled at Mudge's anxious tone. "Just don't leave for Myriam without me."

Mac set her 'screen to hover beside her face as she strode briskly back to her quarters, preset at the angle permitting her to squint at it without walking into a wall, and the exact distance to stop her poking herself in the eye while manipulating the 'screen's display. She'd managed both wall-walk and poke-eye before now, when in a hurry to be somewhere while getting things done.

As now. She dictated in a steady whisper, ignoring any quizzical looks or neck flares from those she passed in the long white corridors. Instructions. Finishing lists. Those tripped off her tongue automatically. Moving to the field? *She could do that in her sleep.*

Harder were the private messages. On the lift ride up, Mac fumbled through, erasing more than she kept. Cautions to 'Sephe about Emily, when she wasn't sure what the Ministry agent already knew. Hints, suggestions—outright pleas for cooperation to Kammie, when there was no guarantee the other would do any of it. Kammie was being imposed upon here. Big time. In effect, Mac was asking the entire season, everything, be warped around Emily's needs. And she couldn't even predict what those might be.

Or that they were even real.

No matter friendship or professional courtesy, Kammie would have a fit. A quiet, professional, no-holds-barred-stubborn fit.

Mac wiped her latest recording. *Too needy.*

The lift opened, and she shifted well to one side to let Rumnor and four companions have the floor space the larger aliens required, particularly given the knife-encrusted bandoliers crisscrossing their torsos. "Good morning, Dr. Connor," the alien intoned sadly as the door closed. Thick yellow tears slipped down his facial hair, barely missing her feet. "I trust your bleeding went well."

Oh. That. Mac squirmed inwardly. *It had seemed brilliant at the time—could have been the beer.* "About that, Rumnor—" she began, intending to clear the confusion.

"You missed a fine cider," Rumnor interrupted, the others rumbling a doleful: "Wonderful." "Exquisite." "Never better." "Remarkable."

Then it was Mac's floor. She swallowed her explanation and patted his arm as she squeezed by to exit. "Next time," she promised.

"Is there cider on Myriam?"

Mac froze halfway through the lift door, turning to look up into those peppered brown eyes, rimmed in yellow crystals. "Why do you ask?"

"Dr. Connor. The lift cannot continue while you stand there."

Mac put one hand on the edge of the door. "What about Myriam?"

Five gloomy giant teddy bears stared down at her, none offering a word.

Seconds ticked by. Minutes. Mac made herself comfortable

against the lift doorframe, crossing her arms across her chest, eyes never leaving Rumnor's.

A Grimnoii at the back made an uncomfortable sound.

"Myriam," she suggested.

Rumnor snicked his teeth together. *Threat or exasperation?* Mac wondered. It could just as well be a nervous habit. She smiled.

Low, almost a growl. "Our people have an interest."

In Myriam or her going there? Mac had thought the Grimnoii neutral to indifferent, here to serve the Sinzi-ra somehow.

She should know not to make assumptions by now.

"What kind of interest?"

More snicking. Then silence.

"Well, if you're planning a trip, bring your own cider," she said pleasantly, and stood back to let the door close between them.

Aliens.

She filed the question of Grimnoii on Myriam for another day, almost running to her quarters. Once there, she closed the door behind her, wished for a lock, then headed for the terrace.

Where there were chairs she could move. Stripping off their cushions, Mac wedged two under the handles of the doors after she closed them, considered the arrangement, then added the remaining two chairs on top. She threaded the beads hanging to either side—her own personal Ro detectors—around the legs and backs of the chairs, twisting the ends together.

It wasn't a lock. But it was a demand for privacy even the too-helpful consulate staff should be able to figure out.

The faint shimmer of the membrane kept out the wild sky, with its rain and now gale force wind. *She would,* Mac decided, *have preferred the weather.*

She took the chair cushions to the corner where the wall curved out to meet the railing, and sat on the pile. Then she pulled off the *lamnas* and held it between her fingers—fingers which trembled ever so slightly until she frowned at them.

"It's not as if you know what kind of message he'd send," Mac reminded herself. " 'Feed my cat.' 'Tell Sing-li blah blah blah.' 'Forgot to mention . . .' " Here she stopped, unwilling to guess what Nikolai Trojanowski might have forgotten to say in their final, stolen minutes before he'd left.

Mac grinned. *Not that they said much.*

Whatever he wanted to tell her, using this strange method, she was willing to hear. More than willing. Mac brought the small ring to her lips, feeling foolish as she kissed it, then blew gently through the loop. *Nothing.*

Finally, slowly, she raised it to her right eye.

- CONTACT -

IS THIS EVEN WORKING? I feel . . .
        . . . like an idiot, staring at this thing . . . /determination/
"Paging Dr. Mackenzie Connor."
Where did . . . come from? No. Nothing formal . . . here . . . /warmth/ Never with Mac . . . safe with Mac . . .
"Hi, Mac. Bear with me. Anchen . . . better with practice." /doubt/ *Concentrate . . .* "Hardest part . . . time . . . busy." /anger/doubt/ *. . . can't trust anyone here . . . except maybe the Vessel . . .* /concern/ambivalence/ *. . . doesn't lie . . .* /belief/surprise/
Concentrate . . . "I'll . . . reports. Here . . . sharing . . . With you, I . . . pretending you're here." /heat/desire/need/ *Calm it down, fool . . . she doesn't need . . .* /need/longing/emptiness/ *. . . even if I do . . .* /effort/ *. . . Concentrate . . .*
". . . Vessel . . . more . . . the programming . . . complex personality, hard to pin down. Misses you. We share that." *Concentrate . . .*

* layered over *

—She smells metal—
The Vessel's voice was sad but resigned. "I wish Mackenzie Winifred Elizabeth Wright Connor Sol had come with us."
"She had other duties."
"Emily Mamani Sarmiento. Have you news? Is she recovering?"
I wish I knew the truth. Mac . . . so worried . . . I wanted to stay, hold her, make it right . . . all I could do was walk away . . . /tired guilt/ *. . . not my job.*

"The Sinzi-ra felt confident. It's going to take some time, Vessel. Our species doesn't recuperate as quickly as yours."

" 'A Dhryn is robust or a Dhryn is not.' We must be able to heal ourselves, Nikolai Piotr Trojanowski."

/curiosity/ "Why?"

"The Great Journey." As if humoring a child. "To stop for the lame or wounded would be to risk the Progenitor. She is the future."

"The Progenitor. We haven't heard from Her ship. Our captain has a valid point: we should confirm the rendezvous coordinates. What if She's left?"

"Then She's left." A hooting laugh. "What a strange face you make, *Lamisah*. Rest easy. The Progenitor will be where She has said. That is why I was sent. To find and bring the truth to Her. She will not leave without it."

* *layered over* *

—She tastes cinnamon and nutmeg—

"You shouldn't meet with that Dhryn alone." Cinder's voice was cold. "It's against procedure."

/sympathy/ *Hardest on her . . . losing so much to the Dhryn . . . resolve/* Need her eyes, use her hate . . . the Vessel only seems harmless . . .

"The vids were running. I knew you kept watch."

"I watch. As well I do—in all the years we've worked together, Nik," the Trisulian's tone turned to anger, "this is the first time I've seen you willfully blind."

"Blind to what?"

"This mission. The Dhryn with its so-convenient coordinates. We're being led into a trap. Can't you see it? I swear that female's turned your head inside out!"

rage/ How dare she . . . /caution/ *Not the only one on board who doubts the Vessel . . . who doubts Mac . . .* /effort/patience/icy calm/ "That's why I depend on you, Partner. What say we work up a few scenarios?"

/effort/ *Good little spy . . . lie to them all . . . lie to those closest . . . lead them where they must go despite their fear . . .* /pity/dread/patience/

* *layered over* *

—She feels weight—

Concentrate . . . " . . . does this work, Mac? There's no one else I can talk to . . ."

/loneliness/

I never knew I'd miss you like this . . .
fear/vulnerability/anger/
I can't . . . Not and do my job . . .
What have you done to me? /despair/
". . . go . . . doesn't . . . sense, Mac . . . better next . . ."
/emptiness/

- 5 -

PLOTS AND PERMUTATIONS

MAC SLIPPED THE RING back on her finger, turning it slowly around and around.

"That was—" She paused, considering. "Different."

Different. The Sinzi might refute any claims to telepathy, but what Mac had just experienced had to be the closest possible facsimile. Her mind hurt, as if pierced by shards of thought. On a more physical level, a headache brewed behind her eyes, promising worse to come.

In sub-teach, imposed images and impressions were organized; upon waking, they floated into the recipient's consciousness already part of memory and function. Useful.

This?

Emotion. Raw, uncensored. Nik's. That was the easiest to sort from the rest.

Mac wiped tears from her face, yawned to ease the knot of tension in her jaw. She'd clenched her free hand so tightly while looking through the *lamnas* the nails had left purple impressions in the palm. *Had to be the real one.* She rubbed it over her thigh, doing her best to stop reacting, to process instead.

As if that was easy. Mac blushed. *She'd felt what he'd felt.*

Which brought up an interesting question. Had Nik realized the Sinzi device would record his feelings as well as whatever words he tried to convey?

Probably not, Mac concluded. The man elevated privacy to a survival skill. This level of exposure couldn't have been what Nik intended.

It did promote a distinct realism . . . Mac closed her eyes, waiting for her treacherous body to settle to more reasonable expectations. *No time for a cold shower.*

The message—*what else could she call it?*—had been far more than Nik's words and emotion. It was as if she'd heard other voices as Nik must have heard them: the Dhryn's. The Trisulian's, Cinder. Overlapping and confused. Recollections. As if the *lamnas* had made a copy of specific memories. She focused, trying to sort out the babble. *Yes. Two different conversations.*

Not random choices. Nik must want her to understand or learn something from each. Or those conversations were important to him.

Or upsetting.

Mac chewed her lip in sympathy. *Still, nothing she didn't already know.* The Vessel was acting as its nature. So was Cinder. Her grief over the destruction of her species' males had been plain enough before they'd left Earth.

And Nik would use it.

Chilled, Mac opened her eyes. An insight she didn't want. *It wasn't the only one.*

There'd been fear to the point of dread mixed with his warmer feelings for her. Not fear for her sake; for his own. "Bet it was the salmon," Mac muttered. She clambered to her feet, then tossed the cushions on the table. "Give a guy a carving, next thing you know he's having nightmares about shared household bills and who drives the skim."

For a long moment, she stood staring out over the tumble of dark water and white caps.

Then Mac's lips softened into a smile.

"Cinder was right," she told the storm. "He's blind about one thing."

Caring for someone else might be inconvenient and damn distracting.

It wasn't a weakness.

"Where are my things?" Mac asked, doing her utmost not to sound aggravated or alarmed. Nursing a throbbing headache she blamed on the alien ring around her finger wasn't helping. Walking in from the terrace to find her quarters stripped of anything Human was distinctly not helping. "And who said you should take them?"

Two, the only individual among the consulate staff Mac could identify with any reliability, would, when they were alone together, show some emotion. *Usually disapproval of Mac's tendency to dig holes in the sand floor with her toes.* Now, she gave a small frown, one of several practiced Human expressions Mac suspected staff employed at will. "Your things, Dr. Connor, have been packed into a shipping container. Myriam is a restricted environment. All materials brought to the planet must be catalogued and sterilized according to IU protocols. Charles Mudge III sent a very clear memo."

No doubt. Mac absently scuffed one toe in the perfectly raked sand where her desk had been. She'd already looked into the closet. Its outer door had been opened—she could tell by the raindrops on the floor. The transport lev had probably docked alongside and loaded up while she'd been staring into the *lamnas*. Staff were efficient, she had to give them that.

Too efficient for their own good, this time. "Sorry, but you'll have to bring it all back," Mac informed the alien. "I have to sort out what goes with Dr. Mamani."

"Dr. Mamani earlier identified her belongings and equipment. They have been packed for shipping to Norcoast Salmon Research Facility."

"Base," Mac corrected automatically. There must have been a constant stream of traffic through her quarters while she was gone, every footprint carefully erased from the sand. *Emily could be too efficient as well.* She pulled out her imp and waved it in the air. "I'd made a list." Out loud, the protest was a little more petulant than she'd planned.

"Which we accessed and followed. The few items not on your list we included for your comfort, knowing your excellent care with budget. The IU will cover all transport costs." Two hesitated. "Was this incorrect, Dr. Connor?"

Picturing crates of wooden salmon now accompanying her to

Myriam, Mac gave up. *Maybe they'd let her sort out what should be shipped back to Earth during the trip to the transect gate.* "Did you leave me any clothes?"

A hint of smug in Two's otherwise composed face. "We are informed as to your schedule, Dr. Connor. There is a bag packed for your trip to—Base. As well, we have set aside all of the personal items you most commonly access for use during your journey."

Efficient and thoughtful. Mac shook her head. Although, by that criterion, Two likely packed the hockey puck she liked to roll between her hands while thinking, instead of her comb. *As for clothes?* She refused to imagine. *Aliens.* "You win, Two."

"I wasn't aware of a competition, Dr. Connor."

Mac grinned. "I don't suppose you'd consider coming to Myriam? You know what a mess I'll make without you."

The other being shook her head just so, an accomplished mimic. "Our duty is to the Sinzi-ra and her guests, Dr. Connor." Two brought both hands to her throat and bowed, deep and low, to Mac. Rising, she lowered her hands and gave a short lilting whistle through her pursed lips.

This was something new. Mac wasn't sure whether to imitate or ignore the gesture. She compromised by ducking her head quickly and giving a self-conscious *chirp.*

"You have been reasonable," Two announced. "May your journey be a safe and successful one, Dr. Connor, so we may have the privilege of serving you once more."

With that, she turned and walked from the room.

A compliment, Mac decided. Though if that was Two's honest opinion of her, she assuredly did not want to meet any guests the staff considered unreasonable.

Left alone, Mac considered her options. She could slump in one of the Sinzi's jelly-chairs. She should be able to force her eyes to read Mudge's detailed notes. *That's what she should do.* Her stomach reminded her she'd missed another meal.

She caught herself turning the ring around and around on her finger. *Not going there again.* Not soon. Anchen hadn't really looked into her own *lamnas* while demonstrating its use, something Mac now thought she understood. That experience, if at all comparable to hers, was disturbing on every level.

Intimate didn't begin to cover it.

Perhaps explaining why the rings stayed on Anchen's long fingers?

She refused to speculate about what Anchen—or any of her disparate personalities—saw or felt.

"And I'm not sharing either," Mac decided aloud.

Problem was, this close to leaving? She couldn't sit still. Especially in an empty room. Mac grabbed the small round bag Two had left for her in the washroom. Time to go. Somewhere.

After one last peek.

She pulled Nik's glasses from her pocket—it had become a habit, carrying them with her—and held them in front of her eyes. They'd fall off her nose if she tried to wear them properly.

Through the innocuous-seeming lenses, the walls of her sitting room revealed themselves as anything but plain and white. Lines, varying in thickness, scrolled over their surface like intricately woven threads. Among those threads, some behind, some in front, gleamed creatures small and large. Mac knew many, or their Terran equivalents. Shrimp and hydra, corals and urchins, sea cucumbers and squirts, curly-shelled oysters. Others were hauntingly strange. Floating orbs with tentacles spiraled around their girth. Eyes that glittered in their threes and sixes. Ribbons and segments, differently proportioned from any on Earth. The artist who created this had loved sea life, and known more oceans than hers.

Mac had never thought to wonder why she'd been assigned this room, of all the rooms in the guest wing, until seeing it through Nik's glasses.

It hadn't been for her benefit—the Sinzi-ra knew Humans couldn't see this range of color unassisted. A recognition of her specialty, perhaps, or her interests. A visual signal to inform the staff of what might suit this particular Human best.

Regardless, her being housed here held a subtle rightness of the sort Mac was coming to believe Anchen enjoyed for its own sake, a generosity without the Human need for a recipient. *Important,* she decided, *to remember that.*

And unfair—having to leave when she was finally making some progress.

Mac tucked the glasses away and the room was white on white once more.

Since arriving, she'd kept a mental list of all the things she would do before leaving the Interspecies Consulate. With an impossibly few hours left, Mac sat under a dripping tree and tallied what she'd missed, which was most of it. "The aquatic delegates," she sighed, taking a bite of tart apple. Not that they'd cooperated. Their portion of the consulate had been out-of-bounds to air breathers, they'd left meeting attendance to representatives who did breathe air, and, to be frank, spent much their time sightseeing in the ocean itself. She'd hoped to casually bump into one of their groups doing just that. "Seen any groupers?" she grinned to herself, imagining herself trying to communicate underwater.

She pulled the hood of her raincoat farther over her head, strangely content despite her list. The storm had abated, but the leaves held sufficient drops to be a nuisance for a while yet. Moisture polished tile and stone; there were busy new brooks alongside the paths. With the settling wind, a chill mist rising under the trees added a nice touch of drama.

She couldn't imagine why staff had put up such a protest to her spending time out here. She grinned. In the end they'd provided both raincoat and picnic, almost shooing her into the garden.

Not that Mac had initially planned anything so restful while waiting for the lev to Base. No, she'd intended to be useful.

There'd been only one problem.

"No one needs me." She tossed the core into a shrub large enough to hide it from frantic gardeners, but not, she trusted, from anything hungry. "Imagine that."

Like old times, having Emily wave a distracted greeting from where she stood surrounded by crates and attentive staff, giving instructions in a staccato blur. Although at Base, Mac thought with amusement, those in attendance would have been worshipful students and a certain tidal researcher. The wave sent the same message. *Later, Mac. I'm busy.*

Mudge and Lyle had been much the same, and the Sthlynii

downright stammering in their panic. She could have hung around to watch, but the harried looks of those still packing weren't as amusing as she'd hoped.

"You'd think they'd never expected to move from here," Mac told the chubby pigeon, or whatever, pecking near her feet. Another miss on her to-do list for this amazing place: learn the birds.

Picnic finished, she lay back on the bench, using her bag for a pillow. Most of her fit. She didn't mind leaving her feet on the ground. For now, at least.

The leaves overhead were tossing this way and that in the gusty wind, revealing glimpses of cloud doing the same. "That's me," Mac whispered, squinting upward. "Macthisaway, Macthaddaway, Macwhoknowswhichaway." Who'd have guessed the day would come when she'd be more anxious about a quick trip to Base than an indefinite stay on an alien world?

With Mudge. "Good old Oversight," she murmured, catching a cold drop on her tongue. That much of home, she'd have.

She'd wanted to say good-bye to Anchen. To thank her. Maybe dare ask questions about the *lamnas.* But no staff would say where the Sinzi-ra could be found, and Mac had to trust the gracious alien would find her before she boarded the lev.

"So now I'm relaxing," Mac reminded herself. "Everyone says I should. No one needs me right now. It's a gift."

She spent an eternity staring up at the leaves, determined to enjoy the peace and rustling quiet.

Then checked the time again.

"Gods. That was two minutes?"

She sat up and shrugged off her coat, tying it around her waist. The two bags, hers and the picnic remnants, she stuffed into the crook of a low branch. "Exploring this place," she explained to the pigeon, "was on my list, too."

Then Mac started walking.

She let her feet and the lay of the land dictate her choice of paths, which meant little more than avoiding the larger puddles. Two hadn't packed extra shoes in her bag. As for getting lost, Mac was sure if she did, staff would appear from behind a tree to tactfully suggest the correct direction of the consulate. This wasn't wilderness, despite the undergrowth and moss-coated trees. It was a politely dressed fortress, designed to protect those here as much as ensure their privacy.

Still, the illusion was pleasing, the footing deteriorating in a manner that promised something special to the intrepid hiker, be there two feet marching or more. Whistling happily under her breath, Mac came up with fourteen species she'd met who could manage this uneven ground without help, even if one didn't have feet so much as a slime-bedecked undercarriage she'd tried to examine without success. Multispecies social events, she'd discovered to her chagrin, brought out the same annoying proprieties as any Human affair. Crawling under a chair while in evening finery, though in the interest of scientific curiosity, still collected disapproving frowns.

She ducked a low branch. The minor obstacle reduced her list to twelve. Mac grinned, almost wishing the chance to test her new-found ability to predict who she might meet, eyeball to nasal orifice, while enjoying the less tidy path. Almost.

There was something to be said for tramping alone, she admitted, taking a deep breath.

And gagging on a smell.

"What the—"

Stopping where she was, at the base of a small rise in the path, Mac took a more restrained, scientific sniff. *Not one of her twelve.* She scowled, knowing what, or in this case who, was responsible for that cloying, expensive musk. And the only way *se* could be here, was if *se'd* flown.

Mac didn't mind Frow as a rule. *Except this one.*

"*Se* Lasserbee," she shouted. "I know you're here."

The forest continued to rustle and drip overhead and to the sides. A bird, unseen but loud, expressed a similar opinion of the intruders. Quieter, more distant, Mac caught the low snarl and thump of breakers against the cliffs. She'd gone east then, away from the landing field.

She continued to watch the path ahead.

Se's hat appeared first, a multipointed affair that marked, according to Mudge, both military rank and present dominance mind-set. *If that was the case,* Mac decided, seeing more points than usual, Se *Lasserbee was going to be a royal pain.*

The Frow were a stratocracy, their military forming the government as well as holding most civil service posts. This state had existed through so many generations of idyllic peace and prosperity that ranks were now inherited and uniforms were exaggerations of style totally without function in combat. The species itself was famed for its unique biochemistry and a certain unfortunate stress response, hence Emily's joke. "Why don't you put a Nerban and a Frow in the same taxi?" Mac mouthed the words. "Because the former sweats alcohol and the latter sparks when upset."

Despite paying very close attention, she hadn't seen any sparks fly yet. *The day was young.*

Under the unwieldy hat came the rest of *Se* Lasserbee, *se's* uniform a somber blue bedecked with thumb-sized silver springs, each marking the appropriate spot for one of *se's* family's honors—said honors being kept safely in the family vault at all times. Two other Frow appeared over the rise behind the first, their hats having a mere three points. *Lackeys,* Mac judged, but kept part of her attention on them. A little too easy, in her opinion, to don a misleading hat.

Se Lasserbee's cloud of musk proceeded *se* down the path and Mac sneezed before she could stop herself. Perfume, food choice, or medication, it had to interfere with more respiratory systems than hers. Just as well for interspecies' tact this was the only Frow who wore the stuff. Why, no one would explain.

Probably covering up something personal. Or some type of olfactory camouflage, however overdone to Human senses. *Or assault?*

"*Se* Lasserbee. To what do I owe this effort?" Mac felt constrained to acknowledge the obvious. The Frow body form was far from ideal for a narrow, irregular footpath like this. There had to be a large custom-equipped lev on the other side of the rise. They should have waited for her to come to them.

But no. The three continued toward her, each with eyes fixed on the path. Every step had to be premeditated and carefully taken. It was like watching a slow-motion accident.

She found herself flattered. *The Sinzi-ra must have rubbed off on her.*

Mac had seen vids of Frow scampering down the vertical cliffs of their home world, long arms outstretched to grab the tiniest holds.

The membrane of leathery skin and fine bone from finger to ankle joint made them the closest to a flight-capable sentient encountered by the IU, other than the Dhryn feeder form. Close, but not close enough. A Frow who lost a fingerhold fell to *se, ne,* or *sene's* death as easily as the next being. She had noticed the membrane let Frow hide what they were eating from one another, presumably a critical need before they invented social dining or cooperative daycare.

Their heads sat on stiff necks that bore accordionlike ridges on either side. Those worked independently, in Mac's limited experience, to tilt the head an extraordinary distance one way or the other. There were two eyes with slit-pupils, four nostrils, and a fanged mouth without lips but still capable of forming understandable Instella courtesy of a thin flexible tongue. These features were tightly grouped in the lower left quadrant of the front of the head, giving a Frow the appearance of never really looking right at you, even when doing so. The rest of the face and the top of the head was kept beneath a hat, itself secured by a strap below the protruding chin.

The head and neck were set below the shoulders, but where Sinzi shoulders rose with delicate flare, those of a Frow were great lumps studded with spines that shot from the base of the fine bones supporting their membrane. Mac kept waiting to see the spines move in some display—they seemed flexible—but the Frow of her acquaintance hadn't done anything interesting with them. The fabric spikes on their hats mimicked the real thing. Already top-heavy in appearance, given their slender torsos, short legs, and long arms, the spikes made a Frow appear ready to tip over and impale the ground at any moment.

Which was the truth. On land, flat land, they moved on two widely splayed legs and only when forced to do so, greatly preferring to lurch into position when no one was looking to assume a dignified, upright posture as if they'd been there all along. It was only polite to let Frow arrive first to any meeting for this reason. As for chairs, they were pointless. The beings didn't sit; their torsos couldn't bend.

Or fit inside a taxi. *Ruining a perfectly good joke.*

Mac's visitors kept their arms wrapped tightly around themselves, as if protecting their uniforms from a possible fall was more important than using them for balance. She couldn't help putting her arms out in anticipation, though her chances of catching one if it toppled were remote. *Provide a softer landing, maybe.*

Se Lasserbee staggered to a halt, much to Mac's relief and *se's* own, then took a moment to compose *se-self.* As *se* wrapped *se's* arms proudly around *se-self, se's* membrane thus becoming a handsome mantle, the last of *se's* companions planted a foot on an upturned root and began to leave the vertical. From that moment, disaster was inevitable. All three collided and went down in a mass of silver-sparkled blue, membraned arms flailing and hands clutching whatever was closest.

There was a plaintive rattle as they settled.

Mac froze, not knowing if it would be a breach to try and help, or if she should look into the distance until they pulled themselves apart. She compromised, staying close enough to assist if they asked, but looking, mostly, away.

Between peeks to see how they were managing.

Not well. One of the lackeys had a grip on a tree. Another had *ne's* long, strong fingers wrapped over most of Se Lasserbee's face, while that worthy had *se's* hands firmly on the first lackey's leg. They didn't seem able to let go.

Great instinct for a cliff dweller, Mac thought with interest. "May I help?" she offered at last.

Se Lasserbee's mouth wasn't covered. "Ah. Dr. Connor," *se* said in *se's* metal in bucket voice, the words preceded by a breathless pant. "Ah. What a pleasant surprise. You might want to move away."

About to comply, Mac noticed wisps of smoke coming from beneath the motionless tangle of aliens. "You're sparking," she commented and then winced, having floundered yet again on the rocks of interspecies' protocol. *Never mention bodily functions.* "I don't mean you personally," she qualified. "But . . . there is something burning under—" an inclusive wave, "—you."

"Yes. Ah. Most observant. We aren't at risk, Dr. Connor. Please. A moment."

Although this close their skin looked more like flexible blubber than leather, their uniforms didn't appear flammable. *Sensible pre-*

caution, Mac judged. Doing her best to keep a nonchalant expression, she tried to spot the source of the tiny sparks, clearly visible in the growing shadow of late afternoon. *Particularly,* she observed, *around the poor Frow on the bottom of the pile.*

The likeliest candidate appeared to be a narrow channel in the skin underneath the arms themselves, from which the tips of thick solitary hairs protruded like a comb's teeth. Might be some kind of spark-generating organ.

Or it could really be a comb, Mac chided herself. The spikes on the shoulders looked to require a bit of buffing. Who knew what lay under the uniforms themselves?

Let alone the hats.

With agonizing deliberation, the three Frow sorted themselves out. Mac found a flatter root than most for a perch and watched, fascinated. They acted as if a false move could plummet them all into some abyss. The simplest shift of a finger involved a great deal of discussion, some of it loud, in their own language. Several times, one grip was replaced in favor of shifting another.

It took, from Mac's surreptitious checks of the time, seventeen minutes and twenty seconds before *Se* Lasserbee stood free and proud in front of her once more.

Better safe than sorry had to be a Frow maxim, she decided, adding that to her knowledge of their kind.

The other two spent an alarming few moments lurching around to stamp out any smoldering spots where they'd lain on the path. Not that there were many, due to the storm's moisture. Mac held her breath until they were safely still again.

"Ah," began *Se* Lasserbee, dignity reclaimed. "Dr. Connor. What a surprise to encounter you in this—" *se* glanced around at the forest, as if lost for the word in Instella, the IU's common tongue, "—place."

"Forest." Mac stood, brushing shreds of bark from her pants. "What do you want, *Se?*" *Not that she couldn't guess.*

"Want? Ah. A moment of discourse with you would be pleasing, as always, Dr. Connor."

She did her best not to scowl. The beings were sadly out of their environment. The other two had unfolded their neck ridges to lean their heads left, in order to stare at the trees. *Maybe they hoped some would be climbable.* The occasional spark continued to flash.

"A private discourse," the Frow elaborated. "On a matter of great importance."

They might have watched for her to leave the consulate, or simply asked any staff where she was. Mac hadn't left instructions to be undisturbed. *Something to remember for next time.* She should have expected to be contacted by someone from the idiot faction before leaving. A pithy message she couldn't read, perhaps. An appointment she'd somehow miss.

Hardly this ambush by the woefully unable.

Clever, she acknowledged, and decided to oblige, curious despite good sense telling her it would be nothing she'd want to hear. "Of course, *Se* Lasserbee. Why don't we go back inside, find a meeting room—"

Se drew *se-self* up to full height. "What is wrong with this fine place, Dr. Connor?"

Fair enough. "Nothing," Mac said blandly. "Here it is. Now, what are we to discuss?"

Before *se* replied, the three Frow went through a great deal of neck ridge unfolding and looking about, which made them totter like broken twigs about to fall. Apparently satisfied they were alone with their quarry, they stopped and looked at Mac. "You are escorting Dr. Mamani to her new place, Dr. Connor," *se* said. "I must accompany her. Take me with you."

To Base? "You know I can't," Mac replied far more mildly than she felt. *Damn aliens.* At least here, this time, she had the rules firmly on her side. "The IU must petition the Ministry for Extra-Sol Affairs for any nonterrestrial to leave the consular grounds."

"We've filed such petition. Ah. But these things take time, Dr. Connor. We are aware you leave tonight. You can include me. I have a cloak."

Mac blinked. "A cloak," she repeated.

One of the lackeys volunteered: "A large one."

If the Frow thought a cloak, large or otherwise, could disguise their shape or movement for an instant, they'd been reading the wrong brochures. *Or a certain Myg was involved—*Mac stopped her train of thought right there. *This was serious.* "I might be willing to convey a message to Dr. Mamani on your behalf, if I judge its contents worth her time—and that's generous, *Se* Lasserbee. The Sinzi-ra set strict protocols for future interviews. Emily's been through enough." This last with a ferocity Mac couldn't help.

Whether this particular species, or this individual, could detect the emotion in her voice was debatable. Not that she could detect any change beyond volume in *se's* tone either. Still, she had to believe those representatives sent to Earth were given some training in humanity.

"Ah," another of those breathless sounds, this time more pronounced. *A request for attention? New topic? Gas?* "Indeed generous, Dr. Connor," the Frow told her, "and we thank you. But we have no message. We do not wish to talk to Dr. Mamani. What recollections she has of the Myrokynay have been passed to our superiors by the Sinzi-ra. And, as you say, she's been through a significant ordeal. Ah. We would not wish to be responsible for causing her further stress in an effort to recall more."

Mac tilted her head to better line up *se's* angled eyes with hers. The pupils were black, slicing through an iris of pale green. Attractive eyes. In fact, without the black spiky hat, the Frow was quite a handsome being, in *se's* own gaunt way.

And a politician.

She couldn't afford to trade subtleties. "If you don't want to talk to her," Mac growled, "why do you want to come with us?"

"Ah." All three Frow repeated their look-around behavior before *se* continued. "Above all else, we desire contact with the Myrokynay. We believe they will take advantage when Dr. Mamani leaves the protection of the Sinzi—"

"Never!" The alien staggered back a step and almost fell. Se *obviously understood* that *Human tone.* Mac took a breath and calmed herself, though her hands shook. "You misunderstand," she said more quietly. "Dr. Mamani isn't bait. She remains under Anchen's protection—and ours—no matter where she is. More to the point, *Se* Lasserbee, the Ro aren't interested. She was a tool they used and discarded."

"In your opinion of events," *se* countered.

"My—" Mac's mouth fell open. Then she sputtered: "They did their best to murder her!"

"Ah. Conceivably a miscalculation. We Frow believe the Myrokynay could be beyond life and death as we experience such things. Ah. They could represent the next stage of all our futures." *Se* touched two points on *se's* hat. "How can we interpret their actions, using only our limited knowledge? How can we possibly guess their great plan?"

"The Ro's 'great plan' is to be the last ones breathing," Mac ground out. "Not interpretation. Not guesswork. That's what they told me, *Se* Lasserbee, while they waited for me and all of us to be killed by their Dhryn."

"Ah. The conversation not recorded by any means at the Sinzi's disposal."

"I heard it." Mac silently dared the alien to utter one more breathless 'ah.' That was all the excuse she'd ask to turn on her perfectly path-adapted heels and leave. Quickly.

The Frow did have a point. She'd wished for a corroborating recording every day since. But the Ro's terrible 'voice' had somehow been focused inside her body and Emily's.

And Emily didn't remember.

"I don't doubt you, Dr. Connor," *Se* Lasserbee said, unwittingly prolonging their conversation in the woods. "Don't take offense. I'm a soldier, not a mystic. I know protocols and procedures. Forms. Any form you like. I have a talent."

Mac's lips twitched at this.

"I have difficult—nay, impossible orders," the Frow went on. "I'm to go where I will have the best chance of encountering one of the Bless—one of the Myrokynay. Encounter invisible beings who live in no-space? That no one else can find? Yet my superiors expect me to succeed. You have been gracious to listen to me."

Se stretched out *se's* long arms and flapped the membranes from finger to hip, then dramatically wrapped *se's* arms to hide *se's* face. The others exchanged a look Mac couldn't interpret, but stayed as they were.

Se *did appear miserable.*

Mac frowned, aware she was extrapolating from Human. *Always a mistake.*

None of them moved or spoke. The minutes dragged. *Bad as relaxing,* Mac thought. "*Se* Lasserbee," she prompted finally. At this rate, they could be here past sunset. "*Se.* Please. There's nothing I can do. I've my own questions, believe me, but I don't know how to reach the Ro. No one does." The Atrium had an entire section devoted to analyzing the modification to their communications system provided by the Ro. Linguists from the original Gathering were working on the code used to convey the instructions for that modification.

Without success; so far, the Ro kept their secrets.

As for replaying the call that had brought the Dhryn to Sol System? Anchen had reassured Mac that the IU had sent a blunt warning to the Trisulians, the only ones outside the Gathering to possess that ability, not to employ it. They weren't ready to set a trap they couldn't, as yet, safely spring. The Trisulians had obeyed.

So far, Mac echoed, wishing again that Cinder had stayed behind. Nik was the alien expert, no doubts there. But he hadn't been the one Cinder had begged to take her weapons because she hadn't trusted herself not to commit murder.

In Mac's opinion, said weapons shouldn't have been given back, but Cinder had been as fully armed as her partner when they'd departed.

Not a topic for current company on any level. Mac knew better than to mention Trisulians to the Frow, both former military powers, both edgy where their historical spheres of influence now overlapped. Long memories. Their partnership within the IU rested on peace and prosperity, not friendship.

A little louder. "*Se* Lasserbee. Did you hear me?"

"Ah." A green eye peered over a fold of membrane. "Dr. Connor? Why are you still here?"

He'd dismissed her?

Mac didn't know whether to stamp her foot in frustration or laugh. She'd been given a polite exit and missed it. *Next time,* she vowed.

Now, however, she was stuck and hurriedly fumbled for something non-committal. "What will you do now?" she ventured.

"Do? Ah. I do have an alternative in mind, but I hesitate to reveal it at this time."

Fine by her, Mac sighed with relief. Then she frowned, remembering a certain elevator full of cider-obsessed Grimnoii. "You do know Myriam is flat," this with a suggestive kick of her foot along the path.

Silence.

Mac's frown deepened as she tried to read anything but polite attentiveness on the part of the Frow. "With no trees," a gesture to their surroundings. "It's a desert. A flat desert."

"With the most magnificent rift valleys, Dr. Connor," one of the lackeys burst out enthusiastically. "Sheer, comfortable cliffs. We've seen stunning images—"

"Let me guess," Mac interrupted, eyes on the individual with the most points on his hat. "Your government has an interest."

Se Lasserbee answered. "Every government has an interest in the origin of the Dhryn plague."

Mac resisted the urge to pull at her hair. *Gods only knew what that gesture might mean to a Frow.* "Of course they do," she acknowledged. "But this is a scientific expedition."

"I'm sure, Dr. Connor, you don't mean to imply Frow lack qualified experts to contribute."

Definitely a politician, Mac decided. Given shouting was statistically unlikely to be diplomatic, and she had nothing worth saying that didn't involve volume, there was only one reasonable response.

Mac untied her coat from around her waist, took her time shaking it out, then draped it over her head.

And waited.

There was a hush she gleefully thought of as shocked.

A hush followed by rapid stumbling footsteps. Mac crossed her fingers. The way back to their transport was uphill. If they fell again, it could be messy. Sparks at the very least.

Not to mention she'd have to hide under her coat until they untangled.

She counted to a hundred after the last clear footstep, in case the Frow had stopped to see if she meant her dismissal.

At last, Mac pulled off the coat, taking a relieved breath of cooler air. A few sunbeams raked low through the trees, catching in the mist. No sign of the Frow. She was either getting the hang of this interspecies' communication thing . . .

Or the Frow had thought she was nuts and left.

"Whatever works," she muttered aloud.

First the Grimnoii and now the Frow implying they, too, were heading for Myriam. It was as if her decision to move to the field had been a signal to everyone else around here.

Mac started walking back to the consulate, deliberately admiring the plants she hadn't had time to name.

Let them come along.

If any of them thought they'd interfere with her team, they didn't know this Human very well at all.

- 6 -

FAREWELLS AND FINDINGS

THE REST WOULD LEAVE in the morning via the walkways outside, joining their equipment and supplies on the consulate's landing field. Emily was already in the more protected launch hangar, overseeing the stowage of her gear. Mac, after her walk under the trees, had decided on a different route.

"You could tell me why we're going this way," Sing-li protested half under his breath as they rode the lift to the basement. Mac, her hand on the wall control, grinned and shifted her bag to her shoulder. He gave that a glum look as well, having tried, unsuccessfully, to take it from her. "And why I have to wear this?"

Her grin widened. "Looks good on you."

He plucked the fabric. "There had to be something else."

"Blame Fourteen," Mac replied. "I just said cheerful." *And anything but black.* Everyone knew the Myg regularly shipped Human clothing back home—and not just any clothing.

"I'm a dessert tray."

"And a very cheerful one," she assured him, admiring the parade of dancing cake slices, happy-faced cookies, and improbable grapevines now stretching across the large man's ample chest and shoulders. True, the overall color scheme was painfully flamboyant and, to top it off, the artist had filled any gaps with dots of bright orange-red, making it appear from a distance that Sing-li had recently been splattered with overripe tomatoes. "At least you're inconspicuous."

"In what possible sense of the word?" he sighed, plucking at the offending shirt again.

The lift door opened. Mac paused before walking out, searching for a tactful answer to his question. Sing-li laughed ruefully before she could find it. "What am I worrying about?" he said. "We'll be at Base. I'll blend right in."

And can't possibly loom. Mac kept that satisfied thought to herself as she shot him a grateful smile. She had one day. Was it asking too much to try and make that time as normal as possible?

As for their destination, she wasn't sure herself why she'd had to come down here, only that she needed to walk this long white corridor once more. Not to the Atrium, with its preoccupied researchers and reconfigured spaces. She passed those access doors, Mac taking little hop-steps to keep ahead of Sing-li's longer strides, both of them nodding automatic greetings at the varied aliens stationed at security checks along the way. Fewer than there had been, she noticed. The consulate had other defenses now.

Here. Mac paused in front of another door. Sing-li didn't say anything as she reached for the control and pressed it.

The room was empty, an expanse of Sinzi white that might never have held a cage, might never have sheltered a Dhryn guest. Stepping inside, Mac glanced upward, seeing only an unremarkable ceiling that might never have opened into the Atrium itself, that might never have supported a mass of recording and transmitting equipment, so every move, every word could be seen and heard across the Interspecies Union, by more beings, and types of beings, than she could imagine.

There might never have been blood, Dhryn-blue, Human-red, on the floor.

She shivered, though the room was pleasantly warm. Parymn Ne Sa Las had been difficult and opinionated, but left all he knew to sacrifice himself in service to his Progenitor. The Vessel he'd become had harbored a new personality, Her personality, charming and strangely comforting.

Who was the Vessel now?

Mac sighed. She hadn't had much luck with Dhryn. She hoped Nik was doing better.

Sing-li had entered with her. He didn't say a word, but his fingertips brushed her elbow so lightly she might have imagined it.

He was right. No point lingering. Mac shook her head at herself and led the way back out to the corridor, heading for the next. The underground complex on this level twisted with the cliffs beyond, eventually connecting to the hangar.

She would have come here even if it hadn't, Mac realized, her feet slowing to a stop again in front of another door. It was closed. *Likely locked.*

"Mac. You know we can't go in there."

She frowned, but not at her troubled companion.

"Mac."

She thrust her bag at him. "Here."

"Dr. Connor. The lev's waiting." More resigned comment than complaint. Sing-li had learned to read her by now.

"This won't take long," Mac promised absently, putting her hand on the door itself and giving a tiny push.

For some reason, she wasn't surprised when the large door swung noiselessly out of her path. She stepped inside and closed the door behind her, muffling Sing-li's unhappy protest.

Her eyes needed a few seconds to adjust from the brilliance of the corridor to this shadowed place. Impatient, Mac lifted her hands as she walked forward in case they'd rearranged the walls, something the consulate was prone to do. She'd rather not arrive at Base with a red nose or black eye to explain.

Although that would be easier than anything else from these past weeks.

This had been the tank room, a simple name for an extraordinary feat of engineering. Here, in this cavernous space, the Sinzi had built the first known permanent and accessible enclosure of no-space, a dimension beyond, behind, above, or after—whatever confusion you liked—normal reality. For no-space allowed certain liberties with time and distance, including winking a ship and its contents between connected star systems.

With Sinzi practicality, they'd used this marvel to house a block of shrimp-rich ocean, so their favorite delicacy could be instantly accessed from any room with a connected table tank. With Sinzi forethought, this not coincidentally provided an immediate demonstration of this breakthrough's potential for selected consulate guests.

The shrimp? Although tasty, they hadn't fared as well—direct exposure to no-space still meant what went in alive, came back dead. Albeit fresh.

The Sinzi were working on that.

No-space was at the core of everything Ro, who had no difficulties surviving it, or bringing along friends. The Ro hadn't, until encountering the Sinzi's little demonstration, found a way to directly observe areas of real space from inside their realm.

Small wonder the Ro had been drawn to the Sinzi's toy.

Mac's nose twitched. They'd cleaned up the flood of water and its dying life, released when she'd fought to save herself from the Ro. Destroying the main tank had been an inevitable side effect, but no one blamed her. To everyone's relief, the table tanks had been replaced overnight with burnished slabs of local stone, presumably spy-proof.

She hadn't been here since.

Her eyes caught a glimpse of light and Mac moved in that direction, hands still up.

They met something cool and slick and hard.

And familiar.

"Gods, no," she breathed as she stopped. Mac stared ahead until her eyes burned, gradually making out details.

She might have been looking through a porthole into abyssal depths. The lights she could see were indicators on shapeless panels, pulsating greens and blues and yellows. They were stacked in a pyramid arrangement, the other sides and top beyond her view. The dim flickers reflected from the waving arms of anemones, the lacy fronds of sea fan and tube worm, flashed from the back of a small white crab. They were residents of a rising mound of pale bone, stacked before the pyramid like an offering.

Whalebone, Mac identified, sagging with relief.

Some of the glow marked the edges of swaying spirals of kelp. The immense plants grew up into the darkness. Between, darker shadows teased, sending back glints of moving green or blue or yellow, as if the artificial lights caught knife blades slipping through the forest.

Salmon.

Mac pulled back, only now aware of the throb beneath her feet, and braced herself.

The Sinzi-ra had rebuilt her tank.

She'd counted on it.

"I'm here," she announced, proud of her clear, firm voice. "Mackenzie Winifred Elizabeth Wright Connor Sol." She wasn't talking to the trapped things. She was talking to what she couldn't see. *Yet.*

Silence. A curious octopus tiptoed toward her, its huge eyes unblinking. After a long moment of mutual scrutiny, the mollusk made its decision about the Human and suddenly jetted backward into the dark.

"You talked to me before. Here I am." *Talk?* Mac's hands became fists. She remembered all too well how the Ro's version of speech had seemed to rip through her skin and burn itself into the flesh beneath. "In case you're confused on the topic, I'm not dead." She replayed that last bit mentally. *Another gem of interspecies communication.*

The darkness developed chill fingers, pressing against her face, working their way down her throat. Mac wrapped her arms around her middle and cursed her imagination. "What do you want from us? Answer me!" she ordered, careful not to shout, but her voice echoed.

An echo complete with the tinkle of small silver rings.

Mac turned as far as she dared, unwilling to put her back to the tank and what might—she dreaded as much as hoped—might be hiding inside. "Anchen?"

A ball of translucent red ignited between them; Mac assumed it was some kind of portable light. It cast a warm pink glow over the Sinzi-ra's white gown and skin. The great topaz eyes remained in shadow. "Hello, Mac," Anchen greeted her.

"What are you doing here?"

"Waiting for you. I'd be a poor host indeed if I did not wish you well on your journey."

Mac swallowed, keeping a wary eye on the dark tank. "How did you know?" The consulate was clear of the vidbots annoyingly prominent in Human public places. Mac had grown rather fond of believing she could skulk at will. *Had that changed?*

The light was enough to see Anchen's half bow. "We are alike, Mac, in several respects. I felt confident you would revisit those places of meaning to you before you left, as would I. I confess, I hadn't expected to find you conversing with the past." A thoughtful pause. "Or do you truly believe the Myrokynay have slipped past our watch and returned? And, if so, that they will reveal themselves to you if you shout at them?"

Put that way . . . Mac winced and stopped there. "I thought it worth a try," she shrugged. "Everyone else thinks I matter to the Ro. And you did rebuild the tank," this last a half question. *Why?*

The Sinzi-ra moved to stand beside her, taller and more fragile, yet with an otherworldly grace even the shadows couldn't disguise. One fingertip, with its stiff useful nail, tapped the dark glass. "Like you, I thought it worth a try," answered the alien.

The *lamnas* slid along Anchen's long finger, sending glints of rose from the light she carried. Mac wondered what each might reveal. *If a Human brain could make any sense of it,* she added honestly, considering she wasn't sure how much sense she'd made of Nik's and they'd started with similar wetware.

Then she shook her head, more concerned with something else, something far more important. "Anchen. Don't make it easy for them. Don't invite the Ro back here."

"We cannot begin to understand one another if we do not converse, Mac."

"I'm all for conversation. Just let it be somewhere and someone else." Mac didn't bother being dismayed by her own bluntness. The Sinzi-ra was used to her by now. "I mean no insult, Anchen," she continued in a low voice. "I—" *Only the truth.* She took a deep breath and flattened her hand over the place on the tank where Anchen had tapped, feeling the cold. "I'm afraid. For you. For all Sinzi." *The whole truth.* "For us, if anything happens to you. You must be more cautious."

"I need not remind you, Mac, that all life is currently at risk from the Dhryn. It is inappropriate to fear for one species—or individual—over another."

"The rest of us don't stand in the Ro's way, Anchen. Your species maintains the Interspecies Union. Without you, the transects fail and we're each alone."

"If," the alien stressed the word, "the Ro are a threat."

"You can't take that chance!" Mac insisted, turning to face

Anchen. The red glow danced back, as if courteously avoiding her face. She couldn't tell if it was somehow tethered to the Sinzi or floating free like a vidbot. In either case, its light enclosed them both in a bubble that might almost have been privacy, if not for the ominous tank and its instruments. *An audience to this was fine by her.* "You don't dare, for all our sakes. Please, Anchen. Tell me you'll be careful."

"Following your example?"

Mac snorted. "I'm not important."

Cool fingertips coated in dancing silver reached to her face, one tracing the line of Mac's jaw, another lifting a curl of regrown hair. It was the first time the Sinzi had touched her other than in Noad's role of physician; Mac's eyes widened in surprise, but she didn't move. "I—all of my selves—hold a different view of your worth."

Friendship as she understood it—or something more akin to the assessment of an experienced diplomat? Mac discovered she didn't care. The warmth inside her was enough. "Then listen to me, Anchen," she urged. "Don't expose yourself to the Ro. Let others do it. At least until we know more." Mac shot a suspicious look at the dark tank. "That includes not coming here by yourself again. Protect yourself. Promise me."

The Sinzi-ra didn't answer immediately. Her fingers wove themselves into something complex and troubled, hard to make out in the low light. *Answering,* Mac thought irrelevantly, *the question of whether the alien held the glowing globe.* "A promise is a connection between those involved," Anchen said at last. "Across any distance."

Mac grinned. "That it is."

"We do not make promises lightly."

"Neither do I," she assured the alien. *Never let go.*

Anchen gave an almost Human sigh. "I may have shown you too much of the Sinzi view of the universe."

"Fair's fair," Mac replied. "You know more about Humans than most Humans do."

That shivering laugh, then the other seemed to come to some decision, for her fingers unfolded with blinding rapidity. "Then we shall exchange promises, Mackenzie Connor, for such a connection must be forged both ways."

Uh-oh. "What would I have to promise, Sinzi-ra?" Mac asked, wary at last.

"To bring me something for my collection."

Somehow, Mac knew the wording was precise. *Bring.* Had Anchen elicited the same promise from Nik every time he'd ventured on her behalf? Complete the journey. Come back where you started.

The Sinzi ethic.

That to do so meant surviving whatever might intervene was in a sense incidental to Anchen. It was finishing the cycle that mattered.

The distinction, to quote Fourteen, was irrelevant. Mac didn't hesitate. "I promise."

Anchen leaned forward, tilting her head so the eye Mac associated with Casmii, the judge, faced her most directly. "What is promised will bind us both, Mackenzie Connor. Are you sure?"

"If you promise to protect yourself from the Ro, I promise to bring you something for your collection," Mac stated, content to finally encounter common sense when dealing with aliens. "I'm sure."

She could just make out Anchen's half bow. At no command Mac detected, the light from the floating globe increased until she had to narrow her eyes. The Sinzi-ra lowered her long neck so they were looking directly at one another before she raised her fingers, their tips curling inward to form a ring like *lamnas* in front of each pair of eyes. "I so promise," she said, holding that posture. "We are bound."

Then: "I promise." "And I." "Over my better judgment, I promise also." "You have my promise, Mac."

Finally: "Promise given and accepted. We are bound."

Every voice the same in tone, the words alone differed. The Sinzi-ra uncurled her long fingers then intertwined them, rings slipping back and forth like raindrops.

Mac realized she'd been addressed, for the first time, by each of Anchen's individual minds. *Not that she had a clue who was who.*

For a fleeting instant, Mac wondered if she'd somehow managed to commit herself to something far stranger than she could possibly imagine. *Again.*

Then she shrugged.

There had to be a tacky souvenir somewhere on Myriam.

"You're quiet."

Mac waved one hand, the other holding her bag. "Thinking," she explained. They were almost at the hangar; she could tell by the way the floor had become a down-turned ramp. The Sinzi-ra had left the tank room with her, bidding them both farewell in the corridor. Sing-li's eyes had been like saucers at the sight of the alien, but he'd asked no questions.

Until now. "Everything all right?"

She glanced up at Sing-li. Seeing the concern in his face, she decided against flippant. "More or less," she admitted. "It's suddenly real—the move offworld, going to Base. Leaving Emily—the rest of you. Didn't feel that way this morning."

He pressed his lips together in an unhappy line. "I should be going with you."

Pinching an errant grape between her fingers, Mac gave his shirt a tug. "If you aren't, you really should change."

"You know what I mean, Mac." The agent shook his head at her. "Some on the IU committee aren't pleased with Dr. Mamani leaving the consulate. They're resisting Hollans' efforts to negotiate clearance for more Humans on Myriam—doubt he'll get a straight answer before you clear the gate. Don't like it, Mac."

She wasn't thrilled either. "Don't worry," Mac told him. "The planet's going to be crowded enough as it is. And I'll have Oversight."

"Oh, that's reassuring," Sing-li said darkly.

"Be fair. He can be scary."

"You don't know what you might face."

"I'm minding a bunch of archaeologists on a lifeless world—what can happen?" Mac stopped and laughed without humor. "Don't answer that."

Before Sing-li could try, they rounded the last corner and saw who was waiting.

"Idiot!" Fourteen called cheerfully, his arm around Unensela, the Myg xenopaleoecologist.

Unensela's six offspring were seated at their feet, looking as angelic as hairless lumps with long necks and big brown eyes could. On seeing Mac, they immediately squealed and scampered at full speed to run up her legs before she could fend them away with her free hand.

Once they were firmly attached by clawholds on her chest and shoulders, a struggle since each had doubled in mass over the past few weeks, Mac recovered sufficient balance to glare at Sing-li. He gave a helpless shrug and appeared to be trying not to grin. "Wasn't me," he vowed, taking her bag.

She'd left orders with everyone imaginable that Fourteen was not to know about her little detour before Myriam. *It had been worth a try.* "He's not coming to Base," Mac muttered under her breath. Four of the Myg offspring excitedly demonstrated their recently acquired ability to mimic sounds, babbling "basebasebase-base" in their high-pitched voices. The remaining two merely howled along.

"You won't believe this, Mac," Fourteen announced as she staggered closer. "We almost missed the flight!"

Mac lurched to a stop by Unensela and waited. The female Myg gave her a sly look—an expression which came naturally, given the sunken Myg eyes and wide expressive lips. She was wearing one of Fourteen's shirts and apparently nothing else. Fortunately, the shirt went down to her knobby knees. Unfortunately, the shirt was a vile orange and turquoise patterned in juggling hamsters.

"Get them off me," Mac said as calmly as she could, given one offspring was gumming her left ear for all it was worth. "Now."

"You should be proud," the Myg insisted. "You're the only Human they like."

"I'm honored. Off."

Unensela pouted, another typical Myg expression in Mac's experience with the species.

Mac took a deep breath.

"Idiot!" Fourteen said hastily, pulling offspring from Mac with both hands and tossing them at his—*what*, Mac wondered, *did you call someone who appeared to dislike you but would have sex with you anywhere, anytime?* She settled for fellow alien. The offspring didn't mind the treatment, each making a "whee" sound as they flew through the air. Unensela didn't try to catch them, letting the small beings latch onto her shirt with their claws wherever they struck. They dropped to the floor at once, cooing contentedly by her feet.

Sing-li was making that strangled noise again. Mac rolled her eyes at him.

Once free of hitchhikers, she pulled her clothing back into some order, ignoring the myriad small holes left by affectionate Myg claws until her fingers found skin through a long tear in previously intact silk. At this, she growled something safely wordless in her throat.

"Hurry, Mac. We'll be late." Fourteen, she noted grimly, was bouncing in place, his favorite, and now-faded, paisley shorts threatening to slip loose.

"Late for—"

"Arslithissiangee Yip the Fourteenth!" A thunderous Mudge came striding up the corridor from the direction of the hangar. "What are you doing here?" He counted Mygs as he approached and amended, "What are all of you doing here?"

"Idiot," Fourteen proclaimed. "The glorious Unensela is here to warm me with her presence as long as possible. I am waiting to board the lev with Mac." The overlooked offspring, following all this intently, burbled "macmacmac."

Mac's "Oh, no you aren't," collided with Mudge's "I think not!" and Sing-li's alarmed "You don't have clearance." Unensela's "But you promised to take them with you!" came afterward, prompting everyone else to stare at her.

"Well, he did," she finished.

"Irrelevant," Mac told her, then looked at Fourteen. "You aren't coming."

The Myg covered his face with his hands. Distress, real or feigned. *Likely real.* She didn't doubt Fourteen's desire to accompany her, or his zeal to be of help. *Strobis*, the Myg version of obligation and promise. She seemed to be collecting a few of those lately.

Mac sighed and pulled his hands down. He peered at her, moisture dotting his fleshy eyelids. "I need you here," she said earnestly. "To find out who else is heading for Myriam—what they want there." She'd left him a message about the Frow and Grimnoii. If there was anything Fourteen relished, it was obliterating the secrecy of others.

"Irrelevant! Why must you go to Base?" he countered. "Charlie can take Emily. They can have sex." He stuck out his white forked tongue and Unensela giggled.

Mudge's face was a study in various hues of red. Mac silenced him with a look. Fourteen knew how to push his rival's buttons, not difficult at the best of times.

"He has abundant external genitalia," Fourteen persisted. "We all saw—"

"I'll see you in orbit," Mac interrupted. She let her tone imply she wasn't worried if Fourteen was inside a ship when she did or not. "Gentlemen?"

She grabbed her bag from Sing-li, who wisely surrendered it, and headed for the hangar doors, pausing only to make sure Mudge was coming, too.

"My apologies, Norcoast," that worthy panted. "He got past me."

Mac glanced at him without slowing. His face glistened with sweat and at least some of its ruddiness looked to be from exertion. The rest, she blamed on Fourteen. "Did you run the entire length of the consulate?"

"A bit more, actually." He wiped the sweat from his forehead with the back of his hand, then took a couple of deeper breaths. "Damn Myg cheated and took a skim."

"I should be the one to apologize," Sing-li offered glumly. "I told Selkirk to keep an eye on him—trickiest being I've ever met. I swear you could hide something at the bottom of the ocean and he'd have it copied and on display by noon."

Mac snorted. "Good thing he's on our side. More or less," this last to mollify Mudge.

"Of course I'm on your side," Fourteen said in her ear.

Mac jumped and swung her bag. Sing-li swore and Mudge simply stopped where he was, throwing up his arms.

Fourteen, having dodged Mac's swing, smiled unrepentantly as he rose from his crouch. "See? I sent Unensela away. It's me now. I was never bringing the offspring."

"Go away," Mac growled.

"You don't mean that."

"Oh, yes, I do."

"You won't win, Fourteen," Emily said lazily.

Mac turned to see her friend leaning against one side of the now-open door to the consulate hangar, arms folded across her chest. Beyond, through the opening, was a line of levs and other transports, beings of various species moving around them at their work. The wide doors to the outside were mere shadows in the distance. The Sinzi built on a generous scale. There were a couple of larger service corridors, as well as this one, leading into the hangar. Not to mention a small, hidden entrance from the surface, for those who preferred even more stealth.

Wouldn't have helped.

"Can you hurry it up, Mac? Pilot's getting antsy."

Mac raised an eyebrow. "I've no doubt." The outfit was remarkable, even for Emily. For her triumphant return, she'd donned a white dress of the Sinzi's favorite fabric that might have been painted over her curved torso, flaring in randomly transparent panels from thigh to ankle. Ropes of black pearls hung from her throat, almost reaching her waist; black satin gloves and sandals completed what was, to Mac, most definitely armor.

She gave her Myg-torn shirt a self-conscious tug and winced as she heard it rip further. *Hopefully she could change on the lev.*

"If he's going," Fourteen pointed at Mudge, "I'm going."

"Oversight's just seeing us off," Mac began. Which hadn't been part of the scheme of things, but she did appreciate Mudge's efforts to intercept the determined Myg—however futile. "Now you both can," she finished brightly. "Good-bye. See you on the transport to Myriam."

A *harrumph*. "Ah. Norcoast. I am coming with you."

At this, Mac's head whipped around so quickly she felt a strain in her neck. "Pardon?"

"Staff's done an excellent job," Mudge explained. "Stellar. No one needs me."

It was like some comedy routine, Mac thought with disgust, with her playing the the innocent victim from the audience. *Had everyone forgotten who was in charge here?* "No, Oversight." This firm and calm. "Emily and I are going. Sing-li is coming with us because I can't stop him without arcane paperwork or a sledge-hammer. You are waiting for us in orbit, making sure everything is ready."

"Everything is ready."

So much for calm. "Then make up a bloody crisis!" Her shout echoed down the corridor and back again, drawing attention from those within the hangar. "I don't care!"

"It's okay, Mac," Emily said smoothly. "I invited Charlie along. Didn't think you'd mind."

Mac looked from one to the other and back again. Mudge's expression was an interesting blend of not-my-fault and uncertainty. *He didn't know why,* she judged. Emily's was pure mischief, her gleaming eyes and wide smile daring Mac to challenge her on this. She might have bought it, but Emily's gloved fingers were locked on her arms, as if to hide their trembling.

The look, like the dress, was designed to misdirect, to make everyone around Emily believe bringing Mudge was some playful whim.

To where the Ro had destroyed part of the Wilderness Trust? *This was no whim.*

Mac gave a nod, more to herself than anyone else, but Mudge visibly relaxed—and Emily? Maybe no one else would notice the slight release of tension in the shoulders, the softening of the smile.

It wasn't, Mac knew, a favor she'd granted.

Meanwhile, someone else had watched this Human byplay with great impatience. "Idiots," Fourteen declared. "Charlie has no reason for going. While I–I–I've—there could be a threat. A risk! Yes. I'm sure of it! There's danger. You need me."

She might ignore Fourteen's protests—and the smell of distraught Myg now filling the corridor—but Sing-li felt otherwise. Mac sighed as the agent loomed over the smaller alien. Who, truth be told, didn't look the least intimidated.

Might be the shirt, Mac judged. "Sing-li," she said. "Sing-li!" sharper when he failed to acknowledge her. "He's making it up."

His voice was threatening despite the shirt. "If there's a potential problem, I need to know what it is."

Mac and Emily traded looks. "Stay here then," Mac suggested.

Sing-li's shocked "Mac!" gave her a twinge of guilt, but only a small one. She was almost dancing with impatience to be gone. By the glow in Emily's eyes, she felt it too.

Home.

If only for a day.

- CONTACT -

"WE SHOULDN'T BE HERE."

Inric didn't let his attention stray from the scanner readout. "No one will know."

His partner, an as yet unblooded Ehztif and thus certified for space travel with other life-forms, continued to pace. She'd taken the usename Bob for its supposed calming effect on Humans, obligate predators being uncomfortable company. Not that Bob was such a predator—not until that first ritual hunt, years in her future, when her digestive system would switch into its mature phase. For now, she drank packaged secretions like everyone else, and expressed a fondness for salted crackers.

Inric pursed his lips and tried to ignore the unsettling click of Bob's talons on the floor plate. It had seemed a good idea at the time to choose an Ehztif partner. No Human-centric games. Enough daring for any escapade but reliably steady.

He would have to find the one Ehztif with an imagination. "Relax," Inric said, leaning back to demonstrate. "Get the data. Get paid. There's nothing here."

Bob stalked—there was no other word for it—to the platform's edge and stared out over the waves. "Nothing. You don't know what that means, do you, Human. But I—I can taste it on the wind." The Ehztif released her prehensile tongue, flipping it through the air before she brought it back into her mouth. She appeared to chew for a few seconds, then sharply expanded her cheek pouches in disgust. "Nothing lives here."

As that was exactly what the Sencor Consortium hoped to confirm, Inric gave a tight smile. "If the scanners are as accurate as your taste buds, Bob, our clients will be pleased."

"Scavengers."

"An essential part of life," the Human replied.

The Ehztif sniffed. Her species shared their home system with the much-despised Sethilak, definitely closer to the scavenger scheme of things. That the two had managed to coexist after encountering one another in space was one of the marvels of the Interspecies Union.

Didn't mean they wouldn't eat one another when the occasion offered.

Inric sat up and leaned over the readout again. The platform's underside bristled with the latest in remote analysis gear, including two prototypes he'd obtained in return for initial field tests and favors to come. And that wasn't all they used to search this world. "Check the imagers again, will you, Bob? They should be close to finishing the latest flyover."

"They're coming," Bob answered, gazing at the horizon. Better vision was only one of the adaptations that made Ehztif useful companions. "Wait. What's that following them? *Ssshhhhssahhsss!*" the Instella dissolved into an impassioned hiss.

Inric lunged to his feet and ran to the rail. "What's wrong?" He stared where Bob pointed, expecting the worst—an IU inspector, come to push them offworld. They had clearances. Just not real ones.

The worlds scoured by the Dhryn were restricted, even ones like this, where there hadn't been a sentient species to leave its accomplishments behind. In the present state of near panic, Inric doubted they'd be fined and sent on their way. Lately, there'd been rumors of entrepreneurs simply disappearing. "Can't be an inspection," he concluded as quickly. The ship they'd left in orbit was to send warning of any approach, as well as being nimble enough to elude almost anything transect-capable given that warning was received in time to retrieve her absent crew of two.

"It's gone. But for an instant, I could see—" Bob appeared to hesitate, cheeks puffing in and out. "Below the incoming 'bots," she said finally. "In the water. There was *sshssah*."

"Meaning?"

"The heat of life."

An Ehztif's ability to detect and react to infrared was the source of a thriving Sethilak industry in camouflage gear, but in this case? The Human exhaled his relief in a low whistle. "Impossible. We've been scanning this world for weeks. The Dhryn weren't interrupted here—they took every scrap of living matter." But Inric's eyes didn't leave the patch of unremarkable ocean.

The water was the only thing that moved on Riden IV. Water, he corrected, wind, and themselves.

"The Dhryn." Bob's head shrank into her shoulders. Her anxious shudders rattled the gleaming armor plates growing across her juvenile skin. When those met and fused, she'd be less flexible and thoroughly deadly to anything her instincts viewed as edible, basically that which generated body heat and wasn't Ehztif. It gave her species a unique perspective on the Dhryn, whose appetite seemed without limit.

They were terrified by a predator higher up the chain.

"We are not safe here," Bob continued, backing away from the rail.

Inric could see the incoming 'bots for himself now. There were a dozen; nothing fancy here, just the same off-the-alien-shelf design Earth had adopted for visual surveillance. They'd recorded mind-numbing images of rock, sand, and water. High ground on Riden IV consisted of chains of weathered islands, few of cloud height, their lee sides dressed in curls of unappealing brown sand. The poles had never, according to IU records, supported life.

The oceans had swarmed with it, fluorescing at the surface by starlight, submerging by day. The slow whorling currents of the tropics had spawned immense mats of jelly, themselves supporting landscapes of towering growth to rival the forests of the equatorial islands. It was said once you heard Riden's singing flowers, released to drift from mat to mat, you could never again enjoy the music of your own species, so intensely beautiful and complex was the sound of their petals on the wind.

The wind only howled now, when it didn't rattle their shelter or *skitter . . . scurry* like invisible mice around the consoles. Inric gave his companion a sour look and went back to his scanner. The consortium wanted assurance the world was lifeless before releasing development funds. Their surveys had cataloged sufficient mineral wealth to justify investment long ago, but Sencor had decided against proceeding. Ore was common; singing flowers, unique. Tourism was the new option.

The Dhryn had forever changed the equation, and the Trisulian hunger for expansion had made it economical for their competitors to take certain liberties with due process.

In other words, if Sencor delayed exercising its mining rights on Riden IV, it might find Trisulian colonists pretending to farm the barren islands and fish the empty seas.

Bringing them to the present situation, and his twitchy partner. "The Dhryn are gone, Bob," Inric stated. "They died in Sol System. Human space, my friend. Human space."

Scurry . . .

"Humans did nothing but cower in their ships. Everyone knows," the Ehztif countered. "And who said all the Dhryn were there? I heard it was only a fraction."

Before Inric could answer, there was a sudden *crack*, as if a whip had snapped across the cloudless sky. Human and Ehztif looked up in time to see the closest 'bot drop into the sea well short of the platform. The rest kept approaching.

"What the hell—"

CRACK!

Moments later, eleven 'bots arrived at their coordinates.

Obedient to their programming, they bobbed in the air precisely where the platform should have been.

Above where the empty sea boiled.

REUNIONS AND REVELATIONS

MAC HAD BROUGHT WORK, too excited to sleep a wink during the trip to Base. She was thus startled, some unmeasured time later, to have something warm grasp her wrist and give her a little shake. "Whaassa?" she asked intelligently.

"Landing in ten, Norcoast," Mudge informed her, moving back to his seat.

Shifting upright, Mac fumbled for her imp, its workscreen having turned itself off after her brain had apparently done the same, taking her closed eyes as its signal. Beside her, Emily's neck was bent at an unlikely angle, the pillows that had earlier propped her head and shoulders now scattered on the lev floor. Her friend snored contentedly, her body catlike in its ability to relax and pour into any shape necessary for rest.

Sunlight was streaming in through the overhead portal. A Human-built machine, but with alien tech and spy mentality. Mac hadn't been pleased to learn she wouldn't be able to gawk out the window like a tourist, nor hunt familiar landmarks as they neared their destination.

She shrugged and tucked her imp into a pocket. *Hadn't missed a thing,* she admitted, rubbing sleep from her eyes. She elbowed Emily. "We're here."

Instead of blinking sleepily at her, Emily sprang half to her feet, her eyes flashing open. "No!" she shouted, arms stretched to their fullest, fingers spread wide.

Mac pulled her back down. "Sorry, Em," she said hastily. She should know better than to startle her friend. "It's okay. We're about to land."

Sing-li had half-risen from his seat across from theirs. She shook her head at him. "We're fine."

"Fine? *Caramba*, Mac. Next time pour ice water down my neck." Emily fussed with her clothing, using the movements to cover how her hands shook. "It'd be less of a shock."

"I'll remember that."

"You do."

Mac wanted to see outside; she didn't need to. She put her head back and closed her eyes. Morning. Late August. Approaching Castle Inlet from the southwest. That meant coming up through Hecate Strait with its whales and long blue swells, closing on the coast where, on a clear day, the snowcapped peaks beyond stole the eye and played tricks of scale, until the forests between tumbling cliffs seemed nothing more than the thin verge along the base of some giant's fence.

When that same eye could make out the surf pounding at the exposed teeth of mountains, could slide up the rocky shore to where the rain forest began, catch a glimpse of a white-headed eagle that threw the trees into perspective . . . then it all became greater than one mind could hold.

A nip over treetops, a plunge down a slope, and the intense blue of Castle Inlet itself would be waiting, tied to the coastal mountains by ribboned rivers, edged in boulders that gleamed like so many pebbles in the hand. Rich with salmon.

Mac's lips turned up at the corners. And there would be Base, swarming with activity, skims and levs being loaded, students and staff trotting the walkways, half with breakfast muffins in their hands. *Possibly green ones.*

"Dreaming about our Nik?" Emily asked, nudging her shoulder.

Mac kept her eyes closed. "Get your own spy."

"Love to."

The ensuing pause was too much for Mac. She opened her eyes to see, as expected, Sing-li squirming beside Mudge, doing his best to ignore the beatific look Emily was bestowing upon him. Mudge, needless to say, wasn't helping, too busy interacting with whatever was displayed by the screen floating in front of his face.

"The man's working, Em," Mac said, getting up to stretch. "Save it."

Emily leaned to look past her. "Nice shirt, by the way."

"She made me," grumbled Sing-li.

"Camouflage," Mac explained, glancing at Mudge as she sat back down.

He didn't look happy. While she could imagine several reasons, starting with Emily's invitation and ending with proximity to Sing-li's shirt, something about his current focus made her gesture to the agent to switch places.

Dropping into the seat beside Mudge, Mac peered at his display. "Something wrong?" she asked, unable to make heads or tails of a tilted three-dimensional flowchart, with inset counters blinking red.

Especially when Mudge stuck his finger in the midst to close it. "Oversight?"

"It's been a while," he said obtusely. "Sims aren't like the real thing anyway. Everyone knows that."

Ah. He'd been working on his piloting. Mac poked him gently in the shoulder. "Planning to take over the lev?" she joked, regretting it as the man flushed mottled red and *harrumphed* fiercely at her.

"I'll have you know the last time I left Sol System I was at the controls."

Twenty-some years ago. "Always good to refresh skills," she said, careful to keep it neutral.

The lev made a swooping turn felt by all aboard. Mac locked eyes with Emily. They were about to land.

Just enough time left to doubt everything she'd planned.

"Hang on, Mac. I go first."

"You've got to be kidding," Mac told Sing-li, trying without success to push by him. Somehow the wacky shirt hadn't diminished the large man's ability to become an immovable object. Frustrated, she tried glaring instead.

With perfect equanimity, he smiled down at her. "It's my job."

"C'mon, Mac," Emily said from behind. "Let him test that cam-ouflage."

Mac threw up her hands. "Fine. But this is the last time while we're at Base you get in my way. Is that clear, Agent Jones?"

Sing-li's smile faded and he gave her the tiniest of nods. The nod that meant, in Mac's experience, that he promised to be discreet. Not that he promised to disappear.

Discreet she could live with. So long as they went through the door.

"You can get in my way anytime," Emily offered from behind.

"Em," Mac muttered in exasperation. "I'm serious."

"So am I." Emily tugged her hair. "It's not my fault you like your men unavailable."

Sing-li wisely chose that moment to open the lev door and step out.

The first thing Mac noticed was the smell rushing in. The con-sulate had been on a seacoast. This was *her* seacoast. She drew a deep breath of cedar, salt, and salmon through her nostrils, feeling as though she drew the air and its peace into her soul.

The second thing she noticed were voices. Many voices.

Too many voices.

Mac moved to the opening and cautiously looked outside.

Sing-li stood to one side of the ramp to the walkway, a big grin on his face. "Welcome home!"

Mac's fingers found and gripped the lev doorframe. She'd stud-ied schematics and images of the pods in their new locale; they looked as she expected. Perhaps a little tidier than before, but then they'd had to take off anything loose, including the impromptu roofing, in order to tow the pods here. Some had been replaced; no guarantees they would last the first winter. There was laundry snapping in the breeze. That breeze could become a gale force wind with little notice here, in the more open portion of the inlet. She hoped someone had warned new staff. The surrounding water, tinted with sediment from the nearby Tannu River, was reflecting the sunbeams coming over the mountains. It was going to be a warm, bright morning.

All this she took in automatically, her attention caught by what, or rather who, was waiting on the walkways.

"What's going on, Mac? Hurry up!" Emily urged impatiently. *Because she couldn't see.*

Sing-li reached for her hand. "It's okay, Dr. Connor."

It wasn't, she thought, staring at the sea of faces. There was a banner draped over the terrace of Pod Three. She couldn't make out the words. The voices—the shouts—died away as everyone gazed back at her. Some were smiling. Others were wiping their eyes.

Her father started walking forward. Her father? And—*gods, her brothers?*

Mac launched herself from the lev and ran for them, somehow noticing a knot of people nearby who suddenly cried out in what had to be Quechua and hurried past her.

Fortunately, she didn't have to try to hug them all at once. She reached her father, buried her face in his shoulder, and felt her brothers' arms go around them both. She sobbed for no reason but joy.

Mac didn't need to ask how or why. All those on Earth she cared about here, now? This was Anchen's parting gift.

Forget interspecies communication.

This, she understood.

"Emily's sister can't stay, but she plans to come back next month for a few days. We'll arrange quarters for her. Meanwhile, if you don't mind, we're thinking of putting Em into your old quarters and office."

Mac did her best to pay attention to Kammie's briefing, but it wasn't easy. Music and laughter permeated the entire pod, not to mention the aroma of grilled salmon. And pizza. Second breakfast or lunch. Her stomach was willing, given it would be early afternoon back at the consulate. Tomorrow. *Time zones weren't such an issue traveling to other worlds.*

"Mac. Does that cover it?"

"Oh. What? Yes, yes. Thanks, Kammie. I appreciate all this, more than I can say." To her surprise, Kammie Noyo had proved more than the Sinzi-ra's equal in grace. *If she'd been the one asked to accommodate changes in August,* Mac admitted, *she'd have dug in and resisted with all her might.* "But—"

"But?"

She couldn't help it. "Why is everyone here? Shouldn't someone be working? It's only August. Surely . . ." Mac stopped, mildly offended when the tiny chemist burst into laughter, clapping her hands together.

"Oh, Mac. Dear Mac," Kammie sputtered as she caught her breath. "If I needed any proof you were yourself again, that would be it. Honestly. People can take a day off. Even here. The world won't end."

Mac frowned doubtfully. "The salmon don't."

"There are monitors. Relax. This is your celebration. Enjoy it!"

"I am," Mac admitted. "But this interruption—"

"Stop, already. We needed it, too," the other told her, abruptly serious. "Seeing you. Seeing Emily. It's beyond wonderful. And after all that terrible business with the Dhryn, the earthquake— well, it's good to know things are back to normal. I can't tell you how much."

Normal? Mac stood and paced around Kammie's office. Hers— hers was gone. She'd peeked in, thinking to show her father and brothers the garden at least, but all that remained was the gravel bed along the floor, like the memory of a dried-up river.

This space was itself again. Piles of paper adorned every surface except for the benches in the attached lab. Even the soil samples Kammie had always insisted line her walls were back, so once more her view outside the pod had been replaced by ranks of silvered vials. Idly, Mac looked to where Kammie had first put the one she'd given her, the one from the Ro landing site.

It was there.

It couldn't just be sitting here, on a shelf, after all that had happened.

Mac had to know. She walked around Kammie's desk, and the curious chemist, to reach and take down the little thing.

It looked the same. Then again, they all did. Mac turned the vial to read the fine precise script on the label. The right date. Collected by Dr. M. W. Connor. Location unknown.

The location had been the outer arm of Castle Inlet, where an invisible Ro ship had touched down, and its passenger had paused before climbing the ramp, perhaps to look at the Human cowering behind a log. A mark in the disturbed moss and mud. A trace. Physical proof the unseen existed.

"Do you need it back?" Kammie asked.

The natural question.

Mac's lips were numb; she strained to hear the *scurry . . . Pop!* of a Ro walker amid the vintage rock and roll from outside. *Her brother Owen would be enjoying that.* "Yes, please," she said, as calmly as possible. "If you don't mind."

Her hand, the real one, wanted to clench around the vial. She'd never meant for this to stay at Base, to be a possible lure for the Ro. She'd believed Nik or his agents here had removed it, to bring to the Gathering and get it safely away.

Why hadn't they?

Mac's eyes strayed to the shelf with Kammie's deepwater sailing trophies. There was a new one taking pride of place. To buy time to think, she went close to puzzle out the print. The Millennium Cup. A regatta across Auckland's Hauraki Gulf.

Last year.

"You were in New Zealand," Mac heard herself say in a strangely normal voice.

"Don't you remember? I went for my holiday in February. Great sailing. I go as often as I can."

Where people went when they left Base had never mattered to Mac. It was how long until they returned to work that she noticed. *She should have paid attention.* "On second thought, you might as well keep this one with the rest. I know you prefer that. Here." She passed the vial back to Kammie. "I have your analysis."

Whatever was in that vial now, Mac had no doubt the soil she'd originally collected was at the IU consulate, where it had doubtless been examined by the experts of the Gathering. *Before she'd gone there herself.*

Kammie had wanted her to take a vacation—had known she was going to the cottage. The cottage where Fourteen and Kay, the Trisulian, had turned up almost immediately because, they'd said, the IU's informant at Base had told them where to find Mac.

How blind had she been? Mac asked herself. No wonder Kammie had accepted any and all changes to have Emily here with such un-characteristic calm. *Anchen had made sure of it.*

Kammie stood very still, holding the vial. "Mac," she said slowly. "What's wrong? You look as though you've bitten a lemon."

There would be listeners. She knew it, even without a vidbot hovering quietly in a corner of the ceiling.

And what evidence did she have? Only that the vial was here, after Nik had assured her it had been removed.

Spies, Mac reminded herself, *told such flexible truths.*

Did it matter if Kammie Noyo watched Base for the IU? *She had,* Mac freely admitted, *superb and disciplined eyes.*

Nik had known who that watcher was. He hadn't told her, so she wouldn't have to pretend.

She was better at it now.

Mac grinned easily. "Just time creeping up on me, Kammie. The lack of, that is," she clarified. "I'd best get back to the party. My dad and brothers leave after lunch. If there's nothing else?" she looked around almost hungrily. "You can contact me by com. I'll leave the—"

"Go," Kammie smiled back. "We've managed fine without you—it's been tough, but I think another few weeks won't sink the place. Although I'm still not sure why they're insisting you go to this planet Myriam. And what kind of a name is that for an alien world?"

Mac made herself shrug. "Free trip. Chance to tie up some loose ends. Broaden my horizons."

The look Kammie gave at this was akin to the ones Mac had already collected from her family members; she met it without blinking. A twinge of embarrassment, however, she couldn't avoid.

She'd done such a thorough job of ignoring the universe until lately.

"Hallo, Princess."

Mac almost shook her head at the incongruity—not of her father and brothers sitting at a table in the gallery, since all three had visited her at Base before now—but of them sitting with Charles Mudge III.

Who looked, she thought, altogether too pleased to be surrounded by Connors.

"You haven't been spreading stories about me to Oversight," she warned her brothers as she sat.

Owen was eldest, the male incarnation of the mother they'd lost when Mac was a baby, complete with premature gray at his temples, a wonderful laugh, and sparkling green eyes. He'd responded to the production of his own family by somehow growing younger himself. Mac enjoyed his company when she could pry him away, which was seldom. Not that she didn't adore her nephew William, but her visits seemed to augment his boundless energy. Her eyes would glaze over by the second day. Nairee, William's mother, was one of those calm, utterly competent people; Mac kept trying to lure her away for a field season, but somehow Owen always caught wind of her attempts before they succeeded. "We'd never tell stories," he said.

"Not and admit it," corrected Blake, their middle sibling. He took after their father in his slight build, being more wire than muscle. He had yet to age or discover responsibility, having a blithe attitude toward life and his own genius that alternately exasperated and charmed the rest of the family. Mac, prone to stick at exasperation, refused to believe her father's frequent assertion they were alike.

She was the responsible one.

Though she'd never forget how Blake had stayed with her after the news came about Sam, not saying a word, not offering futile comfort, just there. As she knew they'd all be, any time she needed them.

On Earth, anyway.

"Oversight?"

Mudge spread his hands. "A gentleman never tells."

Mac dropped into her seat, laughing in surrender. "As long as you didn't mention that damn cat."

Norman Connor chuckled. "You returned just in time," he admitted. "Blake was working up to it."

"Blake!"

"Cat?" inquired Mudge.

"The food smells great," this from Owen, the peacemaker. "I can't imagine why you'd complain about it."

"I like cats," Mac said quickly, to forestall any ideas. Then she nodded at the kitchen, staffed by this year's crop of Harvs. "August. They've learned to cook by this point or given up."

"Mac." Her father lowered his voice. "How's Emily taking all this?"

From here, Mac could see where Emily sat, or rather perched, on a table edge, presiding over a noisy group she'd been told included not only Emily's younger sister Maria, but three aunts, a great-uncle on her father's side, and two cousins, all from Venezuela. They were speaking Quechua, a language perfectly suited to vivid gestures and dramatic expressions. She hadn't a clue what they were talking about.

"I haven't had time to find out," she admitted. Or the chance. Emily's sister, Maria, had turned her back when Mac had approached to say hello in person. She didn't blame her. *Too many calls with bad news or evasion.* "Em's—I think she's lost her taste for surprises."

"Hopefully not for parties."

Mac smiled as she swung around to greet the newcomer. "John! How have you been?"

"Hi Mac, Dr. Connor. Owen, Blake. Nice to see you again. Mr. Mudge." Her former postdoc, now on staff with his own small department, returned her smile as he took the seat the senior Dr. Connor offered. Mac was impressed. When he'd first arrived, Emily's outspoken nature could send John Ward bolting from a room—her record was under five seconds. Mac didn't think that would happen now. He'd somehow grown into himself when she wasn't looking.

Or she was finally looking, Mac chided herself. "Keeping busy," she said. "And you? How's the new department?"

He shrugged. "I'll let you know once Dr. Stewart settles back in. Pretty disruptive, having her take off just when classes were starting at UBC. Kammie doesn't seem worried about a repeat, but I'll let her know she's on probation with me."

John wouldn't have been told how his new statistics prof, Dr. Persephone Stewart, had been recalled from Norcoast to act in her other specialty at the consulate, nor would he know, with luck, that 'Sephe was back to help Emily. Luckily for both agent and budding department head, 'Sephe was delighted to return to academia. *Probation?* With luck, that would be the most danger 'Sephe would need to overcome.

How much of the Human side of things did Kammie know?

To avoid that labyrinth, Mac focused on John. "See?" she said, raising an eyebrow. "I knew you'd enjoy all that power over people."

"Mac!" John protested, and proved he could still blush.

She took pity and let her father proceed to ask interested questions about John's new program. She listened, but not only to the conversation at her table. Her eyes half-closed, Mac let herself bask in chatter, returning to a world where vying approaches to the remote assay of smolt stomach contents were as eagerly debated as the latest hockey trade. The inside of Base, its heart, hadn't changed.

Outside? She gazed through the transparent wall behind Blake's head. Base had been towed from this site, opposite the mouth of the Tannu, almost sixteen years ago. The layout of the pods was the same as before. Mac could believe no time had passed at all, that this was her first field season at Norcoast and her family here to check out the place.

Almost.

Blake's eyes met hers and locked, brimming with questions. Mac deliberately ran the fingers of her new hand over the tabletop. "Let's take a walk, guys."

"Surely we can eat first," Owen objected. His playful expression changed when he looked at her. He understood. She had things to tell them. *Difficult things.*

"Ah, Mac?" This from John. "After eating, there's some other—well—stuff. You know. You should stick around."

Her heart sank. Mac glanced over her shoulder and winced. Sure enough, the head table, usually empty unless there was a game on, was set for the senior staff. *And,* she sighed inwardly, *there were flowers.* Somewhat wilted and prone to lean, but definitely flowers.

She gave John a pleading look. "Tell me I don't have to make a speech."

"You don't have to . . ." John let his voice trail away.

Her brother chuckled deep in his throat. "Oh, this should be good," he predicted. "Remember that time up at the cottage, Mac, when you climbed on the table to lecture all of us about—"

"She's got that look, Blake," Owen warned. "You'd better watch it."

"They haven't served lunch yet." Blake smiled angelically. "She's got nothing to throw."

"Norcoast, no!" this from Mudge as Mac pulled her imp from its pocket. She merely smiled back at her brother as she tossed the device up and down in one hand. "Really, Norcoast."

"Don't worry, Charles," Norman Connor said serenely. "Well, unless shoes come off. Then you might want to duck."

Family, Mac thought, suddenly beyond content.

"Not bad."

Mac, mulling through what she needed to say, gave Blake a surprised look. The two of them were walking ahead, Owen and her father close behind. "The speech?" She'd thought it had gone as poorly as such things usually did. She'd said the expected as quickly as possible and hoped she hadn't sounded like an idiot.

The thank-yous, get-on-with-your-work part had been easy. The brief, supposedly safe announcement about her being temporarily seconded to an offworld research program, and not-quite-desperate plea to keep her updated from Base while she was gone, had brought a startling ovation, with no few tears and horrifyingly proud nods.

She was one of them, she'd thought in a panic. *She hadn't changed; she wouldn't change.*

As a consequence, she'd fumbled introducing Emily's new role as visiting scholar, but Emily herself had stood at the perfect moment to warm applause, thanking everyone here, and Mac, for the opportunity. *Em hadn't lost her touch with a crowd.*

Her brother rubbed her head. "The haircut. I like it. What's his name?"

The ocean was only a rope rail away. *Shame there wouldn't be time to dry him off,* Mac grumbled to herself. The lev taking the Connors back to Vancouver was already docked, doors open, at the end of the adjoining walkway. She scuffed the toe of her shoe into the mem-wood instead. "Think you're smart, don't you?"

Blake laughed. "I know I'm smart. So? Do we get to meet him?"

Mac slowed, trailing her hand along the rope. "I don't know," she admitted finally, looking up at her brother. "He's not in a safe place."

He lost the teasing smile. "I'm sorry, Mac."

She shrugged. "Nik's like you. Smart. He'll manage." She found the spot she wanted and stopped, putting her back to the rail.

Sing-li, whose idea of discreet had turned out to be staying politely out of earshot, stopped too, as inconspicuous as a bear on a beach. He shrugged off her glare, but sat down on the walkway, pretending to study a passing gull.

Her father didn't miss much. "Should I be grateful you have a watchdog or worried, Princess?"

"Both."

At this, the three exchanged looks. "What can we do?" Owen asked simply.

Anchen had given her this, too, Mac realized. No messages to be misunderstood or intercepted. No fake recordings to offer equally false reassurance. These few minutes to talk to her own.

The alien's predisposition with meeting face-to-face had its merits.

"Maybe nothing," she answered bluntly. "I can't see—not yet— how this is going to go. Forget the media release—most of the Dhryn Progenitor ships aren't accounted for. There could be over two hundred more hiding out there. They're still a threat—" She hesitated. *Honesty now, if ever.* "The Dhryn are capable of consuming all life on a planet."

Owen's face set into harsh lines she'd never seen before, likely thinking of William and Nairee. "Can we defend ourselves?"

Mac thought of them, too. Her real hand strayed to the artificial one. *Her wrist dissolving in fire . . .* If the Dhryn returned in numbers?

She shook her head, once, unable to speak.

"Can we stop them?" her father asked, after exchanging looks with her brothers.

"No," Mac found her voice. "Not alone. That's what's worse."

"Gods, Mac," Blake said. "What could be worse than the Dhryn?"

For an instant, she didn't see the faces of her family, or the surrounding landscape she loved almost as much. For an instant, all Mac could see was a seething darkness, reaching for her; all she could feel was that voice ripping through every nerve. She shuddered free of memory. "The Ro—the Myrokynay—you've seen some of the reports. They exist. It's true they killed the Dhryn who tried to attack Earth. What isn't being told is that the Ro called the Dhryn here in the first place. When the Dhryn failed to attack us, the Ro destroyed their ships. There's more." She took a deep breath. "I believe the Ro made the Dhryn into what they are. Made them to serve a purpose. More than a weapon—I'm sure of it. The Chasm worlds were sterilized for a reason. I don't know why. Not yet. I plan to."

Her brothers nodded, accepting what was, in truth, her promise.

Her father looked thoughtful. "Your trip to Myriam. You think the answer's there."

"It's the only place I have to look," Mac amended. "A start."

Blake's eyes narrowed. "You're more afraid of these Ro than the Dhryn. Why?"

"I'm afraid of them both." Mac paused, wondering how far to go. "This isn't about us," she said finally. "It's not about life on Earth or any one world. It's about the transects and all the living things they weave together. The IU. That's what the Ro threaten, because that's the only power we have to resist whatever they want. They'll attack the Sinzi if they must. They'll try to isolate us."

"Destroy the biospace," Blake said. At Mac's questioning look, he shook his head. "Something I read. Compared the species within the IU to a planetary biosphere, but on that unimaginable scale. The sum depends on the interaction of the parts. I thought it pretty simplistic at the time. Now?" He blew out his cheeks and glanced at Sing-li before gazing at her. "Geeze, Mac. What happened to studying salmon?"

"Don't get me started," she said unsteadily. The pilot was waving from the lev. *They were out of time.* "I'll stay in touch. There'll be com packets to and from Myriam. But . . . you should know the risk. The Ro don't need the transects; the Dhryn do. If the Dhryn attack again, there are species who'll lobby the IU to close their gates. If the Ro see our connection as too much of a threat, they could do it for us. In either case, I—" It didn't help that her brothers were looking horrified. "If I can't get home, I don't want you to worry," she fumbled. "I'm pretty good at getting along with aliens, these days. You'd be surprised. I'll be okay."

At that, she faltered and stopped, trying to memorize every detail of their dear faces. Her vision seemed to blur and she rubbed her eyes angrily.

"Solve this, Mackenzie," her father said. "Solve this and come home."

"You should have checked with me."

"Why?" Mac asked, looking up at Sing-li from her seat in the skim. "Don't you like boats?"

Emily laughed. Mudge squirmed. Tie grumbled something about tides and time under his breath, holding onto the stern rope as the little vessel bobbed up and down with the swells.

"I like boats. It's where you plan to go in this one that bothers me."

"You don't know where we're going," Mac pointed out.

Sing-li planted an oversized left boot on the gunnels of the skim. "Exactly."

Although tempted to see how long the agent could keep his balance and stay out of the water, given both skim and walkway were in motion, Mac relented and gave the seat next to hers a pat. "Bit of sightseeing. Hop in. This won't take long."

Tie expressed his opinion of their final passenger by letting go the rope and engaging the engine the instant most, but not all, of Sing-li was in the skim. The man was tossed into the seat, almost falling over it into Mudge's lap. His teeth showed in a wide grin as he righted. "I like boats," he assured Mac. "Better than Tie's driving."

The skim lifted to its cruising height, spending a few moments bouncing up and down as it echoed the choppy surface below. Emily let out a gleeful hoot. Tie sent the machine slewing about to follow the swells instead of crossing them and the ride smoothed immediately. Emily tried to persuade him to change back to the more exhilarating course, without success.

Mac envied Emily's ability to relish the moment. Her own eyes still burned and her chest felt tight and sore. Given the option, she'd have curled up in a fetal position with a large cushion and whimpered herself to sleep.

She'd completed her farewells without blubbering, thankfully. *In part due to Blake*, she smiled to herself. He'd whispered a most unbrotherly comment about her missing beau that would have made Emily proud. *Anything to break the tension.*

Mac missed them all. *At least she'd said good-bye this time, thanks to Anchen.*

She'd found time to change into shorts and shirt—her cottage leftovers, kindly included in her bag by consulate staff. Now, she watched the shore as it flew past. This part of the inlet was an estuarine lowland where the Tannu negotiated for entry into the inlet through a series of braided, changing outlets. The main channel, opposite Base, was a deep turmoil of fresh and salt water, the proportion of each varying with tide and season. The others were quiet, less determined flows, brown and slick between mudflats dotted with sandpipers and other birds already heading south for the winter. Farther in, the channels twisted out of sight behind expanses of reed grass and low trees. Debris from upstream testified that not all days were peaceful sunny ones. Immense logs, bleached soft gray by salt and sun, lay everywhere, as if strewn about by a giant's hand.

The first cliff rose up as if the river was of no consequence. The midday light was deceiving, smoothing out crags and jagged edges until the stone appeared dressed like some castle wall, revealing how the inlet had been named. The next cliff met it at angles, soaring higher, topped by trees and eagles.

Ahead?

"*Aie.*"

The soft, unhappy sound drew Mac forward to her friend, sitting up by Tie. She put her hands on Emily's shoulders. "Bit of a mess," she acknowledged awkwardly.

The outstretched arm that defined the inlet from the Pacific curved westward in front of them, the sun striking harsh glints from exposed rock. The summer hadn't been kind: deep furrows eroded any patches where soil had escaped the tumbling rush into the ocean; any vegetation that had landed roots down and green was now either completely dead or sported bare branches.

Branches with eagles, fair enough. Those bare limbs lined by gulls who were nothing of the kind caught Mac's attention, especially when the tiggers, as one, turned their heads to inspect the approaching skim and its occupants. "You make sure we were cleared to approach," she shouted at Tie.

He grunted something annoyed. Reassured, Mac leaned against the gunnels near Emily. "There's the new station," she said, happy to take her eyes from the ruined slope.

Pod Two didn't quite sparkle in the sunlight. For one thing, it was colored, like the other pods now at the Tannu, to resemble the natural stone of the landscape. *For another,* Mac grinned, *someone had been very busy indeed.* The lead researcher, Martin Svehla, must have been overjoyed by his capital budget, given he loved nothing more than nailing things together.

Now, the roughly oval shape of Pod Two bristled in every direction with floating platforms, some enclosing large amounts of water. A myriad collection of levs, skims, and in-the-water barges were tied up on the lee side. There were cranes hanging from the terrace that spiraled up the outside of the pod. And, Mac squinted in disbelief, a slide dropped in a crazed swoop from the rooftop, ending a formidable height above the ocean surface.

That could hurt.

"I take it you let Marty play," Emily commented, making an obvious effort to keep her eyes from slipping west.

"He seemed the right choice." Mac, recipient of an impressive flow of data from Svehla and company courtesy of the Ministry, wasn't worried there'd been more fun—namely construction—than work, but now she shook her head in mock outrage. "I hope he's planned how to stow all this before winter."

While they talked, Tie brought the skim sweeping into Pod Two's new dock, an elaborate affair with steps as well as ramps. And, Mac noticed with mute admiration, a roof as well as a countertop for sorting gear. She sighed happily. About to climb out first, she paused and turned to Sing-li. "After you." *Only fair to let him do his job.*

The agent was busy whispering into his wrist com, eyes darting back and forth over the docking structure. Mac felt a chill. When Emily stood up beside her, ready to climb out, she lifted her hand to hold the other woman in place. "Something we should know?" she asked Sing-li, mouth dry.

"Do you see anyone here?" Sing-li demanded, getting to his feet. Like Nik, he moved differently when alarmed. *Like a barracuda, effortlessly keeping its jaws and muscular body aligned with the next doomed fish.*

"Why would there be?" An unconcerned Tie shut off the engine and tied off the skim. "Party tonight. Most're back at Base getting a head start. 'Spect we'll find Marty and his crew there." He pointed to the walkway linking the pod to land.

The one place Mac hadn't wanted Emily to go. *She should have called ahead, warned Kammie, done something to prevent this.*

But it was too late. Sing-li, with a nod, accepted Tie's explanation and climbed out. Tie followed suit, Emily going by Mac without a word.

She heard a gentle *harrumph.* "I could stop them," Mudge offered in a low voice, coming to stand beside her. His face was pale and beaded with more than ocean spray. "Make up something about new Trust regulations."

"Wouldn't work." Mac wasn't sure if she was touched or shocked he'd lie for Emily's sake. *Both,* she decided. She met his worried look and shrugged helplessly. "Maybe it's better to get it over with now, while I'm here. If Emily can't handle this . . ." She didn't need to finish. He knew as well as she did that if Emily Mamani broke, she'd be hospitalized again. This time, without Mac. Worse, she could easily end up in a Human facility, where she'd be safe from pestering by the Frow and their ilk, but more vulnerable to the Ro. "Besides," sighed Mac, waving at Mudge to go first, "it's why she invited you."

He frowned and didn't budge. "She told you?" Almost outrage.

Mac hesitated. Tie had led Emily and Sing-li to the junction of walkway and deck, gesturing to something about its construction. *Likely complaining—he approved of change about as much as a*

Sthlynii. "Not in so many words," she said carefully. "But it's obvious, isn't it?"

She'd never seen him smile like this before, a small, quiet smile that reached his eyes and made them twinkle. "I would have thought so, Norcoast, but you can be remarkably obtuse at times."

Obtuse? Interspecies communication suddenly seemed easier. "Oversight—" Mac swallowed, "—why do you think you're here?"

"Dr. Mamani's worried about you. It's going to be difficult—emotionally difficult—saying good-bye. To her. To your other friends. Base. She thought—" he actually blushed, "—she said you'd need a friendly shoulder on the trip to orbit and I'd be the best choice." He *harrumphed* and collected himself. "Not that I expect you'll do anything of the sort, Norcoast," this gruffly. "But I could tell my agreeing to come and offer my support eased her mind."

Mac tried to imagine weeping on Mudge's round shoulder and failed. What she could imagine, all too well, was Emily choosing to lie to him.

To postpone the inevitable.

"Emily's mind is a slippery thing," she said grimly. "Particularly when it comes to moving others in directions that suit her. I appreciate your kindness—really I do—but Emily?" A nod to the ruined slope. "She's brought you here as punishment, Oversight."

Mudge flinched. "Why?" he gasped. "What have I done to her? I—"

"Not yours," Mac interrupted gently. "Hers."

The blood drained from his face, but he gave a short nod before she could say anything more. "I see. We'd best not delay, Norcoast." He started moving.

"Wait." Mac stopped him with a touch on his lapel. *Only Mudge would wear an antique tweed jacket to visit Base in August.* "Damn Emily," she heard herself say. "You don't need to do this, Oversight. You don't need to go through it again. Stay here and wait for us."

"If I do," he countered with remarkable calm, "you know what will happen. Every time she looks at me, she'll blame herself again for what the Ro did here. There's enough guilt going around, Norcoast. None of us should carry more than our share. Especially Emily Mamani."

Each time she thought she knew the caliber of the man, he surprised her. "Probably not a good time for a hug," she decided out loud, her voice unsteady. At his look of horror, *likely feigned,* she patted him firmly on the lapel.

"Let's go."

The original walkway to land was gone, of course, along with the holdfast pillars and gate that had allowed access, if you had the right codes, to the system of suspended paths. It had been built with care so scientists could observe and record without leaving a record themselves. The new walkway was higher, to pass over the debris-crusted shore. If you could call trees larger than a transport lev debris in any sense.

The illusion of walking on air was disarming. Mac gave a tentative bounce, then another, stronger one. The membrane flexed like a giant trampoline.

"Norcoast!" Mudge protested. He looked inexpressibly silly with his fists clenched out from his sides, although Mac's own fingers were wrapped around the transparent rope rail. "What do you think you're doing? Stop that!"

"It's a fable," she explained but obeyed.

A Dhryn fable. Brymn's.

Finally, a memory that didn't sting.

Emily and the other two men were at the new gate, Tie keying in the code. Tiggers on top of each pillar watched him, as if eager for a mistake.

Gulls, Mac thought, *made vindictive watchdogs.*

Over land, the membrane lost its slight give, darkening as their feet approached steps to show the way in the bright sunlight.

At first, Mac noticed what was missing. Shade, for starters. The sun was hot as well as bright. Hot, bright, and unforgiving. The air smelled of dryness and dust. They were lucky, she judged, running her glance upslope to where the ridge overlooked the Pacific. When the westerlies were underway, it must be like a miniature dust storm here.

Life . . . as she looked closer, she realized it wasn't missing at all, simply changed. Every sheltered nook contained its blush of rich green moss, its feathers of fern. Fungi bracketed the lee sides of fallen wood and thrust its way through curls of dead bark. Exposed soil was peppered with sprigs of new grass and the coin-shaped seedpods of fireweed, except for a too-even scar where otters had made a slide to expedite their trip to shore. She smiled.

A squirrel scolded them from its perch on a half-buried tree, one tiny paw braced against an upturned twig, its tail swishing with outrage. Mac saluted before hurrying to catch up with the others.

"Told you," Tie announced. "There's Marty and his crew. Don't ask me what they're doing now."

As it was clear Svehla and his trio of students were ferrying memwood over the crest of the ridge, Mac could make a good guess. The observation deck on the opposite side had been one of his pet projects; she'd expect him to rebuild it as soon as possible. However, given the original construction had resulted in Mudge canceling a third of the proposals for that season—there being no way to remove the deck without more perturbations and him not being the sort to simply throw things at Mac and be satisfied—she also knew why Tie wasn't about to admit it to present company.

Not that Mudge would care today.

He was contained and too quiet, every step deliberate. Emily, on the other hand, flitted up the path ahead of them all like some frenetic butterfly, her long legs flashing through the panels of her improbable dress, waving to Svehla, who had put down his load and shaded his eyes to see who was paying them a visit.

Sing-li waited for Mac. "What are we doing here?" he demanded in a low voice.

She could see the strain on his face; a compliment to their relationship, that he didn't hide it. The Ministry had lost three of its own during the earthquake, men Sing-li knew, perhaps as friends, though she'd never dared ask. "Emily's penance," she replied, equally quietly.

As if the earthquake mattered—as if three lives mattered—against entire worlds lost and threatened.

Where on that scale are we?

Mac shook her head to clear it of Nik's implacable voice. Her companion misunderstood. "You don't approve." Sing-li stared at

Emily, now hugging Svehla and talking so quickly her voice was like a bird's. "Then why did you agree?"

"Think I was asked?" Mac snorted. "Doesn't matter. I wanted to take a look myself. It's one thing to know succession will take place—another to see it happen. It's reassuring."

And it was, Mac realized, taking a deep breath and letting it out slowly. She'd held the image of wrack and destruction tight in her mind for too long, believed somehow it was her responsibility to be here and help fix it.

The reality of regrowth without her lifted a load she hadn't noticed she was carrying until now. *Complete with otters.*

While part of her wanted to stay and see more, Mac could feel time flying by. "This shouldn't take long," she promised, as much for Mudge's sake as anyone else's.

They lengthened their strides to reach the others. Mudge, Mac noticed, had stayed apart. The distancing hadn't reassured Svehla, who was standing somewhat futilely in front of his pile of unapproved mem-wood. "There you are, Mac," Emily sang out. "I told Marty he has to stop all this and get to our party."

The students, dust-coated and sweaty, looked hopeful.

"Hi, Mac." Svehla screwed up his grizzled face, apparently trying not to smile at the radiant woman in front of him. "Em, you know I'd like to, but there's only so many hours of daylight this time of year and we've a spore census to complete—"

Much as it pained her, Mac made herself say: "There's always tomorrow, Marty." His look of astonishment was almost worth it. The students' wide grins, however, made her worry about setting a trend.

His problem. Hers was fiddling with a rope of black pearls.

"Meet you back there, Marty. Em? Lead the way."

She'd guessed correctly. Emily turned with a flourish to take the walkway that now replaced the one she and Mudge had walked that fateful morning in May.

Mudge followed Emily, Mac followed Mudge, finding Sing-li's presence behind their little group no comfort at all, not when she could see the tension hunching Mudge's shoulders, not when she knew as well as he what should be here, and wasn't.

Mercifully, Emily slowed and stopped long before they reached the place where the Ro had last landed, their ship shattering the old growth like dried sticks. She looked confused, as if she'd expected a landmark. Mudge came up beside her. Obeying her instincts, not without pity for both, Mac kept back. Sing-li followed suit.

Emily was taller. The breeze lifted her gleaming black hair, with its streaks of white, and played with the panels of her dress so they brushed Mudge's legs. Her head tilted on her elegant neck to let the sun kiss her high cheekbones and bury her dark eyes in shadow. Her grace was paralyzed, as if she was as much stone as the mauve-gray rock around them.

She was taller, but Mudge, in his shapeless jacket, panting and wiping sweat from his rosy forehead, alive and real, seemed to tower over her.

Their voices carried easily over the desolation. "This was my fault," Emily began, matter-of-factly. "I don't ask you to forgive me."

"Of course not," Mudge panted. "You want to tell me why they did it."

Where had that *come from?* Mac closed her mouth and paid attention.

Emily hesitated, her hands lifting as if warding a blow.

"You want me to understand," Mudge continued, almost stern. "It's important that I know why, isn't it, Emily."

"Y–yes," she faltered. "They were yours, these trees. Mac told me, Charlie. She said you put more value on the smallest twig here than her life's work."

Mac grimaced. *There were some things not worth repeating . . .* "Why did they do it?" Mudge's arm swept outward, but his eyes never left Emily's. "Why did they have to destroy it all?"

She swayed and Mac started forward in alarm, but stopped as Emily began to speak, her voice now reed-thin and gasping. "This world . . . would be cleansed. *They* . . . knew it would be. *They* don't have patience . . . but time . . . time . . . *They* own time. Make ready and wait, make ready and wait, make—"

Emily paused; none of them moved.

Then, "*They* had to destroy the signs . . . signs among the trees that would show what *They* left behind . . . what *They* sent into the ocean . . . destroy the signs . . . sweep it all away . . . those who walked for them . . . the signs . . . your trees, Charlie. Into the ocean. Forgive—" Emily sank to her knees, her arms reaching out to Mudge. "Forgive me."

He sank down with her, gathering her in, holding her tight.

Mac's eyes sought the cove, its dark blue water sparkling in the sun, its depths hiding . . . what? She was aware of Sing-li speaking urgently into his com, doubtless commandeering teams to rip up the recovering slope, to scour the ocean bed, to look for whatever the Ro had left behind for the moment the Dhryn wiped this world of life.

She stood on an empty mountainside, with nothing but open sky, familiar landscapes, and friends in sight, and had never felt so terrified.

And she'd brought Emily here for safety?

- 8 -

PARTINGS AND PERTURBATIONS

IT WAS A MEASURE OF HOW SERIOUSLY the Ministry of Extra-Sol Human Affairs, and Earthgov, took Sing-li's message that convoys of huge black levs whooshed over their heads toward the outer arm of Castle Inlet before Tie finished securing their skim to the dock at Base.

It was a measure of how little attention Base itself paid to the world that they were surrounded upon arrival not by aroused security but by staff and students wearing shirts that made Sing-li's downright conservative, several waving opened bottles, and all smiling.

Run away? Mac wondered numbly as she was hauled from the skim with a roar of welcome, *or grab the nearest beer?*

Sing-li vanished into the crowd, with Tie right behind. None of them had said a word during the ride back. Mac had pulled out her imp and worked. Emily had sat with Mudge, her head on his shoulder, her eyes closed. She'd looked exhausted, but at peace.

He'd looked thoroughly horrified—whether by Emily's revelation or her proximity, Mac couldn't be sure.

For her part, Mac was grateful. Intentionally or by luck, Mudge had asked the right question at the right time, accomplishing what no one else, including Emily, had managed in all the weeks of trying. She'd finally been able to express a memory of the Ro.

Something less disturbing would have been nice.

She burned inside. *What the Ro had done in the past was nothing to this, this violation!*

Hide a threat here? In her ocean?

Mac wasn't sure at what point her fury had turned into something cold and set, her determination into something implacable. She didn't care. All she knew was that she couldn't leave this to anyone else.

Here, she wasn't defenseless.

Of course, the party had begun without them and was now well underway. Mac dodged and ducked her way between gleeful students, keeping an eye fixed on her target, the door to Pod Three and the administrator's office. She had to talk to Kammie Noyo. She wanted—if not answers, then reassurance. Reassurance that others knew, that the appropriate actions were being taken at all levels.

That this time, they'd listen.

It didn't help either her progress or her impatience when students started announcing her presence as loudly as possible. "Mac's back!" "Where?" "Over here!" "Hurry—hide the ribs!!!" "Why do we have to hide the ribs?"

Mac paused to wince.

A chorus bellowed the answer: " 'Cause Mac's back!"

"You'd think they'd forget," she muttered under her breath. "But no." The story of how she'd eaten the last rib on the barbeque one night—quite by accident—had blossomed with retelling to each new crop of students until every rib night began with a chant of . . . she waited for it, resigned. *Easier to stop the tides.*

"No Ribs for Mac! No Ribs for Mac! No Ribs for Mac! Mac gets SALAD and BEER!"

Mac shook her head, an unbidden smile twitching her lips. *Their joy at her expense was irresistible.* "You realize it doesn't rhyme," she complained to those nearest, who only laughed and chanted louder. Someone handed her the beer in question. She waited for it, but this time no one had brought salad. Which usually landed on her head.

Emily put her hand on Mac's shoulder and leaned into her ear. "You should be staying here," she shouted over the din, "not me."

"Not if I want ribs," Mac tossed back. She stopped her futile fight against the human current before Emily could argue, letting herself be drawn with the surge to the line of smoking barbeques on the upper terrace.

It turned out to be the right choice. Mac spotted Kammie's immaculate white lab coat at the top of the first sweep of stairs and struggled, beer in hand, through well wishers to reach her.

When she did, Kammie nodded before Mac could open her mouth to speak, her face somber. "I've heard. Come with me."

"Just a minute." Mac looked around for Emily and Mudge. They were coming up the steps, making slower time than she had—in part because Emily was being accosted from every side. The attention made her sparkle, like a vidstar greeting fans.

"Mac!" Case Wilson had acquired more freckles over the summer, but otherwise the deep fisher looked exactly as he had when she'd left: lanky, muscular, and too young for his years. His wide grin faded as he approached. "What's up?"

Male, breathing, and new. *Perfect,* Mac decided. She grabbed his arm with her free hand and he flinched. "Sorry," she said quickly, relaxing her grip. The prosthesis could be overly firm. "Case, I need a favor. See that woman down there?"

"Dr. Mamani." His pale eyes flicked back to her. "Your friend who went missing. I wanted to say how happy I am she's okay—"

"She's not," Mac interrupted, lowering her voice. "Look after her for me, would you? Just for a little while. Get her a drink, something to eat, breathing space. I have to talk to Kammie. With Oversight," she added, catching Mudge's attention and beckoning him to follow. He detached from Emily's cluster with obvious relief.

"Who's looking after you?"

Mac, her mind already on Ro, ocean floors, and how to snag a savory rib or two on the way to Kammie's office, blinked at Case. "Pardon?"

"You heard me." He was frowning. Not, she decided, in anger, but with his own brand of thoughtful obstinacy. Case would latch on to what he viewed as a problem like a barnacle to stone.

And be about as difficult to dislodge.

Mac frowned back. "I don't need looking after. Emily does."

"Mac—"

"You heard me," she stressed as Mudge came panting to her

side. He paused, giving Case an assessing look. "As I said," Mac continued smoothly, "don't eat all the ribs before we get back. Ah, Oversight. This way. Kammie's waiting for us."

Mac licked her fingers and looked around for a place to drop the small bone. Without a word, Kammie held out an empty petri dish and took her offering.

"The Ministry's expecting your full cooperation." From her tone, 'Sephe wasn't.

Mac hadn't been surprised to find the agent sitting in Kammie's office, although Kammie herself had had something to say about her new statistician invading her privacy—that is, until 'Sephe had pointed out they both represented interests beyond Base, so perhaps they could move on to the topic at hand.

Not a surprise either.

"Let me get this straight," Mac said quietly. She put her sticky fingertips together and studied 'Sephe. "You don't want Base evacuated. You want everything to continue as before." Music thumped through the pod walls and floors. The festivities outside were in full swing. A tiny light was flashing on Kammie's desk—incoming message. More than one. She ignored the display, intent on Mac.

The agent's generous lips thinned with distaste. "This isn't coming from me, Mac. You know that."

"Nor me," Kammie snapped. "The IU committee is not in favor of involving untrained civilians. Most of our people are students, Dr. Stewart. We must send them to safety!"

"Where?" Mac asked, receiving startled looks from both. "If the Dhryn come again," she elaborated in a cold voice, "if the Ro come again . . . where do you think they'll be safe?"

The music outside had stopped. *When would they notice?* she wondered.

Mudge stirred in his seat. 'Sephe leaned forward in hers, dark eyes now inscrutable. "Go on."

"The Ministry wants to keep Base operating as is," Mac elaborated. "Meaning everyone here remains ignorant while you bring in your experts to search for whatever the Ro dropped in the ocean. Base as camouflage. Everything outwardly normal."

"That's the gist of it. Sorry, Mac. I know you're—"

Mac raised her hand to stop her. "We'll cooperate—" and over Kammie's shocked "Mac!" she continued, "—but Base will conduct the search."

"Impossible." 'Sephe shook her head. "We must maintain secrecy—"

Mac's lips twisted. "Secrecy wastes time we don't have. No one knows these waters as well. Searching this ocean is what these people do for a living. Emily can retune her Tracer. You—" a nod to Kammie "—have sufficient genetic coding to differentiate a Ro walker from anything local." The little silver vial on the shelf seemed to wink at her. "It's a running start. Better than anything you have, 'Sephe."

Kammie's eyes were glowing. "We'd have to drop everything else," she warned. "Lose the field season."

Where on that scale . . . "There'll be another," Mac promised, aware she couldn't.

"I'll pass this along, Mac," 'Sephe said unhappily. "But you know Hollans. I can't see him approving."

"I wasn't asking." Mac rose to her feet, Mudge doing the same, his eyes fixed on her. She pulled out her imp and tapped it lightly against the side of her forehead. "On the way back I dumped all relevant information into Norcoast's main system, including a Base-wide message cued to announce itself in every way possible." She indicated the mass of flashing lights on Kammie's desk. "I'd say everyone's got it by now."

"I don't believe it," 'Sephe said flatly. "You're bluffing."

Kammie's mouth worked, her eyes swimming with tears. She made a helpless gesture, and Mac smiled. "Go outside and see for yourself," she told 'Sephe. "Me, I'm leaving the planet."

'Sephe pulled out her own imp and rushed out the door to the hallway. Mac watched her go, then glanced at the ceiling, transparent to the sky and clouds, doubtless filled with embedded eyes and ears. "Thank you," she said in Instella, putting her fingertips and thumbs together in a circle.

Anchen hadn't just sent her here to see her family.
She'd sent her to reconnect herself, and the whole truth, to her home.

The terraces, steps, and walkways were crowded with students and staff. Most sat with their backs to walls. All stared into flickering 'screens, fingers manipulating no-longer-secret data as they talked in urgent hushed tones to one another. The barbeques with their loads of ribs had been turned off, the meat abandoned on the grills.

If it hadn't been for the lurid party shirts, *and the beers in hand,* Mac might have thought them cramming for finals.

She stood on the uppermost terrace, seeing the first impact of what she'd wrought, and trembled. To hide it, she gripped the rail and stared seaward. Two levs were coming into dock. Black ones. *Did they try to be conspicuous?*

"Your people are scientists," Mudge observed. "They'll manage." He leaned on the rail and gave a sad little *harrumph.* "Shame about the ribs, though."

Mac gave him a sharp look. "This isn't funny, Oversight."

"I know." He hesitated, then, in his firm, no-nonsense voice, "You did the right thing, Norcoast. Protocols be damned. In this instance."

She was touched. "You did pretty well yourself, Oversight. Oh, oh." Mac tensed as she saw who was debarking from the first Ministry lev. No mistaking Martin Svehla, although she'd never seen him this disheveled before a party, shirt half torn from one shoulder, hair mussed, missing a shoe. He saw her and began stalking toward Pod Three, shaking off the hands of his students with a rough gesture. "This can't be good," she murmured.

"He won't blame you."

"Trust me, Oversight," sighed Mac. "He will. It's a gift."

Svehla wasn't the only one noticing her presence. Others were starting to stand and migrate in her direction. "Time to go," she decided.

"What? No rousing speech?"

Emily.

Mac froze.

"Or good-bye? *Aie*. Coward."

The last word had bite to it. Mac turned with a sigh. Emily stood there, dark eyes smoldering with outrage. Case was with her, behind and to one side. He looked, Mac judged, equally upset. *Just less dramatic about it.*

" 'Time to go' was a figure of speech. I'm hardly running off, Em," she observed. "Our ride's not here yet." She checked on Svehla's progress. Luckily, he'd stopped to talk to Lee Fyock, who was now staring up at them, too.

Emily waved her pearls at him.

"Lara—from biochem?" Mac said testily. "Stop that."

"You're the one who's stopped everything. This was our party, Mac. There was to be—" Emily gave her hips a frustrated twitch, sending the transparent portion of her dress swirling across territory that made Mudge blush. "Dancing!"

"Dancing?" echoed Case in disbelief. "You're worried about dancing at a time like this? Are you nuts?"

"*Si, Señor!* Ask our Mac."

Given the unlikelihood of explaining to the innocent Case that dancing, preferably sweaty hours of it, was a perfectly normal stress response for Emily Mamani under the circumstances, and equally unable to clarify, in under a thousand words, the state of her friend's sanity to herself or anyone else, Mac settled for a noncommittal grunt.

Charles Mudge III, however, had a definite opinion. *Not that she was surprised.* "You will apologize to Dr. Mamani this minute, young man," he ordered, in his most officious tone. "She's had a very trying day. Very trying."

"Why thanks, Charlie," Emily cooed, trailing her fingers up his sleeve and slipping one gloved arm around Mudge's neck. "We've always been close," she confided to Case. Mudge squirmed free with an incoherent squawk of protest. Emily laughed.

Mac shook her head at the three of them, simultaneously warning off a small group of approaching students. "Have you gone over your gear, Em? We should make sure everything's arrived."

She watched for the transformation. The Emily Mac had known could switch from audacious flirt to preoccupied scientist in the blink of an eye. Broke a new heart every Monday, Mac would tell her. Emily would shrug and reach for her work.

There. Emily abandoned Mudge, to his relief, and gave her a considering look. "I planned a quick assessment and initial power relay check after the party, Mac, but under the circumstances, I can get to it now—be done before you leave."

Mac opened her mouth to agree, then something in Case's face made her hesitate. She paused to take a good look around.

Everyone in sight was looking back at her, those nearest with expressions of confusion and dismay. Six mismatched barbeques stood nearby, stacked with cooling bones, while beer warmed in tubs of melting ice. The breeze caught the edge of the banner draped over the railing, flipping it up so Mac could make out the colorful curves of its lettering, "Welcome Home."

She'd really done it. "Bother."

Ignoring Emily's questioning eyebrow, Mac pulled out her imp, and activated its screen. She drew her finger through the audio control, took a deep breath, then said: "Hi."

The word boomed from every corner of Base and Mac made a face of her own. *She hated loudspeakers. Even more, her voice over loudspeakers.*

"You know how much I love talking like this," she continued, "so I'll make it brief."

She had their attention, no doubt about that.

"Despite what you might be thinking right now, the world hasn't come to an end. Trust me," she added dryly, "you'd know the difference.

"What has happened is that the Ro have made their first mistake. Hiding something here of all places . . . with you lot? What were they thinking?" Mac paused to let the concept trickle through and was gratified to see some half grins and nods. "If there's anything alien underwater, or ever was, who better to find it? You know what belongs—from inlet to strait, from deep reefs to tidal flats. Find what doesn't. And don't let anyone stop you." This last as Mac spotted 'Sephe and Sing-li stepping out on the terrace below.

"I know what I'm asking," she continued, hearing the huskiness in her own voice as it echoed. "It will take years to recover the data you'll lose by abandoning this season, if you even can. Some of your careers will suffer. And it might be for nothing. But, maybe, just maybe, what you do here might help save everything. All of—" she had to stop and settled for a sweeping gesture to include Base, ocean, shore, and sky.

The waves slapping the walkways was the loudest sound as Mac fought to calm herself.

Should have stuck with a memo.

"If ignorance protected you, I've taken that away," she went on. "If staying uninvolved was some kind of defense, I'm asking you to risk yourselves. Not because I don't want you safe—" The word broke. Mac clenched her hands into fists and forced herself to keep speaking. "But because I don't believe there is safety for anyone, or any world, until we resolve this.

"I know what you can do," she finished, "better than anyone. Will you?"

Her heart thudded in the hush. Just when Mac thought she'd have to keep talking, with nothing left to say, someone shouted from a walkway: "Can we have the ribs first?"

The irreverent demand was followed immediately by a distant warbling, "Hide them from Mac!"

As if they'd all been waiting for a signal, the chant began and grew. "No Ribs for Mac! No Ribs for Mac! Mac gets SALAD and BEER!!!"

Mac blinked away tears. An instant later, she was pulling salad out of her hair.

The Ro had waited this long, she reminded herself.

"What, exactly, was that?" Sing-li asked, leaning against a wall. He took a slug of his beer and regarded Mac thoughtfully.

Dusk had come and gone, laying its curtain of darkness everywhere but here. Base was lit from pod to dock, the guide lights along rail and stair upped for the occasion. Mac wondered what passing fish thought of the glow above. *If any approached given the volume of music.*

"Vintage Mac," Emily said, tugging Mac's hair. "Scary, isn't she? I did try to warn you."

He laughed. "Wasn't me who needed warning. Hollans was—well, let's say he was surprised."

"Will he interfere?" Mac asked.

"How? To move your people out of here by force, he'd have to declare an emergency—and prove one exists. Not a good time for false alarms. He certainly can't stop them doing what they normally do. Between us?" He tilted his head back for another slug. "Between us, Mac, I think Hollans and a few others are grateful for the help—not that they'll ever admit it. They aren't supposed to involve civilians, however qualified."

Mac snorted at this, but relaxed. She found another bit of wilted greenery in her shirt and pulled it out to nibble. The party had reached the friendly standing crush of people stage on the terraces, although some dared sit on the steps. There was dancing, but in the gallery—less chance of someone twirling into the ocean. "You'll keep an eye on the place."

It hadn't been a question, but he nodded. "Easier now that stealth isn't an option. Although," he indicated his flamboyant shirt, "there's something to be said for camouflage."

"Mac. You coming?" Emily was half dancing already, those around her clearing a small space and smiling. "There won't be any room left."

"Shame," Mac muttered, but she nodded. A promise was a promise, however onerous.

There was, however, one thing to do first. Before she could change her mind, she stepped up to Sing-li and kissed him firmly on the mouth.

And before he could say or do anything, Mac grabbed Emily's arm and hurried them both away.

"As good-byes go, not bad," her friend commented. "Quick. To the point. A tad public. I think you shocked poor Charlie."

"Shut up, Em," Mac suggested.

"Just giving my expert opinion."

"Didn't ask for it." Mac ran her tongue over her lips, tasting beer, and grinned.

Emily gave a throaty chuckle. "You never do."

Noticing they were about to pass her office, now Emily's, Mac slowed and gave the other a sidelong look. "I'm leaving in an hour. Did you want to check the gear now?"

"Do you?"

Mac lifted the beer she'd nursed since supper and tapped the one Emily carried. "Not really."

"Dr. Connor. You shock me."

A sudden buzz brought three Preds, who'd been sitting against the wall by Mac's door, scrambling to their feet. Mac stepped in front of the first before they could start running. "Turn them off," she said gently.

"What?" said one.

"Mac," protested another. "It's the transient pod off Field Station One. Gotta be. We've been waiting all summer—"

She heard the pain in their voices, saw the anguished curves of their shoulders as the full consequence of what they'd promised came home at last, and couldn't say another word.

"Turn'm off," ordered the third student, tearing free her own wrist alarm and stuffing it into a pocket. "It's okay, Mac. We forgot. Habit, you know."

"Look on the bright side," Emily told them. "You can go to the dance." This notion drew smiles and they trotted away—if not happy, then willing to be distracted.

Mac watched them go. "Thanks, Em," she said after a minute.

"You do realize I'd take all this as my fault—moan, beat my chest, and so forth—except you're doing such a great job of assuming the blame I can't be bothered."

Mac's lips twisted. "Anytime."

Emily tipped her bottle against Mac's. "Let's go visit your fish," she said. "I can dance later."

From the lowermost loading dock, at the end of Base closest to the Tannu River, the sounds of the party, the murmur of voices and music, blended into the restless slap of waves against mem-wood. Sitting on the stern of Norcoast's venerable barge, Mac stretched her bare feet downward and was rewarded by the occasional flip of chill water on her toes. She didn't need to see into the depths to know what swam there. *What the Ro had left was another matter.*

"One day you'll do that and something with teeth will think they're bait."

"Obviously, you've never tried fishing off the dock," Mac countered, wiggling her toes pensively. "I'd be lucky to get a nibble."

"What could *They* have left, Mac?" Emily didn't seem to expect an answer *which,* Mac thought, *was just as well.* "The memory of that day, of the earthquake . . . I know I was there. I know it. I remember being . . . feeling . . . insignificant. No. Small. That was it. I can't trust what I recall of dimensions, Mac. Time, space, they blur together. But this . . . I think I felt small because I was near something much bigger."

"Big could be good," Mac decided, leaning back against one of the huge coils of rope that lined the stern access. She studied the horizon. Black on black. A trace of mauve where clouds hovered over the mountains and caught starlight. Lines of fluorescence straggled across the dark water, rising and falling as if the sea itself was breathing.

"How?"

"Harder to hide."

"*They're* experts."

"So," Mac said firmly, "are we. And we have you." She looked at her companion, nothing more than a darker shadow. "We do, don't we, Em?"

"Looks that way," the other replied, the words spaced apart and thoughtful. "I admit it shook me, remembering . . . what I remembered. But being here, Mac?" Emily took a deep breath and let it out. "How did you know? I feel like myself, for the first time in too long. Oh, I'll be able to work, all right." A low, sparkling laugh. "And I still know the best pubs, for when I've had it with the peace and isolation."

Something for Sing-li to deal with, Mac thought, more amused than worried. "Try not to completely disappear on me again, okay?"

"You, too."

Mac couldn't help looking up, to where stars appeared between the clouds. Some weren't stars at all, she realized, but way stations in orbit, shuttles moving to and fro, the endless traffic of a world whose markets and interests spanned thousands of solar systems beyond its own. *Such a long way from home.*

"I'll be back as soon as I can," she vowed, to herself as much as Emily. "And while I might not have a pub in reach if I get bored, well, there's the Fourteen and Oversight show."

"Poor Charlie," Emily chuckled, then her voice turned serious. "You take care of him, Mac."

"I'll do what I can, but that Myg . . ."

"You know what I mean."

Mac pressed her lips together, then let out a slow breath. "I won't promise, Em. I can't. You saw what I did today. I put Base, all these people, at risk without hesitation. You, too." She shuddered. "What's worse—I'd do it again."

"Don't take too much credit. You didn't put anyone at risk, Mac," Emily corrected. "*They* did. You simply cut some red tape. Although I hope you realize I'm going to continue my work on the Survivors, between helping the others search."

Tossed down like a gauntlet. Mac smiled to herself. "I couldn't imagine trying to stop you, Dr. Mamani."

Instead of the quip she expected, Emily said quietly: "You're the only one who could."

Mac let the words resonate between them, dismayed by Emily's trust. Who was she to judge the value of another's life's work? Who was she to be right—or terribly wrong—about the application of that work to the present crisis?

A salmon researcher, sans fish.

The image struck Mac as funny, for no particular reason, and she relaxed very slightly. "We'll stay in touch. Let me know if you need anything—at least while I'm still in Sol System. After that, it might be more efficient to have Sing-li steal it for you."

"I'll keep that in mind. Handy, having your own spy."

"Until he takes off on some doubt-I'll-return-intact mission," Mac said, then blushed. *Good thing they were sitting in the dark.* She coughed.

"You're blushing, Mackenzie Connor."

"How can you—?" she closed her mouth.

"Too easy." Emily chuckled. "Still, if you think Mr. Jones could disappear on me in similar fashion, I'd better have an assistant who'll stay put. Hmmmm. There were some firm and energetic specimens in the rib queue earlier."

"Now who's too easy?"

"Is it my fault I appreciate the finer things in life?"

"Yes."

They sat in companionable silence after that. Mac didn't need to check the time. Half an hour left. Part of her seethed with pointless advice and all the other things people say when they imagine never having the chance again. *Don't do what I'd do?*

When Emily Mamani never acted on another's impulses?

Stay off the ocean?

When that was where Emily's Tracer would be used?

None of it was worth saying, not now.

The rest of her wanted nothing more than to sit here in the dark as long as possible, cradled by ocean, and listen to Emily's breathing. No need to fill the air with words. They'd spent more time in such peace together than chatter; while working, hours could pass.

Although not working and staying quiet, for Emily, couldn't last seconds. "What was it like?" she began brightly.

Mac bumped her head gently against the rope, twice, before giving up. "What was what like?"

"Meeting the Dhryn female. A life-form the size of a small city—had to be incredible."

"The Progenitor?" Mac ran her fingers through her short hair. "Big."

"Mac."

"Okay," she relented. "My initial reaction? Glee. Those stuffy old biology texts were wrong again. She blew away any prediction on the maximum size of a living being. After that, I got busy trying to figure out how she could be that large: a colonial organism, perhaps a fluid body core with a living skin, a few wilder ideas. But once I saw her face . . ." Her foot was engulfed in a taller wave than most and Mac pulled it up, shaking off the drops. "Once we started talking, I forgot her size. The Progenitor's a remarkable person. I think you'd like each other."

Emily's reply was drowned out by a prolonged *whompf* of wind as a transport lev, a mammoth one, flew by overhead. It was tow-ing sleds, each loaded with an orbit-capable shipping crate. *They'd better not be planning to put her into one of those again,* Mac told herself grimly, but the lev passed Base. They watched as it followed the coast, heading for what had been the Succession Documentation and Research Pod. *The Ministry was apparently done with subtle.*

"Poor Marty," she murmured. He'd avoided her altogether after her announcement. She'd last seen him curled in a corner, nursing a bottle of what hadn't been beer. "He'd built such a wonderful dock. And that slide?"

"Won't be wasted—the dock anyway. And they'll need his survey data and maps." Emily, apparently done with sitting, too, got to her feet. Mac, reluctantly, followed suit. "Hate to say it, but the next one will likely be yours, Mac. You'd better get ready. Unless you're wearing those on the trip."

Mac considered the notion of wearing her very comfortable cottage shorts to Myriam. *Fourteen would love it.*

"I'll change," she agreed.

They climbed up the short ladder and retrieved their respective footwear, Emily's glittering in the dock lights. Given it was August, Mac shook each shoe and, from the second, caught a spider in her hand. She released it on the dock.

"Mac, before you go—" Emily said. "About the Progenitor—"

"Oh. Right. Tell you what." Mac finished fastening her shoe and stood. "I'll record a better description and send it. There'll be plenty of time while we ship out to the gate. Right now, I—"

"Mac." Emily touched her arm. "Please. Listen to me."

She looked up and was warned by her friend's anxious expression. "This isn't another confession, is it?" *There had to be,* Mac sincerely hoped, *limits to even Emily's past.*

"No."

"Oh, good."

"No. It's not good, Mac. Don't you see? It's a pattern with you. This hanging on to the past—this loyalty to friends no matter what. You can't keep doing it. The Dhryn don't deserve it. Your friend Brymn transformed into a feeder and would have killed you. This Progenitor of yours, this remarkable person, could do the same, or worse. You can't trust any Dhryn."

Mac frowned. "We don't know enough about the species to make—"

"We know the Dhryn are a biological weapon, made and wielded by *Them*. Don't go out there believing you can save the ones you like." Emily took her arm, though she hadn't tried to leave. "The entire species has to be exterminated," she insisted. "*They* must be left helpless."

"It's hardly up to me, is it?" Mac said, freeing herself as gently as possible.

"Like it or not, you've become of interest to the people who will make that decision. A word at the wrong time, to the wrong ears? It could mean the wrong choice, Mac."

Mac felt her heart clench. "You're assuming there's a right one."

"There always is. The one that lets us survive."

Was survival a moral choice?

Mac shook her head, but not at Emily. "I'll try not to say anything to anyone. How's that?"

"Unlikely." Before Mac could say a word, Emily's arms went around and held her tight. "Less trust," she urged, her lips to Mac's ear. "I want you back. Hear me?"

"More air," wheezed Mac, doing her own holding. *Too thin,* she fussed to herself. *Her friend was skin over bone.* "No saving the universe without me."

"Deal."

They clung to each other a heartbeat longer, then Emily broke away. She pirouetted on the barge deck, pearls swinging. "Say hi to our Nik for me," she said. Three quick steps took her up to the dock where she dipped in a graceful curtsy, the Sinzi fabric flowing with the motion. "And don't be so serious all the time." Over her shoulder, as she tripped lightly along the walkway toward the music. "*Adios, hermana-muyo.*" Sister-mine.

And Mac was alone.

"Just once," she complained, "I'd like to make the grand exit." The empty barge didn't comment.

She wrapped her arms around herself, holding Emily's fading warmth.

Mac made her way to Pod Four, where two first-floor student rooms had been upgraded to house visitors to Base. The upgrading, from what she could tell, consisted of temporarily moving out the students and most, though not all, of their gear. There was the charming addition of a clear vase filled with pebbles and a dead twig. Since she'd only wanted the room to change from her Myg-ripped blouse and store her bag, she hadn't bothered to ask for a live one.

Striding along the walkway, fingers trailing over the rope rail, she was aware of Sing-li following in the background. He'd more than kept his distance while she sat with Emily. Now, when she could have used the company, it didn't feel right to change the order of things.

Not to mention she'd said good-bye.

The party in and around Pod Three continued without her, a blaze of light and sound that made its own bubble within the surrounding night. *Just as well.* It had taken hours to say hello to everyone; doing farewells, especially after the shock of this afternoon, could take days. Not to mention the beer . . . and arguments . . . possibly maudlin behavior.

Better to slip away in the dark.

Zimmerman, his large head tucked deep into the collar of an orchid-print shirt, stood at the door of Pod Four. Shirt aside, he looked about as casual as the levs continuing to pass overhead. Mac smiled a greeting. "Hope my bag's been behaving itself."

"Hi, Mac." Almost a whisper—but that was Zimmerman's normal voice. "All quiet." He looked wistfully at Pod Three. "Here, anyway."

"Don't worry," she told him. "The students will be rolling home in a few hours and someone always falls in."

"I don't swim." As if fearing this sounded less than professional, he added: "Tie has his skim ready. I'll watch."

"Did you get any ribs?"

His teeth flashed. "Did you leave any?"

"Lies. All lies," she complained, but gestured back at Sing-li, standing in the shadows. "You can grab some while he's here, I'm sure."

"I'll survive. You—some of us should be going with you, Mac," he said glumly. "This isn't right."

Mac smiled. "I'm happier knowing you'll be here, looking after my people—and yourselves, okay? You know Sing-li. He's a troublemaker."

"Sure, Mac." Zimmerman heaved a melancholy sigh that strained the buttons of his shirt. *He'd make a good Grimnoii,* Mac thought. "You'd better get ready. The lev's docked." He opened the door for her.

The pod felt abandoned, as if ready to be lifted for winter storage. Only the posters lining the walls and a pile of rain boots, several large enough to be buckets, proved anyone currently lived here. Stepping around and over the boots, Mac pushed open the door to the guest quarters, so designated by a large "No Students" sign, and looked for the bag she'd dumped on the bed.

What she saw instead were large pale feet, with reddish hairs on their toes. The feet were at the end of equally pale legs, also hairy, which disappeared into a pair of dark blue baggy shorts. Case Wilson's shorts, to be precise, Case himself snoring peacefully, using her bag as a pillow.

Mac walked to the head of the bed and tugged her bag free. Case's head thumped down on the mattress and his eyes popped open, horror on his face the instant he saw her grinning down at him.

She'd never seen anyone scuttle from a bed quite that fast.

Or turn quite that red.

To give him time to recover, Mac took her bag to the desk, pushing aside the vase of pebbles with twig to make room for it. She rummaged inside for something intact and travel-suited. "Never let an alien do your packing, Case," she advised, lifting out the hockey puck to show him. "Even the well-intentioned sort."

"Mac. Dr. Connor. I'm really sorry—"

She found a serviceable pair of Base coveralls and forgave Two immediately. "Turn around."

"I—what are you doing?" he blurted as she began undoing her shirt, then whirled to face the wall.

"Changing," she explained, thinking it was obvious. Dropping her shorts and stepping into the coveralls, Mac added: "What I want to know is what you're doing here instead of being at the party." *Or attending the briefings already underway.* Taking her mind off what she'd started, Mac ran her finger up the coverall seam to fasten the front, then ran a hand through her hair. "Well?" she prompted.

He kept his back to her. *Even his ears were glowing red,* she noted, fascinated. "I . . . I . . ."

"You wanted to say good-bye?" she suggested.

This turned Case to face her, his expression nothing short of desperate. "No. Mac. I want to go with you. To the Dhryn planet."

It had to be something in the air. Or a disease. She shook her head. "Impossible. You can't."

"Why? Sam's going."

She blinked. "Sam who?"

"Sam Schrant. Marin's postdoc."

"Oh." Mac gathered herself. "That Sam. The meteorologist." And more. Schrant was a storm chaser, presently a leader in the field of catastrophic event modeling. She'd asked Mudge to grab Schrant for their group weeks before; the request had been mired in bureaucracy ever since. "I didn't know his clearance had gone through. I'm surprised it has, really." She put back the puck, added shirt and shorts, and closed her bag. "Good for Oversight. Though between us, the man's a menace. In a good way."

Case took a step toward her, his scarred hands open at his sides. "Mac. Listen. I'm good with machines. You don't grow up on a trawler without being able to handle hard work and whatever nature throws at you. And you know I've a level head."

Mac's eyes narrowed thoughtfully. "All true."

"Then I can come?" He edged closer, like some overeager puppy.

Mac edged back, trying not to be obvious about it. He was too tall for her to see his expression from this range without bending her neck an uncomfortable amount. She hit the desk and made it seem on purpose by hopping up on it, which put them at a more even height. *Bonus.* "No."

"But . . ."

"Do you like dancing, Case?"

His sea-washed eyes stared down at her. "What?"

"Do you like dancing?" Mac repeated.

"No. Not really. Why?"

"Even better. I want you to be Dr. Mamani's research assistant."

She might have asked him to jump in the ocean. *With blood-aroused sharks.* "No!"

Mac frowned. "You don't know what her research is—"

He put his hands palm-down on either side of the desk and leaned forward until his nose almost touched hers. "And I don't care."

Barbeque sauce breath. She stifled a giggle, quite sure that reaction would thoroughly offend the earnest young man. Who was, she guessed, upset enough. This close, all she could see were freckles and some patchy stubble.

"What's going on here?"

Mac ducked her head to peer under Case's arm. He lunged back, all the color draining from his face this time. She didn't blame him. Sing-li on his own was intimidating, despite the shirt. Add Zimmerman, nostrils flared and those improbable shoulders jamming the doorway?

Poor Case probably thought he was about to be dropped into that ocean.

"Do you mind?" she said acidly. "I'm briefing Mr. Wilson. He's applied to be Dr. Mamani's assistant."

The expressions as her explanation registered—on all three—were vastly entertaining. *Had she time for it.*

"Briefing," echoed Sing-li, doubt in his voice and the searing look he gave Case.

"I don't want to be Dr. Mamani's assistant," Case insisted.

Zimmerman, not to be left out, relaxed in the doorway and added with a sly grin, "Well, I've never had a briefing like that."

"What are you implying?" The return of his fiery blush didn't help Case's outraged dignity one bit, but Mac gave him credit. He looked willing to take on both agents.

"I have a lev to catch," she reminded all of them. "You three can bond later. Right now, I need another minute alone with Mr. Wilson. If you don't mind?"

Zimmerman half bowed his way out, still smirking. Sing-li gave

Mac his "I don't like this" look but followed, saying only, "We'll be outside."

Once the door closed, Mac put her hands on her knees. "Sorry about that," she told Case. "Where were we?"

"I was saying no to having anything to do with her."

"Ah, yes." She kept her face carefully neutral. "Not the best first impression?"

"I know you've worked together for years." His honesty got the better of him. "But I don't get how. She's a—a—" he stopped there, probably viewing it as wise, and threw up his hands. "She doesn't take anything seriously."

Mac chewed her lower lip for a moment. "Emily Mamani," she said at last, "is a brilliant scientist, an innovative engineer, and can drink someone twice her mass under the table, so don't ever try. She's also a fraud. Not take things seriously? She's so serious— about everything imaginable—it's almost killed her. Despite what I said to everyone today, it's her device, the Tracer, that offers the best chance of finding whatever the Ro sent into Castle Inlet in time to make a difference."

Case sat down on the bed and stared at her. "She's a pretty good actor, then."

"That, too."

"Why does she need me?"

Because firm and energetic is easy. Mac resolutely ignored that memory, focusing on the troubled young man in front of her. "Emily's protected by the Ministry—Sing-li and his lot. Her recovery is being monitored by Dr. Stewart, also Ministry. She's—"

" 'Sephe the statistician? She jams with Sasha's band in Pod Six most nights." He looked incredulous, as if musicians couldn't be spies. "You're kidding—"

Although Mac sympathized, she raised her eyebrow and Case subsided. "Emily was authorized to spend what she must, to use any and all resources here short of disrupting the season. Now that I've done the disrupting, her work will take priority."

"Sounds like she has enough help."

"Help she has, Case," Mac agreed. "All of it complicated. All of it with strings attached. Obligations, expectations. Fear. What Emily needs is someone who won't lie to her, for any reason.

Someone she can trust. Won't be you, not at first. It'll take work. And," she finished with equal honesty, "incredible patience."

His eyes held an odd expression. "You want me to take your place."

"You could say that." Mac slid from the desk, then straightened her coveralls. She absently patted the pocket where she'd put her imp, checking it was there. "Will you do it?"

Case had stood as well, more slowly, as if deep in thought. He gazed down at her and grimaced. "I'd rather go with you, Mac. But if this is what you want—I'll do my best."

Finally, something going her way.

Mac beamed at him. "There is a bright side, Case," she promised. "You'll be heading out to sea. Make sure Em knows your background on trawlers when you apply."

By his look, she'd dismayed him again. "Apply?"

Her lips quirked sideways. "Next lesson about Emily: if she makes a decision, she'll stand by the result. Just tell her the truth— I made you do it. She'll take a closer look. And she'll see what I do." *Integrity, inner strength, and a nice dose of stubborn pragmatism that will annoy her constantly—and keep her sane.* Mac was satisfied.

"What do you see, Mac?" Case asked in a low voice, eyes intent on hers. "I'd like to know."

She might not have Emily's experience with men, young or otherwise, but Mac was reasonably sure Case wouldn't appreciate the attributes she'd listed to herself as much as she did. Instead, she made a show of checking the time. "I see I'm going to be late." She glanced around the room once more, then gave him a nod. "Whatever happens, thank you, Case. I appreciate this more than I can say. Good luck."

"You're welcome," he replied. For an instant, she thought he meant to reach for her, and she braced for a hug, but instead he opened the door. "Good luck to you, too, Dr. Connor."

Relieved, Mac smiled at him and started through the door, already feeling the tug of impatience. *Time to move.* At the sight of her, Sing-li straightened from where he'd slouched against the wall in the corridor.

"Mac?"

She glanced back.

Case, who was much closer than she'd expected, ducked his head and kissed her on the mouth.

" 'Bye," he added, then walked away.

Sing-li snickered. Mac gave him a look and he stopped, but the smirk looked permanent.

"Can we go now?" she asked dryly.

He gestured her ahead with a gallant bow that didn't quite work with the rows of happy-faced cookies on his shirt. "After you, Dr. Connor."

She went out, giving Zimmerman a smile, then strode down the walkway toward the dock, her feet making reassuringly normal sounds on the mem-wood. The music from the party was still thumping. The cool night air smelled of salt and fish and growing things.

The world was as it was.

She could just make out Case, his long bare legs pale against the dark water as he headed for Pod Three, and quickly looked away.

As kisses went, it had been quick and almost clumsy. His lips had been cold.

What it hadn't been, Mac decided with some misgiving, *was the kiss of a friend.*

A somber group awaited Mac at the dock's edge, consisting of Kammie, John, Tie, and, of course, Mudge. A slightly larger and noisier group of students surrounded their fellow who, thanks to Mudge, would accompany them. 'Screens hovered in the air as they hurriedly exchanged critical information at this final moment.

Likely games.

Mac's eyes widened when she saw Tie wearing what appeared to be an oversized flare pistol in a holster belted to his waist. "Where did you get that?" she demanded, keeping her voice down. *Not that the students appeared interested.* There was another sticking out of his pants pocket. "Those," she corrected.

Tie looked abashed but determined. "They're mine. A little old, but they work."

"You don't carry weapons," she objected. "That's their job." A nod to Sing-li

The agent wasn't smirking now, his face drawn in grim lines. "We can't be everywhere at once. We did thorough backgrounds, Mac. Tie, a few others, are qualified and we contacted them. What did you expect, when you made Base a target?"

"But—" Mac closed her mouth on what was, in truth, a meaningless objection. Instead, she gazed at Tie and tried to imagine Base's opinionated mechanic as a warrior. *Having seen him defend what he considered his fleet of vessels from neglectful students,* she decided, *it wasn't much of a stretch after all.*

Tie put two fingers to his forehead in a mock salute. "Did a stint in the military—before you were born, Mac," he told her. "Don't worry. My favorite discussion-closer is still a wrench."

At that moment, Sam Schrant, his friends having left—a couple in tears, walked up and offered Mac his hand. "Hi, Mac. I appreciate this."

His dark hair flopped over his high forehead, almost hitting the tops of his glasses. *She'd tucked Nik's in her bag.* Despite bruises of exhaustion lining his eyes—Sam was infamous for his all-nighters— he looked ready to go. A neon-orange backpack hung from his shoulders, its seams ready to burst.

"We'll see if you thank me once you've been to Myriam," she said, but smiled and took his hand. "Welcome to the Origins Team, Sam."

His eyes, tired or not, gleamed. "I've been doing some prelim work, Mac. That's one incredible orbit. I can't wait."

She could. Mac indicated the waiting lev. "Be my guest."

After Sam said his farewells to the rest and boarded, Mac faced Kammie and John, wondering what to say.

Find the Ro object and you can get back to work?

or . . .

Welcome to my life.

It didn't help that Kammie, always quick to tears, was quietly sobbing into a handkerchief, or that John Ward, for the first time since they'd met, had no expression on his face at all.

A quiet *harrumph* shook Mac from her paralysis. "Schedules, Norcoast, schedules. We can't keep the pilot waiting."

"Yes, of course." She looked toward the well-lit pod and waved. Several of the figures milling on the terrace waved back.

One, standing on the walkway below, didn't.

"Good-bye," Mac said, as much to Emily as Kammie and John, then walked up the ramp into the lev.

She didn't turn around again.

- CONTACT -

THE WINDS CURLED AROUND the standing ones, washing their feet with red sand. Their ranks were legion; their patience greater still.

If patience was felt by stone.

Beyond, where the landscape fractured into a maze of rock cuts and channels, dark eyes watched and measured from the shadows. When the winds paused, when the first rank could be seen through clearing air, then would begin the span of days in which the clicks of poet and penitent could be heard. Only then . . .

Only then, would the Loufta come forth to build.

Others waited, too.

"Remind me how rich we're going to be, *Se* Zali."

The Frow scampered headfirst down the sheer cliff face, fingers finding and releasing holds so quickly *se* appeared to be falling. "Stinking rich," *se* assured *se's* partner on reaching the bottom. Rather than stand, *se* hung like a crawling Myg *sketlik,* albeit with skinlike web stretched taut between *se's* limbs. *Se's* head twisted at an unlikely angle to show *se's* smug expression.

"I don't see why you can't stand up properly. Idiot. You realize you accomplish Numbers Two and Three on my list of why I should never have crewed with a Frow." Oonishalapeel's list was long and still growing, though since his encounter with a Human medic, he now had a word for Number Two, arachnophobia, and a drug to dull the symptoms.

Putting up with the smugness of any Frow came with the territory. "You're sure we're safe from the Dhryn?"

"My *mater's* fifteenth sib-cousin serves the home world station where all incoming data on attacks and sightings are processed, my anxious friend. You read Se Lasserbee's latest report. No attacks. No sightings. No Dhryn. The mighty Myrokynay have destroyed them. Calm your fears, 'Peel." *Se* Zali touched the solitary point on *se's* hat, the Frow equivalent of polite self-deprecation. "You would do well to remember I am a soldier, capable of ensuring our safety at all times."

"Irrelevant. And your irrelevant hat is Number Fifteen," 'Peel proclaimed. "Though I'll keep in mind you're willing to die first."

"Hush." The Frow swung about and scuttled up the cliff in a heave of membrane, uniform, and fingers. Grit rained down. "Do you hear that?" *se* asked, stopping a short distance up.

'Peel made a show of dusting himself. "Making false alarms is Number Ten."

"Forget your boring list, 'Peel. Attend. Is the wind quieting?" *Se* climbed a bit higher and leaned out, neck ridges unfolding. *Se's* eyes closed as *se* listened intently. "Yes . . . I think so."

'Peel opened his collapsible chair and sat down with a thump. "Idiot. You said the same thing yesterday." The Myg pulled out his imp, preparing to add to his list. "Let me see. I'm at two hundred and twenty-four, the smell of Frow breath in the tent. No, Two hundred and twenty-five, the way Frow leftovers always rot. This will be—"

"It's time!" *Se* Zali plummeted to the canyon floor, where he tilted upright cautiously, both hands reaching out in agonizingly slow motion for the support of nearby boulders. He kept shouting. "The winds are dying. The creatures will free themselves at any moment. Call the others!" he ordered. "We must set the nets. Get the processing units ready. They won't stay soft long!"

'Peel glared through his workscreen at the Frow. "Irrelevant. Irrelevant!" Their camp had been made in cooling shadows, but the constant wind-driven grit had made sleeping outdoors impossible. The other five, two more Frow and three blissfully quiet Dainaies, were still in bed. "Wait for the monitoring station to confirm it."

"If we delay, we could be too late. Any emerging Loufta will go through its ascension and be useless."

"Number two hundred and twenty-seven," the Myg crowed. "Making up ridiculous names for alien biology—geology. Whatever it is."

"The name fits."

" 'Ascension?' It's a word about climbing. You climb. Do they climb? No. Idiot!"

"Stop calling me that!"

"Calling you what?"

Neither noticed the wind settling around them, their argument loud in an ominous stillness.

But both felt the rain.

The Loufta sensed the change in the wind as well.

They shuttered their ebony eyes and dug themselves deeper into stone. Perhaps in another thousand years conditions would be right. And they would pull themselves from the veins of the mountains, crawl across the hushed plain, and build the next rank of standing ones from their own hardening flesh in honor of their god.

Another time.

The desperate mouths drank what they could find.

It wasn't enough.

The Progenitor was starving.

The *oomlings* had been sacrificed. All that was Dhryn must follow.

Nothing mattered but that the Progenitor survive the Great Journey.

They hurried to fulfill their destiny.

DELAY AND DIVERSION

"**P**ERFECT TIMING, AS ALWAYS, MAC." Sebastian Jones, Earthgov wildlife liaison for this portion of the remote northwest, grabbed their bags and effortlessly tossed them into the back of his battered skim. He grinned at her. "Chinook've started up the Klondike. Looks to be a big run."

"I'd love to say that's why we're here," Mac answered, fastening her jacket against the evening's bite, "but we're just passing through." *Though why here, in Dawson City, was a question she'd like answered.* The public transit system connecting to the Arctic launch fields stopped in Whitehorse on the way, where there were year-round facilities.

The Ministry lev, for reasons not explained to its passengers, had touched down instead at the business end of the narrow paved strip that had first served Dawson City as an airport. It wasn't that anyone had intentionally preserved the entire strip, although it was handy for keeping levs, freight, and passengers out of the summer mud. It was more that the unassuming length of flat pavement was useful—a place to learn to ride a bike, land a glider, or race skims. What did get removed, regularly, were the signs prohibiting such activities due to the hazard of incoming lev traffic.

The Yukon was like that, Mac remembered fondly. *Regulations subject to reality. And who, or what, could survive on its own was entirely welcome to do so.*

What couldn't? "Thought you had a new skim, Sebastian."

He looked chagrined. "Locked up on me the first time it got

chilly. Took it back to Edmonton for my mom. This one—" he gave the old machine a proud smack that shook something loose underneath, "—keeps going. Shouldn't have let them give me another."

Mudge had been talking to their lev pilot, *no doubt bonding*. After some mutual nodding, he came over to Mac, cautiously avoiding Sebastian's wheezing vehicle. "He's leaving. There's been some delay in our orbit connection," he said, sounding irritated. "We're to be picked up by another lev in the morning, rather than continue to the Baffin spaceport."

"Did he say why?" Mac shook her head to stop his answer. "Of course not." Not that it mattered whether they faced some bureaucracy or mechanical failure. Delay was delay. *Could have lingered at Base.* But the moment that thought crossed her mind, she dismissed it. Longer would only have made it more difficult.

What to do next was another question, Mac thought, looking around. They were standing in the overlapped pools of light that illuminated the landing area, the small building that, during office hours only, housed the ticket office and washrooms, and Sebastian's battered skim. The moisture from their breath fogged in front of their faces. *Not quite below freezing,* Mac judged. She didn't mind the temperature; it kept her awake. Mudge covered a yawn and she sympathized. Being in the dark might suit their body clocks, still on New Zealand time, but Mudge hadn't slept on the way to Castle Inlet and she had only slept a little. They were both down one night's sleep already.

"Where are you taking us, Sebastian?" she asked, stifling a yawn of her own. "Dawson?"

"Unless you prefer to stay here for the night." He made it sound a perfectly viable option, which to him it was, and Sam's eyes widened into saucers.

"Not this time, thanks," Mac said before the poor student thought she'd make them camp out on the tarmac. "We've a long trip ahead and I, for one," she yawned again, "could use a rest. In town would be great."

"But not in that, Norcoast, surely," Mudge protested, pointing to Sebastian's skim. "It's worse than yours."

The skim's engine had settled into an anxious mutter. The skim itself, however, was vibrating up and down—which, since it was floating atop a repeller field and the pavement beneath their feet wasn't moving, was, Mac admitted, somewhat alarming. "Few too many summers over gravel beds," Sebastian drawled. "Hop in. She'll smooth out."

"Don't worry, Oversight," Mac told him, climbing in first. "There are seat belts . . . oh, wait. Not anymore. Best hold on."

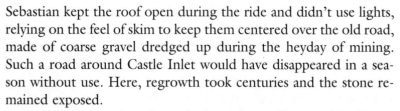

Sebastian kept the roof open during the ride and didn't use lights, relying on the feel of skim to keep them centered over the old road, made of coarse gravel dredged up during the heyday of mining. Such a road around Castle Inlet would have disappeared in a season without use. Here, regrowth took centuries and the stone remained exposed.

The vibrations, though teeth-chattering at first, vanished once the skim picked up speed. She knew the road followed the curved bank of the Klondike River, but the landscape was hidden in darkness. Mac leaned her seat back and watched the sky, picking out old friends. She'd missed the northern constellations.

She'd neglected to look at Myriam's stars, having been a bit preoccupied on the ground. *She'd have time now.*

She heard Dawson City before they got there, and smiled. The ghosts of the past were feverishly reliving their era before summer's end. Player pianos and other antique instruments hammered out tunes from the first, great gold rush; tourists and those who entertained them filled the dirt streets and danced along the wooden boardwalks, swelling the local population a thousandfold. Under a sun that spent most of summer in the sky, and surrounded by a sweeping landscape dominated by ice, water, and rock, it was a party setting like no other.

With one drawback.

"Are you sure there's room for us?" Mac asked doubtfully.

Sebastian gave his quiet laugh. "Not lying down. You'll stay at my place. I've turned out the dogs for the night."

"Thank you." Mac followed this with a gentle kick to Mudge's shin, having heard him take a deep breath as though planning to comment. Their host was a private person, despite his easy charm, more comfortable alone in the wilderness than with anyone else. Mac counted herself fortunate that Sebastian had taken her under his wing since she'd first come to sample Yukon salmon metapopulations a decade ago.

Then again, she thought, *we're both capable of going for days without a word. Not like some.*

At that, she poked her toe into Mudge's other shin for insurance.

Sebastian's home overlooked the Yukon River, downstream from its junction with the Klondike and Bonanza Creek at Dawson itself. Mac, having seen his place in daylight, knew it for a simple, sturdy wood building with a wraparound screened porch, nestled within a copse of twisted conifers. Smaller than her family's cabin, with only two rooms, but more like a home, with every centimeter crowded with personality. She remembered the rafters of the living room/kitchen had been laden with pale wood, waiting to be carved into paddles during the winter night. Two walls had been lined with shelves of physical books, like those she'd read for practice, while the third had boasted a mammoth wood stove, old enough for a museum. But it worked, so it was used. A small counter, with sink and cupboards; a big table, with one chair. For her previous visit, Sebastian had provided a folding stool.

Arriving now, in the dark, all that could be made out was a flickering glow in one window.

And barking. There had to be over two dozen huge huskies in the pack contributing to that enthusiastic part-welcome, part-warning.

"Back into trekking?" Mac shouted over the din. "Didn't think you had the time."

"My housemate's team."

Housemate? Mac shook her head in disbelief. *Leave the planet and look what happens.* "Anyone I know?"

"Not a salmon person." As if this settled it.

A little stung, she defended herself. "I do know people outside my field, Sebastian."

"Gloria McNeal? Polar bear endocrinology?"

"Maybe not that far outside my field," Mac conceded.

Sebastian kicked on the skim lights while they grabbed their bags, the wash of illumination passing over gray stone, swathes of sand, and low tufts of spent alpine flowers. The huskies, silenced as if by a signal, blinked their glowing eyes and yawned to show white gleaming teeth, before jumping back on the roofs of their doghouses. Sebastian had set wider, flat stones in a path leading into the house and they followed these to the porch. Sam's head twisted to look at the dogs. "Think we'll have time to see them run?" he asked her as they climbed the steps.

"Need I remind you, Dr. Schrant, that we're already behind schedule?" Mudge answered testily. "And what's wrong with your power?" This as Sebastian opened the door and the light within was revealed as coming from the stove's banked fire.

Their host lit the lantern on the table before answering. "We don't get broadcast here. Part of the charm."

"Charm?" Sam said faintly, hugging his backpack as if the devices inside were endangered.

Mac grinned. The lantern's rich warm light filled the room, revealing quite a bit of charm as far as she was concerned. Sebastian's housemate had added her touch in the presence of thick braided rugs on the floor, an artful mosaic of pelt samples hanging on the wall by the door, and a second chair at the table.

"Gloria's still in Tuktoyaktuk. You two can sleep there." Sebastian indicated the door to the bedroom. "Mac. Couch. I'll take the porch." He paused. "Anyone hungry? No? Then g'night." With that, he grabbed a blanket from a chest and went out.

Mudge looked at the couch, a sagging tapestried giant almost as old as the stove, then at Mac. She smiled at his expression. "It's more comfy than it looks," she promised, tossing her bag on one end. "Good night, you two."

Sam eyed the dark doorway and didn't move. "I didn't bring a light," he said, still clutching his bag.

Mudge *harrumphed*, pulling one from a pocket. "Come with me."

"Is there—?" Sam looked from one to the other. "Will we have to—"

Mac managed to keep a straight face. The meteorologist wasn't a camper—his data came from remotes and his idea of rough living likely included having to leave his desk to get a drink. *Probably imagined leaves and grizzly bears.* "There's a bathroom off the bedroom," she said, "with plumbing. And a very nice sauna. Sebastian lives independently. He doesn't do without." She didn't bother mentioning the solar panels he'd installed for his imp and skim battery.

A little northern mystique never hurt.

After the others disappeared into the bedroom, Mac turned the lantern down and sat in the new chair. She listened, chin on her hands, to the hushed but clear argument over who would have which side, the brief debate over the best way to light a lantern, and finally the exhausted muttering about trying to sleep and people who needed lights on and there was a schedule. The light under the door went off shortly after the voices stopped.

She smiled and blew out her light.

Outside, the view was forever. Mac sat on the bottom step, out from the porch roof so the stars made a dome overhead, and pulled the thick blanket around her shoulders.

Quietly, from the dark behind her. "Company?"

"Up to you," she replied.

Sebastian came and sat one step above her, easing his long frame back to rest on his elbows. His legs stretched past Mac, ending in white socks.

Without effort, she added him to her overwhelming awareness of the world around her, as intensely real as the long bare hills rolling like waves to the southeast, the black ribbon of water below in the canyon it carved, the crisp cedar-scented air she drew into her nostrils. A dog twitched in its sleep, its feet scratching furiously along the roof of its house. Closer, a scurry as something small dodged their feet to head under the step.

As if to remind her not all things were small or close or needing a roof, a howl sliced the night. The huskies gave low *woofs* of interest, then their heads thudded back down.

"Polar bears," Mac said finally. "How's that work?"

The man beside her gave a low chuckle. "Until pack ice, she helps with the grizzly census. Populations overlap near here."

"Handy." Mac pulled her knees up so she could wrap them in the blanket too, trying not to be envious. Here he was, in an area as remote and isolated as humanly possible in the modern world, and he'd found a fellow biologist to share his life.

While she had—what—an offworld spy who usually wore a suit.

As for sharing anything, that remained part of a future Mac wasn't interested in contemplating. Not now.

Not during her last hours on Earth.

"What's it like?" Sebastian asked unexpectedly. "Out there."

She considered the question. "Like here," she answered after a moment. "You watch your step. And everywhere else becomes—smaller."

He fell silent, as if she'd said enough.

Mac counted shooting stars for a while, then watched a pair of tiny lights trace out the river below. *Probably the ferry making its night run.* She followed the lights until they disappeared around the next sharp bend.

She looked up in time to see a luminescent sheet of green unfurl across the sky. With a gasp, Mac threw off the blanket and started to rise to her feet. She sank down again as pink joined the display, then purples. "Mouse," she lied, her teeth chattering with more than the chill. Ashamed, she fumbled to rewrap herself.

But it was the same color. The same . . .

"Admit it, Mac. You're cold." He sounded amused. "That'll teach you to live in the tropics and lose your conditioning."

Before she could protest she'd done nothing of the sort, Sebastian slipped down to the step she was on and gathered her up, blanket and all, so she could lean back against his shoulder and still see the stars.

Mac let herself relax into his so-Human warmth.

A shame it couldn't take away the fear.

"Dr. Connor."

The strange whisper woke her, but she froze, eyes shut, wondering why her name was the only sound she heard. *Why weren't the dogs barking?*

"Dr. Connor. We don't have much time." The voice became distant, as if speaking to someone else. "Why isn't she waking up? Is there something wrong with—"

She recognized that impatient snap, even muffled. *Hollans?*

Mac opened her eyes, finding herself nose to nose with a hulking silhouette.

"Good," she heard Hollans say. "Would you come with me, Dr. Connor?" The silhouette moved back.

As she sat up, the arm that had been around her fell away.

"Sebas—?" Mac lost the word, her mouth too dry. *What had Hollans done?* She moved her tongue around, found some moisture. "Sebastian!"

She reached out and found him. He was lying beside her on the steps, body flaccid, head back. Mac gave him a gentle prod but he didn't stir, snoring quietly. She glared at the silhouette and didn't bother to whisper. "What did you do to him?"

"Your friend will be fine." A hand appeared in her way, and Mac resisted the urge to slap it aside as she climbed to her feet on her own.

She felt normal. A little cramped and with a sore hip, but nothing that couldn't be explained by falling asleep on a cold rustic staircase. *Except she hadn't fallen asleep.*

No sign of dawn yet. A faint red glow illuminated the ground between their feet. *An invitation.* "This way, please, Dr. Connor."

"I'm certainly not leaving him like this."

"Someone will watch. Please, Dr. Connor."

Hard to argue with someone insistently polite. Giving in, Mac tarried to roll up her blanket and wedge it under Sebastian's head and shoulders, taking in as much of her dark surroundings as she could. No sign of Mudge or Schrant. Hollans must have come for her.

Wonderful.

Using the light to find the stony path, then to avoid larger stones once they'd left it, Hollans led Mac past too-quiet doghouses to the looming bulk of a waiting lev. Its door opened, the interior dimmed so she didn't have to squint to see there was no one wait-ing inside.

"You set this up," she accused, once they'd climbed in and taken seats.

"The delay?" He nodded and pulled off the goggles he'd worn. "Resume normal lighting." The increase was gradual, easy on her eyes. "Would you like a drink, Dr. Connor?"

Kid gloves were never a good sign, Mac decided, now more wor-ried by this midnight meeting than irritated. "Sebastian didn't know," she said.

It wasn't a question, but he answered anyway. "We didn't need to involve anyone else. We can always find you, Dr. Connor."

At the reminder, she involuntarily rubbed her right arm, though the mark from the implant needle had faded months ago. Its result would outlast her bones. *Not a comfort.* "I'll take coffee, black," she said. "What's this about, Hollans? Why the secrecy?"

"Tea." He regarded her levelly. "Dr. Connor, we've had our dif-ferences. I'm aware you don't like me much."

"I wasn't aware I had to," she countered, then flashed a humor-less grin. "You don't like me either. I'm too—" *what was the latest?* "—blunt."

"That part I like." His smile was barely warmer than hers. "If you're going to be wrong, you'll do it in the open. Saves all sorts of excuses and investigations."

Mac shot to her feet. "Is that why we're here?" she demanded hotly. "I wasn't wrong to bring my people into this, Hollans, and I'll defend that to—"

"Sit down. Please. You don't have to defend anything, Dr. Con-nor. Thank you." This to the black-armored agent, anonymous be-hind his or her visor, who arrived from the front of the lev with a steaming mug in each gloved hand. Mac took hers absently and nodded her thanks, eyes on Hollans. She sat and put the mug on the arm of her chair to cool.

Should have asked for ice.

Hollans waited until the agent had closed the door. "And thank you," he told her.

Mac narrowed her eyes, now more than worried.

Bernd Hollans, the Ministry's top official in matters of the

Dhryn and Myrokynay, which meant representing all humanity in the current fight for survival, sat quietly, sipping tea, and let her study him.

A trim, tidy man, Hollans wore his usual suit, as if he'd come straight from a meeting at Earthgov or, more likely, the IU Consulate. He'd added a darker-than-usual shirt, with no cravat at its throat, and, she blinked, very sensible hiking boots. *Prepared, but in a hurry.*

His face gave her no clues. *No surprise.* From their first meeting, she'd thought his features well-suited his line of work: smooth enough to appear vigorous and friendly when he smiled, wrinkled enough to crease into imposing responsibility when he frowned. His eyes were the blue of old ice and missed nothing at all.

He'd been Nikolai Trojanowski's boss once before, and was again. What Mac had seen of that relationship didn't imply mutual liking either, but it held respect.

"You didn't come here to thank me for having common sense," she concluded out loud. Then, thinking over where they were, the way Hollans had drugged or otherwise incapacitated both dogs and people to approach her, the lack of guards, Mac nodded to herself, suddenly chilled. "No one else knows you're here, either. What's going on?" She heard the anxious edge to her voice and deliberately lightened it. "Don't tell me you want to come, too. We're crowded already and we haven't even left for Myriam."

He didn't bother smiling. "You aren't going to Myriam, Dr. Connor. Not the planet, anyway."

"I'm not?" Mac reached for her coffee, then decided against it. *Still too hot.* "Where am I going?" she asked numbly.

"Let me explain the situation, first. Like every species connected by the Naralax, we sent scout ships into the Dhryn System. Haven, not Myriam," he clarified.

Hot or not. She took the mug and a cautious sip. "I take it they found something."

"Several hundred somethings. Ships, empty and drifting. Freighters, transports, you name it. Some sending out automated distress calls—with Dhryn colony idents. We speculate—what is it?" This as Mac nodded.

"The Vessel," she recalled. "When I asked about the colonies, he said they were without Progenitors. That they were lost."

"Seems they found their way home. Looks as though they slipped through the gate in the initial chaos, then settled in a distant orbit to wait."

"No one saw them?" she protested.

"We're talking about spatial distances, not a puddle, Dr. Connor. Do you know how long it takes to sweep even a portion of a solar system for something the size of a Progenitor ship? Forget something a thousandth its size. The surprise isn't that they could hide—it's that we found them at all. The initial discovery was made by the Ar, also surprising—" at her blank look, he skipped what he was going to say. "The Trisulians in the system," his voice became flat, "initially did their utmost to contain the discovery, but the crew of the Ar ship was Human. They raised a fuss, our ships spread it, and details of the find were sent to the IU."

Mac realized she still held the hot mug and put it down, concentrating on keeping her hand and voice steady. "The Dhryn?"

"We don't know." She raised an eyebrow at this and he gave a tiny shrug. "I'm told the ships are nonfunctioning: some damaged, most with their doors open to space. Only three have been found so far intact and powered, but there's been no response from those to any signals. We'll know more when they're boarded. Which hasn't happened yet."

"Why?" She frowned. "What are they waiting for?"

"Reasonable caution, Dr. Connor. Some of the species in the recovery effort believe Dhryn sheathing can interfere with their scanners." He hesitated. "And there have been certain—jurisdictional—issues."

"Idiots." Mac snorted and picked up her mug again. "Let me guess," she told Hollans over its rim. "None of them wants the other to go first. Can they really believe we've time for this nonsense?"

"Some delays are useful," Hollans commented, the corner of his mouth twitching as if she'd amused him. "This 'nonsense' gave our Sinzi-ra time to consult with the IU inner council. As a result, the three intact ships—left that way—are being towed to the gates as we speak. To be brought to Myriam. And you, Dr. Connor."

Mac's mug dropped from her hands, tumbling to the floor. She lunged to retrieve it but missed. The arc of hot dark liquid ended on Hollans' sensible boots.

Bet he's glad he wore them. She made vague shooing gestures at the spill and looked in vain for something to wipe it.

"Leave it, Dr. Connor."

She'd been doing so well, too. "Sorry 'bout that," she muttered, sitting up.

"More coffee?"

"You've got to be kidding," Mac blurted.

Hollans' lips quirked again. "No coffee, then."

"It's bad enough you people have me working with archaeologists on a desert planet," she protested, loudly, ignoring his comment. "I'm not a bloody starship engineer! I study—" Mac stopped there.

"Salmon," Hollans obliged, the quirk fading to something noncommittal. "We've engineers en route to Myriam, Dr. Connor. You know why we want you on those ships."

She glared.

He waited.

Games, even now. "To translate," she snapped.

"To translate," he repeated, giving a smug nod as if she'd pleased him by her startling grasp of essentials. "Until we can produce a full adult Dhryn lexicon, suited to Human sub-teach, we must make do with what we have. Or rather who. You, Dr. Connor."

She should have taken that second coffee, Mac thought grimly. *And aimed higher.*

"Earth orbit to the Naralax gate is a six-day trip," Hollans continued, as if unaware—or more likely unimpressed—by her simmering anger. "You'll be taking something a little faster and more discreet than your originally scheduled transport. I believe you're familiar with the *Annapolis Joy*? Her captain remembers you."

The ship's name was misleading. The *Annapolis Joy* was one of the Ministry of Extra-Sol Human Affairs' less-than-diplomatic dreadnaughts, bristling with armaments normally used to intimidate would-be smugglers before they entered or left orbit. She had had been among those to engage the Ro at Haven.

And the *Joy* had brought Mac home from Myriam.

"He probably remembers the screaming," Mac said under her breath. She'd missed the instant, there on the cold sand, when they'd hurriedly removed most of what remained of her arm to stop the continuing digestion of her flesh. She'd made up for it by regaining consciousness on the way to orbit.

Fortunately, the *Annapolis Joy* had the sort of medical facility that specialized in battlefield trauma, right to replacement parts. Though she hadn't made a friend of the ship's surgeon. *He should have asked before preparing skin she didn't want.*

"Speed isn't the point, is it?" she countered. "If it were, we'd be at the spaceport instead of here." Travel between systems might consume no time, but crawling along a planet's surface did.

Why else send a ship of war?

Because someone else was.

"Oh, no," Mac said as this crystallized. "Don't tell me those 'jurisdictional issues' are coming with the derelicts. Don't even think about dropping me in the middle of a squabble between alien governments. Hollans—you of all people should know better!"

"You won't be involved in any—"

"Wrong," she interrupted. "If everyone, Human or otherwise, is expecting me to translate whatever records, trash, labels, or vids the Dhryn left on those ships, how can I not be involved? Bah!" Mac tucked her knees against her chest and wrapped her arms around her legs. "I should pretend I can't read the stuff. I really should. Starting now."

Hollans appeared to hold back a smile. "You won't be on your own, Dr. Connor."

She rested her chin atop her knee to regard him. Hollans was still the image of calm civility, mug of tea in one hand, coffee-soaked boots neatly aligned.

Who'd waylaid her in the midst of the Yukon for this conversation.

"You could have told me all this by message, too," Mac accused. "It's not as if I've a choice." She lowered her voice. "Why are you here, Hollans? No more games."

His almost-smile faded. "I need your advice, Dr. Connor."

"My—" Mac's eyebrows rose. "Really." She tried, and failed, to imagine what possible advice she could offer Earth's Person-in-

Charge other than to avoid Frow in parks. She tilted her head. "Was this Anchen's idea?"

"The Sinzi-ra respects your insight, Dr. Connor. As do I, in this instance."

"Our esteemed Sinzi-ra also collects rubber fish," Mac pointed out somewhat warily. "All this time at the consulate, you never once asked for my advice. Why now?"

"We're alone."

The implications of that sent a shiver running down her spine. Mac refused to take the bait, *if that's what it was.* This man had been Nik's boss. She was not in that league. *And didn't want to be.* So she simply nodded. "I'll do my best."

After a deliberate sip of tea, Hollans gazed into the liquid, as if considering how best to phrase his answer. A familiar habit. He'd sip and stare innumerable times per meeting. *Came close to getting her imp in his mug once.* Before she had to resort to that tactic, he looked up. "It concerns Trojanowski's latest report."

Mac lowered her feet to the deck and leaned forward, her impatience forgotten.

"The Dhryn—the Vessel—" he continued, "has directed them to enter a region which poses a significant natural hazard to several species on board, Humans included." He pursed his lips for an instant. "I can't identify that hazard without risking their security. I'm sure you understand, Dr. Connor."

As if it would help her *find them on a star chart.* Mac didn't bother saying that aloud. She burned to ask if there'd been a message for her, another ring, but knew better. The *lamnas* was the most private form of communication she could imagine.

Nik had chosen it for a reason.

Love letters, Mac thought wryly, *hardly needed alien tech.*

She twirled one finger in the air. "Can't they go around?"

"The Vessel claims his Progenitor is inside this region—that Dhryn can withstand it."

"A hiding place," Mac concluded and started to relax until she took in Hollans' bleak expression. "You think it's a trap?"

"It could be. The Vessel assured Trojanowski those on board can be protected in evacsuits long enough to reach the Progenitor's ship, where they'll be safe. What if he's lying?" He held up his hand to silence her instant objection. "Yes, Dr. Connor. According to you, Dhryn don't lie. Say I believe you." His tone made that improbable, but he didn't belabor the point. "Could the Vessel be wrong about Humans surviving this? Dhryn have made mistakes about alien biology before."

"I've noticed. What do you want me to say, Hollans?" Mac asked, abruptly weary. *Should have had that second coffee.* "Trap or Dhryn miscalculation. They can't stop now. There's too much at stake." *Where on that scale . . .* "I shouldn't have to remind you." The words left a bitter taste in her mouth.

"You don't." He put down his tea, then laid his hands palm down on his thighs. They were thick-fingered hands, with prominent knuckles and mottled skin. She'd asked Sing-li what Hollans had done before becoming a thorn in her side and been surprised to learn he'd grown up a miner, working first on Earth, then Saturn's moons. *He'd have appreciated the Progenitor's underground home,* she thought irrelevantly.

His blue eyes bored into hers. "I need to understand the risk I've asked my people to take. How far do you trust that Dhryn, Dr. Connor? How far can I?"

"Irrelevant." Mac shook her head. "The Vessel's a biological interface; a way for the Progenitor to disperse and collect information. As well trust your imp."

Hollans' face developed that look, the one he'd get at meetings when she went off on a technical tangent. *Usually,* Mac admitted, *when he'd been sipping and staring and she couldn't in good conscience throw anything physical.*

"What you can trust," she explained, emphasizing the word, "is this Progenitor's will to protect Herself and Her species. She's resisted the Ro. She sent Her Vessel to find us and learn the truth. To bring it back. And . . ." Mac shut her mouth.

"And what?" Now Hollans' eyebrows drew together, resulting in what Mac privately labeled as his don't-mess-with-me wrinkle set. "Dr. Connor," he prompted when she didn't immediately speak. "Please."

. . . *"Run while you still can!"* . . .

"She warned me," Mac said reluctantly. "She warned us all. At the time, I took it as the Dhryn fear of the Ro. They'd gone to such lengths to protect their *oomlings*. Since? I think She had some inkling of what might happen to the Dhryn themselves. Maybe something from their oral history. Maybe more."

"I—see." His stern expression eased into something closer to puzzlement. "Where are you going with this, Dr. Connor?"

Mac shrugged, uncomfortable speculating. "I'm not sure. This Progenitor's behaved differently from the beginning. She called Brymn and me to meet with Her, to commit *grathnu*—a bonding ritual, as much as a reward for service. When I was there . . . something about Her . . . a presence . . ." Mac let her voice trail away, her cheeks warm with embarrassment. "I doubt it matters."

Hollans sipped tea, his eyes locked on her. "Continue anyway, Dr. Connor."

"What about Sebastian and the rest? The shuttle to orbit?"

Hollans glanced at the closed door to the pilot's compartment. "Status of our sleepers?" he asked.

A disembodied voice answered. "Everyone's safe and comfortable, sir."

"Now, Dr. Connor. Indulge me."

It wasn't a request.

Mac thought of those vast underground spaces, home and safety for beings at the heart of their kind. *The breeze, a breath.* "Presence wasn't the half of it," she sighed, frustrated by mere words. *The landscape, a form.* She made herself focus on that small ship, heading into whatever additional hazard space had to offer—as if vacuum and radiation weren't enough. "The Progenitor wants Her Vessel back, with answers." *The warmth, a smile.* "Anyone who helps accomplish Her will? They'll be considered Dhryn. I'm not saying that guarantees their safety, but it has to be less risky than approaching Her ship uninvited. Best I can do, Hollans."

They'd called her Dhryn.

Mac touched her new arm, and made herself remember that, too. "None of us are safe anymore."

"No. But I'm encouraged. Thank you, Dr. Connor."

She gave him a searching look and, for an instant, saw only a man worried about others. *Someone should,* she thought, inclined to envy. "Mac."

Gods, a full smile. It threw his dignified wrinkles into disarray. "Mac."

"If you didn't trust the Dhryn before," she asked quietly, "why agree to go in the first place? Besides the chance to get close enough to destroy a Progenitor's ship." Her voice came out calm and level, as if it had become routine to talk about the annihilation of hundreds of thousands of beings, including the person currently inhabiting a large part of her heart.

Hollans lost his smile. "Remind me to stay on your good side."

A year ago, she'd have shocked herself. *Where had that Mac gone?* "If it comes to that," she said, flat and cold, "Nik will know."

"Not his call," countered Hollans. "IU mission. He'll have to get the other representatives on board to agree."

Mac frowned. Cinder, the Trisulian. Her reaction to the Dhryn should be predictable. Dr. Genny P'tool, the N'not'k. Despite the alien's advanced age, Anchen had asked her to go for her knowledge as a no-space theoretician as well as to continue her work on the Dhryn language. Apparently linguistics and esoteric physics were a logical combination for the N'not'k, though Mac suspected this was Anchen's way of finding something useful for her friend to do. An obligate pacifist. The Imrya. A recorder of events, as well as a renowned designer of servo translations. She wouldn't have any problem making a decision. *Probably would take a while conveying it, though.*

Mac didn't know who else had scrambled aboard the shuttle with Nik and the Dhryn. Couldn't have been many.

Didn't matter.

"This isn't about the Dhryn at all," she said abruptly. "A Trisulian ship at Haven, causing trouble . . . you're worried about Cinder, aren't you?"

If she'd thought she'd seen Hollans' face wrinkled into grim lines before, she'd been mistaken. His eyes were like sparks set in pale, eroded stone. "This goes no farther, Mac."

She hated being right. "I've had the talk. What's going on?"

"What do you know about Cinder?"

Mac hadn't reported how an impassioned Cinder had begged her help to keep from murdering the Dhryn. She'd bet Cinder hadn't shared that moment either.

Some things weren't about saving the universe.

"She's Nik's partner," Mac hedged. "However that happened."

"Was," corrected Hollans. "The Ministry pairs field operatives with other species whenever possible. Experience for us, exposure to our ways for them. Trojanowski and Cinder were an exemplary team until his retirement."

She didn't think she imagined the slight hesitation before "retirement," but nothing in Hollans' expression or this situation encouraged her to ask about the past. "Things change," Mac observed cautiously. *Secrets went both ways.*

"Indeed. Cinder is, to all extents and purposes, now a widow, as is her species. Which is nothing new." At her startled look, Hollans nodded. "That's right. Floods, disease, war have decimated their male populations before now. Mated females respond by impregnating themselves, then seek out new, safer territory before their offspring are born. By whatever means necessary. Wherein lies our problem. The Trisulians are looking outside their systems. And the means . . . ? They stole it from you."

She could be shocked after all. "You think—they'd use the Ro signal?" Mac sputtered. "Call the Dhryn?"

"Yes."

She licked dry lips. "Have they?"

"Not yet. Not that we know," he clarified soberly. "And the posturing by the Trisulians at Haven could be nothing more than heightened territoriality—to be expected."

He didn't look like a man who believed that.

"What does Nik say?"

"That, I need you to tell me, Mac."

She could almost feel the *lamnas* on her finger and resisted the urge to touch it in front of those keen eyes. "You read his message to me, I'm sure. 'Continuing as planned; situation nominal.' I could have used more." She managed a stiff shrug. "That's a spy for you."

"There was more."

Mac froze in place. "What do you mean?"

Hollans turned his hands palm up. "The Sinzi-ra didn't send me to see you, Mac. Trojanowski—Nik—did. Before he left orbit, he urged me not to trust even secured channels, concerned we don't have a handle on the Ro's capabilities. He said he'd arranged a safe way to reach you." He reached into a pocket and brought out a small wooden salmon, holding it out on his thick, callused palm. "I was to show you this."

Betrayal . . .

Or the most profound trust.

Mac found herself too tired to guess. She took the carving from Hollans and put it away in her pocket, then held up her right hand. The *lamnas* gleamed. "Did he send me another of these?"

"Yes." Hollans looked relieved as he took a gleaming circle from an official-looking envelope. He passed it to her. "I was hoping this was the message, but my people couldn't find anything on it."

The silver didn't show any damage, so Mac refrained from pointless comment about private gifts and privileged information. *After all, who had the coffee-soaked socks?* "You wouldn't. The *lamnas* is for me."

"What's a *lamnas*?"

Mac lifted an eyebrow. "You don't know?"

"Nik was consular liaison. He's been deeper in the Sinzi-ra's confidence than any other Human—until you, Mac." Hollans glanced at the ring she held up between two fingers. "It's some kind of communication device, isn't it?"

She considered him for a long moment, then snapped her hand closed over the ring. "It's more. And less. It gives me fragments of Nik's memories, layered one over the other. Hard to sort out; not random. Memories that matter to him. It's—" She took a deep breath and let it out, eyes roving the inside of the lev compartment. Their two seats, a door, curved blank walls. *And Hollans.* "I have to go outside." She stood.

"But—"

Mac headed for the lev door. "You do want me to try to read it now, don't you?"

"Yes." He rose to his feet as well, but seemed to change his mind as he met her eyes. "How long will it take?" he asked quietly.

"I don't know." Staff had packed her entire apartment while she'd peered through the first one. *Either they were incredibly efficient, or it had taken a while.* "It might depend on what's in here," she speculated, lifting the fist with the ring.

The door didn't open to her touch on the pad. *What did he think she'd do? Run?* Tight-lipped, Mac let Hollans reach past to key in a code. "You're sure?" he asked in a low voice, giving her a look she couldn't interpret.

"About going out, yes. I have to be alone. The rest?" She shrugged. "These days, I make it up as I go."

"That's hardly reassuring, Mac."

His aggrieved tone made her laugh. "I thought you liked it when I was blunt."

"I prefer my experts wallowing in self-confidence." Hollans gestured to the now-open door.

"So you," she rejoined, "can leave them stuck in it when they're wrong? Politics. No thanks. I'll stick with blunt and 'hardly reassuring.' "

Mac stepped down the short ramp to the mossy ground, doing her best not to shiver at reencountering the cool Yukon night. She paused to let her eyes adjust, a task made easier as the light from the compartment dimmed to a faint glow behind them. There'd been an old tipped stump not far from the lev. She spotted the dark mound that marked it and walked along until she found a more-or-less level spot within its dry exposed root mass. She sat on top, wiggling to settle herself between bristled sprouts of new growth, and took out the ring.

She was startled when Hollans, who'd followed, took off his suit coat and laid it over her shoulders. It was heavier than it looked, and warm. "Thanks," Mac said, pulling it close. "Now . . ."

"Alone," he acknowledged. "That much, okay?" A brief shaft of light from his hand slid over black armor: a guard stationed at the nose of the lev. *Doubtless,* Mac reminded herself, *equipped with night vision.*

"No." With regret, she took off his coat and passed it back. *Probably bugged.* "I get privacy for this, Hollans, or you can leave."

She couldn't see his face, but she heard his quiet order. "Expand the inner perimeter by fifty meters." And the result. An astonishing number of footsteps moved away in every direction, *doubtless snapping twigs and scuffing sand for her benefit.*

"You, too," Mac insisted, the ring warm in her hand.

"Of course." He took two steps away, then stopped. She could hear him breathe.

"What?"

From the dark. "I trust you saw the final report on the Ro attack on Haven."

"I saw it," Mac admitted. *Which was technically true.* She just hadn't read the thing, given it was jammed with jargon and offered footnotes on particle physics. "The Ro fired some weapon at the planet. Your ships disrupted no-space around the Ro ships, exposed them, and they left. I was," she reminded him dryly, "there."

"Whatever else they accomplished, it's clear now the Ro wanted that one Progenitor dead. The targeting was precise. They almost succeeded."

"As I said. I was there." Despite the bite to her reply, Mac winced. If she closed her eyes, she'd see it. *The immense flame burning through buildings and pavement, penetrating deeper and deeper underground . . . the death cries of a world.* "She escaped."

"The point is that She attracted the Ro's attention, whether through Brymn's actions or yours. She has ours now. This being may be our only chance to negotiate with the Dhryn. This has to work, Mac. We must have a reliable source of information the Ro can't intercept."

A rustle from somewhere beneath the log made Mac hold her breath; only when frenzied squeaks added punctuation did she let it out again. "What if they're here, listening?"

"That," Hollans declared with surprising confidence, "we'd know. Trust me, Mac."

That word again. "Reliable, maybe," Mac said quietly. "Information? That I can't promise," she warned, running her fingers over the ring. "The last time—there wasn't much, Hollans. Things were the same. Everyone was the same." *Nik's despair at his own feelings was her business.* "Nik understands Cinder. He's—he's willing to use her anger at the Dhryn. I saw that."

She thought he nodded, but it was too dark to be sure. "Maybe this time," he said "there'll be something more. I'll wait in the lev. If you're sure about being out here alone?"

"I'm sure."

Mac waited while Hollans' red light traced his path back to the lev, the even fainter glow from inside the craft marking the opening and closing of the door.

She waited an instant longer, stroking her palm along the corded smoothness of the wood. It was like muscle, frozen beneath her hand.

Finally, she brought the *lamnas* to her lips, breathed once, and lifted it skyward until she saw three stars within its circle.

And then . . .

- CONTACT -

INDECISION/
  "Mac . . . I have to believe this . . . working . . . I will believe it." /determination/ *Need you . . .* /loss/ concern/

  Concentrate, fool. "Hollans . . . Hollans . . . he's got to know, Mac." /shame/ *Couldn't tell you . . . not then.* /heat/confusion/effort/ "Forgive . . ." *Doesn't matter. Nothing else matters.* ". . . tell him."

  Concentrate. " . . . sabotage . . ." /rage/frustration/fear/ "Ship okay . . . casualties . . ." *friends, colleagues . . . part of me still slips away . . . what if it were you?* /despair/emptiness/

  /effort/ "Vessel safe . . . systems okay . . . suits . . . most gone . . ." /irony/ ". . . same boat . . ."

* layered over *

—She smells soap—
  The Vessel hooted. "Do not worry so, Nikolai Piotr Trojanowski. We shall soon be with the Progenitor and safe from harm."

  I'll believe that when we head for home . . . but Mac believes . . . /wistful/ *. . . wish she was here.*

  "You're sure about the protocols."

  "Yes, yes. They are simplicity itself, my *lamisah.* Your ship will approach and dock, I will offer greeting, all will be well. You'll see."

  /resignation/ *Those of us who live that long. Glad Mac isn't here. Radiation's not a graceful death.*

"Here. This is a recording of what I'd say to your Progenitor. I want you to keep it with you at all times."

A distressed *thrum*. "Do you fear more violence?"

I fear dying too soon. /determination/ "A precaution."

"All will be well. You'll see."

* *layered over* *

—She tastes blood—

"Hurry!" "This way!" "Aiiiiieee!!" "I'm hit!"

/agony/

The words merged with thudding footsteps, explosions, and anguished cries, a staccato sequence.

Followed by silence.

/calm/focus/ *Don't reply . . . don't reveal . . .* /flutters of pain/endure/

"Nik! Where are you?" Cinder's voice, anxious and sharp. "Anyone?"

/patience/

Footsteps. A sharp *ping*. Then another. And another.

/emptiness/ *It's come to this . . .* /dread/

"Stop!"

A roar, followed by a splatter. A crunch.

/pain/

* *layered over* *

—She feels blood, slippery and wet—

Concentrate . . . "Hollans has to know, Mac. Lost . . . Murs . . . Larrieri . . . dead." /urgent/need/denial/ *Can't tell you, Mac . . . can't let you know what I did . . . had to do . . .* "Cinder . . . dead. Saboteur . . . dead."

A piece of me slips away . . . /anguish/grief/

"Ship okay . . . next stop . . . the Progenitor."

/guilt/ *She couldn't help herself . . . I should have known . . . stopped her somehow . . .* /failure/despair/ *It's only the beginning . . . will fall apart . . .*

Concentrate. "The Vessel misses you . . ." /need/loneliness/

/resolve/

- 10 -

JOURNEY AND JOLT

MAC SLIPPED THE RING on her finger, to join its mate. It was dark; the lev door was closed. When she eased to her feet, her left leg tried to fail, afire with pins and needles from hip to toe. *Answering the question of time,* she thought ruefully, rubbing her thigh.

Her cheeks were ice-cold. Drying tears, she discovered when she touched her face.

The message . . . "Gods, Nik," she whispered out loud as the horror of it surfaced. *What had he done?*

Fought a battle. Killed a friend. Made a decision to risk all their lives.

Day on the job, she told herself, and didn't believe it.

Again, the *lamnas* had revealed more than he'd intended. Far more. "He's hurt," she whispered to the dark. *Outside and in.* Mac didn't need to try and imagine what it had cost Nik. She could feel it, like a fever eating at every part of her body; taste it as ash in her mouth. " 'Part of me slips away,' " she repeated, without making a sound.

She stumbled toward the lev, hands out in case she fell. Before she'd taken more than a few steps, its door opened and Hollans came striding down the ramp. Before he reached her, forms materialized from the darkness on either side and swept her up between them. Mac wondered if these were people she knew.

Were they her friends?

Were they Nik's?

She rested her hands on their armored shoulders and silently wished them safe.

"I was hoping for information, Mac." Hollans' responsible wrinkles had settled into tired and old. "I didn't expect anything like this. Are you sure?"

Mac shrugged, feeling tired and old herself. "How can I be? Whatever words Nik wanted to pass along are mixed up with conversations he remembered. I could be mistaken about a great deal. What seems clearest? An unsuccessful attempt to sabotage their ship. Some of your people were killed." *She'd given him the names she had: Murs. Larrieri. Cinder.*

"The evacsuits." He circled back to that again. "Were all of them damaged?"

That was the crux of it. And she didn't know. "There was something about the suits. It—it wasn't good. Nik's sending the ship in anyway. He wanted me to tell you that."

"It'll reduce their safety margin. They won't all make it." He rubbed his face with one hand, then looked at her. "This is a disaster. Was the Trisulian responsible?"

Mac felt like one of her salmon. *Fish ladder or waterfall?* Without seeing the top, it was a leap into the unknown. The wrong guess meant failure and death.

She had the ear of a powerful individual. A wrong word in it now could precipitate a crisis—perhaps start a war. Emily'd warned her. *So,* Mac realized, *had Anchen.*

And what did she know? Only those fragments of Nik's memories and feelings. He'd done his utmost not to reveal more.

That should tell her something.

Mac held up her hand, the pair of *lamnas* sparkling around her ring finger. "From this? I can't say."

He gazed at her. Done talking, Mac slumped deeper in her seat and yawned so broadly her jaw cracked. *Exhausted biologist at your service,* she quipped to herself. *Just try getting me to make sense much longer.*

The last time Mac had left home, she'd been tossed into orbit in a box, caught by a freight shuttle, then ferried to a warehouse in one of the great way stations. Despite all this clever misdirection, the Ro—and Emily—had almost ambushed her there.

Which probably explained why there'd been no arguments made to an upgrade from box to proper passenger shuttle, complete with viewports and the in-flight vid of her choice.

Now, thanks to Hollans and some abandoned Dhryn ships, they were sealed in a compartment of a Ministry courier shuttle, with no view or entertainment.

Yup. Another box.

Schrant was curled in his seat, sound asleep. *Not a side effect of Hollans' little ploy,* Mac decided, since Mudge was anything but sleepy.

"This is most irregular, Norcoast," he announced. *Again.* With *harrumph.*

She closed her eyes and wiggled a little deeper into her seat.

"Norcoast!"

Mac cracked open one eye. "What?"

"I said, this is most irregular. We had prearranged transit. I don't understand why we aren't using it."

"Are you going to keep repeating that all the way there?" she asked wearily.

He gave her a strange look. "I fail to see why you don't find this all very irregular, too."

Much as she'd hated doing so, she'd agreed to Hollans' insistence that his visit be kept secret, even from Mudge. She'd gone back to the cabin, sat on the step beside Sebastian, who, true to Hollans' word, was sleeping soundly, and had waited while her visitors left. After a few minutes, to no signal Mac could detect, the dogs had stirred enough to stretch and roll over on their rooftops. Seconds later, Sebastian's left foot had dropped off the stair and his eyes had opened.

They'd gone to their respective beds as if nothing had happened.

She'd dreamed of interstellar war.

And now Mudge, who had every right to know and who knew her well enough to sense she was hiding something important from him, was pressing for answers.

Spy games. Mac was growing acutely aware of their cost.

"I'm sure something's come up," she said, as close to the truth as she dared. "Their budget, not ours. We should both try for some more sleep."

His eyes glittered. "I'm not tired. Amazing how quickly we all fell asleep last night. I was sure this young fellow's squirming about would keep us awake for hours."

"That Yukon air," Mac offered, but her own yawn spoiled it.

Mudge fell silent and she settled back into her seat, head back and eyes shut. Mac could feel his reproachful stare through her closed eyelids, but refused to do anything but pretend to sleep. After a while, pretense gave way to reality and she drifted off.

"Mac."

"Not here," Mac mumbled, curling into a defensive ball.

"Yes, you are," the voice insisted, "and so are we. We've docked with the transport ship. C'mon, Mac. Rise and shine."

While she had no intention of shining anytime soon, Mac peered at Sam Schrant's eager face, registered the flaming orange backpack already slung over his shoulder, and decided rising was likely inevitable. "Where's Oversight?" she asked, her mouth feeling as though she'd acquired a layer of barnacles. *Probably snored for the last hour.*

"It's not as if I could have left, Norcoast," came the caustic reply.

Man was consistent, she'd give him that.

Mac sat up, rubbed her eyes, and looked around. *They'd docked?* Nothing had changed within their tiny compartment, except for the stiffness of a certain salmon researcher. She rose to her feet and edged through their stack of luggage to reach the space between the pairs of inward-facing seats. Once there, she began stretching as best she could without hitting either of them on the head. "How long was I out?" she asked, bending left. "And how do you know we've docked?" Right.

"Long enough. Mr. Mudge timed it." This with distinct admiration.

Mac stopped stretching to give Mudge a look that was anything but admiring. "Why would you do that?"

He *harrumphed* and crossed his arms over his chest, eyes narrowed with disapproval. From the bags under those eyes, he hadn't slept at all.

The meteorologist replied happily, "Mr. Mudge has a complete list of the capabilities of orbital shuttles. There's a grav unit on this one, so the only way to tell when we'd reached orbit was to figure out travel time. And he was right. We just heard the clang—Mr. Mudge told me it was the clamps locking on to our air lock."

By this point, "Mr." Mudge was doing his utmost not to look overtly pleased with this thorough description of his cleverness. Mac lifted one eyebrow, but refrained from saying anything. *After all, she'd slept through the "clang."*

She climbed back to her seat and made sure her own bag was close at hand. She wasn't sure how she felt about returning to the *Annapolis Joy.*

That wasn't exactly true. Her stomach was busy informing her. *As if nausea was helpful.*

Mac swallowed hard, doing her best to push away the past at the same time. So what if the *Joy* had remained in orbit instead of rushing her home? They'd established a firm Human presence among the species scrambling to explore the Dhryn home world. So what if she'd spent those weeks in a haze of loss and pain, her questions buried under the urgent onslaught of everyone else's? She'd made it home eventually.

Where no one could know where she'd been.

Done was done, Mac told herself. She swallowed again, relieved to find it easier. *She'd take anything positive at the moment.*

"Will you hurry up?" This from Mudge, who was fuming as Sam repacked his belongings. Mac grinned. It looked as though the meteorologist had wanted something from the very bottom of his pack during their flight and had taken the easy route, dumping the contents over Mudge's neat stack. "Who knows how far we'll have to walk through the way station?" that worthy continued dolefully. "Our original plans took us into the same loading dock as our transport. Now? We could be facing a considerable journey. Perhaps requiring a skim."

Mac made a face. *Really should have told him before snoring.*

"This isn't the way station." *Oh, she'd seen* that *look before.* Before Mudge could launch into full volume accusation, likely involving a litany of her past indiscretions at Castle Inlet and *how could she be trusted?* she said calmly, "You've heard of the *Annapolis Joy,* Oversight?"

"The *J*—" His mouth formed a perfect 'o' and his hands groped in midair, as if trying to grab the name to look at it for himself.

The side of their compartment chose that moment to slide aside to reveal a sunlight-bright hangar, the *Joy*'s half of the air lock equation. Complete with welcoming party.

"Mac!"

She froze with her hand about to close on the handle of her bag, then recovered, hoping no one had noticed. "Doug. Kaili," she greeted. "Nice to see you again."

In a sense it was. The two orderlies in light green coveralls had cared for her during her stay. They'd been kind, efficient, and friendly. *Not their fault her stay had been* . . . Mac found a smile. "Doug Court. Kaili Xai. Charles Mudge III and Sam Schrant."

The four exchanged hellos. Doug resembled a sturdy, younger version of Mudge, with an upright brush of red-blond hair and a neatly-trimmed mustache above his wide smile. Midnight-black Kaili was taller and willow-thin. Mac remembered her as the quieter of the pair, rarely expressive. Now she was beaming with pleasure.

"This is the *Annapolis Joy,* dreadnaught class," Mudge then informed them, seemingly oblivious to the name embroidered in gold on their uniforms. "The very latest. Top of the line. Twinned Ascendis-Theta in-system drives, multiplexed transect-capable sensor arrays. Why she's capable—"

"Oversight," Mac interrupted. "You're drooling."

He shot her a desperate look. "I simply must see her bridge, Norcoast. I must—"

While having Mudge reduced to this state had its plus side, Mac was too unsettled to enjoy it. "Later. Are we supposed to have a medical?" she asked the orderlies, curious why these two had been sent to meet them. She grimaced. "I do know the way."

"Nah. We're surplus at the moment, Mac," Kaili grinned. "Off shift."

"And we asked," Doug added. "Wanted to be the first to welcome you back. How are you?" His eyes flicked to her left hand.

Guessing what he wanted, Mac pulled up her sleeve and held out her prosthesis for inspection. "Been through a bit," she explained, although it was unlikely even these two could see any of the repairs without a scope. Noad, Anchen's physician self, had done a superb job of reinstalling the finger she'd broken fending off the Trisulian male. Then there was the touch-up to the burns where she'd caught spit from their visiting Dhryn.

Maybe she should have asked for souvenir scars.

She glimpsed Mudge's stunned expression as he realized which ship this had to be and kept her voice steady. "Doug and Kaili were my coaches." Mac wiggled her fingers. "See? Haven't lost my touch."

"Cayhill has some new—" She shook her head, just once, and Kaili stopped, finishing with, "If you want, I'm sure he'll take a look."

"We're here on other business."

"You're right." Doug snapped to attention. "Sorry, Mac. We'll catch up another time. This way."

For a ship whose external purpose was to intimidate, the interior of the *Joy* had surprised Mac with its attention to comfort—until she'd learned a typical patrol could keep the crew in space for months. The lighting resembled that received on Earth, from its spectrum to the length of a shipday. The air temperature varied accordingly. Doug had tried to convince her that on very long hauls the captain would occasionally drop it below freezing for a week or so, with everyone reporting to duty in mitts, but Mac hadn't swallowed that one. She had admired the lightly scented breezes that would randomly rush down certain corridors. What furnishings she'd seen were covered in a wide range of materials, having in common functionality as well as variety to the touch.

Sound was the only Human sense the ship's designers had seemingly neglected in their search for ways to stimulate the crew. Then again, the first and possibly only warning of a serious problem would be the shriek of an alarm or the cry of orders.

Mac, Mudge, and Sam followed the two orderlies from the hangar to a corridor, then to where a sequence of arched doors marked internal transit tubes. They were reserved for crew; in all her time aboard, Mac hadn't used them. Now, she shot a questioning look at Doug, who'd stopped by the first.

"Captain's in a hurry," he said in answer. "Wants you and the rest stowed as quickly as possible."

"The rest?" This from Mudge. "Do you mean to say all of our people and gear are aboard?" His eyebrows were on a collision course. "They were waiting for us at the way station. By whose authority—"

"I wouldn't know, sir," Doug replied politely.

Mudge turned to her. "Norcoast?"

Mac indicated the tube door. "We'll find out faster if we go, Oversight."

What she found out first was why the tubes were usually reserved for crew. Once they entered, a process requiring both a code and recognition of one of their escorts, Mac climbed into what felt like a stomach. The space had no straight lines, or rigid walls. Instead, her feet sank ankle-deep and her hands, as Mac groped for support, disappeared within whatever pale substance they'd used. There was something solid a few centimeters in, but it took an effort to reach and even more to free her hands.

She sniffed. *Clover.* "Nice touch."

The others climbed in with her, the crew adeptly bouncing their way to the far side where they leaned their backs against the wall. Mac copied their position, seeing her companions do the same. "What about our bags?" she asked, having dropped hers to the floor in her first startled step.

"Leave it there, Mac."

The door didn't so much close as the walls flowed together where it had been.

"How does—" Sam began to ask, eyes bright with curiosity, when the flexible wall beside him suddenly developed a pronounced curve, as if it were being sucked away.

The sensation of movement came at the same instant. Mac felt herself being pressed deeper into the yielding surface. The others were, too, as was her bag. Doug grinned. "It's called a bolus."

As in lump of food being digested? Mac laughed. "Perfect."

"Thought you'd appreciate it," he said. "They bud from each

entrance to the tube system." Just then, the bolus turned sideways and dropped, but Mac felt only an instant of vertigo. Her
body stayed firmly in place, as though the wall was now holding
onto her. *Which it was,* she realized, after attempting to pry free
her hands. Doug kept lecturing, presumably to keep the novice
passengers distracted. "The tubes themselves are part of the recy-
cling system within the ship. A constant stream of water, heat,
wastes, you name it, travels through. Any freed bolus is whisked
along with the rest until snatched from the flow at the next transit stop."

Mac grinned back. "Gotta love biology."

Doug chuckled. "The engineers will bend your ear about hy-
draulics and closed systems, but we know the truth."

"A flush a day," piped up Kaili.

"The bolus itself applies interior suction when in motion. The
ride can get a little bumpy, but once you're used to it? Nice break
from walking corridors, believe me."

"Fast and secure even if gravity fails," Mudge commented. "And
practical, given the type of ship. A web strung with beads, Norcoast. Remarkably flexible design. How many pods is the *Joy* carrying now?"

The two spoke in unison. "You'll have to ask the exec, sir."
"Really can't go into details, sir."

"You'll have four days. You can ask all the questions you want,
Oversight," Mac said without thinking, then winced inwardly.

Mudge's face glowed with that familiar "gotcha" expression. "I
wasn't aware you were privy to information about the capabilities
of a Ministry dreadnought, Norcoast."

Before Mac had to cover her tracks, Doug spoke up. "Oh, Mac
knows the *Joy*. We brought her home."

She'd counted every hour from the gate to orbit.

"Home from where, Mac?" Sam asked, eyes wide.

Mudge *harrumphed*. "This isn't the time for trading memoirs,
Dr. Schrant. You'll meet your colleagues on the Origins Team
shortly. I trust you were able to familiarize yourself with their work
beforehand?"

Grateful for the distraction, if not for the questions Mudge was
no doubt stockpiling to fire at her when they were next alone, Mac

listened to Sam's animated listing of Kirby and To'o's work, all of which sounded more than familiar to him. *Enthusiasm was a refreshing switch from desperation,* she thought.

The bolus snapped to a full stop between one breath and the next, shuddering along its every surface. The shudders conveniently slid passengers and bags to what was now the floor. An arch formed a new door, the original having melded into the rest of the spongy wall surface sometime after they'd "budded" and joined the waste stream. She smiled to herself at the image.

"Status check?" Doug asked Kaili, who went to the arch and flipped open what was now a control panel.

"Other side's secure," she said after a second. "Clear and opening, now." With that, the door slid aside on an expanse of warm yellow.

Doug, moving nimbly, picked up her bag then offered his hand. Mac smiled and shook her head. She stepped out, pulling one foot at a time free of the tender grip the bolus still had on her feet, and managed not to stagger. "I can see it takes practice," she told him.

That wide, ready smile. *She'd seen it every time he'd arrived to check her new arm.*

It wasn't Doug's fault seeing him brought back such vivid memories. Mac made herself smile back. "Which way now?" she asked, glancing around.

"Idiots!!!" The bellow echoed from wall to ceiling. "I told you she would be coming!"

"Let me guess," Mudge said dryly.

The Origins Team was very glad to see them. The climatologists had swept away Sam Schrant, having arranged to share quarters so they could begin working on his model systems. They'd hurried off in a rosy glow of incomprehensible math. Mudge was accosted by all the Sthlynii at once, who over-voweled at him in anguish about the changes to the schedule they'd originally anguished about at the consulate. Not to mention the risk of lost equipment and did he notice they now had to change their quarter assignments? The *Annapolis Joy* was much larger than the transport the Sinzi-ra had promised, but their portion of it was smaller. It was all too much to bear.

If Mudge hadn't looked so thoroughly officious, Mac might have felt sorry for him.

The Origins Team had been put in an area of the ship unfamiliar to Mac. *Not hard, considering she'd spent most of her time in the medlab.* Meant for passengers, beyond doubt, though there was no evidence of who the *Joy* might normally carry. *Maybe they used her for conferences,* Mac decided, remembering that the ship hadn't seen combat until the attack on the Ro.

Their section was separated from the rest of the ship by a pair of heavy bulkheads that could be air locks at need. Once past this point, the long, gently curving corridor was lined with a series of identical doors, each leading into compact and efficient living quarters with their own biological accommodations. The walls between were removable, allowing some quarters to be larger than others. Mac counted fourteen doors on the left-hand side of the corridor, seven on the right, but was advised to knock first. The Sthlynii remained unsettled about their quarters and were turning up anywhere.

To the right, after the first two doors, the corridor bulged outward to provide a common space, itself split into dining and recreation areas with mem-wood tables. Someone well-versed in transporting scientists had further divided the recreation areas with sound and light screens, creating four workrooms, already in use. Past that point were the remaining five living quarters. The corridor ended in a closed bulkhead.

Feeling oriented, if not truly here yet, Mac munched on a sandwich, contents unknown. She'd joined Lyle Kanaci in the dining area, at a corner table. He wasn't happy about the change either.

"I tell you, Mac, I've been afraid to ask why we rated an upgrade." Always pale, he leaned so close Mac could see the delicate vessels pulsing beneath his skin. He pitched his voice to her ears only. "Can't be good news."

"It's not bad," she assured him, swallowing. "They've found ships from the Dhryn colonies."

He sat back, lips pursed in a silent whistle. "Haven?"

Her people weren't slow. Mac smiled and toasted him with a bottle of juice. "Haven. The ships are derelicts. Abandoned."

"We could use a look," he said eagerly. "We don't have much in the way of modern technology references—trade items, some catalogs. The modern Dhryn didn't export much of their own manufacture."

"Shouldn't be hard to arrange. They're bringing the best preserved to Myriam. Should arrive before we do."

Lyle looked startled, then frowned at her. "Why?"

Mac shrugged. "If I said it offers exquisite congruence to the Sinzi, would that help?" At his blank expression, she cupped her hands on the table, forming an enclosure. "The IU wants all valuable Dhryn artifacts in a place where they can't be claimed by any other species."

"Like that, is it?" Lyle pressed his lips together in a thin line, then nodded. "Explaining this ship. I had my doubts it was because the Ministry had suddenly realized the value of its crack team of archaeologists. Politics."

"We've done pretty well avoiding them so far," Mac shrugged. "Bound to happen. So long as it doesn't interfere with our work." She rubbed a spot on the tabletop with one finger, wondering how best to tell him the rest. "There will be a change, Lyle," she began.

"They'll take you off Origins. To work on these ships."

So much for how to tell him. She nodded, lowering her voice. No one was close by, but she'd noticed the Cey had superior hearing. *Probably the wrinkles.* "To start anyway," she admitted. "Ship controls and systems should be IU standard, Instella, but they're hoping for Dhryn records, vids. You should go ahead and take charge. I'm not sure how long this will all take."

Just then, the Sthlynii contingent went storming past, Mudge in their midst, tentacles and vowels flinging. There was the sound of doors whooshing open and a shout.

"You might want Oversight," Mac added thoughtfully.

"Definitely," Lyle agreed, whose eyes had followed the group out of sight. "Oh, here. You'll find one on yours." He pulled out his imp and activated his 'screen, setting it between them. It displayed their present location within the ship. Mac studied it, unsurprised to see most of what surrounded them left blank. *They were passengers, not crew.* Lyle ran his finger through the image, highlighting various areas in turn. "Down this corridor is the section entry station—where we can access additional stores, pick up an escort to the medlab, hangar etc."

Mac nodded. They'd passed the clear-walled room with its trio of crew sitting at consoles on the way here. Doug and Kaili had waved—likely so their group hadn't needed to stop and check in. *Escorts and guards.* She shook off a sense of being trapped. *Same side, remember.*

"Here we are. These are your quarters, Mac. We're all doubled up, so you'll be sharing with—" He consulted a text list Mac didn't bother to read. "Oh."

"Oh?"

The pink blotches deepened on his cheeks. "This has to be wrong. Someone's made a last minute change. I'll look into it."

Mac dismissed his concern. "Doesn't matter, Lyle. It's only four nights. I'll probably work through two anyway. Who is it, anyway?"

"We're too cramped," he fussed. "It's not just this ship. It's all the—" a sweep of his fingers illuminated the adjoining set of rooms "—others."

"Others? What others?" Then it dawned on her and her eyes widened. "Don't tell me the Grimnoii talked their way into coming with you."

He nodded, as glum-faced as one of the heavyset aliens. "Along with some Frow."

Mac wasn't sure if she should laugh or throw the rest of her sandwich at him. "Anyone else?"

"That's it."

"Should make for an interesting trip." She finished her drink.

"About your roommate, Mac—"

Before Lyle could finish, dozens of tiny claws fastened into Mac's back and shoulders. She yelped. Six Myg offspring cheerily yelped with her, then began gumming her neck, scalp, and ears with painful enthusiasm. *They'd missed her.*

"Er, that would be roommates."

Eyes watering, Mac glared at Lyle as she struggled with the Mygs. "You can't be serious."

He pointed at the text. "Says here Fourteen took a vow of celibacy when we boarded. He's sharing with Da'a. That leaves—"

"There you are, Mac!" Unensela swooped up to their table, completely disregarding her offspring or their current preoccupation. "I hope you aren't a noisy sleeper. I need peace and quiet at night. I must be able to concentrate on my important work."

What she needed, Mac decided then and there, *was to beg enough Fastfix from Doug and Kaili to keep her awake until Myriam.*

An offspring found her chin and began to chew.

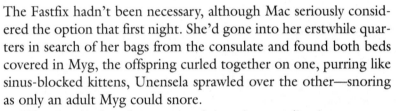

The Fastfix hadn't been necessary, although Mac seriously considered the option that first night. She'd gone into her erstwhile quarters in search of her bags from the consulate and found both beds covered in Myg, the offspring curled together on one, purring like sinus-blocked kittens, Unensela sprawled over the other—snoring as only an adult Myg could snore.

What was it about her quarters being given to aliens?

With the ship's lighting dimmed to night levels, she'd hunted another option, prowling up and down the deserted corridor twice before spotting the glow from one of the workrooms. Sure enough, the climatologists—Kirby, To'o, and now Sam—had been huddled in front of their 'screens, talking in excited whispers. She'd poked thoughtfully at their stash of food, then asked when they planned to sleep. Their appalled looks had been most convincing.

Of course, they'd used their beds as equipment tables, but she'd cleared sufficient flat space on one for herself.

From all signs to the contrary, Mac thought with amusement when she woke the next morning and truly saw her surroundings, *the three intended to stay awake the entire journey.* Possibly fine for the Cey, but the two Human males would eventually crash somewhere.

They wouldn't be sleeping in their shower, she discovered moments later. *And didn't plan on washing either.* Their shower held their outdoor gear.

Something to mention before bodily odor became an interspecies' issue.

Mac made her way down the corridor to her assigned quarters, ignoring anyone awake and functioning—all of whom wisely ignored her as well. She was relieved to find the room Myg-free. Locking the door, she headed for the shower, then stopped.

Was she sure?

Five minutes later, having looked in every conceivable—and a few not so much—place where an offspring could wait to pounce, she headed for the shower again.

There was something essential about being saliva-free first thing in the morning.

Showered, in clothes she hadn't slept in at least once, and hungry, Mac whistled to herself as she followed the promising smell of coffee to the mutual dining room.

Her whistling stopped as she saw who filled the seats.

Grimnoii.

With mugs of—she sniffed and scowled—*cider.*

"Dr. Connor!" "Dr. Connor." "Glad we found you."

It was like walking into a funeral. Albeit a drunken funeral.

"Morning," she greeted, looking wildly for any escape.

There was a coffeepot. Mac focused on it, cautiously weaving her way between large humped backs and bandoliers studded with sharp objects. *Were they allowed to have such things on a starship?* Presumably so, unless the beings had smuggled them in to wear at breakfast.

With the cider.

"Going to be an interesting trip, don't you think?" This from the other non-Grimnoii in the room, Mirabelle Sangrea. Mac poured a mugful and weaved through more backs, feet, and sharp objects to squeeze in beside her.

"I had that feeling," Mac admitted.

Mirabelle pushed over a half-full bowl of fruit. "No use trying to reach the kitchen until they leave, Mac. Trust me, I've tried."

Mac scowled at the Grimnoii. The Grimnoii able to notice lifted their mugs to her and swayed from side to side, very slowly, altogether. "Dr. Connor." "Glad to see you."

"They're plastered," she observed.

"I'd say so. And exhausted. They've been working on their quarters nonstop since we arrived. You'd think, putting that much effort into modifications, they'd have stayed in them, but no. We get them." Mirabelle shrugged.

Mac grabbed an apple and took a ravenous series of bites, considering the situation as she chewed and swallowed. "Who gave them cider?"

"They brought their own."

Which would be her *fault,* Mac sighed to herself. Peeling a banana, she did her best to pretend it was toast. "Here's hoping they remember the way to their own bathrooms."

Mirabelle's eyes twinkled. "Bait them with a jug? Lock all the other doors? Install traps?"

"I've said it before," Mac grinned. "You are an evil yet brilliant woman."

They both sipped their coffee and munched fruit, watching the Grimnoii sip cider and, one by one, settle their huge heads on a forearm or tabletop. *A new spectator sport.* "How's Emily?" Mirabelle asked after the third passed out. "We got the report about the Ro—how they'd hidden something at the landing site." Always thoughtful, now she seemed to pick her words with extra care. "It must have been difficult for her."

"Em?" Mac thought of the fury in Emily's eyes, her defiant spin and exit on the walkway, and smiled. "She's back to work. She's good."

The other woman gave a self-conscious laugh. "I know what you mean. I can't wait to get back to my ruins. I've lost so much time."

If salmon are running the Klondike, they'll be passing Field Station Six.

With no one there.

Mac shook her head, but not at Mirabelle. "You'll make it up," she said firmly, as much to herself as to the archaeologist. "They've promised to set up full access to all the sites this time. That should help."

"Oh, it's going to be amazing. The data—I'll have to grab sleep now, I swear."

A Grimnoii slumped, then slowly fell off the table to the floor to form a boneless brown lump. The gleaming axes through his belt somehow missed puncturing either fur or cloth.

"Maybe that's their plan," Mac mused. "Sleep for four days."

"What's going on here?" The volume of the shout was almost as impressive as the level of outrage.

And before breakfast. "Oversight. Good morning." Mac waved.

Rumnor raised his mug before dropping nostrils first to the table.

After his shout, Mudge became speechless. He tugged at the nearest unconscious alien, succeeding only in spilling the contents of the mug the being wouldn't let go.

"We'll lock up their supply," Mac assured him. "Might as well let them sleep it off."

"This is unacceptable, Norcoast. Unacceptable!"

She surveyed the room. "It could be worse," she judged, having seen it firsthand. *Why the Grimnoii drank a substance that caused them such vile bodily reactions was beyond her.* "It will be worse," she amended. "You'd better contact the crew for a cleanup."

Mudge made unhappy noises every step of the way to their table. Mac was reasonably sure he could have missed treading on the alien at their feet with a little more effort, but she wasn't about to say anything. Sleep and a shower had done wonders toward restoring her sense of balance.

And drunken aliens first thing in the morning weren't a crisis, on the scale of things.

"Have my seat, Charles," Mirabelle offered, standing up to leave. "I'll stop by the station and pass the word about our friends."

"Thanks. There you go, Oversight." Mac grinned at him. "Apple?"

"You seem in a better mood this morning," he half accused. Rather than squeeze in beside Mac, he took the seat opposite, somehow wedging himself between the Grimnoii behind and the table. He shook his head at the fruit. "I had oatmeal and tea in my quarters."

"Foresight," she admired, smiling at her own wit, then proceeded to eat the apple herself, washing down the bites with her now-cool coffee.

"Experience, Norcoast." Almost a *harrumph*. "This hasty change was not part of my arrangements for our journey. I don't expect, nor have I seen, competence."

"Mmmfphlee," she said around a bite. *He was welcome to interpret that as he pleased.* Once her mouth was empty, Mac gestured with the apple. "All this looks pretty competent to me. It's not as if there was much notice." As far as she was concerned, drunken Grimnoii came under the heading "unforeseeable."

"It's the notice that troubles me, Norcoast." He put his hands together, just so, on the table and stared at her. Immobile and much too awake for comfort.

"How so?" She paused with the apple at her lips. *Oh, she knew that look.* She put down the apple. "I told you, Oversight. I received a message about the Dhryn derelicts being taken to Myriam and that the Ministry would help hurry us there."

"I'd like to see it."

So would she. "It was a read-once message," she said promptly, patting the pocket with her imp. "My guess is we'll get a briefing onboard. Maybe—" *she had no shame,* "—on the bridge."

Unfortunately, Mudge on a trail was as distractible as a wolverine. "For all we know, Norcoast, this is some ridiculous collusion between Earthgov and the Ministry. An ill-thought effort to put additional Humans on Myriam, flaunting the IU's per-species restriction. Who knows what problems could result?" A definitely troubled *harrumph*. "What assurances did you receive about the source of this message?"

"Enough, believe me." Mac's eyes rested on the silver rings around her finger. She'd hidden the carving deep in her luggage. "Were you always this suspicious, Oversight?"

"I could ask if you've always been this naive, but the answer would be obvious."

Mac opened her mouth to argue, when something caught her eye behind Mudge. Trying not to be obvious, she leaned to one side to better see it.

The kitchen proper was set aside from the dining area by a temporary wall, only chest high. *There.* Something small, and black, and pointy was hooked over the top, just above the table with the coffeepot and fruit bowls.

A claw?

She squinted. *Definitely.*

"I would have expected you to at least pay attention, Norcoast. This is a serious conversation."

"Oh, I am," Mac murmured, leaning the other way to follow as the claw slid sideways. It was abruptly joined by a second, slightly longer and bearing nail polish. Both pressed their tips deeply into the material of the wall, as if their owner hung on for its life.

"Norcoast?"

Mac focused on her companion. "Sorry. Insufficient coffee."

"I don't understand you," he complained, heaving a sigh so deep the nearest unconscious Grimnoii echoed it.

She chewed her lower lip for a moment, then made a decision. "How I found out isn't the point, Oversight." *Well, he'd disagree about the part where he was drugged unconscious for a good hour or more.* As Mac didn't intend to share that bit, she continued. "There's been—" she searched in vain for a euphemism remotely relevant and had to settle for, "—some difficulties on the ship with Nik and the Vessel. They're fine," *unless the radiation or whatever has killed them,* "but the—difficulty could also be related to some confusion over investigating the derelicts."

The claws, Mac noticed, were still in place.

Mudge pursed his lips and considered this for a moment. Mac took the last swallow of her coffee. Then he gave a brisk nod. "Sabotage to delay them; jurisdictional issues to slow crucial information; a rush to get us—or rather you—to Myriam. Someone's on a clock."

She forgot about the claws and gaped at him. "Pardon?"

"Really, Norcoast," Mudge pointed his forefinger at her. "It's the obvious conclusion. Do you have any idea who?"

None that she'd be willing to discuss here, surrounded by possibly conscious aliens and a set of interested claws.

"Isn't it time you were busy adding competence to something?" She said it half jokingly, but didn't smile. Instead, Mac deliberately glanced around the room and then back to Mudge.

"Ah. Yes. You have a point," he said, waggling his eyebrows with dramatic flare. "Understood."

They were, she judged fatalistically, *the worst spies ever enlisted.* Good thing there were professionals on the job.

He rose from the table as she did. Mac hefted her empty cup and nodded toward the kitchen. "I'm going to try my luck. Meet you later?"

"Later, Norcoast," with enough emphasis to make any eavesdropper pant and follow.

Once he was gone, Mac spent a moment planning her approach, walking back and forth to get different angles on her problem. As luck, or the social mores of aliens would have it, the opening to the kitchen area was behind a table with too many Grimnoii. They appeared to have started their binge facing outward. They'd ended it slumped shoulder to shoulder to shoulder, their abundant back ends lined up to form a complete barrier.

All of the aliens were comatose by this point; a few snoring, *if that's what the faint whistling sound was.* Mac put down her mug and gave the nearest a gentle poke. *Nothing happened.* A firmer one. When that drew no response, she looked at the group blocking the kitchen and assessed the slope.

Climbed worse.

It wouldn't be long before whomever Mirabelle sent to retrieve the Grimnoii showed up.

The claws hadn't budged. If anything, their hold on the wall appeared more desperate than before. Small flecks of paint were coming loose.

Mac took off her shoes, on the premise that climbing a fellow sentient while wearing them was somehow more rude. *She doubted the Grimnoii would notice.* Using a chair, she climbed gingerly onto the table in front of the kitchen, stepping through the maze of outstretched hairy arms and hands. Her right foot landed in a puddle of what she hoped was spilled cider and she wrinkled her nose in disgust.

Three of the Grimnoii were in her path, but only one had a pair of blunt wooden handles thrust through the bandolier that went around his torso. *Useful,* Mac decided.

Before she could reconsider, she grabbed the handles, one in each hand, then put her right foot on the most muscular part of the being's shoulder. When this didn't elicit a reaction, she slowly increased the weight on that foot until she was supporting herself on it.

She lifted her left foot and brought it forward, finding her balance.

Not bad.

The Grimnoii sneezed.

With a shriek, Mac went flying over its backside. Somehow she tucked herself into a ball as she landed and slid along the floor on her rump—until her rump hit something that rattled but didn't give way.

The back wall of the kitchen.

Fighting the urge to giggle, Mac stared up at her feet, then rolled her head to take a look at her surroundings. The first thing she saw was the owner of the claws.

"*Se* Lasserbee."

The Frow was clinging to a set of storage bins as well as the half wall. Like Mac, he was upside down. *A position,* Mac thought, *that looked better on him.*

She turned herself over, staying on the floor, and studied the situation. *No sparks at least. Se* appeared calm enough, though *se's* membranes were in a confused jumble concealing most of *se's* silver-sprung uniform. She decided *se'd* twisted while grabbing for handholds. The pointy hat was now under *se's* chin, exposing a plain, rounded head.

Se unfolded *se's* left neck ridge to turn that head to look at her, more or less directly. "Ah. Dr. Connor." A strained whisper. "Are they gone? Is it safe?"

Now a spark, luckily landing on the bin and not the carpeted floor. Mac hurriedly climbed to her feet, hissing as her rump expressed its opinion as to her means of arrival in the kitchen. "The Grimnoii?" she guessed, leaning over to see where the Frow's other limbs were. "They're sleeping it off."

"They were boisterous!" *Se's* pale green eyes looked almost humanly anguished.

"I'm sure they were."

"I sought refuge!"

Smart creature. "Well, you're safe now," Mac promised. "Let's get you out of here, okay?"

"Ahhh."

No more than the exhalation, but Mac thought she understood. "You're stuck?"

"I am not stuck!" This with considerable passion. Then *se* added more calmly, "The furnishings of this room are unstable and cannot be trusted."

Mac touched the nearest bin, which rocked slightly. The Frow's hand scrabbled for a better hold on it, further rocking the bin, and sparks began to fly in all directions. "Calm down," she soothed, doing her best to hold the bin steady against *se's* frantic movements. "Don't move!"

That, the Frow understood.

Once she was sure *se* wouldn't move—*likely ever*—and the sparks had subsided to a few forlorn glints, Mac slowly let go of the bin. She walked to the other end of the row and noticed all the bins were sitting on a wheeled trolley, presently locked.

She put her hand on the locking mechanism and stretched to look over the bins at the paralyzed Frow. "*Se* Lasserbee. I want you to trust me."

"What are you planning to do?"

"You told me you like protocols and procedures." Mac flipped open the cover on the lock.

"Ah. Yes." *Se's* voice lost some of its panicked edge. "I am expert in many formats."

She eased the lock a half-turn and braced her foot against the trolley. "So you know how important it is to be thorough. To follow steps in sequence."

"Yes, Dr. Connor. But what has this to do with the dreadful instability of this furniture?"

"I want you to count to three with me," Mac said. "One . . ."

"Dr. Connor!"

"Two . . ."

"What are you—" The bins shuddered wildly.

"Three." Mac unlocked the wheels and gave the trolley a shove with her foot.

"Aiee!!!!!"

The bins and trolley parted company with a loud clatter. She jumped out of the way as the nearest bin lost its lid, spilling what looked like precooked spaghetti on the floor. The noodles writhed together for a few seconds before setting off across the floor, apparently drawn by the dark shadow under the half wall.

Not noodles.

Other bins deposited more sedentary masses, including puffs of white powder which drifted down to coat the now-collapsed Frow. Mac watched as *se's* clawed hands grabbed weakly at the smooth floor. "*Se* Lasserbee?" she called softly.

"Ah. Dr. Connor. Please. A moment."

Moving much more slowly than the freed spaghetti, *se* began to sort *se-self* out.

"No rush," she assured *se*, eyeing the cupboards thoughtfully.

Just then, a Human head, above a tan uniform, peered into the kitchen. "Is everything—what's going on here?"

Mac brushed powder from her hair and smiled cheerfully. "We're making breakfast."

"Where are the boisterous ones, Dr. Connor?" *Se's* neck tilted as if a Grimnoii might be hiding in the room that constituted the Frow allotment of the *Annapolis Joy*. "Are we safe?"

For a soldier, the being was remarkably timid. *Which made sense,* Mac reminded herself. *If she could be knocked over as easily as* Se Lasserbee, *she'd be timid around giant drunk teddy bears, too.*

Se'd explained *se'd* come to the dining area to wait for her, having been told every Human would appear in that room eventually. When the Grimnoii had arrived instead, *se* had prudently retreated to the kitchen to wait. Prudently yet quickly. That would be the kitchen with highly unstable furnishings, resulting in *se* being trapped.

Mac had had to help *se* file a formal complaint with the captain before *se'd* calm down enough to converse on any other topic. *In a Human,* she decided, *the being's outward reaction would mean humiliated pride.* Just as well *se* hadn't mentioned her rather crude assistance.

Of course, acknowledging help meant admitting the need for it.

She'd stayed in the kitchen, eating breakfast amid the mess, to let the Frow make *se's* way here in privacy. A very long, slow breakfast. And she'd stayed to help the crew clean up. *Still almost beat* se *back here.*

"We're safe. The Grimnoii are in their quarters." Without, Mac had checked, the remainder of their cider.

"Ah. Excellent. And are you comfortable, Dr. Connor?"

The Frow had managed to bring their own, more trustworthy furnishings with them. More impressively, as far as Mac was concerned, they'd managed to turn their combined rooms into an artificial forest.

Not that there were trees. Instead, everything Human had been removed, replaced by tall supports that filled the available floor space, leaving barely room for a Human to walk between, let alone a Grimnoii. The supports were identical in construction, each made of five burnished metal poles that approached but didn't quite touch the ceiling. The poles were held together by struts, again of metal. These mostly horizontal pieces were wrapped in padding at inexplicable, to Mac at least, intervals. Each support arose from a base that fit snugly against all others like a puzzle piece.

Someone had jammed rolled blankets along the edges next to the room walls, presumably to make up for a difference from expected dimensions. *Thoughtful.*

The supports were fixed, but their bronze poles had octagonal faces, catching and reflecting the ambient light depending on the angle of viewing. It gave the illusion of constant movement. The strung pads varied in color from yellow to deep red. *To Human eyes,* Mac reminded herself. The overall effect was of entering a landscape dominated by verticals and inhabited by perching lumps.

All three Frow were present, but the other two clutched poles as close to the ceiling as possible, their eyes closed. *Asleep or offering privacy?*

Se Lasserbee, hat in its proper place, had wrapped *se's* claws around a support at the room's center. Unlike *se's* lackeys, *se'd* climbed only as far as necessary to keep *se's* feet off the treacherously flat ground. *Courtesy to* se's *guest,* Mac judged it.

Arms resting on soft padding, she leaned her chin on a handy puff of bright red. She'd already discovered a convenient rail for one foot. *Not bad.* "I like what you've done with the place," she told the Frow.

"This?" *Se* Lasserbee tilted *se's* neck farther to the other side, as if there was something new to see in their surroundings. "These are portable *clocs,* convenient and secure, yes, but hardly admirable. I hope you have the opportunity to see one of our true homes, Dr. Connor."

"As do I, *Se* Lasserbee." Her lips twisted in a grin. "And my compliments. I'm impressed you managed to catch a ride on this ship."

"Ah." The metal to every side made it hard to see which glints were from *se's* eyes. "Unlike you, Dr. Connor, the other Human was gullible."

Poor Kanaci. Mac laughed. The lackeys overhead shifted positions with a click of claw to bar. One, she noticed, wound up upside down. *Didn't seem to matter.* "Why did you want to see me?" she asked.

"I have received most disturbing information, Dr. Connor. I didn't know how to handle it until you arrived."

Mac lost any inclination to laugh. "What do I have to do with it?" She lifted her chin from the pad and studied the Frow, whose offset eyes were apparently fixed on her left shoulder. "Couldn't you contact your superiors?"

Se drew *se's* left membrane half over *se's* face, allowing *se* to peek at her from its shelter. "I am a mere passenger. Those in charge of this ship permit me incoming messages only." *Se* revealed more of *se's* face. "Even if I could," this very quietly, as if trying not to be overheard by the sleepers, "I would not. This is my first field assignment, Dr. Connor. I am expected to act appropriately. And I have. I have found you. I will give you this information."

She was going to regret this. "What is it?"

"A report from our contingent at the Gathering. They were given an assignment by the Sol System Sinzi-ra, Anchen, to—are you aware of the condition of the Dhryn world, Haven, when the Sinzi first contacted them?"

"I—" Mac hesitated, thinking hard. *Was she?* "Beyond urbanized, with in-system space travel? Nothing specific. My team's been more concerned with the conditions on their planet of origin."

"Haven was stripped bare," the Frow revealed, *se's* left membrane flapping against the side of *se's* face in emphasis. *Or a nervous twitch.* "The probe found the Dhryn struggling to feed an exploding population, their resources almost gone. The building of the transect gate gave them trade as well as access to systems with worlds to colonize. We believe this saved their species."

"Good timing," Mac commented. "Hardly seems a coincidence, now, does it."

"No." *Se* clicked *se's* claws along a rail. *Approval?* "The Sinzi had received information concerning the existence of Haven and the Dhryn, information which led to their probe. Because of their dire situation and apparently peaceful society, the decision to offer the Dhryn a transect gate was hurried through the IU council. With hindsight, as you say, the significance of these events becomes painfully evident. Our researchers were asked to trace the original source of that information. It turned out to be a daunting task." He stopped.

Apparently their species shared a fondness for melodramatic pauses, Mac thought testily. "Did they find it?"

"They believe so." *Se* brought out an imp, wider but clearly kin to Mac's, and triggered a display.

Not words, was her first grateful thought. The display was a schematic of the worlds connected along the Naralax. Many were pulsing an angry red. As Mac puzzled over the now-familiar map, she began to see the pattern.

Oh, no, was her second thought.

"*Se* Lasserbee," she said, her voice unsteady. "Are those planets that have been attacked by the Dhryn?"

"Several, yes, including ravaged Ascendis. N'not'k. Regellus. Riden IV. Thitus Prime. Others have not suffered any recorded assaults."

"Yet." She clutched the bars on her *cloc*. "Multiple sources for the same message? Wasn't that unusual?"

"Ah. We thought so, too. The Sinzi of that time considered it congruent and thus somehow more credible. Between us, Dr. Connor, I don't think they are as smart as everyone thinks."

Mac didn't think *Se* Lasserbee was as smart as *se* seemed to believe, but refrained from comment. "Let me get this straight," she said, her heart starting to thud within her chest. "The location of Haven was sent to the Sinzi by all those different species. At the same time."

Se's claws tickled the metal struts, producing something remarkably like tinny fanfare. "Even from those worlds lacking the required technology. There can be only one conclusion, Dr. Connor." Another pause, but shorter, as if the being was too eager to wait for her prompting. "The Myrokynay!"

Mac heard the word and felt nothing. *It was as if she'd already known.* But a gut reaction wasn't enough. "Do you have any proof?"

"They have their agents, do they not? It's a pattern of behavior, to act behind others."

"So no proof. *Se* Lasserbee—" Mac shook her head.

"Who else could it be? Doubtless they were trying to warn the species of the Interstellar Union to avoid the Dhryn System, in hopes the Dhryn would die out on their own. The Sinzi misinterpreted. Interspecies communication," *se* announced firmly, "frequently involves such confusions."

"That it does," Mac agreed wholeheartedly, clenching her hands around the pipes until her knuckles ached. "What did Anchen say? Has she raised—" the alarm, she wanted to say, then remembered who she was talking to. *Idiot faction.* A waste of breath to argue; worse, he might stop talking to her. "Has she taken action to confirm all this?"

The Frow opened *se's* neck ridges to bend *se's* neck left, as if seeking another angle to view her. "Why would I tell Sol's Sinzi-ra before you, Dr. Connor? You are the ranking individual of our group. It has been confusing, I'll admit, but your promotion is now evident."

When interspecies communication fails, shut up. Having made this new rule, Mac followed it. She hung onto the Frow's idea of a chair and tried feverishly to piece together any sense from this.

If she believed *Se* Lasserbee's conclusion, the Ro had arranged for the Dhryn to join the Interspecies Union. *Which meant . . .* a shiver trailed down her spine . . . *the Ro had been on those red-marked worlds* before *Haven had been connected to the Naralax.*

Humanity hadn't joined the IU that much sooner than the Dhryn. The Ro had already been there, existing outside of normal time.

How old were they?

Mac deliberately pushed all such thoughts far to the side, for now. *Not helpful to reduce oneself to gibbering terror.*

"Ah. Dr. Connor? Have I said something incorrect?"

If se only knew. Aloud, "The Frow contingent from the Gathering reports solely to you," she ventured cautiously.

"I am the assigned nexus for all Frow reports on this subject. I handle the forms. There must be order." This last as though blindingly obvious.

It might be to someone in a pointy hat, Mac thought grimly. She plowed forward. "And you're part of my group, not Anchen's. Now."

"Yes. Yes."

"Reporting to me."

"Have I been confusing, Dr. Connor?"

Not the time for an honest answer. "Of course not, *Se* Lasserbee," Mac asserted, leaning forward as if relaxing. That every muscle in her body felt more rigid than the poles supporting her was beside the point. "I'm only—surprised—you didn't report this to Dr. Kanaci in my absence."

Or anyone else! The time se'd *wasted,* she thought with a mix of horror and disgust.

"Dr. Kanaci is subordinate," the Frow proclaimed. "All those immediate are subordinate. I am observant. You make decisions. You talk louder." A flutter of membrane. "And he was gullible." *Se's* dazzling list of evidence complete, *se* settled *se-self* more comfortably on the support and gazed at her.

Mac was beginning to suspect a certain inflexibility of thought in the Frow, or rather a channel *se's* thoughts preferred to travel. Find the individual of greatest authority. Give that individual the form. Congratulate oneself. The form's contents weren't as important as making sure it was handed up. *Probably saved time,* she mused, *but only if a reasonable chain of command was maintained.*

Abandoned on Earth, ordered to find the Ro by any means, and receiving information *se* had to know was crucial? Poor *Se* Lasserbee had made a truly stunning leap of faith to transfer *se's* upward obligation to the most likely alien.

Though se *should have picked Mudge.*

Someone more experienced in dealing with other cultures—or brighter—might have grasped the rudiments of Human hierarchies and told the ship's captain. Se *wasn't likely to get a second field assignment,* Mac judged.

She pulled out her imp and set its 'screen to intersect with *se's*. "Please transfer the relevant forms."

Se's claw tips scratched through the displays as if *se* couldn't wait to obey. Once finished, and their respective imps put away, *se* climbed partway up *se's* support and swung to hang upside down. "You will attempt to contact the Myrokynay at these locations?" *se* asked from that vantage point. "You will let me come, too?"

Mac stepped down to the floor, one hand on the nearest pole as she looked up. *Did one admit to having superiors or hold onto perceived power?* She compromised. "I must consult. You'll be informed. Thank you."

The Frow must have taken this as confirmation of all *se's* aspirations, because the next thing Mac knew, Se Lasserbee was scampering effortlessly from support to support, the close spacing of the furnishings now making perfect sense as *se's* hands and feet loosened and grasped one after the other. *Se* rushed up to the sleeping lackeys and yanked hard on each in turn. One almost fell, grabbing to save *se, ne,* or *sene's-self.*

Once awake, they immediately joined Se Lasserbee, all three flinging themselves up and down and around the room. Mac twisted her head to follow. It was like watching birds' flight, or fish darting through a clear stream. *No wonder they hate walking,* she thought, inclined to envy. Their claws made *tings* of varied pitch against the metal; their feet thumped against the pads; their membranes fluttered. The dance overlapped into melody.

To her ears anyway, Mac cautioned, smiling to herself.

She leaned on a pole, not daring to move until they stopped. A Frow at full speed took up a daunting amount of space.

Did explain the chin strap on the hats.

"Dr. Connor."

"Captain Gillis."

"Dr. Connor." With more weight, as if her name constituted some problem.

"I know who I am," Mac offered helpfully. "May I send the message?"

Captain Michael Gillis gazed back at her from his seat behind his tidy desk. He was a tidy man, his uniform impeccable, his silver hair trim and in place. He obviously ran a tidy ship; all she'd seen of the *Annapolis Joy* and her crew could be described as gleaming.

Mac, in their brief encounters together, had come away convinced he most likely folded his socks.

"To the Interspecies Consulate on Earth," he repeated her request, his tone making it clear this was as much a problem as her name. "Not the Ministry. A personal message to a Sinzi. From you, Dr. Connor."

She had no reason to believe he was hard of hearing or obtuse, so she restrained herself with considerable effort. "Yes, from me. Surely I was given authorization."

"That part was left out." Gillis' executive officer, Darcy Townee, stood to one side of her captain's desk. She was a small, round woman who might have been anyone's favorite grandmother, if you ignored the lines of muscle up her neck, the fingers missing from her left hand, and the parade-ground snap to her voice that made even Mac's shoulders itch. "We received orders to get you to the rendezvous in the Dhryn System, Dr. Connor, with all speed and stealth. Stealth, for your information, includes no outgoing signals from passengers we can't admit we have."

"Myriam."

Townee looked taken aback. "What?"

"The system and planet," Mac explained, feeling helpful. "They've been named. Myriam. It's official. You can look it up."

The exec declined to argue. "We will arrange to transfer any and all messages to a Ministry courier ship when we reach the gate."

"I'm surprised you didn't get along with *Se* Lasserbee," Mac said blandly.

"We're not in the habit of taking requests, Dr. Connor." The unspoken implication behind that being she should be grateful to be heard at all.

Mac, having argued her way past what seemed the entire complement of the *Joy* to reach this small antechamber—as close as they'd let her to the bridge—wasn't about to stop now. She leaned forward, eyes on Gillis. "We won't be at the gate for what—another two days? I assure you, Captain. This can't wait."

"You'd help your case, Dr. Connor, if you'd tell us what was so urgent." The captain raised his eyebrows. "An imminent threat to Human security? Some risk to the safety of this ship, perhaps?"

That the Sinzi themselves might have been manipulated by the Ro from the beginning? She owed Anchen the right to hear it first.

Mac pressed her lips together and glared. "Our leaving for Myriam was hardly a secret. You had to specify an approach path to move this thing safely through commercial traffic, so everyone knows you're heading to the Naralax, not another gate. What could possibly happen if anyone learns we're traveling together—a media scoop? Oh, I can see it now. 'Warship offers scientists free ride.' The demands will come pouring in—next will be physicists, mark my words. I know their kind."

Their expressions didn't change from polite attention. "Will two days alter the consequence of your message, Dr. Connor?" asked Townee.

That the Ro had been on those worlds long before the Dhryn?
That they could still be there?

Supposition. She had no proof—only the Frow's eager belief and her fear.

"Let's hope not," Mac told them pleasantly, giving up. *It was that, or a tantrum she couldn't explain.* She put her palms on the arms of the chair and pushed herself to her feet. "I appreciate your time, Captain."

Captain Gillis stood as well. "We're subject to orders, Dr. Connor." *Almost an apology.* "I trust you and your people are finding the accommodations satisfactory, the crew helpful?"

"As always," Mac acknowledged, involuntarily flexing the fingers of her left hand. "Thanks. About that message—" she looked to Townee.

"You'll want something more secure than the usual packet?" At Mac's nod, she added, "Then I'll stop by with the protocols, Dr. Connor. Is there a time you prefer?"

Mac opened her mouth to reply . . .

The alarm sounded.

PASSENGERS AND PROBLEMS

"GET HER BELOW!" Gillis snapped, already on the move toward his bridge.

"I can—" Mac began, but Townee took her arm in a tight grip, urging her toward the door to the main corridor.

The ship's alarm cut off as suddenly as it had started.

A not-so-calm voice replaced it. "Standing down. Captain, we've a confirmed friendly on docking approach. A bloody fast approach. Permission to synchronize?"

Gillis and Townee exchanged looks. "Who is it, Ming?" she asked.

"You won't believe this, Exec." The voice developed a note of awe. "By the spec sheet, it's a Sinzi transect dart. I've never seen one before. No idea how it surprised us—Jim's looking into it. Could have been tucked behind a freighter we just passed. Sucker's bending the laws of physics—"

There was a sharp, short whistle.

"Ah, Captain—?"

Gillis shook his head. "I take it synchronization would be redundant."

"Yes, sir. They've docked themselves, sir. Hangar 1A."

With an unnecessary brush at his uniform and an uninterpretable look at Mac, Gillis headed for the bridge. When the connecting door opened, Mac could see nothing past him but stunned-looking faces.

Even after it closed, Townee remained where she was, eyes

swimming with suspicion. "Impeccable timing, Dr. Connor," she said slowly. "Care to comment?"

Mac tugged her arm free, arranging her face in its best *how should I know?* expression. She'd practiced it often enough with Mudge. "Not really."

Townee's eyes hardened. "To my knowledge—and it's one of those things I would know, Dr. Connor—no Sinzi craft has ever approached and docked with one of ours. To my knowledge," she emphasized, "the Sinzi have only made appearances on planets, well-planned and prearranged appearances, with the right people in attendance. They don't sneak around other species' systems."

"*Sneak?*" The officer's choice of words made Mac snort. "I thought they were 'friendlies.' "

Townee gestured toward the door. "Everyone's friendly," she stated dryly, "until proved otherwise."

Word spread on board a ship even faster than on Base. *Due no doubt,* Mac decided, *to those on a ship not having to dry off and run up stairs first.* "Sinzi? That's what they said?"

"Would I make that up?" she said somewhat testily. "Can we get back to the business at hand, people?"

With the Grimnoii in their quarters and the Frow in theirs, Mac had hoped for some time with the seniormost members of Origins. *Gods knew, she had enough to tell them.* It didn't help that they were having difficulties concentrating, between the alarm itself and its cause. Therin kept puffing, the air setting his mouth tentacles in motion. The Cey, To'o and Da'a, poked fingers into their wrinkles as if searching for lost change, a nervous habit that made Mirabelle, sitting beside them, hold her hand beside her eyes to block the view. Busy writing his next novel, Wilson Kudla wouldn't leave the quarters he shared with his two acolytes, much to everyone's relief.

To make up for it, there was Fourteen, who shot up to pace around the table again, drawing yet another glare from Mudge.

"Would you please sit down?" she begged, rubbing her neck. "My head isn't built on a swivel."

"Irrelevant," he grumbled, but dropped back into his chair.

They'd taken over the dining area, Mac and Mirabelle taking turns looking under the tables. All was gleaming, including the kitchen. *A tidy ship.* "We need answers!" the Myg declared, his eyes peering from their fleshy lids.

"For once, I agree with Fourteen," Mudge announced, his frown apparently set in place and now directed at her. "If you don't have them, Norcoast, we should call one of the ship's officers for a briefing."

Townee would just love that, Mac thought. She rested her fingertips on the table and looked at each of her colleagues, seeing trouble or concern on every face she could read, imagining it there on the ones she couldn't. "We've two days to prep for Myriam," she reminded them. "Whatever else is going on, you're heading for the planet surface, to continue our work. Important work. It's unfortunate there have been some—distractions."

"Distractions?" Lyle burst out in a laugh. "There's a Sinzi ship where it shouldn't be, the Ro have dropped something into the Pacific, and we're losing you."

"While gaining *Se* Lasserbee," she said, her lips curving in a wicked grin. "And friends."

Lyle made a negating gesture. "You can't blame me. They told me you authorized them to tag along."

"Explain to me again why you didn't request proof of any kind." This from Mudge, who had yet to forgive the lead archaeologist for what he referred to as a logistical nightmare. Lyle turned a flaming pink and half rose in his seat.

"Let it go, Oversight," Mac ordered, sorry to have brought that up again. "Lyle. Lyle! Thank you," as the man sank back down, still scowling fiercely. *Academics and turf wars,* she sighed to herself. "The Sinzi are the captain's problem, whatever the Ro might have left is Earth's problem, and I'm hardly lost. For one thing, there could well be features on the derelict ships requiring your expertise, not just someone to read labels. If so, believe me, I'll be in touch. But before all that—I've a question for all of you. About Haven."

"We—ee are no—ot—" Therin shook from his head down and started over. "We are not experts on modern Dhryn, Mac."

"We're the other team, remember?" This from Lyle, obviously still smarting.

"You're here," she said. *Likely not making him feel any better.* "What was the state of the Dhryn world when the transect first connected them to the IU?"

By now, they'd learned her stranger questions had a purpose. They looked at one another, unease on the Human faces. Fourteen stirred first. "There are some numbers," he volunteered. "I will look at them, of course. But . . . Irrelevant? Important? Depends what you are looking for. Can you be more specific?"

"How close to extinction were they? How long—" Mac swallowed, "—how long would the Dhryn have lasted if the Sinzi probe hadn't arrived when it did? A rough estimate will do."

"A rough estimate?" Lyle looked flabbergasted. "Where's this coming from, Mac?"

"Perhaps from perception as much as reality."

Mac rose to her feet with all the others as they were joined by— her eyes widened and she heard Mirabelle gasp—not one, but two Sinzi.

Behind the tall aliens came Captain Gillis and Executive Officer Townee, both pointedly looking at Mac.

Not everything was her fault, she thought, rather resentful.

Please.

At first, Mac was struck by how much these Sinzi resembled Anchen. The same willowy form and grace, the same deceptively plain white gown, the same rapt attention to everything around them. Even Fourteen was silent.

Their differences gradually registered and she saw them as individuals. A lesser rise of shoulders, with more of an inward bend, made the one male. His fingers bore rings—*lamnas*—of red, their shimmer as he moved disturbingly like blood pouring from several unseen wounds. *Not that it likely looked that way to a Sinzi,* Mac scolded herself. His two great complex eyes were made up of five pairs. *Five minds.* He regarded her solemnly, offering a slight bow at her attention. "Dr. Connor. I am Ureif."

The second Sinzi bowed as well. Her rings were silver, set with flecks of green. Her eyes were two by two, and not quite aligned with one another. *Probably not the time to ask,* Mac decided, restraining her curiosity. "I am Fy," the female Sinzi said.

Mac hastily remembered her manners. "May I introduce—"

"You are known to us," Ureif said smoothly. "Greetings."

Now what? The Sinzi made the dining room seem cramped and overly—*Human,* sprang to Mac's mind, and she smiled involuntarily. "Are you from Anchen?" she asked.

Both raised their fingertips, forming a complex pattern, and gazed through them at Mac where she stood between chair and table.

"We participate," Fy said unhelpfully.

"Participate in what?" asked Gillis. "I'm still waiting for an explanation. Why are you on my ship?"

The Sinzi showed no sign of being offended. They lowered their long fingers, the sound of their rings an incongruous rain on water. "We participate in the promise," Ureif said, as if that should explain everything.

This couldn't be her fault, Mac told herself, despite the sinking feeling it most likely was. "So. You're here to—to help out," she said brightly. "How thoughtful."

Gillis and the rest looked perplexed. The Sinzi looked solemn.

The Frow who'd just clawed *se's* cautious way around the corner flung a membrane over *se's* face and moaned.

While the three massive Grimnoii who crowded in behind, forcing Townee and the captain to move or risk their toes, and sending the poor Frow tumbling out of sight with a squeal?

They gave a brisk salute and announced: "Sinzi-ra Myriam. Sinzi-ra *Annapolis Joy.* Your quarters for the voyage are prepared and ready."

There were times, Mac decided, *you just had to roll with it.*

She offered the beleaguered captain a cheery smile.

The *Annapolis Joy* did have a proper meeting room, Mac discovered sometime later. Like all meeting rooms of her experience, the victim was put at one end of a ridiculously large table, while all others took seats where they could stare at said victim. Although she'd never been able to prove it, she was also convinced such rooms tweaked environmental controls to create a zone of lower oxygen and temperature. *As for the sacrificial chair?* Mac thought grimly as she took her seat. *Its comfort wouldn't last.*

Mudge sank into the first seat to her right. "This is amazing, Norcoast," he whispered in a husky voice. "Simply amazing. What a privilege."

Mac glanced at the source of his ecstasy. The left wall of the meeting room was transparent, giving them a full view of the *Joy's* main bridge. Which could have been, so far as she could tell, any assortment of consoles, hovering 'screens, and intent operators from the Atrium.

Okay, there was the tree.

The tree, looking as embarrassed as foliage in that setting possibly could, stood guard beside the door to what Mac assumed was the captain's office. From here, she couldn't tell quite what kind it was. Healthy. Its upper branches had grown into the ceiling panels, leafy tips poking back out seemingly at random. Its irregular shape implied judicious trimming was all that kept it from blocking the door.

Was the tree a revelation about Gillis, she wondered, *or a legacy he's had to endure?* It might be helpful to know.

She could use any help possible. The captain hadn't been impressed to learn his visitors were now passengers. After the Sinzi left with the surprisingly alert Grimnoii, he'd scowled at her.

And all he'd said was, "Dr. Connor." *In that voice o'doom.*

Townee had jerked her head for Mac to accompany them as she'd walked out with Gillis.

Without being asked, Mudge and Fourteen had appointed themselves her escorts and tagged along. *Moral support or morbid curiosity.* A couple of crew had met them at the entry station, then all five had squeezed into a bolus for rapid transit here. The captain and his first officer had taken their own, apparently having another stop to make first.

Making their victim wait.

The Myg, uncharacteristically silent, now sat to Mac's left. He'd immediately busied himself with multiple imps, setting up palm-sized 'screens which he continued to study intently.

Out of habit, Mac felt her pocket for her own, making sure it was there. Fourteen hadn't changed his light-fingered ways. She'd asked him once why he continued to acquire the more portable belongings of others, especially since each would shortly turn up in a pile on whatever work surface he was using. *Where everyone learned to look first for missing socks.* The Myg had only smiled. The rest had grown resigned to him.

Except Mudge. Occasionally his outrage would overcome his better sense, and he'd dart in, sweep up the pile, and return the spoils to their rightful owners. Such recoveries held their unique risk, since the Myg, delighted by Mudge's fury, began hiding a noxious surprise in each pile and lurking nearby to watch. The results had been pretty entertaining, although she'd had to speak to Fourteen about permanent dyes.

Mac sighed. *Those were the days.*

"Sorry to keep you waiting." Captain Gillis and Townee entered with quick strides, as if to prove they'd hurried from wherever. Another Human came in behind the officers, not a member of the crew by his casual clothes and instant Mudge-like attention to the bridge.

Mac waited for them to take the opposite end of the table, to obtain maximum impact from glaring at her down its polished length, but the captain of the *Joy* sat beside Mudge instead. Townee took the seat beside Fourteen. Meanwhile, the stranger wandered to the transparent wall and stood gazing at the activity there, as if he wasn't part of the meeting at all.

That was an option? She wished she'd known.

"Our new passengers are making themselves at home," Captain Gillis began. He now appeared more preoccupied than upset. *Something had changed,* Mac thought. "We've received some clarification," the captain confirmed. "Ureif—more specifically, his Iode-self—is a transect ship engineer of note and will assist Dr. Norris," a nod to the man still gazing out at the bridge, "in determining what happened to the Dhryn derelicts once we reach Myriam. We're told this Sinzi has particular expertise with their technology."

"Ureif is the Sinzi-ra for Myriam," Mac guessed.

Townee was frowning, but not at her. "Fy assumes that duty. She'll be assessing the state of the gate and monitoring all traffic. Ureif is apparently Sinzi-ra over . . ." she waved her hands to encompass their surroundings ". . . the *Joy.*"

"Not," Gillis said rather glumly, "that anyone in the Ministry can tell us precisely what that means."

Fourteen looked up, his pudgy hand slicing through all his 'screens to close them at once. "The presence of a Sinzi contingent establishes your ship as a place of significance, Captain Gillis. Ureif will not assert any control or interfere with you—but all Sinzi will pay very close attention to what happens here."

"He's a spy?" Townee pressed her palms flat on the table as she surged to her feet. "Captain, we can't permit any passenger to report on internal ship business, let alone how we carry out our orders!"

"Those orders include full cooperation with the IU and the joint investigation into the Dhryn," Gillis said mildly, tapping the table with his forefinger. He appeared thoughtful.

Although she sat back down, from her scowl Mac doubted Townee was finished. *Sure enough.* "Captain. At least let me make adjustments to our security—"

"Idiot!" Fourteen interrupted. "The Sinzi have never taken such a bold step before. That should tell you how high the stakes have become. These are beings of immense *strobis*! Your security is irrelevant. Bah! You are irrelevant!"

"Not helping," Mac whispered at him.

"Dr. Connor?"

She swung her head back to the captain, feeling like a student caught peeking at a fellow's exam. "Yes?"

"But, Captain . . ."

"Enough." Said quietly, but Townee subsided without another word. "Dr. Connor," the captain continued, "clearly Rumnor and his people knew the Sinzi were coming."

"I didn't," she said warily, guessing where this was going.

"I could tell." Gillis smiled. "No one's that good an actor." His smile faded. "Yet this is the second time today I'm faced with an unexplained connection between you, Dr. Connor, and arguably the most important species within the IU. No offense, but what's going on? Aren't you just a translator?"

"So I'm told," Mac agreed, beginning to see the poor captain's dilemma. Like the Frow, he was doing his best to find and navigate a rational chain of command. *Shame she couldn't offer one.* "Though most of the time I'm a biologist. This is only my second trip away from Earth."

Norris turned to face her. "Your first was aboard the Dhryn freighter *Pasunah*."

Part of the meeting after all.

"Yes. I provided a description."

He had a long face, the sort that finished puberty with middle-aged jowls and, in some personalities, laugh lines. *Didn't appear to have any of those.* His thick black hair was mussed, as if he hadn't noticed it yet this morning. His clothes were creased in odd places, implying they'd spent too much time packed.

"I've read your account, Dr. Connor," Norris said in a dismissive voice. He took a seat one away from Townee, as if needing space—*or a stage,* Mac grumbled to herself. He leaned back and steepled his fingers. "We'll have to see if you can recall anything useful."

Mac's lips twisted. "Have you been on a Dhryn ship, Dr. Norris?"

"I'm thoroughly conversant with the technical specifications of every transect-capable—"

"That would be 'no,' " she observed, her tone pleasant.

Mudge gave her a stern *not helping* look.

Mac ignored it. She recognized Norris' type. Academia let them flower in high-ceilinged rooms, with coffee machines down the hall. They published like clockwork and judged those around them accordingly. Fieldwork? That was for unproven grad students, who somehow never made it on the final author list.

Last conference, hip-checked one into an ornamental pond, she remembered fondly. *Landed knees up, covered with mud and lily pads.*

With frog.

"Is the *Pasunah* one of the derelicts?" she asked, fervently hoping not.

"You'll have ample time to discuss Dhryn ships later," Captain Gillis interposed. "What can you tell me about the Sinzi on my ship?" His eyes locked on Mac.

She quickly lifted both hands to show they were empty.

Gillis nodded and shifted his attention. "Arslithissiangee Yip the Fourteenth?"

"You may call me Fourteen, good captain," the Myg replied expansively, the forks of his white tongue showing briefly, as if savoring the sound of his full name. "Of course I know a great deal more. Ureif? By reputation. Don't insult him. Fy? Appalling youth for a post of importance; her selves—transect engineer Faras and student Yt—at their first accommodation. She must possess unusual gifts and/or experience to be so trusted. But Ureif?" His half buried eyes assumed their sly look, the one Mac knew meant he was anticipating their reaction. "You have on board, Captain Gillis, the former Sinzi-ra of Haven—and the Dhryn."

There had to be one, she thought numbly. The Sinzi not only maintained the gates, they acted as interspecies' oil, easing potential frictions, soothing conflicts before they escalated.

But on Haven? "I was there," she blurted. "There was no mention of a Sinzi-ra." She wasn't sure why she felt betrayed.

"Idiot," Fourteen said fondly. "Once the Dhryn had established a colony in another system, they applied to the Sinzi to exclude alien traffic from their home. Other species do the same . . . some to protect their biology, some because they realize their boring homes are not worth visiting and they wish to avoid embarrassment when tourists want their funds returned. Idiots! Never advertise a 'remarkable dining experience' when you can't cook—"

"Fourteen," Mac growled.

His pale lips formed a charming pout. "Always so serious."

She'd strangle him later. "Please."

"The Dhryn stayed within their systems, with only minor trade outside their territory. One consulate was more than sufficient. The office of Haven's Sinzi-ra was moved to the Dhryn's first and ultimately largest colony. A consulate Ureif closed when it became clear the Dhryn had abandoned their worlds for good."

Mac's lips formed the name she couldn't bring herself to say. *Cryssin.*

Brymn's home.

"Seems you're in luck, Dr. Norris," Townee observed. "Ureif will have firsthand knowledge of your derelicts."

Ureif must have known him, Mac thought feverishly. Brymn had been one of the very few Dhryn who regularly traveled to alien worlds; his research had been widely published in Instella. *There would have been discussions, arrangements, briefings on alien—on Human—behavior.* Brochures.

She had a brief, dizzying insight into how being with her, the last one to see Brymn before his transformation, might feel to Ureif. Add to that traveling with her to the site of Brymn's death, in the presence of ships from Haven?

How could a Sinzi resist?

Mac allowed herself a moment of smug. *It wasn't* all *her fault.*

Captain Gillis drummed his fingers lightly on the table, as if encouraging them back on topic. *It seemed his habit.* "Fourteen. What do you know of Ureif's selves?"

"Ulor, Rencho, Eta, Iode, and Filt," Fourteen listed promptly. "Ulor is the transect engineer. Rencho, consulate administrator and a sculptor of some renown, among Sinzi at least. Eta is a mathematician—not up to my brilliance, of course, but formidable. Iode, the ship engineer, you know. Filt?" Mac wondered if she were the only one to catch the slight hesitation before the Myg concluded, "The one to watch."

"Why?"

"Because, Captain, you host none other than the newly elected Speaker for the IU Inner Council."

If Gillis had wanted to establish a chain of command, he had one now. *Judging by the green hue to his cheeks,* Mac thought, *its links were a little bigger than he'd anticipated.*

Fourteen was doing his utmost to appear bored. Not believing that for an instant, Mac took a cautious sniff. *Ah, someone else wasn't too calm about this "Filt" on board.*

"And you just happen to know all this," said Townee, trading glances with her captain. "How?"

"Irrelevant," Fourteen answered, folding his arms over his chest.

"Captain," she continued, ignoring the Myg, "we're having more than enough security issues. I strongly recommend we wait for confirmation from a more—official—source before we act on any of this."

Mudge, beside Mac, rubbed his nose, but stopped short of covering it. "Confirm, of course," he said, "but, much as it pains me, I must vouch for our colleague's ability to find the most obscure or private information in minutes. I wouldn't delay necessary actions because he's obnoxious."

"Charlie!" Fourteen crowed with laughter and bounced in his chair, arms waving. " 'Obnoxious!' That's wonderful. As for you—" he snapped his fingers at Townee, a recent accomplishment of which he was very proud, "—and your security?" *Snap.* "Irrelevant! Irrelevant! I had your ship's logs and records open within five minutes of boarding. Idiots." He sat back with a smile that could only be called blissful.

Really not helping, Mac winced.

She glanced at the *Joy's* most senior officers and saw the stunned, then furious expressions she expected. Even Norris looked alarmed.

"Don't worry. He's with me," she said, before the uproar could start. *Or armed guards arrive to cause an interstellar incident.*

Or Fourteen release any more anxiety into the room.

"I was hoping not to need this," she added, almost to herself.

Mac took a blue-and-green envelope, barred in gold, from her pocket. She flicked it along the polished table.

Captain Gillis stopped it with a slap of his hand. She watched him stare at the words crawling over the face of the envelope. *Her name.* Giving her a very strange look indeed, he showed the envelope to Townee before sliding it back.

Mac put it away, along with any hesitation. "Whatever else you've been told about us—about me, Captain—we aren't subject to Human, or Myg, or even Sinzi authority. All on my team have agreed to work for the Interspecies Union. While Fourteen should have asked before dipping into your files—" she said with a glare at the being in question, who grinned back, thoroughly unrepentant, "—he did nothing outside our mandate. Earthgov and the Ministry have pledged full, unquestioned support of IU efforts to resolve the crisis, have they not?" She waited for and received Gillis' slow nod. "Those would be our efforts, Captain, among others. As for what that means to you and your ship?"

Her lips found the smile that gave grad students fits before a test. *She hated meetings anyway.*

"Thanks for the lift," Mac told the commander of the Ministry's newest dreadnought. "We'll let you know what else we may need. Now—I'm sure we all have to get back to work." She stood.

"Wait! Who do you think you are?" Norris blustered, rising to his feet as well. "You can't give us orders!" He looked from face to face, as if seeking support. Finding none, he glared at Mac. "You're just the translator, damn it!"

"Actually," Mac replied calmly, "I'm just the salmon researcher. But I'll do my best. I expect the same from you."

Townee appeared to hide a smile behind her hand. *Norris hadn't made any friends,* Mac observed without surprise.

Captain Gillis stood and offered a slight bow. "My apologies for any confusion, Dr. Connor. You will, of course, have our full co-operation."

After a thorough check on her claims.

"Tell the Ministry I'm behaving." She flashed a grin. "They worry."

"I'm beginning to see why," said Townee.

With nods to collect Fourteen and Mudge, Mac turned and left the room.

"Well, Norcoast," Mudge allowed once the door whooshed closed behind them. "That was impressive."

Mac sighed and shook her head. "I think I'm going to be sick."

"Idiot."

"And this would be your fault," she accused the happy Myg. "I was hoping for a nice, quiet, oh-who-cares-about-Mac, inconspicuous trip, but no." She poked him in the muscle of his arm with one finger. "Someone had to show off."

"Inconspicuous," he informed her, "is boring."

Boring was so much simpler, Mac thought wistfully as they followed their crew escort back to the transit system.

As well as holds full of gear, Lyle had brought himself, the original twenty-six from Myriam who'd come with him to the Gathering—Human except the five Sthlynii and two Cey—and two Mygs, Fourteen and Unensela (plus the offspring). He'd been flummoxed into adding the three Frow and five Grimnoii.

Mudge had provided Sam Schrant.

But even if the Sinzi were her fault, Mac decided, hands on her hips and glaring, *she wasn't responsible for—this.*

"How long has it been going on?" she asked finally.

Doug Court shrugged. "Since I got here, at least. You'll have to ask them."

"Them" being the Grimnoii, currently on all fours. From what she could see, their backsides tending to vast, they had their faces pressed to the base of the closed door to their—or rather the Sinzi's—quarters. As many as could. Since only two and a half Grimnoii could successfully press-face at a time, there was a slow-motion struggle underway involving far too much heaving and collision of weapon-based apparel for Mac's peace of mind.

"Might not be the best time for a question," she ventured.

The individual closest to her toes, and farthest from the desired door crack, chose that moment to burrow his way past the others. His huge padded feet worked frantically against the smooth floor until finding purchase against someone else. He disappeared beneath his fellows.

There was a great deal of moaning and one heavy thud, but, to Mac's fascination, he surfaced at the door, promptly plunging his face to the crack.

While it was all well and good for aliens to be, well, alien, this was the only corridor through the section allotted the Origins Team. Mac traded waves with those stranded on the far side of the scrum, and considered the problem.

"It's always about sex," Unensela offered, coming up beside her. She was dressed in a lab coat, open to let the offspring clinging to her chest see what was going on. They stretched their long necks and echoed, "Sexsexsexsexsex!"

Someone behind Mac snickered.

"That's not how—" Mac thought she'd best forgo the lecture and finished with, "that's not what they're doing."

"Irrelevant! The most glorious female ever to breathe must be right, Mac!" This from Fourteen as he joined them, while admiring Unensela from head-to-toe and back again. *Apparently his present celibacy was of the look, don't touch, variety.* The female Myg preened. "This is not the act," he continued, "which is highly improbable even for large mammals and must hurt—but its essential precursor. Romance!"

The Grimnoii happened to groan loudly at that moment. Mac was reasonably sure she smelled fresh vomit.

Well, they should all be hungover.

"Ship's corridors have to be kept clear, folks." Court backed a step as if to let her know he wasn't volunteering more than the regulation.

"Romance," Mac repeated. "You're kidding."

With a last longing look at Unensela, who stuck out her forked tongue, Fourteen took Mac's arm and led her a short distance from the mass of struggling fur. "The Grimnoii admire the Sinzi," he whispered.

"You don't mean—" Mac gave the pulsing mass against the door a shocked look. "They aren't trying to—With the Sinzi!"

"Idiot. You read too many brochures. Get a mate. The Grimnoii are a passionate, physical species. They suffer from—I believe the Human equivalent is an inferiority complex. A little too much passion. A little too physical. They break things," Fourteen summed up neatly. "They have come to admire the Sinzi above all other species. Since part of a Grimnoii's education is to observe the social behavior of accomplished adults, many Grimnoii instead send their unbred males to observe Sinzi." Fourteen shrugged and gave Mac his sly look. "Like Humans at this stage, they tend to be hopeless romantics."

More thudding, accompanied by cheers from the Humans on the other side. *At least one Grimnoii had acquired fans.*

"How is this romantic?" She held up her hand. "Wait. Wrong question. What do they accomplish by wallowing at the door?"

"They demonstrate their admiration for the Sinzi by doing their utmost to capture their scent." Fourteen smiled widely. "Stimulating display, isn't it? I've only seen discreet sniffing of footprints— pretend to drop something, quick nose to pavement, that sort of thing. Until now. Well, I've heard of attempts to bribe staff for used laundry, but they say that about any species."

She wasn't going to ask who "they" *were.* "Thanks. I'll take it from here."

"Idiot! They're quite fixated. And large. Wait, Mac. What could you do?"

Ignoring the sputtering Myg, Mac searched for and found their chemist on this side of the Grimnoii clot, just leaving the dining area. "Henri! A word please?" she called, walking over to him.

"Yes, Mac?"

After she told him what she wanted, his eyes gleamed. "I'll be right back," he promised and took off at a near run.

Court noticed his departure and raised his eyebrows in question. Mac grinned and gestured to him to follow the chemist. "He'll need your help."

"Idiots." Fourteen had watched all this. "Help with what? They cannot be distracted by tricks. Trust me. I know."

Mac merely smiled and went back to where she could see the Grimnoii. She found a convenient bit of wall and leaned on it.

All five appeared near exhaustion, still except for the occasional deep shuddering breath or hopeful wriggle of a shoulder. Some of the bandoliers had snapped; others were snagged together. *Reminded her of the fallen Frow, unsure how to sort themselves out.*

The audience was getting bored. *Not to mention the air in the corridor was growing reminiscent of* The Feisty Weka's *bathroom.* The lucky ones on this side could go back to the workrooms or dining area. On the other, the choice was limited, since the Frow had the last two rooms to the left, the Mygs two of the five on the right.

Mac wondered what the Sinzi thought of the ruckus outside their quarters. Was it a familiar downside of working with Grimnoii—or did they put it down to something Human? Something to ask when she finally talked to them alone. *Among so much else.*

She hadn't asked the captain to send her message to Anchen. Considering she'd made one miscalculation with the Sinzi-ra already, it didn't seem the right time to stick her neck out. *Atta girl,* she praised herself. *Retroactive caution.*

"Got just what you ordered, Mac." Henri and Doug Court looked inordinately proud of themselves as they returned. Henri held up a pressurized vial, about the size of his little finger. "Ethyl mercaptan. Our little low-tech trick to locate surface openings in ruins."

Mac considered the Grimnoii, still locked in their slow struggle to stick their fleshy nostrils into the door crack and sniff Sinzi. "It won't hurt them?"

"I checked. Cleared for all species presently on board. No one's going to like it," Court's wide grin was wicked, "but it's safe. Should dissipate almost immediately, but I've advised environmental to mop up the air through here."

She held out her hand. Henri looked crestfallen and Mac chuckled. "Do you want them to blame you?"

"Point taken." He put the vial in her hand. "It's potent, even dilute. One pump." He and Court covered their noses and mouths with medmasks. Unensela, who'd been hovering beside Fourteen, squealed something Myg and dashed down the corridor, the offspring squealing an octave higher. Fourteen followed at a more dignified pace.

"I thought you said it was safe," Mac protested. "And where's mine?"

Henri laughed, the mask muffling the sound.

Chemists, she muttered to herself.

This little byplay hadn't gone unnoticed. By the time she turned to face the clump of aliens on the floor, vial outstretched and ready, the corridor had emptied of all save Mac, the five Grimnoii, and the two men with masks. *Who could have brought her one.*

"One pump."

"I heard you the first time," she snapped, and pressed. *Once.*

The spray might have been next to invisible, but its result was immediate. Mac gagged as the world became one giant rotten egg. The odor lodged in her sinuses and coated the inside of her mouth. She thrust the vial back at Henri and blinked at the Grimnoii.

Who were peacefully blinking back at her. All five had sat up, their large noses—a couple scraped and bleeding—busy twitching in her direction.

"I thought Humans couldn't cook," said one mournfully.

"Someone can," sighed the next, as all began rising to their feet, loosened pointy objects clanging to the floor around them. Where they didn't land with a *splot.* As bodies uncovered the floor, it became clear there were a large number of deposits in which to *splot.*

Too much romance. Mac kept breathing through her mouth, hoping the Sinzi stayed in their rooms a while longer.

"Dr. Connor's here." "Dr. Connor."

To Mac's horror, the Grimnoii started walking toward her, arms out, nostrils working.

Feet *splotting*.

To limit the spread of the mess, she stepped to meet them, wishing she had a hose.As she got closer, she could smell the cider on their breath. Among other things.

There was something unavoidably familiar about all this.

Students on a binge.

"It isn't even Saturday," she began in disgust.

"Dr. Connor! You're here!" Before she could evade him, Rumnor grabbed her in a pungent, sticky hug.

Argh. Mac pushed free. "Glad to see you, too. Now, I want you back in your quarters."

A chorus of doleful voices: "Have supper with us first." "Come." "Smell that?" "Yum!"

"No!" she ordered firmly. "Wait! Stay where you are!"

Too late. The romantic five, apparently now famished, turned as one and shuffled into the dining area, their feet leaving prints no one would want to sniff.

Those already in the dining room rushed out, complaining noisily as they encountered deposits.

Mac sighed and turned to Court. "We'll need another cleanup in there, please."

Court and Henri kept their masks on, although the rotten egg smell had faded to a hint of decay. Henri, mute, pointed at her torso.

She didn't need to look. The damp was soaking through in several spots. "I'll be right back," Mac said. "Keep an eye on them. Please?"

A day into the trip, and she already felt sorry for Captain Gillis' tidy ship.

When it was time for a strategic retreat at Base, Mac would take out a skim and drift for a while, listening to the restless ocean. At a field station, she'd hike just far enough along the river to be out of earshot, should anyone decide to call her, and wade in the shallows to turn over rocks. Even the consulate had offered her a terrace, with its view of the deep sound and possibility of whale.

Water made everything simpler.

On the *Annapolis Joy*? Grateful to see Unensela back at work, Mac fled to their shared quarters, left the offspring pouting on the beds, and locked herself in the shower.

Good enough. With the bonus of removing Grimnoii bits.

There was only one problem with water, Mac discovered after a few moments spent relaxing in the sprays.

It coaxed unbidden thoughts to the surface.

Without asking her first.

Nik's memories intruded first, laced with pain and guilt and remorse. She wasn't surprised by the tears running down her cheeks, merely unsure whose they were.

If he were here, now, she thought with a betraying rush of heat, *they could both forget.*

But what might be happening now—what might have already happened—dissolved any warm fantasy. Mac dug her fingers into her scalp harder than necessary. Could you trust a being capable of consuming a world's life?

She should have gone.

Then who would have cared for Emily? Mac put her head under the sprays, holding her breath until her heart pounded.

Emily was in harm's way again, as much as any of them.

She should have stayed.

Fighting free of the past, Mac found herself facing her current dilemma.

"We participate in the promise."

She shivered despite the steamy water. "Only one Sinzi promise I know of," Mac whispered through the drops hitting her face. *What had Anchen promised?* "To protect herself from the Ro. While I'm to come back, with something for her collection."

Harmless enough.

Which it obviously wasn't, not if it meant other Sinzi—particularly very important Sinzi like Ureif—were "participating."

"Bother."

As a mutual language, Instella was showing some flaws.
"Norcoast?"

So much for her retreat. "Idiot!" she grumbled in a low voice, hoping he'd think she was Unensela and leave. A chipper chorus of "Macmacmacmacmac" demolished that notion.

She pressed her forehead against the shower door. "Go away, Oversight."

"We need to talk."

She'd expected him to track her down eventually, if not this fast. Mac sighed to herself and shut off the water by way of surrender.

She pressed moisture from her hair with her hands, slicking it from her skin out of long habit, although the *Joy* offered both air dry and large fluffy towels. She went for the towel option, wrapping one around her torso and securing it before opening the door to step out.

Mudge was sitting on the bed closest to the door, offspring cautiously investigating his back and arms. They had their feet and bottoms planted well back, in case he proved a hazard to young Mygs. At the sight of her, they swung up their long necks, huge eyes glowing. "MacMacMac!" they sang, with the exception of the one who couldn't yet articulate. He warbled along.

"Your cheering section," Mudge observed.

Mac sat beside him, absently collecting offspring in her lap. They'd finally grasped that she didn't enjoy having them climb on her head. *Most of the time.*

"I didn't know the Sinzi were coming, Oversight."

"But they are here because of you." An offspring charitably fell against Mudge's leg and stayed there, looking up hopefully. He offered it his fingers to gum. Another noticed and hopped over to the now-interesting Human.

"Keep them off your ears," Mac advised. She sighed, glancing at his somber face. "I think so," she agreed. "Anchen made me a promise. I had no idea—"

"What did you say?" he interrupted, twisting to stare at her. The new arrival, enjoying the game, fastened claws in his shirt and burbled. His face turned ashen. "A 'promise?'"

Not the most reassuring reaction she could imagine. "It seemed like nothing at the time," Mac defended. "We were saying good-bye. I asked her to be more careful of the Ro. She asked me to be careful, too. I promised; she promised. I thought that was it."

He blew out his cheeks, then shook his head, cradling the offspring in one arm. "Norcoast, if I didn't know you better, I'd swear you did this sort of thing to age me."

"What did I do?" Mac objected. *This time at least.* "Besides," she continued testily, "I assumed Anchen wouldn't let me do anything—complicated. She knows me pretty well." She subsided, rubbing small heads.

Mudge shook his head again, but sat back. The shock on his face gradually eased into something more fretful than alarmed. "True. The Sinzi-ra—our Sinzi-ra—is a courteous being. She understands us better than most. Not surprising she'd follow your lead—attempt to reassure you with a Human expression. Yes. I'm sure you're right." Fretful disappeared beneath a hint of chagrin. "My apologies, Norcoast."

"Don't be too sure, Oversight," warned Mac reluctantly. "There wasn't much Human about it. Her selves promised. Each in turn. By name."

"Oh, no." The shock was back in full force again.

When he didn't say anything else, only sat staring at her while hugging baby Mygs, Mac snorted. "Please don't leave it at that. If you know something, tell me so I can worry too."

"I know that Sinzi promises—the real thing—are infamous, Norcoast," he said, each word measured and careful as if to ensure she appreciated how much trouble she was now in. "They bind the individuals within a body, but it doesn't end there. To start with, any Sinzi who wishes to participate in an existing promise can arrange to do so."

"I was afraid of that," she said. "Ureif and Fy." *Did that mean extra souvenirs?* Mac wondered inanely. "Wait. You said . . . 'to start with'?"

Mudge nodded, his eyes wide as an owl's. Mac was sure hers matched. Not to be outdone, the offspring responded to the seriousness of their tones by sitting perfectly still, huge limpid eyes on whomever spoke. "Other Sinzi who share a—" he seemed to search for a word, finally saying "—who share a desire to accomplish a certain thing will also participate in a promise made by the originator of that desire."

"Anchen said they didn't make promises lightly," Mac recalled. "Now I see why."

Mudge *harrumphed*. "Excuse me, Norcoast, but you don't. Not yet. The Sinzi don't talk about promises either, but the Imrya keep excellent records. A Sinzi engineer once promised an anxious Imrya merchant his ships would always pass safely through the new transect system, a promise, I must add, made just before maintaining that system became the focus of the entire Sinzi species." He frowned. "I should mention Imrya ships were also given remarkable safety features, now standard throughout the IU."

"There are any number of perfectly reasonable explanations for the evolution of useful technology, let alone the Sinzi's focus on the transects," Mac insisted. "One promise? You can't seriously believe that, Oversight. The Imrya embellish grocery lists, let alone their own history."

Mudge *harrumphed*, his eyes sober and considering on hers. "What I believe, Norcoast, is that this promise of yours means a great deal more to the Sinzi than you appreciate."

"Maybe," Mac conceded morosely. "Aliens," she complained, "should come with manuals. Stop that!" An offspring had discovered the water drops on her back and was licking them vigorously.

Mudge took the Myg and put it on his lap with the other two. "And you should be more careful."

"That's easy to say now—" Mac stiffened.

"Norcoast?" After their years of scrapping, she wasn't surprised he could read her face as easily as she read his. "What is it?"

"Why would she do it in the first place?"

"Anchen."

"Yes. Why make me a promise, knowing it would draw in other Sinzi?"

An offspring was making its way, very slowly, up Mudge's chest, eyes fixed on his left ear. He pulled it down. "Tell me the wording. Exactly."

Belatedly, Mac thought of possible listeners and pointed to her own ear.

Mudge shook his head, the motion followed intently by the off-spring. "Nothing we can do about it. What was the promise?"

"We each made one."

"No, you didn't," he said in that maddening *I'm always right* tone. "You exchanged them. Halves of a whole. The Imrya merchant promised to send ships through the transect, the Sinzi to keep those ships safe if he did. The words, Norcoast."

Mac shrugged. "I said to Anchen, 'If you promise to protect yourself from the Ro, I promise to bring you something for your collection.' She collects these tacky souvenirs," she explained, feeling foolish. "Anchen said, 'I so promise. We are bound.' She held her fingers like this." Mac mimicked the gesture, making rings in front of her eyes.

Always willing to participate in a new game, two offspring jumped for her hands. Mac hurriedly grabbed her towel.

Mudge didn't appear to notice. Putting aside his share of Mygs, he stood and began to pace, managing two and a half steps each way in the small room. Mac and the offspring sat on the bed, watching.

Finally, he stopped and gave a frustrated *harrumph*. "I've no idea what that could mean to other Sinzi, Norcoast. Are you sure you have it right? It's not like them to take such personal interest."

"Word for word," Mac confirmed. "Maybe we're reading too much into this."

"When the Sinzi-ra of the IU Gathering commits to viewing the Ro as a potential personal threat, despite there being no consensus from member species? And then the new Speaker to the IU Inner Council shows up and declares himself a participant?"

Put that way . . . Mac sighed and shifted. "I need to get dressed and talk to them. Straighten this out."

"Don't you dare!"

"I beg your pardon?"

Mudge did his impersonation of an immovable object. "You heard me, Norcoast," he said fiercely. "The last thing this situation needs is you trying to 'straighten it out.' You or any of us." He stressed the last word.

Not us? Mac tilted her head. "Then who—"

"Oh, there you are!" Unensela squeezed through the door

before it fully opened. "Idiots! Starting without me!" She promptly dropped her lab coat, revealing far too much anatomy.

Literally, Mac observed, her eyebrows rising.

The Myg, or someone, had painstakingly drawn Human-ish body details on her torso. In hot pink. "I've wondered about external genitalia," she coaxed, stepping closer. "Show me yours, Charlie!"

The offspring, obviously familiar with the warning signs, dove under the bed.

Mudge, already crimson, gasped something unintelligible and fled out the door. As if part of the trap, the discarded lab coat caught him on the way and he almost stumbled, recovering to stagger out into the corridor and disappear.

"Get dressed and apologize to him," Mac said quietly, in the voice she reserved for certain students. *The ones who either straightened up or were gone.*

"Oh, come on, Mac," Unensela pouted. "Did you see Charlie turn color?" She collected her coat and pulled it over her "Human" paint job, leaving the buttons undone. "Besides, what else were you two doing, hmmm? It's a long trip and Fourteen's being tedious. You Humans must manage some fun despite your physical shortcomings. We are sharing quarters." This with that sly look.

Mac's lips pulled back from her teeth.

"Not anymore."

In the end, it was Mac who wound up with her bags in the hall. She didn't mind in the least, having discovered while hunting a shoe that the offspring had been going under the beds for more than shelter.

Never room with a procreating alien, Mac decided, making it her next new rule.

"Mac! There you are," Lyle exclaimed, jogging toward her. "I've been looking all over for you."

"Next time check the shower like everyone else," she said. "What is it?"

He pulled out a sheet of mem-paper. "I've been working on

some projected needs, based on the data that came with the Sinzi. There've been some developments on Myriam we should take advantage of before—"

Mac held up her hand to slow him down. "What data, Lyle? Did the Sinzi come from Myriam?"

"This?" He flexed the sheet. "No. The data was received at the consulate—the relay from the regular Myriam courier. Always takes a while for them to remember we exist and could use the latest reports." The bitter words were habit; Kanaci seemed as pleased as she'd ever seen him. "Good luck for us the Sinzi were coming. The courier wouldn't have caught the *Joy* before the gate and Gillis refuses to lift that ridiculous transmission blackout."

The Sinzi had traveled to Earth first. She wasn't sure what it signified, but tucked away the fact. "Did they bring anything else?"

He snorted. "Your student's boots. Seems he'd left them— Mac?" as she wheeled around to rush down the corridor.

He'd left his boots at Base.

"Where are you going? Don't you want to see the list?"

"Lists go to Mudge," Mac reminded him over her shoulder.

"Okay. Just don't forget to check your messages."

She stopped in her tracks and looked around. Lyle held up his imp and waved it back and forth, grinning.

Mac reached into her pocket for hers. "We're connected to the ship?"

"Fourteen doesn't waste time. Whatever's come in on the com squeal from the Sinzi dart's been routed per recipient. Although he's probably peeked. You know what he's like."

Mac nodded absently. *A message from Emily.* "I'll go take a look," she told him, walking backward with each word, then abruptly stopped, at a loss where to go. Privacy was nonexistent now that everyone was awake and working.

"This way," Lyle offered gently, no longer grinning at her. *She looked that desperate, did she?* "The Grimnoii did us a favor by annoying the captain—not to mention Charles has been sending memos every half hour since boarding. They've opened the level above this one for us—more quarters. Should be ready any time." He picked up most of her bags. "You've got your own, Mac. I'll take you."

Oversight comes through again.

Relieved, she grabbed the rest of her things and followed Lyle.

She wasn't the only one on the move. The end of the corridor was stacked with belongings, if not people. "We're taking advantage of the new space to reorganize," he explained. "Charles' and my roommates are heading upstairs. And we've put the Grimnoii closest to the entry station. In case the crew has to clean. And—" Lyle opened the hatchlike door that had previously been sealed, revealing a vertical shaft and ladder, "—they don't like climbing. So far, there's been only one glitch in the new assignments."

A flicker of shadow in the shaft and a pointy hat protruded from the top of the doorway. "Ah, Dr. Connor!" *Se* Lasserbee said happily. "Isn't this wonderful?" *Se* turned and disappeared upward, the click of claw on metal echoing in the shaft. Not echoes, Mac realized, so much as companions. *They must all be in there.*

"That would be the glitch," she guessed.

"The Frow won't leave the shaft," Lyle admitted. "But there's a bright side. Watch." He tossed one of her bags into the shaft.

Before Mac could do more than reach out in a futile reflex, her bag reappeared in the firm grip of one of the lackeys, who swarmed up the ladder using three limbs. Another Frow appeared from below and hung in front of them, membranes fluttering as if eager.

She obliged, lobbing a bag into the shaft. The alien snatched it and was gone. Mac could swear *ne* chortled with glee. "Handy, that," she said.

"To a point. They'll bring everything back down again if you let them. And—they don't share well."

"Share what?"

Lyle gestured to the ladder itself.

"You've got to be—"

He shook his head. "Hold on tight. You'll be fine. It's only one level. Take one rung at a time."

The ladder ran through the center of the circular shaft, its rungs an easy step from the opening. Mac glanced down and swallowed hard. "It's more than one level," she told her companion, stepping back. *At least cliffs ended in rocks you could imagine hitting.* The shaft appeared to go on forever. For all she knew, it ran through the ship's interconnected arms.

"The rest are sealed to all but crew—unless there's an emergency." Lyle, apparently having no height or falling issues, leaned into the shaft. "If we need to evacuate, this is our closest exit. There's an evac drill scheduled before we enter the gate. Hey!"

A flurry of blue uniform and dark membrane swooped past, and Lyle dodged back into the corridor, the little hair on his head now mussed. There were whoops from inside the shaft. "They think it's a game," he said unnecessarily, running his hand over his head.

Did they? Mac wondered, but didn't bother to comment out loud. Far be it from her to disturb the archaeologist with things like territorial imperatives and the type of physical signals likely important to a species that clung to walls. *Sometimes, blissful ignorance went a long way in interspecies communication.*

Her own approach to the ladder was somewhat grim. Knowing she couldn't match the Frow in speed, she didn't bother letting them know she was coming by looking first. Instead, Mac stepped out and took hold. Firmly.

The *Joy* did have internal breezes, almost imperceptible but distinct. Mac quite liked them. But the wind that buffeted her seconds after she wrapped her arms around the ladder had nothing to do with any circulation system. All three Frow had plummeted by her, membranes expanded to move as much air as possible.

Cute.

Mac glanced up at the open door. *About twenty rungs,* she estimated.

The Frow had stopped some distance below, waiting, no doubt, for her to start climbing. That was what a Human would do.

Is that what a Frow leader would do?

Without stopping to consider the consequences if she were wrong, Mac closed her eyes and let go, spreading her arms out wide.

"Mac!" Lyle shouted as she began to tip backward and fall. "Mac!"

But even as her feet left the ladder, each of her arms was taken in a remarkably strong, but gentle clasp. Mac opened her eyes again to find herself rising, borne by the two lackeys. *Se* Lasserbee was climbing the ladder in front of her, *se's* limbs moving so quickly *se* was a blur.

Within a matter of heartbeats, they'd put her down on the next level up.

"Thank you," Mac said rather breathlessly to the aliens, now hanging upside down in a small cluster to look at her.

"Mac!"

"I'm fine, Lyle," she shouted, hearing him climbing below. One of the lackeys unfolded *ne's* neck ridges to look down and she added quickly, "He's with me."

The Frow subsided, although she thought *ne* appeared disappointed.

Maybe not a game, but certainly entertainment, she judged, and smiled to herself. "I hope you aren't tired," she told them, picking up her bags. "There's more luggage to come up."

"Your quarters are last on the right," Lyle said, stepping out beside her after a wary look at the Frow overhead. He wisely didn't ask any questions, but his eyes wondered at her.

Fair enough, Mac thought. *She wondered, too.*

"I'll go settle in," she said, impatient to check her messages. "I'll be fine," this when Lyle looked inclined to accompany her. "See you shortly."

The corridor was much shorter than the one below, with only four doors per side. Most were open, with crew from the *Joy* busy making beds. Mac assumed they used the sealed bulkhead at the corridor's end. She had no problem with being isolated from the rest of the ship. Not if it gave her privacy.

Her room was ready, almost identical to the one she'd briefly shared with the Mygs, but with a worktable instead of the second bed.

Mac dropped her luggage on the floor, closed the door behind her, and sat down at the table. She pulled out her imp, turning it around in her hands as she waited for her heart to calm down.

She'd made the right choice with the Frow. *A fifty/fifty shot.*

Now to find out if she'd made the right choice for Emily.

Taking a deep breath, Mac activated her imp and searched for messages. *There.* She touched the 'screen to open the first and found herself staring at her friend, as though they sat across from one another.

Then Emily spoke.

- CONTACT -

"SO THIS IS some Ministry *cabrón's* idea of keeping us in touch?" Dark eyes flashing, Emily made a rude gesture. "I hope they do better when you get to Myriam, Mac. This is ridiculous."

She ran a finger along her trim bangs. "*Ai.* All they'll give me right now. I'd better use it. But you know I hate making recordings. If I played this back, I'd erase it all. Then you'd be mad, wouldn't you? The things I do for friendship . . .

"First. Status check." She *tsked* with her tongue against her teeth, her tone growing businesslike. "I've rebuilt my Tracer. Bit of a trick. Whoever took it apart wasn't careful and I'm guessing you tried to put it back together. *Tsk.* But . . . gave me a chance to tweak things, make some improvements I'd come up with at the consulate, so no heads need roll." A flash of that wicked smile, then serious again. "Haven't tested it. Kammie's working with a few of the others to produce a better sample for the 'bots to sniff. We need to know what I'm looking for, right, Mac? Now that it isn't you."

One long finger began to tap.

"I'm giving your young friend a try. He knows his way around a deck, I'll grant you. We're installing the Tracer on one of the harvester levs this afternoon and, I admit, he's had some good ideas about that. Otherwise, he's a thorough pain and utterly, utterly boring. You did that on purpose, didn't you?" This without rancor. "I supposed I asked for it."

The finger kept tapping, a quiet, regular percussion.

Emily's lips stretched in a wide grin. "Zimmerman, though? He's been fun. Turns out to be quite the dancer. You know what they say about big feet—or maybe you don't. Poor Mac."

Tap tap.

"I hate making these. You're going to owe me, Dr. Mackenzie Connor. Where was I?" She nodded. "They're a third done with the sweep of the inlet floor—not that any of us believe we'll find anything that easily, but we have to start somewhere. The harvs and preds have a betting pool on the side. Who'll be the first to find it—whatever 'it' is. You'd think we were looking for sunken treasure. I'm the odds-on favorite, by the way."

Tap tap.

"Treasure." Emily's pupils dilated. "We know better, you and I. If we're exceptionally lucky, it'll be something we can destroy. They're outfitting the harvester with the latest and deadliest. If we aren't that lucky? Well, at least you're off-world." With a mercurial shift in mood, she laughed. "There's a switch, Mac. You gallivanting, me stuck here. Hope you're enjoying yourself. Met anyone interesting? Oh, that's right, you have. I don't have to worry about your sex life, or lack of, anymore. Whew. That's a load off my mind."

Tap tap.

"Otherwise, not much new. I haven't had time to do more than select a group to collate the latest info on the Survivors. 'Sephe's helped there—she's picked out the best statisticians among them. I'd like to bring in someone from Sencor, but that's a no. They're keeping the lid on pretty tight. I can't get onshore for lunch, let alone invite company." A pause. "That's okay. We're going to ship out as soon as the hookups are finalized. I've an idea or two for our search grid. It's a big ocean. I told you. *They* knew where to hide something, Mac. That can't be good for us."

The tapping stopped.

Emily lowered her head, showing her cap of shiny black hair, streaked with white, then looked up, a faint smile toying with her lips. "Don't worry so much. I'm fine. Recovery, scans, etcetera etcetera, better than expected, blah blah. That's what having a goal does, Mac. It keeps you moving in the right direction." Her face hardened. "You remember that, next time you look a Dhryn in the eyes.

" 'Bye for now. Stay tuned for your next exciting message from home. Whenever they let me send one. I'll expect some juicy details from you. *Adios.*"

"Hello, Dr. Connor." Hands behind his back, Case was standing on a walkway or deck, the horizon behind him delineated by the rise and fall of ocean swells. *Afternoon.* "They told me you wanted updates on everything here. From me that means news about Dr. Mamani." His cheeks reddened. "First, I want you to know

I'm not going to apologize. When you get back, if you don't want to talk to me, that's fine. But you might not be back. So I did—well, what I had to do."

He coughed and moved his face away from the sun, his cheekbones growing shadows. It added years. "Dr. Mamani. Emily. You were right, Mac. She's not like anyone else. She's—" a frowning pause, "—she's like the ocean. Shows her surface to anyone. Calm one minute; stormy the next. But her depths? You'll only know those before you drown. Trust me. I'll stay clear. She scares me almost as much as she scares herself.

"Dunno if that made sense to you." A self-conscious shrug. "But I've seen the faces of people who want that one big catch so badly they'll gamble their lives— put out despite storm warnings. Emily has that look.

"Mind you," he continued, "she could be the one to do it. I doubt she's slept since you left and it doesn't show. I don't know where she gets her energy, but the rest of us catch naps when she's not looking.

"Anyway. I'll do what I can to help her. We'll put to sea tomorrow," this with transparent longing.

"You take care of yourself, Mac."

- 12 -

MESSAGES AND MEMORIES

MAC'S FINGERS STROKED through her 'screen, opening and then closing the remaining messages. Most were brief. A hello from Tie. A comment on the weather from John. A promise for more with the next courier from Kammie. The longest was a text list of indefinitely postponed projects, prepared by Marty Svehla.

Maybe it made him feel better, to share his loss.

She didn't bother reading it, past the venting stage herself.

Case's message was better than she'd hoped. She'd expected him to be perceptive, but to see Emily so clearly and still stay? "I did well by you, Em," Mac said out loud.

Emily's message?

With a sense of dread, Mac replayed it, muting the sound and enlarging the section of image that included Emily's fingertip on the desk. She slowed the replay and counted the rapid taps, recording each with the movement of her own finger within another field of the workscreen. When done, she closed the message, and brought up the results.

"Oh, Em," she whispered. "No."

Throughout her message, Emily had tapped eleven times, paused one beat, then tapped eleven times again. Over and over.

With the precision of a machine.

They'd tried—*all of them*—to find some significance to the number. Emily had been unaware. When finally shown recordings of her obsessive counting, she'd been disturbed but could offer no explanation. She'd listened with disbelief and considerable embarrassment to her own quiet complaints about the inadequate reconstruction of her fingers. Mac had stopped mentioning any occurrences. There seemed no point in upsetting her friend.

Yet the number persisted, as if from a wound that wept instead of healing.

Alluring as the idea of real privacy was, Mac didn't plan to waste time sitting in her new quarters. She had too much to do, starting with the Sinzi.

Too much to do, but she caught herself hesitating as she made to leave. Her lips curled to one side. "Why not?" she said, and dug into her pocket for what she'd carried since that night in the Yukon.

The little carving fit along the palm of her hand, its tail flexed to give the body a line of muscular tension. The pale blue of her pseudoskin might have been the waters of a river, the salmon surging upstream.

Her first gift, and he'd returned it. *Seemed her luck with men hadn't improved.*

There was a transparent shelf over the narrow desk, the desk itself beside the bed. Mac placed the carving so she would see it even when lying down.

He'd returned it because he needed her help, and knew she'd give it.

She'd never had patience for romance. *Her fault,* she admitted. But what was the point in not speaking your mind? Not to mention she failed to find pleasure taking forever over an elegant candlelit meal when there was data waiting.

To Emily's outspoken disgust, Mac usually found a way back to her data. Without her date.

Her eyes rested on the little carving. She pressed her lips to the rings on her finger.

Candles were irrelevant.

Promising herself a locked door and her own bed, Mac went in search of aliens.

The first she encountered was the Cey, Da'a, dragging a roll of fabric through the door nearest the shaft. "Hello, Mac," he greeted, both arms around the roll. She knew it was used as part of the Cey's mode of worship, although not how. The fabric was intricately woven and faintly aromatic, with more than enough in the roll to make a full-sized tent for the two Cey who'd come with Lyle. The other pair had stayed on Myriam, joining a Cey expedition. *Had enough of Humans or not invited by the IU to the Gathering?* she wondered, then thought it just as likely they'd simply preferred to stay with their work.

"Let me help with that," offered Mac.

As well she did, for the heavy roll was slightly longer than the room and it took both of them to finally wedge the thing inside so the door would close.

"Thank you," Da'a said when they were done. "My *au'us* fit in the other room. I didn't anticipate this problem."

"Why did you move?"

Impossible to read a face made of heavy, overlapping wrinkles, but Mac had come to some conclusions regarding a Cey's body language, when she had context. A slight hunch of the shoulders during a discussion signified agreement; the same posture while working alone, concentration. A gentle nodding while another spoke was the Cey equivalent of wild impatience; nodding while speaking himself, emphasis. And the ball of a thumb rolled just so against the other palm?

Amusement, at any time.

Although exactly what Cey found funny? She was still working on that.

"I changed rooms, Mac, because I was sharing with Arslithissiangee Yip the Fourteenth."

Aha. "Gotcha," Mac grinned widely. "I've heard Fourteen snore. He shook the rafters of our cottage."

"Snore?"

She hesitated. *Confusion about the word or the act itself?* "My mistake, Da'a," she said, which it likely was. *If anyone should know not to jump to assumptions . . .*

"Perhaps, Mac." His shoulders hunched agreeably. "Unless we both refer to our colleague's lovelorn poetry. Another stanza about

Unensela's tongue, and I might have run shouting into the hallway like some well-nipped *sralic*."

"Poetry."

"So he claimed. I myself judged it painful. The object of his obsession might disagree. I urged him to go recite to her, but he insisted on inflicting his verse on me. I spoke to Charles about new quarters, and took the first available."

Mac grinned. "You've made a wise choice, Da'a." She had to ask. "How did you find climbing the ladder?"

"I had no difficulties. But I believe Charles will be sending the Frow a very long and detailed memo on the subject."

She winced. "He tried to come up?"

Da'a hunched his shoulders. "Tried would be the operative word. He used uncharacteristic language. Loudly. It did not convince the Frow."

Mudge was going to blame her *for this.*

"Why would I blame you, Oversight?" Mudge asked mildly.

Too mildly. Mac waited for the rest.

The Frow had snatched her from the ladder and carried her down faster than falling, then skittered out of sight before she could so much as open her mouth to chastise them. *They probably knew full well they were in trouble.* Lyle had only shaken his head and pointed down the corridor when she asked where Mudge might be.

She'd gone straight to his quarters—or rather his sanctum. Since losing his roommate, he'd managed to create a full office, complete with an intimidating desk facing the door, and chairs for supplicants. His bed was now a pull-down attached to the back wall. There were no personal belongings in sight. *Like Emily, he armored himself with his space.*

A *harrumph* as Mudge settled deeper into his chair, having greeted her at the door as if she was late for one of their 'discussions' about the Trust. "Just because you dragged me into this in the first place, made me spend a less-than-memorable night in a Yukon cabin, and have since failed to adequately explain even one of the events that have transpired since we left the consulate? Why would I blame you because the Frow tried to kill me?"

Mac raised a brow. "Don't exaggerate, Oversight."

He used his finger to describe a drop, then flattened his palm with a thud on the table. "Two levels before they deigned to stop my fall. Two! I could have died, Norcoast."

"You know perfectly well they were just—" Mac hesitated. *Fooling around?* wasn't quite the term for it. *Setting you beneath them?*

"Even when I insisted I was to meet with you, they refused to let me climb one rung. The only good to come of it all was that Da'a was able to use the ladder without torment. I have," he pronounced, "formally expressed my displeasure to the Frow representative."

Who'd been one of the beings tossing Mudge around. Mac frowned, afraid she understood too well why Mudge hadn't been allowed up. The Frow had established their chain of command, putting her at the top. It wasn't much of a stretch to imagine they'd given themselves a similar promotion by appointing themselves in charge of access to her.

Alien hierarchies were as abundantly awkward as Human ones.

"*Se* Lasserbee likes forms and protocols," she said at last, planning to have a private chat with the Frow concerning *her* chain of command. "As for explanations?" Mac leaned her chair back and stared at the ceiling, going through the list herself. The promise? The Sinzi on the ship? Mudge knew more than she did. What was happening with the Vessel and Nik? He knew as much.

Hollans?

One day, she cringed. *Maybe.*

"I wish I had some, Oversight," she said finally. "Back on Earth I could hunt my own answers. At least make the motions and feel useful. Right now? All I can do is worry about what might be happening."

"Which is out of our control, Norcoast." A pause. Then, quietly, "It doesn't help. Being here, on this ship."

Mac dropped her gaze to his too-knowing one. "It doesn't," she gave him, her hand, *that hand,* curled in her lap. "But we've enough real demons to keep us busy. What happened here . . . there was never ill will, Oversight. I was—" a rueful smile twitched her lips, "—just a fish out of water."

He didn't look convinced.

Time to change the subject, she decided. "Now, Oversight, what's so important you risked death by Frow to tell me yourself?"

Mudge sat straight, his face assuming a grimmer cast. "I believe there's been a discovery in Castle Inlet."

She tensed. "There was nothing in my messages." Then she remembered, like a bad dream, how Nikolai Trojanowski and the Ministry had produced vids purportedly from her to cover her absence from Earth—vids so realistic they'd fooled her family and friends. "They wouldn't dare," she snapped, ready to march straight to the bridge and demand to speak to Hollans himself.

"What, fake communiqués?" Mudge shook his head. "I see no point—we're supposed to work with Base on any data. But your people aren't the only ones looking, Norcoast, are they?"

The whoosh of giant levs overhead, the steady stream of equipment and personnel heading to Pod Two. "The Ministry?" she hazarded. "What makes you think they've found something? Not that they'd rush to tell us." *Perhaps for good reason,* she thought, remembering Nik's caution to Hollans.

"There are other channels," Mudge announced, a hint of smugness on his face. "I've maintained contact with staff at the consulate, of course, to ensure our group will receive full support on Myriam. To save time, I requested an updated inventory of materials of interest—on hand and in transit. Which I've received." He held up his imp. "It makes for informative reading, Norcoast."

Mac touched finger to forehead in salute. "I've always said you were a dangerous man, Oversight. Go on."

He didn't blush. *That serious,* she thought uneasily. "The consulate received an urgent request for equipment to be delivered to Castle Inlet. Specifically, Sinzi devices to inhibit the formation of a no-space transect, as well as their most advanced stasis chamber."

Mac leaned forward, her breath catching in her throat. For a wild moment, she imagined some pitched battle along the walkways of Base, with an intrepid Tie bringing down aliens with his trusty antique flare guns. Then she shuddered, knowing any such confrontation would be in the dark, with an enemy heard, not seen.

And involve blood.

"Do you think they've found the Ro?" she asked Mudge, unable to keep a tremor from her voice.

"The Ro seem to work through others wherever possible," he said soberly. "Dr. Mamani said they'd swept 'those who walked for them' into the ocean, along with whatever they were hiding there. My guess would be they've found one or more of those bodies. Or what's left of them. It's been months, Norcoast. You know as well as I do how efficient ocean scavengers can be."

The normalcy of crabs and bacteria steadied her nerves. "They may not be a factor," she pondered aloud. "The 'walkers' were swept down in the landslide." Sing-li had said they'd found the bodies of their agents within mud and stone. *The cold comfort of recovery beacons.* "They could have been buried." Mac's heart began to beat faster. *A look at what the Ro really were—or as close to it as possible?*

His face mirrored her own growing excitement. "And be virtually intact. If that's so—we might have gained our first advantage, Norcoast."

"I must contact Anchen. Hollans. Both of them." She rose to her feet. "I have to see the scans—get samples sent here."

He held up one hand. "Nothing can happen right away, Norcoast. The captain's right to maintain a com ban. It's just a day and a half till we meet the courier at the gate. You'll have to wait."

"Pointless waste of time," Mac muttered, but sank back down.

Mudge gave her his stern look. *The one where he planned to refuse a perfectly reasonable request on grounds that would make no sense to her.* "The point, Norcoast, would be to prevent anyone in this system confirming your presence on board until we've left for Myriam."

"Use codes. Do secret stuff." She gestured wildly. "It can't be that hard." *She wasn't that important.*

She didn't want to be.

"The risk isn't justified, not to satisfy our curiosity."

Mac scowled. "I don't see who would care."

"Do you want me to name all the species connected by the Naralax, or stop with the Ro?"

She pressed her lips together and glared at him as if this were all his fault.

Mudge *harrumphed*. "Whatever's going on, Norcoast," he mollified, "we'll learn more when we get the next batch of messages. Old-fashioned, but secure."

"I don't like waiting in the dark."

"Come now. You're capable of appalling patience, Norcoast. Use it."

Mac snorted. "Is that supposed to be a compliment?"

Mudge sat back, fingers laced together, and gazed at her.

She wasn't the only one, Mac realized with familiar frustration. "A day and a half." She made a face. "Fine. I'll start preparing my messages. Townee's going to show me their procedure for secure mail."

"Their procedures?" Mudge grimaced back at her. "That wretched Fourteen already broke those. Much as it pains me, Norcoast," he heaved a sigh in demonstration, "we'd better give everything private to him for encoding. I can't imagine anything more secure. Except for those." He nodded to her rings.

Mac shifted her hand below the table, then felt her cheeks warm. *Could she be more obvious?* "You know about *lamnas*?"

"*Lamnas*," he repeated, as if, like Hollans, he fixed a new word in memory. "I didn't know, Norcoast. But I observe. You never wear jewelry, yet you leave the consulate wearing a ring identical to those on Anchen's fingers. It could be a token or gift. But before we leave Earth orbit, one ring has become two. Am I right to suppose you anticipate a third when we meet the courier?"

Only if Nik survived to send it.

Something of her despair must have shown, because Mudge grew very still. "These *lamnas* aren't from Anchen."

Mac gave the tiniest shake of her head.

"How dare he—?" The words were fierce and low. "It's unconscionable. Is there anyone who isn't using you in some way, Norcoast?"

"There's you, Oversight," she replied unsteadily.

"Totally unacceptable," he blustered. "Do you hear me? Unacceptable!"

"I'm not arguing," Mac said, comforted by his honest outrage. "But I'd rather know—be used—if that's what it will take to resolve all this and make sure everyone's safe."

Harrumph. "And at that time, I plan to tell a certain someone exactly what I think."

She wished Nik luck. "You do that."

Mudge *harrumphed* again, angrily, but calmed. "I suppose we must be satisfied that things are underway, Norcoast. The Dhryn ships, our going to Myriam, whatever the Ministry's uncovered . . . the other ship . . ."

That was what they called it between themselves, the "other ship," to be sure they weren't the ones to inadvertently discuss Nik's so-fragile mission.

If there was a ship the Ro would want to find, Mac knew beyond doubt, *it would be the one carrying the Vessel home to his Progenitor.*

Mac and Mudge spent the better part of an hour talking around what was to come. Neither could be sure what to expect in Myriam System, so they made contingency plans to the best of their ability. He didn't argue when she said he should go to the planet with the archaeologists; she didn't argue when he told her Fourteen should stay on the *Joy* with her. It was a measure, she thought, of how seriously Mudge took their present difficulties in communication that he wanted her to have the one being able—and fiendishly delighted—to circumvent ship's security.

When she left his quarters, she felt if not in control, at least prepared.

A feeling that lasted as long as it took for Mac to take two steps toward the dining room.

"Dr. Connor. Why haven't you reported to the simulation lab?"

Few people became this *annoying on second acquaintance,* she decided, wheeling to confront Norris.

"What are you talking about?"

He'd added a hovering 'screen to his attire, set to hang above his line of sight, so his eyes constantly flicked up to it.

Mac, considerably below, waited for him to look back down at her, mentally giving him a count of three.

At two, Norris returned his attention to her. *Disappointing.* "I sent you notification. Surely you read your mail."

"Not if I can help it," Mac said truthfully. "Is this something that can wait, Dr. Norris? I'm about to check on my team."

"Team?" His eyes lifted to the 'screen, as if seeking confirmation. "You've been reassigned to me. You have no team, Dr. Connor."

Before Mac could settle on what she would actually say in response to this, *it being early in their relationship for her to kick his skinny shin,* they were interrupted by the arrival of Sam and his new colleagues, To'o and Kirby.

"Mac! There you are. You have to come and see this."

She threw Norris a triumphant look. He didn't appear impressed. "Dr. Connor is busy," he said.

Mac wasn't sure which reaction was more telling: the sudden silence, or the way even the Cey's eyes opened wide as all three climatologists stared first at Norris, then her.

Too easy, she decided regretfully.

"Dr. Norris, why don't you grab a coffee and we'll continue this later," she advised, keeping it civil, then walked past them all, heading to the work area.

First to move wins.

But she'd underestimated Norris' ability to miss a cue. "Dr. Connor," he exclaimed. "Our time on the ship's simulator is not limitless. And Dr. Cayhill is waiting."

Mac's hand twitched. Despite her instinct to keep on walking, preferably until the entire bulk of the *Joy* was between them, she stopped and turned around. "What could Cayhill possibly have to do with some simulation you want to show me?"

Norris' show of surprise was a little too studied. "Aren't you aware of safety requirements when a subject is immersed? A physician must be present. Dr. Cayhill, being familiar with your physiology, kindly volunteered."

Familiar with what's left of my arm, she nearly said aloud, but knew too well how someone of Norris' type would respond. Instead, she gave him a withering glance before saying to the now-worried climatologists. "Oversight's in his quarters. Fourteen's somewhere in the work area. I want them both here, please. Now."

They hurried off, glancing back at her with questions in their eyes. Mac crossed her arms and stared up at Norris. "The *Pa-sunah*," she said.

"A working facsimile, yes." He looked insufferably pleased. "I knew this class of ship carried a complete suite of training sims."

"Is this really necessary?"

"It wouldn't be if your 'firsthand' account had been at all adequate."

She felt her right leg tense and deliberately eased her posture.

"Mac?"

"Norcoast?"

From different directions—*and different-shaped windpipes*—came identical tones of disapproval.

"They'll be coming, too," Mac informed Norris.

Dr. Gordon Cayhill was a middle-aged man of average height, average mass, and—in Mac's estimation—above-average tenacity when it came to what he viewed as the most appropriate medical treatment for his patients. No doubt he'd performed miracles for those in his charge.

The only problem? He'd wanted to perform one for her as well. She'd said no. Loudly. Repeatedly. And with all the apparent impact of water rushing over a barnacle glued to stone. The only plus had been to leave the ship knowing they'd never have to deal with one another again.

Funny how things worked.

She didn't bother to smile. "Dr. Cayhill."

"Dr. Connor." He didn't smile either.

"Charles Mudge III," that worthy introduced himself, pressing forward into what was patently a conversation going no further without help. "I presume you are qualified to supervise such a procedure?" His voice implied anything but.

Now Mac almost smiled.

Fourteen wasn't to be left out. "Irrelevant. We presume nothing." He drew out an imp and set a 'screen up between them, muttering under his breath as he worked. Then, "Ah! Oh. You are."

He closed the screen and gave Mac a shrug. "At least he hasn't let anyone die."

"There," Norris pronounced. "Can we get on with this?"

No? Mac swallowed, aware she'd gone as far as she could in terms of protest. More and Norris was capable of tossing Fourteen and Mudge from the room. *She didn't want to be alone here.*

Norris, with the inevitable escort of *Joy* crew, had brought them to this distant part of the ship. It was an area without the warm colors and natural light tones seen elsewhere; the corridors were lower, cramped, their walls curved in as if reinforced. Mac remembered it vaguely—she must have been carried through here when brought on board.

Screaming.

She made herself focus. The simulator lab was more of the same, function and form. The presence of life was mocked by sullen gauges and flickering displays. The center was taken up by a long, low box.

Great, Mac thought, licking dry lips. *It would have to look like a coffin.*

"Do you understand the procedure, Dr. Connor?" Cayhill asked.

She made herself walk to the box. "Incoming feeds supply the simulated environment I'm to experience. The firing of my nerves to move muscle will be translated into that environment seeming to move past me." She shrugged. "Everyone's played games on a sim."

"This is far beyond anything you've seen within a game platform," Cayhill stated dryly, opening the lid. Mac stared down into what appeared to be a nest of dark wire and somehow managed not to leap back. "We use a combination of sub-teach and other neural methodologies to induce a totally convincing experience. Your own memories will fill in any blanks. You'll believe you are again inside the Dhryn ship, Dr. Connor."

Wonderful.

She'd briefly explained what Norris wanted to Mudge and Fourteen on the way here. Neither had offered an opinion. *Not out loud.* She could read their disapproval; she knew they understood why she wanted them there. Now Mudge stepped up, his shoulders squared. "Given you will shortly have three Dhryn ships at your disposal to examine, Dr. Norris, I fail to see how this is anything but an imposition and a waste of Dr. Connor's valuable time."

"And who are you again?" Norris demanded, sneering at Mudge.

"Idiot!" bristled Fourteen. "To begin, he is someone immensely more important than you, and obviously of greater intelligence. Bah. This entire process is irrelevant. You are irrelevant!"

Mudge looked astonished; Mac hid a smile. Dr. Cayhill showed no expression whatsoever. "It's my understanding the captain requested this process, Dr. Connor," he said. "I'm aware you do not always follow regulations or recommended procedures. However in this instance I must warn you failure to oblige this request will not be taken—"

"Shut up, Cayhill," Mac suggested, turning back to the coffin. "I'm here." She poked at a wire. "Let's get this over with, shall we?"

"As you wish." He indicated one of the doors lining the near wall. "You'll find a jumpsuit through there. It contains the necessary receivers and contacts. Put it on while I get ready."

She nodded and took a few steps, only to be intercepted by Mudge. "Norcoast," he whispered, "are you sure about this?"

Fourteen was with him. "Idiot." His hands hovered near his face, as if he wanted to cover his eyes. "This procedure is intrusive. It could be dangerous. You should refuse."

Not helping, Mac thought, but reached out to touch both of them. "That's why you two are here," she said, not in a whisper. *Let Norris and Cayhill know she had brought not reinforcements but witnesses.*

Mudge understood—or else he read her determination in her face—because he stood aside and let her go.

Reality was a dream.

Mac ran her finger around the viewport, skin catching on the tiny burr of metal she'd found there once before. Her breath again fogged over stars and Earth and Moon. The air entering her nostrils was familiar, metal-tainted and dry.

The *Pasunah*.

Much as she hated to admit it, Cayhill had been right in this much. It wasn't like any vid game she'd tried.

The jumpsuit had clung to her skin, from fingertip to toe, the inside of the fabric prickly and uncomfortable, like shorts worn too long at a beach. That awareness had vanished the instant she'd lain in the coffin, swamped by overwhelming sensations of pressure and cold. She'd muttered something about improper calibration, only to have the words trapped as a mask was placed on her face. A moment of suffocation and utter darkness, then . . .

. . . she'd been here, in her quarters on the Dhryn freighter.

"Impressive."

Mac would have been more impressed if Cayhill had told her how to get out of this. But no, he'd insisted her vitals would be monitored and that waking her—*not that she felt asleep*—would be done automatically should it be necessary.

"Hopefully in time for lunch," she grumbled.

Her quarters looked exactly as they had when she'd first seen them. Walls met at angles closer to seventy degrees than ninety, well suited to the slant of an adult Dhryn's body. The middle of the large room was filled with an assortment of Human furniture. She remembered breaking much of it.

Funny how she now saw it intact.

"Guilty conscience," Mac decided, heading for the door.

Starting her in this place, if there'd been a choice, could be Norris' first and last mistake. The Dhryn, frantic to escape the Ro who'd penetrated the way station, had rushed her on their ship and locked her in here for the duration. "Not going to explore much if that's still the case," she commented, hoping Norris could somehow hear her.

Then Mac spotted something new, a palm-plate beside the door. It hadn't been there before, at least not on the inside, where a passenger could reach it.

She studied it, oddly nauseated by the deviation from memory. *What else had Norris meddled with in the simulation?*

There was one way to find out. Mac stretched her left hand toward the plate, only to freeze in mid-reach.

Her hand was flesh.

"Of course it is," she scolded herself. She was experiencing the *Pasunah* as she'd seen it.

So much had been different then. She reached behind her head and touched the loose knot she'd half expected. It was still a shock to free the braid and bring it forward over one shoulder, to run the length of hair through her hands.

Mac shoved it back. "Move on," she warned herself. Her thumb rubbed the emptiness of her ring finger. She wasn't interested in reliving the past. *The present was sufficiently complicated, thank you.*

She touched palm to plate, determined to get this over with as quickly as possible. Norris wanted a Human perspective on the corridors and hangar deck, particularly where they would be entering the derelicts. It shouldn't take long, if she could get out of here.

To her pleased surprise, the door retracted upward to reveal the brightly lit corridor beyond. "Nice," she commented, stepping out. The corridor was more spacious than she remembered, which likely had to do with the Dhryn proclivity for carrying her from place to place like so much luggage.

Mac picked left and started walking, dutifully observing the occurrence of closed doors—*three*—and inset light strips—*continuous*. She counted her footsteps, on the premise that the more data she gave Norris, however trivial, the less argument he'd have for a return trip.

Which she wasn't making.

The freighter wasn't the *Annapolis Joy*. Thirty-one steps took her to the end of the corridor and the large doors that led into the hangar.

Mac frowned. It had seemed farther. Of course, being clutched by a running Dhryn tended to distort one's sense of distance.

And she hadn't been feeling observant at the time. In fact, she'd been shouting at the top of her lungs. They hadn't answered her questions. They hadn't spoken to her at all.

She hadn't been Dhryn then.

Mac opened the hangar doors.

The space inside was empty except for a few cables along the floor and a large skim, crumpled nose-first against the near wall. Its front end wasn't badly damaged, but apparently whomever had piloted it hadn't bothered to slow down before entering. *Or they'd used the wall for brakes.*

Mac walked over to it, recognizing the skim. *There'd been a jolt,* she recalled. She'd put it down to alien driving, it being her first such experience. Norris must have made his own interpretation.

They'd been terrified. Mac ran her hand along the silent machine, walking toward its end. No matter what others thought now, the Dhryn she'd known had feared the Ro. "With good reason," she said aloud.

"What are you doing, *Lamisah?*"

"Just looking around," Mac said absently, reaching out to pat Brymn's warm, rubbery arm. "There's this annoying—"

She froze, whirling to look into those large golden eyes, their curious pupils like sideways eights. Violet sequins dotted the bony ridges above them, more traced the rise of cheek and curled above the ears. His lips, currently a rich fuchsia that matched the bands of silk wrapping his blue torso, shaped a cheerful smile as familiar as breathing. His hands were whole. *Brymn, not Brymn Las.*

"You're dead," she told him.

A hoot of amusement. "And why would I be dead, Mackenzie Winifred Elizabeth Wright Connor?"

He wouldn't be, she realized. "Damn Norris," she said. "He added you to the simulation."

"Why would 'Damn Norris' do that?"

"I—" she closed her mouth and thought about it. "You're right. He wants to know about the *Pasunah.*" Then, she knew. "Cayhill." The word came out like a curse. This had all the hallmarks of his well-intentioned interference.

When she'd become a "difficult" patient, he'd fixated on her inability to read and apparent lack of grief, believing her suffering from stress, if not outright brain damage. He'd declared her unable to make clear decisions and requested permission to take complete charge of her care.

She'd clearly decided to leave his care for good, Mac recalled. She'd stormed out of the medlab and refused to go back. *There might have been some broken glass.* Cayhill had been overruled not so much by Mac's own fury as by the needs of the IU investigators, who desperately wanted her full cooperation and weren't interested in inter-Human squabbles.

She had a great deal to thank aliens for . . . starting with this one.

Simulation or not, her eyes swam with tears as she looked at him, whole and blue and vibrant. "It's good to see you again, Brymn," she told him before she thought.

The golden eyes glistened, too. *They shared that response.*

"Have you missed me, *Lamisah*?"

The question caught her unprepared. *Did it come from the simulation program or her thoughts?* "We're both on this ship," she countered.

"Do you still grieve for me, Mackenzie Winifred Elizabeth Wright Connor?"

The form was perfect, from the curious tilt of his big head to his padlike feet. The words weren't.

Cayhill's Brymn, not hers. Mac edged away until her back hit the skim and she was pinned.

The Dhryn with his dear face loomed closer. "Why do you not answer, *Lamisah*? Is it because you are about to run? You know you should. You should run as far and as fast as you can."

Gods, no!

She covered her mouth with one hand, holding in a scream.

His eyes grew smaller and sank back. The intense blue of his skin faded, as if washing away with every pulse of his blood.

Mac lowered her hand, reached it out even though it trembled and her mind gibbered with fear. "Stop, Brymn," she begged. "This isn't what you were supposed to be. You were to be one of the glorious ones. A Progenitor. This—this is something the Ro did to you."

The bony ridges that defined his features smoothed back into his skull.

Mac couldn't get enough air. It was a *simulation*. She fought to see something else, *anything else*. She tried to imagine his arms growing larger instead of thinner; she tried to see his eyes as warm and gold and real.

She smelled rot.

His mouth opened, the only feature left to recognize. "Gooooooo."

His hands had become mouths, his shoulders and sides grown shimmering membranes. He inhaled and soared from the deck.

Green rain struck her face and upraised hands, dissolving flesh as she finally started to run, washing away her back as she fell.

Fell into a pool of liquid.

Then the mouths began to drink.

- 13 -

POMP AND PROMISE

MAC AWOKE, SURPRISED to find herself whole. She opened her eyes, not surprised to find herself in the medlab.

For a series of deep slow breaths, she considered Cayhill. Specifically, she considered the most practical way to dismember his body before feeding the bits to young salmon. *Who were,* she thought with satisfaction, *always hungry.*

Aware she'd never inflict such a fate on any fish, Mac regretfully abandoned her fantasy and sat up.

"Norcoast!"

"Morning, Mac." This from Doug Court, who gave a series of gauges by the cot a professional look before taking her wrist to check her pulse for himself. "How do you feel?"

Mudge hovered at the orderly's shoulder, his face paler than she'd ever seen it. "Rested," she said for his sake, looking around to see who else might be here. She relaxed when she saw the three of them were alone.

"Dr. Cayhill wants to be called when you wake up," Doug said carefully.

Meaning he hadn't made the call yet. Her hands found the sensors attached to her forehead and neck. She yanked them off. "Be my guest," she said, swinging her legs around and sliding from the cot in one more-or-less easy motion. The easy part was the swing; standing without obviously tilting was harder. Mac focused on Mudge. "I'm done here."

Without a word, he held out his arm.

"Your clothes." Doug went to a cupboard and brought out her things. Mac glanced down, only now realizing she wore one of the ill-fitting blue gowns Human medical practitioners felt obliged to inflict on the sick.

Maybe she would just feed his fingers to the fish.

"Ah, Norcoast?"

Mac looked at Mudge, whose face looked more pained than she felt. Immediately she eased the tight grip her artificial hand had fastened on his wrist. "Sorry about that." The *lamnas* were still on her other hand, she noticed with relief.

"What happened in the simulator?"

Cayhill kept recorders running in this room. She'd learned that lesson long ago. Mac arranged her face in its closest approximation to dazed confusion, *not hard,* and pretended to give Mudge's question some thought. "Not a clue," she said finally. "All I remember is falling asleep. Quite peaceful, really. Guess it didn't work."

Choke on that, she wished her listeners.

"There you are!" Fourteen came close to knocking Mac down when she arrived back at the Origin Team's section of the ship. He settled for bouncing up and down on his toes, shirttails flapping. "The idiots wouldn't let me stay while you were without clothes. I suppose one has to have external genitalia. Sexism. I left Charlie to enjoy the view."

Mac saw the moisture along his eyelids, and the way the Myg couldn't stand still. Beneath the foolery lay sincere concern. She was touched.

Mudge was insulted. "I did no such thing."

"Enjoy or view? That makes no sense. Idiot!"

Mac slipped her arms through both their elbows—Fourteen's being thicker and lower than Mudge's—and steered them away from their interested escort. She'd lost enough time. The corridors had brightened to daylight shortly after they'd left the medlab, meaning she'd been out of commission for over fourteen hours. Time she should have spent working, eating a couple of meals, followed by a night in her own new bed.

A strike against Norris and Cayhill.

"What's been going on?" she asked her companions, loath to let go. She didn't want to admit, even to herself, how good it felt to hold them, how much she needed to know she still had arms and it had been nothing but a simulation.

No nightmare had been as real. Strike two.

If she was kind to Cayhill—*unlikely*—she'd try to believe he couldn't have known how much memory she could bring to his little role-play, how accurate her sensory awareness of death by digestion would be. No physician would willingly put a patient through that, for whatever reason. *Would they?*

If she was paranoid—*getting there*—she'd believe he'd done it under orders to reinforce her fear of the Dhryn, to further taint her memories of Brymn so she'd view his kind as the prime threat instead of the Ro.

The idiot faction had Human members.

Unaware of her dark turn of thought, Fourteen rambled on, giving a typically personal answer to her question. "—I ate with the gorgeous Unensela, discovering that the most tasteless pap is exquisite if she is near me." He gave a huge smile. "After that, I returned to the task of encoding innumerable boring messages. You Humans spend too much time reciting your irrelevant daily routines to one another."

"And you don't?" Mudge snapped. He'd pressed the elbow wrapped by her fingers gently to his ribs, as if promising that support as long as she needed it. "Are you psychologically incapable of giving a simple status report?"

"Idiot!" Fourteen stuck out his tongue at Mudge, its forked tips flailing the air in front of Mac's nose. "Nothing. How's that? Everyone spent last night worrying about our Mac. There was no work done at all."

Strike three.

"Norcoast!" This as Mac tugged free her arms and started walking more quickly. The other two hurried to catch up.

"Find space and assemble everyone concerned—ten minutes," she said over one shoulder. "Including the captain."

It took forty-five minutes: sufficient time for a furious biologist to shower and change, albeit into an amber-and-blue silk suit the consulate staff must have deemed travel wear; abundant time for the vagueness of "everyone" when said to a certain Myg and a zealous memo-happy administrator to sink in.

So Mac was not completely surprised by the sea of faces that greeted her when she followed Lyle Kanaci into what must be one of the larger meeting rooms on the *Joy*.

New rule, she vowed, *be specific.*

However, their arrangement stopped her in her tracks.

The Sinzi had set up court.

It looked like nothing else. Grimnoii stood at slouching attention to one side. The Frow, desperately straight and balanced, stood to the other. Humans and other aliens formed an interested mass in front. While the two Sinzi, Ureif and Fy, were slender white pillars to either side of—

She was not *sitting in that chair.*

"Macmacmacburblemacmac!!!"

Any potential dignity afforded by the now-appropriate silk suit vanished under the onslaught of anxious offspring, who clambered up her as if she'd been a tree. She winced as fabric tore.

Mac carefully shifted the one nuzzling her neck to her shoulder. Again able to breathe, she gave a small, resigned sigh and took the few strides needed to bring her closer to the Sinzi, but not the chair. *At least there wasn't a table,* she told herself. "Hi, everyone."

"What's this all about, Dr. Connor?" Captain Gillis' face was set in neutral. She decided that wasn't because he didn't have a strong opinion about being hauled from his bridge to this—*whatever it was*—but rather was waiting for her to give him the opening to express it.

She was going to lock Fourteen and Mudge in a closet and . . .

"Hello, Captain," Mac said, setting her voice to confident. "Just a final strategy session. To—" There being no discreet way to stop an offspring from burrowing into an armpit, her smile became somewhat fixed. "To be sure we're all clear on what's going to happen post-transect. We are going through the gate this afternoon, are we not?"

"Eleven hundred hours shiptime." Executive Officer Townee's

opinion was easy to read, her thinned lips and scowl cues to all Humans in the room. Mac appreciated that clarity. *There was something to be said about dealing with your own species.*

But Humans, in so many ways, weren't the issue. "We find congruence in Dr. Connor's desire to meet at this time," Ureif said, dipping his long head in Mac's direction. "This is a critical juncture, Captain. To all here, our thanks for coming."

Mac brightened. *Maybe the crowd in this room wasn't completely her fault.*

"Dr. Connor," Rumnor came forward and indicated The Chair.

She was being punished anyway. Seeing no way to avoid it, not without offending the Sinzi, Mac sat. With the offspring, who promptly started rearranging their holds on her clothing to better see what was happening.

Ureif leaned over and, without moving his lips, made a *chipchirrup* sound. The offspring swung their faces toward him and echoed it, eyes wider than usual. A second, more emphatic *chirrup* from the Sinzi, and the offspring climbed off Mac and scampered into the assembly, presumably seeking Unensela.

Despite being relieved her clothes would now stay intact, Mac found she missed their warm little bodies. *Probably because now she faced "everyone" without support.* She checked her posture and swallowed, hard.

There was a soft tinkling of ring to ring as each Sinzi rested the tip of one long finger on Mac's shoulder. Startled, she glanced up at them, but both were looking toward the captain.

Whatever its meaning, the gesture didn't go unnoticed. To'o's wheezing inhalations—the Cey being congested since morning—were the loudest sound in the room.

"We wish to hear your suggestions as to the deployment of personnel and resources, Captain Gillis," Ureif said, his voice soft and mellow. "I will, with your consent, establish a consulate within your vessel to service those involved with the Dhryn ships. I anticipate ongoing negotiations. I trust you can accommodate any who need to stay on board? Three staff—" a finger lifted to indicate the Grimnoii, who shuffled proudly, "—will be available to liaise with your crew."

"Two will travel with me." Fy's paired eyes caught the light as she nodded graciously to the remaining Grimnoii. "My dart will be insufficient. I trust you can provide additional small craft to convey us and our equipment to the transect station as well as to the planet surface."

Fingertips pressed gently into Mac's shoulders. *Her turn.* She coughed and gave the plainly astounded captain a sympathetic look. "The Origins Team will be divided during the investigation of the derelicts. I trust—" she deliberately echoed the Sinzi phrasing, "—you can provide those who remain on board full and independent communications with those on Myriam."

When someone opens the spillway, she thought smugly, *you swim.*

She saw the captain's hesitation, his quick glance to Townee and back to her, but couldn't guess which way he'd go. Her experience with Human government and bureaucracy had tended to be of the "maybe, if you shout long enough" variety—*no offense to Mudge.* Her experience with the military mind-set? Based on Emily's old thriller vids. *Likely unrealistic.* Her recent stint with the Ministry had been—*confusing.* Something of a blend of anxious bookkeepers and overprotective relatives.

The captain had the ability to stop the Sinzi from playing a role at Myriam. *He could,* Mac realized, dry-mouthed, *turn his ship around and take them back to Earth.* Or he could cooperate on every level. She didn't see any middle ground. Either he honored the intent of his orders, to assist the IU as it sought an end to whatever combination of Dhryn and Ro threatened life, or he retreated behind the doubtless innumerable regulations designed to keep a Human ship on Human business and under Human control.

Been there, Mac reminded herself. *"Where on that scale . . ."* The grim reality applied to individual species, as much as to individuals. *None of them were safe.*

As if he knew she understood, Gillis' eyes burned into hers. She dared a slight nod.

After twelve heartbeats, he returned it.

"Your trust honors us," Captain Gillis stated, his voice sure and strong. Townee's scowl vanished, as if she'd only needed a decision. "The *Joy* is at your disposal, Sinzi-ra. My exec will work directly with your staff. Dr. Connor, expect modifications to your working space. We'll have to install the equipment you need."

The fingertips lifted from her shoulders as the Sinzi performed one of their elaborate gestures. Framed by such grace, Mac stayed absolutely still. *The moment called for some dignity,* she decided.

Which again lasted only until the irrepressible Sam Schrant shouted "Hey, Mac! Ask for ribs!" from the safety of the crowd.

They might have stirred an ant nest, Mac decided two hours later. She dodged against a wall to avoid being run over as a pair of Grimnoii rushed past behind wheeled carts loaded with dark Sinzi bags.

The establishment of a formal consulate, or the best facsimile possible in the time before reaching Myriam, consumed the *Joy* crew as well. Ureif would remain in the quarters he now shared with Fy, but he'd provided an extensive list of requirements for the other space he would need. Mac heard bits and pieces, mostly from Mudge. Despite the bags under his eyes and her own guilt, she'd asked him to keep involved. Not only had he agreed without hesitation, he'd already managed to justify two trips to the bridge.

Among the more urgent Sinzi requests had been those for meeting rooms and accommodations with direct access to docking ports.

Expecting company.

The Grimnoii were a bustle of efficiency, when they weren't saying good-bye to one another. Mac spotted a couple rubbing noses outside Ureif's quarters. They seemed overcome by the urge to stand and sniff at regular intervals.

She assumed the Sinzi-ra were aware and had factored the trait into their schedule.

For a schedule it was. Sandwich in hand, Mac made her way to the work area, once split into four, now divided into three. The combined, larger space was being filled with consoles, displays, and chairs. Gillis was as good as his word. A shifting number of crew had taken up floor plates and were installing various feeds. Fourteen hovered excitedly, pocketing tools when no one was looking, producing one with an innocent smile whenever an irate Human shouted for it.

The waiting courier ship would dock with them within the approach funnel leading into the Naralax. A lesser gate, in terms of volume, but most of its traffic still required tugs to reach final approach positioning. The dreadnought was among the few permitted to enter on her own. Mac hoped that meant they went faster.

She didn't like waiting.

"Dr. Connor!"

She was pretty close to not liking Norris either.

"Over here." She sat on the nearest empty table and waited, taking the moment to finish her sandwich.

Norris wove his way through a confusion of bags and people to reach her side. "I sent you a—I've been looking for you."

"You've found me."

His imp was in his hand. "Have you had a chance to think more about your sim experience? Dr. Cayhill suggested some recollections might begin to surface."

Mac understood the almost pleading note to his voice. She'd been his hope for more data on the Dhryn ship; it wasn't his fault she'd explored so little of it. *Thirty-one steps, three doors, one friend.*

And death.

"Sorry, Norris," she said, surprised to mean it. She'd written her own memo to Gillis, copied to Hollans. It sat waiting with the rest of the messages Fourteen had, in his terms, "brilliantly convoluted." Cayhill, regardless of his motivations, would no longer be a factor in Mac's life.

Though dismemberment had its appeal.

She didn't believe Norris had anything to do with the perversion of the sim. He was too focused on his own work to care about anything else. *Something she could appreciate,* Mac admitted. "If I get a minute, I'll go back over my original statement. Might jog a memory," she offered. "Though the Dhryn didn't let me see much."

"You would?" His eyes widened. "I'd appreciate that, Dr. Connor."

She slid off the table. "Anything else? It's a little crazy at the moment."

"Yes. Please." Norris leaned over her, his free hand reaching as if to make sure she stayed.

Mac sidled to avoid the touch, trying not to be obvious. *Civil*, she reminded herself. "What?"

He lowered his voice. "I understood this was a Ministry operation, Dr. Connor. There was no mention of aliens being in charge."

Or biologists.

Nonetheless, she had a fair idea what troubled him. "You're worried they won't let you on the ships."

"Ureif knows more about Dhryn designs than I do."

Mac smiled at what seemed an honest complaint. "I can't see the Sinzi-ra exploring in person. You should be able to do all the crawling about you want. But if there's any problem, let me know."

"Why do they listen to you?" Norris looked perplexed, his voice plaintive. "Who are you?"

No one you'd know, she felt like saying, but settled for, "When we've time, I'll do my best to explain. Right now, I suggest you finish whatever prep you have to do. Once we're in Myriam, it's likely to be pretty hectic. First ready," her grin was the one that gave new students fits at the start of the field season, "first out the door."

From his expression, she'd presented him with a new concept. *Bet you've made plenty of others wait on your timing*, Mac thought less than charitably. But she'd done her best. Time to finish her own preparations. "See you on the other side," she told him, and walked away, aiming for the one work area where scientists were still actually working.

"Kirby, To'o," she greeted, stepping over piles that hadn't been there yesterday. *It was as if clutter found them.* "Dr. Schrant." She wasn't ready to let him off the hook—yet—for shouting her name in the meeting. *At least he hadn't done the entire chant*, she shuddered.

"Hey, Mac." The three looked up through their 'screens. "You got a minute now?"

She checked the time. "About that." The courier must dock soon. She planned to be first in line, not last. But these three had been at her heels since yesterday. "What is it?"

To'o grabbed a paper-laden chair and tipped its contents to the floor. "Have a seat, Mac."

"Corrupted by Humans," Mac observed. As she sat, Kirby hurried to reposition one 'screen in front of her face. She squinted at the now-familiar outlines of the planet Myriam. "What am I look-ing for?"

"Watch, Mac," Sam urged. "We've run this umpteen times. Here's the way this world should be."

" 'Umpteen' is not a—" Mac closed her mouth. The world in front of her had transformed, the upper hemisphere blue-green, white at its pole, the southern brown and yellows. The image flick-ered, showing the world going through its annual seasons. Winter storms, dust clouds, cyclones. The pace of change increased, until a new pattern appeared. Over time, the seasonal changes shifted closer and closer toward one another, change coming now quickly until, like a flash, the moment came when greens appeared at the lower pole, while at the upper they faded to brown and dull yellow. *Triggering the Dhryn migration.* "I've seen this," she reminded them. "Myriam experiences a periodic shift in tilt, affecting the overall climate."

"Did you notice the oceans?"

Mac looked at the image, now flickering so rapidly the change from north to south was like a pulse. Myriam's oceans resembled narrow ribbons. Much of the planet's water had been under-ground; it had never been as moist as Earth. "What am I to notice? They look normal enough."

"Exactly." The three exchanged proud looks, then gazed happily at Mac. "Isn't it great?" Sam asked.

She'd utterly missed the point. Mac frowned at them. "Explain 'it.' "

"Oh." Kirby and Sam looked a bit too contrite. To'o, as if un-aware the wrong Human might understand the gesture, rolled his thumb along his opposite palm.

They were laughing at her.

Mac sighed. *Students.* "Remind me to show you geniuses some comparative physiology one of these days. What's so great?"

Kirby poked his finger into one of the oceans hanging in midair in front of Mac. "This should still be here."

Sam took over. "Nothing we've done . . . no scenario we've input, no even more catastrophic climatic change or the loss of liv-ing matter . . . nothing removed the surface water in this way. And you know how good I am at catastrophe." He folded his arms, looking pleased with himself.

Mac nodded absently, staring at the image of a world that should be, and wasn't. "So it was a weapon of some kind. The Ro. We were assuming as much."

"Not so fast." Kirby leaned forward. "We checked with the other Cey group. They've been looking at the planet surface for signs of some kind of attack. Nothing."

She frowned. "Then where did it go?"

"Away." The three shrugged in unison, a gesture the Cey copied perfectly, then sneezed.

" 'Away,' " Mac repeated. "What kind of answer is that? Away where? How?"

"We need more data," To'o stated. The others nodded. "Further samples from the ocean floor could tell us if the water was destroyed on site."

"If not, maybe it was collected and carried off somehow." This from Kirby. "There are water miners—"

"Way too sudden for that," Sam objected. "I keep telling you . . ."

Mac stopped listening, her mind filled with a dark tank, boiling with life; she could feel that voice etched along nerve endings. "Or it was drained," she said very quietly.

"To where?"

"Anywhere. Through a no-space opening within the ocean. The Ro could be capable of that. Maybe they put some kind of device or gate underwater. In an abyss."

"Mac?" She hadn't realized Sam had freckles, but he'd grown so pale a smattering of them appeared on his cheekbones. "Do you think that's what they left in Castle Inlet?"

For an instant, it was as if she could see it happening . . . the low tide that didn't end, the drying continental plains and estuaries, the snap-crack of settling ice, the last-ever flows rushing down sea canyons, the belching of released gas as the floor itself was exposed . . . the tremulous few gasping in exiled pools, to die by sun instead . . . the rains that failed . . .

Mac tightened every muscle to hold in her shudder. "Good

question," she said, making it brisk, rising to her feet. "Do you have all this ready to send to Base?" They nodded. *Your chance to save the world, Em.* "Give it to Fourteen. Tell him to mark it top priority. And Sam?"

His eyes were as haunted as hers must appear. "Yes, Mac."

" 'How' isn't as important as 'why.' There's a reason for all this," she promised, herself as much as the frightened climatologists. "It's our job to help discover it."

Mac left them to it, considering an addition to her own message for Emily. *Doomsday device. Have fun hunting.*

She shook her head. While she didn't doubt Emily would be exhilarated by the challenge, neither of them had believed the Ro would leave anything less.

And what she really wanted to ask, she couldn't. Not without undermining Emily's fragile self-confidence. Not without cueing those who'd doubtless scan all incoming messages that Emily might not have recovered enough to be trusted.

Mac intended to know, some day.

Why eleven?

Mac was halfway up the ladder to her quarters when the courier arrived, the Frow apparently otherwise engaged. *Maybe they preferred to spend transect in their quarters.* She wasn't quite sure who on board ignored passing through no-space and who fussed in a corner. Kudla, it turned out, was one of the latter. He and his disciples had locked their doors and asked not to be disturbed until safely through to Myriam.

She'd set her imp to an audible alarm, cued for that announcement from Mudge, waiting on the bridge. When it went off, she paused, hands tight on the rung. *Up or down.*

"Down."

Admit it. Her heart wasn't hammering in anticipation of a transmitted message.

Mac's feet and hands thudded against the rungs as quickly as she could move them, her left palm making a slightly crisper sound.

The one time she could use the Frow. One rung . . . two . . . three . . . her right foot slipped on the fourth and she recovered. Five . . .

Chime!

One rung . . . two . . . three . . . her right foot slipped on the fourth and—

Mac stopped and held on, breathing more quickly. She knew what that moment of déjà vu signified.

They'd gone through the gate.

She resumed climbing down, trying not to estimate how long it took to dock a ship and cycle through an air lock, for someone from that ship and air lock to hand a small package over to the right authority, for that person to return through the air lock into that ship and for that ship to remove itself and move to a safe distance. Because if she did . . .

Mac stopped and rested her forehead on the cold metal.

She'd know it hadn't been long enough.

"As if I know anything about starships," she scolded herself, and started moving again. "Maybe they throw things at each other."

But Mac no longer hurried, afraid of what might not be waiting.

"You should have seen it, Norcoast." Mudge was practically aglow. "A splendid maneuver. Simply outstanding."

Executive Officer Darcy Townee preened. *The only word for it,* Mac thought, fascinated. "We work on our precision."

"And it shows." He seemed about to bow, but turned it into a more restrained duck of the head. "I was privileged to be on the bridge during the event."

"Anytime, Mr. Mudge," offered Townee.

"Charles, please."

"Darcy."

Gods. The woman was blushing.

Mac took a deep breath and let it out. She'd wandered up and down the section of the ship open to passengers in search of a courier package, trying to not to appear too eager while asking anyone likely. Intercepting these two on their way back to the Origins area had been promising—until she'd realized neither was carrying any sort of pouch.

"I guess there's no mail," she said. *And Nik was dead.*

"Pardon?" asked Townee.

"She means messages," Mudge translated, remorse wiping the smile from his face as he took in Mac's expression, which mustn't have been the "don't care" one she'd attempted.

"We entered the gate too soon," she managed, looking only at Mudge. *What had it been—radiation, the Dhryn, his wound . . . some other danger no training or technology could avoid . . .* "There couldn't have been time."

"Now, Norcoast, there's no reason to—to think the worst," he told her, as if hearing her thoughts, not her words. "The *Joy* didn't rendezvous with a courier, she took one on board. It's sitting in the ship's hold now. The maneuver I praised was the *Joy* scooping up the waiting ship while launching another to stay in Sol. It will transmit our messages to Earth."

"While incoming messages were sent immediately to their recipients on board, Dr. Connor," Townee explained, looking puzzled. "Don't you have yours on your imp?"

Mudge *harrumphed* for her attention before Mac had to gather her wits to reply. "Darcy, there would be some delay releasing physical items, surely. Security and safety checks?"

"You're expecting freight?" She sounded mildly offended, as if the Ministry's fleet of couriers was being subverted to carry stuffed salmon.

Mac shot Mudge a look of pure gratitude, uncaring if the officer saw it. "Something like that," she said. "How soon—"

"Dr. Connor." "Dr. Connor." Rumnor and another of the Grimnoii came up behind, moaning her name.

Mac felt like moaning herself. *Aliens had the worst timing.* "Now's really not the best—"

"Now is when the Sinzi-ra must see you."

"Ureif?" Mac asked. "But—"

"Ureif's busy on the bridge, Dr. Connor." Townee's eyes narrowed. "We arrived into a situation. Com traffic's heavy and I'm sure he can't be—"

"Sinzi-ra Myriam." "Fy awaits. Hurry."

They might sound and look miserable, but Mac recognized determination when she saw it. *Along with significantly greater mass.* "I'd better go, then," she sighed, but gave Mudge a look she hoped he could read. "Oversight?"

He gave that brisk *man-on-a-mission* nod, and she felt a surge of relief.

To think, she used to find it annoying.

Mac resisted the urge to hug him.

The Grimnoii took up positions to either side on the way to the Sinzi's quarters. Given their bulk, and the variously jutting points that glinted menacingly with each ponderous step, their little procession effectively wiped the hall of other pedestrians. Mac grimaced an apology to those ducking into doorways or backing up. *It would take longer to argue with the Grimnoii than to get there.*

They stopped in front of the closed door, waiting. Mac waited, too, sneaking sidelong glances at her escort. Their eyes had stopped producing the congealing yellow tears, so obvious at the consulate. Without them, and the crust they produced, the hair on their faces and chests was a clean, shiny brown. *Much more appealing.* She couldn't resist. "Rumnor? Your eyes are much—" she sought a neutral term, "—drier."

"You noticed." He heaved a sigh that rattled knives. "They itch, too. We ran out of drops last night."

"Drops?"

The other Grimnoii lowered his voice to a confidential bass mutter, his breath vaguely floral. "We're allergic."

"To—" Mac realized both were looking at her, blinking, *now that she knew to pay attention,* their swollen and red-rimmed eyes. "Oh. To me?"

"Humans. Mygs. " Deep and sad. "Everyone we've met."

Feeling a quite extraordinary guilt, Mac tried not to breathe in their direction. *Nothing she could do about shed skin.* "I can ask the captain," she offered. "Maybe the medlab has something you can use."

"No need." "The Sinzi-ra knows and will care for us."

"Speaking of the Sinzi-ra," Mac ventured, eyeing the still-closed door. "Shouldn't we let her know we're here?'

The Grimnoii looked at one another, then at Mac. "There is a difficulty," Rumnor admitted.

"Faras wishes to see you," his companion whispered. "Yt is unsure."

"Hush!" Rumnor growled.

A Sinzi, with disagreeing selves? Whatever else, it didn't bode well for Fy as a Sinzi-ra. "When in doubt," Mac decided. She knocked firmly on the door.

The Grimnoii drew back in apparent horror.

The door opened on darkness. A long finger appeared in the light from the corridor. It stroked the air in a beckoning gesture, its rings of silver and gold tumbling up and down, before it disappeared again.

Mac stepped inside the room, unsurprised by either the white sand underfoot or the failure of her escort to follow.

The door closed, and she couldn't see a thing. From the restless tinkle of metal to metal, the Sinzi was to her left. *Somewhere.*

Mac considered the situation and hadn't a clue. *When in doubt,* she reminded herself again—as she had many students—*ask.* "Do you not want me to see you, Sinzi-ra?"

"You have eyes, do you not?" The calm gentle voice might have allayed concerns about being locked in the dark with a crazed alien; the underlying assumption gave Mac pause.

"Human eyes are adapted to use our sun's peak output, Sinzi-ra. I require light between four hundred and seven hundred nanometers."

"So narrow a range. Remarkable. How do you manage?"

A flashlight helps, Mac almost said, but restrained herself. She heard the Sinzi moving in the sand, her long-toed feet lifting and pressing down, the brush of her gown along the fine grains. Then she blinked in ship-normal light. "Thank you," she said at once.

Fy arched her neck and tilted back her head, a posture Mac had never seen Anchen perform. Her eyes glinted. She held this position for five seconds, then returned to normal, her mouth pursed as she studied Mac. *As if she'd been expecting something in return,* Mac decided. *What?*

"My apologies, Dr. Connor. I do not know about Humans. In fact, I do not know much about any non-Sinzi life-forms. My work has not involved you. Until now." A gesture with two fingers. "I feel woefully inadequate."

She *felt inadequate*? Mac wasn't sure whether to run from the room or not say another word. *She wasn't qualified for this conversation.* "Please, call me Mac. Anchen does," she added, waving her hand in a vaguely Earthward direction.

With startling speed, Fy rushed toward her. Mac held her ground and her breath, but the taller alien stopped short of contact. Instead, one finger lifted to indicate Mac's right hand. Or rather what she wore on that hand. The *lamnas*.

"These are not yours."

Was that a problem? Running became a serious option, but Mac kept still. "They're from Anchen," she agreed. "A gift."

"Yes. The other promise." The Sinzi leaned over as if to study her, head swiveling to bring one set of eyes after the other to bear.

"What other . . ." Mac's mouth snapped shut. *Of course.* "What promise did Nikolai Trojanowski make to Anchen?"

Fingers flashed to loop before her eyes and the Sinzi answered. "To find the truth about the Dhryn and bring it back to her."

Mac licked dry lips. "And—Anchen's?"

"To maintain his connection to you, regardless of distance. An interesting challenge."

"You were involved?"

The Sinzi dropped her fingers from her eyes. "Of course. A promise reliant on our system affects every transect engineer. In this case, we agreed to supply Nikolai's ship with six explorer probes, each capable of opening a temporary no-space passage to return home."

Handy, Mac thought numbly, aware it was far more than that. As far she knew, no other species had been granted access to the Sinzi's cherished probes. They were used to contact and assess potential new members of the Interspecies Union.

When not carrying her mail.

"Home," she echoed. "To Earth."

Pursed lips. Then, "Was that an inappropriate word, Mac? I mean no disparagement to Human theological or historical beliefs but I refer to N, the system of Sinzi biological origin. From there, your *lamnas* and any other information are transferred to waiting Human courier vessels and sent to Sol System."

Human ships, in the famed Sinzi home system? *The Inner Council must have had polite fits.* The oldest friends of the Sinzi, the systems first connected by their transects. The powerful.

She could just imagine Hollans' glee when he'd learned of the plan Nik had arranged.

With more of that disconcerting speed, Fy went to sit in one of the room's four jelly-chairs. When Mac didn't move, the Sinzi again pursed her lips before speaking. *Confusion,* Mac judged it. "Don't Humans use chairs, Mac?"

A Sinzi with no experience with aliens, she reminded herself, missing Anchen. Mac sat in the jelly-chair nearest Fy, sinking in with an involuntary smile. "Oh, yes," she said.

"You must tell me at once if my behavior is offensive," the Sinzi urged. "Ureif believes I can manage, but—" Her left fingers trailed in the sand while the right formed a tense knot on her thigh. "Yt is disconcerted."

She knew that feeling. Empathy warmed her voice. "And you must ask me if you find anything about Humans confusing."

"I have been given brochures," confided Fy. "I plan to study them carefully when time permits."

Was no one safe from Fourteen? Mac shook her head. "You'll get more reliable answers from me, Sinzi-ra. Believe me."

"Anchen did state this. Which is why I asked staff to bring you to me, Mac. I will soon leave for the transect station and then the planet." The knotted fingers visibly tightened on one another. "I will be alone."

"I'll have access to communications—you can call me any time," Mac promised, bemused to be the one offering comfort and advice. "Before you go, Fy, I'll introduce you to Charles Mudge. He's going to Myriam as well. You can rely on him."

Fy's head went back, but only for an instant, as if she'd realized the gesture meant nothing to Mac. Meanwhile, her entwined fingers loosened, but kept moving with a slow fretfulness over the fabric of her gown. "I am grateful. But, while we remain congruent, I have questions, Mac."

"Please." Mac sat back and hoped for something easy. *Like external genitalia.*

"Why am I here?"

Okay, not easy. "What were you told?" she hedged.

"I participate in both promises Anchen has made with Humans. To fulfill my duty to yours, I was told I was needed here. That you would explain why."

"Me?" Mac said incredulously. "Anchen said I would?"

"Can't you?" The knot began to re-form, joined by the left fingers.

Mac tsked her tongue against her teeth. "You know about transect systems," she hazarded. "Myriam has one."

The fingers flew apart, dancing frantically in midair, rings tinkling like so many castanets. "I'm an archaeologist, not a traffic analyst! I should be back at my work!"

"But Fourteen said you were a transect engineer," Mac countered, then corrected herself: "Faras, that is. And Yt is your student. Oh. Sorry." *Don't identify the component personalities,* she scolded herself. "I didn't mean to be rude, Fy."

A lift of fingers that had to be surprised laughter, from what she knew of Anchen. "A transect engineer who studies the remains of alien technology discovered in the Hift System. And whose student is the inestimable Yt, a historian of promise. Our field is not one of wide interest. The Sinzi moved beyond the partial clues left by the Myrokynay long ago." Not pride, but certainty. "However, there remain interesting questions about the originators of the technology I hope to answer one day."

Mac could hardly breathe.

She'd asked Anchen to protect herself from the Ro.

And been sent the Sinzi's expert on Ro technology.

"You must have attended the IU's Gathering on Earth," she ventured.

Fy brought two fingers close, but not touching. "Anchen accessed potentially relevant data from all Sinzi, including mine. I study molecules of metal, Mac. I analyze dust for alien components. I interpolate design from pieces found in congruence. My work has nothing to do with the living."

"You'd be surprised," Mac said, feeling suddenly old. "Correct me if I'm wrong, but it's my understanding the transects within the Chasm don't use Sinzi technology, but were reactivated when the Naralax was—" *What did you call it when a nonexistent worm burrowed through no-space and left a hole that wasn't there?* "—made."

"Through the Hift System, yes. But it would be incorrect, Mac, to say the Chasm worlds continue to rely on alien technology. The first act of the Sinzi upon discovering the Chasm was to replace all existing transect stations. The originals were destroyed, of course."

"Why?" Mac asked, startled.

A look that in a Human would be astonishment. "They were less stable. We could not permit unsafe connections to our system."

The promise to the Imrya freighter? She wanted to ask, but thought better of it. *Really didn't want to know.* "So the remains at Hift are all you have to study."

"Yes. Which is why I am confused to be here." Distress. "How can I serve the promise?"

Fy's *lamnas* caught Mac's eye. The rings were bolder than Anchen's, their mix of metals reflecting unsteady white-and-yellow flecks that ran down the walls.

Like water.

"There might be more remains," she told Fy. "We—the Origins Team—are exploring the hypothesis that the Ro—the Myrokynay—used no-space technology to somehow drain Myriam's oceans, very quickly. If they did, there should be some physical trace of their technology. Like Hift." She didn't let herself think about a working version. *Not yet.*

"Why would they do this?"

"We're looking into that as well," Mac said grimly.

With the swift grace of a pouncing cat, Fy lunged to her feet. She began to pace, the panels of her gown fluttering. "I must go down there. At once! I must have samples, scans." She lifted all six fingers before her eyes, as if searching for a *lamnas* to set it all in motion.

Though loath to leave its comfort, Mac extricated herself from the jelly-chair. "On that front, I have good news. Myriam's been a very busy corpse. I daresay every centimeter's been mapped and surveyed. Enough data for a start."

Fy stopped pacing to look right at Mac. "Even if your hypothesis is correct, Mac, there may be nothing to find. Much of the Hift site was left intact for us. There's no reason to assume any other Myrokynay site will be as cooperative."

"Left intact for *you*." *She didn't like where this was going.* "You think the Ro meant you to find it?"

"There is no proof." The Sinzi-ra spread out her fingers, then pulled them into her body. "However, our more recent history has become of concern. Anchen has brought forth the possibility that the timing of our discovery and its implementation as the transect system suited the purposes of the Myrokynay. The findings of how we were 'shown' Haven and the Dhryn only underscore this."

"You've heard." Some tension she'd carried until now released, and Mac smiled. "The Frow were so adamant about following their own chain of command." *To her.*

"Of course. We have arranged to hear everything of interest that travels the transects."

Mac blinked. "I don't understand," she said, fearing she did.

A graceful sway left, then right. "I do not know how it is for a Human in these times, Mac, but the current lack of consensus among the IU species on this situation deeply disturbs us. We do not easily comprehend such a state as sane. Though I am arguably closer to it during this difficult phase of my life, even I cannot imagine the ability of others to function while in disagreement." Fy ran the tip of one fingertip down the rings of another. "When disturbed, all Sinzi listen. Very carefully."

The Sinzi-ra in every system of the IU were eavesdropping? Mac had no problem imagining a unanimous reaction to that revelation from both sides of the Ro debate. "Please don't talk about this to anyone else, Fy," she warned uneasily. "It's important. You can ask Ureif, if you wish."

"I do not need to ask. I trust you, Mac. Do you require a promise?"

"No, no," Mac replied hurriedly. "I trust you as well. Focus on the problem—leave the politics to others." *Her own plan.* Fortunately, the problem was bigger than any politics. "Before we jump to any conclusions about Ro motives," she went on, "keep in mind their sense of time isn't like ours. I've a feeling they understand biological timelines, but there's no evidence they grasp how long it takes other species to change culturally." *Or care,* she added to herself. "Including the time it took you to develop no-space technology. I believe they were surprised by the Sinzi application at the consulate. The display tanks?"

"I will keep this in mind. Yet there is admirable congruence in their actions."

Mac hesitated, leery of misinterpretation. *Between her assumptions and Fy's Human-naïve enthusiasm, probably not much could be worse than the two of* them *talking.* "How so?" she asked finally.

"They return to you, do they not?" The pacing resumed, as if Fy were too excited to stand still. *Or she thought better moving.* "Demonstrably, Mac, you have come to occupy a rational nexus of attention, being of significance to both past and current Dhryn, and to the Gathering of the IU, while reestablishing your own connection to their former agent, Dr. Mamani. To be in your presence must be a powerful attraction for the Myrokynay."

Now there was a horrifying thought. Mac shook it off. "I appreciate the compliment," she told the Sinzi, turning in the sand to keep watching the alien as she paced around in a circle. "But it's a Sinzi perspective. Other species don't necessarily think in such terms."

Fingers swung from side to side. "What other terms are there?" Fy demanded, moving around the room faster and faster, her long legs flying.

Shoes full of sand, Mac began to get some idea of the effort Anchen had expended to learn to interact effortlessly with Humans. "Would you please stand still?"

Fy might have turned to stone. Sand drifted down around her hem.

"Thank you. And here's some advice about being around Humans. Fewer, slower movements. We get dizzy."

Fy's fingers twitched at their tips. "This is unnecessary with the Grimnoii."

"The Grimnoii," observed Mac, "shove their noses under your door. You could probably dance on their heads and they'd like it. Which reminds me," she continued, having a suspicion of what might constitute "necessary." "You do know about their eyedrops? They expect you to provide them."

Fy sat down again. Considerably more slowly, this time. "What are eyedrops, Mac?"

Interspecies communication fails again. Mac decided life was too short to keep score.

"We'll put Oversight on it," she said. "But first, let's take a walk. I've some colleagues you'll want to meet."

Prioritize.

Mac left the huddle of Sinzi, Human, and Sthlynii to its work. They'd plunged into the more esoteric realms of molecular archaeology, opening overlapping workscreens replete with jargon. She'd become unnecessary; Fy confident. *Leave it to a mutual passion to get past the little things.*

"Prioritize," she repeated under her breath, wondering what to do next. The hall and rooms were still buzzing with activity, but with an anxious underlay. Arrival in Myriam had revealed some complications.

Rumor, the fastest briefing, held that a Trisulian warship was on approach to the *Annapolis Joy,* demanding some kind of clearance from the Humans. Mind you, rumor also held that Dhryn Progenitor ships had been sighted in any of thirty systems, tonight's menu would include fresh N'not'k clams in mint, and Wilson Kudla had sold a new book which would detail his successful mystic battle with the Myrokynay.

Of that list, she'd go for the clams.

"Couriers can carry clams," Mac muttered, pausing to give a Grimnoii right of way. Yellow liberally stained his cheeks, chin, and clothing, and he looked as close to content as one of his kind could. *Mudge was a force.*

He'd been waiting for her outside the door to Fy's quarters. One look at his face, and Mac had known. There hadn't been a package for her.

Since, she'd gone through the motions. *Easy to be calm, when you don't dare think.* Mudge had wanted to talk; she'd sent him after eyedrops.

She felt enclosed in a bubble, detached from the conversations walking by with their preoccupied owners, their urgency. *She needed work.*

"Prioritize," she said again, forcing herself to examine the 'screen floating beside her face, using the effort of reading to stay focused.

Cayhill's entreaty for her to come to the medlab she deleted. The current set of complaints about Fourteen she grouped into one, forwarded to the Myg. *He'd enjoy that.* Mac frowned. Norris had sent her several messages, all marked, of course, urgent.

Spotting him coming down the busy hall, she deleted those, too.

"Dr. Connor!" He halted to let Da'a go past, then had to dodge around three intent Humans and their cart. *The man had a gift for finding traffic.* "Dr. Connor, a moment please."

Mac closed her 'screen. "Got your messages," she informed him. *Technically true.*

He came close and lowered his voice. "Can you be ready?"

Might have been a bit hasty on the delete, she realized. "Ready for what? When?"

"I've obtained clearance." He didn't appear to notice her admission of ignorance, perhaps used to her. *Or too intent on himself,* she judged. "The *Joy* is closing on the first derelict. We should be in range within the hour."

"They've settled the jurisdictional issues?" Mac felt a shiver of caution. *Nothing was this smooth with aliens.*

"We've permission for an external survey. A start. I want you to come. Please. I'll send someone from the crew to bring you to the hangar bay when it's time."

She was nodding before realizing she'd made a decision. *Fine, then.* "I'll be in my quarters."

Mac sat on her bed, knees and feet neatly together, hands in her lap. Her hands, palms up, cradled the carving she'd given Nik, and he'd sent back to her through Hollans.

"You've been around," she told it.

The wood took warmth from her skin, as the living version

would from the water around it and the rays of sunlight penetrating the surface. She rubbed her thumb gently over the black lines representing the connections between life and world, aware she should find other things to do, unable to do them.

She closed her eyes briefly. They were dry and hot. Tears would have helped, but she wasn't ready to cry—not yet. *Not without proof.*

A knock on her door, too soon to be Norris' summons. Mac raised her voice. "Not now, Oversight."

"It is Ureif, Dr. Connor."

The one being on the ship she didn't dare refuse. *Had to be an alien conspiracy,* Mac told herself as she rose to unlock the door. *She couldn't always have this kind of luck.*

Unexpectedly, Ureif was alone in the hall. "Greetings, Dr. Connor." She glanced toward the ladderway. He gave a very Human smile and gestured in the opposite direction, to what had been a sealed bulkhead and was now an open door to another corridor. "The captain has granted me access throughout his ship."

Including a back door to her part. Mac somehow returned the smile, and stood aside to let the Sinzi-ra enter. "To what do I owe this honor, Sinzi-ra?" she asked, somewhat hysterically trying to gauge if her only chair or the bed would better suit the lower anatomy of the Speaker to the Inner Council of the Interspecies Union.

The chair. She pulled it out and offered it.

"Thank you, but I cannot stay, Dr. Connor. I've come to deliver this."

His finger uncurled, its coating of red rings ending in not one, but two of purest silver.

In slow motion, Mac reached out her hand. The Sinzi let the rings slip into her palm. She stared down at them, then up into his great complex eyes. "Forgive the delay," he asked, bowing his long head. "These came to me first, an unintentional error in procedure, and I was unable to leave the bridge until now."

He'd left the bridge—and whatever situation brewed among the species at Myriam—to bring her these himself. She closed her fingers around the rings. *A Sinzi could do nothing less,* she realized with some wonder. *Not even one as important as this.* "Thank you."

He produced a folded sheet of mem-paper from a pocket she hadn't noticed in his gown. *Nice trick.* "There have been more incidents, Dr. Connor, not as widely reported as we could wish. You should have this information."

Mac took the sheet with some trepidation. "What do you want me to do with it, Sinzi-ra?"

"Use it as you see fit. Although I would advise care discussing its contents with the Frow. They are a volatile species."

Great. Mac opened her mouth to ask for details, but Ureif gestured to the door. "Excuse my haste," he said. "But the good captain was not calm about my departure. I should return."

Tucking the sheet in her own pocket, the rings tight in her other fist, Mac went to open the door. As she stood close to the Sinzi, he lifted a curl from her forehead with one fingertip. "It was with this you committed *grathnu*?"

Hair or hand. Mac still blushed. "I didn't have much choice," she explained.

"The Dhryn." Ureif released the curl. His head tilted to focus his lowermost pair of eyes on Mac, his fingers meeting in a complex shape that reminded her of Anchen. *By far, more sophisticated than Fy.* "I found them pleasant. Industrious, courteous, with a playful humor able to cross many species' lines. Blind to the larger universe, yet the individuals I knew best sought nothing more than to be happy and contribute to the well-being of their kind."

Mac nodded. "You watched them leave for home, didn't you?" she dared ask. "The colony ships. You knew they were at Haven, all this time."

"They were devastated by news of the Ro attack," he answered without hesitation. "As the word spread, everyone put down what they were doing and went to the spaceports; nothing mattered but to return to their Progenitors as quickly as possible. They believed they were needed."

The Progenitors had already left—what had that been like, to arrive home to nothing? "What could they do but wait?" she observed sadly. "Until they died."

Ureif's fingertips twitched. "I am disturbed by their fate, Dr. Connor. By that of all Dhryn. I see no potential circularity. Do you understand this?"

"I think so," Mac said, leaning her shoulders against the wall. "You see no future for the Dhryn as they are now." She sighed. "I'd like to disagree. I valued them, too. But I don't see any hope either."

" 'As they are now.' " Ureif straightened his head so all of his eyes looked at her. "What does this mean, Dr. Connor?"

"Mean?" Mac hesitated. "I suppose, being a biologist, I see the Dhryn as the culmination of two processes. We have ample evidence they evolved and were successful on their own world—and mounting evidence that those Dhryn, the original form, were acted upon in some way by the Ro to produce the Dhryn you and I know. A biological weapon."

"I see why Anchen spoke of your peculiar insights, Dr. Connor." While Mac puzzled at that, he went on, "Are you aware Sinzi regard no process as inherently linear? That there will always be circularity discovered, if the viewer is sufficiently discerning?"

"Not until now." *But it explained a few things.* "I don't feel at all discerning in the present situation."

"Nor do I, Dr. Connor."

"Mac."

Definitely a bow. *Ureif should teach that to Fy.* "Mac. Until our next meeting."

She locked the door behind him and leaned her ear against it. Once sure there wasn't another alien ready to knock, Mac opened her fist and gazed down at the rings. "An 'open me first' tag would have been useful," she told them. Her heart thudded in her chest. Now that she had news from Nik, she felt oddly reluctant.

Alive. That was the easy part. *The good to the soul part.*

What else he had to tell her remained to be seen. *Literally.*

Sitting in her chair, she stood the rings on the surface of the desk, holding them in place with the thumb and forefinger of each hand. She gave them a spin.

The left ring revolved twice, then fell with a faint clatter. Mac reached for it, then changed her mind, watching the still-spinning ring. "That eager, huh?" She took that ring to her bed, kicked off her shoes, and lay down.

She brought the metal to her lips.

Then looked through it.

- CONTACT -

/EFFORT/

"Mac . . . we made it . . ."/resolve/ . . . *so tired* . . . /doubt/

Concentrate, getting easier. "All of us . . . left . . . safe. Can't go back . . ." /fear/ "Ship . . . damaged . . . contaminated." *The darkness almost claimed us. I could taste . . . death.* /determination/ "Made it this far . . . matters."

Concentrate. ". . . Vessel introduced us . . . You were right . . . Progenitor . . . amazing sight . . ." *You did this alone, Mac . . . I have to be as strong as you were . . .* /awe/pride/

Concentrate. "She listened . . . we must wait . . . Mac, she's weak . . . starving . . ." /pity/fear/horror/ *She's consuming her own to stay alive . . . are we next?*

Concentrate. ". . . She saw me alone . . . asked . . . you. How we . . . Where . . ." *Where are you . . .* /longing/ ". . . have a place . . . must convince Her . . ." /resolve/

* *layered over* *

—She smells mint—

"Nikolai, I cannot endure—" Genny P'tool's beak closed, moist bubbles forming along the junction of top to bottom.

How do you talk to someone already dead . . . /anguish/ . . . *I would have spared you this, old one.*

"Rest, Gorgeous. The Progenitor ship found us in time."

Time for everyone else. /rage/frustration/

"Take—take my work. Others can keep . . ."

/despair/resignation/ *Be the last breath . . . I can't stay . . . do us that grace . . .* /pain/ *Die while I'm here.*

"You'll do it yourself. Just stop making Mac jealous, okay?"

The damned Dhryn have no doctors, no medicines . . . save us and let her die.

"Hah. Saw you first. My pretty Nik."

"You say that to all the . . ."

/grief/relief/guilt/

Good-bye, Genny.

* layered over *

—She tastes salt—

"Is She not magnificent, *Lamisah*?"

/disbelief/fear/ *I'm standing on a hand . . . a hand . . .*

"Magnificent is an understatement."

"I have told Her of your service to that which is Dhryn." A soft hoot. "And of your daring to argue with Mackenzie Winifred Elizabeth Wright Connor Sol."

/wry amusement/ *Even the Dhryn know . . . unfair . . . those eyes of yours could melt stone . . . only flesh, Mac . . . landed me in the drink . . . too busy daydreaming . . .* /despair/resolve/ *. . . like now.*

"Will the Progenitor listen to me?"

"She will listen, but we must not tire Her. The Great Journey takes its toll on all that is Dhryn."

/hope/resolve/ "You'll have to help me. She must learn the truth."

Another hoot. "But of course, *Lamisah*. Is that not why we are here? Although," a sigh, "it is not a truth anyone would want."

/pity/determination/

"One step at a time, my friend."

* layered over *

—She feels silk—

Concentrate . . . "Let Anchen know . . . Genny P'tool . . . dead." *With Murs . . . Larrieri . . . Cinder . . . who next . . . doesn't matter.* "We couldn't save her."

/anger/futility/

Vessel and I . . . only ones left who know . . . /determination/ *. . . must survive . . .*

"Quarters fine . . . She remembered you . . . water in the shower." *You made an impression, Mac . . . not surprised . . .* /warmth/ "Wanted to know . . . everything. Searched . . . feeders touched me . . ." /horror/

Concentrate . . . ". . . tried to send more . . . didn't seem . . . work . . ." We're underway as planned . . . easy part . . . tell Hollans . . ."

/resolve/

- 14 -

TOUCH AND TEMPTATION

HER PILLOW WAS SOAKED. *Tears.* Her clothes were as well. *Sweat.* Mac slipped the new *lamnas* on her middle finger and ignored how both hands trembled. She looked up at the next ring, sitting like harmless jewelry beside the salmon carving, and fought for the courage to touch it.

Nik's messages, Nik's memories, were startlingly vivid now. *Practice makes perfect.* "His or mine or both." The information might be easier to sort through and understand—at least, she thought so.

But the emotional load was growing worse. Between his passions and her reactions to them, she felt as exhausted as if she'd somehow run a complete marathon in the last few minutes.

Her eyes swam with tears again; she let them run down her face and over her ears. *Poor Genny.* She'd been the most frail. Likely a factor.

Honest grief, honest joy. Nik was alive. The Vessel was alive.

And they were with the Progenitor.

The "easy part." Mac reached for the second *lamnas.* She had the impression Nik doubted it had worked. *Using a broken one couldn't be good.* "I'm not feeling braver," she warned it, "but you know what they say about curiosity and biologists."

She brought the ring to her lips, then looked.

- CONTACT -

SHE HEARD THE OCEAN—
Waves crashed against cliff; seabirds screamed overhead; thunder rolled along the shore . . . under it all drummed a word.
"Lamisah!"

* *layered over* *

—She tasted bile—
Her teeth drove into her brother's flesh; her mouth flooded with heat; she swallowed life . . . within it all pulsed a word.
"Survival."

* *layered over* *

—She felt the cells of her body—
Stomach, ridged and acid; muscle tight with power; skin, the boundary line of who and what she was . . . through it all hammered a word.
"Truth."

REACTION AND RESOLVE

MAC FLUNG HERSELF to the side of her bed in time for the first uncontrolled spew to hit floor, not fabric.

By the fourth, she no longer cared where it went. She hung from one hand on the desk, her other having found purchase somewhere on the floor. The ship spun in huge looping circles and she was about to fall off. Her head pounded with a blinding white pain. Her gut persisted in its belief she had more to vomit.

Dying would be nice.

Between spasms, Mac counted each successful breath. When she reached five, she concluded she wasn't going to die after all. *More's the pity.* When she reached ten, she opened her eyes.

Big mistake.

A few arduous moments later, she managed five again. Ten. But this time she waited for twenty peaceful breaths before peering between almost closed eyelids.

No vomit.

That worked.

If she didn't count the stabbing sensation behind her eyes. *Sensitive to light.*

Working toward simple goals such as continuing to breathe, avoiding direct light, and hoping the ship would stop moving soon, Mac managed to sit up. Swaying in that position, she congratulated herself.

Then realized what had happened.

"She knew . . ." A whisper that hurt her poor head. *The Progenitor must have talked to Nik about the* lamnas, *what they were.*

Then used one.

The proof clawed its way through Mac's every pore. Dhryn thought and memory fought for space within her mind, as if she'd been turned inside out.

And the proof of that . . . ? She cracked open her eyes a smidge more to see the disaster she'd made of her new quarters. "Bother."

First things first. With one arm tight around her abused middle, and her hand shading her eyes, Mac staggered to the shower and stepped inside. Once there, she pushed her head into the jets and kept the water and soap running—first over her clothes, then over each subsequent layer as she stripped to skin. With regret, she kicked the once-lovely suit to the side.

Offspring holes in it anyway.

Next, she turned the room lights to minimum and used her wet clothing to mop most of the mess from the floor, slipping the sodden mass into disposal sacks. Moving at the mindless task worked some of the knots from her neck and abdomen. *Though she'd feel those muscles tomorrow.*

Mac set the air refresh to maximum, crossing her fingers the reek of almost-dead biologist wouldn't simply be pumped to some other room and noticed. Gooseflesh rose on her skin and she rooted through her bags to find something that wasn't silk or suit.

At the bottom of one, plain coveralls—similar to those worn by the crew. "I'll never complain about your packing again, Two," she promised the consular staff as she pulled the garment on. Wanting to be quite sure to remember which was which, she put the fourth ring on her left hand. *Quite the collection.* Mac considered putting the *lamnas* on a chain around her neck. But they weren't jewelry. They weren't an imp or mem-sheet. They were pieces of Nik, intimate and hers.

Plus that other. She explored those memories with care, like probing a sore tooth with her tongue. And found a question.

Had the Progenitor spoken Dhryn?

Being unable to tell scared her. Mac rested two fingers on her lips and mouthed, "The rain at Base . . . two three four." First in English, then Instella. Last, and with reluctance, Dhryn. *Oomling Dhryn.*

The oomlings. She sank into her chair, the words in Nik's voice blending with that perverse mix of hunger and desperate remorse until she knew, beyond doubt, one truth. The Progenitor, the future of her kind, was sacrificing the existing generations in order to survive.

Even She would break, Mac realized. No matter this Progenitor's desire to avoid killing others, instinct would rule before the end. And what of the other Dhryn, hiding within the transect system? "That which is Dhryn must survive," she whispered.

They were all running out of time.

Their crew escort left them at the door. Norris continued to give her sidelong looks as they walked through the *Annapolis Joy's* hangar deck. Finally, Mac couldn't take it any longer. "What's the matter?"

"You look awful."

No surprise there. She felt awful. Having a Progenitor try to stuff meaning inside her head through a Sinzi device had produced a headache that continued to mock the heavy-duty painkillers she'd gulped on the way to meet him.

Mac wanted to explain, but "Dhryn brain" was too dangerous and "simulator hangover" was petty under the circumstances. "Lunch didn't agree with me," she said, which was undeniably the case. *The mere thought of eating . . ."*

She'd chosen to intercept Norris on his way to the Origins section. It had given her time to begin to sort through her new thoughts, and, more importantly to Mac, removed any possibility of him appearing at her quarters before they were cleaned.

Avoiding the person sent to clean her quarters had been a bonus.

After passing several large, promising craft, with uniformed crew bustling around them, Norris stopped by what looked to Mac like an ordinary transport lev, about the size used to ferry weekly supplies to Base. *With,* she noticed, *dents.*

Norris opened the door and climbed in. "C'mon," he said impatiently.

Without committing her feet to the ramp, Mac leaned forward to look inside. Other than mismatched seats for pilot and passen-

ger, there was nothing but recording equipment—some mounted
to the walls, some loose. There was also no other person, and Norris was climbing into the pilot's seat.

So not always behind a desk. "You're the pilot?"

"Of course." He busied himself with an alarming number of
switches. Lights came on and a complex 'screen activated to hover
in front of him. "It's my ship."

Mac pointed toward the hangar's launch bay. "It's space out
there." She thought that came out nicely matter-of-fact, but he
stopped what he was doing to gaze down his nose at her.

"We have a slim margin of opportunity, Dr. Connor. If you
don't feel capable of accompanying me, stay here."

She rested her hand on the side of the lev in apology. "It seems
a little small."

"To maneuver around obstacles." His hand caressed the console. "Are you coming or not?"

He didn't appear suicidal, she told herself. As reassurance, it did
nothing to steady her nerves, but Mac climbed up the ramp and
took her seat, tossing her pack underneath. "Of course."

Norris closed the door behind her. As he continued his final
checks and preparations, Mac glanced around.

This "lev" was different from those that moved through air. For
one thing, the roof wasn't retractable. *Brilliant,* she scoffed at herself. For another, there were no windows. It was really like being
inside a box.

She could handle being in a moving box. She'd done it before.

She concentrated on relaxing in the passenger seat, leaning back
with her eyes closed. The position—or the painkillers—began to
make progress on her headache. After a few minutes, it faded into
a sullen throb.

The craft lurched forward. *The tow to launch.*

She didn't bother watching Norris deal with that either. Her
stomach gave a gentle gurgle, the kind that meant it was willing to
try something when she was. *Progress.*

The lurching ended in sudden smoothness, then Norris gave a
satisfied, "There we are. Take a look, Dr. Connor."

Mac opened her eyes. She didn't scream, but the sound that did come out of her mouth before she closed it had a good deal in common with that made by an offended mouse.

She was *in* space. *Without a ship!*

Hands tight on the armrests, Mac took a deep breath. *Something wasn't right. She was getting air.*

But the roof and walls she'd found so comforting had become transparent. Mac glanced down and looked up again quickly. *So had the floor.*

Norris' little craft had transformed into a bubble containing themselves, his packed equipment, and what bits of console he needed to consult. Interior lighting was reduced to that provided by his 'screen.

"Not a box," she said rather glibly.

"Warn me if you're going to be sick. I've bags."

She had nothing left.

Mac began to take in what was around them, twisting her head to see more. "I'm fine."

They weren't alone. Dwarfing the stars, Myriam's sun, and the world itself were ships. *A mixed school,* thought Mac, trying to find some frame of reference.

From their perspective, the *Annapolis Joy* lay below. The ship resembled a lacework coral, rounder buds held within a network of thick lines, but more random and three-dimensional than creatures bound by tropisms to sun and gravity and wave. If Mac hadn't known something of the *Joy's* inner dimensions, she'd have judged the ship fragile. Lights and reflections teased her complex shape from the darkness beyond and revealed other shapes—probably shuttles—moving over her surface like small crabs. Others moved farther away, difficult to follow at this range, but she spotted one set of lights that seemed to parallel their course. "Who's that?"

"Your escort," he stated. "The captain insisted."

She liked the captain.

To either side and—Mac looked up—above were other much larger ships. While she mentally tagged them as eel, octopus, grouper, sea cucumber, and so on, Norris abruptly noticed her interest and began to spout numbers and model years as if he'd checked a list before coming out. *Probably had,* she thought.

"Which is the Trisulian?" she interrupted.

He called up something on his 'screen, the changing glow doing unfortunate things to his long nose. "Nadir to the *Joy*—plus thirteen or thereabouts."

"Point," she suggested.

Norris got up and came to stand behind her right shoulder. He leaned down so their cheeks almost touched, then gave a *huff* of satisfaction that caught in Mac's hair. "That," he said, his arm reaching out, finger ending at a dim shape. "We'll get a better look when we're at the derelict."

He sat again. Mac stared into the darkness. "Do they see us?"

"I hope so. Otherwise, they'll believe we're violating our approved flight path to *Beta*."

"*Beta?*" She looked at him quizzically. "I thought we were doing a pass over the *Uosanah*."

Norris worked some controls before answering. When he did, his voice was subdued. "I prefer not to use real names for the dead."

Mac, who affectionately nicknamed turkeys before shoving them in the oven, decided not to comment. "How close is the Trisulian ship to *Beta?*"

"Close as it gets without being docked. They towed her here."

Lovely. "How—"

"Dr. Connor," Norris interrupted, sounding rather exasperated. "I've preparations to make that will take every minute before arriving at our destination. If you could please be quiet until then?"

Mac grinned. "Sure."

She leaned back and gazed out at a vista she'd never imagined seeing for herself. Dozens of ships, from as many or more species, hovering in space like a cloud of plankton. She'd have to coexist with Norris until Mudge could take a ride. Not to mention get the specs from the engineer. *Base could use something like this.*

"I need music," Norris muttered, jabbing his finger in the workscreen's upper quadrant.

Mac nodded, though he hadn't asked, ready to listen and relax.

Sound blared through the little ship and she winced. "What's that?"

"An accordion. From my personal collection. You don't hear

music like this anymore." Norris began whistling along, slightly
off-key. Whistling to . . . Mac closed her eyes and shook her head.

As she'd feared.

It was a polka.

Surrounded by vacuum, trapped in a bubble with an engineer
who collected polkas. On cue, her headache throbbed anew.

A ride for Mudge in this thing was not, she vowed, *worth this.*

Specs for the bubble lev might be.

If it was a very short trip.

"Dr. Connor!"

"Wasn't asleep," Mac grumbled, opening her eyes. *Not for long,
anyway.* The inside and outside of her head were blissfully quiet.
Rubbing absently at the lingering ache at the back of her neck, she
straightened and looked around. Beside her loomed not so much a
shape but an absence of anything but darkness. *"Beta?"* she
guessed.

"That's the Trisulian battle cruiser." Norris pointed downward.
"There's our target." He stood and went into the back. "I'll show
you."

Light flooded the floor, and Mac moved her feet to get a better
look. The *Beta—Uosanah*—gleamed bronze against velvet where
Norris had illuminated it. Unlike the *Joy,* she appeared capable of
entering an atmosphere, if sleek curves and a lack of external protrusions counted.

Norris resumed his seat. "We'll head for her belly."

The bubble rolled to reorient with the derelict overhead, then
plunged toward it. Mac held her breath, but her stomach didn't
react. At the instant a crash became inevitable, the bubble leveled
out to travel forward along the Dhryn ship. She sent a searing look
at Norris, but he was too intent on flashing displays to notice an
irate passenger. *Probably never had one before.*

The belly of the *Uosanah* was studded with what looked like
cranes and other handling equipment. *So much for her attempt to
decipher ship design,* Mac thought, wondering if these were to take
in orbital boxes, such as Earth exchanged with her way stations.

Her wonder turned to concern when Norris immediately took them into that maze of metal. Their lights flashed against girders and wires and giant hollowed plates. *Too close for comfort.* Mac held onto her armrests, planning exactly what to tell Norris when it was safe to distract him. From his look of concentration, he was hunting something.

He directed the bubble deeper and deeper until the irregular machinery closed around them like a trap. About to protest, *distraction or not,* Mac noticed their pace slowing and closed her mouth.

Just in time. The lights washed over what lay directly ahead. A series of large round doors. *Closed doors.*

Doors Norris continued to approach, although now with caution.

Enough was enough. "What are you doing?" Mac demanded.

"I have to concentrate." One particular door began to loom. Norris' fingers sped across the console.

The door filled the front view, reflecting so much light Mac squinted as she half rose from her seat. "Norris!"

"Hush."

Like a yawning mouth, the door slid open, the lights from their craft plunging within to reveal a launch bay almost identical to the one they'd left.

Of course. Standard technologies, Mac thought inanely. *Trust the IU.*

Trust Norris? *Only as far as the ride home.* "Nice trick, opening that," she said as calmly as possible.

He swung his head to look at her. The determination in it froze her in place. "Here's a better one, Dr. Connor." He did something to the controls.

And the bubble leaped forward to enter the bay.

Almost instantly, the great door closed behind it and the little ship lurched. Mac recognized the motion. They were being towed into the hangar.

Inside the dead Dhryn ship.

"This is why you brought me along," Mac said, furious with herself. *It beat being terrified at what now held them.* "You never intended to just fly by."

"You said it yourself, Dr. Connor." Norris seemed short of breath. " 'First ready, first out the door.' "

"That didn't mean ignoring protocols! What about our escort? What about the Trisulians?" She lowered her voice from full shout; it didn't lose its hard edge. "You'll never be allowed on one of these ships again."

"There was no guarantee I'd be allowed at all. Don't you see? This is my one chance. To show I can contribute. That Humans should be involved." He surged from his seat and went to an instrument apparently suspended in midair near where the door should be. "Don't worry, Dr. Connor. Didn't you see the material lining the bay? It's the Dhryn stealth cloth. Can't see us here. Couldn't see us on approach either. I put us in on *Beta's* far side." Now he looked at her, pale yet defiant. "I've set a buoy to produce a false image of us crisscrossing the surface. Our flight plan gives us three hours' minimum before the *Joy* notices. More than enough time to discover what happened to this ship and the others. There."

Before Mac could do more than cry out in reflex, the lev regained its walls—and an open door.

The cold smell of death flooded in.

"Air's breathable," Norris promised, gathering up bags which he slung over both shoulders. "Bit dry."

Mac wrinkled her nose. "Bit rotten," she amended. Normally, she appreciated the smell for what it signified. *The annual carpet of dead and dying salmon, aswarm with feasting eagles, gulls, and bears. Waters enriched for the generation to come.* Here and now, on this ship?

"I'm guessing the Dhryn never left."

Norris had his back to her. "Ships don't die empty, Dr. Connor." Supremely nonchalant, except she could see his hands shaking as he snugged a belt around his waist, how they fumbled to clip tools to it, dropping one. "Are you ready?"

She couldn't let him go alone, Mac realized, though sorely tempted. For all his bold talk, he knew what he'd done. His career was over if this gamble didn't pay off. *If he didn't incite a war first.* "Remind me to introduce you to Emily Mamani, if we get out of this," she growled.

Mac pulled her pack from under her seat and fitted it on her back. "First I want your promise to get us out of here before the Trisulians—or anyone else—come looking."

"Of course. I do know what I'm doing, Dr. Connor. You read the labels; I'll do the rest. It shouldn't take long."

Save her from theorists loose in the field. "Three hours," Mac repeated, making a show of checking the time.

The hangar was improbably normal. Lights on standby raised to daytime levels as they left Norris' ship, a little brighter than Human norm, but Dhryn liked it that way. *Normal, but too quiet,* in Mac's opinion. The *Joy's* had been full of moving people and machines, rang with voices and mutters and vibrations. *Uosanah's* service shuttles sat silent and still.

Norris began taking scans of everything in sight, as if no one had ever seen a freighter's hangar deck before. She was no starship engineer, but Mac was reasonably sure this wasn't going to provide any answers as to what happened to the colony Dhryn in Haven. She walked ahead, hoping to lead by example, when she noticed the pool of congealed blue under the second shuttle in line.

"Norris!" she called, squatting to look underneath.

Three arms hung down, their ragged ends evidently the original source of the blood pool. Mac frowned and moved closer. *Grathnu* severed a limb cleanly. There'd been no massive blood loss when Brymn had given his to the Progenitor. These—She pulled out her imp and poked the nearest arm out of the shadows. "Wasn't *grathnu,*" she pronounced, studying the dried shreds of skin, flesh, and bone. "What do you make of this, Norris?"

Careful to avoid the pool, Norris went on his knees, one hand over his nose. "I don't know what grath—whatever is. But he must have been desperate to squeeze in there. This—" he pointed to the underside of the shuttle, through which Mac glimpsed portions of blue skin and brown fabric, "—is part of the tow mechanism. If anyone had tried to launch her, he'd have been torn apart."

Mac straightened and glanced around. All quiet, all peaceful. *All empty.* "So he wasn't trying to leave the ship."

"Or he tried," the engineer disagreed, climbing to his feet, "but didn't have time to climb into the shuttle before having to hide."

Hide from what? "We could leave," she suggested, holding back a shudder. "We could leave right now and let a team come back." The look he gave her was very likely the one she'd given Kammie when told to abandon the field stations because of a mere earth-quake. Mac sighed. "Fine. But this never ends well in vids."

"I don't watch them."

"I'm not surprised." She sniffed the air. "C'mon. There are more here."

More wasn't the right word, Mac decided a moment later, as she and Norris stared down at what had been Dhryn. "Three," she guessed, using a toe to shift what remained of a leg so she could see underneath. There was clothing. Bone. Little else. "They've been eaten," she added helpfully.

"I can see that." To his credit, Norris was stone-faced and calm. He raised his scanner, passing it over what was left. "Cannibalism," he concluded briskly. "There have been cases."

Mac raised her eyebrows. "There have?"

"Asteroid miners. Pre-transect deep space missions. Not uncommon."

"You're making that up."

He pulled out his imp with a challenging look. Mac shook her head, feeling again the Progenitor's remorse. *And appetite.* "You could be right," she admitted grudgingly. "Sure we can't leave now?"

"Of course not." Norris nodded to the hangar exit. "We've two and a half hours left. The only danger here is ignorance."

"I'll remind you you said that," she told him, but followed anyway.

The engineer knew the ship. *Knew the floor plan,* Mac corrected, watching Norris closely. He made the right turns. He announced, correctly, what would be behind doors before opening them. She was less impressed that he expected her to go first through those doors.

Sure, let the biologist find the icky bodies.

Although, to Mac's unspoken relief, they found no more corpses. The doors led to nothing more exciting than intersecting corridors and holds. Many holds, crammed to their ceilings. The *Uosanah* had been an active freighter, fully loaded with goods bound for Cryssin Colony, likely en route to Haven before the Ro attack had changed everything.

Norris was hunting for a link to the ship's data systems, which, he claimed, should be available within the holds. If they found one, they wouldn't have to go all the way to the *Uosanah's* bridge. On that basis, Mac was happy to tag along, but so far, they'd had no luck. *So much for floor plans.*

The latest hold was the largest yet. Norris cheered, convinced it must hold an access panel. While he checked his 'screen for details on this part of the ship, Mac pulled aside the wrapping on the nearest crate and picked apart packing material until she uncovered its contents. "Ah."

"You've found something?" Norris demanded, hurrying over.

She lifted out an umbrella and opened it for his inspection. Bold stripes of red, green, and orange ran around it. There was a second handhold, farther up the handle. Well-suited to Dhryn. "They don't like rain."

"Dr. Connor, we're looking for ship's data. There's no time for—"

"Speaking of which, it's suppertime on the *Joy.* I don't know about you, but I missed lunch." *Missed breakfast and lost lunch,* but the difference didn't matter to her empty stomach. Mac leaned the umbrella against the crate and pulled open her bag. From it, she drew two nutrient bars, one of which she passed to an astonished Norris. She found her bottle of water and took a slug. "I've learned to travel prepared," she said, biting into the bar. "Go ahead. I've more."

He sniffed it, then took a bite. He made a face. "This is awful."

"Stops you eating too many." Her stomach growled and Mac took another, bigger bite. She waved her stick at Norris. "We could use a ship like yours at Base—my research station. Any chance of getting the specs? When we get back," she qualified, handing him the water. "We have transparent membrane, of course, but to go to any depth we need something that can take pressure."

He gave her a strange look. "My ship? Oh. You mean the projector. It's just a fancy internal display, Dr. Connor. What—did you think my ship somehow turned transparent?"

Touché. Mac laughed. "Biologist," she quipped. "But the end result is extraordinary. I'd really like to have it."

"You're welcome to the schematics," he replied, tucking the rest of his bar into a pocket. "We should—"

"Get going. Yes." Mac finished hers and put away the water bottle, feeling almost normal again. *Amazing what a little sustenance could do.* "What now?"

"There should be a panel in here." Norris checked the time and shook his head. "It's taking too long. We'll have to split up to check along the walls. You know what to look for—"

"Not really."

"Any panel that has the outline of the ship on or beside it. Call me if you find one."

"No com." At least, none that he'd given her. *Fieldwork amateur.*

Norris grinned and shouted, "Hello!"

The echoes reverberated throughout the hold.

"Point taken," Mac said, grinning back. She looked around. In keeping with all Dhryn structures she'd seen, the hold walls were at angles less than perpendicular. Racks laden with crates lined both sides. Here, the left wall angled sharper than the right, its first rack barely above her head. Norris would have to duck. "I'll take this side," she offered.

On impulse, she grabbed the umbrella.

The center aisle of the hold had been bright and open. Along the wall, the light was lessened by the overhead rack. Worse, Mac found herself passing through the shadows cast by huge boxes. Each band of darkness was regular and sharp. Five quick steps took her back into light.

Two slow steps took her back into the dark.

It wasn't pitch. She could see well enough to know there weren't panels of any description, but to be sure, she trailed the fingers of her left hand over the cool metal. Her right clutched the umbrella. An unlikely weapon; uncertain comfort. She considered dropping it, but couldn't find the right spot. *Mustn't leave a mess.*

Within the next patch of shadow, her foot kicked something small and sent it skittering forward into the light. Mac bent to pick it up. "Well, I'll be . . ." she murmured. It was a Dhryn food cylinder. She held it up and peered inside. Not empty. Its contents had dried and shriveled into a lump.

There were more. The swathe of light at her feet was littered with them. "They weren't starving," she whispered uneasily. She followed the refuse into the aisle and found herself in front of an open door.

Mac stepped inside what could only be a storage unit. Its shelves were lined with tidy rows of food cylinders, thousands of them. Only near the door were any disturbed. There, a shelf was smashed and cylinders were scattered everywhere, as if . . .

She backed out of the unit, hand tight on the umbrella. "Norris!"

. . . as if someone or something had discovered they weren't edible.

"Norris!" Mac put her back to the hold wall.

Something *scurried* along the overhead rack.

Her breath caught. *It couldn't be.*

Scurry, scurry.

She could hear running footsteps and didn't dare call out again. Didn't dare do anything. Sweat trickled down her forehead, evaporating to chill in the dry air of the hold. She didn't dare shiver.

Skitter, scurry.

There. Above and to her right. The direction Norris would come.

An ambush?

Mac didn't think, she exploded into a run, weaving between crates, heading away from the Ro—*the walker*—and the man. As she ran, she found her voice and shouted. "The Ro are here. Go back, Norris! Call for help!" The words were punctuated by her thudding feet.

Spit! Pop!

Loud, but not as close. If the walker understood what she'd said—had chosen to chase Norris—they were in worse trouble.

There was worse? "Hurry, Norris!"

She'd run into the far wall of the hold soon. Mac began search-ing for a hiding place, cursing the tidy habits of Dhryn under her breath. Each crate was neatly aligned with its neighbor, offering nothing that would shelter a speck of dust, let alone a desperate Human.

Wait. Just ahead two crates overhung their pallet, as if pushed. Tearing off her backpack, Mac flung herself on her stomach and wiggled into the tight space beneath. She squeezed back as far she could, pulling the pack and umbrella under with her.

Then did her best to be invisible.

- 16 -

ENCOUNTER AND EFFECT

NOTHING TO SEE here. Mac did her best to believe it. *Maybe the Ro would, too.* Her legs were already cramping and her right arm, caught beneath her body, would shortly be asleep. These minor discomforts were welcome distractions. She wanted to avoid thinking about the corridors of the Dhryn ship—of Norris running back—of what it would be like to try and remember the way when something was chasing you, something you couldn't see . . . holding your breath so you could listen for any sound . . .

Stop that.

She hadn't heard anything more, from the Ro or Norris. She might have been wrong. Norris would have a comment or two about that.

For once, she'd love to take the blame. She took slow, light breaths.

Something stank. Mac took a deeper sniff and almost gagged. She knew that smell.

Dead Dhryn.

All her senses must have been shut down by fear to miss it. Mac only now appreciated that her shoulder and hip weren't pressed against another crate, but into something yielding.

She didn't panic. *Nothing wrong with sharing space with a corpse,* she assured herself.

Unless it was warm.

Mac held the air in her lungs, listening over the frantic thudding of her heart. No doubt about it.

Something else was breathing behind her.

She exhaled slowly and gently, resuming her own breathing. *After all,* she reasoned wildly, *she'd been fine so far. Why suffocate?*

She lay on her stomach, her right arm pinned beneath, her head turned so she could look out of her hiding place. *As if she'd see the Ro walker.* Now, gradually, Mac lifted her head and rolled it on her chin, eyes straining at the black shadows behind her.

A small piece of shadow moved closer, tentatively, slowly. She made herself stay still as a three-fingered hand formed in the light. It reached toward her face then withdrew, reached again and stopped in midair, trembling. Its skin was puckered and seamed, the digits twisted. Dark drops fell from the palm.

She'd seen a hand like that before.

Mac looked harder and made out the glint of an eye in the darkest shadow. *Just her luck.* She felt profoundly abused. *The only hiding place from the Ro, inhabited by the Dhryn version of insane.*

When adult Dhryn failed to Flower into their final metamorphosis, it was called the Wasting. Those trapped within their degrading bodies were shunned, and set aside to die. Brymn had feared that fate. Ordinary Dhryn "did not think of it." Mac had been . . . curious.

Really not curious at the moment, she decided. A Wasted was dangerous. Brymn had been emphatic in his warning. They were known to attack other Dhryn. Mac's heart began to race again.

The gnawed remains of the *Uosanah* crew . . . the available but ignored food within the storage unit . . . *yummy fresh Human.*

Just as she tensed to squirm away as quickly as possible, *Ro or not,* the hand fell to the deck, palm up. The fingers spasmed once, as if in entreaty, then were still.

Mac hesitated, remembering more of that conversation with Brymn, another lifetime ago. She'd told him she sought the truth. She'd claimed it was part of being Human to act . . . to help.

She'd watched him Flower into something far worse.

Her left hand was touching her pack. Moving very slowly, Mac reached inside until her fingers closed on a nutrient bar. She brought it out, bringing her left arm over her head until her hand was near the Wasted's. "This is our food," she whispered as quietly as she could. She laid the bar on its palm.

The fingers curled closed. The hand withdrew. She could see the glint of the eye, then it was gone; the head had changed position. *Trying her offering?*

The hand reappeared, empty and palm up. *Didn't bother to chew.* Mac reached into her pack and found another bar. It vanished in turn. When the hand came out a third time, she whispered, "I'm sorry. That's all I have."

A vibration she felt through the floor. Distress.

It understood?

"I'm Mac—" *Dhryn formalities seemed even more pointless than usual.* "Who are you?"

The voice was faint but clear. "I do not exist."

Aliens. Mac lifted her head until it touched the crate above, trying to see more of the Dhryn. "We can discuss that later," she told it. "Can you walk?"

Her first fear, that the Ro would be waiting for them, proved unfounded. Her second, that the Wasted was wedged under the crate for good, proved uncomfortably close to the truth. It was too weak to struggle free on its own. She'd finally had to lie down and pull at whatever emaciated limbs she could reach. She did so as gently as possible, gradually working the Dhryn free.

During this process, they'd been sitting ducks. *Proving the Ro was otherwise occupied.*

Doing her best not to think about how, Mac sat beside the Dhryn, letting it recover. In the light, the reason for calling this state the "Wasting" was apparent. The being was little more than fracturing skin over bone. She was astonished it still breathed. The arms were sticks, the legs not much better. *The hands* . . . she leaned closer. Three were missing, severed neatly. This had been a Dhryn of accomplishment, thrice honored by his Progenitor. No other clues. Its—*his,* she told herself—his body bore no bands of cloth. *They probably wouldn't have stayed up anyway.*

The rotting flesh smell came from the fissures in his skin. There was nothing she could do about those, not here, and the fluid they leaked was going to leave a trail.

"You need to stand," she said. *Where was Norris?* She saw the umbrella and offered it. "Use this."

"Why?" The Wasted lifted his face to hers. The yellow of his eyes was sallow and pale, the flesh pulled away from the bony ridges of his features to show her the precise shape of his skull. His lips barely moved. When they did, they bled. "I do not exist."

"The Ro do," she said deliberately. "There's one on your ship. We have to leave, now."

When his eyes half closed, as if in defeat, she sharpened her tone. "I am Mackenzie Winifred Elizabeth Wright Connor Sol. That which is Dhryn must survive. Do you understand me?"

"You are Human," he whispered in perfect Instella, "I do not exist. The Progenitors are gone. What is Dhryn now?"

Not a Haven Dhryn. *A more worldly creature.* Mac knelt beside him. "Not all the Progenitors are gone," she pleaded, using the *oomling* tongue. "Come with me. Don't let the Ro win."

His eyes closed and she thought he'd given up. Then, slowly, one hand reached for the umbrella. She hurried to put it in his grasp and help him stand.

If it hadn't been for his wheezing breath and halting, but steady steps, she might have walked with the dead. Certainly the smell was there. Mac ignored it. Normal Dhryn body posture, slanting forward at almost forty-five degrees, worked in her favor. Her right shoulder fit nicely under his left uppermost arm, which lacked a hand. He gripped the umbrella in his right upper and middle hands. As for his mass?

Right now, it was less than hers. She supported a body that shouldn't be alive. And they made progress. The Wasted knew the ship and didn't hesitate as he led her back to the hangar. The trip was shorter than she remembered, without side trips to investigate every door.

Where was Norris?

Mac listened for the Ro, the skin at the back of her neck crawling with fear. No way to hide or outrun the creature now. Not with the Wasted; not in these open halls.

They turned a corner and Mac gave a sigh of relief, recognizing the final stretch of corridor. "Almost there," she said.

A voice in her ear, strained with effort. "Why are Humans at Haven?"

"Long story," she temporized. "Let's get out of here first."

She hadn't remembered the door to the hangar being open, but Norris could have left it that way, to help her get through quickly. *No choice.* Mac and the Wasted shuffled forward.

They passed the pile of cloth and rotting bone, neither glancing in its direction.

The lev came into view. *Nothing had ever looked so good,* Mac decided, trying not to hurry. Her blood pounded in her ears, making it hard to listen for what might be hiding between the shuttles as they passed.

"That is your ship?" said the Wasted.

"Yes—" Mac's voice broke as she saw the form crumpled in the lev's shadow. "Wait here," she said, disentangling herself from the being's hold as carefully as haste allowed.

Then she ran to Norris.

He'd almost made it, she realized in horror, dropping to her knees beside the body at the foot of the lev's blood-splattered ramp. Her hands didn't know where to touch. There was hardly anything of him not sliced apart, hardly anything but his face still recognizable. Red arched in all directions.

Slime glistened.

"Human!"

Mac whirled, unable to credit that deep bellow had come from the Wasted, amazed to see him rushing toward her, using his hands and stumps as well as feet. He reared up, drew in a deep breath, then retched. She flung herself away and back as acid spewed forth from his mouth, to coat a nightmare from thin air.

A nightmare that screamed!

Mac writhed on the floor, hands tight over her ears, but it made no difference. The sound penetrated her nerves until she could barely think. She tried to see what was happening.

The Wasted had dropped flat on the deck, limbs outstretched.

While some*thing* died.

The sound finally stopped. Mac took a shuddering breath, then two. She rose to her knees, her feet, and staggered forward. All the while her mind tried to deny what she saw.

This was a walker?

Mac didn't see how this thing in front of her could have walked at all. Its body, if there was one, was hidden beneath a convulsion of limbs, all distinct, drawn into fetallike curves. Tatters of material, glittering metal flakes, fibers—all drifted in the air above it, as though not ready to succumb to gravity and fall with the body they'd once wrapped. She saw no head.

There were the claws, though, long, straight, and needle sharp. *Scoring moss and soft wood like a fork; slashing through furniture, fabric—and flesh.* There were limbs like wings or fins within the mass, others thin and knotted on one another, fingertips and bony clubs and cable-thick hooks . . .

With utter calm, Mac turned her head to one side, threw up the nutrient bar and water, wiped her mouth with the back of her hand, then returned to examining the Ro's servant.

None of it made sense. It shouldn't function, not with this tangled, nonsensical structure. The strangest alien form—the weirdest Earthly ones—at least looked as though they could work. *This?*

"Human?"

How could she forget the Dhryn? Mac hurried to his side. He was trying to rise and she helped as best she could. "There could be more," he warned her, his voice barely audible.

"You're right. I know." She passed him the umbrella and they made their slow way around the two bodies.

The short ramp took the last of his strength. She managed to get him inside before he collapsed on the floor of the lev. Mac took the umbrella and used it to methodically sweep the air inside the craft. Once sure they were alone, she closed the door and threw the lock to keep it that way.

She rested her forehead against the door. "We won't leave you here, Norris," she whispered.

Could they leave at all? Taking the pilot's seat, Mac stared helplessly at the console. The console stared back, its dozens of winking machine eyes giving no clue as to their purpose, daring a mere biologist to guess and blow herself up.

"Are you a pilot?"

"No." She glanced at the Wasted in sudden hope. "Are you?"

"I do not—"

"Exist," she finished impatiently. "Yes, I know. Before that. Can you operate this ship?"

"Before . . ." The word was accompanied by a mournful vibration Mac felt through the floor. "I was, in your terms, captain of the *Uosanah*."

Finally, trapped with someone who had the right skills. "Then you can use this." She waved her hands over the incomprehensible console.

He pulled himself to a sit on his lowermost arms, his head beside hers. It drooped from his neck, as though too heavy for it. As he studied the console, she watched a new fracture open behind his ear and ooze blue. "No," he said at last. "Even if I could decipher these controls, they are locked."

"Oh."

"The ship is transmitting." A sticklike finger moved forward and pressed a button. A shaky voice filled the lev.

"This is Dr. Norris, on board the derelict *Uosanah*. Mayday. Mayday. We're in the central hangar. Dr. Connor has confirmed the presence of Myrokynay. Repeat, we have Ro on board. Mayday. Mayday. I'm setting this on auto and going back for her. Please hurry. This is Dr. Norris—"

The Wasted pressed the button again to silence the voice.

"He made it here," Mac said numbly. *And went back for her.*

"Was Norris all his name?"

She shook her head, trying to wrap her grief and guilt around an alien point of honor. "We hadn't been properly introduced. Not yet."

The Wasted lifted his head very slightly—*a bow*. "Then you must—" a gasping pause, "—learn all of his names, Mackenzie Winifred Elizabeth Wright Connor Sol."

"I will," she promised.

He sagged down where he was, between the seats, his face half under the console. Mac moved her feet to make more room for his left arms. She looked around, but couldn't see anything on the small ship to use to make him more comfortable. Norris had thrown his bags in the corner, but they were too small to be useful bedding.

Norris. Mac pulled up her knees and wrapped her arms tightly around them.

Had he hurried to his ship on her word, sent the signal, gone out only to be ambushed within reach of safety?

Or had he run all the way here, the Ro close behind . . . heard that horrible sound nearer and nearer . . . reached the shelter of his ship . . . yet gone back for her?

Mac looked at the locked door, thinking of what lay beyond. *How didn't matter.* "You saved our lives," she whispered. "Thank you."

She cocked her head, listening for any sign of life, hearing only the labored breaths of her companion.

Then dropped her head to her knees.

"Is anyone in there? Dr. Norris. Dr. Connor. Are you in there?"

Mac raised her head, looking to the door, but the voice was inside the lev. *The console.* Lights were flashing in various patterns, more lights than she imagined simply receiving a transmission would require. "This is Dr. Connor," she replied, hoping she didn't need to activate any control to be heard. "Who's this?"

"Your escort from the *Joy.*" *Nothing could have sounded as good.* "Lieutenant Lee Halpern. Dr. Connor, is Dr. Norris with you?"

"No. He's been killed." Mac checked the Wasted. Given the proximity of the Trisulian ship, she wasn't about to announce his presence on an open com. He showed no signs of consciousness but was breathing.

"Are you in immediate danger?" Sharp and to the point.

"No. I don't think so," Mac qualified. "You can get me out of here, I hope?"

"Already on it. Intersystem craft have an auto retrieve function—safety feature. The captain asked Dr. Norris for his remote codes before you left. Ship's systems will reverse your course and head back to the *Joy.* Stand by."

Mac sat by, relieved beyond words. But as time continued to pass with only the same light patterns taunting her, that relief faded. *If she counted the number of times auto-anything had failed in the field* . . . She leaned over the console. "Halpern. I'm guessing there's a problem."

"We're working on options, Dr. Connor. The codes activated the retrieval of a probe, Dr. Connor, not your ship. Where are you exactly?"

Norris had made sure he wouldn't be stopped short of his goal, Mac realized, feeling more pity than anger.

"Inside the *Uosanah*. Parked in a hangar," she sighed, leaning back in the chair. "We entered through the middle of a row of round doors inside a mass of what looked to me like container-handling equipment. But I'm no engineer."

"Is there any way for you to determine the presence of hostile forces?"

The Ro? "The one I know of is dead. And," Mac took a steadying breath. "Dr. Norris is outside the ship, too."

"Is the area secure?"

"Of course it's not secure. That's why I'm locked inside!" Mac glared at the lights, then shook her head. *She wasn't at her best.* "I'm sorry, Halpern. It's been a little—I'm out of my depth here. I don't know if there are more of them. I'd really rather not go and look, if you don't mind."

"I don't want you to, Dr. Connor—may I call you Mac?"

The situation was that *bad?* "Yes."

"Mac, I don't want to alarm you—" *Didn't people realize how terrifying that statement was?* "—but things are a bit complicated out here as well. The captain launched tacticals at your distress call—they could get inside the derelict, deal with whatever—but the Trisulian commander won't let them approach. The Sinzi-ra is doing his best to change that." The tone was matter-of-fact. Mac winced, well able to imagine the furious negotiations. Everyone in the system probably heard Norris' distress call—including the part about Ro on board.

The idiot faction, trying to send diplomats; the rest preparing to blow up the Uosanah *and the other derelicts.*

And one trapped biologist.

She wasn't the only one at risk. Halpern's tiny shuttle was a provocation to all sides, simply by being near the Dhryn ship. "How about you?" she asked. "Can you stay?"

"Not going anywhere, Mac. Not without you." A pause. "I don't suppose you're a pilot."

"No. Why?"

"Oh." A pause. "If you were, and if you could find and access the protocols Dr. Norris used to enter the hangar, you could set the bay to auto. You'll drift out and I'd snag you and take you back to the *Joy*." Halpern grew enthused. "Maybe I can talk you through it."

And if she could breathe vacuum, she could walk. Mac sighed. "Norris locked the controls. Even if he hadn't, you should see this thing, Halpern. It's modified from standard. There's research gear, scanners . . ."

A hand brushed her foot and Mac stopped to glance down. The Wasted was still unconscious. *But breathing.*

"Wait." She bit her lower lip, then nodded to herself. "There's someone with me who might be able to make sense of it."

"Who?"

A dying Dhryn who'd survived this long on the bodies of his former crew? Mac thought fast. "Charlie. Charlie Mudge. He wanted to come along and we snuck him on board." Dead silence. Mac prodded the Wasted with her toe. "I know it was against regulations," she babbled on, "but he's flown starships."

"Regulations be damned. Let me speak to him."

"Give me a minute. He's—he's been hurt." She reached down and shook the Wasted, obtaining a low moan. "Charlie," she urged, careful to use Instella. Her hands slipped over fluid and flaccid skin. She gripped harder. "You have to get us out of the hangar. Do you understand? I need you."

"I—do not—exist."

"He's not himself," Mac said loudly. She got out of the pilot seat and crouched as close to the alien's head as she could. "Listen to me," she whispered. "This is your ship. You must know how to launch a shuttle—please, *Lamisah*."

An eye opened and regarded her, its yellow almost white. " '*Lamisah?*' " His bleeding lips twisted in what might have been scorn. "You are not-Dhryn."

"And you don't exist." Mac rested her hand on his chilled shoulder. "A great pair. Can you do it?"

"Mac? How's Charlie?"

"Oh, getting there." Halpern sounded anxious. *Good thing there wasn't a vid link.*

The Wasted sucked in air and held it. He rose, gripping the chairs and her knee for purchase, then almost fell again. She wrapped her arms around him, trying to avoid the larger fractures. As he leaned against her, she could barely make out his whisper. "Internal com. Command . . . I can command . . ."

She raised her face to the lev ceiling. "Charlie's accessing the codes." *He didn't need to know which ones.*

"Hurry," Halpern responded, distinct stress in his voice. "It's a little busy out here, if you get my drift."

"Can you do it from here?" Mac asked the Wasted. She took his slow reach for the console as yes.

A little busy?

Jurisdictional issues.

"I can't believe I'm doing this," she muttered and put her hand over the Wasted's to stop him. "Wait."

Halpern heard. "Doing what, Mac? There's no time—"

"Stand by."

Moving quickly, Mac dumped the tools and scanners from one of Norris' bags, slinging it over her shoulder. She grasped the umbrella firmly and went to the door. The Wasted turned his big head to watch her unlock it. "I'll be right back," she promised, and threw open the door.

Once again, the odor of decay and death filled her nostrils. This time, instead of being hidden, the bodies were steps away. Before she could hesitate—*as in come to her senses*—Mac walked down the ramp. She took her time and poked the air around and in front with the umbrella, feeling like a fool but unable to move unless sure she wasn't walking into a Ro or its invisible servant.

The silence should have been reassuring. *It made it hard to breathe.*

"Way too much imagination," she panted.

She reached Norris, and gently laid the umbrella beside him. *He'd said "Ships don't die empty."* She didn't think he'd mind resting in this one for a while longer.

Mac put the bag over her real hand and headed for the other

corpse. Every second counted. "Just another specimen," she told herself, hunting for something to grab that wouldn't cut through the fabric. One of the clubbed limbs looked promising. Both her hands shook so badly she couldn't touch it on her first try. "Call yourself a biologist," she muttered. "It's another dead specimen. Doesn't even smell. Much."

A lunge and her fingers wrapped around what felt harder than ordinary flesh. Without pause, she pulled back, her artificial hand clenching so tight she felt something give. The body resisted, then moved, sliding along the deck, remaining limbs waving aimlessly.

scurryscurry

Mac froze, then realized the sound had come from the corpse, as if parts rubbed together. "You're dead," she reminded it, and pulled. *scurryscurry* She took a step and pulled, wishing for more slime. "Wait . . ." And again. "Till . . ." She grunted a word with each effort, as much to keep herself company as to cover the sounds from the corpse. "They . . ." The thing outmassed her, though not by much. "See . . ." Keeping it moving was easier, though her arms were already aching with strain.

"You!"

Her foot hit the end of the ramp. Stepping up, she blinked sweat from her eyes and heaved. The corpse came partway, then stuck fast.

Was a little cooperation too much to ask?

Abandoning her prize was unthinkable. *They'd never be given a chance to examine it.*

Then Mac smiled. She'd loaded and unloaded levs in the middle of blizzards. *There were a few tricks.* "Wait here," she told the corpse, and ran into the lev.

The Wasted hadn't died while she'd been gone. *One relief.* "Be ready, Charlie," she told him, then went to the ramp control, tossing the bag from her hands. The air moving into the lev made her shiver despite the warmth of exertion. The open door was like an invitation.

But, at long last, Mac-friendly technology. With a cry of triumph, she reversed the closing sequence, overrode the load safeties, and hit the emergency retract.

With a machine protest, the ramp snapped itself up against the ship before the door could shut.

And with a *skitter . . . scurry . . . POP!* the corpse answered momentum and rolled into the lev, Mac jumping out of its way.

"Always works," she said with satisfaction, turning to her companion.

The Wasted's eyes were huge and his limbs trembled so violently they clattered against the console.

"Don't worry," Mac soothed. "I can fix the door." She let the ramp back down, reset the controls, and let the door close properly.

"That—that—" The Instella stopped and the floor vibrated. Not that there was much floor left, the corpse having sprawled into a nasty mass of appendages, several either broken from her handling or with implausible joint structure. Or both.

Leaving no room for a panicked Dhryn.

"We do not think of it," she told the Wasted, slowly and clearly, making sure his eyes were on hers. "Do you understand me?"

"Mac!" Halpern's disembodied voice was close to a shout. "What's going on? Where did you go? Charlie didn't answer—has he passed out on you?"

"Lamisah," she whispered. "This one thing and you can rest. I promise."

Eyes blinked at her, then shifted to the console. "I am—here, Halpern," the Wasted said, the effort to speak at all plain to Mac. Her throat tightened in sympathy. Withered fingers touched a blue button among the dozens, slowly input numbers, methodically pressed a sequence of other controls. *How well could his mind function, given the wreck of his body?* Mac judged this an unproductive line of thought and dropped into the passenger seat.

The ship gave that characteristic lurch and she leaned with it, as if encouraging it to continue moving. *Last chance to stop us.*

"Sending us into the bay now," the Wasted said. "I've—I've set auto launch to put us—put us beyond the freight area."

"I'll be waiting for you." Halpern, quick and sure. "Good work, Charlie. Can't wait to shake your hand."

The Wasted gave Mac a look she had no problem interpreting at all.

- CONTACT -

T HE FROW HUNG HEAD DOWN, the better to see the small black object lodged at the base of the crevice. Its surface was nonreflective. It might have been water-polished stone, heaved from a distant riverbed during the annual floods. *Se* Ferenlaa checked the signal detector once more to be sure. "Record this as number sixty-three and destroy it."

Se's lackey, *Ne* Liani, was perched on the opposite wall. *Ne* dutifully recorded the number. "Sixty-three. How many more are left?"

Ne was an individual of undeniable beauty in uniform, with the intelligence of drying moss. Why *ne* had been assigned to *se* when *ne* would have shone hanging at a ceremonial post or as a display model for a hat store, was beyond *se's* comprehension. *Mater* must be slipping. And now, when routine had become crisis, *ne's* blithe incompetence was a risk.

"I've told you before, sib-cousin, it doesn't matter how many remain. They must all be found. Now, be quick! Once this one is destroyed, I'll be able to tell if another lies near our position."

Quick movement was thankfully among *ne's* skills, along with—*se* was told—a finely developed moral sense. Both virtually guaranteed success as either a snatchcross referee or pet retriever. After all, was not a family's highest goal to advance the next generation through the ranks? As *Ne* Liani fumbled with the acid pack attached to *ne's* chest, *se* mused on how best to broach the subject with *mater* when next home. If they had a home to return to, *se* corrected.

Ne struck a pose with the spray nozzle in one hand, membranes set to advantage. "Ready, sib-cousin."

"Just destroy it," ordered *Se* Ferenlaa. As the first blast bubbled its way through the object's outer casing, *se* monitored the signal detector. "Again. Good. It's silenced."

Se flipped *se-self* around and flowed up the crevice, pausing beneath the signs citing rates and regulations, ignoring the agitated flutters from the banished tourists clinging overhead. The Teinsmon Trickle was always busy, being one of the must-do wonders of this region. It wasn't *se's* fault that those waiting for the all-clear had paid a truly ridiculous sum for the privilege of hanging for an hour within its mineral-laden sprays.

Missing one of the transmitters would be.

Their Sinzi-ra had made that clear. The outgoing signal must be stopped.

The Trisulians—*may their offspring rot within their bodies*—had arranged for an unknown number of the devices to be strewn about the Frow homeworld. Most had been sold as landscaping ornaments, their black polished into a smooth hemisphere that could be affixed on a wall among rooted flowering climbers. Quite fetching, if cheap. Those had been easily traced and destroyed.

But the rest were of the type *se* hunted, dropped into shadows by Trisulian tourists. They'd known where to start looking—no Sinzi-ra let aliens wander a homeworld unremarked—but they hadn't found them all before the transmissions began.

Calling the Dhryn.

It had become a race against death. While ordinary citizens went about their business, unaware their world was at risk, those with the right training were given detectors and ordered to climb wherever a device might be hidden, to find and destroy it. *Se* Ferenlaa installed home com systems, with *se's* sib-cousin's dubious help. Close enough, they'd told him.

Se held out the detector, hoping they'd found the last here. *No. Another signal, nearby.* "Come!" Relieved *Ne* Liani hadn't noticed the admiration of the spectators—such things turned a young Frow's head—*se* led the way as rapidly as *se's* older limbs could move, leaving safer paths in favor of any shortcut that beckoned.

A planet-wide evacuation was impossible. Those of highest rank were told, but refused to leave. *Se* shared their pride. Frow clung fast and would not willingly fall.

When no handhold offered, *se* threw *se-self* forward and down in hopes of one, membranes out and humming, sulfur-stained rock flashing past. *Se's* claws snatched at one grip, then another, finally latching on to a barely perceptible crack. Making sure all four limbs were secure, *se* looked for *ne.*

"Right here, sib-cousin," came the reply. *Ne* Liani passed *se,* moving with easy grace.

Se checked the detector. "It's above us. There. Sixty-four."

The Trisulian had shoved the transmitter in a fissure near one of the larger trickles, the rocks to either side carved by the claws of the generations of Frow who'd sought miracles from the spring.

Ne recorded the number. "Sixty-four. Shall I destroy it now?"

Se wanted to grab the acid pack and do it *se-self.* "Yes, yes! But climb above it first, fool!"

"There's no need to be insulting, sib-cousin."

Ne even pouted beautifully. *Se* clung to the rock and swore to talk to *mater* if they survived this. "Just do it. Please. Quickly."

Ne Liani pumped the spray.

Se Ferenlaa stared at the detector. "Again."

Were they too late?

"Again. Hurry!"

It was silenced. *Se* climbed higher and checked. *Nothing.* Hardly daring to hope, *se* went to where cliff ended in the deadly flat land above and held out the detector.

Nothing.

They'd done it. Here at least.

Se put away the detector and climbed down to where *ne* waited. Without a word, *se* carefully stripped, hanging hat and uniform on the provided hooks. *Se* slipped into the nearest glistening trickle of water and relaxed.

"Sib-cousin. We haven't paid!"

Se Ferenlaa sighed. Maybe *ne* had a future in ticket sales.

At least now, ne *might have a future.*

Consternation . . .

The Call ends. The path is lost. The Great Ships pause.

All that is Dhryn is endangered. There is no life but that which is Dhryn.

The Progenitors call for Vessels, seek accommodation.

But that which is Dhryn understands the Truth.

One must survive the Great Journey.

Even at the cost of another.

- 17 -

PRESENTS AND POLICY

MAC WASN'T SURE if she was escorting one corpse or two to the *Annapolis Joy*. The Wasted, now curled at her feet, had grown quieter and more still throughout the journey. She hoped it was *hathis*, the Dhryn healing comalike sleep. She feared it was simply the end.

The lev continued, attached somehow to Halpern's shuttle. She couldn't switch to the surround view Norris had installed, which meant she sat in a box for the duration. *A very quiet box.* She'd told Halpern "Charlie" was sleeping. In turn, he'd expressed concern over who else might be able to listen. They'd agreed on silence.

Not even a polka.

The return didn't take as long as she'd remembered, despite having napped on the way out. Halpern's relieved, "about to dock, Mac," announcement startled her.

Mac sat straight. "And me without a shower," she muttered to herself, wrinkling her nose. Most of the stink came from her clothes. Sweat and vomit. *Lovely.* A brush of one hand did nothing for the overlapped stains of Human and Dhryn blood. *The hand was bloody, too.*

Her knees glistened with slime. The corpse didn't. She frowned at it thoughtfully. *Useful stuff, slime.* A healthy salmon wore a protective coat of it. Salamanders breathed through it. Slugs glided on a road of it. Nothing quite matched her observations. *Can't assume it's natural slime anyway,* she scolded herself, postponing any investigation until much later.

Moving around the lev was awkward, given the need to avoid contact with alien parts. Mac tiptoed and sidestepped to her backpack. Once there, she took out her water bottle and used what was left in it to wet her face and hands. She used the backpack itself as a makeshift towel, having to trust the end result wasn't worse.

Physically, she was in better shape than her clothing. Food was a distant concern; just looking at the corpse made her queasy. Emotionally, she was numb and content to remain so for a while longer.

Mentally, though, she'd reached the state Emily referred to as "crabby" and Mudge had frequently decried as "utterly unreasonable."

In other words, she'd had enough.

She'd ordered Halpern to bring them into the hangar set aside for Ureif and his consulate, using the premise the Sinzi would want to meet her anyway so it saved time and travel.

Hollans might have found a walker on Earth. He might even plan to share.

She'd make sure more than Humans would have a crack at this one.

Halpern, concerned about "Charlie," assured her he'd called ahead for a med team to meet them.

Mac's lips stretched in what wasn't a smile. *Weren't they going to be surprised?*

"Unlock the door, Dr. Connor."

Mac hugged her knees and didn't budge from the passenger seat. *All well and good to have a plan,* she thought ruefully. *Until no one listened.*

Halpern, either doubting the sanity of a certain biologist, or following the orders of someone whose sanity he did trust, had ignored her request and returned them to the same hangar from which Norris had left. The Human part of the ship. And now a very familiar voice shouted at her through the com system.

"Dr. Connor," Cayhill said, for the fourth time. "Open this door! Let me attend to Mr. Mudge!"

Funny how the best lie could come back to bite you, sighed Mac. She supposed he knew better than to pound his fists on metal, realizing she wouldn't hear it, but the image had its charm. "I've told you, Cayhill. I'm waiting for the Sinzi-ra," she said, for the fifth time. "It's not a hard concept."

A new voice. "Norcoast!"

Mac winced. "Oversight."

She waited for it.

Right on cue. "Charlie Mudge?" The words came out in a sputtering bullroar that had to hurt the man's throat.

The answering *harrumph* was that signature mix of dignified offense. "I am not 'Charlie.' "

"And you aren't on this ship with Dr. Connor, gravely injured."

"Idiot! Of course he's not."

Hearing the odds in the hangar shifting her way at last, Mac grinned. "Hi, Fourteen. Is Ureif there?"

"This is Captain Gillis, Dr. Connor."

Or not. Her grin faded. "Captain. I'd like to get out of here." She put aside her body's sudden agreement on that point. *There was a bottle handy.*

"Then unlock the door." Reasonable.

Mac put her hand on the Wasted. *Not dead yet.* She glanced at the corpse. *Still dead.* "Once Ureif is here."

Reason gave way to official outrage. "The Sinzi-ra is busy trying to keep the Interspecies Union together in this part of space, Dr. Connor!"

"So," she replied coolly, "am I."

She wasn't surprised by the ensuing silence, well able to imagine their faces as they tried to decide if she'd been through too much at last, or this was as serious as she claimed. Cayhill would be shaking his head sadly, but with a triumphant "I warned you about her" in the look he'd give his captain. Fourteen would have his hands over his eyes, worried about her and unable to do anything about it. The captain would appear thoughtful. While Mudge . . .

. . . *he'd know.* Maybe not what she had on board, but that she did have something—someone—with her she wouldn't risk being revealed without the Sinzi-ra's authority at hand.

There was, of course, a point beyond which she couldn't push Gillis, not on his own ship. If this had been one of the *Joy's* shuttle fleet, he'd have already ordered its door opened and have the codes to do it. Because this modified lev was Dr. Norris' pride and joy, a man he must believe was dead on his watch, she didn't think the captain was prepared, yet, to order his crew to cut their way inside.

Mac estimated she had no more than a half an hour left. She eyed the bottle.

"I am here, Dr. Connor."

Ureif's voice. Mac checked the time. Twenty-one minutes. *He'd cut it tight.* Something else had been occupying him; whatever it was, she was about to complicate it.

"Sinzi-ra." As she went to the door, she ran her fingers through her hair, finding a patch of something sticky. *So much for personal grooming.*

She opened the lev door.

Captain Gillis hadn't taken any chances. A semicircle of armored and armed guards posed threateningly, so close they had to shuffle back when Mac sent down the ramp. Both Sinzi, accompanied by Grimnoii, stood beyond that barrier with Gillis and Townee; Mudge and Fourteen beside them; Cayhill and a small knot of orderlies relegated to some distance away.

This well-thought out arrangement lasted only as long as it took her appearance to register, then Ureif and Mudge were on the move, Gillis only a step behind. The guards took the hint and lowered their weapons, stepping out of the way. Not fast enough for Fourteen, who shoved the nearest aside with both hands.

Mac lifted her hands to slow the stampede. "Nothing a shower won't cure," she said quickly. "I wasn't hurt."

Whether she convinced them or not, protocol paralyzed them at the base of the short ramp: the Humans unwilling to get in Ureif's way, the Sinzi-ra attempting to defer not to the captain, but to the ashen-faced Mudge. *Exceptional awareness,* she judged, relieved to be right. Not to diminish Fy, but this was a Sinzi of Anchen's caliber. *They all needed that.*

And while manners sorted themselves out, Fourteen ran past them all and thundered up the ramp, shouting, "Idiot! Idiot!" He stopped short of grabbing her in a full hug, perhaps realizing that would ruin his favorite paisley shorts, and settled for patting her shoulders. "There are others to take such risks," he scolded all the while. "Others of less value or interest. You should not have gone."

"Glad to see you, too," she said.

Then Mudge was in front of her. Fourteen stepped aside without a word.

Judging by his expression, she looked worse than she thought. If he'd offered concern or sympathy, she might have faltered, begun to react to the past few hours. Instead, a calm question. "What do you need, Norcoast?"

"A stretcher," Mac said immediately, having made her own plans. "Medical facilities within our portion of the ship. Guards and vids for that. And one of those bigger parts bins." Mac pointed down the hangar to where crew had stopped pretending to work on another shuttle while such interesting events were underway in their area.

Mudge nodded and, collecting Fourteen with a look, went back down the ramp. The two moved apart to allow Ureif to advance, the captain close behind. The captain spoke first, eyes wide. "You're sure you're all right, Dr. Connor?"

As she nodded, Ureif lifted one graceful finger to indicate her shoulder, his mouth turning down. "This is Dhryn blood."

Mac backed into the lev, mute invitation. There wasn't room for the other two to fully enter, but she doubted they'd want to anyway. Not once they saw what waited.

The captain's hand flew up to cover his mouth and nose, eyes staring. He managed not to retch, but beads of sweat formed on his forehead. For an instant, the Sinzi's fingers trembled, their blood-red rings sounding like the first hit of freezing rain on dry grass, then they stilled.

Both looked at her.

"Don't worry. The walker's dead," Mac assured them, well aware their reaction wasn't to the Wasted. She gestured to the unconscious being. "He killed it before it could attack me." *Learning how was high on her list.*

Gillis spoke through his hand. "Dr. Norris?"

"We were exploring the *Uosanah* when I heard the walker in one of the holds. While I hid, he went to call for help." Her voice came out flat and strange. *Just the facts.* "When he tried to come back for me, the Ro's thing ambushed and killed him." There was a rise in the sound levels outside. *Mudge and Fourteen.*

Gillis' hand dropped away. His mouth worked before he spoke. When he did, the words were harsh and accusing. "You left Norris there—"

"He's got company," Mac replied wearily. "The rest of the Dhryn are dead."

For an instant, she thought he meant to strike her. Then Gillis shook his head, the blind rage in his face subsiding into something more rational. His eyes flicked to the corpse, his throat working as he swallowed. "How the—never mind, I don't think I want to know. Good work, Dr. Connor. Good work." Real warmth. "What now?"

She wasn't surprised by his self-control. *This* was *the captain of the Ministry's latest and greatest.* "We need to preserve the body. And," she gazed up at the so-far silent Sinzi, "to invite IU scientists on board to learn everything they can from it. From both factions," she emphasized.

This was the key, Mac thought, hardly breathing. *Let those who still believed the Ro were the IU's saviors see this nightmare of flesh for themselves.*

Let them try to imagine its masters.

Gillis' eyes took on a gleam.

A cool finger's tip traced Mac's cheek. "I am overcome," Ureif said, and bowed his head, the white gown whispering with the movement. "What you propose . . . it offers profound congruence."

"I thought you'd like it," she grinned.

Mac didn't like where she had to spend the next hour. Instead of following either Wasted or corpse, or even providing a full briefing to someone, she was sent to decontamination and abandoned to the overzealous ministrations of orderlies with a hose.

Cayhill's revenge, she judged glumly, lifting her arms for yet another spray. She wore her rings, nothing more. Her imp and the little salmon carving sat in a bag, waiting where she could see them.

Humans hadn't been members of the IU long enough—by millennia—to be acceptable hosts for anything worse than Nerban shoe fungus. *And that only stuck to soles for a ride elsewhere.*

When they were done scouring every centimeter of her skin with pointless biocides, Mac thanked the orderlies for the cleanup. *No denying she'd been filthy.* She thanked them for providing clean crew coveralls and slippers. *Her latest clothing having been sent to disposal.* Though she hadn't much else anyway. Consular staff hadn't fully appreciated the rigors of life in space.

She didn't bother to thank them for the sandwich she pilfered on her way out.

Kaili Xai was waiting to escort her wherever. Mac smiled with relief, glad to see someone familiar. "Be honest," she said lightly. "Did they leave me a face?"

Kaili smiled back, then made a show of peering closely. "I think you've lost some freckles."

Mac shrugged. "More where they came from—and where are we going?"

"Where do you want to go?"

The calm question took her aback. *Returned with corpse and guest from a disastrous unauthorized mission, complete with loss of its leader?* "I thought," Mac ventured, "there'd be some yelling."

"Oh," Kaili's expression turned serious. "Enough of that going around. Half the ship is being turned into a consulate and the captain has his hands full fielding delegations to the Sinzi-ra already." A dimple. "I'm sure he'll yell at you eventually."

"No hurry," Mac said. "In that case, I know exactly where I want to go."

As she and Kaili walked to the Origins section, Mac wolfed down her sandwich and then began peppering her companion with questions. The orderly might not be an officer or have bridge access, but Mac doubted even Townee had as thorough a grasp on what was happening on board.

Kaili, who'd taken a certain homesick biologist under her gentle wing the year before, was happy to share the latest gossip. "Oh, no one minds," she replied, when Mac asked about the crew's reaction to the sudden changes. "Might be different if it weren't the Sinzi, but, gad—isn't it amazing, seeing them walking around? Everyone's sending mail home about it. I never thought I'd see one in person." She gave a shy smile. "I even spoke to Fy. She came with Charlie to the dispensary for eyedrops. Graceful. Polite. Quiet. She made me feel special."

"Charlie?" Mac's lips twitched. *Poor Mudge.* Aloud, "I tend to feel I'm wearing my work boots around them." They turned a corner and she waited until a couple of crew passed them before continuing. "What do you mean, everyone's sending mail? I thought there was a ban."

"Just while we were gatebound." Kaili made a rude noise. "You can bet that wasn't popular. The *Joy* may look like a warship, but we're more a glorified customs inspector. Sure we've all simmed on combat rigs, but the tightest we've had to play it was that business with the Ro. At that, the most we did was orbit Myriam and wait on the scientists. I'd expect a mutiny if the captain tried to shut us up here." She laughed. "Or my parents'll register a complaint."

"I'd like to call to my dad," Mac said before she thought.

"It's not quite talking," explained the orderly. "One stream of newspackets goes into the gate, addressed to Earth or wherever. Another set returns. They squeal at close to light when they hit the system. The bigwigs can arrange for sequencing, which is close. If both speakers are near a gate, the time delay can be seconds. But regular folks like us make do with a two- to three-hour swing. Still, keeps you in touch. Last I heard from . . ."

Mac let Kaili's voice drift by, nodding at the right places. *Plenty of time for some judicious editing,* she thought, almost appalled to feel reassured.

They didn't use intership transit, the medlab not being that far. Kaili made Mac laugh with tales of her newly retired parents' efforts to coax an Earth-type garden from their yard on Mars. For her part, Mac talked about her brothers, finding unexpected peace sharing Owen's fall from dignity upon fatherhood and skirting like an abyss how much she could use Blake's advice.

"Not taken, hmm?" Kaili's teeth gleamed in wide smile. "You should introduce us, next pass by Earth. He sounds yummy."

Blake? Mac considered her brother, trying to see it, and shook her head. "I'll introduce you, but then you're on your own. He's the type the family likes to call 'an individual.' Translates as royal pain, sometimes."

"But not always."

"No," Mac said softly.

The Origins part of the ship was deserted. Gillis had merely expedited the move to Myriam. *Probably like releasing a flood.* Everyone, she'd been told, had willingly packed and were now busy checking the transfer of their equipment to planet-bound shuttles. *Leaving her behind,* she sighed to herself, then wondered how she'd become so attached to archaeologists and their work. She'd see them before departure. *Doubtless the time to become maudlin.*

They stopped outside the door Kaili indicated as the Wasted's quarters, both nodding a greeting to the guard stationed beside it. "Thank you, Kaili."

"I'll be around. Stay out of trouble for a while, Mac. Hear me?" With that, Kaili left.

Mac steeled herself and entered the room.

For an instant, she was sure Kaili taken her to the wrong place, even though she'd been told they'd used a portion of the newly abandoned work areas.

There'd hardly be a guard at any other door.

Implying this was the right room. But there were candles burning beside the bed, albeit a bed with an unconscious Dhryn on it. And the last person on the ship she expected to find seated beside that bed looked up at her, dipping his head in acknowledgment, while Doug Court rolled his eyes at her from his station by the monitors.

"Dr. Connor," Wilson Kudla said quietly. "Have you come to join our vigil?"

"Our?" She took a step sideways in order to see Kudla's disciples sitting cross-legged on the floor behind their leader. Their eyes were closed and their lips moved in silent unison, their habit when forced to chant outside their tent. *Small mercies,* Mac thought. "Who let you in here, Kudla?" she demanded, keeping it low.

"Are we not part of this mission? Do we not have the same clearance as the rest?"

Only because you didn't go anywhere, so no one thought to cancel it.
Mac fumed, eyes flitting between the Wasted, who wasn't dead yet, and the insufferable Human at his side. "Of course," she gritted out between her teeth. "May I ask why you're here?"

He swept both arms around to include the Wasted, ceiling, and a portion of the deck in the gesture. "This is one of the Lost Souls. Those who cry to me from the past." His gaze sharpened. "I describe them most clearly in Chapter Thirteen."

"Chapter Thirteen," echoed the disciples in an ardent monotone.

Doug coughed in the background.

Mac forced a smile, the tightness in her jaw warning her the result was probably unpleasant. "I'll have to look that one up again." As if aware he was being deleted, Kudla routinely messaged fresh copies of his opus, *Chasm Ghouls: They Exist and Speak to Me.* "You shouldn't neglect your writing," she ground out. "There's nothing you can do to help here—at the moment, anyway."

"We're doing no harm." Kudla had a forgettable face that tended to park itself at vaguely preoccupied. Mac was startled to see him frown with determination. "We wish to stay."

Ready to have the guard haul them out, her curiosity got the better of her. "Why?"

"He should not be abandoned."

"The med staff—"

His narrow-set eyes actually flashed with outrage. "Would you wish no other companions while awaiting your destiny, Dr. Connor? I think not!"

She sent Doug a helpless glance and he mouthed, "It's okay."

It did keep the author and his disciples busy.

"Stay," Mac agreed. "But you won't touch him. Get rid of the candles. Obey every order you're given by Doug here, or those who replace him, and do not—" she stressed the word, "—engage the Wasted in conversation if he wakes. I'm to be called. These aren't negotiable, Kudla."

"Lost Soul," he corrected.

She sighed. "Call him what you want. Just don't interfere with his care. Understand me?"

He stood and half bowed, sweeping back the voluminous brown

robe he affected. It would have looked dignified except the fabric was caught under his stool and he lost his balance, the disciples scrambling up to save him from a fall.

Mac sighed again.

Humans.

"Thank you for coming." Mac stroked through her 'screen, storing her work. For the first time in a while she was struck by the blue tinge of her fingers. *He brought it out in her,* she thought without resentment, watching Cayhill's approach.

He took his time, his eyes darting around the room. She let him.

It looked liked a hospital room. *Or pending morgue,* Mac reminded herself. The former captain of the *Uosanah* lay on his side, festooned with machinery more alive than he appeared to be.

Cayhill's eyes passed over Kudla and his disciples, now happily huddled together in one corner, touched on the orderly station, now empty, and stopped at the Wasted. "I thought it would be dead by now."

"Nothing we've done," Mac admitted, rising to her feet. There'd been no change, no breakthrough. The nearest possible help? *She was looking at him.*

Giving her a glare as if to imply this was all her fault—*true*—the *Joy's* head physician wandered around the room, hands hovering over various instruments. *Most appropriated from his medlab.* His path wove with seeming casualness closer and closer to the unconscious being, until finally, he halted by the bed. "What's wrong with him?" Almost reluctant.

"A Dhryn can undergo a second metamorphosis," Mac explained, moving to the other side. "The change from *oomling* to adult form? They all do that. The second, the Flowering, changes an adult into something more specialized."

He flinched back. "The feeders."

"Yes. But not in this case." She laid her hand on the blue-stained sheet. "This is the Wasting. I was told it happens when the second metamorphosis fails. Ordinary Dhryn shun such individuals, ignoring their existence even when a Wasted is driven by hunger to attack the living, or feed on the dead. They don't live long, regardless."

"I can see why." Cayhill gazed down at the alien. "The skin is degenerating at every point of stress. The resulting fluid loss— What are you doing for his pain?"

"Nie rugorath sa nie a nai." At his puzzled look, Mac realized she'd spoken in Dhryn. " 'A Dhryn is robust or a Dhryn is not.' They have no medical databases, Dr. Cayhill. There's nothing we can do."

His pale eyebrows drew together. "That's absurd," he snapped. "At least get him off this bed and into a suspension chamber—take the pressure off skin and bone."

"Anything else?" she asked innocently.

Cayhill's frown deepened into suspicion. "Oh, no, you don't. I can't be involved in his care. I told the captain. I can't deal with alien patients, Dr. Connor. It's another specialty altogether. I'm not capable—"

"Not even the Dhryn are capable of dealing with this patient," Mac pointed out. "I could dissect him—hopefully figure out the percentage of the population that ends up this way and why. My team is researching his past, the life on his planet—hopefully they'll figure out how the Dhryn came to be as they are." She could no longer decipher his expression, but kept going. "This Dhryn believes he no longer exists, Cayhill. What he needs is someone who won't let him die." She took a deep breath. "Please."

His fingers reached out to the bed, but he continued to hold Mac's eyes with his. "Why do you care?"

The question echoed hers of Kudla, who watched all this from his corner. She chose to take it at face value, as honest rather than more probing after her hidden motivations or unresolved guilt.

The truth, then.

"I'm not like you, Dr. Cayhill," Mac said quietly. "My work deals with species, not individuals. I follow changes in populations over time, how they interact with others, their environments. Bear with me, please." This as he scowled his impatience. "I want you to understand something. The drives acting on living things— that's what I do. And right now, all around us, those drives are colliding. The result will be extinction. The only real question left is who goes first. I can imagine destroying the Dhryn." Mac looked down at the Wasted and shrugged. "But when I stand here, all I see is someone as trapped as we are."

Without a word, Cayhill took a scanner from the nearby table and passed it over the Dhryn. As abruptly, he stopped, closing the instrument in his fist as if the results offended him. "I won't put up with interference," he informed her almost fiercely. "Not even from you. I want that understood, Dr. Connor. If he's my patient, I'm in charge."

Mac carefully didn't smile. "Of course. Just let us know what you'll—"

"I have my own supplies and staff," he interrupted. "Let me get to work. For what good it will do."

With a nod, she went to the Wasted's head and leaned over his ear, purposefully speaking Dhryn. "You'd better listen to him, *Lamisah*. He'll make your life miserable if you die under his care."

When she straightened, Cayhill was staring at her, patentedly dismayed. "He doesn't speak Instella?"

"He does," she assured him. "And he seems used to Humans. But don't expect a typical doctor-patient conversation. Dhryn don't discuss biology, including their own bodies. If you need me, I'll be available. Anytime."

He stiffened. "I won't need you, Dr. Connor."

"If he needs me," she modified, very quietly.

Cayhill waited for a few seconds, as if to make sure she knew he wasn't giving in, then nodded.

"Dr. Connor! Dr. Connor!"

"I know I'm late," she told the Grimnoii shambling up behind her, making sure to give it room. The creatures managed to sound twice as large as they were, even inside a starship. *Useful technique,* Mac thought, remembering the packed corridors of Base in spring.

There'd been nothing more from Emily or Case in the mail from the courier. *Nothing personal,* she clarified. The detailed reports waiting in her imp had gone a long way to easing her alarm. Emily

Mamani at full throttle could give Kammie lessons in data dumping. None of it came sorted or annotated or indexed, just an "Oh, right. Mac wanted updates," tossed her way, loaded with schematics and Em-only jargon and the occasional salacious cartoon.

Annoying and utterly normal.

"Normal's wonderful," she said out loud.

"Pardon?"

Mac shrugged an apology. "Talking to myself. Human thing." She glanced at the alien, recognizing the array of curved knives. Grimnoii facial features were sufficiently distinct to Human eyes to set them apart as individuals, but she found it quicker to tell them apart by their hardware. It would have helped if they had names, but Rumnor was the only Grimnoii on board who had—or would admit to—one. *For all she knew, the Sinzi required their staff to go nameless and Rumnor was a rebel.*

Equally likely, she reminded herself, *"Rumnor" wasn't a name at all, but a some kind of rank, like "pack leader" or "cider enabler."* About the only sign of precedence was that he tended to speak up first. But then, the others usually caroled in with their contribution pretty quickly.

Undeterred, Mac had applied her own mental labels to keep them straight. This one was Fy-Alpha, Fy-Beta's belt sporting barbed darts. The other Sinzi had Rumnor, plus the two Mac called Ureif's Alpha and Beta, fond of axes and spears respectively.

Not that she'd use the names to their melancholy faces. She was becoming more diplomatic. *When she remembered.*

"Is Fy already there?" Mac asked.

"Of course." This followed by a sigh so heavy and prolonged it implied the universe itself had ended yesterday and they'd been left behind. Mac, taking the hint, picked up the pace. "I bring her the latest newspackets through the gate plus more data from the planet."

More data? "Anything I should know?"

"Do you perform comparative studies on reconstructions of technological remains based on molecular analyses, Dr. Connor?"

"Every Tuesday," she said, straight-faced.

The Grimnoii shook his head ponderously. "You are a tricky one."

Since they met their escort to the meeting at this point, Mac was left to wonder if being "a tricky one" was a desirable reputation to have among well-armed aliens.

Their escort, a tall friendly woman named Elane, walked them to the by-now familiar tube door, coding the request to send them on their way. Another escort would await them at the other end. *Dump the tourists in the river and net them downstream.* Although Mac and Fy-Alpha would have fit within the same bolus, to her relief it had become practice for the weapon-festooned aliens to travel alone.

Plus crusty bits from their happily weeping eyes tended to stray.

The door closed after the Grimnoii and it was Mac's turn. "Have a nice trip," Elane told her as she stepped inside.

"See you later." Mac grinned, finding her balance despite the way her feet sank in at first. *Getting to be a pro at this.* The walls flowed together behind her and she turned to press her back against the far wall, waiting for the bolus to move. Today's scent was fresh cut wood, most likely a crew suggestion.

She felt her body press into the yielding surface and relaxed, ready for the odd sensation as the bolus dropped away and flipped over.

... scurry ... scurry ...

Only knowing she had to be able to hear stopped the scream in her throat.

Nothing.

The bolus merrily swooped and whirled its way toward its destination.

Nothing.

Mac took small, careful breaths, forcing herself to think instead of panic. *Panic was so much easier.* She ran her eyes over the rest of the inner surface, studying every pink centimeter. There were no dimples or other marks to imply something else was along for the ride. She was alone.

Except for her imagination.

"Bah." She didn't need false alarms.

At this rate, she'd be imagining she and Norris had brought the Ro's walker to the *Uosanah* in the first place. That they'd flown together, its telltale sounds conveniently masked by argument and accordion.

That they were on the Joy, *not the derelicts.*

"Stop that," Mac told herself, aghast. The Gathering had developed ways to detect the Ro and their walkers; Dhryn fabric screens disabled them.

Screens that hadn't worked on the Uosanah.

"New rule," she said, fighting to keep her voice steady. "No thinking in a bolus."

But she couldn't hold back one more.

Just because something was terrifying didn't make it stupid.

"Take a seat and wait over there, Dr. Connor. Thank you."

Mac didn't want to sit. She wanted nothing more than to jump up on the captain's long polished table and shout for them all to listen. *Stamping her feet.*

And having gained their attention, she wanted to insist this mass of civilized, responsible beings stop whatever they were arguing about—said argument having continued despite her arrival—and convince her she was wrong.

The Ro couldn't be on board.

Mac sighed. Being a civilized and responsible being herself, she walked over to the row of chairs indicated, now lining the transparent wall overlooking the bridge, and sat beside Mudge.

She took a quick census. The large room was doing its best to hold over thirty individuals, and Humans, despite the furnishings, were in the minority. Herself, Mudge, a member of the crew by the door, and the captain, standing at the shoulder of the Sinzi-ra at the far end of the table. *A waste,* thought Mac, noticing the chairs suited very few of the posteriors presently planted in them. From where she sat, she could see a bench with cushions, but it was occupied by someone's feet.

She felt sorry for Ureif, if he took his guests' comfort as personally as Anchen had.

If this was a meeting, she had to wonder at the agenda. Several were speaking at once—*okay, with grunting and one off-key whistle*—and the room's air was being overscented with mint to compensate for odors it was never intended to handle.

Mudge tapped the back of her hand. "When did these arrive?" he whispered.

She could wish he was less observant—or had better timing. "Ureif brought them."

"And? Any news?" His anxious whisper attracted frowns or their equivalent from those nearest. She leaned over and put her lips to his ear. "Not now, Oversight. What's going on?"

If she'd hoped for reassuring calm, it wasn't here. The voices and body language of all species in the room showed tension, if not worse.

He returned the favor, ducking and twisting his head. "There's been an incident reported, Norcoast. The Frow home world, Tersisee."

Oh, no. Mac looked for, and found, the Frow. *Se* Lasserbee and his lackeys were backed firmly—and securely—against the far wall. From the grips they'd latched on one another, no one was going to fall alone.

"The Trisulians," she whispered.

Representatives of that species sat to the left of Sinzi-ra Ureif, bodies and limbs wrapped in red leather, paired eyestalks fixed on the Frow. Their broad, haired, and faceless heads revealed nothing to a Human observer. The weapons slung on their backs gave reasonable indication these weren't diplomats or scientists. In fact, few here looked obviously academic. *Not that she'd any idea what that meant once you left bipedal motion behind.*

The purple beadlike tip of the uppermost eyestalk on the nearest Trisulian abruptly swiveled to point at Mac. The lower, being male and blind in this light, remained lidded.

As proof she wasn't the only one who noticed such things, everyone in the room fell silent and turned to look at Mac.

Moments like this, she thought glumly, *were why she really hated meetings.*

"Dr. Connor." Ureif rose, fingers lifting. Fy was at his right. "On behalf of everyone here, as well as the Inner Council of the Interspecies Union, may I express our gratitude for your courage and quick thinking. You have provided us all—" *did she imagine "all" was stressed,* "—with our first advantage against the Myrokynay, at great risk to yourself. Thank you."

Mudge elbowed her ribs and Mac shot to her feet. "Any of you would have done the same," she blurted.

"Not me. I'd have expired on the spot," rumbled a well-dressed Nerban, waving his proboscis at her, his single eye almost closed.

"Tell her! Tell Dr. Connor!" *Se* Lasserbee shouted, rocking his trio of support. Sparks flew, and those beings in range of the Frow moved away. From the look on the captain's face, she wasn't the only one hoping the ventilation system could keep up with the Nerban's sweat. *The things one had to worry about around aliens.* "Tell her!" the Frow shrieked. One clawed hand daringly freed itself to point at the Trisulians. "Confess your evil to our Hero!"

Okay, a completely new reason to hate meetings.

"It is common knowledge," said the Trisulian who'd looked at Mac, "that Frow are inclined to paranoia, particularly in their dealings with other species. They scream collusion over regular freight runs; now they rant about innocent tourists. We have, Sinzi-ra, matters of *nimscent*—of future significance—to discuss."

Tourists? Mac wondered if she'd heard the right word.

"Villains!"

"Dr. Connor," the Trisulian continued smoothly, her—*his,* Mac corrected, counting eyestalks—powerful voice overriding the now-incoherent protests of *Se* Lasserbee. "It has come to our attention you may have news of our liaison with your Ministry, Cinder. We are most anxious to know why her communiqués have stopped prematurely."

She bet they were. Mac's hands wanted to curl into fists. She put them behind her back, rubbing her thumb against the rings on her fingers.

"The only matter before us is whether your entire misbegotten species should be sanctioned at the highest level!" *Se* Lasserbee roared. "The highest level!"

For improper tourism? She knew better than to hope that was all it was.

Since the aliens were again shouting at one another, Mac turned to Mudge, standing beside her. "What happened?" she whispered.

"The Trisulians are accused of planting transmitters on Tersisee. Some disguised as harmless ornaments, others left hidden in tourist areas. When the Frow found them and began destroying them, the remainder activated." Mac gasped and Mudge shook his head gently. "It's all right. They were removed in time. But their Sinzi-ra did confirm they were sending the Ro signal—the one that summoned the Dhryn to Sol System. Outside the IU Consulate on Earth, only the Trisulians have that technology."

Mac stared at the three Trisulians, trying to imagine how they could sit there and protest. These had to have been senior staff from the warship at Haven—perhaps the commander. Surely they would have known about the attempt to eradicate the Frow.

She narrowed her eyes. It was difficult to be sure, given the abundant thick strands of red and gray flowing over their shoulders and chests, but she thought the upper third of their torsos were enlarged, beginning above the opening to their stomach, the *dous-cent*.

Pregnant.

More to the point, territorial.

Argument wasn't going to overrule that state of mind.

She'd seen the mammoth Trisulian ship, sitting like a boulder in the flow to and from the gate. They weren't alone—every species in this room represented another ship, had another viewpoint. Mac took a step forward and raised her voice one notch above the rest. *Helped having spent summers talking over the roar of a river.* "Have you compared our Ro walker to the one found on Earth?"

Another pause, this one incredulous. Then, "What did you say?"

She didn't bother looking for the speaker; she kept her eyes on the Sinzi. "This is the group studying the corpse I brought back, isn't it? Surely you'll want to check it against the Ministry's specimen." Mac also ignored the strangled *harrumph* from behind her—she wasn't planning to explain how she knew. For that matter, she and Mudge could be completely wrong. For now, she had the rest of the room thinking about something else, something that faced them all. *Good enough.* "Unless of course you've started exploring the remaining Dhryn ships," she went on, taking advantage of their silence, "and found more for yourselves."

Ureif's red-coated fingers gleamed as they made a complex knot in front of his chest.

That one meant "difficulty," Mac judged, and wasn't surprised. She'd guessed the result of her explorations would be a standstill, with everyone reconsidering the stakes. The newspackets and couriers must be flying through the gate.

Speaking of messages . . . Fourteen should have voiced an opinion by now. She tried to see past those in front of her, searching for him without success.

The Sinzi-ra spoke. "A helpful suggestion, Dr. Connor. We will obtain the required data."

"With due respect, Sinzi-ra," this from the Nerban. "We haven't settled where the examination will be conducted. Given the Humans possess their own specimen, why should they keep this new one?"

A few other suggestions were shouted or grunted. The Sinzi-ra unraveled his fingers and lifted their tips to his shoulders. "This is no longer a Human ship, but a declared consulate of the Interspecies Union. As such, it is the recognized venue for research and discourse that may impact more than one species along the transects. Do you wish to petition the Inner Council for a change to that policy? I will entertain a vote."

Checkmate, Mac thought with admiration.

The Sinzi-ra's offer produced, if not a mellower mood, then a more thoughtful one. The Frow, while continuing to glare across the table at the Trisulians—something they did quite effectively, since it involved lowering a shoulder ridge and extending their necks—stopped sparking. The Trisulians, for their part, oriented their eyestalks on Ureif, as if setting themselves apart from the rest of the room.

Mac was grateful for eyes that weren't so blatantly obvious.

The discussion resumed, this time about establishing an agenda to continue various aspects of the business at hand. Mac and Mudge sat down again.

A *harrumph.* She glanced at him. "What?"

"Nothing."

Mac frowned. *She knew that tone.* It was the one Mudge used to make her think she'd won an argument, when she hadn't come close. "Someone had to say something."

"And you did, Norcoast."

Same tone.

"If you're wrong about the Ministry, it doesn't matter. If you're right?" She shrugged. "What's the worst Hollans can do?"

"Before we get back to Earth, or after?"

"After," Mac leaned back with a shrug, "I don't plan to care."

- 18 -

BOTHER AND BIOLOGY

THERE WAS ONLY ONE thing worse than a meeting where she was on the spot, Mac decided, stifling a yawn. *A meeting where she wasn't.* The discussion had droned on for over an hour now and showed no signs of ending. *Good thing the corpse was in stasis.*

"Stop fidgeting, Norcoast."

"I'm not—" she began to protest, when the door opened.

It was Fourteen. He waved an urgent summons but not, to Mac's astonishment, to her. Instead, Fy bowed graciously and left her place with Ureif without a word of explanation, walking past everyone to join the Myg.

Trundling in her wake, Fy-Alpha nearly knocked over the poor Frow.

The discussion continued without pause, the Cey delegation holding forth on the need for more derelicts to be brought to Myriam so everyone could explore their own and was there going to be lunch?

No one was looking. Seeing her opportunity, Mac grabbed Mudge's wrist and pulled him to follow the Grimnoii out the door, keeping them both low in case Captain Gillis spotted the escape of his fellow Humans and tried to interfere. *He'd begun to glaze over, too.*

Once the door closed between them and the meeting, Mac let out a *whoof* of relief.

Mudge shook off her grip and straightened with a glower. "Do you even know what dignity means, Norcoast?"

"If it means being stuck there when I could be working, I'm not interested."

Fourteen and Fy were deep in conversation, walking rapidly down another corridor, Fy-Alpha in tow. "What's that all about?" Mac wondered.

"With him, it could be anything." At her look, he relented. "The Sinzi-ra requested his help earlier. I presume something to do with the message traffic. They're headed to the bridge," he nodded after them.

"While we're going back to Origins." Mac started walking to the tube door. "I want to check on our guest."

"Surely you should be packing, Norcoast." Mudge hurried to keep up.

"Why?"

"The drop to Myriam."

Mac snorted. "I'm a little busy right now to help you get ready, Oversight. Get Sam."

"I don't think you understand. You're coming, too. You need to pack."

She stopped in the middle of the corridor to stare at him.

Mudge backed up a step. "Now, Norcoast, surely you expected it. Only military personnel will be boarding a derelict until any and all risk has been removed. Sinzi-ra Ureif and the captain were quite sensible about that. Quite firm, in fact. No one disagreed. Civilians—including you—won't be put in danger. Losing Dr. Norris . . ." He tsked sorrowfully. "Too high a price to discover the Ro have been with the Dhryn all along."

"That's what you think?" She gestured at the closed meeting room door. "What they think? That the walker came with the Dhryn?"

"What else?"

That she'd brought it with her? Facing Mudge's puzzled look, Mac couldn't bring herself to say it. He'd think she was certifiable, and everyone would agree.

Besides, she chided herself, *why would a walker hide all this time on the* Joy *and then sneak a ride to a dead Dhryn ship?*

To follow her? Despite Fy's belief that Mac was *"a nexus of interest,"* for the Ro, Mac couldn't see what the aliens would gain from a trip to the *Uosanah*. They had to realize she'd bring back any findings. *Why risk discovery in the tiny space of the lev?*

If the walker had been on board with them, it would have had to dodge around Norris like a dancer. *Or clung to the ceiling.*

Mac shuddered.

"Norcoast?" Mudge's puzzlement turned to concern. "You're safe now. A terrible ordeal. Terrible. But a good night's sleep . . . you'll be fine." Having come to his own conclusions about her hesitation—*and how to deal with it,* Mac smiled to herself—Mudge scowled ferociously. "Norris had no right taking you on that ship. None!"

"I don't need to board the *Uosanah* again, or any other ship," she assured him. "We have her captain. Once he regains consciousness, we can ask him what happened to them."

Mudge shook his head. "Conscious? I thought he was dead already. He certainly looked dead," he modified.

"He does that," Mac nodded. "And he probably won't last the night, which is why I can't leave. If he wakes, I may be the only one he'll answer." She smiled. "Besides, Oversight. I have my own quarters, with a nice new bed I haven't used yet."

Harrumph. "In that case, I'm staying, too." He wagged his forefinger under her nose. "I'm not letting you out of my sight again, Norcoast." His lower lip developed a slight quiver. "I should have been with you—"

She put her finger to his, stopping its movement. "I wish you had." She dropped her hand. "On the bright side—" *before either of them grew more emotional,* "—there should be a record of Norris allowing Base to have the schematics for his ship. Full surround imaging, Oversight. Except for the seats," she added.

His eyes popped open, concern forgotten. "You saw the exterior of the *Joy*?" With awe. "What was she like?"

"Big," Mac offered, pointing to the tube door. "Reminded me of coral."

"The wonders of technology are wasted on you, Norcoast," he muttered. "Simply wasted."

"Origins, please," she told the crew waiting by the controls. "What more do you want, Oversight?" she asked him as they settled inside the bolus. "You've been on the bridge—how many times?"

"It's not the same," he said with unusual petulance.

The bolus sucked them against its walls and bounced into the stream.

Mac gradually relaxed.

It wasn't the same, she echoed to herself.

She'd been rattled, that was all. *Not the first time.* At Base, late at night, she'd wake to that sound, paralyzed with fear until she found its source. Dried reeds in her garden. Sleet against the walls. A disoriented bat. There'd been a crab . . .

"Norcoast."

She focused on him. "Yes?"

"Your new rings."

Mae sighed. "They've made contact. It's a waiting game now." *She didn't bother with the rest.*

"That much success. Good." But he frowned.

She knew that look. "What?"

"You say this is secure. But I'm concerned how the Trisulians would know to ask you about Cinder."

Mac would have shrugged, but her shoulders were stuck fast. "They asked," she disagreed. "Nothing says they knew. Their culture thrives on secrets, layers of them. Who knows what . . . who has information to trade for influence. It wouldn't surprise me if they presume we're all like they are and act accordingly." *Hairy spies,* she thought. *Disguises would be a snap.*

"But you do have information they'd want."

She sent him a cautioning look, *although presumably any eavesdroppers here would have faces.* "I wouldn't call it 'information,' Oversight."

He might have persisted, but the bolus snapped to a stop. The door opened almost immediately and Elane greeted them with smile. "Good meeting, Mac?"

"As always," she answered, pulling free of the walls. Mudge did the same, and they staggered their way out together.

Mac could almost feel Mudge fussing as they walked into the Origins section. *Never a good sign.* "What now?" she asked once they were alone.

"You should eat something."

"Sleep. Eat. You're worse than my dad." Mac's stomach gurgled and she threw up her hands. "Fine. I'll eat."

He ducked his head so she only saw the corner of his smile. *Which meant he didn't see hers.*

"You call that eating? Bah."

"I call it efficient." Mac sipped through the straw, trying in vain to identify the taste of the warm, thick liquid. She waved her tall cup at him enticingly. "You could have had one, Oversight." The ship's version of e-rations had turned out to be a soup, packed with nutrients and sealed into a container suited for zero-g. *Perfect for the biologist on the move,* she thought, taking another sip. "I should take some of these home."

Shaking his head in disbelief, Mudge bit into his carrot—or facsimile—then continued working his way through the mass of salad on his plate. "I prefer to recognize what goes into my body, thank you very much. And you," he jabbed his loaded fork at her hovering 'screen, "should learn to relax."

Mac blinked. "I'm relaxing." They were sitting in the empty dining room, and had been for some time. She'd only opened her 'screen to check for new messages, been scrolling haphazardly through the list. *Nothing from Emily.* She'd marked Kammie's for later reading. "What makes you think I'm not?"

Mudge shook his head again. "Never mind."

"I can do small talk," she offered, giving him a wicked grin.

He held up his hands. "Save me. What's come in?"

Mac set her list between them, two-sided so Mudge could read it at the same time. "I'd expected something from the Ministry by now," she complained.

He leaned so she could see his frown past the display. "Why?"

"Hollans should realize I'd want to see their results."

Mudge's face disappeared behind rows of text. She could hear crunching. *Opinionated crunching.*

"Well, he should." Mac closed the display and put away her imp, aware she sounded petulant. *She had a right to be.* "We have to understand these walkers—what they are—what they're capable of—how to detect them—how to—" *be safe*. She took a long sip.

"I'm sure, Norcoast, the scientists busy with the specimen you and your friend obtained will provide a report when they're ready. Including any comparative results. Copied to those who will act on it."

She grimaced. "In other words, it's none of my business."

"I didn't say that." Mudge divided his remaining beans into neat rows. "There are, of course, ways to work within any system to obtain timely documentation." One bean was moved from one row to the next. "Protocols, etcetera."

Mac sorted that out, then beamed at him. "Great!"

A sheepish *harrumph*. "I'll do my best, Norcoast. I can't promise—"

"You'll be my hero," she interrupted. "No matter what."

Almost a smile. "Have a carrot."

"Thanks." She helped herself to two, eyeing his plate. *At the rate he chewed, even with her help this was going to take a while.* "You don't have to finish all that. Unless you're hungry." She made it sound unlikely.

"If you're ready to go, Norcoast," Mudge said dryly, "I'll meet you there when I'm done."

Mac looked around the empty room and felt a twinge of guilt. "No problem. I'm relaxing," she claimed, tipping her chair back to prove it. She took out her imp and rolled it from one hand to the other. Back and forth. "See?"

He *harrumphed*. "I see you'll give me indigestion. Go. Please."

She leaped to her feet, cup in hand. "You know where to find me."

Mac was steps away when Mudge called after her. "Norcoast. Remember what he is."

She nodded without turning around.

Mac walked into the Wasted's infirmary and stopped, astonished. The bed had been banished to a corner. In its place was a large wheeled platform, in turn supporting what looked like a miniature escape pod.

"The Lost Soul rests within," Kudla said helpfully. He and his disciples were the only ones in the room. They'd pulled chairs around a table and were, Mac blinked, playing cards. As ordered, the candles were gone. Now the room held dozens of knee-high brown statues of what appeared to be frogs, mouths open. *Didn't anyone check their luggage?* she thought wildly. "Take a look," he suggested, pointing at the pod.

She began to frown, but went to peer through one of its windows.

The Wasted was floating in midair, tubes connected to various parts of his anatomy. His body, bathed in a pinkish light, had lost more flesh, something Mac would have deemed impossible. Only the barely perceptible rise and fall of his torso hinted at life.

So much for shaking him awake, she thought.

"Where's Cayhill?"

"He and the Myg went to commune with the planet. I assured them we could help, but they weren't interested. Can you imagine?"

The disciples exchanged glances and shrugged at one another as if to show they certainly couldn't.

She could. "Where's the orderly?"

"The doctor said it was a waste of personnel and set up remote monitors instead. We," this with great dignity, "would not abandon the Lost Soul."

As the "Lost Soul" appeared unlikely to notice a fire, let alone the existence of other life in the room, Mac merely nodded and left.

She found Cayhill where she'd expected, leaning over the shoulder of the officer assigned to the new communications room. *The room she hadn't been able to use yet.*

"MacMacMacMacMac . . ." Five offspring warbled a greeting and scampered toward her from several directions. The sixth sat down on the floor, its eyes scrunched with effort. Just as Mac worried about the carpeting, it opened its eyes and let out a triumphant "Mac!" of its own, running to her.

Oh, good, she thought wryly. *Now they can all talk.*

"Dr. Connor." Cayhill studied her for a moment, then looked back at whatever engrossed the com-tech. "About time."

Mac settled warm bundles of offspring on shoulders and hips, resisting the urge to toss a couple his way. *The offspring didn't deserve it.* "He looks more comfortable. How long does he have?"

Cayhill glanced up again, this time with a frown. "What are you talking about?"

Was she in the wrong room? Even the com-tech was giving her an odd look. "Before he dies," Mac clarified. "The Wasted."

"Idiot!" Unensela breezed by Mac, heading for Cayhill. "About time you got here."

The offspring, perhaps feeling the tensing of every muscle in Mac's body, chose that moment to launch themselves toward the female Myg. She, now busy at the console, expertly shoved them aside with one foot.

"I'm guessing there's something you two want to tell me," Mac said firmly, walking around to the other side of the console to confront them. At their blank looks, she pointed to the wall behind which the Wasted floated in his pod. "About him."

"I'll take a break," offered the com-tech, beginning to rise. Unensela and Cayhill took a shoulder each and pressed the poor man back into his seat.

"Stay on it. We need this data." Cayhill nodded to the side, and Mac followed him.

"Dr. Connor," he told her in a low voice. "I found no signs of injury, beyond the old amputations and present skin damage. I found no signs of illness. My patient isn't sick. He's starving. There's no reason to believe with a proper course of nutrients—"

"With all due respect," Mac interjected, not bothering to keep her voice down, "You don't know what you're talking about. This isn't some malnourished infant, Dr. Cayhill. This is a failed metamorphosis."

"Says who?"

She stared at him. "Pardon?"

"You heard me." Cayhill did smug as well as any Myg of Mac's acquaintance. "You told me yourself there isn't a medical database for this species. I see no justification for invoking some—some species' superstition over normal diagnostic procedure. All indicators show my patient is suffering from a lack of certain key nutrients. Unensela has been assisting me to identify those, with the help of a team of paleoecologists on the planet."

Mac shook her head. "Dhryn metamorphosis is no superstition, Cayhill."

He lifted an eyebrow. "I didn't say it was. If you insist we assume this individual is indeed undergoing a fundamental reorganization of his physiology, my argument only becomes stronger. Developmental deficiencies arise in Humans if there is an insufficiency of particular nutrients during that growth period. We could be seeing this pattern in the patient. Thus his metamorphosis isn't flawed—it is incomplete." When she didn't look convinced, he continued, "You work with fish, don't you? Do they eat the same food at every stage of their growth?"

She had an immediate mental image of a salmon eft fastening its tiny mouth on the fin of an anchovy five times its size and looking wistful.

Mac chewed her lower lip for a moment. "Say I accept your hypothesis—for now," as his eyes gleamed triumphantly. "How are you going to discover what he needs? You may know all there is about Human nutrition—that's not the same as Dhryn, believe me." She pulled a nutrient bar from her pocket and pointed it at him. "To be blunt, these went right through."

Implying the Wasted's show of life after consuming the bars had had more to do with fearing the Ro than digestion or alien acts of kindness.

"The only data I've seen has come from modern colonies or Haven itself. They consumed highly synthesized materials. What about their natural diet?"

Natural diet? Mac clenched her artificial hand. "That would be us, Cayhill."

"Ah, but this one didn't eat Human when he had the chance, did he?"

Mac bowed her head for a moment, then looked up, all antagonism gone from her voice. "Listen to me, Cayhill. Make no mistake. The Dhryn consume every organic molecule on the worlds they take. We can't pull anything specific from that."

"Is that diet necessary for all forms of Dhryn, or just the Progenitors?"

"We don't know—" She paused, thinking it over. *Could he be right? What would it mean?* "I'll admit it's a good question, Cayhill, but it doesn't affect this Dhryn."

"You don't know," he said flatly, his face set and stern. *She'd seen that look.* "Why does that make me wrong?"

This had been a bad idea, Mac realized. " Dr. Cayhill, I want to thank you for all you've done," she began.

"I have it!" Unensela crowed. "ItItItItIt . . . Mac!" echoed the excited offspring, the sixth stuck on its first word. "Come. See this."

Mac followed Cayhill's rush to the communication console. The com-tech moved aside to let them all see the 'screen. "What do you have?"

The 'screen held an image of a collection of seeds, turning to show them from every side. From the scale below, most were larger than Mac's palm. She leaned closer. Their thick cases were scarred and burned, but intact.

"What am I looking at, Unensela?"

"These were found within the Dhryn havens of the southern hemisphere—the one our findings show was beginning to regenerate. They represent these major families of—" she began to rattle off a series of names.

Mac held up her hand to stop the list. "Not a botanist."

"Neither am I," Cayhill joined in. "But these look damaged."

"Idiot! They've been bathed in feeder goo and passed through a gut. You'd look a little rough yourself."

" 'Feeder goo?' " Mac repeated, raising an eyebrow.

"Not a biochemist," the Myg said archly.

" 'Passed through a gut.' You're sure."

Unensela pointed at the names on the bottom of the image. "They are."

The Dhryn, moving across a dying landscape, consuming everything. Carrying inside them the seeds of the future, to be left where they would grow and one day again support the migration of the Dhryn . . . mutual adaptation . . .

Then, one day . . . agriculture . . .

"We get these seeds brought to the ship and feed them to . . ." Cayhill's voice turned sharp as Mac shook her head at him. "Why not?"

"They weren't digested. For all we know, the inner material is poisonous to the Dhryn."

"Irrelevant! Irrelevant!" Unensela jumped up and down. "It gives us a viable course of action." She pointed at a new image, showing lush, green-blue vegetation. Chemical formulae danced among the leaves.

Cayhill looked between the two, his face blank. "What?"

Mac looked at the Myg, whose grin widened to show all four yellowed teeth, gum ridge, and white forked tongue. "The analysis of these plants," she reluctantly explained, "has produced a reasonable reconstruction of their physiology and structure when grown. If—*if*—some Dhryn ate them whole as a food source, you might be able to work out a nutrient regime suited to a present-day Dhryn to try using substances available on board."

"Idiot. There is no 'might.' Yes!"

The offspring ran up Mac again, warbling "YesYesYesYes . . . Mac . . . Yes!"

Unensela beckoned the amused com-tech back to his machinery, the two of them immediately occupied sending messages to her collaborators on the planet. Cayhill stood gazing at Mac and the offspring, a question on his face. "They aren't mine," she informed him. "They just think they are."

"Still going to fire me?"

"Oh." The corner of her mouth twitched up. "That obvious?"

"I thought so."

They did have history. Mac rubbed the back of an offspring; the creature responded by digging its claws into her chest. "No," she said to both man and claws. "I know you won't let him die if you can help it. As for this idea of yours? If I had a better one, believe me, I'd say so." She glanced at the Myg. "Just keep in mind that Unensela and the rest of them deal with the Dhryn of the past. We know the current generation has been extensively modified—the modern diet may be part of that."

"There you are, Norcoast," Mudge exclaimed, hurrying through the door. "Is everything all right?" His look to Cayhill vowed memos otherwise. "How's the patient?"

"Not dead," Mac answered.

"I couldn't tell."

"Notnotnotnotnot . . . Mac!" In the midst of this random enthusiasm, two of the offspring leaped from her to Mudge, not quite tearing fabric, though she'd have some marks. *Bonus for the uniform.*

Mudge caught them on his arm, wincing as they made sure of their landing. "I imagine they'll enjoy having room to run around."

On Myriam. Mac's hands sought the ones still clinging to her. She'd forgotten the offspring were to leave the *Joy,* too. "I'm not so sure that's a good idea," she began. "The situation in-system isn't as stable as it might be and—"

"Irrelevant." Unensela breezed by Mac, Mudge, and the offspring. "Everything's set. We're packed. I must work with these people, find out more about the recent plant life. First, my goodbyes to Fourteen. I shall break his hearts. It's his fault, sticking to his own bed the entire trip." She marched out of the room, but they could hear her as she went down the hall. "We could have had sex fifty-seven times by now . . . twice that if he'd keep in shape . . ."

Cayhill smothered a laugh. Mac shook her head. "I wouldn't doubt it."

"We should head to the hangar as well, Norcoast. It's time."

"I'll be back as soon as I can, Cayhill," she promised. "Good luck."

Already preoccupied with the names in the image, he grunted something noncommittal.

Mac made sure the offspring planned to stay with her for the trip, welcoming the distraction.

She hated good-byes.

The hangar being used by the Origins Team wasn't the one where Norris had kept his lev. This was far larger, wider, and populated by vessels that dwarfed those walking the suspended access way.

Yet Norris was present, Mac discovered. She, Mudge, and the offspring arrived at the departure platform as the captain of the *Annapolis Joy* stepped behind a podium placed there for his use. Beside him, looking as real as if he'd never left, stood Norris.

His simulacrum, she told herself, noticing the differences. The three-dimensional projection was accurate, but carefully positioned so the face gazed back at no one. The feet stood on another surface. By the clothing, this was an image Norris had supplied. *She'd have guessed he'd own a tux; just the thing for those academic fundraisers.* He'd likely held court and awed the donors; Norcoast usually asked her to hide in the back.

Tuxedo, no 'screen hovering by a distracted, busy eye, a too-careful pose from smile to shoulders.

She focused on Gillis' somber face. This Norris wasn't the man she'd known.

This wasn't the man who'd died for her.

"Like many species within the Interspecies Union," Gillis began, "Humans respect the remains of our dead. We are negotiating to recover those of Dr. Sigmund Eduardo Norris as soon as possible without risk to others. We leave no one behind."

Mac judged this as much a promise to the Origins Team and the shuttle crew, gathered around the podium with them, as to Norris. *Might not be having the desired impact on civilian scientists.* Mirabelle and Lyle looked more worried than reassured. She understood completely. The last time they'd been at Sencor's research outpost on Myriam, their biggest concern had been sandstorms and funding. Suddenly, they had the promise of the captain of a dreadnought to stand by them in case of emergency. They had to wonder what he was anticipating that to be.

Captain Gillis said a few more words. Mac and the others listened. She was impressed. He didn't pretend to know Norris as more than a passenger, nor did he dwell on the manner of his death. Instead, the captain read from Norris' curriculum vitae, listing awards and accomplishments, inventions and discoveries—defining his life by his work.

What Norris himself would have done, Mac decided, and her estimation of the captain rose again.

She was, however, slightly disturbed to think he'd have done much the same had it been her.

When the brief service was done, Gillis came over to her. "Not my favorite part of the job, Dr. Connor," in a quiet voice.

Mac laid her hand on his arm, the nearest offspring reaching out to do the same with a tiny paw. Gillis looked down and smiled. "You did it well," she assured him. "I found what you said—" She blanked and finished with more honesty than tact, "I didn't know his full name until now. Thank you."

He appeared pleased. She withdrew her hand and gathered in the offspring.

Gillis surveyed the group waiting to board, several lingering nearby for a chance to talk to her. "Important to give them a chance to pay their respects."

Mac half smiled. "And they got your point, Captain. Though I can't say it will make them happy to think they might need a warship."

"I wouldn't be either," he said soberly. "Perilous times, Dr. Connor."

"Mac."

His eyes smiled. "Mac. I'll leave you to your farewells." With a hint of a bow, Gillis walked away.

She hefted the offspring into the crook of her arm, looking around for Mudge and his load.

Lyle came up to her, eyes gleaming. "I can't believe we're finally heading home," he said. "I won't believe it until I smell the dust."

Mac chuckled. "I know the feeling—although for me it would be cedar and sea." She grinned. "Okay, and rotting fish, but don't spread that around."

He rolled his eyes, grinning back. "Trust me. I'll keep your secret." A more considering look. "Charles says you two will be joining us shortly. Pleasant surprise. Thought they'd be keeping you busy with the derelicts for weeks yet."

Mac shrugged. "Politics."

"Should have guessed." The archaeologist's smile widened. "But if it gets you downworld sooner, that's fine with me."

"Thanks, Lyle." She was touched. *They'd come a long way.* "You'd better go," she added, understanding why his eyes kept flicking to the loading platform. *Heading to the field.*

She could feel the pull herself.

He leaned forward and kissed her on the cheek. "Will do. And you behave." Others came up even as Lyle left, swamping Mac with handshakes and kisses and hugs. The offspring clung to her, wide-eyed and excited, patting anyone who came close enough with their paws. Their claws they kept firmly planted in her and Mac began to worry if she'd get them off when the time came.

Out the corner of her eye, she could see Mudge doing his utmost to fend off such overt affection, nodding gravely to each well-wisher before they came too close and holding his pair of offspring to his chest like a shield.

The initial crush worked its way past; everyone was as anxious as Lyle to get on board. *Maybe they thought the captain would change his mind.* Mirabelle, having waited until now, came up and gave Mac a hug. " 'Bye, Mac."

Mac shook her head. "Archaeologists," she complained. "I might see you tomorrow, you know."

The other woman didn't smile. "And you might not. Don't underestimate how we feel about you. We've been through so much together, Mac, and you've done—well, you've done more for us than we could say."

Mac scrunched her face. "I seem to remember making you work all hours on crazy questions."

Mirabelle laughed but there was a suspicious brightness to her eyes. "Crazy questions that made us—and our work—significant. Whatever we've accomplished to help all of us survive, Mac, we did through you. And we won't forget that."

Speechless, Mac watched the woman walk away. Mudge came over. "Glad to see they recognize your contribution, Norcoast," he said quietly.

She snorted, shifting offspring. "They need to get back to work. We all—" Mac stopped to pull off the one gumming her chin. "Where's Unensela?" She hadn't spotted the Myg during the ceremony or good-byes. "Is she already on board?" She wasn't in the line to enter.

"She is late." Two of the tall, shaggy Sthlynii approached, Therin and Naman, his—with their complex, overlapping families, Mac had yet to figure out if Naman was an uncle or son. *Maybe both.* Naman and the remaining two Sthlynii in Origins rarely spoke aloud to anyone but each other. They were, to Mudge's delight, expert memo writers. Therin blew out his tentacles with annoyance. "We maaaaaaay nooooot waaaaiit."

As if his voice had been a signal, the offspring dropped from Mac and Mudge to climb up the Sthlynii, disappearing within their thick tunics as if they'd done it before. *Into pockets,* she realized, as six big-eyed heads popped back out, paws holding what appeared to be candy to their mouths. "YumyumyumyumyumMac!" they sang happily around the treat.

"That's bribery!" Mudge accused, his hands still raised as if holding the small creatures. He dropped them to his sides at Mac's grin. "Well, it is."

Therin's tentacles milled in what Mac had learned meant amusement. "We miss our younglings, Charles. Caring for these sweet beings—" his hands patted several purring lumps, "—is a privilege. We mind them for Unensela as often as we can."

Mudge swallowed whatever objection he thought he had, perhaps, like Mac, relieved the offspring would have someone responsible watching over them on Myriam.

Speaking of Unensela . . .

"There she is," Mudge said, then gave a sharp *harrumph.* "I knew it."

His tone warned Mac. Sure enough, two Mygs, not one, were walking down the accessway toward the loading platform. *No,* Mac squinted, *make that one walking and the other jumping from foot to foot as if avoiding hot coals.*

The shouting became audible as the couple closed on them.

"IDIOT! IDIOT! IDIOT!" This from Unensela, who shouted the word continuously without turning to look at Fourteen.

He was the one hopping—and babbling. "Please, Glorious One. Your eyes are hidden chips of wet agate. Your tongue—let me tell you about your tongue . . ."

"IRRELEVANT!"

Needless to say, everyone else in earshot stopped what they were doing. Well, except for Kudla and his disciples, clutching bags Mac hoped contained frog statuettes. They used the distraction to move to the head of the boarding line and enter the shuttle. *Presumably anxious to resume communing.*

She looked forward to his next book.

Meanwhile, they had a problem.

Fourteen had finally managed to stop Unensela. The tactic of falling flat on the floor in front of his ladylove was perhaps not original, but Mac gave him points for drama.

The focus of all this was less impressed. Unensela kicked him in the midsection. "You are without *strobis*!" she shrieked. Fourteen curled his arms around his abused middle and kept his mouth closed. "There is nothing I want from you! Nothing!"

Aliens. Mac sighed and stepped forward. Mudge gave her a horrified look. She made a face at him, then turned to the Mygs. "Do I have *strobis*, Unensela?"

Unensela stared at Mac "Irrelevant. You don't know our ways. Don't interfere. This—" another kick, "—is worthless."

They weren't, Mac noticed, *particularly hard kicks.* Nor was Fourteen complaining, as if any attention was better than none. *More telling*, she sniffed, *the air was free of Myg distress.* "Does my life have value to the whole?"

"Idiot." The female Myg's mouth turned sullen. "Of course it does. We would not all follow you if it didn't."

"Which would be why Arslithissiangee Yip the Fourteenth offered his allegiance to me last year, before you two met."

She might have sprouted a second head and startled the Myg less. *Unless that was in a brochure, too*, Mac chuckled to herself.

"You . . ." Unensela dropped to her knobby knees beside Fourteen. Her hands hovered over him. Perhaps wary of her mood, he remained in a defensive curl. "Is this true, Tickles?"

A cautious nod.

Unensela's hands covered her face and she dropped backward to land on her rump, the picture of misery. "All is lost!"

So much for that plan. Mac sighed. *She really should leave aliens alone.*

Mudge *harrumphed.* "I believe," he said in his "officious" voice, "there is some confusion here. If I may, Norcoast?"

"Please," she told him.

" 'Tickles,' " he used the nickname with obvious relish, "vowed himself to Dr. Connor's service in lieu of any other suitable offering. At a time when his circumstances were, *ahem,* somewhat less complex. I believe, if you ask her, she will tell you his service is no longer required."

"Absolutely," Mac agreed, having no clue where Mudge was going.

Fourteen rose on one elbow, the aim of his tiny eyes shifting from Unensela to Mac and back. "You no longer need me, Mac?" he asked in a heart-wrenching voice. Beads of moisture dotted his eyelids. "It is because I failed you, isn't it? I will do better next time. I have been studying sabotage techniques in my spare time. And explosives. You will see! I will throw myself into danger's mouth for you!"

Wonderful. Mac glared at Mudge. His lips shaped the words "trust me." "Irrelevant!" he shouted, in a perfect imitation of Fourteen at his most obnoxious. *He'd heard enough of it,* she realized. "Insufficient! Insulting! Dr. Connor requires the ultimate sacrifice."

She did? While Mudge on a roll was a thing of beauty, as evidenced by the rapt attention of those around them, Mac was growing concerned by the direction this seemed to be going. *Was the man after revenge for all those practical jokes?*

Then she noticed Unensela, who had moved her hands just enough to give Fourteen a wistful look.

" 'The ultimate sacrifice,' " Mac echoed, putting some gusto into it.

Fourteen clambered to his knees, dividing his earnest pleading look between Mudge, Unensela, and Mac, as if unsure who needed to be influenced most. "I would if I could," he exclaimed. "But I've no offspring of my own."

The offspring already present sucked candy noisily, seeming entertained by it all. Mac spared a moment to wonder at the sheer chaos that must be a Myg family night.

"You could have." Unensela's hands fell into her lap. "If you were free to devote the appropriate effort, that is." This with a sly look at Mac. *The scamp wasn't the least confused by the Human-Myg interface.*

Mac felt a certain sympathy for Fourteen. *Still, he was the one who'd rapturously compared Unensela's beady little eyes to wet agate.* "Oh, he's free to do whatever it takes," she proclaimed. "So long as *strobis* is maintained." One of the crew arrived and stood looking anxious in the background; when he saw she'd noticed, he waved and pointed to the shuttle. "Perhaps we could move this along? The captain," Mac added, "would like the shuttle to depart on schedule."

Fourteen rose to his feet, then gave a deep bow from the waist. He put both hands over his eyes. "I, Arslithissiangee Yip the Fourteenth, can never hope to repay you, Mackenzie Connor of Little Misty Lake, for saving my valued life, more than once. If service to your *strobis* is not enough, then I, Arslithissiangee Yip the Fourteenth, can only offer my firstborn offspring to you, Mackenzie Connor of Little Misty Lake."

"That's really more than I—

Hands went down. A stern look. She closed her mouth.

Hands up. "But to fulfill this obligation, I, Arslithissiangee Yip the Fourteenth, however unworthy, must now apply to the inestimable, the glorious, the—"

The shuttle? Mac wanted to say, but restrained herself. The forks of Unensela's tongue were hanging out.

And growing pink.

"—brilliant Unensela to accept my allegiance, flesh, mind, and spirit, so long as I may live." His hands came down, one reaching out. "Will you accept?"

The brilliant Unensela took his hand and pulled herself up, pausing to brush at her coat. "Took you long enough." This with an affectionate push at Fourteen's chest.

Both Mygs, Mac thought, *looked remarkably smug.*

And the waiting member of the crew looked remarkably desperate.

"You'll make your grandsires very happy," she hazarded. "Now, sorry to rush you, but those heading to the planet should go—"

She was talking to thin air. Both Mygs turned and started walking toward the shuttle, arms around each other. Therin and Naman, with the offspring, followed behind.

Leaving her and Mudge alone.

"What just happened?" Mac asked, throwing her hands in the air. "Where's he going? He's supposed to stay on the *Joy*—he was working with Fy—he can't just go with her!"

"Think of it not as losing Fourteen's expertise, Norcoast," Mudge suggested, looking smug himself, "but of gaining their firstborn."

"That's not funny, Oversight."

"You should see your face right now."

"I am not adopting or otherwise accepting any child of theirs! What?" This as he shook his head and smiled. "They can't make me," she insisted, then sighed. "Can they?"

Mudge laughed. "Norcoast, don't you know the Myg life cycle?"

Mac eyed him suspiciously. "Beyond wanton enthusiasm and sloppy parental care? Not really." *Given that enthusiasm, she'd half expected to have the results joining the offspring in ruining her wardrobe.*

"The firstborn of any fertile pair is a *nimb*." Mudge held out one hand and mimed putting something in it. "Myg literature variously refers to it as "the love lump," "the ideal gift," or more crudely as "proof the plumbing works." They aren't the most lyrical species."

"Lump of what?"

His cheeks turned pink. "I'll let you look that up. Suffice it to say, caring for one requires a jar, not a room and education."

Why that . . . "Fourteen knew perfectly well I'd assume—" Mac's outrage turned to reluctant admiration. "He got me, didn't he?"

Mudge whirled one finger in the air. "Welcome to my world, Norcoast."

Mygs might boast they had no external genitalia, but their bodies possessed a number of effective contact points to compensate for a lack of pinpoint accuracy. Mac hurriedly scrolled through the known, presumed—*and highly unlikely*—sexual positions involved, to the physiology of pregnancy.

The pre-*nimb*, it turned out, was a plug separating the birth channel from the lower digestive tract, its eventual connection to the outside world. A male Myg's sperm not only impregnated his partner, but began the process of crystallizing that plug into a *nimb*, which the female would pass before discharging her embryos. The embryos came packaged in membranous sacs of six each, completing their growth outside the mother's body. Birth was officially declared when a sac split and offspring began climbing and warbling on the nearest adult or facsimile.

The *nimb* itself received somewhat better treatment, being considered a family heirloom as each pair could produce only one. *Not to mention,* Mac realized, *it was the only product of a successful mating that stayed put.* The birth sac was traditionally stuck up in a tree or, in urban centers, hung on a hook outside the door. The hatched offspring were quite capable of finding and adopting their own surrogate parent, who apparently couldn't refuse.

She grinned, imagining Unensela packed and on her way to the spaceport, only to become a Myg-mom by walking down the wrong street.

Ambush by cuteness. Somehow it suited the Myg personality.

Mac poked her finger in the 'screen to find an image and found a catalog of display containers instead, ranging from ornate to obnoxious. Apparently, one did not bother to look directly upon the *nimb.*

No surprise. "That is not going on my desk," she stated.

Cayhill looked up. "What isn't?"

Mac closed her 'screen and stretched. "Fourteen's firstborn." She got up from the table and walked over to the pod.

"I don't want to know." Cayhill went back to his work.

"Good choice." Mac peered into the window. "How's it working?"

The physician had come up with an ingenious, if low-tech, way around their lack of experience with Dhryn anatomy. Rather than hunt for a blood vessel or internal organ, he'd simply fixed tubing inside the pod so one end, with a self-closing nipple, rested against the Wasted's partly open lips. The other end of the tube came out of the pod, where a bulb and clip arrangement allowed Cayhill to test-squeeze a drop of his latest concoction into the being's mouth. The idea was that a preferred taste would make the lips close on the nipple, then the Dhryn would either suck on its contents or they could force more in from outside.

For this to work, Cayhill had had to reduce the repeller field to minimum. Even that slight press against the sheets below had caused more skin to fracture, more blue fluid to leak out.

It had to work, Mac thought, appalled. The Wasted was now more skeleton than flesh.

After leaving the hangar, Mudge had headed for the bridge, gleeful at having been invited by Townee to watch the shuttle launch. Mac had returned here to find Cayhill trying one mixture after another. The source? Bins and carts loaded with the remnants of fresh vegetables and ornamental plants filled one side of the room. A workbench with extraction equipment was in the center, lines of fluid-filled vials at one end. Piles of shredded leaves littered the floor. She assumed a technician had helped dismember and extract. No one person could have made that much mess so quickly.

Though it smelled quite wonderful. *You just had to ignore the undertone of rotting Dhryn flesh.*

Mac watched as the next glistening drop formed at the nipple's tip, fell away to land on a cracked lip, then slid inside. *No response.*

"Which one was that?"

He checked the 'screen hovering over the pod. "Aloe and soy."

"Hand cream?"

A shrug. "Components fit the list." Cayhill pointed to the bench. "Bring me the next please, Dr. Connor. There."

Mac found the vial he wanted and brought it. She chewed her lower lip as he poured the liquid into the dispensing apparatus.

He glanced at her. "You have a comment?"

"He'll be dead before you can try all the combinations." *They all would.*

"If I were substituting," Cayhill agreed. "But I don't care about negative reactions." He squeezed to release a new drop. "Only to find a positive one. I'm adding a new pair of nutrient sources each time. Should be done with the lot in another hour."

So much for scientific method. Mac shrugged, willing to go along. "Why not do them all at once, then?"

"Some of these items are in short supply, but contain essentially the same elements as the rest. So I'm trying the abundant ones first."

Okay, some logic. "Let me help."

"Wait." His face lit with triumph. "Look!"

Mac pressed her nose to the window.

The Wasted's lips had fastened over the tube. She could see the muscles of his neck working as he swallowed. *Again.* She scarcely breathed. *Again.*

"Hold this," Cayhill ordered, thrusting the tube and bulb at her. He hurried to the table, his 'screen going with him. "I'll make more."

"Hurry," she advised. The swallows were coming faster; the level of liquid in the tube dropping apace.

A vibration rattled the pod and the Wasted's eyes cracked open. Mac fumbled for the com switch with her free hand. "It's okay," she said. "You're safe. You need to stay still. This is—" *Dhryn had no medical terms* "—a rescue pod." His eyes closed again. She couldn't tell if it meant comprehension or collapse.

"Move." Without waiting, Cayhill shouldered her aside. He sat a beaker of liquid on top of the pod and began tearing apart the bulb and clip. Mac helped, taping in place the funnel he'd brought in his pocket. Cayhill threw more than poured, somehow managing to add more liquid into the tube before the Wasted drained it.

Once they were sure the Dhryn was swallowing steadily, Mac leaned her back against the pod and surveyed the damage. Pale green liquid coated the side of the pod and puddled the floor. They both had streaks of it down their clothing. "Toss you for cleanup."

Cayhill frowned. "Call someone. I have to make more broth." He went to the table, his left foot leaving damp prints on the floor.

Mac looked inside. The Wasted had closed his eyes, but his fingers were now wrapped around the tube as if to make sure it stayed in his mouth. He swallowed regularly. "We could be killing him," she commented uneasily. *Or not helping at all.*

"Do we have a choice?" Cayhill gave her that unreadable look. "Sometimes you have to trust the patient."

An apology? Mac let it go. She filled her cheeks, then let the air out through her teeth. "I'll clean up." There was a bag of wipes and a vacuum mop by the door. She set to work on the pod, sniffing at the spill. "Is that tea?"

"Green tea. And macadamia nuts."

Herbivore? Fits the migration profile, she pondered as she cleaned the floor. A trip across most of a planet might take a couple of generations of ordinary Dhryn to accomplish on foot, even if the Progenitors could live that long. More rapidly moving prey would elude them.

She helped Cayhill pour—more carefully—another dose of broth into the tube. "We need something better than this," he decided. "Wait here."

Between looks at the Wasted, Mac moved on to sweeping up the discarded leaves and other debris from around the table, putting those into the bins. It was the closest thing to gardening she'd done in years, and she found herself enjoying the feel of stems and peel, the delirious smells of what grew.

Cayhill backed through the door, pulling something with him.

"Don't you ever ask for help?" inquired Mac.

She could read that look all right. *Annoyance.* "It's the middle of the night, Dr. Connor."

Sure enough, she glimpsed night-dim lighting in the corridor before he was through the door.

Time flew when tending aliens.

He wrestled what turned out to be a stand festooned with empty bags over to the pod. "We fill these," Cayhill announced, "connect them in sequence, and he can drink all he wants."

"What about the—ah—consequence?" Mac ventured.

A pitying look. "The catheter was the easy part."

For whom?

Working together, they produced enough broth to fill all but one bag. Once he'd checked the system for leaks, Cayhill declared himself satisfied. "Nothing to do now but wait, Dr. Connor," he finished.

And stood there looking at her.

Mac sighed, giving up her untouched bed. "I'll stay. I've reports to read."

His eyes strayed to the equipment attached to the pod. *Not about to let a mere biologist handle* his *patient,* Mac decided. "No, no," Cayhill said at last. "I should stay. You go."

"I won't touch anything," she promised. "You've hooked it all to remote monitors, right?" At his hesitant nod, Mac grinned. "Get some rest, or we can play cards. Kudla left his deck."

"Call me if there's the smallest change," said Cayhill hastily. "And watch for gunk in the tubing. The filters were coarse."

"Change, gunk, got it. Go." Mac let her grin fade. "And thank you, Doctor. Whatever happens."

Her gratitude seemed to startle him. "Whatever happens," he replied gruffly, "I expect to be notified without delay."

After Cayhill left, Mac amused herself by walking around the room a few times, straightening this and that. Noticing the bed had fresh sheets, she rolled it from the corner and positioned it along-side the pod, in case she needed a nap. She stared in at the Wasted, seeing no change at all. In case, she switched on the com so they could hear one another.

Out of excuses not to sit down and work, she stood in the middle of the empty room and closed her eyes to listen.

The barely heard, self-conscious hum of machines. A drip from within the pod.

Satisfied?

Mac checked the door again, then stared up at the unblinking vid in the corner, hating to think this would be public record. *So she was obsessive.* It wasn't the first time.

Despite feeling a thorough idiot, she disconnected the handle from the vacuum mop and used it to carefully sweep the room, including pokes at the ceiling and finishing with a lunge under the pod.

Done, she positioned two chairs so she could sit in the one and see blue flesh through a window. The other was for her feet.

She pulled out her imp and set up her 'screen, looking first for updates from Mudge. Nothing. *Probably going to stay on the bridge till they kick him off,* she thought, glad he was happy.

There were a few notes from members of the Origins Team, mostly dealing with what had been left behind, or for when she came down. Mac shunted those to Mudge and looked for anything from a little farther afield.

Finally. She smiled as she called up a set of newly arrived vid messages, from the latest newspacket or courier. She didn't care which.

Mac settled deeper in her chair and cued the messages to play.

- CONTACT -

EMILY WAS STANDING outside, lit by sunshine, framed by intense blue. Her head was covered in a large fluffy mass, more like a growth of bright red hair than a hat; a scarf of the same improbable fabric traced the underside of her jaw and cheek. Her nose was distinctly pink and her breath left little puffs as she spoke. "Hi, Mac! Got your message. You sound the veteran spacer. Proud of you, girl.

"Guess where we are!" The image briefly tilted sideways, catching the ice-rimmed prow of the harvester lev, a flat expanse of sea beyond. "Two tries. Whoops! Wrong!

"Tracer's working, Mac. It's working," this with passion, her face close. "I knew it would. I'm on its tail—or whatever. Sneaky bastard. It's been leading me around . . . playing some tricks . . . thinks it's clever. But I'm not going to lose it. Not now."

Quiet, intense. "You should be here, Mac. This is where the answers are. I feel it. Forget that ball of dirt. This is where we'll learn how to stop *Them*, once and for all."

The image tilted again, this time spinning in a circle as if Emily had grabbed the 'bot for a dance partner. Behind her, more blue sky and ice, frozen metal, distant others wrapped against the cold.

"C'mon home, Mac," she urged, becoming still. She brought the 'bot to her eyes, as if trying to see inside, turning the image into a confusion of lashes and dark, dilated pupils. "*They've* never been in a hurry before. *They've* never made mistakes. Something's started the clock. Not—not at noon. It's eleven. Mac, it's eleven. Remember that."

The 'bot swung up, as if she'd tossed it, then leveled out and returned to its original position. Emily tucked her chin into her scarf. "Gotta go, Mac. Can't leave the Tracer for long, not even with Casey-boy.

"Just . . . come home as soon as you can. Okay?"

Case was sitting, his back against a curved wall that might have been anywhere along the lev's inner hull. He'd tanned, or gained freckles; aged, by the fine lines beside his eyes and mouth. But he looked out from the image with assurance. "Hi, Mac. We've been at sea a while. Feels good, you know. Being out here. You likely expected that.

"Em's gadget is hauling us all over. Sing-li's always on the com getting clearances. Part of my job is warning civilian harvesters we're coming through. A couple learned the hard way Em isn't going to divert course. You ever been on one of these big harvs when it ramps up and over another lev? Whoot! Don't worry. No one's been hurt." A grin. "Maybe a few feelings. Handy having Earthgov and the IU on our side, that's for sure."

The young man rubbed one hand over his jaw, the grin disappearing. "I guess I'm the one to tell you. Em—I caught her taking 'fix. She laughed—boasted 'Sephe was getting it for her, that no one cares, long as she finds their monster. I think—I know she's right, Mac. Everyone's too quiet, too focused. Feels like we're in a whirlpool and don't know how long till the bottom.

"About Em . . . I don't want you to worry. I'm making her take supplements, got her promise not to up the dose. I've seen guys 'fix for weeks, Mac. They weren't good for much by the end, but they pulled their weight for the harvest."

Case's lips quirked sideways and his eyes glowed. "With or without, none of them could keep up to Emily, though. She's on the trail.

"Hope you're okay, Mac. As I said, don't worry. We'll find this thing. You can trust us."

Hard to tell if Hollans had aged. His wrinkles contrarily defied it. Instead of looking at the 'bot, he stared out over a wide patio, edged by trees; one hand rested on the stone wall that edged the terrace. He took a deep breath before speaking. "Dr. Connor. Mac. They told me what happened on the *Uosanah*. I never meant you or Sigmund to be in any danger. I want you to believe that." A pause. "I've spoken to Katie, his wife. Those things—doesn't matter how many times I do it,

I never know what to say. But I made sure your family knew you were okay. The media's got more than I'd like about the whole business. No help for that now."

His fingers worked at the stone. "What you did . . . what you both did . . . I've decorated agents for less." A low laugh. "You know, I can picture your face right now. Don't worry, Mac, I'd never make you accept a medal.

"I'd like to know how you found out about the walker before we sent the specs to you, but I'm learning not to be surprised by anything you and your people accomplish. Dr. Mamani, for instance. She's already chasing whatever the Ro left in Castle Inlet. None of our sensors detect a thing. She's either crazy or our best shot. I'm inclined to the latter."

He turned to face the 'bot at last. "I hope you've had news from our mutual friend. I know you've heard about the mess with the Frow. 'Mess.' " Hollans made a face. "A tragedy, that's what's coming. Earthgov's expelled the Trisulian ambassador. We aren't the only ones. But you know being politically isolated will send the wrong message to the Trisulians. I feel like a voice shouting in an empty room. We should be finding them opportunities to colonize, maybe even the Dhryn worlds, if it comes to that. Help them believe their coming generation is safe. But you get politics within species as well as between. Anchen's conducting negotiations around the clock." He looked away again. "Maybe they'll work. Regardless, now every species in the IU knows the Trisulians tried to summon the Dhryn. It's not much of a step to realize the only way to end that threat is to eliminate the Dhryn themselves.

"So we're back to that, Mac. The Ro or the Trisulians. Both now hold the Dhryn over our heads." His voice became very quiet. "You know what I'm asking. You know, I hope, what you must do if you have the opportunity. What Nik must do.

"For all our sakes."

REBIRTH AND RESUMPTION

MAC CLOSED HER 'screen, hand trembling. The rest of her messages could wait.

It wasn't as if any of it was a surprise.

She'd known. Deep inside, in the place where nightmares festered while she was awake, she'd known Emily was expendable. And the Dhryn.

And everyone else.

So long as they stopped this.

It was hard to remember normal, to think about the way the IU had been before this fundamental threat to its very nature. *Not that she'd paid attention to it then,* Mac mocked herself.

She walked over to the pod, and put her hand on its cool surface. "It's not even your fault," she said.

Ureif had seen no circularity.

Numb, Mac walked to the lighting controls and accepted ship settings. The room dimmed to twilight, the shadows softening the edge of machine and pod, the aroma of crushed plants teasing at the senses, a pretense of life.

She climbed on the bed and laid down, rolling to face the Wasted through his windows. He no longer swallowed, the nipple stuck to a lower lip as if abandoned. Perhaps he was dying.

Perhaps he was lucky.

Mac closed her eyes and wept.

She'd dimmed the lights.

Mac squinted, opening her eyelids the barest amount possible. The glow wasn't much, but it was right in her face.

For an instant, she believed it was a flaw in the pod, its internal lights jumped to some higher setting, ready for an autopsy.

Then, as she came fully awake, she realized it was something else entirely.

The Wasted was . . . *glowing.*

She slid from the bed, tiptoeing closer, and gasped. Her hands caught at the pod to keep her upright.

Okay. Not just glowing.

The creature inside the pod wasn't what she'd left there. It was no feeder, no normal adult . . .

Warm, golden eyes gazed back at her.

"*Lamisah.* What am I?"

Luminescence.

"I don't know," Mac breathed.

The Wasted had . . . changed. *Cayhill was right,* she thought. *An arrested metamorphosis, not a failed one.*

The Dhryn before her was still blue, but that blue was almost painfully vivid. What had been fractures in his skin were now connected into bands wrapping his torso and limbs in softly glowing white. His face and body had fleshed again, the body thicker than before, stronger. The eyes. The eyes were everything Mac remembered about Dhryn, warm, alive, vibrant.

With a beseeching look. "Can you release me, *Lamisah?* I no longer fit inside."

Her hand reached for the control and froze. *The voice!* It was higher pitched, with a different cadence.

It was no longer male.

"*Lamisah?*"

Mac shook off her paralysis, aware the being was right. He—she—now more than filled the inside of the pod. No matter what else, getting out was a priority.

First, Mac went to the door and locked it from the inside.

Then she went to the table and picked up the closest thing to a weapon she could find, a thin metal rod.

Aim for the eye.

Last, she went to the pod, pushed the release, and moved back.

There was an alarm. *Of course.* Lights in the room shot up to normal day, then strobed orange. No sound here, but doubtless abundant bells and shrieks elsewhere. *She didn't have long.*

The pod lid opened and fell back with a clang, knocking over Cayhill's stand of bags.

The *creature* sat up and smiled. "Thank you." He—she climbed out with ease, power and grace in every movement.

When she stood on the floor in front of Mac, it was on four sturdy legs, not two. The uppermost arms were now legs, the middle set thicker, more muscled. They'd regrown something almost like hands at their wrists but these were broad, almost webbed. *Feet.* At the moment, those middle arms were bent at the elbows and carried up against her midsection. When she bowed her head and shoulders back in gratitude, Mac saw the seventh limb, now muscular and with a three-digit hand.

And when she came upright again—taller now, and solid—and settled to regard her Human companion, skin and eyes aglow even against the brighter light, she was nothing less than glorious.

Mac dropped her would-be weapon.

"What are you?"

The delicate mouth smiled, as if they now shared a secret. "Hungry."

"Dr. Connor. This is the second door you've locked on me. This is my ship, you realize."

Mac winced. Captain Gillis sounded infinitely more reasonable and calm than Cayhill, who'd been first to arrive and shouted himself hoarse at her while waiting for the rest. "Sorry about that," she said "Hang on." She unlocked and opened it, but kept herself firmly in the way. "I wanted you to be here," she explained, trying not to look at Cayhill. *He deserved better.* "All of you," this with a nod to Ureif and Mudge.

Mudge looked as grim as she'd ever seen him. She'd expected that.

She'd expected the armed guards, too.

"If you'd come in, calmly." Now she did look at Cayhill, doing her best to plead with him without saying a word.

His face was flushed with rage, his eyes fierce. But he gave a curt nod.

Mac backed slowly, controlling the entry. Not that any of them wanted to run in—they'd seen on the vid, she was sure, what waited. A new kind of Dhryn.

Or maybe something else. Her heart hammered as she considered the possibilities.

She'd done her best to provide a suitable setting for the introductions. *Not that she'd had much to work with,* Mac reminded herself. She'd shoved the wheeled platform to one side, the bed with it. The worktable joined them, its mass of vials and equipment hidden under a sheet. That left the table and chairs, plus the bins. The bins of used plants were now out of the way. Along with the all-but-one empty bags.

She'd put the table in the middle, fished out a plant sufficiently intact—*in her opinion* —to serve as a centerpiece, and arranged the chairs on one side. There weren't enough, but the Dhryn didn't need a chair. Neither did she.

It no longer looked like a hospital room.

A point not lost on Cayhill, whose lips pressed tightly together. Then he saw his patient and wonder flooded his face. "I don't believe it."

The Dhryn raised her head in a bow. "I am told you are responsible for my current state." She indicated herself with her flexible limb, the movement as graceful as any Sinzi. "I would give you my name, Human-*erumisah,* but I do not exist."

"Erumisah" *was a rank earned through* grathnu. Mac supposed providing food qualified. "This is Gordon Matthew Cayhill," she introduced, having taken a judicious look at the ship's crew list.

"Ah." The Dhryn paused, as if considering how to clap without paired hands. Then she dropped what Mac thought of as her mid-legs to the floor, their flatter feet making a reasonable smack. "Most distinguished. I take the name Gordon Matthew Cayhill into my keeping."

"The captain of the *Annapolis Joy,* Michael—Rupert James

Gillis." Mac hadn't found his middle names, so she made up a few. Gillis didn't even blink.

Another vigorous smack. "Outstanding. I am honored to take the name Michael Rupert James Gillis into my keeping."

"Charles Jean Mudge III. *Erumisah.*"

The Dhryn passed her golden gaze over Mac for an instant at this claim, but dutifully smacked the floor to acknowledge Mudge.

Mac then gestured to the Sinzi, feeling ridiculously formal. *Should have ordered pizza and beer,* she thought. But this was what she had. "Sinzi-ra Ureif." She watched the Dhryn closely. If there was an alien face she read as well as her own, it was Dhryn. Now, she thought she saw a flicker of recognition.

"Sinzi-ra Ureif."

Ureif tilted his head to bring his lower eyes more in line with the Dhryn, but didn't speak. *How much did he know?* Mac wondered. *About this Dhryn, a former ship captain from Cryssin Colony. And about the Wasting.*

"If you'd have a seat?"

The Dhryn moved to one end of the table, going down on her four larger legs. Seated, she was taller than any Human in the room. Intimidating by size, awe-inspiring by her very existence, but there was something gentle, something warm about her—*don't Humanize,* Mac warned herself. It was hard. The Dhryn even smelled good.

Mudge waited for the captain and Ureif to choose seats, but not for Cayhill. Mac tried to catch his eyes, but he seemed to deliberately avoid hers. Cayhill took the last seat without hesitation.

Mac felt better pacing anyway. "I assume you've all seen what happened?" she asked, nodded at the vid.

Now Mudge looked at her. "You took an unconscionable risk, Norcoast."

Before she could reply, the Dhryn leaned forward. "I would never harm my *lamisah,* Charles Jean Mudge III."

"You ate your crew."

Mac gritted her teeth, but the Dhryn nodded gravely. "They sustained me." There was no remorse or regret in the voice. *That which is Dhryn must survive.*

Even one who "did not exist."

"What about us?"

"Mr. Mudge, please." Mudge subsided, with a scowl at Mac. The captain put his forearms on the table and leaned forward on them. "Dr. Connor. This is your party."

Really could use the beer. Mac nodded. "Thank you. I asked you here to meet the Progenitor."

"Is that what I am?" asked the Dhryn, sounding thoughtful.

"I believe so."

"But I do not exist."

"That was before—"

"Dr. Connor." Mac turned from the golden eyes to meet Ureif's topaz ones. "Use great care."

A warning from the former Sinzi-ra of Haven, or the Speaker of the IU Inner Council?

Or both.

Regardless, it was excellent advice. The being was like a new student, intensely curious, soaking up information without discrimination. Mac had done her utmost to avoid saying anything beyond simple commands, "move here," and reassurances, "there's more food coming." *She could do more harm than good.* "Yes, Sinzi-ra. I concur. That's why I need all of you—" she paused, like the rest watching as the Dhryn, unself-conscious, reached across the table to the centerpiece, fastened her fingers on the closest leaf, and pulled the ragged mass to herself.

But once she had the plant, the Dhryn seemed puzzled. She stared at it, her fingers toying with the leaves. A piece came free. She put it into her mouth, her lips working. After a moment, her mouth opened. The piece was clearly intact. She pulled it out and held it toward Mudge, a *thrum* of distress rolling through the floor underfoot. "*Erumisah,* this will sustain me. Why can I not eat it? I must have it. I hunger."

Mudge *harrumphed,* but there was no denying the confused hurt in the Dhryn's voice. He looked at Mac, who tipped her head toward Cayhill. "Dr. Cayhill," Mudge coughed. "If you'd be so good as to examine your—patient?"

Cayhill went pale. *Probably dawned on him unconscious dying aliens were the easy part,* Mac decided. She walked over to the

Dhryn and rested her hand on the being's shoulder. "He must look inside your mouth," she explained.

Seeing Mac there, *uneaten*, Cayhill stood and approached, taking a scope from his pocket. When nothing more alarming happened than the Dhryn opening her mouth, he shone the light inside.

And frowned.

Without warning, he pushed the scope between her lips. The Dhryn shied back like a draft horse stung by a fly. Cayhill reacted by throwing himself in the opposite direction. He collided with his own chair and spun around to dive behind Mudge who, like the captain, had jumped to his feet.

The Dhryn sat. She picked up another leaf. "I must have this," she insisted, as if nothing had happened.

"The esophagus is gone," Cayhill blurted. He rose to his feet, apparently reassured, but stayed behind Mudge.

"What do you mean?" the captain asked.

"It's sealed off. There's only the airway left."

Explaining why the Dhryn had stopped before finishing the last bag.

"What is an esophagus, *Lamisah?*"

"Something you need." Mac chewed her lower lip, considering the Dhryn. The glowing white bands merged along the back, the entire area now appearing to pulse with every breath. *Like the puffer form*, she realized suddenly. *Display or support for a growing body mass?*

Later.

She laid her palm on the nearest band, feeling the membrane shudder delicately in response. The Dhryn did not object, merely turned her great head as far as possible to watch. Mac smiled at her, then kept examining the band. At the verge of band and blue skin, she spotted a small ridge on the blue and leaned in to see. A dimple, such as all Dhryn possessed, but this felt different. Without taking her eyes from it, Mac said, "Cayhill, I need your scope."

She didn't pay attention to the ensuing protest, but wasn't surprised to have Mudge pass her the device and stay close.

Magnified, the dimple became a tiny, lipless mouth; its opening, when she pressed gently, no greater than her fingertip. She aimed the scope along the blue skin. Sure enough, all of the dimples had been modified in the same way.

Mac stood up, her hand lingering on the Dhryn. "You can no longer feed yourself," she said, unable to keep the regret from her voice. *The end of individuality. Did the Dhryn feel it?*

"Then you are correct and this is a Progenitor," concluded Ureif, rising slowly to his feet. "Reliant on her people."

"I am hungry." There was overwhelming trust in the look the Dhryn gave Mac. "My *lamisah* will provide for me."

And she'd worried about adopting a Myg offspring.

Mac was nodding before she knew she'd made the decision. "Dr. Cayhill's broth. Some eyedroppers. We'll figure something out." *For now.*

"Dr. Connor. I think we need to discuss a few things first." Gillis' jaw was clenched.

She'd wondered how long it would take him to begin to see the problem of hosting a rapidly growing Dhryn Progenitor on his ship. *Let alone what the neighbors were going to say.*

"Wait, Captain. If you would." The Sinzi stood away from the table. He swept his fingers stiffly from his shoulders, then brought them together in that complex knot. Finally, he bowed deeply to the Dhryn. "I welcome you home at last, She Who Is Dhryn, on behalf of the Interspecies Union. The Consulate of the *Annapolis Joy* is at your service." The fingers trembled, setting up a chime from their rings. "May I say, I am humbled to bear witness to this epic congruence, your return through space and body to the birthplace of your kind. It is the pinnacle of my life." The Sinzi collected himself, saying more calmly, "Captain, I rely upon you to expedite suitable accommodations."

She really didn't like the sound of this. From his pallor, neither did Gillis. Mac licked her lips. "Sinzi-ra, forgive me, but surely this is the best place right now for our—guest. While she requires medical care." *And eyedroppers.*

"I must make an immediate announcement that She Who Is Dhryn will receive representatives from other species. She cannot do that in here." The topaz eyes seemed to glitter. "This ship will accommodate her needs, or we will move to another."

"I am hungry," the object of these lofty plans reminded them.

Mac looked at Mudge, whose dumbfounded expression likely mirrored her own.

Even Sinzi could be trapped by their own nature, she realized, feeling a sick foreboding. *Those representatives weren't going to be happy.*

Still, she thought more cheerfully, *looked like she'd have help with the eyedroppers.*

The new Progenitor's appetite proved unexpectedly useful. Not only did it keep the being herself preoccupied to the point of total compliance to everything around her, Mac thought some time later, but Cayhill had roused to oversee the entire project.

Probably because he finally had a patient who didn't talk back.

"Are you listening to me, Norcoast?"

Mac stifled a yawn and nodded. She could sum up Mudge's response to recent events—*he thought she'd lost her mind*—but it would be impolite to stop him now. *Not to mention impossible without help.* "The Sinzi-ra is confident," she pointed out. *Again.*

"And the captain is not. Nor is Earthgov, or the Ministry, or any level of government represented in this solar system. Or on their way!"

There had been a steady flow of traffic through the gate. *Not surprising.* What had been a surprise was how quickly and thoroughly the Sinzi-ra managed to disseminate word of the presence and condition of their new guest. *Even her family should know by now.*

There was a basic consideration that transcended the Sinzi rapture at the physical journey of this individual. There could be other Wasteds lurking in the holds of the derelict ships, individuals innocent of the crimes committed by the rest of their species, individuals who needed immediate rescue.

Though immediate was unlikely. Any rescue attempt was now being debated by the Inner Council, Ureif—or rather Filt—participating from here. They also debated the future of the Dhryn on the *Annapolis Joy.*

Good luck with that, she wished them.

"Norcoast!" His fist thumped down on the table.

She rested her fingers on top of it. "Peace, Oversight. It's done. Whatever happens now is out of our hands."

He *harrumphed* at this, then sighed. "You could have left the room."

"You," she pointed out, "could have stayed at the Trust."

Mudge wasn't ready to smile. "And I suppose you would have managed without me?"

"It would have been difficult." *Being dead*. She didn't say it; she didn't have to. She could see the memory passing over his face. Mac patted his fist, then rubbed her eyes. They were waiting on Captain Gillis, who'd left orders they weren't to go anywhere until he'd clarified a few things.

In her experience, that implied yelling.

Or, harder to ignore, "how did you get me into this," looks.

Since Gillis had left to produce accommodations for his now-illustrious guest that wouldn't offend the Sinzi but would satisfy his security staff, she shouldn't have to face either for a while. "What time is it?" she asked Mudge, yawning again.

"Too early for breakfast, too late for a night's sleep."

Mac got up and went to the transparent wall that separated Gillis' meeting room from the bridge. The tree kept its vigil to the side. The rest of the space was as incomprehensibly busy as before. "Can they see us?" She waved at one of the crew looking this way.

"Of course not." Mudge joined her. "Too distracting."

"There's Fy." Mac pressed her finger on the wall to indicate the Sinzi. "Is that the com?" Hard to tell, given the cluster of Humans, Grimnoii, and hovering 'screens.

"Yes. If it hadn't been for the new traffic, she'd be running checks on the gate station by now, but there hasn't been a break." At her impressed look, he preened ever so slightly. "Darcy keeps me up to speed."

As the station in question was little more than an orbiting box of monitoring equipment, connected remotely to the myriad other orbiting boxes that together coaxed the gate out of no-space, Mac thought the Sinzi should be quite happy to be able to work from the comfort of the ship. " 'Darcy,' is it?" she teased, looking for the woman in question.

Mudge *harrumphed*. "There's no need for that tone, Norcoast," he began, when the lighting on the bridge went red.

Several other things happened at once. A klaxon went off, varying in volume but impossible to ignore. The organized confusion on the bridge became frantic, with some personnel diving for seats and others moving out of their way. The captain appeared through his door, one hand brushing the tree trunk as if by habit. Guards came through every other door, weapons at the ready.

Including this room. Mac and Mudge whirled together at the sound of the door opening and heavy feet.

"What's going on?" she demanded, but the armored man shook his head.

"There'll be an announcement," he told them, taking up his station by the now-closed door.

To keep them in or . . .

Mac whirled to Mudge, her hand tight on his arm. "The Ro. The walker. It didn't come with the derelict—"

"What are you talking about?"

She was shaking. "It came with us," she shouted, desperate to be understood. "They're on the *Joy*—"

"No, they aren't." Mudge took hold of her shoulders, eyes intent on hers. He spoke deliberately, as if making sure she heard every word over the alarm. "You weren't the only one who thought of that possibility, Norcoast. Security's run constant checks, accounted for all sounds and mass within the ship. They mist the corridors and hangars at night, looking for signs. The *Joy's* clean. We're safe."

"Could have—told me—" she hiccuped fiercely.

"And have you supervise that, too?" He gave her a small shake, looking more worried than he sounded. "I'm sorry, Norcoast. I didn't want you to think about them anymore. I should have told you."

Mac hiccuped once more, and shut her mouth. She took a deep, slow breath through her nose, Mudge nodding encouragement, then let it out. "At least we weren't asleep in bed," she said faintly. She found herself wondering how much, if anything, of the captain of the *Uosanah* remained to help the Dhryn understand the alarm.

Mudge's hands squeezed her shoulders, then dropped away. "Shouldn't be long."

Sure enough, the wailing alarm stopped, leaving an expectant silence. The red lighting switched back to normal. Mac could see Gillis preparing to speak—he looked her way, perhaps remembering they were there. She began to relax.

Then she heard his voice, level and devastatingly calm.

"We have Dhryn incoming. A Progenitor ship has arrived through the transect gate. Repeat, we have Dhryn incoming.

"Battle stations."

- 20 -

RISK AND REUNION

WHICH PROGENITOR?

W Mac turned to Mudge.

He took one look at her face, then grabbed her wrist and pulled her with him to the door control leading to the bridge. He had it open before the startled guard could do more than shout, the two of them stumbling down the stairs to the bridge floor.

Captain Gillis appeared to be one of those rare beings unaffected by sudden entrances or emergencies. *Or was at his best under pressure.* He greeted them with a gracious nod, waving away the guard. "Dr. Connor. Mr. Mudge. Good timing. If you'll join me?" He led the way to the com area, where Fy had taken over the controls of three consoles, her fingers flying through their displays with that inhuman speed. Mac averted her eyes, queasy enough.

Townee was there. She looked at them with a frown. "We're having difficulty establishing a link, sir. Their equipment isn't IU standard."

"Keep on it. Sinzi-ra. Any more coming through?"

Were they outnumbered?

"Not yet. There has been—maneuvering—on the part of ships in a direct line. I have asserted the need to avoid provocation at this point."

Who'd fire first?

Mac rubbed her thumb over the rings on her fingers.

Gillis might have been asking about the weather. "Show me."

The air above them darkened until she might have looked

outside the ship, into space itself. *The ships were too small,* she thought, but that was to include present company.

They were otherwise accurately rendered. She found the Trisulian, now at the far side of the group from the *Uosanah.* Many ships were in motion relative to one another, *moving away,* she realized. The *Joy* was still, sitting above the dotted oval representing the event of the gate, between all the others and the oncoming Progenitor Ship.

"Enlarge."

The image of the Progenitor Ship grew larger. As it did, there were gasps. The silver hull had been *eaten* away; vast portions were little more than dribbles of what had been solid, but had somehow melted and then congealed. The rest was deformed and pitted. *A wonder the thing flew at all . . .*

Mac's pocket chirped.

To be accurate, the *salmon* in her pocket chirped.

She pulled it out with numb fingers, then looked up to see she had the full attention of those around her.

The chirping, now louder, became an arrhythmic clicking. One of Fy's fingers reached toward Mac, the tip beckoning. She offered the carving—*whatever it was*—and the finger wrapped around it, while the Sinzi's other fingers darted and danced furiously within the com system display.

A loud crackle, then a voice. "Do not fire. This is Nikolai Trojanowski, Ministry of Extra-Solar Human Affairs, attached to the IU Gathering. Do not fire. Our intentions are not hostile. Please send a shuttle with adjustable docking clamps to these coordinates. Repeating. This is Nikolai—"

Mac listened to the words, hearing the triumph as well as exhaustion, and smiled.

The man knew how to make an entrance.

Mac thudded her fist into her pillow. She considered the situation and thumped it again.

She'd been the image of a calm, cool professional.

"Of course, there have to be negotiations," she told the cowering bit of foam. "Yes, I quite understand that means delays." *Thump!* "Why should anything involving aliens ever—" *Thump!*"—be— "*Thump!*"—easy?!" *Thump!*

The pillow succumbed, coughing up fluff and going flat at one end.

She'd been exceptionally understanding.

But hadn't fooled Mudge. He'd hovered a little too overtly, offering her drinks and running interference when she'd tried—*time after time*—for some answers.

At least he'd recovered her salmon from Fy. Mac threw herself down on her stomach, then rolled over to stare at it on the clear shelf.

"Some salmon you are," she scolded. The device within the carving had been Sinzi, a little something they'd provided Nik in case he'd been taken aboard the Dhryn ship, with its pre-IU technology. He'd had its partner, ready to coordinate com signals or whatever at the right time. Fy had been very pleased.

Mac wondered what other little surprises a certain spy had left in her life.

She pulled the blanket to her chin and stretched out her toes, yawning. The new bed was as comfortable as she'd hoped, the room private and peaceful. *And clean, right to an apologetic hint of lilac.* The Frow, while not talkative, had been on duty in the ladderway, lifting her with their accustomed flare. The Dhryn was resting, having—according to Cayhill—consumed most of the ship's supply of raspberries and cashews, shells included, in a new broth. *The man was in his element with tubing and a perfusion pump.*

She eased her hips and shoulders, almost hissing with the delicious pain of relaxing muscles. Tense muscles. She needed a good run.

Or a certain spy.

Mac smiled wistfully, but pulled her thoughts firmly from *that* direction. *He'd get here when he did.*

She shut her eyes, let her mind drift, intent on that too-brief clarity between committed to sleep and committing it. This was when threads wove themselves together without effort, when intuitive leaps came like breath. She'd learned not to waste it.

She let her thoughts go where they would . . .

. . . *a Progenitor the size of a blue whale moved across a sere landscape, six powerful limbs churning their way forward. She was less massive than Her bulk suggested, much of Her body composed of immense sacs of gas lighter than the surrounding air. Around Her flew a ceaseless pulse of others, attracted to the glow of her skin, jostling to be next to offer their store of digested nutrients to Her body. Beside her marched others, stout and capable, well-organized. Their low voices communicated well across the landscape. These carried the youngest under their bodies, as well as seeds.*

There was laughter, at the beginning of the Great Journey. The triumph of a species moving how it could, when it must, in a world that relied on its passing for renewal.

Mac's eyes shot open. *It fit.* A body plan that would have worked for the Dhryn. Not that glut of a form, suited only to producing millions more *oomlings* than one world could sustain.

She tossed until she found a less comfortable position; she needed to think.

A reversion to type.

She felt rigid as the idea took hold. "Is that what you are?" she breathed. *They'd need to run the genetic material, see if the* Joy's *Progenitor was a match to the current form, but with a different sequence of genes active.*

But some would always be born. The "lost souls."

"They'd have to forbid biology," she whispered. "They'd have to create the myth of the Wasted, shun them, let them die. They'd need a diet that wouldn't support the final metamorphosis of the original Progenitor."

Had this been the terrible price the Dhryn had paid the Ro, for admission to space?

Or had oomlings been stolen, changed, their own kind unaware until it was too late?

What did it mean now?

Ureif promoted this one Dhryn for all the wrong reasons. Non-Sinzi would see that.

Could there be a right one? Could she be fertile? Could the original form of Dhryn be restored through her and those like her?

Should it?

Mac fell asleep before she had answers, dreaming of limbs become hands, of hands become mouths, of mouths counting to eleven and dripping with green, while *something* laughed.

Fourteen had sent her three hundred and fifteen messages.

"Must have cut into their time for sex," Mac commented, scrolling the list. "And me waiting for my nugget."

"Norcoast!"

She opened one at random. "He's groveling. But busy."

"Good."

Mac raised her eyebrow at Mudge. "Good he's groveling?"

"Good he's busy." Mudge took a sip of tea. "Keeps him out of trouble."

She *tsked* at him, but kept opening messages. No need to rush through brunch. Every reason to keep busy here, too. *No news.*

And presleep thoughts weren't for the light. *She needed data.*

Mac opened another. "Whoops."

Mudge paused, a cracker halfway to his lips. " 'Whoops?' "

"Wasn't meant for me. I hope. 'The pale forks of your writhing tongue flutter the tent of my passion?' " She slid her finger through the 'screen to close that one. "Hello." This as she skimmed the next message, then reread more slowly. "I'll be . . ." She read it again. "You wouldn't believe what they had for supper."

"I hope you appreciate, Norcoast, that there is very little as annoying as being a forced spectator to message reading. Particularly," Mudge waved today's carrot, "your message reading."

"Sorry," she said without looking away from the 'screen. Sorting the messages by topic didn't seem to work. *Typical Fourteen convolutions.* "Don't mind me."

"You can eat while you read," he fussed, pushing more vegetables on her plate.

"This is odd." Mac squinted at the display hovering between them. The list of messages showed as lines of simple text—*simple for someone else*—but those three hundred and fifteen lines now formed a perfect zigzag to the right. "See this?" For emphasis, she followed the pattern through the display with her finger.

It shouldn't have done anything.

But the display changed immediately. The text list disintegrated and re-formed into an image—a vid recording. "Look! It's Fourteen." Mac moved the 'screen so Mudge could see as well.

And only Fourteen, his face so close no background showed. He wasn't moving or talking. "It's not working," Mac said.

"If it's a private message, Norcoast, he'll have encoded something to activate it, a way for you to control when it plays."

"Oh. Of course." Mac leaned toward the 'screen.

"You know what it is?" Mudge sounded surprised.

"I've an idea," she replied, giving him a wink, then said firmly, "External genitalia."

Fourteen's image animated into a smile. "Idiot! I have none!" Then the smile was gone. "I knew you'd find this, Mac. You're more clever than you think. Not as clever as I am, but that's why you need me.

"You asked me to uncover the purpose of those rushing to Myriam. A simple matter. Boring, boring, boring. The same rush when a new restaurant becomes the trend. Everyone wants to be seen there, even if they hate the food. Irrelevant. Boring scientists and those who want to be boring scientists. With boring messages and no sex. I ignore them all. So should you. Any data of substance is moving freely."

His hands came into view, hovering near his eyes. "The Trisulians. I found additional proof of their infamy, of their plot against the Frow. Revolting species, but if we eradicated species for their looks, where would you Humans be, hmm?

"I gave this to the Sinzi. Fy asked my help in deciphering messages intercepted after the Frow were safe. The Trisulians are resentful beings. They blame the Sinzi, not themselves."

Beads formed on his eyelids. "There have been those who answer, privately, secretly. Only I could have found them. Words of fear. What do we know beyond the systems connected by the transects? How do we know the Sinzi aren't able to travel beyond those limits? What if we are trapped, not freed, by the transects?"

His hands flattened over his eyes. "Words of distrust. That the Myrokynay and their history are an invention, that the Sinzi are the Ro, that the unseen walkers are simply more new technology they haven't shared; that the Dhryn are the Sinzi's pawns and always have been."

Fourteen's hands moved away. His tiny eyes glistened. His mouth worked. "Words, Mac, from only a few. But now the Sinzi produce a new kind of Dhryn and permit a Progenitor ship to join us here. The Ro couldn't have done better themselves. For many, it's a thin line between admiration and envy. There should be no denying the *strobis* of the Sinzi. Idiots.

"We cannot survive the loss of the Sinzi. Yet we may be their destruction.

"In this dark time, I have the comfort of my life's love, Mac, and I thank you for that. Look after Charlie.

"I fear for us all."

The image fragmented back to the list of harmless messages.

Mac closed the 'screen, surprised her hand was steady. *Surprised her plate held green-and-yellow vegetables.*

Surprised to be sitting still when everything inside screamed in denial.

"We have to warn the Sinzi," she told Mudge.

His head was half bent, his eyes shadowed and fixed on her. "To what purpose? They have no weapons, no fleet of warships. Their protection from the Ro was in being scattered. One, maybe two per system; a homeworld that's little more than a stopover; the rest in perpetual transit. The Sinzi will be helpless if the IU turns on them."

"And without them, the transects will fail."

"There are those who might consider that the only way out—safety in isolation." His palm turned over on the table to rest open and empty.

Mac's lips tightened. "Until they discover the Ro are real after all."

A miserable *harrumph*. "Norcoast . . . what if . . ."

"Don't say it, Oversight." She reached out with both hands to take and hold his. "Don't think it. Trust me. I know the Ro are real. I've seen one—felt its voice burn inside me. Emily has, too."

His free hand came down on hers, pressing gently. "Then we must find one to show everyone else."

The corridor lighting was midday bright. There was a gentle breeze laced with cinnamon and no crush of impatient archaeologists to block it. The temperature, Human perfect, was doubtless set to keep the crew comfortable, regardless of activity. The *Annapolis Joy* was putting on her best inside face.

A shiver coursed down Mac's spine, raising gooseflesh on her real arm. *Could cut the tension with a knife,* she noted as she walked toward the Sinzi's quarters. She knew her reasons and it wasn't hard to guess why the crew she passed failed to smile. *Battle stations, then a Progenitor ship for a neighbor might do it.*

She didn't want to know why the Grimnoii ahead were standing in a clump in the midst of the corridor, instead of standing at attention by the Sinzi's door.

But she had to know. "Rumnor," she greeted, making sure to smile as she approached. "Anyone home?"

"Mac." For once, only he replied. The other three, Fy-Alpha and -Beta, plus another of Ureif's, continued to pace. *Pace wasn't the right word,* Mac decided, noticing the Grimnoii weren't picking up their feet, but rather slid each one forward in turn. *Slow-motion skating?*

They were polishing a circle in the already gleaming floor, but otherwise she couldn't see the point. She looked back at Rumnor.

"Sinzi-ra Fy is 'home,' " he answered, his expression more doleful than usual. "Ureif is—" He stopped.

"Ureif is . . . ?" she prompted.

The others halted, turning as one to look at her.

They'd always been large and carried more weapons than they had hands to use, but she'd never viewed Grimnoii as menacing. *Gloomy bears with allergies who drank too much, yes.*

Mac changed her mind. There was nothing but menace in their present posture and attention. Nothing but the clearest possible signal even to an alien that the wrong move or word would precipitate something she was unprepared to face.

The Sinzi's door opened. *Monitoring the hall?* Mac thought, inclined to be grateful. "Mac," Fy said, beckoning her within. "I am pleased to see you. Come in."

"Gotta go," Mac told the Grimnoii, walking confidently, if quickly, past.

When the door closed, she let out a relieved breath. "Thank you, Fy. The Grimnoii seem a little—tense—today."

"They have withdrawn their service." Fy touched fingers to shoulders—*mild distress*. "Now they protest."

The polished floor . . . *they wiped the Sinzi's scent away.* Mac sank into the nearest jelly-chair. "The Dhryn."

Fy took another chair, her fingers restless. "How can they not appreciate the congruence, Mac? Is it not the most obvious of joys? Do you not feel it?"

How could the Dhryn not know a Human needed water . . .

At least this Sinzi asked the question. "I can understand that a Sinzi would be affected by this Dhryn," Mac said, careful of every word and its impact on the mind behind those glittering eyes. *Minds.* "I've had practice. But I also understand why the Grimnoii protest. They are—concerned—that Sinzi enthusiasm here means less for the goal of protecting the IU and its species."

"Why?"

"I'm not qualified to explain it," she hedged.

"I have no other!" Fingers flashed, rings sliding like a river of gold and silver. "Consider me your student. Do your best."

"We're both in trouble," Mac muttered, then pursed her lips in thought. Her student was an engineer and an historian who studied technology. *Perhaps if she tried something surely familiar to both.*

Mac climbed from the chair to kneel in the sand before the Sinzi. She swept a patch flat with her hand, then drew a straight line in it. "The Grimnoii." She drew a second line, parallel to the first. "Humans." She drew three more then stopped. "The IU. What do you see?"

"I see failure," Fy said cooperatively. "Isolation. Stagnation."

Mac added an arrow to each of the lines, all at the same end. "And now?"

"Directionality. Purpose. But isolation and stagnation remain." A fingertip came down, as if the drawing were irresistible, and drew a complex spiral that crossed all the lines, then met itself. Fy withdrew her finger. "There. Complex, interwoven, interdependent. Is this not better?"

"That's not the question." Mac drew another straight line outside the rest, adding an arrow. "You must remember the components.

The IU is made up of cultures who view their progress as linear and isolated, who appreciate the role of the Sinzi and Sinzi technology, but as aids to one thing." She drove a thick, deep furrow through the complex spiral, putting an arrow at the end. "Survival. Together, or apart."

Fy pulled herself back as if the line were threatening, then leaned forward again. Two fingers explored the air above the drawing. "Remarkable. But if true, we are fundamentally different in our understandings and approach. How do we ever communicate properly?"

The mild complaint made Mac smile. "We keep trying," she said. "It's easier when dealing with similar goals. Biology's helpful that way—living things have a great deal in common."

"Technology also." Fy nodded. "There are rarely protests against physics."

She'd fit in at Base. Mac laughed, returning to her seat. "So you get my point?"

"We shall see." The Sinzi tilted her head one way, then the other, as if her two minds considered Mac separately. Then she straightened. "The Grimnoii see Ureif's support of this Dhryn and the Progenitor ship as an indication that all Sinzi could move away from their—direction." Fy touched the heavy line. "They fear we make a different choice. That we would abandon them, in favor of the Dhryn."

Mac was impressed. "And not return. There would be no circularity."

The Sinzi shuddered, rings glinting. "No future. They must be so afraid." Her voice rose. "I must share this with Ureif."

Who probably knows and moves ahead anyway, Mac told herself, *gripped by the tighter connection, perhaps believing he sees the right course.* "He was Sinzi-ra to the Dhryn, Fy."

"He bound himself to your promise," Fy said, as if Mac should realize this by now. "It takes precedence. We must preserve the Interspecies Union."

Her head hurt. "That's part of my promise?"

"How will you get home if the transects fail?"

As this was a question she tried to avoid on the principle of there being no good answer, Mac let it go. "There's another problem,

Fy." She took a deep breath and plunged. "It's come to my attention—" *there was a good euphemism for having a code-breaking,
moral-free Myg in your pocket* "—that some within the IU believe—
it's ridiculous, of course—but rumors spread. What I mean is, some
believe the Sinzi are—" Mac stopped, staring at the graceful being
across from her. *She couldn't say it.*

"They believe we are the Myrokynay?" Fy's fingers shivered in a
Sinzi laugh. "Ah! I am learning your face, Mac. It opens like a
flower when I surprise you."

Mac shook her head ruefully. "Consider me in bloom. You
knew?" *Had Fourteen sent his message to the Sinzi as well?*

"The site at Hift has been the focus of debate and controversy
long before I began to work on it, Mac. Some groups claim we
found the inspiration for no-space technology elsewhere, moving it
to Hift to hide other discoveries. Others claim there was no ancient
technology to be found, that we planted clues to cover the theft of
vital components from other species." A dismissive gesture. "And,
yes, there have always been those who say we are the Myrokynay's
descendants, that Hift was a long-lost outpost rediscovered. How
else would we have known where to look? And so forth. My work,
in part, laid those claims to rest. The devices at Hift were made of
materials previously unknown to Sinzi."

"But they are materials used by the Ro?"

"That remains in question," Fy replied with an almost Human
shrug. "We have had none to compare. The Chasm transect stations were replaced before this was a priority. I await an opportunity to examine samples from the ocean floor of Myriam."

Mac chewed her lower lip, then nodded. "I think there's something closer."

"No."

"That was pretty quick. You could at least think it over."

Darcy Townee snorted. "What I think, Dr. Connor, is that you
should have had enough shuttle rides for one lifetime. And realized
our current situation means no travel, no exceptions."

Fy rested a fingertip on Mac's shoulder. They'd contacted the consular hangar deck, to find they'd need the captain's authorization to release the Sinzi's tiny ship. The next step had been a trip to the bridge, only to find Gillis tied up in a meeting. *Probably looking at them through the wall right now,* Mac thought with irritation.

"Surely I may be permitted to take out my dart? I should inspect the transect station."

Among other things. The Sinzi-ra had been galvanized by Mac's suggestion she investigate the construction of the Progenitor's ship, so conveniently nearby.

Not that they had to specify all their stops.

Or all their reasons.

"That's not up to me, Sinzi-ra. I'm very sorry."

"Then get him." Mac pointed to the wall.

Townee gave her a very strange look. "I beg your pardon, Dr. Connor?"

"You heard me." She took a step and wrapped her hand around the tree trunk, not for support but as warning she was prepared to hold on and stay. "You're interfering with the business of the Sinzi-ra of Myriam. We're not leaving until you release the Sinzi-ra's dart, or get Captain Gillis in here to do so."

Standing beside her, Fy let her fingers swoop around in a gesture that, while impressive, Mac was reasonably sure meant nothing in particular. *Quick study.*

Townee, confronted by insubordinate behavior on her own bridge, by individuals she couldn't do more than sputter at, turned a dusky red. *Mudge could do it better,* Mac thought rather cheerfully.

They should have stopped by his quarters to collect him. *Nothing like officious moral support.*

"Dr. Connor. We are at alert. I will have you removed."

Mac tightened her grip, the artificial fingers indenting the bark. "You can try," she offered politely.

"My money's on the biologist."

She reacted to that voice before she named it, her heart thudding helplessly in her chest. *Handy tree,* she thought, holding on for dear life.

Nikolai Trojanowski stood at the top of the stairs leading to the meeting room, within the opening left by its sliding door. Captain Gillis and Ureif were with him, as well as Cayhill.

They'd invited Cayhill and not her?

Mac's resentment vanished in a flash of understanding. Cayhill was supporting Nik, his arm around the other man's waist, his shoulder under Nik's arm. *He'd been hurt.*

She could still feel it.

That was how they came down the three wide stairs. Slowly. So slowly she had time to loosen each finger in turn, then walk forward to meet them.

"We wish to leave this ship," Fy insisted, having come along also.

Mac was close enough to see the amused look Nik gave her. "You do?"

Close enough to see the crusts of burns on his skin, the way his clothes hung loose, how Cayhill was keeping him upright.

She stifled a cry behind her hand, eyes filling with tears. Nik said something she couldn't hear, pushing free of Cayhill to reach for her. She hurried to take his weight, inhaling sweat, sickness, and pain as she pressed her cheek against his. His hand cupped her head, then slipped. Warned, she held tighter. "Cayhill!"

"I've got him. Here." They eased Nik to the floor, Mac going down first to support his head and shoulders. "I warned you," Cayhill snapped furiously at no one in particular. "Get a stretcher up here, stat."

"Is he dead?" This from Fy.

Mac ignored everything but Cayhill, kneeling beside Nik. "How bad is he?"

He gave her a quick look, then resumed going over his new patient. "Until I do a scan and blood work, I won't know. Doubt he's slept in days. Signs of dehydration. Those burns—healed, maybe, but look like radiation. Stayed on his feet by will, nothing more."

"Here." Mac held her hand over Nik's lower left rib, drew it up and over to his right side. "He was hurt here. In a fight. About a week ago. I don't know the weapon."

Cayhill opened Nik's shirt, giving a short grunt at what he saw. "I do. Handheld disrupter. Doesn't look too bad. More direct or prolonged, though . . ." He looked at her. "How did you know?"

Because she remembered the pain as if it had been hers . . . "We've been in touch."

The stretcher arrived. Mac hovered nearby, finding it strange to watch the smooth practiced motions of Cayhill and his orderlies from her feet, not her back. *As Nik had watched when she'd come on board.*

No one spoke to her. There'd been a look or two. A whisper to the captain. The Sinzi stood by, Fy silenced by confusion if nothing else. Mac didn't have room for her now.

He looked . . . spent.

When the stretcher left the bridge, Mac followed.

As he'd followed.

No one tried to stop her.

By the time Nikolai Trojanowski opened his hazel eyes, Mac had spent a lazy eternity reminding herself of the strong lines of his jaw, the shadows below cheekbone and eyebrow, pooled in the hollow at the base of his throat. She'd already met the wound on his body, now washed and sealed with the rest of his scars.

Yummy.

By the time his eyes focused and puzzled at the ceiling, she'd adjusted the fine chain around his neck, with its paired rings. Each time, she'd practiced what she'd say when he awoke, and changed her mind as often. She'd flushed and paled and finally settled to content.

So by the time his head finally turned on the pillow and those hazel eyes found her, she just smiled. "Took you long enough. Trust Cayhill." The physician hadn't asked anyone's permission before pumping Nik full of sedative as well as nutrients. *Crisis or no.*

But when Nik didn't smile, or speak, or do anything but look at her—his eyes like someone drowning—Mac understood. "I'm really here," she whispered. "I can prove it."

She took off her clothes. Careful of the tubes and healing wound, she slipped in beside him, and pressed her body along his. "There. I won't let go." She held him while he shook.

And held him after he stopped shaking.

Mac opened her eyes and found Nik looking down at her. "Took you long enough," he said, his hand resting flat and warm on her hip. His cracked lips twitched into a half smile. "I can't believe you got Cayhill to put me in your quarters."

"We've reached an understanding." His hand strayed and she frowned. "An understanding, Mr. Trojanowski, which included you resting."

That dimple.

"Define 'resting,' Dr. Connor."

She wanted nothing more than to stay like this, the door locked with them hidden inside, his arm, sleep-heavy, across her stomach. Mac admitted it, then drew her fingertips down the side of his face, smooth one way, catching in stubble the other. "No more rest," she said when Nik opened his eyes.

Their hazel darkened as he gazed at her. His arm lifted, but when she started to move away, it came down to hold her in place. "We need to talk," his breath warm on her cheek.

As meeting venues went, Mac thought, snuggling closer, *this had merit.* "Who starts?"

His hand captured hers; his fingers toyed with the rings she wore. "I see they made it." A question in his eyes.

She nodded. "And worked. Those three," she amended, touching the one exiled for safety to her artificial hand. "This—I'm guessing the Progenitor wanted a close look."

His expression could only be described as dumbfounded. "She imprinted a message?"

Mac winced. "Let's just say I appreciate Her situation."

A pause. "So you got most of what I wanted you to know."

And more. She tensed involuntarily.

"What's wrong?" A flash of concern. "Did the *lamnas* hurt you? Mac, I would never have tried them if I thought there was a risk."

Okay, a potential disadvantage to bed meetings. She made herself relax. "Have you ever received a *lamnas*?"

He shook his head slightly, his lips brushing her ear. *Distraction.* Mac wasn't entirely clear if that was a disadvantage or not. "Anchen and I practiced, but I couldn't make sense of what she tried to send me. I had to rely on her belief that another Human—you—would be able to detect words, if I concentrated on them."

If they hadn't been like this—the dim light, huddled together under a sheet—Mac might not have said it. *Not without a few beers.* But Nik deserved to know. "To be honest," she said, "your messages weren't just words."

His turn to tense, which under other circumstances she would have found intriguing. "What do you mean?"

"I—felt—what you were feeling."

"Oh." His lips curved beside her eye. "I suppose that explains the lack of small talk, even from you." His hand rose to cup her breast in its warmth. "I can't say I mind."

"Not just those feelings," she clarified. "And not just feelings. I received memories. Your memories. As if I'd been there. Been you."

He might have turned to stone. Mac pulled away reluctantly, sitting up and crossing one leg beneath so she could look at him. Nik's stricken expression as he stared back was more than she could bear. "It's okay," she said, feeling clumsy. "No one else knows."

"Anchen—she didn't say anything about memories."

Mac didn't flinch from the growing outrage on his face. *She'd feel the same.* "How could she know what would happen between Humans? And how do we know she'd make that distinction at all?" *Words, feelings, memories—what had to pass between the individuals inhabiting one body?*

Nik sat up, ripping free the tubing that had somehow stayed in place. *Not for want of trying,* Mac thought, tempted to smile despite everything else. "What memories?" he demanded harshly, eyes dark.

Anyone else, she'd doubt. Anyone else would recoil from her, from such exposure.

"Your worst," Mac admitted without fear. "At a guess."

"Oh." His face paled and she watched him swallow. "And you still . . ." A hand waved vaguely at the bed.

She frowned. "Why wouldn't I?"

"Gods, Mac." Nik took her in his arms, pressing his lips to her forehead before burying his face in the hollow where her neck met her shoulder.

The man was *in a weakened state.* She put up with it for another thirty seconds, then tapped him on the back. "Saving the known universe?"

Nik lifted his head, his anguished expression wiping whatever else she might have said from her mind. "We have to talk about this," he stated. "All of it. I have to explain—"

From somewhere, Mac found the strength to deny him. "Later," she promised, very gently. "If we live that long. If it still matters." Before he could argue, she tightened her arms around him once, then stood. "Right now, there's someone the Progenitor needs to meet."

"She isn't here."

Mac blinked. "I saw the ship—"

"A negotiated sacrifice." Nik eased his legs over the side of the bed, wincing only slightly. His hand rested on his stomach, where Cayhill had applied mem-skin over the almost-healed but tender wound. *Habit,* Mac decided, well able to imagine trying to get medical help from the Dhryn.

There must have been others. "Who else survived?" she asked, feeling guilty not to have given the rest of his companions a thought. Then what he'd said sank in. " 'Negotiated sacrifice?' "

The corner of his mouth deepened. "We came out better than expected. The *Impeci* 's crew of five made it, as well as the research staff other than Genny P'tool. A bit worn, but nothing worse. The Progenitor broke from hiding to come to us; we docked and so escaped most of the radiation. As for the sacrifice?" He shook his head. "I wouldn't have believed it, Mac. Another Progenitor had taken shelter in the same system. Both were starving. They discussed the situation through their Vessels and the other—well, I don't know what argument was used, but all the Dhryn, including the Progenitor, from the other ship agreed to be consumed in order for our Progenitor to survive."

Mac tilted her head. " 'Our' Progenitor?"

Nik looked up at her, his eyes like transparent green glass. "I learned a few truths myself." He rose to his feet with almost his usual grace. "I've come in the empty ship, with a skeleton Dhryn crew, to act as Her Vessel." He paused. "Skeleton crew. There's truth for you. How long can they fast? I never saw one eat. They were skin on bone, Mac. Haven Dhryn. None spoke Instella—whenever one looked my way I'd say *lamisah* and hope for the best."

Mac fastened on what caught her attention. "You're Her Vessel? What happened to the Dhryn Vessel?"

"He disappeared the second day we were on board," his face grim and set. "Along with all the Dhryn not directly engaged in operating Her ship. There was no explanation."

"No need." Mac wasn't sure if what she felt was sympathy for the being who had been Parymn Ne Sa Las, or admiration for Dhryn communal will to survive. *Likely both.* "She told me." She held up her hand and touched the fourth *lamnas.* "The Progenitor's running out of time."

Nik looked stunned, but didn't ask. *Just as well,* Mac thought. "That's why I'm here. She sent me to prepare the way. She's following, to meet with the IU and negotiate a truce through the Sinzi. While we rested, Ureif's been setting up the protocols."

"We need a shower," Mac announced bluntly. "Now." She took his arm in a firm grip and pulled him into the stall with her, turning on the sprays. Once sure they were surrounded by the noise of water, she burst out: "Are you trying to destroy the IU? To ruin any credibility the Sinzi have? Because you couldn't have found a better way to—" The rest was smothered by his mouth.

When the wet, passionate kiss ended—*too soon and not soon enough, under the circumstances*—Nik held her close. She felt his sigh. "There's risk on all sides, Mac. But you said it. She doesn't have much time left. None of the Dhryn do. And we need them to defeat the Ro."

Brain damage? Mac considered it, as well as the option of having Nik sedated. "The Dhryn are the Ro's weapon," she pointed out.

"A weapon that almost destroyed them."

She shut off the water. They stood toe-to-toe, dripping in unison, Nik waiting for her to speak. *Which might take a while,* Mac thought wildly.

As if sensing this, he reached out and plucked a towel from the rack. "Our Progenitor sent Brymn Las looking for an answer." He began drying her off, starting with her hair. "What is the minimum genetic diversity required in a population to respond to evolutionary stress? Could this number be predicted for a species? He discovered your work on evolutionary units in salmon. Which, Dr. Connor," the towel progressed downward, "I found riveting reading, given our situation."

Just her luck, Mac grumbled to herself, *to be toweled by a handsome man in a shower and have* him *want to talk salmon.* "Brymn Las was worried about his people," she said, taking the towel and her turn drying him.

Thoroughly.

He put his hands against the tile behind her head as she worked, eyes warm. "That wasn't why his Progenitor asked the question, Mac. She wanted to know if they'd killed enough Ro in the Chasm to doom that species—to finally be safe from them."

Mac dropped the towel. "The Chasm?" she breathed, staring up at him.

"The Chasm. It's been the puzzle all along, Mac. The key to solving it isn't how, but why those worlds were laid waste." His smile was faint, but triumphant. "And that it happened twice."

"Twice." Now she let him hear her skepticism. "Why didn't the Origins Team—or any other—find a result like that?"

"There was nothing to find. The Ro used the Dhryn to wipe the life from those worlds, Mac. What happened next? The Progenitor had stories, legends, bits of information passed down from the three Progenitors who made it to Haven. Who were taken to Haven," he corrected, nothing warm or calm in his eyes now. "From these, and what She learned from Brymn Las and others—including what we told Her Vessel—She pieced together the rest. They were changed by the Ro, used by them to destroy other life in the Chasm, including their own homeworld. But there's more."

"Go on."

"Ro attention was fixed on those empty worlds—why, no Dhryn knew. The Dhryn were preoccupied themselves, desperate to find food for their now-starving Progenitors. Some broke the Ro conditioning. Whether they then realized what they'd been made to do and rebelled, or whether they were simply trying to survive—it doesn't matter now. The Dhryn attacked every world in the Chasm again, this time obliterating the Ro. Or so they thought."

"They were wrong."

"Yes. My guess is that some Ro were in their ships. All they had to do was wait for the Dhryn to turn on one another. Rather than lose such a useful tool," his voice had an edge, "they collected the last three Progenitors and took them to Haven, locking them into one system. The Dhryn could do nothing but breed and wait. The Progenitors kept their dreadful secrets from the new generations, hoping they'd done so much damage to the Ro that they'd never return for them, always afraid they would. They did their best to forget. And almost succeeded."

The defense of ordinary Dhryn: 'We do not think of it.' Mac shivered. "The Ro did return. The IU even helped, giving the Dhryn access to the Naralax."

"Just what the Ro wanted. Only this time, when the Dhryn rebel, they'll have allies. The IU."

She frowned with concern. "Who else knows all this?" The question of his sanity she kept to herself.

"The Sinzi-ra, the captain, the Inner Council, the Ministry. The decision makers." Nik's fingers traced her jaw, lingered on her lips. She gave a startled protest as he turned on the shower. "No one needs us quite yet," he assured her, his voice low and husky. "You remember how dry a Dhryn ship can be, don't you?" He leaned his head back until water ran over his closed eyes and burned skin. It streamed from his chin and down his chest, glistening on his shoulders.

"Definitely yummy," Mac murmured, following the drops with her hands.

Good thing she'd locked the door.

- CONTACT -

"LOOK!"

"This may be a tedious and menial posting, but those are insufficient to excuse failure to fully utilize the excellent protocols established and prepared for our use." The seniormost Imrya relished this opportunity to elaborate in a meaningful yet sensitive manner appropriate to the youth and inexperience of her younger compatriot. "To properly request my attention," she began, "you must first—"

But her younger compatriot wasn't listening. Instead, his nostrils were pressed to the viewport. "Have you ever seen anything so glorious?" he gasped. "I must record this. I must write at least a stanza—no, I will surely dedicate the rest of my days to an epic work worthy of this moment, this spectacle, this—*oof*—"

The seniormost Imrya, notepad in hand and having successfully deposed her younger compatriot from the only viewport on this side of the station using her ample rump, settled in to see what was worth a life—such moments coming rarely even to a species devoted to the pursuit of literary perfection.

Slivers of light were converging on the Naralax gate, a region of space both infamous and lately well-explored by playwrights. Other traffic gave way, as was the custom when encountering a Sinzi courier dart.

But so many darts. They had been flowing in from other gates for weeks now. None had questioned their movement. Frankly, Imrya weren't roused to attention by the hasty, too-brief messaging of other species. Any news of import required, to their way of thinking, a minimum of ten thousand words to properly introduce the topic. Anything less simply couldn't matter.

Yet the flow of information represented by so many darts at once was on a scale to grab even an Imrya by the wattle. The beauty of the small, sleek ships. The way they followed one another, in perfect sync and sequence.

The seniormost scribbled down adjectives as quickly as she could, hearing her younger compatriot vainly attempting to do the same.

Neither bothered to wonder where the darts were going.

That which is Dhryn must make the Great Journey.

That which is Dhryn must *move*. It is the Way.

As before, as before, as too many times, the Call is heard. Insistent . . . dominant . . . *demanding*.

That which is Dhryn resists . . . resists . . . then succumbs.

The Call is the only hope left.

INVESTIGATIONS AND INVASION

M AC MIGHT HAVE LOCKED the door to her quarters. *Didn't mean the universe would pay attention.*

The com panel was flashing. Someone less patient was knocking. *There was probably mail on her imp marked "urgent!"*

Mac glanced at Nik as they dressed and was oddly comforted by his wry grin. "It's probably Oversight," she warned, smiling back.

He pointed to the abandoned tube on the bed. "My money's on Cayhill." He closed the neck fastener of the pale green crew fatigues left for him, then deftly checked its pockets, pulling out to show her, in order, an ident chip, an imp, and one of the palm weapons she'd last seen him use on Earth. At her look, he grinned. "I always leave spares behind."

She reached into hers and brought out imp, nutrient bars, and the little salmon. "I take mine with me."

The knocking, now more like hammering, stopped for a moment, then resumed. *Given there was no shipwide alarm, whoever it was could wait.*

"Speaking of Cayhill," she bent to pull on her shoes, "how do you feel?" This with a twinge of guilt. Somehow she doubted the physician had included certain activities as part of her promise to look after his patient. *Though she could testify that the patient was fully functional.*

"Afraid."

The word, however matter-of-fact his voice, made her look up in surprise. "Of Cayhill?" *This seemed unlikely.*

His face showed unfamiliar strain. "Of waking up in a few minutes. Of finding none of this was real. I know that's ridiculous."

Still shaky, despite the bravado. "If I were you," Mac replied lightly, "I'd be more afraid of Cayhill. You're likely to be grilled on our time together."

"And me not at my best." *That wicked dimple.*

Mac raised a noncommittal eyebrow. "I've no complaints."

With a laugh, Nik captured her hand and brought it quickly to his lips. "When you've had my best, love, you'll know the difference. Trust me."

She felt the rush of heat in her cheeks, and elsewhere. Words failed her. *Banter like this was Emily's turf.*

Nik reacted at once. He knelt, still holding her right hand and collecting her left, all amusement gone from his face. "Mac—" The hammering intensified. Nik sent the door a baleful look, then turned back to her. "I didn't mean—damn it, Mac, you know what happened was—" He stopped there.

Had words failed him, too?

Mac almost smiled. "I know," she told him, turning her hands to hold his. Then she did smile. "You do realize, Mr. Trojanowski, that as a scientist I can't accept any hypothesis without thorough experimentation."

His smile was every bit as wide as hers. "Of course, Dr. Connor."

The door actually creaked. "I'd better get that," Mac said. She had to tug her hands free and pretended to scowl at Nik. *Who didn't look the least repentant.*

Mac opened the door. "What is it, Over—" She stopped and stared at Rumnor. The Grimnoii tucked his—*yes, he'd been using a hammer*—into its sling and bowed slightly.

"The Sinzi-ra requests you attend Her Excellence, the Progenitor." As Nik came to stand by Mac's shoulder, the alien blinked slowly, yellow crystals raining on the floor. "Both of you."

"She's arrived?"

Wrong Dhryn. "In a sense," Mac cautioned, relieved to see at least one of the Grimnoii had returned to the Sinzi's service. *Or was spying.* She disliked the notion; she didn't avoid it. "The Progenitor has recently undergone metamorphosis. Remember?"

They hadn't had time for much more conversation, but she'd

made sure Nik knew about the Wasted and the corpse of the Ro walker. Captain Gillis had provided him with a somewhat skewed version of the entire business. She'd eventually need to add all the details—*given Gillis hadn't thought to mention her being on the* Uosanah *in the first place*—but at least the Ministry's man on the spot was aware of the players.

And had no reason to berate her for taking risks. *There were,* Mac decided, *distinct benefits to being anonymously foolhardy.*

"Ah, yes," Nik said smoothly. "Please tell the Sinzi-ra we'll be there shortly. We're expected at the remains first, you see. To provide final identification." He pronounced this last with such intense melodrama it was all Mac could do not to react.

Rumnor seemed to find the emphasis convincing, for he nodded and left without argument.

" 'Final identification?' " Mac asked, once the alien disappeared down the ladderway.

"Even modern, space-faring Grimnoii follow tradition," her companion informed her. "The perished must be named in order to rest. Those who could identify the dead are not impeded in any way." His expression turned grim. "And I want to see the enemy."

"It's a walker, not a Ro." Mac made a face. "What's left of it."

"You've seen it?" Nik raised a rakishly singed eyebrow. "Do you know where it's kept?"

"Yes. Wait. The com was flashing. Let me check. I'm trying to be better about messages." Mac slipped back into her quarters—*funny how pleasant memories warmed a room*—then pressed the button.

It was a sequence of voice messages: Mudge, Cayhill, Mudge, Cayhill, Cayhill, Mudge, and so forth. A nice "hope you feel better soon, Nik" from Court, whom she guessed knew the spy from his earlier sojourns aboard. More Mudge, Cayhill. Both men sounded terse, as if they suspected why they weren't being answered but hoped she didn't know they knew and so would answer her com regardless.

Nothing more urgent. Mac recorded a quick "we're heading out" reply to any and all, then rejoined Nik in the corridor.

"Not that way," he said when she started toward the ladderway. "Through here." He indicated the door through the bulkhead to the rest of the ship.

"We're not allowed—" she objected, then watched him key in the door code. "Okay, I'm not allowed."

Her spy grinned. "After you, Dr. Connor."

Captain Gillis' accommodating crew had done a superb job of transporting the Origins Team, despite the quirks that came with archaeologists. They'd risen to the occasion when more aliens were added to the mix, and relished the challenge when one of those aliens turned out to be a Flowering Dhryn. No requirement had seemed too great, not even the need for more rooms and a private hangar for the new Interspecies Consulate on board.

But they must have been hard-pressed to find secure autopsy space for the Ro walker. Mac surveyed the result with some dismay. *No way around it.* It was a tent, tucked against one wall of the Sinzi's hangar. "This was the best they could do?" she asked the nearest of five guards stationed between the cable supports.

He shrugged. "Handy to the scientists' transports, Dr. Connor."

In her experience, convenience for scientists was a secondary motivation. "And they don't have to be escorted through the *Joy,*" she guessed.

A flash of teeth, but a carefully neutral, "I wouldn't know about that, Dr. Connor."

Nik was heading for the open flap, so Mac nodded good-bye to the guard and followed.

To be fair, it was quite a tent. Mac was inclined to envy. Beyond the flap was a nicely rigid doorframe, complete with transparent door. Through it, she could see what appeared to be a well-lit metal cage, its upper surface head-high. Nik produced some kind of ident to wave at the guard at the door, gesturing her to follow as he passed that barrier.

Mac made clucking noises with her tongue, then took a deep breath and followed.

If an intent focus and the carrying of small, blinking instruments were the hallmarks of scientists, then the inside of the tent was packed with them. Otherwise, there was nothing to distinguish this group from one of Anchen's outdoor gatherings. *Less ventilation.* Mac wrinkled her nose, attempting not to breathe through it.

The cage wasn't to keep something in—*not that she'd any doubt the corpse was exactly that*—but an all-species' access mechanism. Frow clambered across the top. Something for which Mac had no name was fastened to a horizontal bar by curved teeth, its trio of tentacles poking through at the stiffened black remains suspended within the cage. Mac quickly moved her eyes from the corpse. While underneath? She bent over to watch a Nerban on its back, working with apparent comfort, a face shield protecting its proboscis from drips.

Group insanity or interspecies' efficiency. She hadn't made up her mind.

Nik had stopped, his eyes wide with shock as he stared at the walker. *There hadn't been any way to prepare him,* Mac thought sympathetically. At least he didn't look about to vomit. She had a feeling his default ran more to fight than flight.

Not that there was anything wrong with flight.

Especially from a nightmare.

"Mac!" Fy came forward from where she'd been in conversation with a heavier-than-most Imrya, moving through the crowd with that unexpected speed. "I am pleased you are here. I have made the most remarkable discovery with the help of these fine—ah." This as she noticed Nik. "You have improved."

Nik bowed, almost as gracefully as a Sinzi. "Greetings, Sinzi-ra. My name is—"

"You are Nikolai." Fy brought her fingers up to form rings in front of her great eyes. "My apologies for not recognizing you sooner. I participate in your promise as I do in Mac's."

"Mac's?" Nik turned his head to give her a look that could best be described as appalled. *Answering the question of whether he knew what a Sinzi promise meant.*

Mac replied with a helpless shrug.

Aliens.

"Your discovery, Fy?" she asked brightly.

Fy launched herself back to a console beside the cage, leaving the two Humans to make their way through the cluster of researchers.

As they did, Nik whispered urgently: "You made a promise with Anchen? Do you have any idea of the possible consequences?"

"You did it first," she shot back.

"I—" He closed his mouth but not, she was sure, because he didn't have more to say on the subject.

"Here, Mac. Nikolai. See?" Fy's delicate fingers were wrapped around a grotesque serrated hook, about the size of Mac's forearm. The dull black of its surface was scored by regular holes. *Sample cores,* she realized, even as a more primitive part of her mind gibbered at her to either throw up or run, whichever reaction came first. *Simultaneous might work.*

Instead, Mac reached back until her fingers found Nik's wrist. "What did you find?" Her voice sounded normal, given the background of alto grunts and tenor mutters, but she felt his hand cover hers.

"Remember our discussion—concerning the Hift artifacts? This—" a triumphant wave of the hook came close to landing on Mac's nose, "—this is of the same material!"

"It's a machine?" This quick and sharp from Nik. "Some kind of construct?"

"Machine, no." The Nerban who'd been with Fy spoke up. His long eyelid was opened to its maximum to admit more light in the—to his kind—dim room. The eye itself lay hidden deep within the revealed cavity. Mac didn't know their features well enough to be sure if this was the individual from the meeting. *The silver-and-emerald bangle circling his proboscis was new.*

"Construct? Most definitely. The biological portion consists of conjoined body parts, no two of which came from the same source organism. Despite this, there appears an underlying logic to the result. The sum did have life, as the IU defines it. The technology, the tools, were melded into the flesh. If only it hadn't been so damaged, we'd know more."

And she'd be dead. Mac shuddered and let go of Nik. "Have you compared this one to the one found on Earth?" she asked. The man beside her stiffened in shock. *Right. Full briefing overdue.* "Buried by the earthquake," she told him quickly. "The Ro used the landslide to cover the tracks of whatever they put into the ocean. Em's on its trail." *News at six,* she thought inanely.

"Yes," the Nerban said. "The components are identical."

She'd expected a match. That didn't make it any more pleasant. Mac closed her eyes for an instant. *One of those things had been on Earth, on the slopes of Castle Inlet.*

How many more?

"Have you identified any of the components?" Nik asked. "The organisms."

"Others are working on that. It will be difficult. The genetic material is severely distorted. Mutations, damage, manipulation at the molecular level. For now, all I can say is we've found no match to existing species within the IU, but—"

"There she is!"

Mac hunched her shoulders, somehow knowing that shout boded nothing good.

The shout announced the Trisulian who surged through the rest. This one was wrapped in red leather but with a belt of scanning equipment and probes instead of a weapon. *Not pregnant,* Mac noted, belatedly counting only two eyestalks. Female. *And going to stay that way.* "You," the alien continued without pause. "You are Mr. Mac, Mr. Connor. I have a question."

Quiet spread outward from their little group. *She hated it when that happened.* Having no other option, Mac nodded. "What is it?"

"There are inexplicable marks." The Trisulian lifted the black limb she carried. "Here. And here."

Were they cutting off souvenirs?

Somehow, Mac kept her feet from moving backward and made herself examine the limb. Easy to see what had puzzled the Trisulian. "Oh. Those are mine." Without touching the limb, she held her left hand over the marks, spreading her fingers and thumb to show how each fit into one of the indentations. "It's a prosthesis," she said, wiggling the fingers in case the aliens mistook Human strength. "I was in a bit of a hurry."

"In a— What the—" Nik switched to English for a few choice and impassioned phrases before recovering to think of their audience. "Mac? You were there? On that ship?"

"You could say that," Mac hedged.

"Alone, Mr. Mac captured it. At great risk to herself."

Nik's response to this was thankfully lost as the Frow from atop the cage structure chose this moment to plunge almost to the floor. "You will treat Dr. Connor with the respect due her rank!" he shouted at Nik. Then he noticed the Trisulian and snapped his membranes threateningly. "How dare you approach Dr. Connor! How dare you be in this room! How dare you be on this ship!"

The Trisulian cowered behind her share of corpse, the Frow kept shouting—*the Nerban sweating*—while other aliens either paid rapt attention, ignored the fracas completely, or began to edge to the exit, all in their own unique ways.

Mac shook her head at Nik. "You could have waited," she mouthed.

He said something she couldn't hear over the din—*probably just as well*—then jerked his thumb at the door. She nodded.

Time to find somewhere else to cause an uproar.

"This is a closet."

"I know."

Mac put her back to a convenient shelf and sniffed. *Cleansers, even in space.* "Why are we in a closet?"

Nik had taken her by the hand—her real one—and marched her into the nearest corridor from the hangar, along it past several doors identical to this one, then in here. *He knew the layout of the ship remarkably well,* she decided.

Or it was a spy thing. The ability to hunt out closets. Doubtless useful.

"Ureif's waiting for us," she commented.

"I know that, too." Nik stood in front of the now-closed closet door, close enough to touch. He'd tried to cross his arms, but had winced and left them at his sides. She guessed his wounded abdomen didn't appreciate the pressure. Now he leaned his shoulders against the door. "You've been busy, Dr. Connor. Care to save me finding out in bits and pieces?"

Not accusing, she judged. *Truly curious.* And there were things he should be told. "How do you want it? The abridged 'things I want you to know' or the really long 'it's too late to argue with me even if you could' version?"

"How about the 'I trust you' version." *Almost that dimple.*

Ah. Mac fastened her eyes on his and began at the beginning, with Emily.

Nik was more than a patient listener, he had that rare talent of drawing confidences from others. *Handy in a spy.* She'd noticed that about him before. He became absorbed, as if he processed every word. She could see it now, in how the hazel of his eyes responded, growing darker or lighter, and in the expressive lines of his mouth.

Those lines had settled into conviction by the time Mac finished.

"Emily keeps repeating 'eleven,' " Nik echoed in a low voice, eyes hooded. "Could it be that simple?"

She stared at him. "It means something to you?"

"Maybe." Nik frowned in thought. "We've wondered all along—why so few attacks? Why no more? It's not the Dhryn's choice. The Progenitors starve waiting for the Ro to 'call' them to feed. Why the delay?"

"Not because we've scared them," she said bluntly. "Not because we can stop them."

"The Ro do seem to hold all the cards." Nik lifted his head. The closet light caught fire in his eyes. *If she didn't know better, she'd swear he looked triumphant.* "Why would they let the Dhryn die now, after all they've done to start them in motion?"

"You expect me to explain the Ro?" Mac snorted, but Nik only raised a challenging eyebrow. *He was going someplace with this,* she realized. *Play along.* "The Dhryn are tools," she said slowly. "You discard a tool once you finish a job. Or if you find a better one. Or if it's defective," she added, remembering a certain unloved power screwdriver and a cold, wet night trying to repair an autosampler. *The screwdriver had skipped perfectly over the waves.*

"Or you put it down, so you can pick up something else. After all, you only have two of these." Nik lifted his hands and wiggled the fingers at her.

"Your point being?"

"Assume the Ro aren't finished. What if they've put the Dhryn aside, not because they want to, or it's convenient, but because there simply aren't enough Ro to be everywhere or do everything that's necessary to control them. Not enough hands, Mac."

He liked the idea. Mac chewed her lip, wanting to like it, too. But she'd learned caution the hard way. "Go on," she prompted.

"After I heard what the Progenitor had to say, about the Dhryn turning on the Ro in the Chasm, how close they'd come to defeating them—it dawned on me we could be dealing with the survivors of that battle. Emily said the Ro abandoned a planetary existence millennia ago." Nik reached out and took her by the arms, his eyes aglow. "Mac. Those survivors could be the last of them. I think that's what Emily discovered. What if she's been trying to tell us how many Ro are left?"

"Eleven?" Mac's hands tightened on his wrists. "Gods. That simple? Poor Em." *It made a terrible sense.* Through the confused and distorted memories, the well-meant efforts to cure her obsession, she'd clung to that one bit of vital information. She'd tried to tell them.

Without context, without Nik's new information about the Dhryn, it would have been for nothing.

He'd kept talking, the words staccato quick and sure. "The Ro paid no attention to us until the Progenitor began searching out the truth. When She rediscovered enough to be concerned the Ro could return, when She contacted a Human—you, Mac—that's when they took notice." Nik's voice turned grim. "They tried to identify and silence Her. One ship. Remember? Maybe . . . maybe one Ro. While the rest moved on to bigger things, directing the Dhryn against entire planets. One at a time. Why? Did one of them need to be there?" He looked distinctly annoyed, that familiar crease beside his eyes. "Too many damned questions."

She stood on tiptoe to kiss his nose. "So I'll add mine. Why did the Ro strip the oceans from the hundreds of worlds in the Chasm?"

Nik got that look. *The one she'd learned meant something she wasn't going to like.*

"What is it?"

"Are you sure they did?"

Mac frowned. "It happened."

"Yes, but was it intentional? Think about it, Mac. The Dhryn kill the Ro on those worlds. Without the Ro, their no-space technology fails—technology they could have located deep underwater. And then?"

"I don't like where this is going, Nik."

"If the Ro lived or hid in oceans before, they could be doing it again." Nik's eyes burned into hers; she had the feeling he didn't see her at all, caught by nightmare. *She shared it.* Then his expression smoothed into what Mac thought of as his public face, his noncommittal, do-what-it-takes, face. *She wanted to shake him.* "What cost do you think the IU would be willing to bear," he asked in a light, pleasant, how-are-you voice, "if it meant the Dhryn destroyed the last of the Ro before dying themselves? To end both threats? Would they vote to accept the cost of a world?"

Not their world. "Not Earth," Mac heard herself say. She let go of him, backing into the shelf. *Half a step—small closet.*

"A backwater planet," Nikolai Trojanowski reminded her, implacable, cool. "A transportable, adaptable intelligent species. A small price, isn't it? If the IU can trap so much as one Ro there? Better yet, get them all? Save the transect system. Save themselves?"

Mac glared. "You aren't serious. Nik. You can't possibly—"

" 'Where on that scale,' Dr. Connor. Remember?" His mouth twisted abruptly, his voice losing its calm. "Oh, the IU would owe humanity. Those who survived would be compensated, resettled. Our species would gain a seat on the Inner Council. A brand new world."

Salmon, surging into the air, water falling from their silvered sides. The great trees leaning overhead, green and gold and mossed with life. A slug, crawling towards the taste of sex and food.

The shivered cry of eagles.

"There is no other world," Mac said, knowing it was the truth. *Not for them.*

Not for her.

"There's no other world," Nik agreed. He opened his arms. When she stepped into them, he put his lips to her ear. "We'll need another way."

Nik took them to the nearest communications station. Once there, he dropped his ident in front of the crew. Whatever it said, the three didn't hesitate, immediately standing and moving well back from their console, letting Nik take their place.

She could use one of those. Mac considered it, then changed her mind. She'd seen the cost of that kind of power. She waited, silent, while her spy composed several missives. *If anyone could send secrets, it would be this man.*

Those secrets sat inside her like a meal her body already regretted. *Hollans would get more than he bargained for,* Mac thought. Fact and speculation. The former might be scattered; the latter fit too well. *Neither were comforting.*

"I can't set up a give and go with Earth," Nik said abruptly. "Have you been having equipment problems?"

"Not at our end, sir," answered one of the crew. "But there've been sporadic delays with incoming packets for the past few hours. Sinzi-ra Myriam is monitoring the gate."

Nik swiveled the chair to look at the crew. "Outgoing?"

Two of them glanced at the third, a woman with specialist bars on her arm. "From our side, outgoing reads nominal, sir," she replied.

Even Mac could hear the unspoken doubt in her voice. Nik rose to his feet, every line of his body tense. "Traffic is moving through the gate?" he demanded.

"Of course, sir." All three looked astonished by the very idea. *They were lucky,* thought Mac, who wasn't. "But until the incoming rate returns to normal," the specialist pointed out, "we won't know if outgoing messages are being delayed as well."

"We'll notify you once the problem's rectified, sir. Shouldn't be long."

Nik nodded. "Thank you." He turned to Mac. "Shall we go meet your guest?" Warm smile, easy tone. If she didn't know better, she'd think it was an ordinary day and he was proposing to visit a mutual friend. *A Human chameleon,* she decided enviously. Anyone looking at Nik would think nothing was wrong with the world.

Anyone looking at her? Mac snorted. *She didn't need a mirror.* The crew they'd encountered in the corridor had given her second glances. *Worried ones.* These three had been no different.

"Let's go," she agreed.

The length of corridor leading back to the hangar and beyond turned out to be consular space, bustling with activity. *None of it Grimnoii,* Mac noted. They found the Wasted's luxurious new

quarters without difficulty—just a little early. Crew were still installing slanted false walls. *Humans only.* Mac hoped it was convenience. *It didn't bode well if only the Sinzi and Humans could bear
to be near a Dhryn.*

The Progenitor, they were told, was still holding court in her
room in the Origins corridor.

"They'd better hope she doesn't grow too big for the door
first," Mac muttered to Nik as they retraced their steps. "Gillis
won't be happy if they cut into a permanent wall."

Nik chuckled and took her hand. "Mikey's not so bad."

" 'Mikey?' " She gave him a sidelong look. *Captain Gillis?* "Do
I want to know?"

"We went to school together." Nik grinned at whatever he saw
in her face. "What? Did you think I never went? I did, you know.
Learned to read. Math. How to torment the new teacher. All that."

"I never thought of your life before all this—" Mac waved at the
corridor. *Tactful as always,* she chided herself and tried to cover it.
"Were you one of those daring kids whose parents came to know
the principal?"

"Orphan."

Could she be worse at this? "I'm sor—"

He silenced her fumbling apology with a quick kiss, making her
blush and gathering far too much interest from passing crew.
"Doesn't matter. I wasn't old enough to know them. Mining accident took most of the adults that year. As for the principal?" Nik
paused. "I managed to stay off his scanner."

They reached the door to the Origins upper level and he keyed
in the code. "You do know I have brothers," she commented as
they went through the door. "No staying off theirs."

An inscrutable look. "Should I be worried?"

"Not about Owen," Mac grinned. "Blake? Now he'll be—"

"Norcoast!"

Easier to face than a furious Mudge?

"Oversight," she greeted warily, taking in his decidedly rumpled
appearance. "Been here long?" "Here" being outside the closed
and locked door to her empty quarters.

"No. I've spent most of the last hour getting past those infernal
Frow!"

Oh, dear. Mac winced. "I'll speak to them. This is—"

But Mudge had already transferred his glare to Nik, his entire body shaking with rage. "As for you, Mr. Trojanowski, I would expect a man of your responsibilities to not only appear in timely fashion at scheduled meetings but to have a care for others. Your treatment of Dr. Connor has been nothing short of appalling. Appalling!"

"You're absolutely right, Charles," Nik said solemnly.

Mac coughed. "Could we discuss this on the way, please?" *Or never?*

"On the—" Mudge sputtered.

"We're late, right?" she said, her eyes pleading, *not now.*

Mudge *harrumphed* fiercely, but subsided. "You were late," this with emphasis, "an hour ago."

"Then we'd best be going." Nik waited for Mudge to lead. Mudge gave a meaningful glare at the ladderway and stayed where he was.

Mac shook her head and walked past them both.

Probably the best approach with the Frow, anyway.

The Frow had wisely chosen discretion, perhaps remembering Mac's reaction to their previous Mudge-tossing escapade. Their presence was a mere shuffling in the distance, a glow of alert eyes. She waved as she stepped off the ladder at the lower level, as much to remind them she was watching while the others climbed down, as to say thanks.

The guards at the door were still crew. While steps away, Mac felt the touch of Nik's fingers on her wrist and stopped. "I'm not sure we should mention the other Dhryn," he told them both. "Not until we understand the dynamics better."

Mudge *harrumphed.* "Which would make perfect sense, except it's too late. While you were recuperating, Ureif made sure Her Glory was fully apprised of the situation. And myself." This last with a somewhat smug look. Mac could well imagine Mudge wearing down all authority in reach to find out what was happening.

" 'Her Glory?' " She raised an eyebrow.

"We've been informed that's the appropriate address by a non-Dhryn."

"Haven Dhryn don't acknowledge the existence of non-Dhryn," she pointed out. "How could there be such a thing?"

"Makes sense," Nik countered. "The necessities of interacting with the IU. Sinzi-ra Ureif dealt with colonial Dhryn, true, but he would have needed to communicate with the Progenitors if only through their *erumisah*." He looked ahead to the guarded door. "I might as well pull what rank I have as the Vessel for—for the other Progenitor." He rubbed one hand over his chin thoughtfully. "Her Glory was a ship's captain, right? Brymn Las was a traveled scholar. Makes you wonder about the early experiences of the other Progenitors, doesn't it?"

"They're likely diverse individuals," Mudge agreed. "It could be difficult to predict their behavior, should they begin to act outside the influence of the Ro."

"Late, remember?" Mac rolled her eyes and started for the door. Her companions hastened to follow.

There'd been some effort to improve the Dhryn's temporary quarters. Another of the work area walls—*the one to her precious communication equipment*—had come down. The communication gear itself was no longer in sight. The floor was half sand, with a pair of jelly-chairs, the remainder a soft red carpeting. On the carpet was an immense padded chaise lounge affair, also red. From its proportions, it hadn't come from the *Joy*. The thing was propped to support its occupant.

An occupant who hooted with delight at the sight of Mac. *"Lamisah!"* shouted Her Glory. The floor underfoot thrummed with whatever else she said.

"Please don't move," Cayhill said, hovering over the recumbent alien. The Dhryn bristled with curved tubes, as if a clear spray was shooting from her body in all directions. *The other way around*, Mac realized, tracing the tubes back to where they connected to an apparatus. *Perfusion pump*, she grinned to herself. *Knew it*.

Ureif had risen from his chair, fingers flowing in a graceful welcome. His blood-red rings matched the carpet perfectly. *Nice touch*, Mac thought, although she was reasonably sure that "red" wasn't the color to the Sinzi it was to her eyes.

Nik acknowledged the Sinzi-ra, but his attention was fixed on the Dhryn. From his expression, he was every bit as amazed as she'd expected. He nodded to the physician. "Dr. Cayhill."

Cayhill ran his eyes over Nik and grunted. "I see you've recovered. When you get around to my messages, Mr. Trojanowski, do pay attention to the one listing your nutritional requirements." He turned back to his task.

"You look wonderful," Mac told the Dhryn, ignoring Cayhill. And she did seem the image of health, her blue skin almost fluorescent, the glow from her bands soft and steady. There seemed no further increase in size; perhaps growth occurred in spurts. *Must not help Gillis sleep better.*

"I feel wonderful! These are wonderful beings! All is wonderful!" Each "wonderful" was accompanied by a heave on the lounge, producing a fluttering of the tubes that sent Cayhill into frenzied action.

"You know you must keep still, *Lamisah*," Mac said in Dhryn.

"Where's the fun in that?" One golden eye winked at her. Her Glory, no longer bouncing, switched back to Instella without effort. "He is a marvel, my *erumisah* Gordon Matthew Cayhill."

The voice, the phrasing, was warm and friendly. Confident. Even charming. *All things the Wasted hadn't been.* Somehow Mac doubted this personality had belonged to the former captain of the *Uosanah*. Here was a new individual, suited to lead her kind.

Or, at the moment, four Humans and a Sinzi. Mac turned to introduce Nik. He shook his head slightly and she closed her mouth, glancing at Mudge who looked equally puzzled.

Without a word, Nik walked up to the massive Dhryn and knelt near her head.

For her part, Her Glory looked as confused as Mac felt. She leaned forward as if studying Nik, her mouth slightly open, lips working as if she spoke without sound. Then she suddenly reared up, her handed arm coming up before her face, her other limbs tensed. Cayhill scrambled to corral the tubes. "I taste Her! I taste Her!" shouted the agitated Dhryn. "Where is She!?"

It seemed clear Nik was in imminent danger of attack—*the Dhryn could smash his skull with that arm,* Mac realized—but he remained motionless and in reach. When Mudge moved forward, she stopped him. "Nik knows what he's doing," she whispered. *Hopefully.*

"My Progenitor has sent me, Her Vessel," Nik said in Instella, calm and collected. "I am to speak with you on Her behalf."

"You are not-Dhryn." But she eased back down and lowered her hand. Cayhill growled something under his breath and shot Mac a dirty look as he hurried to reinstall now-dripping tubes.

How could this be her fault? Mac thought indignantly.

"These are unusual times."

A forlorn *hoot*. "As I am proof." A long pause, in which gold eyes met hazel. "Speak, then, Vessel."

She could almost feel the tension ease from Nik's shoulders. "My Progenitor would have me tell you of the Great Journey," he began. "How That Which Is Dhryn was perverted by the Ro. And how That Which Is Dhryn must follow the path of the truth."

Mac held her breath, waiting for the Dhryn's reaction, but Her Glory must have been made of sterner stuff than others of her kind. She merely said, "Go on."

"These things and more you should hear before my Progenitor joins us."

The glow from the bands around her torso pulsed with more intensity. *A display?* wondered Mac. "She returns to Haven?" asked the Dhryn.

Guess no one thought to correct that small confusion, Mac winced. But Nik didn't blink. "She'll be here soon," he answered smoothly.

In Dhryn. "Will She ask for my flesh?" The warmth was gone from Her Glory's voice. Mac felt the vibration through the floor, saw it shake the fountain spray of tubing. "I am younger, stronger. More fit, more deserving. That Which Is Dhryn must survive." Louder. "I will ask for Her flesh! My *lamisah* will be my Vessel. She will demand it!"

No doubt about it. That imperative finger was aimed her way. Mac sighed inwardly. *Salmon researcher. Would no one remember?*

"I can't be your Vessel—" she began.

"Why not? He claims to be one."

Mac's eyes narrowed. *Her Glory was as new to this as they were.* "Do you even know what a vessel is?"

That was a pout. "I know what a Vessel does—speak for a Progenitor. You must speak for me! She cannot have my flesh!"

Nik rose to his feet. "Don't be afraid," he said, making an accurate guess at what was going on. "My Progenitor means you no harm. She seeks a truce, a way for All That Is Dhryn to survive. She offers the truth."

"Why will he not speak Dhryn?" Her Glory asked with disdain.

She had a few choices here, thought Mac, *most of them complicated.* She'd learned not to trust complicated, when it came to aliens.

Mac stepped closer. "Because Her Vessel has good manners. It's rude to speak any language but Instella in the presence of other species." This, in Instella, as firmly as she'd ever chastised a student. "These fine beings will not take you seriously unless you behave to your station."

She was acutely aware of those fine beings, and how they were, each in his own way, staring at her in disbelief.

Her Glory, meanwhile, began to hoot. "Ah, my excellent Vessel," she said *in Instella.* "Again you guide my path correctly. I apologize to all. But—" her head bent to regard Nik, "—I remain of decided appetite."

To his credit, the Ministry's liaison with aliens bowed gracefully and took this strange comment in stride. "I will convey your words, of course."

"Tell me what I should hear," Her Glory requested, her small mouth smiling. "But first, *erumisah*? I crave something. Perhaps what you called grapes? And those delightful little leaves."

"I'll arrange it." Cayhill went to the com and barked orders, presumably to the crew now assigned to liquefying Her Glory's diet. He'd done a magnificent job so far. *Not that they had a reference,* Mac told herself. *For all they knew, she was supposed to have turned orange by now.*

"Sit, Vessel. Be comfortable, as I am. Is this not a wonderful seat?" Her Glory made a tiny bounce, smiling at Mac. "Is everything not wonderful?"

The door opened and Fy slipped in, her fingers tightly knotted. *Distress or other strong emotion,* Mac guessed, looking to Ureif for clues. His fingers hung still. *Too still. Distress, then.*

Not wonderful.

Ureif swept one of his Human-like bows to Her Glory. "Please excuse us. We must confer."

Mac looked to Nik; he nodded to the Sinzi. "Come on," she told Mudge, and led the way to the corner where the two aliens now swayed in earnest consultation, their voices too low to hear.

"—was anticipated," Ureif was saying. When the two Humans came close, he made a welcoming gesture. "Great news. The Progenitor's ship has come through the gate."

Timing was everything. Mac resisted the impulse to look over at Her Glory. "What's the situation?"

Fy's fingers moved restlessly, silver and gold jingling down their lengths. "There is discord. Ships are moving without authorization. A small number have aimed themselves at the gate, but wait. More from fear of the Dhryn than from respect for protocol. I fear a collision, should they not resume orderly behavior."

"Are any moving to open vectors?" This from Mudge, whose face was pale and set. "The Trisulians have a formidable ship."

"At my request," Ureif said very quietly, "Captain Gillis has repositioned our two ships within thirty minutes of the gate mouth. None are closer. We have asked the arriving Progenitor to station Her ship alongside, toward the gate."

"So they'll have to go through the *Joy* and the other Dhryn to reach Her." Mudge sounded quite pleased by this. "Or She can leave through the gate before any weaponsfire could catch up."

"Of greater importance," Ureif corrected gently, "all must come to meet Her Glory here. It forms the most exquisite congruence." Both Sinzi swayed back and forth at this.

Mudge was pleased. The Sinzi were patently ecstatic.

Mac couldn't believe it. "Did you learn nothing from the Gathering?" she snapped. "You've made us into a single target!"

"We are in communication with the Progenitor," Fy soothed. "If there are any hostile acts, we will warn Her."

Who warns us? Mac kept that to herself. "How? I thought their ships didn't have IU technology."

Fy managed a fair approximation of a Human smile. *She'd been practicing,* Mac judged. "Ah, but remember this Progenitor's ship carries a Human craft in its hold. Nikolai's ship remains inside, crewed by his associates. Now that we are within the same system, this gives us the means to communicate."

Maybe she was wrong.

Mudge was studying her. He *harrumphed* uneasily. "What is it, Norcoast?"

Maybe she wasn't. Mac shivered.

"There's some problem with newspackets," she told him, feeling her skin crawl. "Incoming are delayed. We couldn't set up a dedicated exchange at all."

Fy touched her fingertips together. "There is a great deal of traffic. I am not the most experienced, Mac. I suspect a flaw in my scheduling. I have asked for assistance."

Mudge was still looking at Mac, eyebrows lowering in a frown. In the background, she could hear Nik's steady, calm voice as he kept briefing the Dhryn.

Did he feel it, too? That time was running out.

She backed a step away without thinking, needing space, her feet sinking in the sand. "Something's not right." She hadn't meant to say it out loud, but once she did, she believed it.

Nik was at her side in a heartbeat. She held up her hand to silence him, to silence them all.

She held her breath and closed her eyes to listen.

Nothing. The shift of sand under a long toe. The whisper of fabric. The steady thud of Cayhill's pump.

Okay, she was an idiot. Relieved, Mac smiled as she opened her eyes and turned toward Nik.

The ceiling fell.

Scurry, scurry.

Spit! POP!

- CONTACT -

GILLIS PATTED HIS TREE. It wasn't his, technically, having been a gift to the *Annapolis Joy* on her official launch. Some publicist's bright notion; a touch of the home planet heading to the stars. The little thing had outlived its day-of-launch purpose to become the ship's mascot. He was well aware its trimmings wound up in their own pots in crew quarters. They'd have a forest at this rate. He should look into some birds.

"Status, Darcy."

Townee glanced up from the scan console as the captain approached. "She's behaving."

"Amazing. Show me." Gillis sank into his chair, staring as the display revealed the massive bulk of not one, but two Dhryn Progenitor ships. He whistled through his teeth. "Ouch."

The new arrival was more intact than the first, but heat had melted and scored her prow into lumps of black slag. Proof, if they needed any, that this ship had been the focus of the Ro attack at Haven. Otherwise, her hull reflected white and silver wherever Myriam's sun reached, its curves and dips familiar to anyone who'd studied the images captured in Sol System. Every ship had been identical; this was another of the same.

"Sir. There's something strange going on with the gate."

"End display," Gillis ordered, blinking as normal lighting was restored. "What is it?"

"We had nominal to heavy packet traffic up to a moment ago, sir. Incoming from all over the IU. Now—the only incoming packets are from Sol," the tech said. "I can't explain it, sir. If I didn't know better—"

"Go on."

"It's as if the transect itself's been modified, sir. What could do that?"

This drew looks from around the bridge. *Anxious ones.*

Townee walked to the station to check the readings for herself. After a few seconds, she turned to nod at Gillis. "Confirmed. In fact, now the Sol packets are slowing to a trickle. Damnedest thing."

"Sir!" This from the system-tech, her voice raised but calm. "We have a ship-wide mass shift. The grav generators are compensating but—"

The scan-tech broke in: "Something's just—appeared—on the hull. Out of nowhere. Another aft. Sir, we've multiple contacts. I repeat, multiple contacts on the hull."

"Battle stations," Gillis snapped, surging to his feet. "Now!" The alarms began wailing.

"We've breaches," the system-tech reported, her voice shaking. "Repeat, multiple hull breaches. Fields holding—"

Spit! POP!

A hot spray struck Gillis in the face. He scrubbed it from his eyes with a startled curse.

He realized it was blood when the screaming began.

Scurry, scurry . . .

- 22 -

SHOCK AND SACRIFICE

HER GLORY HEAVED herself off the chaise lounge with a roar, the tubes snapping away. Their liquefied contents flew in every direction, to strike and stick in glistening lines against surfaces, moving surfaces, crawling surfaces.

So many . . .

Mac froze as forklike footprints scarred the sand before her. *Scurry, scurry . . .*

A weapon fired near her head. The Dhryn retched and spat. *Settling the question of whether the acidic spit came from the stomach or somewhere else,* Mac helplessly noticed.

Something died. Someone shouted.

Spit! POP!

Her arm. *Something had her by the arm.* She came to life, screaming and struggling. "Let go of me!!!"

"Mac! Come on!"

Scurry . . .

Nik. It was Nik. Mac shut up and tried to think past the terror. There were Ro walkers here. *Now was not the time to even think she'd told them so.* They were on the ship.

They were in the room. *So many . . .*

Some were dead, hulking masses of darkness, steaming with acid burns or flame. The Dhryn moved like a great blue-and-white panther, circling the huddled Humans and Sinzi on all six legs . . . Something unseen ripped through her skin, blue pouring out. Nik fired and it fell to the sand, revealed in death. He swung and fired again, shouting as he did. "Charles, take her! We have to get out—" The words were overwhelmed by the shrill of the ship's alarm.

Mudge's face blocked the carnage. Mac focused on it, breathing in shuddering gasps. "Now, Norcoast," he said with remarkable patience. "I want you to take a step for me. I'll help you." His hands took hers and pulled gently, as if nothing mattered but that first step. "That's the way."

In a sense nothing else did. If she didn't move, she'd die. On some level, Mac understood and fought to move her foot, even as the rest of her did its best to shut down completely. *It would be so much easier, so much quieter.*

"Come, Norcoast. We have to get back. The salmon won't wait. You've work to do. I may not always approve but since when did you listen to me? Just take a step. One step."

Mudge was babbling.

Shocked, Mac took two steps before she realized it.

Then, as if that motion burst some inner dam, her feet were driving through the sand as she ran with Mudge to the door, his arm around her. "Nik!" she twisted to look back.

A hard shove from behind. "Here. Go! Go!"

She hit the wall of the corridor and spun around wildly. Nik and the guards stood in the open doorway, firing into the room methodically and quickly. *They knew to aim at the torn ceiling.*

Mac shuddered and looked away, numbly aware the corridor was intact. *Nothing to attack them here.* The two Sinzi stood nearby; they seemed shaken, but unscathed. The Dhryn paced behind the Humans still firing, as if she wished to take part. Mudge was with her. She reached a hand toward him. "Where's Cayhill?" she whispered.

Despite the ongoing alarm, the Dhryn must have heard the question. She turned her head to look at Mac, yellow mucus bubbling from her nostrils, then resumed pacing. *Dhryn tears.*

Mac didn't need the short, grim shake of Mudge's head.

The weaponsfire ended. While the guards closed and sealed the door, Nik came to Mac, weapon still in his hand, and leaned close to be heard. "Are you all right?" His eyes were like flint as they searched for wounds, his mouth tight.

"I couldn't move. I couldn't—" she flushed as her voice broke. With an effort, "I thought I could handle it."

"You warned us, remember?" He laid his free hand along her cheek. "You did just fine, Mac. Now we'd better get—"

"Sir. Head for your quarters and stay there," one of the guards ordered. "We have to report to stations." With that, the two ran off toward the main portion of the ship.

"We can't stay," Mac said, her voice that of a stranger. Her hand shook as she pointed to the Dhryn. "They want Her dead, they want the past dead. They know She's here. They'll keep coming."

"We participate in the promise," Ureif said solemnly. "Our dart rests in the consular hangar."

Nik looked at Mudge. "If Ro think at all like us, that was an advance group with a specific target. The rest will go after ship's systems, create chaos. We could have a window. Remove what they're after. They might back off."

"Dart's transect-capable," Mudge agreed, then *harrumphed* firmly. "It's the best choice. I'm familiar with the specs."

"So am I." Something seemed to pass between the two men, then Nik nodded. "Let's go, then."

Someone had to ask, Mac thought. She turned to Her Glory. "Can you climb a ladder?"

"The Dhryn are attacking!"

Mac bumped her head against the ladder rung for the second time. "No. The Ro are attacking, *Se* Lasserbee. And this Dhryn is on our side. We need to climb the ladder. Now." *And if the Frow didn't get out of their way within the next few seconds, she was going to let Nik shoot him somewhere.*

That wasn't her first choice, but the appeal was growing. The shipwide alarm had subsided to a background drone, hopefully implying the captain and his crew were taking charge. *That didn't mean they were safe.* "Now," she repeated, smacking her artificial hand against the ladder.

"We saw the dead one." This from a lackey, hanging head down near Mac. "Is that what attacks?"

Mac shuddered. "Yes. There could be more on the ship. Many more. It's not safe. You should be in your quarters. And we," she said firmly, "need to climb the ladder."

"We will take you to your quarters!" This with a snatch for her arms she narrowly avoided. "To safety!"

"No. They're chasing us. Do you understand? We can't stay on the ship."

"You are in danger?"

"Yes! We all are. Please. Get out of the way."

Two scampered down, past the lower level entrance. *Se* Lasserbee climbed above her. "Then we shall protect you," he announced, his hat bobbing with each movement. "It is our duty."

So long as they got out of the way, she thought with relief.

Mac waved to the rest to follow, then climbed to the next level and turned to watch. The muscles between her shoulders seemed permanently knotted. *Turtles had the right idea,* she assured herself, wishing for some body armor and the ability to pull in her head. *They were only guessing the Ro hadn't infiltrated the entire ship already.*

The only evidence in favor of that hypothesis was that they continued to breathe. *She'd take it.*

First up was Her Glory, who climbed the vertical ladder much the same way as Brymn had managed to swim—by using the power of her limbs to overcome mechanical deficiencies. Once she was safely off the ladder—requiring some contortions and a leaping skid much like the landing of an albatross—the rest followed. The Sinzi climbed as dexterously as any Frow, their beringed fingers perfectly adapted to grasp and release in rapid sequence. Mudge was next, then Nik, weapon still out, brought up the rear.

Not quite. Claws appeared around the doorframe, followed by the pointy tips of hats, followed by feet, followed by . . . *Oh, no.*

The Frow were coming with them.

"You should go to your quarters," she said desperately. "Please. It's not—we're not safe."

"Which is why we must attend you, Dr. Connor," *Se* Lasserbee informed her, slowly working his body through the opening. Luckily for the Frow, there were hand grabs to either side. The corridor, however, loomed as a slick wasteland, its walls broken only by closed, smooth doors.

They'd be helpless.

Nik touched her shoulder. "Mac. We have to go." He didn't wait for her answer, half jogging to the bulkhead door at the end of the corridor to input his code, the Dhryn moving easily by his side. *Ran like a grizzly.*

Fy and Ureif stayed with Mac, as if they wouldn't move until she did. Mudge waited, too. Muttering under her breath, with a last look back at the Frow—who had made it to the cling-to-handrail stage and were regarding the floor—she went to Nik.

He had the door unlocked, but motioned them all to wait. "I'm going to scout ahead," he explained, slipping through the opening.

He moved like a predator, she thought.

He paused before closing the door behind him to take one last look at her, his eyes full of everything they didn't need to say to one another. *That distraction could get them killed,* she realized with a chill, finally comprehending Nik's dread of loving her.

Biology always wins, she reminded herself. Her spy might be distracted, but she could—*almost*—pity anything that threatened her.

Her Glory sat abruptly, supporting herself on upper and lower-most legs, the middle two—*that had supported her bulk in movement*—tucked up. "I am hungry, *Lamisah.*"

Mac rested her hand on the Dhryn's upper shoulder. "I know," she said gently. "How long—?" *Can you survive* was the part she didn't say. They couldn't feed her now. Later was past a gulf Mac couldn't imagine.

The golden eyes held boundless warmth. "If you can endure my complaints, *Lamisah,* I believe I can endure my hunger quite a while."

Mac snuck a peek at the Frow. They'd made it to cluster in the first doorway, feet splayed and holding onto one another. *Se* Lasserbee, ever alert, saluted, the movement almost knocking them down.

The door opened and Nik stepped through, keeping his hand on the doorframe. One look at his grim-set face and Mac's heart lurched. "They've been," he said without preamble. "No way to know how long we have. Let's go." His hand lifted to beckon them forward; Mac stared at the bloody print it left on the wall. His eyes followed hers.

"Watch your step," he added.

Mac learned a great deal about herself over the next few minutes. She could put her foot into a pool of blood without hesitation. *There was no floor free of it.* She could step over body parts, black, red, or glistening with slime. *None were identifiable.* And she could think about survival. *The body looked after itself.*

Emily's room had been nothing like this.

The corridor beyond the door was a slaughterhouse. The violence of the walkers had left nothing remotely recognizable. Perversely, their corpses—for the crew hadn't died alone—were intact, obstacles to pass.

She learned a great deal about Nik and Mudge as well. The former led, weapon out, muscles taut and body poised for action, using himself to test the way. Mudge had methodically checked every pile of intestine and bone until finding a weapon of his own. Now, he followed behind, a solid comfort.

The aliens were silent, except for the mutters of distress from the Dhryn, whose body was too wide to avoid brushing against the walkers. The Sinzi's gowns soaked up blood and became streaked with slime and ash. They walked with Mac, a finger each on her shoulder as if needing to be sure they remained together.

Once they made it this far, the Frow fared better, their claws finding ready holds. *Was it easier for them?* Mac wondered numbly. She'd lost count of the number of times she'd walked on the bodies of dead and dying salmon, more intent on her footing than the savage toll. *But they'd left eggs behind. They'd found a way for their kind to survive.*

Unlike the *Annapolis Joy,* gutted from the inside.

The consular area was no better. Nik paused beside the com station to let them catch up. She didn't look into the door. "Not far to the hangar now," he said. There were deep, harsh lines beside his mouth, but his voice was steady. *You could take strength from it.*

"Ship's systems are still functioning—I could call for backup. They won't know anyone's alive here."

Mudge *harrumphed*. "If there isn't anyone else alive, you'd reveal our location for nothing. I say keep going."

"And if there is," Mac said, surprising herself, "they'll live longer with us gone."

The low drone of ship's alarm suddenly stopped, leaving a dizzy emptiness behind. The lights flared, then died to a flicker lower than night mode. Runnels of slime continued to fluoresce for brief seconds, marking the ceiling and walls as well as the dead.

As Mac's eyes adjusted, she realized the soft glow from the Dhryn's torso now pooled around them all. Just beyond, in the shadows, random sparks marked each Frow. *Useful adaptations,* she thought, unable to stop herself from trying to understand, even in a universe falling apart.

"Magnificent," exclaimed Fy. Her fingers lifted toward the Dhryn. "Mac, have you seen anything to compare?"

"Humans cannot see as we do," Ureif said.

Fy's "Oh," was accompanied with a look to Mac. "My apologies."

"We can discuss eyes later," Mac suggested. *That word again.*

"Ready?" Nik didn't wait for an answer, but led the way into the dark.

Mac supposed it was too much to hope that darkness would matter to whatever eyes the Ro walkers used.

The Dhryn's glow, however faint, proved a mixed blessing. While it helped Mac plan her next step—*and made it possible to ignore the rest of the corridor*—she felt as if she traveled inside a spotlight. Nik, Mudge, and the Frow stayed well out of it, likely for that reason.

The entry to the hangar was damaged, as if forced from the outside. *Explaining why the ceiling had been intact.* Nik went ahead to scout.

Mudge came up to Mac. "How are you managing, Norcoast?"

"Better," she said honestly. "I guess you can get used to anything."

What little she could see of his expression looked aggrieved, as if she'd presented an application to hang laundry from his precious trees. "He shouldn't have involved you in all this. I've said it before."

"Nik?" Mac found herself smiling. "Come on, Oversight. Surely I get some of the credit." Then she lost her smile. "I'm just sorry I—"

A *harrumph*. "None of that. I knew what was ahead. Better than you did."

"I wouldn't doubt it," she replied.

Nik returned. "I heard something," he said quietly. "Could have been broken equipment giving way. Could have been them."

"Guide us, Vessel." Her Glory reared to tower over them all, incidentally lighting some things Mac didn't want to see. "I long to destroy more."

A gleam of teeth. "You may have your chance," Nik said. "But let's try to do this tight and secure, all right? Sinzi-ra, I want you to lead. You'll need to get your dart open and running. Don't look back or hesitate, no matter what happens."

"We honor the promise," Ureif said solemnly. Mac thought Fy looked a great deal less certain.

They started moving, but when Mac would have gone through the door in turn, Nik pulled her against him and found her mouth with quick bruising force. Mac licked her lips, tasting blood. She stared at him, wide-eyed, her hands trembling against his shoulders.

He'd kissed her like that once before.

It had been good-bye.

"Oh, no," she whispered. "No," this time louder. Her hands formed into fists and pounded his shoulders.

Nik caught her right fist in his hands and opened it, pressing a ring inside. "Made it while you slept," he said in that matter-of-fact tone she hated. "In case."

"No."

"We have our jobs to do, Mackenzie Connor. Go. Save your fish." *That dimple.* "And the rest of the planet, if you don't mind."

"How?" Her voice cracked.

"You'll think of something." He backed away. "Time to leave."

Mac could have closed the distance with a step. *Could hold him. Could beg.* Instead, with a bone-deep shudder, she nodded.

"Where on that scale . . ."

The hangar was better illuminated than the corridor, by virtue of emergency lighting tracing the paths to the launch bay. At first, Mac thought the place untouched, then she saw the bodies clustered around two areas, a dark gaping hole in the side of the hangar—*the source of the walkers?*—and the examination tent. The tent had collapsed, hiding whatever lay inside. *Small mercies,* she thought as they passed it, not wanting to see what remained of the busy scientists.

The dart was closest to the launch bay. *Fy's request?* Mac thought, aware of the irony. Easy to spot among the squared shapes of the *Joy's* shuttles—a slim bit of silver and black, its design like the curved tip of a Sinzi finger, its surface etched with intricate designs.

They hurried together across the floor, a desperate drum of footsteps in the silence. *Almost together,* Mac corrected, glancing up to see the Frow scuttling a parallel course underneath the meshed walkway overhead. The Sinzi arrived at the dart first, as planned. Fy placed her fingertips into six places on the lower surface. Seams widened within the design, pulled away from the dart's side to become a graceful stair that lowered itself to the hangar floor without a sound.

Spit! Pop!

From in front—*and above*!

"Hurry!"

She didn't know who shouted, or if they all did. Everyone moved. Fastest of all were the Frow, who dropped down on the dart, their claws moving faster than her eyes could follow. For the first time, she saw they had weapons. One fired toward the end of the dart, and a heaving mass of darkness slid down its far side.

Scurry, scurry . . .

Se Lasserbee shouted something incomprehensible, pointed aft. The other lackey tried to fire, then *split* along *ne's* middle, dark red splashing over the dart.

As the Frow fought, the Sinzi urged the Dhryn inside, despite her loud and vocal protests. Backs to the little ship, Nik and Mudge were firing at seeming random. With success—shapes formed and died.

Spit! Pop!

A hat drifted down beside her. Mac reached for it in horror.

"Get inside!" Nik shouted. "Move!"

Startled back to sanity, she ran up the stairs and began to go in, then stopped, having almost run into Her Glory's anguished face. "I can't move back, *Lamisah*," the Dhryn cried. "It's too small inside."

Mudge had known the specs, Mac thought numbly.

Nik had kissed her good-bye.

She fought to see past the bulk of the Dhryn. The dart was meant for a pilot and one passenger—both Sinzi. Now, Her Glory took up most of the floor and one of the forward seats. There might be space in front of her for one small, folded Human-sized body. *That didn't take into account providing air.*

Mac whirled to find herself facing Ureif and Fy. "There must be another ship—"

"Only this one can travel the transect and take you home, Mac," Ureif said calmly. "We participate in the promise." He touched fingertips with Fy, making a shivering motion that sent several rings cascading from his fingers to hers. "Fy will ensure you travel safely, and that all know what has transpired."

Fy was silent and trembling, but she slipped past Mac to enter the dart, climbing over Her Glory's back. Ureif then touched his fingertips to Mac's cheek. "I, who once failed the Dhryn, now find circularity. Thank you."

Stunned, Mac watched Ureif go back down the stairs, for the first time showing the astonishing speed of his kind. He wrapped three long fingers around Nik's shoulders and pulled him toward the stairs. "You must honor your promise as well," the Sinzi insisted. "You must go home."

Nik's eyes were wild. "No! No!" But before he could struggle free, Mudge calmly stepped up, took careful aim with the butt of his weapon, and struck Nik's head with a short, quick blow.

Scurry, scurry . . .

Spit! Pop! Skitter!

Hearing walkers from all sides now, Mac ran down the stairs, Fy behind her. Mudge and the Sinzi were already dragging Nik to them. "Take him," Ureif ordered.

"We can all go!" Mac cried as she took Nik's arm and felt Fy take the other. They hurriedly backed up the stairs, pulling the half-unconscious man. "Oversight! Come on!"

Mudge smiled at her.

Then he turned, raised his weapon, and resumed firing into the emptiness of the hangar.

It was like swimming in a nightmare, feeling the current pulling her down, feeling the drag on her legs, the loss of light as she sank.

"Oversight?"

Even as her mouth shaped his name, Ureif activated the stair controls from outside. Fy tugged at Nik; Mac roused to help. Somehow they squeezed themselves inside, Her Glory helping as best she could.

Mac caught a last glimpse through the closing door.

She saw Ureif fall, fingers still outstretched as though to deny the walkers with his dying flesh.

She saw a small, fussy man be a hero.

Then the door snapped closed.

- 23 -

ESCAPE AND ENCOUNTER

MAC HELD NIK, HER GLORY held them both, and Fy—somehow Fy climbed over her alien cargo to reach the controls.

Could the Ro still stop them?

Was Oversight watching them leave him behind or was he already dead?

Mac pressed her face into Nik's hair. He groaned and tried to move. "Don't," she said huskily. "You'll kick Her Glory."

He stilled. "Who?" Just the word.

She knew what he meant.

"Fy's here. She's flying the dart."

"How did . . . ?"

Mac lightly kissed the side of his head. "Hopefully you aren't concussed. Oversight—" she took a breath, "—he seemed to know what he was doing." *Odd skill for a man prone to memos.*

"We are in the launch bay," Fy announced. "They have not attempted to stop us."

"Yet," rumbled the Dhryn. Mac could feel her voice against her side and through the deck. Not that she had much feeling left in her legs or rump. Her spy had significant weight.

Better to think about that.

"I hunger, my *lamisah*."

And there was the distraction of a starving Progenitor.

Unlike Norris' modified lev, the dart was silent, vibration-free except for its passengers. "Launching now," Fy announced.

Mac closed her eyes.

When she was still breathing a moment later, she opened them again. "Are we okay?"

"Seems that way," Nik whispered. Louder: "Sinzi-ra, we should learn what we can of the situation before leaving Myriam for Earth. Can you tell if the Ro are attacking other ships? The planet?"

Mac shifted in alarm. Nik's hand found her thigh and squeezed it gently. "I doubt they've gone after anything but the Dhryn."

"All Dhryn?" This from Her Glory. "We must stop them!"

"That's the plan," he said, his tone leaving no doubt of the outcome.

Making doubt her job, Mac realized.

"There are transmissions," Fy announced. "Garbled, confused. They do not follow emergency protocols." She sounded faintly offended.

As Mudge would be. Mac pressed her cheek against Nik's head, careful to avoid where he'd been struck. Her eyes were dry; the way they'd get late at night after trying to read too many reports.

"Keep at it. Any information would help."

"Distress calls. Human. I think for the *Annapolis Joy,* not because of other attacks. Newspackets—heading into the Naralax. None arriving."

"We can't worry about the rest of the IU," he pointed out, remarkably sensible, Mac thought, for someone currently crushed between an overhead bin, a woman, and a Dhryn. "What about the other Progenitor? Can you reach Cavendish?"

"Tucker Cavendish?" Mac whispered. She remembered the Ministry agent she'd first met on the way station. *A lifetime ago.* Tough, ex-military, face covered with implants. *A survivor.*

"Yes."

"*Lamisah.* My Vessel. I require the other Progenitor. You must negotiate with Her Vessel." A muscular shudder passed through the Dhryn's body.

And tried to pass through hers. Mac squirmed for breathing room, Nik trying to help. "You must stay calm," she urged. "Don't move."

Very faintly, in Dhryn. "Must I die, *Lamisah?*"

Mac stared into the eye near her head, saw her face in its large, figure-eight pupil. *The eye of a being who'd commanded a starship and knew the Interspecies Union,* she reminded herself, wary of underestimating Her Glory. "I don't know," she replied in the same language. "The not-Dhryn have reason to fear your kind."

A vibration through her flesh. "Sinzi-ra Ureif told me. Our Great Journey has been perverted by the Ro; That Which Is Dhryn used as a terrible weapon, aimed by their will. If we are freed from the Ro, *Lamisah,* will we still be feared?"

There was no time left for lies. "Yes. As long as That Which Is Dhryn is capable of consuming the lives of others, you will be feared."

"Mac," asked Nik quietly. "What's going on?"

The Dhryn switched to Instella. "My apologies, Vessel. I seek to understand how I, who was Wasted and doomed, can have value to That Which Is Dhryn. The Sinzi-ra spoke of circularity, of my being the future. My Vessel speaks of the fear of not-Dhryn, a fear which may demand our extinction. I require the wisdom of your Progenitor. I must know which of these paths to follow."

Instead of answering, Nik spoke to Fy. "Sinzi-ra. Have you raised Cavendish?"

"There is a difficulty."

Mac felt him tense. "Explain."

"The belief spreads that the Progenitor's ship brought the Ro. Several warships are moving to open vectors. Cavendish is broadcasting a denial, but his signal clearly comes from a Human source, causing further misunderstanding." Mac could hear the rings on Fy's fingers, as if the Sinzi made a gesture of exasperation. "I continue to signal the truth, that the Ro seek to prevent our truce with the Dhryn, but I fear there is more reflex than reason at work around us."

"How close are we to the Progenitor?"

"We have already passed beyond her ship. The gate is ahead."

The Dhryn rumbled distress.

"Turn around," Mac urged. "Take us back."

"We cannot remain here, Mac. The promise—"

Nik's hand tightened on her thigh. *My turn.* "Fy. The only safety lies in stopping the Ro for good. The Progenitor is the key to the promise. We have to save her, too."

"I require the other Progenitor," Her Glory said, adding her vote.

Votes wouldn't matter, Mac realized. *The Sinzi worked by achieving consensus, not majority.* Fy had to want this for her own reasons.

"Listen to me, Fy," she said. "I shared *grathnu* with this Progenitor, the first and only alien to do so." *As far as she knew, anyway.* "I am the Vessel for Her Glory, who I believe is the original form of Dhryn. You will move away from profound congruence unless you bring us together. The drawing in the sand, Fy. Sinzi join the lines. Please."

Another squeeze. *Approval or caution?*

Either applied.

Every second added distance, which added risk, but the three of them waited in silence to let Fy think it through.

"I, Faras, am unsure," the Sinzi said at last. "I, Yt, am not."

It had to be a talent, Mac thought bitterly. *She'd paralyzed the Sinzi's selves with one well-intentioned argument.*

She decided not to say anything else for a while.

Nik took over. "Consider the sundered connections, Sinzi-ra. I know of your work with the Hift artifacts, yet you have never been able to view working Myrokynay technology. What if, as we believe, the Progenitor's ship was built by the Ro? I am apart from the crew of my expedition and would return to them. Mac would return to the Progenitor who sought her out on Earth. Her Glory is apart from her kind and requires her Progenitor's council. Should these connections not be attached, one to the other?"

Mac could hear the tinkling of rings. Then Fy's voice, subdued but clear. "Are you sure you are not Sinzi, Nikolai?"

"Quite sure." She could hear the smile in his voice. "If we now understand one another, Fy, all credit goes to Anchen as my teacher and Mac as my guide."

The man was good, Mac noted, smiling herself.

While Fy retraced their path to the Progenitor's ship, Mac, Nik, and Her Glory rearranged themselves in the cramped space. *Lucky*

none of them was claustrophobic, Mac thought. At least the air remained fresh.

The rearrangement was a precaution. Nik couldn't vouch for what they'd face when the hatch opened—it made sense that both Humans be at least able to walk. Mac had lost touch with her feet some time ago.

Her Glory stayed put, being quite comfortable as she was. Nik managed to prop himself up so Mac could rub life back into her legs, hissing as awakening nerves merrily fired their displeasure. Once she could move, Mac crawled on top of the Dhryn, leaving the area directly before the hatch to Nik. The glowing bands were cool, the blue skin warm. She did her best to avoid sticking a finger into any of the tiny mouths.

Not bad. Mac stretched, careful to keep her feet from the Sinzi's back. She watched Nik bring out his weapon, holding it concealed in his palm. "You expecting a problem?"

"They got on the *Joy.*"

No need to ask who "they" were. "They don't need to board a Progenitor's ship to destroy it," Mac pointed out. Based on the fragments recovered in Sol System, the working hypothesis was that the Ro had somehow moved portions of their technology from the Dhryn ships into no-space, opening them to vacuum.

They'd stripped their technology from Emily's flesh at the same time.

"No Hift materials were found in the wreckage," Fy offered. "It was a great disappointment."

Nik sat on the deck, easing his legs straight. He looked up at Mac where she leaned her chin on the Dhryn's forehead ridge. "The Ro attack on the Progenitor's ship at Haven fried quite a few systems, including what my people deduced were long-range communications. That's why they hadn't replied to our signals in the first place. We stopped the Dhryn from repairing them. A gamble, I admit. No way to know if that's how a Ro destruct signal is picked up and distributed throughout the ship."

Mac rose and fell with Her Glory's sigh. "Surely the proof is that the ship remains intact," the Dhryn suggested.

"Something of a comfort, yes."

Mac frowned. "Not really."

"What are you thinking?" he asked. The Dhryn shifted and tried to turn her head to see Mac, forcing her on her elbows to protect her nose.

"She was hidden from the Ro," Mac pointed out. "Now She's not."

Nik jerked his thumb aftward. *Fy was listening.*

Mac grimaced but nodded.

They'd know soon enough.

The Progenitor's ship remained intact. The Ro either couldn't, or didn't, destroy her.

Maybe they didn't have to, Mac thought with a shiver, looking around.

What had hummed with life and light now seemed filled with the silent desolation of a graveyard. *Worse,* she decided, following Nik. *A graveyard implied mourners.*

From inside the dart, their approach and entry into the Progenitor's great ship had had all the high drama—*for passengers at least*—of taking a lift to another floor. Once inside the ship, they'd stepped out into this dimly-lit hollow cave. The space resembled the busy holds of the *Annapolis Joy* or the *Uosanah* only in being big enough to hold shuttles and their like. There were no guides along the floor. No lines of waiting empty craft. *No crew.* Lighting from above failed against the black, anti-Ro fabric lining ceiling, floor, and angled wall. Behind them, the Sinzi dart glittered like exotic jewelry, dropped and abandoned on velvet.

"There's the *Impeci.*" Nik's quiet voice echoed into the distance. He pointed to an ordinary shuttlelike craft, larger than those on the *Joy.*

Mudge would have known the specs. Mac took a steadying breath. The Human ship looked normal. "What's wrong with it?"

"Nothing a thorough scrub and filter replace wouldn't solve. Without that, you'd need an evacsuit to survive the radiation inside for more than a few hours."

"Where is everyone?" Her Glory was subdued; her body hunched low over her legs. "I've been here before. There should be workers here. Those to greet us. Other ships."

"There were when I left," Nik said. Mac, hearing that slight edge, glanced at him. His face was expressionless. *Never a good sign.* "My people will be in their quarters. We set up a com relay there. That way." He pointed to a door, its frame askew with that characteristic Dhryn slant.

Just then, a side hatch opened on the *Impeci,* sending a wash of brighter light outward along with its ramp. A figure appeared, calling out even as he began to stumble in their direction. "Nik? Is that you?"

"What the hell—" Nik took off at a run. "Tucker!" She understood the horror in his voice as Cavendish drew close enough for her to see clearly.

No suit!

The man staggered more than walked. When the two met, Nik grabbed and held him. Mac and the two aliens hurried to join them.

Nik had had isolated burns, already healing. The face Cavendish turned to greet them with was a mass of weeping sores and hanging implants, as if the flesh beneath the skin was dissolving away. His eyes were the only thing sane within that madness. Sane and, when they fell on Her Glory, filled with wonder. "What are you?" he asked, his lips bleeding with the words, enunciating with care.

Because he'd lost most of his teeth, she realized with a sick shock. Mac eased her shoulder under Cavendish's other arm, helping to support his weight, careful of what she touched. "We have to get you home—"

"What were you doing in there? Where's your suit?" Nik interrupted furiously, though his hands were gentle. "I gave strict orders to stay away from the ship—"

"Had to . . . come back. Stay inside. She can't control . . . warned . . . us . . . stay in the ship." Cavendish gasped between each burst of words, but didn't stop. "She's running out of Dhryn. Feeders . . . entered our quarters. Took . . . took . . . we've lost a few. Rest of us . . . figured . . . better the radiation . . . wouldn't be long before we got off . . . share the suits. Now you're here." This with a trusting look.

From where she stood, Mac could see how Nik's free hand

clenched into a tight fist, but when he answered, it was warm and reassuring. "You'll be fine, Tucker."

Others appeared at the hatch, walking down the ramp. One, two Humans, an Imrya. Then no more.

Was that all? Mac watched Nik mouth names as they approached, his face growing pale.

Only two wore protective gear. She suddenly remembered Nik's battle with Cinder, her mind now filling in the rest. *Cinder's sabotage—she'd gone after the suits.* None looked as gravely ill as Cavendish. Mac looked her question at Nik. "You stayed on the coms all the time I was gone, didn't you, Tucker?" he asked, his voice soft. To Mac, "Even in a suit, exposure adds up."

"Thought you might call," Cavendish said, then convulsed in a cough.

"There are medical supplies on my dart." Fy took over from Mac and Nik, using her fingers to form a slinglike seat for the ill Human. Cavendish leaned back in that support, his head lolling against the stained white of her gown. "Sinzi," he managed.

Though all from the *Impeci* had suffered radiation burns, the two remaining researchers, especially the Imrya, were in far better shape than the ship's pilot. He needed help to walk, and exhibited more burns to his skin. Mac guessed he'd traded shifts at the *Impeci's* com with Cavendish. He'd been the ship's pilot. Now, he couldn't stop looking over his shoulder.

A reflex she understood very well.

Grim-faced, Nik told them what had transpired on the *Annapolis Joy.* Mac watched the hope of rescue fade from the faces of those who'd been waiting for it. There was no protest, only quiet questions. *A measure of Nik's colleagues,* she judged.

While this went on, Cavendish and the pilot, Bhar Dass, were made as comfortable as possible in the Sinzi's tiny ship. Nik ordered the Imrya—*whose name Mac couldn't pronounce*—and her Human colleague, Fiora Parrish, to stay and care for them. "We may have to run for it," he told them when they protested. "I want you here, ready to go. We'll keep in touch." He showed them the remote links the Sinzi had provided. "You're sure you can use the com system?" This to the Imrya. "It's not quite IU standard."

The alien looked at the Sinzi, who nodded. "We Imrya are honored to be the first recipients of improvements by the gracious Sinzi. I am familiar with this system."

Nik didn't look surprised. "Monitor what's happening outside and keep us posted."

"Should I broadcast a detailed advisement not to fire on this ship, given the presence of the Sinzi-ra?" The Imrya clutched her recorder tightly, as if she'd like to mention the presence of that as well.

Hand over proof to those already worrying about a Dhryn/Sinzi connection? Mac touched Nik's sleeve; he met her eyes and nodded before turning back to the Imrya. "Given the situation, let's not get specific. Just say this is a nonhostile ship, under truce."

The pilot raised his head, his eyes haunted. "Is it?"

"We'll find out," Nik promised.

The tiles, colored and bright, hadn't changed. The soft green carpet, the woven silk panels in rainbow shades, the floor rising in great steps were familiar. But nothing bounced on the carpet, or slept within the paneled pens, or cooed sleepily. The tiles surrounded a crèche emptied of life.

Mac stepped back from the lookout with a sigh. The Dhryn with her seemed less affected. *Perhaps because these hadn't been her* oomlings.

More likely, she reminded herself, *this sacrifice was part of being Dhryn, too.*

"This way," Nik said, pointing down the right-hand tunnel.

These tunnels had their own ghosts. "Did you see any Wasted while you were here?" Mac asked as she rejoined Nik. *Not that they could feed the one they had.*

He shook his head.

The Progenitor must have consumed their faint flickers of life, too.

Fy trailed their small line, her attention repeatedly caught by this or that about the walls or exposed controls, holding up one of the recorders she'd attached to a belt before they'd left the dart. Mac supposed the Sinzi was happy, in the way a researcher could find joy with her subject.

She couldn't remember it.

"Almost there," Nik told her. His fingers laced with hers. "No sign of trouble yet."

"As if that's a good thing to say," she complained, only half joking.

They watched for Ro, even here, where the shroud material of the Dhryn should provide protection.

As for Dhryn . . . "Could the entire ship be this empty?"

Nik shrugged. "We couldn't estimate the minimum crew requirement to keep things running. A lot's automated, as you'd expect." A pause. "When I was on board, She was working Her way through one section at a time."

Spy School 101: Euphemisms for All Occasions, Mac said to herself, not fooled by his tone. "I'm sorry," she offered. "If it helps, I felt Her grief through the *lamnas*. She consumed Her own children first."

Another shrug, this sharp and tense. "Feeders don't discriminate. We'll need to be careful."

"The Mouths of the Progenitor do not think," Her Glory agreed, her voice full of warmth and longing. "They only provide."

Of course she'd want to find feeders. Nik's fingers tightened around hers. *Not the only one worried.* "Can they provide for you?" he asked the Dhryn, as casually as if he inquired after her favorite color.

"Among the many things I don't know, Vessel. This state—" a quiet hoot, "—is new to me as well." Her Glory paused. "I'm reassured Haven remains after all. Even in this form. Something of my old life."

"Have you reached accommodation with your other self?" This from Fy. *Understandable curiosity from someone having a little trouble in that department.*

"Accommodation?" The Dhryn appeared to consider the question as they walked, the taller Sinzi leaning over to listen. "Those memories have no taste, no power. I simply know what happened. We arrived at Haven to find it destroyed. We waited for nothing, hiding ourselves from the Ro, from all that were not-Dhryn. The time came when some chose to die. I know I chose to survive, despite having no purpose or value. For that, I await the judgment of the Progenitor."

As if on cue, a figure appeared ahead. Standing, Mac noticed with relief. Nik's other hand eased back to his side. *He'd been ready to fire.*

"You were told to stay in your ship, not-Dhryn. Why are you here?" A Dhryn voice, male, older, his Instella flawless. He stepped forward into the light. *Two hands missing—someone of importance.* As if in emphasis, his eye and ear ridges were traced in vivid turquoise, more of that color on his lips and in the silk banding his torso.

The effect would have better, Mac decided, *if he hadn't needed strings to hold the hands around what was close to a match for a Wasted's body.* The strings had a second function, being beaded with the Dhryn version of imps. *Odd decoration,* she puzzled.

"Deruym Ma Nas," Nik greeted. "I've returned, as promised."

The Dhryn leaned forward, slight threat. His remaining hands, Mac noted, held weapons, though not pointed at them. *Yet.* "Which not-Dhryn are you?"

Something about the attitude of what was obviously a cloistered Haven Dhryn, albeit an educated linguist, stiffened Mac's spine. "You know perfectly well he's Her Vessel," she stated in Dhryn. "We come on urgent business for That Which Is Dhryn and the Progenitor expects us. I am Mackenzie Winifred Elizabeth Wright Connor Sol."

His stumps and hands came together in a startled clap of respect. "I didn't see you. Or—" Words in either language failed him as Deruym Ma Nas finally caught sight of Her Glory.

She was worth a look, Mac thought with poignant pride, easily half again the size of the Haven Dhryn, her body robust and full. The dulled lighting only emphasized the golden luminescence banding her torso. Her Glory needed no silks—*or were the brilliant silks of modern Dhryn an echo of what they'd lost?* she wondered abruptly.

"Deruym Ma Nas," Her Glory said in that warm, loving voice. "A most admirable name. I take it into my keeping, though I've none of my own to exchange." She held out her single hand. "Know me by this, *erumisah.*"

The other Dhryn rose in a bow, then brought his mouth close to her palm, lips working at the air above the skin. His eyelids lowered and he began to sway in what seemed ecstasy. *Or a seizure,* Mac cautioned herself.

Never assume with aliens.

An old rule, but a good one.

With Deruym Ma Nas as escort, their group moved quickly to the wide, downsloping ramp that led to the Progenitor's Chamber, more precisely as quickly as his frequent backward looks at Her Glory permitted. Mac glared at the Dhryn as he did it again, almost stumbling.

The lush carpet quieted their footfalls. There were more spirals of silver than she remembered along the black shroud lining the walls. *More names added.* She wished for time to try and read them. But time they didn't have.

They should be running.

It wasn't only fear, though Mac didn't understand her eagerness to reach their destination until they stopped in front of the vault-like door to the Progenitor's Chamber.

It felt like coming home.

Did she think the Progenitor could fix things?

Make things right?

Bring back the dead?

Mac shook her head, hard. *The Progenitor was as endangered as the rest of them.* She followed Nik through the door, seeing Deruym Ma Nas glance up at the last minute. Curious, she did the same.

Before, the holes around the great door had been empty, inexplicable. Now, a pale feeder Dhryn squatted in those above, as if waiting for strays.

Mac dropped her gaze, her nerve endings remembering what her mind refused.

"This one will remain here." Deruym Ma Nas pointed at Fy.

The Sinzi's fingers clenched in shock. "But I must see the Progenitor!"

No surprise, Mac thought. *To a Sinzi, a physical meeting was paramount.*

Deruym Ma Nas, surprised or not, wasn't about to be swayed. "She does not have to see you. You are—" he paused and blinked one/two at the tall alien, as if lost for the right word, then settled for: "—unfamiliar."

Fy looked to Mac, who could only shrug, thinking of the days she'd spent waiting for the Progenitor to be ready to meet her first Human. "I'll ask," she offered.

"Isn't there a safer place to wait?" Nik didn't need to point at the lurking feeders.

"It is all right." The Sinzi made an graceful come-hither gesture toward the silver-sparked walls. "I would prefer to stay here. These appear the oldest engravings. I would be grateful for the opportunity to record them."

Nik looked uneasy. "Are you sure, Sinzi-ra?"

Mac had learned to read Fy's fear and saw it now, in the tremble of fingertip, the distracted focus of the topaz eyes. To the Sinzi's credit, she remained steadfast. "Will it matter where any of us are if the Progenitor chooses to feed?" She faced the Dhryn and lifted her recorder. "Deruym Ma Nas, may I have your permission?"

"You need none," he told her. "These walls are meant to be read by all who come here, throughout the generations." For an instant, Mac thought she detected something sad and resigned in Deruym Ma Nas' expression, before it returned to impatient. "We must go."

The Haven Dhryn disappeared within the archway, Her Glory with him.

Nik nodded to Mac, who began to walk with him after the Dhryn. She couldn't help glancing back at the Sinzi. The willowy alien stood in the black-walled corridor, watching them leave her. She appeared composed, but her fingers were locked around her recorder. The lower half of her gown was stiff with dried Human blood. "Fy," Mac suggested, "you might want to ignore what I said about moving slowly around aliens."

An almost Human smile. "I understand."

"Mac?"

"Coming."

Fifteen steps through the arched door itself. Mac counted each, smelling metal, feeling the chill. Then the passage. Nik and their guide—still the only normal adult Dhryn they'd seen—led the way. Her Glory and Mae followed them.

Mac lifted her face, knowing the reason for the rhythmic pulse of warm air over her skin. She sniffed, disturbed by a faint decay.

Then they were out, into that world where flesh and biology ruled.

- CONTACT -

HUMANS WERE FAMED for their ability to grow accustomed to any marvel, to take the strange in stride. It made them easygoing crewmates on alien ships, although a frustrating market to satisfy.

But not even Humans could grow used to this.

"Current count?" Hollans requested, sipping his tea. None of them left the Atrium these days. He had a cot near Telematics, took his meals within sight of the screens monitoring traffic through the transect.

And what traffic . . .

Day after day, Sinzi had been pouring into Sol System through every gate. Polite, noncommittal Sinzi, following protocol to the letter, requesting only a designated orbit for their ships to stay out of the way of whatever else moved to and from Earth.

Saying nothing else.

"Two hundred and fifty-three thousand, four hundred and two personal darts, five hundred and twelve liners." The tech consulted a smaller screen. "That accounts for the entire registered Sinzi liner fleet, sir. I don't have a reference for darts."

Hollans shook his head. There wasn't a species in the IU whose delegate hadn't hammered—or the equivalent—on his door, demanding to know what the Humans were doing. Not a species who wasn't desperately afraid the Sinzi were leaving its system for good, the transect gates on automated settings only. Traffic had virtually stopped.

The Sinzi were abandoning them to the Dhryn.

That was the latest.

"Sinzi-ra?" Hollans asked quietly, as he had so many times. "What are your people doing?"

Anchen, as she had each time before, smiled her perfect Human smile.

"They participate in the promise."

24

RETURN AND REACTION

THE LANDSCAPE HAD AGED. Mac stared out over a grayed blue, its surface puckered and wrinkled by furrows deep enough to hide a starship. There were no wide ponds of shining black, no frosting of new life. The few feeders lay flaccid, their arms tipped into drying puddles.

With the others, she rode that improbable hand to the incredible wall of flesh, hollowed by nostrils able to engulf a lev as well as barges. Mac's eyes dismissed what was irrelevant, seeking the face embedded in the wall.

And found it.

"Welcome, Mackenzie Winifred Elizabeth Wright Connor Sol." The same quiet, so-normal voice she remembered, with its familiar kind warmth. The same gold-and-black eyes.

No sequins. Perhaps the Progenitor spared her few remaining Dhryn that service. *Seemed a shame.*

"My previous Vessel told me you had served in *grathnu* again."

"What?" *Oh.* Mac held out her artificial arm. "Not quite. You know what happened to Brymn Las?"

Those eyes could become cold. "The Ro interfered with That Which Is Dhryn." The hand underfoot shook. "They must never do so again."

"That's what we hope," Nik said.

"Ah. My Vessel. Welcome. You have done well. Very well. I had no doubt."

Nik gave a deep bow. "Thank you. But, Progenitor—forgive

my haste. We must leave this system at once. I'll explain as we travel."

"Of course." A soft hoot, higher-pitched than other Dhryn. "We already answer the Call, my Vessel." Her eyes moved to Her Glory. "Tell me, what is this?"

"Answer the Call?" Before Mac could do more than exchange looks of alarm with Nik, she felt a nudge against her back. From its direction, it had to be from Her Glory's hand. *Right, Vessel.* "Well," she began helplessly, "this is—"

"What do you mean—'answer the Call'?" Nik interrupted, stepping forward. Deruym Ma Nas drew his weapons and moved to block the Human's way.

"Do not threaten my Vessel," the Progenitor chided her *erumisah.* "And do not fear." This in a more gentle tone to Nik. "The empty ship receives the Call and responds; my Dhryn who crew her would otherwise never disobey me. We follow by my will."

Mac's heart pounded. *Not good,* she babbled to herself. *Not good.*

If Nik shared that choking fear; he didn't show it. "I urge you to reconsider, Progenitor." Calm, reasoned. "What we've done to your ship—it may not be enough to protect you from the Ro. We don't know."

"We will know, my Vessel," She replied, as calmly, as reasonably, "when I attack them. We will know when I scour the Ro and its contamination from whatever world it has chosen. The Call will end. If others answered? You, my Vessel, will speak for me to those Progenitors. We will protect them, too. Together, we will continue until there are no Ro left alive."

As the Progenitor spoke, feeder-Dhryn rose from Her surface, like pastel petals caught by Her breath. Some came so close Mac could see their oblong clear bodies, their boneless arms. *Their mouths . . .*

She froze in place; Her Glory heaved a wistful sigh.

Those eyeless faces seemed to acknowledge their Progenitor before all of them turned, using the fins on back and sides to stroke the air. They began moving toward the walls and ceiling of the vast chamber. *Thousands,* Mac realized numbly. Far less than she remembered. *Far too many.* As they reached their destination, they disappeared through holes in the walls she hadn't noticed in her first visit. *Doors—but to what?*

The Progenitor smiled. "I will destroy my enemy."

There were certain unavoidable ramifications to standing on a giant hand. *Of course, even if there'd been time,* Mac told herself, *tact had never been her strong suit.* "You know," she ventured, "this might not be the best plan."

Eyes of gold and black fixed on her. "It is my will." She sounded more surprised than upset.

"The Dhryn are not alone, Progenitor." Nik came to stand by Mac. "Others oppose the Ro. Let us bring warships from other species. End the threat of the Ro together."

"They are our enemy—"

"Don't you understand?" Mac couldn't stop herself. "This Call—it won't just be Ro on that planet! There'll be other life!"

Were they watching the catastrophe of the Chasm unfold again?

The vivid blue underlid flashed over the Progenitor's eyes, twice. *Stress.* Mac tensed, but the hand supporting them might have been carved from rock. When the great creature spoke, it was still in that reasoning-with-aliens tone. "Of course. The Ro require it."

"For what?" Nik asked, silencing Mac with a look. "Why do the Ro require other living things, Progenitor?"

The first frown. "We do not think of it."

The first evasion. For safety's sake, Mac only imagined stamping her foot. *They were close to something vital here, something that would finally make sense.*

Nik must have sensed it, too. "They interfered with That Which Is Dhryn," he pursued relentlessly. "Made you consume the life from worlds at their command. Why would they require life on those worlds, if they planned to remove it?"

For a moment, Mac didn't think the Progenitor would answer. Her small lips worked as she remembered Brymn's would do when he was disturbed. The breath moving past was deeper, with more force.

Was that a tremble in the hand?

She resisted the urge to grab Nik. *They'd only fall together.* "Please, Progenitor," she said gently. "We seek the truth."

"As do I," came the response. Mac discovered she'd been holding her breath. "Bear with me, *Lamisah*. The fragments I have gleaned from the past resemble *oomlings*, precious because they represent continuance, but these never Freshen to the wisdom of adulthood. The most whole are the gifts from my predecessor, and She from Hers." A sigh that shook the barren landscape below and whistled past the hand. "Yet they answer no more questions. My predecessors wished That Which Is Dhryn to survive the Ro—not understand them."

"Trust me when I say we must understand them to survive," Nik urged. "Let us try. Tell us, tell your *lamisah,* everything you can about living things and the Ro. You sent Brymn Las and your Vessel to Mackenzie Winifred Elizabeth Wright Connor Sol for that very reason." He put his hand on Mac's shoulder, pressed gently as if in warning. "She's here, now. Earth's foremost biologist. She can help."

Nothing like an unearned promotion, Mac winced to herself. She attempted to be positive. *Maybe salmon would have relevance.*

"That's me," she said brightly.

The Progenitor's gold-and-black eyes regarded her. "Will we need to find and kill them all?"

A perfectly reasonable question. Mac wished it wasn't the one going through her mind about the Dhryn. *Emily'd warned her.* "I'll need to know more about their life cycle," she evaded. "How many it takes to reproduce—to make *oomlings,*" this as the Progenitor looked perplexed.

"I make *oomlings.*" With a low hoot—*presumably at bizarre alien notions*—echoed by Deruym Ma Nas and Her Glory.

Obviously the topic of Dhryn sex, or possible lack thereof, wasn't going to help. Mac picked another tack. "What do Ro make?"

"Tools."

"Machines?" Nik suggested. "Ships. Devices?"

The Progenitor pursed Her lips for an instant. "Servants. Servants of flesh and bone. Such as attacked you, *Lamisah,* and poor Brymn Las. The ones who hide within shields. The ones we learned to keep away from our world."

Nik looked disappointed; he'd doubtless hoped for something, anything, new.

But Mac felt the stirrings of curiosity. "Why do the Ro make servants?"

"How else can they reach beyond their chambers?"

"Chambers?" *An expression for no-space?* "What do you mean?"

The hand moved away from the face and swiveled to give them a view of the Progenitor's vast cavern. "Chamber," She said with a gentle hoot, returning Her hand, and guests, to their original position.

More than living quarters, Mac thought. *The only place She can survive.* "The Ro have to stay there," she guessed.

"Where are their chambers?" asked Nik, his eyes almost glowing. "Within their ships? On the worlds they choose?"

"They are not like us. Their chambers have holes, doors, to many places at once, places that flow together. The stories claim a Ro must open such a door to begin a world. Once opened, That Which Is Dhryn can reach in to kill it." Her voice held immense satisfaction.

"Explaining why that opening to no-space might stay open," he mused, "but why for only so long? A failsafe . . ." He frowned. "I could see something set to grab an attacked Ro back inside—but why take away the oceans, too? We're missing something." He looked at Mac.

As if she'd know. She obligingly frowned back. "You said a Ro opens its chamber to 'begin a world.' " She pounced on the odd phrase. *Ominous was more like it.* "What does that mean?"

The hand trembled again. "I do not think of it. We do not think of it."

"You must, Progenitor," Nik insisted. "Time's running out."

No need for a reminder. Mac shuddered. They were on their way to the next target. *She was not going to think about where or what.*

As if in echo, the Progenitor said, "I do not think of it." Her lips began to quiver; Her eyes flashed blue.

Before Nik could press Her further, Deruym Ma Nas put away his weapons. "Rest," he rumbled in Instella. "Allow me to answer your Vessel, my Progenitor."

"My *erumisah* is wise." This with a breathlessness that had nothing to do with the pulses of air through the great nostrils.

"Do you know what the Ro are doing?" Nik asked him.

"We do not know," an emphasis, "anything beyond the evil nature of the Ro. My Progenitor has directed our search of the archives. I am," a graceful bow, "the Senior Archivist."

Mac spared a moment to wonder if he knew of her and Brymn's ruthless foraging through the oldest of the Haven Dhryn's textiles, then decided it couldn't matter now.

Sure enough, Deruym Ma Nas gave a forlorn hoot. "A meaningless title, since no others remain." He touched a few of the imps decorating his torso. "I keep their trust."

Mac blinked. He could easily have over a hundred of the devices on those strings. *The amount of data that implied?*

But they had no time. "Could we hear your informed speculation on the Ro, Deruym Ma Nas?" she asked courteously.

Judging from Nik's face, he'd settle for a wild guess, so long as it moved them closer.

You couldn't rush Dhryn. She'd learned that lesson.

In response, Deruym Ma Nas folded his arms, the severed wrists outward, in case they forgot his earned rank. "We discovered forty-nine references concerning the Ro and taste."

"Taste? What does—" Mac frowned and Nik subsided. "Taste," he echoed. "Please continue."

"I'm hungry," Her Glory whispered in Mac's ear. She patted the huge Dhryn, but kept her attention on the archivist.

"In these references to taste," Deruym Ma Nas continued, his eyes not leaving Nik, "there is commonality. Whether embroidered within fabrics, or placed into mosaic, even within the stories remembered by my Progenitor, each refers to the foul taste of the worlds contaminated by the Ro, of how this taste was deemed unfit for the Progenitors to share."

"Because this was your enemy," Nik guessed.

Human bias. As she shook her head, Mac abruptly grasped the import of what Deruym Ma Nas was trying to tell them. *The taste of what?* "The Ro used the Dhryn to remove the original life from chosen worlds," she thought out loud. "But when the Dhryn rebelled and attacked the Ro, those worlds still had a taste, but now so different the Progenitors couldn't consume it." Her voice rose with excitement. "Don't you see? It means those worlds didn't stay barren. The Ro had put life on them. Their kind of life."

"Why?"

"The oldest imperative of them all." *Did they feel the rightness of it?* "Individual survival isn't enough—your kind must continue.

The Ro aren't adapted to no-space. Maybe nothing is." *Just passing through it with the Ro had made her sick; repeated trips had damaged Emily's mind.* "We know they came from a planet. Those who left it were committed to live in no-space. We've seen time flows differently there—they could have lost touch with their previous existence almost at once. They might have thought they could exist like that forever, only to discover they'd become impotent, damaged, maybe even dying.

"What would they do? Give up the future?" Mac shook her head. "Not the Ro I met. They could make biological machines, but that wouldn't be good enough. They'd want the real thing, to rebuild themselves. Time here would mean nothing to them. They had the tools. All they needed were living worlds to host their regeneration—fresh, sterile worlds, free of alien life to compete or contaminate. Then they find the Dhryn, the perfect—"

Stop right there, Mac thought, suddenly remembering where she was.

Too late.

"More Ro!" roared the Progenitor. "They used us to make more?"

Her hand spasmed, toppling them all. Nik threw his arm over Mac as they fell, holding them flat against the palm.

- CONTACT -

"WE HAVE INCOMING SHIPS, SIR," the transect technician reported, smoothly, professionally.

"Finally!" her supervisor burst out. "You'd think with the Sinzi here, everything would run like clockwork. But no, traffic's off and if we get one more complaint about missing newspackets, I'll—"

"Sir. Sending to your station." Only someone standing close by could have seen her hands tremble. Or someone who'd been there when the Dhryn had arrived.

"Got it." One look at the display and her supervisor reached for the emergency com control, then thought better of it and reached for the secure line to Earth.

"This is Venus Orbital," he announced. "We've unannounced warships coming through the Naralax Transect. Repeat, incoming warships. Species—?"

"Trisulian, sir. They aren't broadcasting idents, but I'd know those profiles in my sleep. Fifty, another group of twenty, still coming."

"Going by profile, the intruders are Trisulian," he sent. "Venus Orbital, standing by." He began punching in the codes to lock the facility behind blast doors, for all the good they'd do against ships capable of smashing planets to rubble.

The technician swiveled her chair to stare at him. "Standing by for what, sir?" she asked in a low, urgent voice. "What the hell's going on?"

Her supervisor looked up at her question.

"Let's hope it isn't war."

"The Trisulians are demanding the Sinzi immediately submit to their authority, disband the Inner Council of the IU, and relinquish all information on no-space technology and the transect system."

Hollans picked up his teacup. "Anything else?"

"Did you not hear me?" The Imrya ambassador was a remarkably succinct individual for his species. *Doubtless why he'd been posted so far from home.* "You must allow me to request the immediate deployment of the Imrya fleet here."

"And escalate what is currently rhetoric into a battle?" Hollans sipped his tea. "No, thank you, Ambassador."

"We must stop the Trisulians! We must protect the Sinzi!"

"Our forces were already en route to the gate."

"Forgive me, Mr. Hollans, but your forces wouldn't give an Ar pause. We've had peace between systems because the Sinzi were scattered, everywhere. Now too many are here, vulnerable to attack or capture. They have made themselves too tempting a target."

"Something I've told the Sinzi-ra," Hollans replied rather testily, "several times. We all have. They persist in providing no information whatsoever."

"Do they wish confrontation? To what end?"

Hollans put down his teacup. "I think it's something far more dangerous than that, Ambassador. I think the Sinzi seek a congruence, here. If that's the case, the Trisulians?" He lifted his hand and bent one finger down. "They're merely the first to accept the invitation."

25

PREDICAMENT AND PERIL

A N ETERNITY LATER, the shuddering ended, the hand stopped moving, and no one was dead. During that time, while waiting to fall, be thrown, or survive, Mac noticed the little things. The skin beneath her hands was warm, although loose and dry, no longer as elastic as she remembered. The smell? She wrinkled her nose and tried to keep her face away from the surface. The Progenitor's circulation was failing; the hand itself likely septic.

Really not a good thing to think about while on that hand.

Although Her Glory appeared content to stay prone, Deruym Ma Nas struggled to his feet almost at once. "The evil of the Ro has no limits," he exclaimed.

Which would sound more impressive, Mac decided, peering at him, *if he wasn't still shaking.*

She was surprised not to be. The combination earthquake-with-potential-plunge would once have had her gibbering with fear.

New standards.

"Your idea about the Ro," Nik whispered. "It fits, Mac. What we know so far; what we've guessed. Good work."

"Desperation," she whispered back.

In answer, he kissed her nose.

They rose to their feet, the hand having remained stable throughout this exchange. The process entailed what Mac considered a responsible amount of clinging to one another.

A shame to let go, she acknowledged as her fingers left Nik's sleeve.

"Please forgive me," the Progenitor said quietly. "I could take such dreadful news when I was strong. I could endure." Her eyes held inexpressible weariness. "Now, I fail. And That Which Is Dhryn fails with me."

She had a choice, Mac realized. Something that seemed to be happening all too often lately.

She hated having a choice.

Nik simply raised an eyebrow when she sent him a pleading look. *Up to her.*

Mac glowered but nodded.

"That Which Is Dhryn may not be failing," she told the Progenitor, stepping aside so Her Glory was no longer hiding half behind her.

The Progenitor's eyes glanced at Her Glory, who stood up literally ablaze with joy, then back to Mac. "What is this?"

Mac thought of the *lamnas.* The Progenitor had done Her stomach-turning utmost to convey not only her despair, but her need. *A need she understood.* "What you asked of me," she said. "The truth."

The Progenitor's lips quivered and Deruym Ma Nas lowered his body in warning. Nik looked poised to—*do what? Tackle the bear-sized alien and toss them both off the hand?*

Mac didn't see much future in that.

"Explain," the Progenitor said at last.

Mac coughed. *In for it now.* "You spoke of the Ro's interference, Progenitor," she said carefully. "They've done more to That Which Is Dhryn than you know. Without them, I believe you would be like this. A little bigger," she added, giving Her Glory a considering look.

Or a great deal bigger, she suddenly realized, *once the migration had ended and the Dhryn population entered a stationary rebuilding generation—a variability within the norm the Ro could have exploited.* "The Ro didn't just take you from your home world into space," Mac went on. "They didn't just find ways to control your behavior. They made changes to the Flowering itself."

"Continue," the Progenitor said, her small mouth turned down at the corners, yellow drops forming on her nostrils. Otherwise, she appeared reassuringly calm. "Why would they do this?"

Calm for how long? Mac swallowed. "The Ro wanted Progenitors who could produce more *oomlings*. They wanted as many feeders, Mouths, as possible. Those are their weapon. That meant Progenitors so large they could no longer move by themselves. They knew how to change the pattern of your growth and development." *Another piece snicked into place.* "And Ro technology produced food to sustain you. These ships? They were essential. Not just to bring you where the Ro Called, but because—as they made you—you can't live anywhere else."

When the hand didn't immediately tip, she relaxed very slightly and continued. "They could alter the Flowering process, too. Remember Brymn Las? He didn't become what you predicted, a Progenitor, because the Ro—" she forced the words past the memory, "—made sure he didn't."

She indicated the silent Dhryn at her side. "This is what I believe you both would have become without the Ro. The original form of Dhryn Progenitor."

"Where did she come from?" Still to Mac. *Protocol between Progenitors, or a refusal to acknowledge what stood before her?* Without knowing which, all Mac could do was press ahead. She noticed Nik taking advantage of the Progenitor's attention to turn slightly away and lift his wrist to his mouth, likely contacting those left behind. *Warning them the ship was on the move.*

Where was anyone's guess.

"Where?" This from the Progenitor, when Mac failed to answer immediately. Gentle, but insistent. "Our home world? A colony of Dhryn who escaped the Ro?" There was a distinct and growing excitement in her voice.

"A little closer," Mac said. "Her Glory was once captain of the Cryssin freighter, *Uosanah*. He Flowered into what you've been calling the Wasted."

Deruym Ma Nas scuttled as far away from Her Glory as the hand permitted. *Almost too far.*

"I do not wish to doubt you, *Lamisah*," responded the Progenitor graciously. "But this is not possible. The lost ones fail and die. It is the Way."

"It's the Ro's way," Mac countered. "All they had to do was make it possible for your bodies to synthesize certain substances, things once obtained from what you ate on your home world. Any Dhryn without this ability would starve to death on Haven or on board your ships." *The whole truth.* "They might survive a little longer by eating other Dhryn. That's why the Wasted attack their own kind. To save one? All we had to do was provide this Dhryn, who was dying, with food as close as possible to what would have been available to your ancestors. Look at her."

"I hunger," Her Glory offered, less than helpfully.

The Progenitor's eyes shifted to her. "As do I, little one."

Before this could become a negotiation about who should eat whom, Mac jumped back in. "The point is, the diet you've been producing for yourselves on Haven—" *however clever the fungus,* "—was part of the Ro's plan. It couldn't meet the needs of any Dhryn born who reflected the original type. That was one way they've controlled your population. Any Dhryn whose body threw off their conditioning and reverted to the ancestral form would starve to death at Flowering instead of becoming a Progenitor. Wasted." *Had some Progenitor* known *to call them that?* "You would continue to produce the kind of Dhryn that suited the Ro."

"They came—they came and touched the *oomlings* until we found ways to keep them out." Deruym Na Mas had risen to a more conciliatory posture and was watching Mac intently. "Is that why, Mackenzie Winifred Elizabeth Wright Connor Sol?"

Why did everyone think she understood the damned Ro? Mac shrugged. "I don't know. They could have been making further modifications. They might have been monitoring something about you. Or—" She hesitated and looked to Nik. He nodded, still trusting her with this. *Great.* "Maybe the Ro were waiting for something. A sign your population was ready to migrate."

"The Great Journey. Even that they would pervert?"

"Especially that," Mac agreed.

"Have the Little One approach me."

Mac turned but Her Glory was already walking forward, her movement powerful yet graceful. Fit.

Could the Progenitor see it?

Her Glory stopped when she could walk no farther. She lifted her sole hand and spread her strong, delicate fingers against the wall that was the Progenitor's cheek, then rose on four legs so their eyes met at the same level.

Gusts of warm air moved outward, cooler air returning. Nik stopped talking into his com, watching the new and the old. *Or rather,* Mac corrected herself, *the original and the perversion.*

Though to call the gracious Progenitor a perversion seemed as wrong as anything else. Especially when Her face, suspended in the wall like an image of who she really was, formed an expression of such kindness. "Can you speak so my Vessel can understand?"

The Progenitor had used Dhryn, but Her Glory didn't hesitate. "Yes," in Instella. "I ask your wisdom, She Who Lights the Way." Her luminescent bands shone more brightly, as if activated by emotion. They cast shadows on the great palm and attentive face. "I wish to know how I can serve That Which Is Dhryn."

The Progenitor squinted. "Commune with me. We shall sing the *Gnausa.*"

Deruym Ma Nas drew in his arms, leaning back in a Dhryn bow. *Just what they needed,* Mac thought. *Ro on the attack and a pause for another alien ceremony.*

She was not *providing a body part.*

And neither was Nik, decided Mac, having grown fond of his as well.

Singing implied voice, to a Human at least, but the Dhryn kept silent. *To Human ears,* Mac cautioned herself. She watched in fascination as Her Glory leaned forward, slowly, carefully, as if to offer the Progenitor a Human-style lover's kiss. She stopped a few centimeters short of contact. They remained thus, their lips parted, close but not touching.

A long minute passed. Then another.

Mac eased left for a better view.

Nothing.

Another minute. Two more. Deruym Ma Nas remained in his bow, although his limbs were now trembling with strain. He had a decidedly desperate look, as if he'd rather fall off the Progenitor's hand than stop bowing.

Mac glanced at Nik. He was studying Her Glory and the Progenitor. Catching her eye, he nodded toward the two, mouthing, "Look."

She dared step nearer and finally saw that something was passing between the open mouths. Moisture glistened on their lips and the surrounding flesh. *A fine spray?* Whatever it was, Her Glory's eyes had half closed in apparent rapture. The Progenitor's remained open and fixed on the other Dhryn.

This could take a while.

Mac walked over to Nik, careful to avoid the edge. "New to me," she whispered. "Have you seen anything like it before?"

Deruym Ma Nas' turquoise lips turned down in disapproval. *Haven Dhryn.* Mac smiled at him.

"No," Nik answered as quietly. "But when I agreed to be Her Vessel, She said it would be in spirit only, since Humans couldn't sing. Could be part of that process."

Mac turned to look outward, her shoulder against his. "Any idea where She's taking us?" *More exactly, where the Ro were leading them?*

"I had Fy contact the dart, to have Bhar check sensors. We're tractored to the other Dhryn, heading for the gate. From there?" She felt his shoulder move. "Any number of choices, Mac."

She sighed. "None of them good."

"No." A pause. "We've a couple of probes left on the *Impeci*. Once through the gate, we can at least let the IU know which system is under attack."

Mac reached into a pocket and brought out a nutrient bar. She snapped it in half. "Here."

Nik tapped his to hers. "Cheers, Dr. Connor."

She smiled. "Now you see the extent of my culinary skills."

"We won't starve." Nik's arm stole around her waist. "I can cook."

"Another experiment?" Mac leaned her head against him. Although her stomach objected, she ignored it, methodically chewing and swallowing the entire morsel.

Water would have been nice, but there was some on the dart. *They weren't desperate.*

Yet.

"Incredible, isn't She?" Nik murmured.

Mac gazed out at a vista holding all the beauty of a desert at twilight. "You should have seen Her whole." *Before She began to die.*

Before so many did.

She took an uneven breath and Nik's arm tightened. "You didn't see him fall," he said with that uncanny perception. "That's what you told me. That's what you need to remember."

"I feel appallingly selfish," Mac confessed. "Hoping for one among all the rest. With what's happening—"

Nik gathered her against him. "Then I'm selfish, too."

"Mac."

Didn't mind the sound of her name this way, breathed into her ear with such tenderness. Not about to wake up. But the sound . . . that was nice.

"I think they're about done. C'mon, Mac." The tenderness remained, but there was an added note of urgency that didn't intend to be ignored.

Mac opened her eyes, immediately realizing two things. First, she was tucked very comfortably within a nest composed of Nik's lap, arms, and body. Second, they were in . . . "This is the Progenitor's Chamber." She flushed and struggled to her feet. "You let me fall asleep on Her hand?"

In front of aliens?

"Guilty, though in my defense there was no 'letting' involved." Nik grinned unrepentantly as he stood. "Should I mention snoring? Guess not." This at her glare.

Mac rubbed her eyes. "What did I miss?"

"The Progenitors communed." Deruym Ma Nas sat nearby. His hands fussed with the strings holding his silks and the imps. He looked exhausted. *Not only the prolonged bow,* Mac judged. He was too thin, malnourished, and worn with care. "*Gnausa* is complete."

She looked at Her Glory. The large Dhryn leaned against the wall of the Progenitor. Glistening liquid streaked her jaw and upper chest, as it did the flesh beneath the Progenitor's mouth. Her bands glowed and her eyes were vivid gold. The Progenitor's eyes were closed, as if She slept.

"What is *Gnausa*?"

"It is how a Progenitor anoints Her Successor," Deruym Ma Nas told them. "No one else knows what passes between them." His lips moved and he folded his arms as if overcome by emotion. "But I—I can feel the result; I know I am in the presence of not one, but two of Those Who Light the Way." A hint of a bow to Mac and Nik. "An unexpected joy."

"Forgive me, but you don't seem joyful," Mac observed.

"After what you've revealed?" The archivist sighed. "I would like to believe there will be more accomplishments by That Which Is Dhryn to remember and record, but I am no fool, Mackenzie Winifred Elizabeth Wright Connor Sol. A Progenitor alone is doomed. A Successor without a future cannot save us."

Her Glory had been listening. Now, she came over to Deruym Ma Nas and bent to look the smaller Dhryn in the eye. "Despair cannot save us," she corrected.

This close, Mac could see that the liquid had spilled out of Her Glory's mouth—*which made sense, since the being could no longer swallow*—yet was viscous enough to stick to her skin. She looked closer. It was collecting in a maze of fine cracks in the thick blue. *Or had produced the cracks,* she realized, thinking of the potency of Dhryn spit. "How do you feel?" she ventured.

"Hungry." Her Glory smiled, as if asking Mac to share the humor in that admission. "Ambitious. Determined." She rose to her full height. "Is this not a glorious day? Who could not feel wonderful?" This as a shout that echoed far below.

"Hush. Leave me, Daughter." The Progenitor didn't open Her eyes. "I must rest before we reach our destination and defeat the Ro." There was no room for debate; as She spoke, Her hand moved away from Her face.

And so did they.

Fy was waiting for them within the long arched doorway. "May I see the Progenitor now?" she asked eagerly as Mac stepped from the hand.

"She fails," Her Glory said, her voice implacable. "I endure."

She brushed by the Sinzi and headed up the ramp, Deruym Ma Nas following behind with a clatter of imps.

Move on. Survive. Mac understood the impulse. Part of her applauded it.

Part of her was already grieving. *No matter what happened next, the days of the Progenitor—Brymn's, hers—were numbered.*

Nik was shaking his head. "Blunt. I fear accurate." He touched the thick metal wall. "The ship will only last as long as there's crew."

Fy zipped around the two Humans, stopping in front of Nik. "I could examine the control systems," she said quickly, her fingers writhing. *Hopefully this was the excited anticipation of a scholar hoping to be set loose on the real thing,* though Mac didn't rule out a nervous twitch. "I would be willing—"

"We may need your help, Sinzi-ra," Nik assured her. "First, we need to check on the situation outside the ship. Anything new?"

Mac watched the two Dhryn, the old and the new. They'd stopped in the open, just beyond the arch. Deruym Ma Nas bowed to Her Glory and moved out of sight. Her Glory sat on the cushioned floor, her ridged back toward Mac, and began to rock from side to side.

What was she doing? Mac walked closer, curious.

Suddenly, a mass of tentacles appeared in one of the holes around the door, then three feeders dropped to where Her Glory sat, helpless and oblivious.

Mac let out a cry and broke into a run, *not that she had any idea what she could do.*

"Mac! Wait!"

She slowed, not because of Nik's shout, but because the feeders had continued to drift downward until they rested on the floor before the Dhryn. Mac moved to the right-hand wall and edged forward to a good vantage point.

"You have the worst bloody reflexes—"

"Shhh." Mac grinned at Nik's fervent complaint as he hurried up beside her. "Look."

The feeders were not attacking Her Glory. *Far from it.* Instead, their tentacles were delicately exploring her face and chest. "I think they're after the liquid from the Progenitor," Mac whispered. The mouths at the ends of the tentacles stayed in no one place for long.

She noticed something else. Their clear bodies never stopped pulsating, but now each pulse spread a faint tinge of violet.

"They've friends," Nik cautioned as another pair joined the first three.

Fy's finger rested on Mac's shoulder. "Is this something to fear?"

Yes! Mac quelled the impulse and settled for a tight-lipped, "I don't know."

Her Glory had excellent hearing. "These are mine now, *Lamisah*. They will seek the Taste that I require. Which would," she added with the hint of a hoot, "include walnuts."

The violet was accumulating along the outer rim of each membrane; more drew a faint band across the ventral surface. *Perhaps coloration unique to each Progenitor,* Mac guessed.

Nik pressed his lips to her ear. She felt more than heard the words. "And us?"

He had his weapon out and ready. *He'd seen what a feeder could do to Human flesh.* She put her hand—*the new one*—over his, pressing it down. "Cayhill's work. Her Glory is herbivorous. Plants, Nik. We should be okay."

He resisted. " 'Should be' isn't good enough, Mac."

"There's only one way to know." She steeled herself to walk out there, but Nik beat her to it, heading for the Dhryn and her ghastly company.

"No. Wait!" She rushed after him, only to find Fy coming with her. "Oh, no. Not you," she declared, trying to grab some part of moving Sinzi. *It was remarkably difficult.* Mac wound up with an undignified handful of gown, said gown dragging her forward with it anyway.

Fortunately, the feeders scattered out of the way like jellyfish, their bodies bloating, membranes fluttering almost frantically. Her Glory hooted, her sides shaking. "You should see yourselves, *Lamisah!*"

Mac kept her eye on the feeders, now squeezing themselves back through the holes above the door. When the last tentacle disappeared from view, she looked back at the Dhryn. "I take it they were finished?"

Her Glory rose to her feet—*Her feet,* Mac corrected to herself, quite sure by this point the honorific was required. *Although she'd like to know more about the whole* oomling *production side of things.* "They will come with me. As will my *erumisah.*" She gestured grandly and Deruym Ma Nas scuttled back from where he'd been staying at a safe distance.

Someone not quite so sure, Mac thought.

"Come with you—where?" asked Nik.

"With you, of course. Deruym Ma Nas is right in one thing. I will need help. Your help. The help of the Interspecies Union."

Fy's fingers formed their complex knot. *Distress or confusion.* Mac sympathized "To do what?" the Sinzi inquired politely.

A one/two blink of warm golden eyes. "We shall destroy the Ro together. Then I shall restore That Which Is Dhryn to what we once were." Her Glory beamed at Mac. "Mac promised to help."

The Sinzi appeared paralyzed, then her head tilted, as if to let one set of eyes after the other study Mac's carefully noncommittal face.

Suddenly, her fingers shot upward, before gracefully lowering into circles through which she gazed at Mac. "I, Faras, participate in the promise! And I, Yt!"

Nik put one hand over his eyes and shook his head.

This, Mac told herself, *wasn't her fault.*

"I didn't promise," Mac insisted. "At least, I didn't promise what Her Glory thinks I did."

Nik raised one eyebrow. "Dare I ask?"

"It was more a 'that way to the washroom, I'll be here if you need me' kind of promise."

"That's not how She's interpreted it."

Mac slumped against the side of the dart. "I noticed."

"It could be worse," he said lightly, busy with his imp. It was preset to squeal its contents to a Ministry receiver when entering no-space. Something they were to do very soon, judging by the sensor data, so Nik was recording as much information as he could.

Other ships were on the move behind them; they wouldn't catch up. Starting position was everything in real-space travel. The only good news so far? The Imrya had caught signals from the *Annapolis Joy.* No specifics, not on unsecured channels, but Mac was willing to settle for knowing someone was alive. *For now.*

"Worse how?" Mac grumbled. "Fy wants in on it. Whatever it is."

"Worse if you'd promised the Progenitor."

"Oh." She dropped her head to stare at her feet. *Mistake.* The bottoms of her pants and boots were covered in dried blood and slime. She looked up again, breathing through her nose. *Mistake.*

The feeders had followed them to the vast hangar, rising to disappear into its darkness, only to reappear clothed as small silver ships. All five were now lined up between the *Impeci* and the Sinzi dart. Waiting, they'd been assured by Her Glory, for Her to enter Her chosen transport. At which point, they'd latch on to its hull and accompany Her.

Wherever She went.

Seeing the round doors on the lower half of the small things, Mac guessed where tentacles would protrude, allowing the feeders to digest their target, then suck up the result without leaving their casings.

"What are we going to do about them?" she nodded at the silent row.

This gained her a quick look.

A grim one. She straightened. "Nik? What did you do?"

"Let's just say I've prepared an option."

Her Glory was napping by the feeders, conserving Her strength. She'd stopped complaining about being hungry. *Not necessarily a good sign.* Deruym Na Mas sat nearby, nervously checking his imps, nervously checking his surroundings. He was having some difficulty imagining they were to travel outside the Progenitor's ship.

It didn't help that he'd believed the Progenitor's ship was still part of Haven.

Fy was inspecting the *Impeci,* wearing a Sinzi evacsuit from the dart. Meanwhile, those from the *Impeci*—the Imrya and Fiora, the pilot, Bhar, and Cavendish—remained inside her craft. It kept them away from the newest members of—*what were they anyway?* Mac wondered. *A merry band of adventurers? Or the walking dead, too stubborn to lay down?*

Not something Nik would do. She knew that about him. She didn't ask about his "option," trusting it would save them if the feeders couldn't find sufficient walnuts.

Wherever they went.

"Humans?"

It was the Imrya. Mac and Nik rose to their feet as she approached. "Cavendish," he said.

"Yes. He has expired." The alien lifted her recorder, then let it hang from its strap. "I find myself too full of words, Nikolai. A noble being."

Nik merely nodded. With an effort Mac could see, if no one else could, he fought back any reaction, focusing on the task at hand. "Let's get him on the *Impeci*. I want us all in place before transect. We don't know what's on the other side, or even if this ship will hold together." He went with the Imrya, the thorough professional.

Mac stayed where she was.

One less.

She felt ill. If they had to evacuate the Progenitor's ship, Cavendish, terminal and fading, had improved their chances by dying now. *You could never escape the math.* There had been too many of them for the dart.

There still were.

She leaned her head back against the swirled metal. They had the poisoned *Impeci*. The Dhryn could tolerate the radiation inside the Human ship. *That wasn't the problem.* Her Glory couldn't pilot it, not with only one hand.

Bhar, the *Impeci's* pilot, was slipping in and out of consciousness. Fy was needed to pilot the Sinzi dart. And Fiora knew as much as Mac about flying a starship. *Which was nothing.*

Leaving Nik, who knew too much.

He'd wear an evacsuit. Giving him a few hours of protection.

If that. He'd been exposed already.

"I hate this plan, Em," Mac muttered.

Sacrifice the Dhryn? For all they knew, Dhryn might be the only way to kill the Ro.

Sacrificing Nikolai Trojanowski? *Part of the job.*

"I hate the job, too," she said clearly and with emphasis.

"Why are you talking to the air? Does this serve a purpose?" Deruym Ma Nas shuffled closer. "What is that?" This last as Nik walked by them, his eyes straight ahead, carrying the wrapped form of Tucker Cavendish.

"Nie rugorath sa nie a nai." Mac switched to Instella. "A Human, Tucker Cavendish. Remember his name, Archivist."

"I will." He sat beside her. "I fear I will have more names to re-member, Mackenzie Winifred Elizabeth Wright Connor Sol, than there are living Dhryn."

She looked at him. "What you do is important, Deruym Ma Nas. Remember that too."

"It is my value to That Which Is Dhryn," he agreed, then sighed. Mac felt a vibration of distress through the floor. "Is it true? Will the not-Dhryn help us? The Successor is certain. But I have doubts."

"You're her *erumisah*," she said carefully. "Doubt's part of your duty, isn't it?"

"To an extent." A small hoot. "I confess I lose my reasoned ar-guments within Her Light."

"Write them down," she suggested.

. . . Mac felt a vibration of distress through the floor. "Is it true? Will the not-Dhryn help us? The Successor is certain. But I have doubts."

"You're her—" she stopped there, understanding what had happened.

They'd gone through the gate.

The Dhryn looked confused. "Why do we repeat ourselves?"

"I'll explain later. Stay with Her Glory."

Mac started walking toward the *Impeci*. Nik was already coming back. From his intent expression, he'd felt it, too.

A shout from behind—Fiora, from the open door of the dart. "It's Earth! They've taken us home! We're saved!"

Mac didn't need to see the horror on Nik's face to know.

They weren't saved at all.

- CONTACT -

THE SINZI SHIPS HAD BEEN MOVING into position for days. Earthgov had maintained a politely interested view of these proceedings, there being little else to be done. Earth media, having more options, had launched sufficient remote probes to constitute a significant navigation threat to normal traffic, which was rerouted to other orbits.

However much a nuisance, it was the media who first realized what the Sinzi ships were doing. They were arranging themselves into an immense spiral, the narrow end pointing toward the Earth, the wider toward her Sun. The effect was dazzling, when the Moon didn't eclipse it, and the image became commonplace in homes across the system, complete with identifying logos and associated advertising.

Until problems with newspackets and other shipments made the headlines. The curious artistry of the Sinzi slipped from Human attention.

The arrival of the Trisulian fleet, with its threats, soon consumed it. But not, it seemed, the Sinzi, who refused to discuss the matter.

And so matters stood.

Until matters changed.

Hollans rose to his feet. "Say again."

"It's gone, sir."

"The Naralax Transect," he repeated, wondering what could be affecting the usually exemplary staff of Venus Orbital. *Some Trisulian gas?* "You're telling me it's gone."

"Yes, sir. The approach horizon, the gate—they don't register. It's gone, sir. Pending traffic's sitting in normal space. Yelling for answers."

"Let's get confirmation on that, Venus Orbital."

The voice on the com became somewhat shrill. "You don't think we'd call about something like this without making sure we weren't nuts? Sir." More calmly. "We've confirmation from all possible observation points. It's gone."

A slender fingertip rose before Hollans' eyes, claiming his attention. "I'll get back to you, Venus Orbital," he muttered, staring up at the Sinzi-ra for Earth.

"Sir?"

He closed the connection as Anchen took a seat at his gesture. "Did you hear that?" he said numbly. "The Naralax . . . gone?"

"It is not gone, Mr. Hollans." Two fingers inscribed a spiral through the air, rings tinkling. "We have moved it. Temporarily."

"Where?" Hollans gripped the edge of his desk, trying to understand. "Why?"

Anchen smiled. "Where? To Earth orbit. Why?" Her fingers formed loops before her eyes. "We participate in the promise."

- 26 -

HOME AND HORROR

OF THEM ALL, ONLY FY wasn't shocked. *Which was just as well*, Mac thought, since the Sinzi happily busied herself setting up a tactical display at Nik's hoarse request.

"What do you mean—we're in orbit?" The *Impeci*'s pilot, Bhar, had regained consciousness only to doubt he truly had. They'd made him comfortable in the dart's open hatch. "That's impossible," he insisted. "The gate's inside Venus' orbit. It takes almost a week to get to Earth."

"Apparently things have changed," Mac told him. She felt somewhat vindicated by this evidence the transects were not as foolproof as she'd been told. It brought the technology down to the level of a malfunctioning lev; something to be fixed.

Although there was the issue of crashing first.

The tactical display came to life outside the dart, a larger version of what might be generated by an imp. Earth was to one side, a breathtaking swirl of white over blue.

But like the others, Mac kept looking to the other side, where a rotating spiral of silver ships—*Sinzi ships*—dominated the polar sky.

"We are here." Enlarging the display, Fy put her fingertip on a pair of dots. They were within a cloud of similar dots exiting the base of the spiral.

Aimed at Earth.

"All That Are Dhryn," Her Glory rumbled.

Nik's eyes were fixed on the image, his hands clenched into fists. "I knew it," he accused. "The Sinzi will sacrifice Earth for the IU!"

"We participate in the promise—"

"Stop saying that!" Mac shouted at Fy. "This is our world. Our home! Don't you realize what you're doing to us? Why did you bring the Dhryn?"

"We did nothing but come to Sol and move the Naralax in congruence with Earth."

"Why?" Nik repeated, his voice no quieter than Mac's.

Fy's fingers were trembling. "Surely it is obvious—"

"What's obvious is you've betrayed us!" Her own hand shaking, Mac brushed tears from her cheeks. "I trusted you. We all did!"

"Wait," this sharply, from Her Glory. "Look."

The cloud of Dhryn was dispersing before their eyes; they weren't heading for the planet below.

Even as that relief hit, Mac gasped as she saw where they were going. "They—they aren't—"

Fy seemed to relax. "Yes. You see? As anticipated."

All that remained of the Dhryn turned to close on the spiral of Sinzi vessels.

"The Ro must have Called the Progenitors to eliminate the real threat to their plans," observed Her Glory. "We are too late."

"We're still in this," Nik said urgently. "Deruym Ma Nas. Tell the Progenitor—we must break away from the other Dhryn ships, now." The Dhryn looked startled, but ran for the nearest com panel—at least, Mac assumed that's what it was. "Fy," Nik continued, "show me system-wide tactical. Where are the Human ships?"

The display twinned under the Sinzi's direction, the second half showing from Earth inward. "Your fleet is gathered where the Naralax used to be," Fy said unnecessarily. "With a substantial number of Trisulian vessels. Together they approach your world. They will not reach it for another four days at maximum." A growing list of text appeared. Mac didn't try to read it. "Interesting. A substantial number of nongovernment newspackets are entering the gate from your world. I do not recognize the type."

"Media drones," Bhar volunteered. "I don't believe it."

"There's got to be something we can do." Nik yanked out his com and began spouting code and numbers into the device.

Spy stuff.

Mac was staring at Fy. "This won't accomplish anything," she objected. "You'll only die first. The Ro will use our worlds."

"The Sinzi go!" She glanced around at Bhar's hoarse cry. "They're running from the Dhryn."

They all looked. Sure enough, though a few Sinzi ships appeared to be holding position—*perhaps to control the transect gate*—the rest were now leaving the spiral. The result was like a flower opening.

And about as fast.

"You call that running?" Mac wanted to reach into the display and shove the tiny lights out of danger. The Progenitors were gaining every second. "Can't they go faster?

"If they wish," Fy said calmly.

If she was being pursued by giant ships filled with feeders she'd wish a great deal harder, Mac thought, wondering what the Sinzi were up to—*and why it had to be in her corner of the universe.*

"If . . ." Nik closed his hand over his com. "You want the Dhryn to follow." Flat, sure, *that dangerous tone.* "Your people are bait. For what?"

"We promised to keep Anchen safe from the Ro, and to help Mac return home."

"How?" Mac burst out. "By dying?" The Progenitor ships in the display became haloed with a bright glitter. "Those are feeders." *She probably hadn't needed to point that out,* Mac realized, given there were five sitting on the deck behind them.

The first Sinzi ships disappeared within that glitter. Mac reached out blindly, finding warmth with one hand. It wasn't Human.

Her Glory.

Mac turned and stared into that alien face, those golden eyes. Only, for an instant, it wasn't alien at all, the grief in those eyes so real and familiar it was all she could do not to say his name and weep.

"The Progenitor has broken away as you suggested, Vessel," Deruym Ma Nas told Nik. From his tone, the Dhryn was thoroughly confused by the entire process. *Lucky.*

"Where's She going?" Mac asked, trying to find their dot among the many. *Away from the rest would be a positive step.*

The archivist sat down, as if exhausted by the trot to the com panel. *Which he could be,* Mac realized. "Our mission has not changed. The Progenitor hunts the Ro contamination," he told them. "It will be on the planet."

Nik's eyes caught and held Mac's. "Earth," he said.

Not a positive step.

- CONTACT -

THE TELEMATICS AREA of the Atrium was silent, except for technicians' low voices as they relayed information. Above them all, beyond the curve of atmosphere, Sinzi ran. Sinzi died. And when the rest of the Dhryn were finished, everyone knew they'd turn to follow the Progenitor already on course for Earth.

They'd done all they could for the Sinzi. Now it was time to save themselves.

Hollans turned to his aide. "Dee, do we have anything in range?"

Dee grimaced. "Nothing bigger than a docking shuttle. Unless you want to throw shipping crates at them." She checked the 'screen hovering by her ear. "The Sinzi—at least they're buying us time, sir. Evacuations are underway from every continent. How much damage we take depends on where that first Dhryn strikes."

They'd prepared for this—the way a desperate parent realizes she can carry only one child to safety through the fire and must let go of those other small fingers.

The Human species would survive another day, or however long the Ro left them.

"She hasn't said a word?"

Hollans looked over at the Sinzi-ra. Her great topaz eyes gazed at the display, her fingers quiet in their complex weaving, her gown impeccable. A dark red ring winked among the silver on her third left finger. He'd come to notice such things. "No," he answered. "But that doesn't mean silence."

Dee took a message and grabbed Hollans' arm even as she replied into her headset. Then, "Sir! It's Nik. Trojanowski!" Pure triumph. "He's back!"

"Patch him through. Now."

"Here."

"What's going on?" The familiar voice filled the area, drawing everyone's attention.

To the point. *Definitely Trojanowski.* "The Sinzi are being pursued by the Dhryn. Where are you?"

"On the Progenitor Ship heading for Earth. Don't shoot. She's our contact and free of Ro influence. She's after the Ro. Says there's one on Earth."

"We have no—" Hollans stopped as Anchen came up to him. "The Sinzi-ra is here," he said.

"Greetings, Nikolai," as if her kind wasn't in peril. "How is Mac?"

"Here and worried." Quick and sharp. "Sinzi-ra, what are your people doing?"

"What they must," she replied placidly. "Do you require assistance?"

A pause Hollans sympathized with, then a brisk: "Is Dr. Mamani still following the Ro device? We believe it's some kind of a mobile station—where a Ro interacts with real space. Vulnerable. If we can get to it, stop the Ro, that should stop the Dhryn."

Hollans made an urgent gesture to his aide. "We're sending you Dr. Mamani's current position now," he told Nik. "A force will meet you there."

"Have them stand by," came the surprising response.

"For what? You may have noticed time isn't something we have in great supply, Mr. Trojanowski."

"There's a threat, sir. We believe there's a Ro failsafe on the device. We'll need the Sinzi's help to disable it. Sinzi-ra Myriam, Fy, is on board. She'll pass along the details."

A threat—to Earth. Hollans relinquished his place at the com with a bow to Anchen.

To his aide, "Continue evacuation protocols."

- 27 -

CONSEQUENCE AND CHANGE

MAC HAD LISTENED carefully to Nik's plan. It had been as reasonable as anything else she'd heard lately.

She'd just modified it.

Which was why she was jamming her right foot into an evac-suit. The smell curling up from inside reminded her of dead salmon, which, under the circumstances, seemed almost pleasant. *Almost.*

"Tell me again why you're going instead of me, Dr. Connor."

Mac squinted at Bhar. The pilot was on his feet. *And leaning on the edge of the stairs to stay that way.* "Because I could push you down," she observed pleasantly.

"You're a civilian!"

"That's what I keep telling everyone," she agreed, pulling the wretched garment over her shoulders. "They never listen."

Nik, already in the other suit, sealed his visor. "Ready?" His voice came out with a tinny undertone, reminding her of Svehla in his scuba gear.

"Yes," she said, doing her best with the unfamiliar fasteners as she moved.

"Bhar?"

"On my way, sir. Good hunting."

Mac hadn't asked about the *Impeci*, what it would be like. She didn't care. *They'd only be inside as long as it took to drop from orbit to Emily's last known position.*

Home.

Fy was coming with them, as were the Dhryn. All the Dhryn. The Progenitor—both of them—were insistent. Mac eyed the five feeder pods now limpeted to the upper hull. *Probably should call ahead for walnuts.*

Among the elements Nik was coordinating as Sinzi died and they rushed to Earth?

Walnuts could wait.

The remaining Humans would trust themselves to the Imrya's skills with the Sinzi communication system and Earthgov's ability to track them. Fy had preset the dart to soft land on Earth. Mac wished them luck.

The *Impeci*—more specifically Her Successor—would find and destroy the Ro while the Progenitor waited in orbit. *She'd liked the plan.*

She wanted to like the plan, too, Mac told herself wearily. She nodded good-bye to Bhar and waved to the others.

A shame she couldn't.

Mac entered the contaminated ship after Nik, catching up to him in the wide opening that led to the ship's internal corridors. The *Impeci* seemed entirely harmless and ordinary; she could have been inside any overnight transit lev. *If she ignored the radiation warning that scrolled underfoot, its arrows pointing the way to safety.*

Outside.

Where safety was no more than one being's good intentions.

"Nik. Wait." Her voice echoed inside the visor. He pointed to the com control by her chin. Mac pushed it on, fumbling in her haste. "Nik," she repeated. "We can't leave yet. The Progenitor. She's— We can't trust Her."

His visor angled down so he could look at her, but she couldn't see enough of his face to read his expression. His tone was neutral. "She's promised to leave Earth alone."

"But I don't believe She can," Mac said urgently. "Her feeders—they won't let Her starve to death, not with a planetful of life in reach. You brought—" She swallowed hard. "I know you have the means on board."

"You know what you're asking, Mac?" Still that neutral voice.

Optimist, not idiot, Mac wanted to say. Instead, she snapped: "Of course I know," then regretted her temper. *It wasn't Nik's fault.*

She put her gloved hand on his wrist in apology. "We must be able to stop Her, if it becomes necessary."

His glove covered hers. "Spy, remember? A certain level of mistrust's a job skill." More soberly. "I rigged charges when we first boarded, controlled from the *Impeci*. Two failsafes. One's here. Anything interrupts the signal from this ship, boom."

Mac shuddered inwardly. "The other?"

His hand moved to pat the biceps on his other arm.

Gods. "I really didn't want to know that."

"You might need to." A gesture forward. "Let's get going."

She'd—*almost*—prided herself for achieving a level of ruthlessness she'd never imagined before.

Not in Nik's league.

The *Impeci's* bridge was small and straightforward. Once the Dhryn ripped out the chairs, there was room for all of them. Mac stayed back. Her role, if any, would come once they landed.

That had been the modification to the plan. Emily, and she supposed Case Wilson, had used the Tracer to pinpoint the location of the Ro chamber. Mac was the only other Human qualified to use the device; made sense to have her available.

That wasn't why Nik agreed to take her along.

The Ro had used the same technology to find her once. They had—*how had Fy put it?*—an interest in a certain salmon researcher.

Mac crossed her arms as best she could in the evacsuit. *There was,* she thought with no little irony, *distinct circularity to it all.* If she was Sinzi, she'd enjoy it.

The Tracer could find the Ro—Emily's hunt had proved that. What would happen next depended on luring the Ro from its chamber into the open.

So, like the Sinzi running not quite fast enough from the Dhryn, Mac was bait.

Once the Ro was exposed, Her Glory was more than willing to tackle the creature. *And probably could.* Though to Mac's unspoken relief, Nik had assured them that, if needed, reinforcements would be there.

But dealing with the Ro was only the first step. They had to seal the chamber's connection to no-space before it began draining Earth's oceans.

Fy believed it could be done.

They were, Mac decided, *leaping blind.*

"We're clear of the Progenitor," Nik announced. He cued the main screen. A mass of dim silver rushed by overhead, but Mac stared hungrily at their goal. Earth. Northern hemisphere. Pacific. *Home indeed.*

Deruym Ma Nas peered at the display. "What's that?"

Her Glory hooted. "Another world, Deruym Ma Nas."

"Are you sure? It looks too small," the archivist argued.

A louder hoot greeted that.

Fy came up to Mac. The Sinzi version of an evacsuit was a clear membrane, as if the being was coated with flexible glass. It silenced her rings, but not the restlessness of her fingers. "Mac, I have a difficulty."

Nik heard and frowned. *The man who knew the species.* Mac gave him a slight warning shake of her head, having a little more experience with this particular Sinzi. "What difficulty?"

"I must confer in more detail with Anchen—"

"The connection's open, Fy," Nik said, gesturing to the com panel. "But I thought you'd already discussed what needs to be done with the Sinzi-ra." Mac was likely the only one on board who could interpret his tone as: *don't need a problem, busy saving the world.*

Fy spun in a tight circle, fingers close to her body, then stopped as quickly, her neck bending to bring her face almost touching Mac's. "Instella is inadequate," she whispered miserably. "I must speak as Sinzi do, but that's not permitted in front of—"

"Aliens," Mac said helpfully, when the being faltered. The *Impeci* was plummeting to Earth, they were standing in evacsuits to survive even this brief exposure to the contaminated ship, and—*if she grasped the essentials*—the being who was to help save the planet was worrying over manners while her species faced near-extinction.

Somehow, Mac managed not to laugh, protest, or tear at her hair. Watching this exchange, Nik's frown turned into a look of serious concern and he pointed to the time. *Of which they had none.*

"Tell you what, Fy," this as cheerfully as possible. "Close your eyes and pretend we aren't here."

Now Fy was frowning, too, although in a Sinzi the expression involved a painful-looking knot of fingers.

Plan B. Mac reached into the right side pocket of her evacsuit, pushed her hand through the sealant layer, and fumbled her way into the pocket of her coveralls. *Finally a real use for the damn thing.* "Hang on," she grunted, trying to snag her prize with two gloved fingers. *The world dies because she can't reach a stupid . . .* "There!" With that, she tugged free a blue-and-green envelope barred with gold. Her name appeared over its surface in moving letters of mauve. "By the authority of the Interspecies Union," Mac said glibly, "I demand you speak to Anchen in whatever language will save us." She brandished the envelope like a flag under the Sinzi's eyes. "Okay?"

There was a moment of complete silence on the bridge.

Then Fy bowed, almost as graciously as Ureif. "Okay." She walked over to the com, Nik easing out of her way, and called up a 'screen above the com. "Anchen," she said clearly. "Concerning the procedure to close the Myrokynay's no-space connections within the target area. I have additional thoughts, based on the likeliest materials of construction. We must—" the Instella stopped and something else began.

Mac had edged closer, curious. Now she winced and covered her ears, an action which made no difference whatsoever to the bedlam coming through the speakers inside her helmet. The two Dhryn merely looked startled. Nik waved at Mac, then pantomimed how to control the volume. Mac lifted her hand to do so, but waited.

The sound issuing from Fy's mouth was harsh to Human ears not because it was discordant, she realized, but because it was modulating so quickly and along such a scale it came across as static. *No, more than that.* Multiple tones implied a simultaneous conversation, as if Anchen's reply—perhaps more than Anchen's—in the same tongue overlapped Fy's. Certainly Fy's lips hadn't stopped moving.

They listened and spoke at the same time?

Jabulani would love this, Mac thought. Not to mention what it implied of the usual pace of information exchange between the

Sinzi. *They must think we're snails.* The patience and skill required of any Sinzi who had to talk to another species—*no wonder they invented Instella.* They'd needed it so others could talk to them.

Finished, Fy's fingers closed her 'screen. She turned to Nik and Mac. "Anchen has studied the penetration of the consulate by the Ro. Their technology has not significantly advanced with time as has ours. We concur there is room for confidence our efforts will be successful. If the Ro opens its gate, that is. If it remains inactive, we can do nothing."

Great, up the odds. Still, Mac thought this a positive sign. Nik, however, had that expressionless *nothing good* look. "We'll get it to stick its head out," she insisted. "I'm not the only bait." She nodded at Her Glory.

Her Glory, perhaps fortunately, was preoccupied. She was watching the sensors. *Probably good someone was,* Mac thought.

Until the Dhryn's hand shot forward to adjust one control, then another. No haste, but not slow either. "We have new traffic, *Lamisah.*" The announcement was quiet and sure. "Coming through the gate."

Nik did something to the main screen, changing the display from the oncoming ball of ocean and cloud to a stream of code.

Fy let out a string of Sinzi, fingers moving more quickly than Mac could see. The Dhryn rumbled. While Nik, staring at the code, was muttering: "That's . . . that's . . . I don't believe it . . . how . . ."

All of which didn't help a certain biologist one iota.

"Would someone tell me what's going on?" Mac demanded.

- CONTACT -

EACH AND EVERY TRAFFIC controller, from the Antarctic spaceport to the Moon—and way stations between—reacted by locking down anything remotely near Earth orbit, including whatever sat in launch catapults. Although this meant a disruption in shipping likely to result in more than a few stale pastries, no one argued.

There wasn't room for more.

Ships differing in shape, size, and species were pouring from the gate held above the North Pole by the Sinzi. Hundreds. Thousands. There were no com calls. Protocol didn't exist. The only reason they didn't collide on arrival was that exiting from no-space somehow pushed existing matter aside.

That, and the fact that each ship immediately powered up to chase Dhryn.

"Even the Ar," Hollans observed, shaking his head in wonder. "Outstanding."

The Imrya ambassador was standing nearby. "Our fleet was the first through," he pointed out. "These others? Why, some do not have offensive capabilities! What can they hope to accomplish?"

"The same thing we all do, Ambassador," answered Hollans with a grim smile. "To save the Sinzi. To save the IU. Even an unarmed starship can be a weapon, if you have the will."

Anchen had been with consular staff, about to serve species-specific refreshments. Now she came up to the Human and Imrya, and gestured to the display. "You showed them our need and they have come." A deep bow to Hollans. "Thank you."

Hollans lost his smile. "You knew?"

With every military and government resource days away at the original gate, he'd pulled strings at every level, threatened, begged, and bribed, all to send every orbiting Human media packet and snoop satellite through the new gate, with their vid recordings of the Sinzi spiral—and the attack of the Dhryn. There hadn't been time to add explanations. He'd had to trust the images would be enough, even if the eyes seeing them wouldn't be Human.

"What you did? Of course. That any would answer?" A delicate shrug. "We had hope, nothing more. There comes a time, my friends, when actions speak past any differences of language or form. Observe."

Hollans followed the sweep of finger back to the display.

The spreading fountain of Sinzi vessels, the base already engulfed by Dhryn, slowed, then stopped. Before the Dhryn caught up to them, they began to move again, but this time inward, more and more quickly, the fountain collapsing back on itself.

Into the whirlpool of oncoming ships.

All two hundred and seventy Progenitors' ships slowed, then stopped, a decision echoed by the glittering clouds of tiny feeder ships. Then, as if unable to fathom anything but the Call to consume the Sinzi, every Dhryn turned and followed.

The minutes ticked by, positions shifting, the future becoming inevitable.

As the last Sinzi poured through the newcomers to safety, the display showed weaponsfire—a concentrated, targeted stream from every ship capable of it, at point-blank range.

Within minutes, the Great Journey was over. That Which Was Dhryn became nothing more than glowing debris.

Except for one.

A lone Progenitor's ship, with a slagged prow, still on course for Earth.

"Sinzi-ra Anchen?" Hollans asked diffidently. *There was no longer doubt who had planned this—who now would make the decision.*

"We await the final congruence," the Sinzi said. "Would you care for tea, Mr. Hollans?"

- 28 -

CONGRUENCE AND CONFRONTATION

MAC WAITED FOR THE OTHER SHOE to drop. Nik was busy on the com to Hollans, passing along congratulations and whatever else people said to one another during a victory celebration. *Victory,* she thought numbly. Her Glory, still at sensors, had showed no emotion as the IU destroyed Her kind. Deruym Ma Nas hadn't understood. *His Progenitors did.*

Unlike the Dhryn, Fy was visibly shaken. She hovered beside Mac and her fingers flowed up and down in short flutters, as if she tried to fly.

"Are you all right?" Mac asked at last.

"I'm in accord," Fy replied—*hopefully a yes.* "Other members of the IU now have proof we were as much at risk as they from the Dhryn. Their response—its result? I don't know the Human equivalent to how I feel, Mac. As you see, I cannot move slowly, as you've wisely suggested is appropriate. I shall never forget this moment. It will reshape what I am. Thus for all Sinzi."

Mac frowned. "I don't understand."

"Many of us died today." A fingertip rested on Mac's chest for an instant. "As you go where you're needed, so must we. The transects must be maintained and kept safe for all. My Faras-self is capable and will assume this task." A lift of two fingers, like a Human shrug. "Others will go to do the same."

"What of your research?" Mac asked.

"My Yt-self will continue." Fy's triangular mouth formed a

passably Human smile. "She enjoys the hunt. To answer questions and seek new ones. To disturb the dust. Do not fear I'll—"

. . ."What of your research?" Mac asked—*again!*—then stared at the Sinzi. "What just—"

Her Glory shouted, "On intercept!"

There was always another shoe.

As if outside of panic, Mac considered the situation and snorted to herself. *Okay, with aliens, it could be more than two shoes. Or none.*

Life used to be so simple.

Nik was answering the Dhryn, his voice tense. "I see it. Fy— we'll need to sharpen our approach, get some speed."

"What is it?" Mac started to follow the Sinzi to her console, walking between the two Dhryn to reach Nik. "What's—"

A grip that would have broken her flesh arm. "It's them!" shrieked Deruym Ma Nas. "I saw them. I saw them before! I know that shape!"

Mac's eyes leaped to the main screen, no longer a *to-her* meaningless mass of codes. Instead, it showed a spire hanging in the darkness.

"So do I," she said numbly.

The Ro had stopped hiding.

CONTACT -

CASE RAISED THE VIEWER TO HIS EYES, turning slowly to scan the sea ice. "What I thought. She's gone past the pressure ridge." He pointed to a line of heaved, upthrust white, the sleeve of his well-worn cold weather suit pressed flat by the biting wind. His hair stood straight.

Probably frozen. 'Sephe leaned her chin into her com, tucked inside the warmth of her hood. The former fisher had assured her this was spring. *Hadn't arrived as far as she could tell.* "This is Stewart. Inform Hollans Dr. Mamani isn't back yet. Does he want me to go and get her?"

She waited for the reply behind a dubious shelter of mem-fabric, hoping the answer would be no.

The Tracer had led them to this icy desolation. *According to Emily.* The Ro— or whatever they followed—had stopped. *According to Emily.* They'd been moving the harvester lev in steadily decreasing circles ever since. Now, the good doctor finally satisfied, they waited while she fine-tuned whatever it was. Which required peace and quiet. Without company.

According to Emily. Case hadn't argued. 'Sephe had learned to watch him for signals when Emily Mamani was pushing herself too far. Impossible to tell otherwise. The woman was driven.

So long as she went in the right direction, 'Sephe was happy. *She didn't want to follow her out on the ice.*

"Hollans here."

'Sephe straightened, the wind hitting her back. "Yes, sir."

"This isn't a conversation call. We're about to take out the hostile. Get Dr. Mamani back from wherever she's gone and stand by."

Before 'Sephe could acknowledge, there was a sudden *crack*, as if a whip had snapped across the sky. She looked up in time to see the rear of the harvester drop away.

"We're under attack!" she shouted, then ran for Case.

The sea exploded around them.

- 29 -

ENEMIES AND ENDS

"T HE TRUE BATTLE BEGINS!"
"Stay at your post!" Nik snapped at the aroused Dhryn. Her Glory subsided, but Mac could feel the vibration of her rage through the deck. "It's not our fight," he continued. "We're after the one on Earth. Monitor what's going on. How's the Progenitor?"

This brought an anguished moan from Deruym Ma Nas. Mac put her hand on his shoulder and bent to his ear. "Trust them, *Erumisah*," she said in Dhryn. "As She does."

Did the Progenitor know what Nik had left behind on Her ship? Did she understand what her lamisah *might do in the name of their own kind?*

Mac doubted any answer to those questions could remove the sick feeling from her stomach. She looked for a bright side. *Maybe it was the first sign of radiation poisoning.*

"The Ro do nothing," Her Glory rumbled. Then, "Aha! The Progenitor sends Her Mouths against them. We shall prevail!"

"Why don't they counterattack?" Fy pointed at the silent, motionless Ro ship.

Nik didn't look up from the *Impeci*'s controls. "I think they are," he said. "Looks like we were right—the autodestruct can't affect Her ship. But they'll—"

The display was erased by a blinding flash, then reset itself. Mac's visor compensated. The Dhryns' eyes, she noticed, were now protected by that blue inner lid. Fy had her fingers before her eyes and appeared in distress, but she had no time to check on her.

What was happening was before them all.

The Ro had fired on the Progenitor.

As Her great ship began to glow in wide bands—*almost mim-icry*—Mac held onto Deruym Ma Nas, although the battered older Dhryn did nothing more than thrum his distress. *Finally under-standing what he saw,* she thought, and held tighter.

She'd remembered the Ro ship as a towering splinter of bronze and light, accompanied by other, much smaller splinters. On the *Impeci's* screen, she saw the reality. The main splinter was not a single piece, but three identical shards, like immense crystal fingers. Those, like the smaller pieces, were connected by crisscrossing scaf-folds, their tips toward the embattled Progenitor, as if whatever beam or power had been used originated from those ends.

All the while feeders swarmed over the Ro ship, fastening to its sleek surfaces, corroding through. Despite what she knew, Mac silently urged them on, but it was too little, too late.

The last Progenitor's ship lost its shape and reflection, turning dark as it was liquefied before their eyes. Fragments burst away. *Their contribution?* It didn't matter. She was gone.

Deruym Ma Nas curled into a massive ball of misery, eyes shut tight. But Her Glory began shouting at Nik. "Let me call them! They are mine now!"

At first, stung by grief, Mac couldn't understand what the Dhryn wanted so desperately.

Nik did.

"Stay back!" His weapon flashed out. "I won't let you send them against Earth!"

Mac stared at the screen. The dots that were the feeders now drifted aimlessly away from the Ro ship. *They might be mindless, but they reacted as if they knew their Progenitor was dead and they no longer had function.*

"Fool! I'll send them against our enemy! My Vessel, tell him!"

The Ro ship was tilting. *Aiming at them!*

"Nikolai. The other ships can't reach us before the Ro fire," Fy said quietly.

Why was everyone looking at her?

"All I know," Mac told him, "is we can talk to Her Glory."

Nik whirled and punched a sequence of buttons. "Do it," he

told the Dhryn over his shoulder, his eyes wild. "This should reach them."

Hadn't put down the weapon, Mac noticed.

Her Glory sat on Her four legs, and closed Her mouth. Before Mac could do more than frown with surprise, the Dhryn's sides began moving in and out.

If she'd thought the deck vibrated before, this was paramount to a quake. Mac tore her eyes back to the screen. "It's working!" she cried as dots began moving back to the Ro.

The Ro ship tipped further. Dots winked out in line with its sparkling prow. It continued to turn over, like an immense broom sweeping space clear.

"We're entering the atmosphere," Fy exclaimed.

The Ro ship was almost in line with them.

Nik looked at Mac and shook his head. "We're not going to make it."

Suddenly, a new voice screamed: "We take our vengeance!" The display filled with a black hull even as alarms rang through the small bridge.

"Damn Trisulian almost clipped us! Where'd she come from?" Nik demanded, hurrying back to the controls. The alarm fell away.

Fy's fingers were flying over her console, but it was Her Glory who answered. "Through the gate. They must have vectored in behind the Progenitor. There are more—"

On cue, the speaker blared again, this time with a familiar voice. "Sorry we're late. Got a bit crowded back there. Glad you've left us something to do."

"Welcome to the party, Captain." Nik's smile was a beautiful thing.

Captain Gillis?

Mac sagged against the conveniently still-comatose archivist. "The *Joy*—?" she whispered.

"We're battered and bloody, but we've teeth. The walkers left when you did. Thanks for that." The voice faded, then came back loud and clear. "We'll keep this guy busy. Good hunting. *Joy* out."

Nikolai Trojanowski shut off the display, then looked around the bridge. His head was up, his eyes bright and fierce. He held out his hand to Mac as she rose to her feet. He nodded to Fy. "Sinzi-ra," he said with a slight bow. "Put her down at the coordinates for Dr. Mamani. Mac? We need to change."

The air hit like a drug. Mac drew in a greedy gasp, coughed at the cold, then immediately took another, each feeling as though it went straight to her arteries.

"There!" Nik shouted, his arm raised to point.

Mac was busy looking the other way. "Ah, Nik?"

He turned and glanced up. The five feeders they'd brought were lifting free from the hull of the *Impeci*, their small craft noiseless and quick.

They weren't alone.

A dozen, maybe more, were overhead.

"Do not fear, *Lamisah*!" Her Glory boomed. "These shall drink only of the Ro!"

"Oh, good," Mac replied, for want of anything better to say.

Nik shrugged and pulled up his hood. "Let's go."

They'd only started walking when he touched her arm. "We're expected."

Mac followed his gesture. Coming behind them was a line of Ministry levs, large, black, and thoroughly reassuring.

Less reassuring was the plume of smoke beyond the levs, rising from a crashed hulk on the ice. "The harvester!" Mac gasped. "Emily!"

But she took only one step in that direction before Nik grabbed her. "She's not there, Mac. C'mon!"

"This way!" Her Glory was already on the move, her six legs churning. *Those padded feet were perfect for irregular ice,* Mac couldn't help but notice. Better traction than her borrowed boots, intended for a man half again her size.

It didn't matter. None of it mattered now. She could see their goal for herself: Emily, a dark slim line against the gray-blue ice, her attention on the Tracer.

They stumbled forward, levs landing all around them. Emily's hood was off. Mac saw the flash of pale as she twisted her head to check out the newcomers, then turned back to the machine.

"She's got it," Mac shouted to Nik as they ran. "She's found it!"

Armored figures began pouring from the levs. Some carried equipment. There were shouts, orders. Some at them. Nik slowed as someone claimed his attention. Several someones, like ice-white trees with topaz eyes. *Sinzi!*

Mac kept running, for these last few steps with one hand gripping the Dhryn beside her to take advantage of the larger being's power. Their breath puffed, out of sync.

A final slide and rush, and they arrived.

"Hi, Mac. About time you got here." Emily's lips pulled from her teeth in a predator's grin. Her eyes touched and dismissed the Dhryn. "I see we need to talk. Later. He's coming up." She drew a finger through the 'screen hovering above the console. "See?"

It felt so utterly normal that Mac stepped to the console without a second thought, her eyes reading the status. "The 'bots are under the ice," she said in wonder. And not in a straight line, as they'd used to scan the Tannu River, but closing in a circle like a net. "They've been reliable?"

"Good as your finny friends," boasted Emily. "Case helped with the mod. But can we focus on that, please?" "That" being something large and asymmetrical, rising slowly from the depths.

Not that slowly. "It's underneath us?" Mac shifted her feet.

"We're on top of it," Em countered cheerily. "Perfect! I admit, I was wondering how to get its attention. Seemed set on anchoring to the bottom here. Running into it with 'bots didn't seem to make any difference. But it began moving a moment ago. I should have known you'd bring the right bait." This time, she did look at the Dhryn, a long assessing look. "Interesting."

"Later," Mac reminded her. "Emily, we've a problem. This thing—" she pointed at their quarry. "It's capable of taking the ocean with it. Through some kind of no-space gate."

"Why?"

It was still rising. Mac could hear shouts across that ice and hoped that Nik and the Sinzi were ready with whatever they had.

If they had anything . . .

If the Ro ship had been destroyed . . .

If the feeders knew the difference between friend and foe . . .

Mac shrugged. In so many ways, the future might be measured in heartbeats.

Not her problem.

"The Ro are trying to regrow themselves," she explained quickly. "Here. In the ocean. When they're stopped, they retrieve whatever they've done, including the water. We don't know if it's deliberate or a consequence—but that's why the Chasm worlds are dry, Em. The Dhryn killed the Ro, but their gate took away the water."

"We shall kill the Ro." Ice snapped as Her Glory spoke for the first time. Her hand rose to the feeders overhead.

Emily followed the gesture with her eyes and appeared transfixed. "Gods, Mac. What have you done?"

"Later," Mac said again. "Listen to me, Em. You, too." She smacked Her Glory on a broad shoulder. "We have to do this in the right order. The Ro has to come out first, hear me? We let the Sinzi do whatever they can. Then we—" *hold a meeting, ask its name, check its agenda,* "—then we kill it," she said, cold and sure.

Her species imperative.

"Which means we have to get out of the way!" Mac glanced at the readout. *The Ro was accelerating upward.* "Now would be good," she urged.

Her Glory was moving back. Emily shook her head, staying with the Tracer, her fingers reaching for its 'screen. "Just let me—"

"Em!" Mac reached for Emily and pulled with all her might.

The ice smashed open from below, blocks and crystal shooting in all directions. They were knocked flat.

And a huge writhing mass of *red* reached for the sky.

She'd expected a machine or some obscene blend like a walker. *Not this.* On her back beside Emily, Mac stared up into what was most definitely alive.

Not a tentacle, she decided. More like a rapidly growing tendril or root, pulsing wider every bit as quickly as it expanded in length. Transparent in places, with budlike protrusions also growing. Utter black in others. All of it in motion, yet she could swear she glimpsed stars within those patches of darkness.

~YOU WILL NOT INTERFERE WITH US~

The words tore into Mac's skin, cutting to the bone. She could hear Emily screaming.

The pain wasn't as important as the triumph. *They had the Ro!*

~WE CONTINUE~

Mac writhed, her back arching, but found her voice. "We'll stop you!"

~YOU ARE INSIGNIFICANT. YOU WILL END~

Agony!

~WE ARE WHAT WILL LIVE FOREVER~

The tendril seemed to reach the clouds.

There was a roar that shook the ice. Mac and Emily clung to one another.

Then, gently, it began to rain.

Green rain, the color of growing things, of spring.

The first drops struck the tendril and it flung itself from side to side, succeeding only in spreading the liquid.

More drops fell.

Great suppurating wounds appeared. The tendril flailed once more, then dropped to the ice with a heavy thud.

~WE MUST SUR~

And more drops fell.

Until nothing was left of the tendril but a pool of green liquid on the ice.

Then the mouths began to drink.

- 30 -

FRIENDS AND FINALES

MAC SPAT SNOW.

"You dead?" Emily asked, her tone one of idle curiosity.

Cold. And it felt like someone had pounded nails through her skin. Mac took a cautiously deep breath. "Nope. You?"

Emily Mamani rolled over on her stomach. Her dark eyes shone. There was snow in her hair. "Doesn't look like it."

"What about everyone else?"

The two biologists sat up and looked around.

Floating ice filled the hole torn by the Ro. Crystals were sifting into the cracks. The hole would be gone soon.

The ocean remained.

They'd done it. Mac said it to herself. *Didn't quite believe, yet.*

"Tracer's pooched," Emily commented. Sure enough, all that showed of the device was a bent support strut poking through the ice.

"Looks like it." They helped each other stand, the process complicated more by a tendency to giggle than the freshening wind. "What parts do you—"

"Mac!" She whirled at the voice and immediately lost her footing. It didn't help that Nik slipped as he tried to catch her. They fell to the ice laughing.

Emily leaned over to look down at them. "Gee, that's romantic."

"Get your own spy," Mac said, and proceeded to pay attention to her own.

There were details. *There were always details,* Mac fussed, holding Nik's hand. It wasn't that she didn't care, it was more that she viewed what was done as done.

Time to move on.

She could taste spring in the air, this close to the Arctic Circle.

But no, there were details. Which required standing in what the Ministry apparently viewed as a landing field. *She could tell them a thing or two about the seeming permanence of sea ice.* The levs were hovering, at least. The scattered clumps of people were taking their own chances.

Though a shot of hypothermia didn't seem to worry anyone at the moment.

The crew of the harvester were recovering from it. The few who'd been on board when the Ro attacked had landed in the icy water. They'd all been wearing survival skins beneath their gear. *Base regulations had their reasons,* Mac thought rather smugly.

"What's the situation?" Nik asked a newcomer, another of the armored anonymous in black.

The Sinzi had brought their own equipment. Mac had listened to the edges of that conversation. Something about transect gate management then the Sinzi ran out of words. She'd been mildly entertained by the ensuing charades, particularly as the Sinzi were wearing slim gloves over their muscular fingers, the *lamnas* adding odd lumps. They'd lost her well before the other Humans stopped nodding and looked mutely grateful.

The Sinzi weren't in danger of losing their role as no-space guardians any time soon, Mac thought. Although she suspected there'd be some hard discussions about consulting with their allies rather than simply maneuvering them into a desired location.

The Naralax Transect was as it had been, Sol's gate where it had been, to the relief of Venus Orbital and the now-quiet Trisulian armada.

She wasn't even going to ask. The Sinzi had put themselves at risk to prove a point. The Trisulians—they'd made a point as well. The Inner Council faced a hard decision. *If they asked her,* Mac thought, while profoundly hoping no one did, *she'd wait until after they'd all given birth.* No new mother in her experience had time to make trouble.

And there'd been enough suffering.

She found herself yawning and watched the cloud of breath condense.

Nik's hand abruptly tightened. "Mac. Wake up!"

"Wasn't asleep," she protested, shifting from foot to foot. *Maybe close.*

"You tell her," he ordered, shaking his head and grinning.

The newcomer tapped his left forefinger against his holster and Mac's eyes widened. "Sing-li?"

Up went the visor, revealing a huge grin. "Can't fool you, Mac. Nice having you back."

Her smile was so wide it hurt. "Nice to be back."

Sing-li glanced at Nik, then at her. "I see you're in good hands." *With a wink.*

She tried to scowl, but couldn't. "I think so," she grinned, tightening her arm around Nik's waist.

"The message?" Nik suggested. *She could hear his smile.*

"Delighted, sir. Dr. Connor," semiofficious, "a message for you has been relayed from Myriam." Another wink. "There's only one person I know who could sneak something personal directly here and this fast."

"Fourteen!" *Definitely awake now.* "What's he say?"

"It's not exactly from our talented Myg," Nik warned, his grip firming.

Mac stamped her boot on the ice. "Before I freeze, gentlemen?" she suggested.

Sing-li tried to compose his face into something more serious. *Didn't work,* Mac thought, waiting impatiently. "Here you go. 'There will be a full review of all upcoming projects in the Wilderness Trust before'—there's a line under 'before,' Mac—any such projects resume.' Signed Charles Mudge III.'" A pause. "Oh. Sorry, Mac. I didn't think it would make you cry. We can deal with him," almost grimly.

"Not crying." Mac burrowed her head into Nik's chest and hiccuped helplessly. "Laughing," she managed to say. *If there were some tears mixed in, that was her business.* Mudge was alive! "I can deal with Oversight, Sing-li. Trust me."

She had less to say when, shortly afterward, Nikolai Trojanowski was informed by another messenger that his ship had left orbit some time ago. Along with Her Glory, Deruym Ma Nas, several replete feeders, and one Sinzi.

They'd made it through the gate before the Sinzi removed it from Earth orbit.

Her spy hadn't seemed surprised.

"I hate these things."

"The clothes?" Emily gave her a critical look up and down. "Looks fine to me. Two has good taste."

Mac tugged at the rich blue jacket. "You know what I mean," she said darkly. "These things. These—" She waved wildly.

"Oh, and that's clear, Dr. Connor? C'mon. Get down."

Mac stepped from the platform in front of the Sinzi mirror. "While we're at it," she complained, "why do you get to wear normal clothes?" She looked at Emily with envy.

Emily Mamani wore coveralls, with useful pockets. And shoes that weren't going to trip her. *Not that she wasn't gorgeous*, Mac thought, trying to pin down exactly what gave the other woman that glow. Something in the face, perhaps. Freedom.

Purpose.

As represented by the necklace Emily now lifted between two gloved fingers. "Four down," she said, flipping past those red beads. "Three on the ship. One in the ice." The remaining beads were white. "Seven to go. Which makes eleven." She dropped the necklace savoring the word. "Didn't I tell you?"

"Yes, but you were nuts," Mac reminded her.

The Trisulian warship, with help from others from Myriam, had disabled the Ro ship—*if that's what you called something closer in function to a factory,* she thought. But it had already been crippled; the Progenitors, old and new, had had their revenge after all. Early reports described vast areas used to dismantle and rebuild living

tissue, others as storerooms for completed walkers and other machines. The Ro themselves? They'd been physically bound to
their ship as well as somehow existing outside of it. When the
Sinzi terminated its no-space connection, three had reappeared.
In pieces.

The chamber beneath the ice—what was left of it after the feeders had been called away by Her Glory—had been filled with preserved embryonic cells, all of the same basic pattern as the Ro
themselves. Enough to saturate an ocean. Enough to restart their
kind at the expense of any other.

The IU planned to waste no time tracking down the remaining
Ro, fearing the beings would retreat before they could be found
and destroyed. There would be no more negotiation. It had become apparent even to the idiot faction that the goals of the Myrokynay and the rest of the IU were mutually exclusive.

Survival depended on stopping the Ro while they still could.

Someone else's battle, Mac thought. Speaking of which. "When
do you leave?" she asked Emily.

"The N'not'k await!" That wicked grin. "Don't worry, I'll stay
long enough to catch your speech."

"I am not," Mac gritted her teeth, "giving a speech."

Emily ignored her. "Loved the last one, by the way. Did you
know they'll be broadcasting to the IU?"

"Won't matter," Mac said, heading for the door. *Get it over with.*
"Not giving a speech," she muttered. "Going to sit at the back and
enjoy my supper. Two promised me shrimp. You," she jerked her
thumb at Emily, "give a speech."

"Coward."

Mac stopped at the door and turned. "Behave. And be careful,"
she said. Before it could become emotional, she made herself
frown. "Keep track of the field season. I'll have your gear at the station, but try not to arrive late next time."

Emily tapped her on the nose. "Careful's my middle name. But
Mac?" She shook her head, her eyes warm yet strangely distant. "I
won't be coming back. You can keep my stuff. Oh, I'll visit," this
quickly as Mac's face must have shown her shock. "But I'm kind of
popular right now, if you've noticed. Sencor's begged to renew my
funding. There's that aquatic world out there. I'll be able to do

what I want for some time." Her lips twisted to the side. "After I save the known universe."

"That first," Mac managed.

A hint of worry creased Emily's forehead. "You do understand, don't you? Fish really aren't my thing."

That word again.

Unfortunately, she did. "The Survivor Legend. You haven't given up."

"Never!" A quick hug and that dazzling smile. "It's still a puzzle, Mac. What happened to that one world, among all the rest. *Aie!* Now that we're getting a clearer picture—the mystery only deepens!" Emily laughed. "I'll stop. You don't want to be late for your speech."

"I'm not," Mac said clearly as she opened the door, "giving a speech."

They weren't all here. The realities of in-system space travel being what they were, it wouldn't have been possible to bring everyone. *Someone must have tried,* Mac thought as she surveyed the crowd on the Sinzi's vast patio. Her father and brothers; Emily's family. Hollans, of course, with a quite remarkable number of Ministry personnel. *In truly awful shirts.* She smiled to herself. Fourteen was here in spirit.

Her *nimb,* he'd informed her smugly, was waiting at Base. *Hopefully in a box.*

She counted alien species she recognized, getting into the forties before deciding "all of them" likely covered it—including the ones in the fountain she'd still never met in person. Most she didn't know. *Biospace.* She liked the word.

"Nice speech," Nik commented, his breath tickling her ear.

She gave him a suspicious look.

"No, really." *That dimple.* "Short, to the point. I think the Imrya, maybe a few others, expected more than 'Thank you for inviting me tonight. Support research. Enjoy the party.' But not me." He laid one hand over his heart. " 'Twas pure Mac."

Mac sighed. "I hate these things. My mind goes blank. You,

though?" She bumped her shoulder against his. "Even Blake was impressed. And that's saying something."

Nik had been more than eloquent. He'd stood before them all—vidbots and living eyes—to tell them exactly how close they'd come to disaster. Without naming names, or species, he'd made it plain that only courage and sacrifice had saved them when diplomacy faltered. The silence at the end had been more telling than any applause.

"I hope so. He kept grilling me. I think Owen and your father took notes. I've had easier interrogations, believe me."

"That's a good sign," Mac assured him. "Blake ignores people he doesn't like." She slipped her arm through his, watching as the groups below milled around the various bars and entertainments. Not at random. There were preferences. The weather being what it was, the staff had erected either heaters or chillers on poles throughout the expanse. The resulting pattern was quite fascinating. *She should make notes.*

Later. They'd found this quiet spot away from the rest. *They deserved it.*

"Do I intrude, Mac, Nikolai?"

"Of course not," Nik said immediately.

"Anchen!" Mac grinned with delight. "I wondered when we'd see you."

The gracious Sinzi bowed, her fingers spreading. "I waited. There were many demands on us all. Now, in the pause before departures, comes the right time to complete our promise."

A word that now made her nervous. "Please tell me this won't involve the entire civilized universe."

"Mac!" Nik looked horrified. "Sinzi-ra, there was wine with supper—"

"Giving a speech. Didn't drink," she informed him haughtily.

Anchen's fingers shivered in her laugh. "Always you speak your mind, Mac. I value this even more highly after our absence from one another. You are a joy to me, a nexus who will always be centered within my beings." This with a brush of those fingers through Mac's hair.

She restrained the urge to stick out her tongue at Nik. *Wine, indeed.* "So once I give you my gift, we're done?" *And safe?* "No more promises?" In case the Sinzi took that as a request, Mac hurriedly added, "which doesn't mean I'm suggesting one."

"You have already done so, Mac." Another bow. "I am honored to participate in your new promise."

Oh-oh. Mac glanced at Nik. He, for his part, was looking magnificently noncommittal. *Which meant he knew something she didn't.* "What promise would that be?" she asked warily.

"The promise you made to Her Glory, in which Fy became the first participant. Your Ministry's ship," this to Nik, "will be decontaminated and returned, Nikolai."

"You're sheltering the Dhryn." Mac chewed her lip and this notion for a moment, then nodded. "Thank you."

"Shelter? No. Your promise was to help the Dhryn survive."

Mac could almost hear Brymn's anxious questions. *"How many of us must survive . . . what is our evolutionary unit?"* "Ureif and I—we talked about a future for the species. I don't know if that's possible from one, Sinzi-ra."

"We will search the derelict ships for more survivors. Regardless, there are means to promote diversity," Anchen said with serene confidence. "Trust that we have seen the path taken by the Myrokynay and will tread more carefully, Mac. There is animosity toward the Dhryn, as well as gratitude for their help against the Ro. Her Glory wishes to continue to provide this help while we Sinzi undertake our portion."

"Your portion?"

Nik spoke. "The Sinzi have begun the restoration of Myriam."

Mac blinked. "Pardon?"

"Water is the first concern," Anchen replied, perhaps thinking Mac's shocked expression meant she required specifics. "We will work with experts on that world, including your colleagues. Technology will be in place soonest. The biology will follow apace. My understanding is that there have been caches of viable seeds recovered. Other species will have to be approximated or non-Dhryn substitutes found. The Dhryn will have a future, Mac. We participate in the promise."

The regeneration of an entire world. Unensela would be ecstatic. They'd all be. Her entire team.

She'd have to keep in touch.

"That's quite the promise," Mac ventured, beginning to smile.

"It attracts our interest, too. And now, I believe you have something for me?"

Mac reached into the pocket of her lovely jacket—*staff having realized the necessity of such things*—and drew out the salmon carving. "For your collection." She grinned at Nik, then offered it to the alien. "It's a well-traveled fish."

Anchen's fingertip wrapped around the tiny thing. Her mouth trembled, then smiled. "I'm overwhelmed. It shall have a place of honor."

Nik held out his hand. On the palm was a single *lamnas*. "Thank you," he said, his voice husky with emotion. "This is the last one."

Anchen didn't take the ring. "Surely you still need it?"

Mac felt a stir of worry. "Why?" Then, she looked at Nik and *knew*. "You're leaving." The words seem to come from someone else.

He met her eyes. Seeing the remorse in his, she took an involuntary step back. "You're leaving now. With Emily. To hunt the Ro."

"It's the job."

"You don't have to." Her hands were fists. "Someone else can go." Anchen looked from one Human to the other, but remained silent.

Nik closed the distance between them. "You could come with us, Mac." Low and intense. "Help finish your work."

"My work?" She paused in disbelief, then half smiled, as if to share a joke. "Don't you remember? I study salmon, Mr. Tro-janowski."

"There you are, Norcoast!"

Mudge was climbing the stairs toward them, his cane banging every step. He looked flushed and irritated.

And alive.

"You shouldn't be out of bed," Mac told him.

"There's nothing wrong with me." He squinted at her through his good eye, the line from scalp to jaw over the other being covered with the Sinzi's wonderful bandaging. *He wouldn't lose it.*

Others on the *Joy* hadn't been so lucky.

Mudge looked from Nik to Mac. He *harrumphed* uneasily. "I'm interrupting—"

Mac swallowed and stood straighter. "No. What is it?"

"My lev to Vancouver's arrived early. I came to say good-bye." He hesitated and studied her face for an instant. "There's room, Norcoast," this in a gentle voice, "if you're ready to go home."

Home.

"Unless this is a bad time—"

"No," Mac said unsteadily, not looking at Nik. "It's the perfect time."

Time to return to who and what she was.

- 31 -

RESUMPTION AND REWARD

LATE SEPTEMBER PAINTED the upper forest slopes with orange and yellow, poplar and tamaracks showing off their colors. Eagles and ravens gathered to argue over river shoals. Bears grew fat. And mice collected the velvet from antlers, in anticipation of the cold.

Deeper in the valleys, all remained green and lush, as if to belie winter's approach, while sleek-sided Coho sported heavy jaws and attitude as they rushed up the rivers to spawn.

"You're sure the scanner's in place?" Mac leaned out over the cliff, one hand on the edge.

A dizzying distance below, a Frow danced along the loose rock, humming to *ne-self.* "You worry too much, Mac," *ne* called up. "I've checked it twice."

She was sorely tempted to drop something. *The Frow would only enjoy catching it.* She grinned. Hadn't lost a tool since her latest grad student's arrival.

And once she'd let *Ne* Drysolee pitch *ne's* tent on the cliff face above the field station, she'd slept much better. *Something Mudge didn't need in a report.*

He'd been touchy since Fourteen's last visit. Mac winced slightly. *Though she did see his point.* The now child-sized offspring hadn't grasped that picking her flowers wouldn't go over well— and they'd picked quite a few before she'd noticed. *Including a number of small trees.* Mudge had produced so many forms for her to complete, she'd insisted on finishing at the restaurant. *On his bill.*

Mac got to her feet and headed for her tent. There was rain on the way as much as salmon. She'd left her coat off, the day having been warm and pleasant. One of those gifts.

"You expecting company?" Case asked, standing behind the console, wrench in hand. He'd come for the week to help install a modified version of the Mamani Tracer. *Twitchy in two days.* She wasn't sure if it was the Frow's fascination with his freckles or the cliffs.

"Not unless you've called a ride," she told him, glancing down the valley. It was a skim from Base. With Ty driving, by the look of it.

"Why would I do that? Because you're a slave driver and expect everyone to exist on food through a straw?" He chuckled as she pretended to scowl. "I'm used to it."

Ne Drysolee's two-pointed hat appeared above the cliff edge. "Perhaps they send us pizza, Case! Or ribs! Ribs, Mac!"

No matter the species, students always ganged up on her. Mac shook her head. "Don't even start. Help unload whatever it is, but don't waste time. They should be here today."

She ducked into her tent and retrieved her coat, catching sight of Wilson Kudla's latest on the box by her cot. She winced. *Dedicated to her; really should read the damn book,* she thought guiltily. *Later.*

Mac hunted and found the bag of moss she wanted sent back to her new garden. *No point wasting the ride.*

When she came out, however, Mac let the bag drop.

The skim had landed. Ty leaned against its side, grinning.

And Nikolai Trojanowski was walking toward her, wearing his suit and cravat, carrying his office over one shoulder.

No glasses. *Unless she counted the pair in her tent, tucked in the velvet case along with the one* lamnas *she'd never brought herself to view, having said good-bye enough for one lifetime.*

All she could think of was, "You do know it's going to rain." For proof, she lifted her coat.

He stopped just out of reach. "Hello, Mac."

What was she supposed to say now?

Case nonchalantly tossed his wrench over the cliff to keep *Ne Drysolee* occupied, then went to talk to Ty.

Fine, desert her.

"What are you doing here?" Mac blurted out.

Nik reached into his pocket and drew out an envelope, his eyes never leaving hers.

"Oh, no," she warned. "Don't you even think about it."

Paying no attention, he opened and held out a piece of ordinary mem-paper. "This is a formal complaint, Dr. Mackenzie Connor," in his most official voice. "I suggest you pay attention."

"Complaint?" She frowned. "From who? About what?"

"From the Oversight Committee of the Castle Inlet Wilderness Trust. To the Interspecies Consulate. Regarding the presence of unauthorized aliens within an Anthropogenic Perturbation Free Zone. Class Three."

"He's a registered student!" She snatched at the sheet and crumpled it into a ball. "Oversight's gone too far." *She'd even sent a new pot for his damn plant.* "You can just take this back and—"

Nik's eyes were smiling. "You didn't read it."

She muttered something anatomically unlikely, but opened the ball and gave its contents a quick glance.

Then a look.

Then a longer look.

"If that's okay with you, Dr. Connor?"

It was a request for a permanent on-site liaison from the consulate, to ensure any nonterrestrials interested in pursuing studies with the famed Dr. Connor would be supervised by someone knowledgeable. *In other words, watched like a hawk so they didn't break Oversight's rules.*

"This better not come out of my budget," she said, carefully not looking up. *Did he see her hands tremble?*

"Not at all."

"And this—liaison—stays out of the way."

"Absolutely. He'll even cook."

At this, Mac finally raised her eyes. "I thought you were gone," she said very quietly. She pointed up.

"I tried," Nik said just as quietly, stepping closer. "Then I realized it was time to come home."

Mac opened her arms to bring him the rest of the way.

Below, dorsal fins sliced the dark water, disappeared, rose again with a muscular heave. Rose-black bodies jostled for position, moving ever forward, seeking their future.

The salmon were back.

- CONTACT -

T HE BEADS SLIPPED through slim fingers, one by one, the fingers at the end of smooth bare arms, skin a perfect match to the tanned olive tones of the woman's face and neck. Her fingers stopped at the lone white bead and her teeth flashed in a grim smile. "I'd say we have a lock. Everyone in place, Zimmie?"

Zimmerman checked his console then nodded. "You're sure?"

Emily Mamani let go of her necklace and stroked through the 'screen over the Tracer. "Oh, yes."

Riden IV's ocean wind was more howl than tropical breeze, the air hot, humid, and always in your face. Zimmerman had shed his armor the first week. The big man now worked barefoot, in shorts topped by a fanciful shirt. That shirt was plastered by sweat against his big frame. He'd take it off, but Emily had distracting ways of commenting on the view.

Not that she wasn't distracting herself.

She'd resumed singing in her not-quite Spanish language. He hid a relieved grin, knowing the signs of a successful hunt by now. *About time.* This planet gave him the creeps. The rest had been empty, lifeless. This—despite the sullen dark waves and barren islands—this was something else.

When they'd arrived, their team had conducted the usual assays, checking the results against those from an ill-fated Sencor survey. Something new had indeed appeared, right here, below where their lev hovered. Microscopic, colonial, all of a kind. Coating the rock of deep submerged ridges. Coming free to float beneath the surface. Sticking to the wave-scoured edges of the land.

And it wasn't alone.

"Call the bait," Emily said abruptly.

"You're sure?"

"It's time."

Zimmerman nodded and lifted his wrist to his mouth, spoke once, then lowered his arm. "Done." His hand dropped to the weapon belted over his shorts.

She noticed. "They're allies, now. Blame Mac."

"Right." He moved his hand away, his massive shoulders giving a self-conscious shrug. "Habit."

Emily's laugh blended with the wild wind. "We couldn't do this without Her help," she pointed out. "Nothing draws a Ro from its chamber but a Dhryn. I should know." Her fingertip traced the necklace at her throat.

Six more Wasted had been found clinging to life in ships adrift at Haven. Two had survived and grown to full health. A tenuous, but promising beginning for their species.

As this was the end for another. There'd been no more ships, only dead worlds like Riden IV, each being prepared by an oblivious Ro. And only here had those preparations borne fruit.

"You'd think the Ro would get a clue," Zimmerman growled. "They must have noticed something was wrong by now."

" 'Now,' when it comes to our quarry, is a slippery thing," she said calmly, turning to look over the ocean, her shiny cap of black-and-white hair whipped by the wind. "We've been hunting for what . . . almost a year? In no-space, hardly time for a heartbeat. The Ro have taken advantage of what time does to us. It's their turn, Zimmie, to feel the other side of that knife." A chuckle. "Gotta love the irony. They built an entire world—a fleet of starships—all to keep their so-useful Dhryn safe and nearby. When the Dhryn turned on them the first time, they still saved as many possible. Even now, they blindly reach for the same tool, not noticing it's turned on them again."

A Sinzi dart drew near, surrounded by five smaller silver ships. "Keep in mind, my friend," she said quietly, "no one hunts the Ro with better reason than Her Glory. Not you. Not I. Now, to work."

She returned to the Tracer, her fingers moving rapidly through its hovering 'screen. Zimmerman watched the dart lower itself until ocean spray dotted its sides. Proof there was a Dhryn inside—otherwise, the Ro would react with one of its lightning attacks. *They'd lost a few levs discovering that detail.*

"It's on the move!" Emily shouted. "Get us up!"

He lunged for the controls, sending their lev to join the small fleet of others hovering overhead. The dart did the same.

"Catch of the day." She didn't need to point to the seething boil of water below. 'Bots were zipping from the water like chased fish. They circled once to locate the lev and began their return to their mistress. "Check the Sinzi have blocked the gate, then notify the team."

Zimmerman lifted his wrist again and spoke. The dart dipped once, as if in acknowledgment, then lifted out of the way.

He joined Emily at the rail. They watched as five larger-than-usual levs plunged down to fire their harpoons, cables playing out with a whine louder than the howling wind. The tips disappeared into the froth.

A froth suddenly stained with red.

Three of the cables snapped taut. The other lev crews released their failed harpoons and fired another round, this time hitting their target. All five began to strain upward. A dark shape gradually formed beneath the surface, huge and struggling. More harpoons, these without cables, launched into its midst.

"Messy," Zimmerman commented. Another detail they'd discovered: each of the Ro was somehow rooted into its chamber; much of that structure biological as well. A vulnerability exploited by the Dhryn feeders, but the IU wanted more of the technology left intact for study. *Messy worked.*

The struggle was over almost as soon as begun. More levs approached, sending down nets and divers. The limp shape shifted, but it was only the wind and waves; the cables held firm; the Ro was dead.

"Well," announced Emily. "That's done." She took the white bead in her fingers and pressed just so. Red flowed through it, until that bead matched its neighbors. "Eleven."

"How can we know that's all of them?" Zimmerman stared at the hideous shape being pulled from the sea.

"Here and now? I'm sure." Another shrug. "Anywhere else? Don't care. My job's done. And very well done." Emily slipped her arm around the big man's waist. "Time to find the party."

"There's a party?"

"There's always a party," Emily said, her tone vastly content. "With dancing." She laughed. "Don't look so worried. I'll behave. I promised Mac."

Zimmerman had scrunched up his forehead. Not so much a frown, as an indication of deep thought. "And after that?"

"Oh, that's when life gets interesting, Zimmie. What do you know about the Survivor Legend?"

Life coated rock, broke free to rise and float, struck an edge and stayed. It busied itself with sunlight and chemical reactions.

Bits failed. Bits survived. Of those, bits failed while others succeeded and grew and combined. Of those, some failed while others grew . . .

Without a caretaker's watchful eyes, the seeds of That Which Had Been Myrokynay became something else, many things else.

All new.